PRELUDE TO MARS

BOOKS BY ARTHUR C. CLARKE

Nonfiction

Interplanetary Flight / The Exploration of Space / Going into Space /
The Coast of Coral / The Making of a Moon / The Reefs of Taprobane /
Voice Across the Sea / The Challenge of the Spaceship /
The Challenge of the Sea / Profiles of the Future / Voices from the Sky /

With Mike Wilson

The First Five Fathoms / Boy Beneath the Sea /
Indian Ocean Adventure / Indian Ocean Treasure /
Treasure of the Great Reef /

With R. A. Smith

The Exploration of the Moon

With the Editors of Life

Man and Space

Fiction

Islands in the Sky / Prelude to Space / Against the Fall of Night /
The Sands of Mars / Childhood's End / Expedition to Earth /
Earthlight / Reach for Tomorrow / The City and the Stars /
Tales from the "White Hart" / The Deep Range /
The Other Side of the Sky / Across the Sea of Stars /
A Fall of Moondust / From the Ocean, from the Stars /
Tales of Ten Worlds / Dolphin Island / Glide Path /

With Stanley Kubrick

Journey Beyond the Stars

Arthur C. Clarke

Harcourt, Brace & World, Inc.   NEW YORK

PRELUDE TO MARS

An Omnibus containing the
complete novels
PRELUDE TO SPACE
and THE SANDS OF MARS
and sixteen short stories

TO VAL AND WERNHER
*Who are doing the things
I merely write about*

Contents

III ON THE SERIOUS SIDE

IV THE SANDS OF MARS 315

PRELUDE TO SPACE

FOREWORD

Science-fiction novels are usually short-lived, and the durability of this book is therefore somewhat flattering. It was written in July 1947, during my summer vacation as a student at King's College, London; the actual composition took exactly twenty days, a record I have never since approached. This speed was largely due to the fact that I had been planning the book for more than a year and had made voluminous notes; it was already well organized in my head before I set pen to paper.

Now, one or two things have happened in astronautics since 1947, and inevitably some of the ideas and statements in this novel are more than a little dated. But I have left them unaltered, because they set the book in its historical perspective; if they occasionally jolt you, please ask yourself just what *you* thought about space travel in 1947.

(Also, if the comparisons are not odious, I would point out that both Verne's *From the Earth to the Moon* and Wells's *The First Men in the Moon* are still flourishing, though no one believes in Cavorite or space-guns.)

The chief respect in which reality has departed from my fiction is, of course, in the Russian dominance of manned space exploration. Yet even this is indirectly reflected in the words of one of my English characters: "For some reason, you Americans have always been a bit conservative about space-flight, and didn't take it seriously until several years after us." This statement was still true a decade after I finished the book—when Sputnik I was launched in October 1957. It is now very hard to realize that right into the 1950's many American engineers *in the rocket field itself* pooh-poohed the idea of space flight; with a few notable exceptions, the banner of astronautics was borne by Europeans (or ex-Europeans like Willy Ley and Wernher von Braun).

The modest amounts of money with which I assumed space research could be conducted may also cause some amusement. No one could have imagined, in 1947, that within twenty years not millions but *billions* of dollars would be budgeted annually for space flight, and that a lunar landing was a primary objective of the two most powerful nations on Earth. Back in the '40's, it seemed most unlikely that governments would put any money into space before private enterprise had shown the way. And if we had realized that our cost estimates were out by a factor of approximately a thousand, we should have been so discouraged that we might have dropped the whole idea; so I am not in the least ashamed of misleading my fellow-enthusiasts by overoptimism.

One success as a minor prophet I can claim; I placed the first lunar impact in 1959, and Lunik II hit the Mare Imbrium at 21:01 G.M.T. on 13 September 1959. (I was watching hopefully through my Questar telescope from Colombo, but saw nothing.) The Mare Imbrium was also the region I selected for a landing; that, however, is a long-established tradition.

I was a little more conservative, though no one would have agreed in 1947, in putting the first manned suborbital flight in 1962, and the first orbital flight in 1970. Certainly no reasonable person would have imagined that the *second* feat would have been achieved before the first—and as early as 1961.

In choosing 1978 as the date of the first landing on the Moon, I was guilty of extreme wishful thinking. I did not really imagine that it would happen before the year 2000—but I wanted to feel that I had a sporting chance of seeing it. Today, of course, if I settled for 1978 I should be extremely unpopular around NASA Headquarters.

While writing this novel, I had the great advantage of access to calculations which my colleagues A. V. Cleaver and L. R. Shepherd were making on the subject of nuclear rocket propulsion. These were later published in their classic paper "The Atomic Rocket" (*Journal of the British Interplanetary Society*, September 1948–March 1949), which pioneered this field of studies. Although the atomic rocket has taken longer to arrive than many of us expected, it is satisfactory to record that the first full-power test of such a device took place in 1964.

My little jibe at the late Dr. C. S. Lewis in Part Three subsequently resulted in an amicable correspondence and a meeting at Oxford, where I tried to demonstrate to him that all would-be astronauts were not like the malevolent Weston in his *Out of the Silent Planet*. He cheerfully compromised with the observation that though we were probably very wicked people, the world would be an awfully dull place if everyone was good. Our letters, incidentally, should be appearing in a volume of Dr. Lewis's correspondence now being edited by his brother.

Prelude to Space was written just two years after I had published my 1945 paper on the theory of communications satellites, and so was probably the first work of fiction in which the idea of comsats was advocated. This edition will appear in the year when they go into commercial service—a fact which I still find more than faintly astonishing.

Perhaps still more astonishing is the fact that, after almost two thousand years of such speculations, it will never again be possible to write a story of the first journey to the Moon. All the more reason, therefore, to consider *why* men should wish to explore space, not how. There are still far too many members of the political, business, and even scientific community who can see little purpose in manned space flight; their education remains an urgent necessity.

One of the main themes of this novel was the absurdity of exporting national rivalries beyond the atmosphere—a concept I summed up in the phrase "We will take no frontiers into Space." In the light of recent events, this statement may seem a little ironic; indeed, my friend Anthony Boucher once suggested that it might be the most tragically wrong of all the prophecies of the Space Age.

But I still stand by it. Just before his death, President John F. Kennedy called for co-operation between the U.S. and the U.S.S.R. in the exploration of space; and whatever may happen in the short run, in the long run such co-operation is inevitable. Indeed, in the literal sense my prophecy has already been fulfilled, for the nations involved in the so-called "Space Race" have already declared that they will make no territorial claims on celestial bodies.

That is good news for the Universe. The 100,000,000,000 planetary systems of our Galaxy can breathe a collective sigh of relief. We won't annex them.

Arthur C. Clarke
New York, December 1964

PART ONE

For five miles, straight as an arrow, the gleaming metal track lay along the face of the desert. It pointed to the northwest across the dead heart of the continent and to the ocean beyond. Over this land, once the home of the aborigines, many strange shapes had risen, roaring, in the last generation. The greatest and strangest of them all lay at the head of the launching track along which it was to hurtle into the sky.

A little town had grown out of the desert in this valley between the low hills. It was a town built for one purpose—a purpose which was embodied in the fuel-storage tanks and the power station at the end of the five-mile-long track. Here had gathered scientists and engineers from all the countries of the world. And here the "Prometheus," first of all spaceships, had been assembled in the past three years.

The Prometheus of legend had brought fire from heaven down to earth. The Prometheus of the twentieth century was to take atomic fire back into the home of the Gods, and to prove that Man, by his own exertions, had broken free at last from the chains that had held him to his world for a million years.

No one seemed to know who had given the spaceship its name. It was, in actuality, not a single ship at all but really consisted of two separate machines. With notable lack of enterprise, the designers had christened the two components "Alpha" and "Beta." Only the upper component, "Alpha," was a pure rocket. "Beta," to give it its full name, was a "hypersonic athodyd." Most people usually called it an atomic ramjet, which was both simpler and more expressive.

It was a long way from the flying bombs of the Second World War to the two-hundred-ton "Beta," skimming the top of the atmosphere at thousands of miles an hour. Yet both operated on the same principle—the use of forward speed to provide compression for the jet. The main difference lay in the fuel. V.1 had burned gasoline; "Beta" burned plutonium, and her range was virtually unlimited. As long as her air-scoops could collect and compress the tenuous gas of the upper atmosphere, the white-hot furnace of the atomic pile would blast it out of the jets. Only when at last the air was too thin for power or support need she inject into the pile the methane from her fuel tanks and thus become a pure rocket.

"Beta" could leave the atmosphere, but she could never escape completely from Earth. Her task was two-fold. First, she had to carry up fuel tanks into the orbit round the Earth, and set them circling like tiny moons until they were needed. Not until this had been done would she lift "Alpha" into space. The smaller ship would then fuel up in free orbit from the waiting tanks, fire its motors to break away from Earth, and make the journey to the Moon.

Circling patiently, "Beta" would wait until the spaceship returned. At the end of its half-million-mile journey "Alpha" would have barely enough fuel to maneuver into a parallel orbit. The crew and their equipment would then be transferred to the waiting "Beta," which would still carry sufficient fuel to bring them safely back to Earth.

It was an elaborate plan, but even with atomic energy it was still the only practicable way of making the lunar round-trip with a rocket weighing not less than many thousands of tons. Moreover, it had many other advantages. "Alpha" and "Beta" could each be designed to carry out their separate tasks with an efficiency which no single, *all-purpose ship could hope to achieve. It was impossible to combine in one machine the ability to fly through Earth's atmosphere and to land on the airless Moon.*

When the time came to make the next voyage, "Alpha" would still be circling the Earth, to be refueled in space and used again. No later journey would ever be quite as difficult as the first. In time there would be more efficient motors, and later still, when the lunar colony had been founded, there would be refueling stations on the Moon. After that it would be easy, and space flight would become a commercial proposition—though this would not happen for half a century or more.

Meanwhile the "Prometheus," alias "Alpha" and "Beta," still lay glistening beneath the Australian sun while the technicians worked over her. The last fittings were being installed and tested: the moment of her destiny was drawing nearer. In a few weeks, if all went well, she would carry the hopes and fears of humanity into the lonely deeps beyond the sky.

ONE

Dirk Alexson threw down his book and climbed up the short flight of stairs to the observation deck. It was still much too soon to see land, but the journey's approaching end had made him restless and unable to concentrate. He walked over to the narrow, curving windows set in the leading-edge of the great wing and stared down at the featureless ocean below.

There was absolutely nothing to be seen: from this height the Atlantic's mightiest storms would have been invisible. He gazed for a while at the blank grayness beneath and then moved across to the passengers' radar display.

The spinning line of light on the screen had begun to paint the first dim echoes at the limits of its range. Land lay ahead, ten miles below and two hundred miles away—the land that Dirk had never seen though it was sometimes more real to him than the country of his birth. From those hidden shores, over the last four centuries, his ancestors had set out for the New World in search of freedom or fortune. Now he was returning, crossing in less than three hours the wastes over which they had labored for as many weary weeks. And he was coming on a mission of which they, in their wildest imaginings, could never have dreamed.

The luminous image of Land's End had moved halfway across the radar screen before Dirk first glimpsed the advancing coastline, a dark stain almost lost in the horizon mists. Though he had sensed no change of direction, he knew that the liner must now be falling down the long slope that led to London Airport, four hundred miles away. In a few minutes he would hear again, faint but infinitely reassuring, the rumbling whisper of the great jets as the air thickened around him and brought their music once more to his ears.

Cornwall was a gray blur, sinking astern too swiftly for any details to be seen. For all that one could tell, King Mark might still be waiting above the cruel rocks for the ship that brought Iseult, while on the hills Merlin might yet be talking with the winds and thinking of his doom. From this height the land would have looked the same when the masons laid the last stone on Tintagel's walls.

Now the liner was dropping toward a cloudscape so white and dazzling that it hurt the eyes. At first it seemed broken only by a few slight undulations but, presently, as it rose towards him, Dirk realized that the mountains of cloud below were built on a Himalayan scale. A moment later, the peaks were above him and the machine was driving through a great pass flanked on either side by overhanging walls of snow. He flinched involuntarily as the white cliffs came racing towards him, then relaxed as the driving mist was all around and he could see no more.

The cloud layer must have been very thick, for he caught only the briefest glimpse of London and was taken almost unawares by the gentle shock of landing. Then the sounds of the outer world came rushing in upon his mind—the metallic voices of loud-speakers, the clanging of hatches, and above all these, the dying fall of the great turbines as they idled to rest.

The wet concrete, the waiting trucks, and the gray clouds lowering overhead dispelled the last impressions of romance or adventure. It was drizzling slightly, and as the ridiculously tiny tractor hauled the great ship away, her glistening sides made her seem a creature of the deep sea rather than of the open sky. Above the jet housings, little flurries of steam were rising as the water drained down the wing.

Much to his relief, Dirk was met at the Customs barrier. As his name was checked off the passenger list, a stout, middle-aged man came forward with outstretched hand.

"Dr. Alexson? Pleased to meet you. My name's Matthews. I'm taking you to Headquarters at Southbank and generally looking after you while you're in London."

"Glad to hear it," smiled Dirk. "I suppose I can thank McAndrews for this?"

"That's right. I'm his assistant in Public Relations. Here—let me have that bag. We're going by the express tube; it's the quickest way —and the best, since you get into the city without having to endure the suburbs. There's one snag, though."

"What's that?"

Matthews sighed. "You'd be surprised at the number of visitors who cross the Atlantic safely, then disappear into the Underground and are never seen again."

Matthews never even smiled as he imparted this unlikely news. As Dirk was to discover, his impish sense of humor seemed to go with a complete incapacity for laughter. It was a most disconcerting combination.

"There's one thing I'm not at all clear about," began Matthews as the long red train began to draw out of the airport station. "We get a lot of American scientists over to see us, but I understand that science isn't your line."

"No, I'm an historian."

Matthews's eyebrows asked an almost audible question.

"I suppose it must be rather puzzling," continued Dirk, "but it's quite logical. In the past, when history was made, there was seldom anyone around to record it properly. Nowadays, of course, we have newspapers and films—but it's surprising what important features get overlooked simply because everyone takes them for granted at the time. Well, the project you people are working on is one of the biggest in history, and if it comes off it will change the future as perhaps no other single event has ever done. So my University decided that there should be a professional historian around to fill in the gaps that might be overlooked."

Matthews nodded.

"Yes, that's reasonable enough. It will make a pleasant change for us non-scientific people, too. We're rather tired of conversations in which three words out of four are mathematical symbols. Still, I suppose you have a fairly good technical background?"

Dirk looked slightly uncomfortable.

"To tell the truth," he confessed, "it's almost fifteen years since I did any science—and I never took it very seriously then. I'll have to learn what I need as I go along."

"Don't worry; we have a high-pressure course for tired businessmen and perplexed politicians which will give you everything you need. And you'll be surprised to find how much you pick up, simply by listening to the Boffins holding forth."

"Boffins?"

"Good Lord, don't you know *that* word? It goes back to the War, and means any long-haired scientific type with a slide-rule in his vest-pocket. I'd better warn you right away that we've quite a private vocabulary here which you'll have to learn. There are so many new ideas and conceptions in our work that we've had to invent new words. You should have brought along a philologist as well!"

Dirk was silent. There were moments when the sheer immensity of his task almost overwhelmed him. Some time in the next six months the work of thousands of men over half a century would reach its culmination. It would be his duty, and his privilege, to be present while history was being made out there in the Australian desert on the other side of the world. He must look upon these events through the eyes of the future, and must record them so that in centuries to come other men could recapture the spirit of this age and time.

They emerged at New Waterloo station, and walked the few hundred yards to the Thames. Matthews had been right in saying that this was the best way to meet London for the first time. The spacious sweep of the fine new Embankment, still only twenty years old, carried Dirk's gaze down the river until it was caught and held by the dome of St. Paul's, glistening wetly in an unexpected shaft of sunlight. He followed the river upstream, past the great white buildings before Charing Cross, but the Houses of Parliament were invisible around the curve of the Thames.

"Quite a view, isn't it?" said Matthews presently. "We're rather proud of it now, but thirty years ago this part was a horrid mass of wharves and mudbanks. By the way—you see that ship over there?"

"You mean the one tied up against the other bank?"

"Yes, do you know what it is?"

"I've no idea."

"She's the *Discovery*, which took Captain Scott into the Antarctic back at the beginning of this century. I often look at her as I come to work and wonder what he'd have thought of the little trip *we* are planning."

Dirk stared intently at the graceful wooden hull, the slim masts and the battered smokestack. His mind slipped into the past in the easy way it had, and it seemed that the Embankment was gone and that the old ship was steaming past walls of ice into an unknown land. He could understand Matthews's feelings, and the sense of historical continuity was suddenly very strong. The line that stretched through Scott back to Drake and Raleigh and yet earlier voyagers was still unbroken: only the scale of things had changed.

"Here we are," said Matthews in a tone of proud apology. "It's not as impressive as it might be, but we didn't have a lot of money when we built it. Not that we have now, for that matter."

The white, three-story building that faced the river was unpretentious and had obviously been constructed only a few years before. It was surrounded by large, open lawns scantily covered by dispirited grass. Dirk guessed that they had already been earmarked for future building operations. The grass seemed to have realized this too.

Nevertheless, as administrative buildings went, Headquarters was not unattractive, and the view over the river was certainly very fine. Along the second story ran a line of letters, as clean-cut and severely practical as the rest of the building. They formed a single word, but at the sight of it Dirk felt a curious tingling in his veins. It seemed out of place, somehow, here in the heart of a great city where millions were concerned with the affairs of everyday life. It was as out of place as the *Discovery*, lying against the far bank at the end of her long journeying—and it spoke of a longer voyage than she or any ship had ever made:

INTERPLANETARY

TWO

The office was small, and he would have to share it with a couple of junior draftsmen—but it overlooked the Thames and when he was tired of his reports and files Dirk could always rest his eyes on that great dome floating above Ludgate Hill. From time to time Matthews or his chief would drop in for a talk, but usually they left him alone, knowing that that was his desire. He was anxious to be left in peace until he had burrowed through the hundreds of reports and books which Matthews had obtained for him.

It was a far cry from Renaissance Italy to twentieth-century London, but the techniques he had acquired when writing his thesis on Lorenzo the Magnificent served Dirk in good stead now. He could tell, almost at a glance, what was unimportant and what must be studied carefully. In a few days the outlines of the story were complete and he could begin to fill in the details.

The dream was older than he had imagined. Two thousand years ago the Greeks had guessed that the Moon was a world not unlike the Earth, and in the second century A.D. the satirist Lucian had written the first of all interplanetary romances. It had taken more than seventeen centuries to bridge the gulf between fiction and reality—and almost all the progress had been made in the last fifty years.

The modern era had begun in 1923, when an obscure Transylvanian professor named Hermann Oberth had published a pamphlet entitled *The Rocket Into Interplanetary Space*. In this he developed for the first time the mathematics of space flight. Leafing through the pages of one of the few copies still in existence, Dirk found it hard to believe that so enormous a superstructure had arisen from so small a beginning. Oberth—now an old man of 84—had started the chain reaction which was to lead in his own lifetime to the crossing of space.

In the decade before the Second World War, Oberth's German disciples had perfected the liquid-fueled rocket. At first they too had dreamed of the conquest of space, but that dream had been forgotten with the coming of Hitler. The city over which Dirk so often gazed still bore the scars from the time, thirty years ago, when the great rockets had come falling down from the stratosphere in a tumult of sundered air.

Less than a year later had come that dreary dawn in the New Mexico desert, when it seemed that the River of Time had halted for a moment, then plunged in foam and spray into a new channel towards a changed and unknown future. With Hiroshima had come the end of a war and the end of an age: the power and the machine had come together at last and the road to space lay clear ahead.

It had been a steep road, and it had taken thirty years to climb—thirty years of triumphs and heartbreaking disappointments. As he grew to know the men around him, as he listened to their stories and their conversations, Dirk slowly filled in the personal details which the reports and summaries could never provide.

"The television picture wasn't too clear, but every few seconds it steadied and we got a good image. That was the biggest thrill of my life—being the first man to see the other side of the Moon. Going there will be a bit of an anticlimax."

"—most terrific explosion you ever saw. When we got up, I heard Goering say: 'If *that's* the best you can do, I'll tell the Fuehrer the whole thing's a waste of money.' You should have seen von Braun's face——"

"The KX 14's still up there: she completes one orbit every three hours, which was just what we'd intended. But the blasted radio transmitter failed at take-off, so we never got those instrument readings after all."

"I was looking through the twelve-inch reflector when that load of magnesium powder hit the Moon, about fifty kilometers from Aristarchus. You can just see the crater it made, if you have a look around sunset."

Sometimes Dirk envied these men. They had a purpose in life, even if it was one he could not fully understand. It must give them a feeling of power to send their great machines thousands of miles out into space. But power was dangerous, and often corrupting. Could they be trusted with the forces they were bringing into the world? Could the world itself be trusted with them?

Despite his intellectual background, Dirk was not altogether free from the fear of science that had been common ever since the great discoveries of the Victorian era. He felt not only isolated but sometimes a little nervous in his new surroundings. The few people he spoke to were invariably helpful and polite, but a certain shyness and his anxiety to master the background of his subject in the shortest time kept him away from all social entanglements. He liked the atmosphere of the organization, which was almost aggressively democratic, and later on it would be easy enough to meet all the people he wished.

At the moment, Dirk's chief contacts with anyone outside the Public Relations Department were at meal-times. Interplanetary's small canteen was patronized, in relays, by all the staff from the Director-General downwards. It was run by a very enterprising committee with a fondness for experimenting, and although there were occasional culinary catastrophes, the food was usually very good. For all that Dirk could tell, Interplanetary's boast of the best cooking on Southbank might indeed be justified.

As Dirk's lunch-time, like Easter, was a movable feast, he usually met a fresh set of faces every day and soon grew to know most of the important members of the organization by sight. No one took any notice of him; the building was full of birds-of-passage from universities and industrial firms all over the world, and he was obviously regarded as just another visiting scientist.

His college, through the ramifications of the United States Embassy, had managed to find Dirk a small service flat a few hundred yards from Grosvenor Square. Every morning he walked to Bond Street Station and took the tube to Waterloo. He quickly learned to avoid the early-morning rush, but he was seldom much later than many senior members of Interplanetary's staff. Eccentric hours were popular at Southbank: though Dirk sometimes remained in the building until midnight, there were always sounds of activity around him— usually from the research sections. Often, in order to clear his head and get a little exercise, he would go for a stroll along the deserted corridors, making mental notes of interesting departments which he might one day visit officially. He learned a great deal more about the place in this way than from the elaborate and much-amended organization charts which Matthews had lent him—and was always borrowing back again.

Frequently Dirk would come across half-opened doors revealing vistas of untidy labs and machine-shops in which gloomy technicians sat gazing at equipment which was obviously refusing to behave. If the hour was very late, the scene would be softened by a mist of tobacco-smoke and invariably an electric kettle and a battered teapot would occupy places of honor in the near foreground. Occasionally Dirk would arrive at some moment of technical triumph, and if he was not careful he was likely to be invited to share the ambiguous liquid which the engineers were continually brewing. In this way he became on nodding terms with a great many people, but he knew scarcely a dozen well enough to address them by name.

At the age of thirty-three, Dirk Alexson was still somewhat nervous of the everyday world around him. He was happier in the past and among his books, and though he had traveled fairly extensively in the United States, he had spent almost all his life in academic circles. His colleagues recognized him as a steady, sound worker with an almost intuitive flair for unraveling complicated situations. No one knew if he would make a great historian, but his study of the Medicis had been acknowledged as outstanding. His friends had never been able to understand how anyone of Dirk's somewhat placid disposition could so accurately have analyzed the motives and behavior of that flamboyant family.

Pure chance, it seemed, had brought him from Chicago to London, and he was still very much conscious of the fact. A few months ago the influence of Walter Pater had begun to wane: the little, crowded stage of Renaissance Italy was losing its charm—if so mild a word could be applied to that microcosm of intrigues and assassinations. It had not been his first change of interest, and he feared it would not be his last, for Dirk Alexson was still seeking a work to which he could devote his life. In a moment of depression he had remarked to his Dean that probably only the future held a subject which would really appeal to him. That casual and half-serious complaint had coincided with a letter from the Rockefeller Foundation, and before he knew it Dirk had been on the way to London.

For the first few days he was haunted by the specter of his own incapacity, but he had learned now that this always happened when he started a new job and it had ceased to be more than a nuisance. After about a week he felt that he now had a fairly clear picture of the organization in which he had so unexpectedly found himself. His confidence began to return, and he could relax a little.

Since undergraduate days he had kept a desultory journal—usually neglected save in occasional crises—and he now began once more to record his impressions and the everyday events of his life. These notes, written for his own satisfaction, would enable him to marshal his thoughts and might later serve as a basis for the official history he must one day produce.

"Today, May 3, 1978, I've been in London for exactly a week—and I've seen nothing of it except the areas around Bond Street and Waterloo. When it's fine Matthews and I usually go for a stroll along the river after lunch. We go across the 'New' bridge (which has only been built for about forty years!) and walk up or down river as the fancy takes us, crossing again at Charing Cross or Blackfriars. There are quite a number of variations, clockwise and counter-clockwise.

"Alfred Matthews is about forty, and I've found him very helpful. He has an extraordinary sense of humor, but I've never seen him smile —he's absolutely deadpan. He seems to know his job pretty well—a good deal better, I should say, than McAndrews, who is supposed to be his boss. Mac is about ten years older: like Alfred, he graduated through journalism into public relations. He's a lean, hungry-looking person and usually speaks with a slight Scots accent—which vanishes completely when he's excited. This should prove something, but I can't imagine what. He's not a bad fellow, but I don't think he's very bright. Alfred does all the work and there's not much love lost between them. It's sometimes a bit difficult keeping on good terms with them both.

"Next week I hope to start meeting people and going further afield. I particularly want to meet the crew—but I'm keeping out of the scientists' way until I know a bit more about atomic drives and interplanetary orbits. Alfred is going to teach me all about this next week —so he says. What I also hope to discover is how such an extraordinary hybrid as Interplanetary was ever formed in the first place. It seems a typically British compromise, and there's very little on paper about its formation and origins. The whole institution is a mass of paradoxes. It exists in a state of chronic bankruptcy, yet it's responsible for spending something like ten millions a year (£, not $). The Government has very little say in its administration, and in some ways it seems as autocratic as the B.B.C. But when it's attacked in Parliament (which happens every other month) some Minister always gets up to defend it. Perhaps, after all, Mac's a better organizer than I imagine!

"I called it 'British,' but of course it isn't. About a fifth of the staff are American, and I've heard every conceivable accent in the canteen. It's as international as the United Nations secretariat, though the British certainly provide most of the driving force and the administrative staff. Why this should be, I don't know: perhaps Matthews can explain.

"Another query: apart from their accents, it's very difficult to see any real distinction between the different nationalities here. Is this due to the—to put it mildly—supranational nature of their work? And if I stay here long enough, I suppose I shall get deracinated too."

THREE

"I was wondering," said McAndrews, "when you were going to ask that question. The answer's rather complicated."

"I'll be very much surprised," Dirk answered dryly, "if it's quite as involved as the machinations of the Medici family."

"Perhaps not; we've never used assassination yet, though we've often felt like it. Miss Reynolds, will you take any calls while I talk with Dr. Alexson? Thank you.

"Well, as you know, the foundations of astronautics—the science of space travel—had been pretty well laid at the end of the Second World War. V.2 and atomic energy had convinced most people that space could be crossed, if anyone wanted to do it. There were several societies, in England and the States, actively promulgating the idea that we should go to the Moon and the planets. They made steady but slow progress until the 1950's, when things really started to get moving.

"In 1959, as you may—er—just remember, the American Army's guided missile 'Orphan Annie' hit the Moon with twenty-five pounds of flash-powder aboard. From that moment, the public began to realize that space travel wasn't a thing of the distant future, but might come inside a generation. Astronomy began to replace atomic physics as the Number One science, and the rocket societies' membership lists started to lengthen steadily. But it was one thing to crash an unmanned projectile into the Moon—and quite another to land a full-sized spaceship there and bring it home again. Some pessimists thought the job might still take another hundred years.

"There were a lot of people in this country who didn't intend to wait that long. They believed that the crossing of space was as essential for progress as the discovery of the New World had been four hundred years before. It would open up new frontiers and give the human race a goal so challenging that it would overshadow national differences and put the tribal conflicts of the early twentieth century in their true perspective. Energies that might have gone into wars would be fully employed in the colonization of the planets—which could certainly keep us busy for a good many centuries. That was the theory, at any rate."

McAndrews smiled a little.

"There were, of course, a good many other motives. You know what an unsettled period the early '50's was. The cynic's argument for space flight was summed up in the famous remark: 'Atomic power makes interplanetary travel not only possible but imperative.' As long as it was confined to Earth, humanity had too many eggs in one rather fragile basket.

"All this was realized by an oddly assorted group of scientists, writers, astronomers, editors and businessmen in the old Interplanetary Society. With very small capital, they started the publication

Spacewards, which was inspired by the success of the American National Geographic Society's magazine. What the N.G.S. had done for the Earth could, it was argued, now be done for the solar system. *Spacewards* was an attempt to make the public shareholders, as it were, in the conquest of space. It catered to the new interest in astronomy, and those who subscribed to it felt that they were helping to finance the first space flight.

"The project wouldn't have succeeded a few years earlier, but the time was now ripe for it. In a few years there were about a quarter of a million subscribers all over the world, and in 1962 'Interplanetary' was founded to carry out full-time research into the problems of space flight. At first it couldn't offer the salaries of the great government-sponsored rocket establishments, but slowly it attracted the best scientists in the field. They preferred working on a constructive project, even at lower pay, to building missiles for transporting atomic bombs. In the early days, the organization was also helped by one or two financial windfalls. When the last British millionaire died in 1965, he balked the Treasury of almost all his fortune by making it into a Trust Fund for our use.

"From the first, Interplanetary was a world-wide organization and it's largely an historical accident that its H.Q. is actually in London. It might very well have been in America, and a lot of your compatriots are still quite annoyed that it isn't. But for some reason, you Americans have always been a bit conservative about space flight, and didn't take it seriously until several years after us. Never mind: the Germans beat us both.

"Also, you must remember that the United States is much too small a country for astronautical research. Yes, I know that sounds odd—but if you look at a population map you'll see what I mean. There are only two places in the world that are really suitable for long-range rocket research. One's the Sahara desert, and even that is a little too near the great cities of Europe. The other is the West Australian desert, where the British Government started building its great rocket range in 1947. It's more than a thousand miles long, and there's another two thousand miles of ocean beyond it—giving a grand total of over three thousand miles. You won't find any place in the United States where you can safely fire a rocket even five hundred miles. So it's partly a geographical accident that things have turned out this way.

"Where was I? Oh yes, up to 1960 or so. It was about then that we began to get really important, for two reasons which aren't widely known. By that time a whole section of nuclear physics had come to a full stop. The scientists of the Atomic Development Authority thought they could start the hydrogen-helium reaction—and I don't mean the tritium reaction of the old H-bomb—but the crucial experiments had been very wisely banned. There's rather a lot of hydrogen in the sea! So the nuclear physicists were all sitting around chewing their fingernails until we could build them laboratories out in space. It wouldn't matter, then, if something went wrong. The solar system would merely acquire a second and rather temporary sun. ADA also wanted us to dump the dangerous fission products from the piles, which were too radioactive to keep on Earth but which might be useful some day.

"The second reason wasn't so spectacular, but was perhaps even more immediately important. The great radio and telegraph companies *had* to get out into space—it was the only way they could broadcast television over the whole world and provide a universal communication service. As you know, the very short waves of radar and television won't bend around the Earth—they travel in practically straight lines, so that one station can send signals only as far as the horizon. Airborne relays had been built to get over this difficulty, but it was realized that the final solution would be reached only when repeater stations could be built thousands of miles above the Earth —artificial moons, probably traveling in twenty-four-hour orbits so that they'd appear stationary in the sky. No doubt you've read all about these ideas, so I won't go into them now.

"So by about 1970 we had the support of some of the world's biggest technical organizations, with virtually unlimited funds. They *had* to come to us, since we had all the experts. In the early days, I'm afraid there was a certain amount of bickering and the Service Departments have never quite forgiven us for stealing back all their best scientists. But on the whole we get along well enough with ADA, Westinghouse, General Electric, Rolls-Royce, Lockheeds, de Havillands, and the rest of them. They've all got offices here, as you've probably noticed. Although they make us very substantial grants, the technical services they provide are really beyond price. Without their help, I don't suppose we'd have reached this stage for another twenty years."

There was a brief pause, and Dirk emerged from the torrent of words like a spaniel clambering out of a mountain stream. McAndrews talked much too quickly, obviously repeating phrases and whole paragraphs which he had been using for years. Dirk got the impression that almost everything he had said had probably come from other sources, and wasn't original at all.

"I'd no idea," he replied, "just how extensive your ramifications were."

"Believe me, that's nothing!" McAndrews exclaimed. "I don't think there are many big industrial firms who haven't been convinced that we can help them in some way. The cable companies will save hundreds of millions when they can replace their ground stations and land-lines by a few repeaters in space; the chemical industry will——"

"Oh, I'll take your word for it! I was wondering where all the money came from, and now I see just how big a thing this is."

"Don't forget," interjected Matthews, who had hitherto been sitting in resigned silence, "our most important contribution to industry."

"What's that?"

"The import of high-grade vacuums for filling electric-light bulbs and electronic tubes."

"Ignoring Alfred's usual facetiousness," said McAndrews severely, "it's perfectly true that physics in general will make tremendous strides when we can build laboratories in space. And you can guess how the astronomers are looking forward to observatories which will never be bothered by clouds."

"I know now," said Dirk, ticking off the points on his fingers, "just *how* Interplanetary happened, and also what it hopes to do. But I still find it very hard to define exactly what it *is*."

"Legally, it's a non-profit-making" ("And how!" interjected Matthews, *sotto voce*) "organization devoted, as its charter says, 'to research into the problems of space flight.' It originally obtained its funds from *Spacewards*, but that hasn't any official connection with us now that it's linked up with *National Geographic*—though it has plenty of unofficial ones. Today most of our money comes from government grants and from industrial concerns. When interplanetary travel is fully established on a commercial basis, as aviation is today, we'll probably evolve into something different. There are a lot of political angles to the whole thing and no one can say just what will happen when the planets start to be colonized."

McAndrews gave a little laugh, half apologetic and half defensive. "There are a lot of pipe-dreams floating around this place, as you'll probably discover. Some people have ideas of starting scientific utopias on suitable worlds, and all that sort of thing. But the immediate aim is purely technical: we must find out what the planets are like before we decide how to use them."

The office became quiet; for a moment no one seemed inclined to speak. For the first time Dirk realized the true importance of the goal towards which these men were working. He felt overwhelmed and more than a little frightened. Was humanity ready to be pitchforked out into space, ready to face the challenge of barren and inhospitable worlds never meant for Man? He could not be sure, and in the depths of his mind he felt profoundly disturbed.

FOUR

From the street, 53 Rockdale Avenue, S.W.5, appeared to be one of those neo-Georgian residences which the more successful stockbrokers of the early twentieth century had erected as shelters for their declining years. It was set well back from the road, with tastefully laid out but somewhat neglected lawns and flower beds. When the weather was fine, as it occasionally was in the spring of 1978, five young men might sometimes be seen performing desultory gardening operations with inadequate tools. It was clear that they were doing this merely as a relaxation, and that their minds were very far away. Just how far, a casual passer-by could hardly have guessed.

It had been a very well-kept secret, largely because the security organizers themselves were ex-newspapermen. As far as the world knew, the crew of the "Prometheus" had not yet been chosen, whereas in actuality its training had begun more than a year ago. It had continued with quiet efficiency, not five miles from Fleet Street, yet altogether free from the fierce limelight of public interest.

At any one time, there were not likely to be more than a handful of men in the world who would be capable of piloting a spaceship. No other work had ever demanded such a unique combination of physical and mental characteristics. The perfect pilot had not only to be a first-class astronomer, an expert engineer and a specialist in electronics, but must be capable of operating efficiently both when he was "weightless" and when the rocket's acceleration made him weigh a quarter of a ton.

No single individual could meet these requirements, and many years ago it had been decided that the crew of a spaceship must consist of at least three men, any two of whom could take over the duties of a third in an emergency. Interplanetary was training five; two were reserves in case of last-minute illness. As yet, no one knew who the two reserves would be.

Few doubted that Victor Hassell would be the ship's captain. At twenty-eight, he was the only man in the world who had logged over a hundred hours in free fall. The record had been entirely accidental. Two years before, Hassell had taken an experimental rocket up into an orbit and circled the world thirty times before he could repair a fault which had developed in the firing circuits and so reduce his velocity enough to fall back to Earth. His nearest rival, Pierre Leduc, had a mere twenty hours of orbital flight to his credit.

The three remaining men were not professional pilots at all. Arnold Clinton, the Australian, was an electronic engineer and a specialist in computers and automatic controls. Astronomy was represented by the brilliant young American Lewis Taine, whose prolonged absence from Mount Palomar Observatory was now requiring elaborate explanations. The Atomic Development Authority had contributed James Richards, expert on nuclear propulsion systems. Being a ripe old thirty-five, he was usually called "Grandpop" by his colleagues.

Life at the "Nursery," as it was always referred to by those sharing the secret, combined the characteristics of college, monastery and operational bomber station. It was colored by the personalities of the five "pupils," and by the visiting scientists who came in an endless stream to impart their knowledge or, sometimes, to get it back with interest. It was an intensely busy but a happy life, for it had a purpose and a goal.

There was only one shadow, and that was inevitable. When the time for the decision came, no one knew who was to be left behind on the desert sands, watching the "Prometheus" shrink into the sky until the thunder of its jets could be heard no more.

An astrogation lecture was in full swing when Dirk and Matthews tiptoed into the back of the room. The speaker gave them an unfriendly look, but the five men seated around him never even glanced at the intruders. As unobtrusively as possible, Dirk studied them while his guide indicated their names in hoarse whispers.

Hassell he recognized from newspaper photographs, but the others were unknown to him. Rather to Dirk's surprise, they conformed to no particular type. Their only obvious points in common were age, intelligence and alertness. From time to time they shot questions at the lecturer, and Dirk gathered that they were discussing the landing maneuvers on the Moon. All the conversation was so much above his head that he quickly grew tired of listening and was glad when Matthews gave an interrogatory nod towards the door. Out in the corridor, they relaxed and lit cigarettes.

"Well," said Matthews, "now that you've seen our guinea pigs, what do you think of them?"

"I can hardly judge. What I'd like to do is to meet them informally and just talk with them by themselves."

Matthews blew a smoke-ring and watched it thoughtfully as it dispersed.

"That wouldn't be easy. As you can guess, they haven't much spare time. When they've finished here, they usually disappear in a cloud of dust back to their families."

"How many of them are married?"

"Leduc's got two children; so has Richards. Vic Hassell was married about a year ago. The others are still single."

Dirk wondered what the wives thought about the whole business. Somehow it didn't seem altogether fair to them. He wondered, too, whether the men regarded this as simply another job of work, or if they felt the exaltation—there was no other word for it—which had obviously inspired the founders of Interplanetary.

They had now come to a door labeled "KEEP OUT—TECHNICAL STAFF ONLY!" Matthews pushed tentatively against it and it swung open.

"Careless!" he said. "There doesn't seem to be anyone around, either. Let's go in—I think this is one of the most interesting places I know, even though I'm not a scientist."

That was one of Matthews's favorite phrases, which probably concealed a well-buried inferiority complex. Actually both he and McAndrews knew far more about science than they pretended.

Dirk followed him into the semi-gloom, then gasped with amazement as Matthews found the switch and the place was flooded with light. He was standing in a control room, surrounded by banks of switches and meters. The only furniture consisted of three luxurious seats suspended in a complex gimbal system. He reached out to touch one of them and it began to rock gently to and fro.

"Don't touch anything," warned Matthews quickly. "We're not really supposed to be in here, in case you hadn't noticed."

Dirk examined the array of controls and switches from a respectful distance. He could guess the purpose of some from the labels they bore, but others were quite incomprehensible. The words "Manual" and "Auto" occurred over and over again. Almost as popular were "Fuel," "Drive Temperature," "Pressure" and "Earth Range." Others, such as "Emergency Cut-out," "Air Warning" and "Pile Jettison," had a distinctly ominous flavor. A third and still more enigmatic group provided grounds for endless speculation. "Alt. Trig. Sync.," "Neut. Count" and "Video Mix" were perhaps the choicest specimens in this category.

"You'd almost think, wouldn't you," said Matthews, "that the house was ready to take off at any moment. It's a complete mock-up, of course, of 'Alpha's' control room. I've seen them training on it, and it's fascinating to watch even if you don't quite know what it's all about."

Dirk gave a somewhat forced laugh.

"It's a bit eerie, coming across a spaceship control panel in a quiet London suburb."

"It won't be quiet next week. We're throwing it open to the Press then, and we'll probably be lynched for keeping all this under cover so long."

"Next week?"

"Yes, if everything goes according to plan. 'Beta' should have passed her final full-speed tests by then, and we'll all be packing our trunks for Australia. By the way, have you seen those films of the first launchings?"

"No."

"Remind me to let you see them—they're most impressive."

"What's she done so far?"

"Four and a half miles a second with full load. That's a bit short of orbital speed, but everything was still working perfectly. It's a pity, though, that we can't test 'Alpha' before the actual flight."

"When will that be?"

"It's not fixed yet, but we know that the take-off will be when the Moon's entering her first quarter. The ship will land in the Mare Imbrium region while it's still early morning. The return's scheduled for the late afternoon, so they'll have about ten Earth-days there."

"Why the Mare Imbrium, in particular?"

"Because it's flat, very well mapped, and has some of the most interesting scenery on the Moon. Besides, spaceships have *always* landed there since Jules Verne's time. I guess that you know that the name means 'Sea of Rains.'"

"I did Latin pretty thoroughly once upon a time," Dirk said dryly. Matthews came as near a smile as he had ever known him to.

"I suppose you did. But let's get out of here before we're caught. Seen enough?"

"Yes, thanks. It's a bit overwhelming, but not so very much worse than a transcontinental jet's cockpit."

"It is if you know what goes on behind all those panels," said Matthews grimly. "Arnold Clinton—that's the electronics king—once told me that there are three thousand tubes in the computing and control circuits alone. And there must be a good many hundreds on the communications side."

Dirk scarcely heard him. He was beginning to realize, for the first time, how swiftly the sands were running out. When he had arrived a fortnight ago, the take-off still seemed a remote event in the indefinite future. That was the general impression in the outside world; now it seemed completely false. He turned to Matthews in genuine bewilderment.

"Your Public Relations Department," he complained, "seems to have misled everyone pretty efficiently. What's the idea?"

"It's purely a matter of policy," replied the other. "In the old days we had to talk big and make spectacular promises to attract any attention at all. Now we prefer to say as little as possible until everything's cut and dried. It's the only way to avoid fantastic rumors and the resulting sense of anticlimax. Do you remember the KY 15? She was the first manned ship to reach an altitude of a thousand miles— but months before she was ready everyone thought that we were going to send her to the Moon. They were disappointed, of course, when she did exactly what she'd been designed for. So nowadays I sometimes call my office the 'Department of Negative Publicity.' It will be quite a relief when the whole thing's over and we can go into forward gear again."

This, thought Dirk, was a very self-centered outlook. It seemed to him that the five men he had just been watching had far better reasons for wishing that the "whole thing was over."

FIVE

"So far," wrote Dirk in his Journal that night, "I've only nibbled round the edges of Interplanetary. Matthews has kept me orbiting around him like a minor planet—I must reach parabolic velocity and escape elsewhere. (I'm beginning to pick up the language, as he promised!)

"The people I want to meet now are the scientists and engineers who are the real driving force behind the organization. What makes them tick, to put it crudely? Are they a lot of Frankensteins merely interested in a technical project without any regard for its consequences? Or do they see, perhaps more clearly than McAndrews and Matthews, just where all this is going to lead? M. and M. sometimes remind me of a couple of real-estate agents trying to sell the Moon. They're doing a job, and doing it well—but someone must have inspired them in the first place. And in any case, they are a grade or two from the top of the hierarchy.

"The Director-General seemed a very interesting personality when I met him for those few minutes the day I arrived—but I can hardly go and catechize *him!* The Deputy D.-G. might have been a good bet, since we're both Californians, but he's not back from the States.

"Tomorrow I get the 'Astronautics Without Tears' course that Matthews promised me when I came. Apparently it's a six-reel instructional film, and I've not been able to see it before because no one in this hot-bed of genius was able to repair a thirty-five-millimeter projector. When I've sat through it, Alfred swears I'll be able to hold my own with the astronomers.

"As a good historian, I suppose I should have no prejudices one way or the other, but should be capable of watching Interplanetary's activities with a dispassionate eye. It isn't working out that way. I'm beginning to worry more and more about the ultimate consequences of this work, and the platitudes that Alfred and Mac keep bringing up don't satisfy me at all. I suppose that's why I'm now anxious to get hold of the top scientists and hear their views. Then, perhaps, I'll be able to pass judgment—if it's my job to pass judgment.

"*Later.* Of course it's my job. Look at Gibbon, look at Toynbee. Unless an historian draws conclusions (right or wrong) he's merely a file clerk.

"*Later Still.* How could I have forgotten? Tonight I came up to Oxford Circus in one of the new turbine buses. It's very quiet, but if you listen carefully you can hear it singing to itself in a faint, extremely high soprano. The Londoners are excessively proud of them, since they're the first in the world. I don't understand why a simple thing like a bus should have taken almost as long to develop as a spaceship, but they tell me it has. Something to do with engineering economics, I believe.

"I decided to walk to the flat, and coming out of Bond Street I saw a gilded, horse-drawn van looking as if it had rolled straight out of *Pickwick*. It was delivering goods for some tailor, I believe, and the ornamental lettering said: 'Est. 1768.'

"This sort of thing makes the British very disconcerting people to a foreigner. Of course, McAndrews would say that it's the English, not the British, who are crazy—but I refuse to draw this rather fine distinction."

SIX

"You'll excuse me for leaving you," said Matthews apologetically, "but although it's a very good film, I'd scream the place down if I had to see it again. At a guess, I've sat through it at least fifty times already."

"That's O.K.," laughed Dirk, from the depths of his seat in the little auditorium. "It's the first time I've ever been the only customer at a movie, so it will be a novel experience."

"Right. I'll be back when it's finished. If you want any reels run through again, just tell the operator."

Dirk settled back into the seat. It was, he reflected, just not comfortable enough to encourage one to relax and take life easily. Which showed good sense on the part of the designer, since this cinema was a strictly functional establishment.

The title with a few brief credits flashed on the screen.

THE ROAD TO SPACE
Technical advice and special effects by Interplanetary.
Produced by Eagle-Lion.

The screen was dark: then, in its center, a narrow band of starlight appeared. It slowly widened, and Dirk realized that he was beneath the opening hemispheres of some great observatory dome. The star-field commenced to expand: he was moving towards it.

"For two thousand years," said a quiet voice, "men have dreamed of journeys to other worlds. The stories of interplanetary flight are legion, but not until our own age was the machine perfected which could make these dreams come true."

Something dark was silhouetted against the star-field—something slim and pointed and eager to be away. The scene lightened and the stars vanished. Only the great rocket remained, its silver hull glistening in the sunlight as it rested upon the desert.

The sands seemed to boil as the blast ate into them. Then the giant projectile was climbing steadily, as if along an invisible wire. The camera tilted upwards: the rocket foreshortened and dwindled into the sky. Less than a minute later, only the twisting vapor-trail was left.

"In 1942," continued the narrator, "the first of the great modern rockets was launched in secret from the Baltic shore. This was V.2, intended for the destruction of London. Since it was the prototype of all later machines, and of the spaceship itself, let us examine it in detail."

There followed a series of sectional drawings of V.2, showing all the essential components—the fuel tanks, the pumping system and the motor itself. By means of animated cartoons, the operation of the whole machine was demonstrated so clearly that no one could fail to understand it.

"V.2," continued the voice, "could reach altitudes of over one hundred miles, and after the War was used extensively for research into the ionosphere."

There were some spectacular shots of New Mexico firings in the late 1940's, and some even more spectacular ones of faulty take-offs and other forms of misbehavior.

"As you see, it was not always reliable and it was soon superseded by more powerful and readily controlled machines—such as these——"

The smooth torpedo-shape was being replaced by long, thin needles that went whistling up into the sky and came floating back beneath billowing parachutes. One after another speed and altitude records were being smashed. And in 1959 . . .

"This is the 'Orphan Annie' being assembled. She consisted of four separate stages, or 'steps,' each dropping off when its fuel supply was exhausted. Her initial weight was a hundred tons—her payload only twenty-five pounds. But that payload of magnesium powder was the first object from Earth to reach another world."

The Moon filled the screen, her craters glistening whitely and her long shadows lying, sharp and black, across the desolate plains. She was rather less than half full, and the ragged line of the terminator enclosed a great oval of darkness. Suddenly, in the heart of that hidden land, a tiny but brilliant spark of light flared for a moment and was gone. "Orphan Annie" had achieved her destiny.

"But all these rockets were pure projectiles: no human being had yet risen above the atmosphere and returned safely to Earth. The first manned machine, carrying a single pilot to an altitude of two hundred miles, was the 'Aurora Australis,' which was launched in 1962. By this time all long-range rocket research was based upon the great proving-grounds built in the Australian desert.

"After the 'Aurora' came other and more powerful ships, and in 1970, Lonsdale and McKinley, in an American machine, made the first orbital flights around the world, circling it three times before landing."

There was a breathtaking sequence, obviously speeded up many times, showing almost the whole Earth spinning below at an enormous rate. It made Dirk quite dizzy for a moment, and when he had recovered the narrator was talking about the force of gravity. He explained how it held everything to the Earth, and how it weakened with distance but never vanished completely. More animated diagrams showed how a body could be given such a speed that it would circle the world forever, balancing gravity against centrifugal force just as the Moon does in its own orbit. This was illustrated by a man whirling a stone around his head at the end of a piece of string. Slowly he lengthened the string, but still kept the stone circling, more and more slowly.

"Near the Earth," explained the voice, "bodies have to travel at five miles a second to remain in stable orbits—but the Moon, a quarter of a million miles away in a much weaker gravitational field, need move at only a tenth of this speed.

"But what happens if a body, such as a rocket, leaves the Earth at *more* than five miles a second? Watch . . ."

A model of the Earth appeared, floating in space. Above the equator a tiny point was moving, tracing out a circular path.

"Here is a rocket, traveling at five miles a second just outside the atmosphere. You will see that its path is a perfect circle. Now, if we

increase its speed to *six* miles a second the rocket still travels round
the Earth in a closed orbit, but its path has become an ellipse. As the
speed increases still further, the ellipse becomes longer and longer
and the rocket goes far out into space. But it always returns.

"However, if we increase the rocket's initial speed to seven miles
a second the ellipse becomes a parabola—so—and the rocket has escaped for ever. Earth's gravity can never recapture it; it is now traveling through space like a tiny, man-made comet. If the Moon were in
the right position, our rocket would crash into it like the 'Orphan
Annie.'"

That, of course, was the last thing one wanted a spaceship to do.
There was a long explanation then, showing all the stages of a hypothetical lunar voyage. The commentator showed how much fuel must
be carried for a safe landing, and how much more was needed for a
safe return. He touched lightly on the problems of navigation
in space, and explained how provision could be made for the safety
of the crew. Finally he ended:

"With chemically propelled rockets we have achieved much, but to
conquer space, and not merely to make short-lived raids into it, we
must harness the limitless forces of atomic energy. At present, atomi-
cally driven rockets are still in their infancy: they are dangerous and
uncertain. But within a few years we shall have perfected them, and
mankind will have taken its first great stride along the Road to
Space."

The voice had grown louder; there was a throbbing background of
music. Then Dirk seemed to be suspended motionless in space, a few
hundred feet from the ground. There was just time for him to pick
out a few scattered buildings and to realize that he was in a rocket
that had just been launched. Then the sense of time returned: the
desert began to drop away, with accelerating speed. A range of low
hills came into view and was instantly foreshortened into flatness.
The picture was slowly rotating, and abruptly a coastline cut across
his field of vision. The scale contracted remorselessly, and with a sudden shock he realized that he was now seeing the whole coast of
Southern Australia.

The rocket was no longer accelerating, but was sweeping away from
Earth at a speed not far short of escape velocity. The twin islands of
New Zealand swam into view—and then, at the edge of the picture,
appeared a line of whiteness which for a moment he thought was
cloud.

Something seemed to catch at Dirk's throat when he realized that he was looking down upon the eternal icewalls of the Antarctic. He remembered the *Discovery*, moored not half a mile away. His eye could encompass in a moment the whole of the land over which Scott and his companions, less than a lifetime ago, had struggled and died.

And then the edge of the world reared up before him. The wonderfully efficient gyro-stabilization was beginning to fail and the camera wandered away into space. For a long time, it seemed, there was blackness and night; then, without warning, the camera came full upon the sun and the screen was blasted with light.

When the Earth returned, he could see the entire hemisphere spread beneath him. The picture froze once more and the music stilled, so that he had time to pick out the continents and oceans on that remote and unfamiliar world below.

For long minutes that distant globe hung there before his eyes; then, slowly, it dissolved. The lesson was over, but he would not soon forget it.

SEVEN

On the whole, Dirk's relations with the two young draftsmen who shared the office were cordial. They were not quite sure of his official position (that, he sometimes thought, made three of them) and so treated him with an odd mixture of deference and familiarity. There was one respect, however, in which they annoyed him intensely.

It seemed to Dirk that there were only two attitudes to adopt towards interplanetary flight. Either one was for it, or one was against it. What he could not understand was a position of complete indifference. These youngsters (he himself, of course, was a good five years older) earning their living in the very heart of Interplanetary itself, did not seem to have the slightest interest in the project. They drew their plans and made their calculations just as enthusiastically as if they were preparing drawings for washing machines instead of spaceships. They were, however, prepared to show traces of vivacity when defending their attitudes.

"The trouble with you, Doc," said the elder, Sam, one afternoon, "is that you take life too seriously. It doesn't pay. Bad for the arteries and that sort of thing."

"Unless some people did a bit of worrying," retorted Dirk, "there'd be no jobs for lazy so-and-sos like you and Bert."

"What's wrong with that?" said Bert. "They ought to be grateful. If it wasn't for chaps like Sam and me, they'd have nothing to worry about and would die of frustration. Most of 'em do, anyway."

Sam shifted his cigarette. (Did he use glue to keep it dangling from his lower lip at that improbable angle?)

"You're always agitating about the past, which is dead and done with, or the future, which we won't be around to see. Why not relax and enjoy yourself for a change?"

"I *am* enjoying myself," said Dirk. "I don't suppose you realize that there are people who happen to like work."

"They kid themselves into thinking they do," explained Bert. "It's all a matter of conditioning. We were smart enough to dodge it."

"I think," said Dirk admiringly, "that if you keep on devoting so much energy to concocting excuses to avoid work, you'll evolve a new philosophy. The philosophy of Futilitarianism."

"Did you make that up on the spur of the moment?"

"No," confessed Dirk.

"I thought not. Sounded as if you'd been saving it up."

"Tell me," Dirk asked, "don't you feel any intellectual curiosity about anything?"

"Not particularly, as long as I know where my next pay check's coming from."

They were pulling his leg, of course, and they knew he knew it. Dirk laughed and went on:

"It seems to me that Public Relations has overlooked a nice little oasis of inertia right on its own doorstep. Why, I don't believe you care a hoot whether the 'Prometheus' reaches the Moon or not!"

"I wouldn't say that," protested Sam. "I've got a fiver on her."

Before Dirk could think of a suitably blistering reply, the door was thrown open and Matthews appeared. Sam and Bert, with smoothly co-ordinated motions that eluded the eye, were instantly hard at work among their drawings.

Matthews was obviously in a hurry.

"Want a free tea?" he said.

"It depends. Where?"

"House of Commons. You were saying the other day that you'd never been there."

"This sounds interesting. What's it all about?"

"Grab your things and I'll tell you on the way."

In the taxi, Matthews relaxed and explained.

"We often get jobs like this," he said. "Mac was supposed to be coming, but he's had to go to New York and won't be back for a couple of days. So I thought you might like to come along. For the record, you can be one of our legal advisers."

"This is very thoughtful of you," said Dirk gratefully. "Who are we going to see?"

"A dear old chap named Sir Michael Flannigan. He's an Irish Tory —very much so. Some of his constituents don't hold with these new-fangled spaceships—they've probably never really got used to the Wright Brothers. So we have to go along and explain what it's all about."

"No doubt you'll succeed in allaying his doubts," said Dirk as they drove past County Hall and turned on to Westminster Bridge.

"I hope so; I've got a line which I think should fix things very nicely."

They passed under the shadow of Big Ben and drove for a hundred yards along the side of the great Gothic building. The entrance at which they stopped was an inconspicuous archway leading into a long hall which seemed very remote from the bustle of traffic in the square outside. It was cool and quiet, and to Dirk the feeling of age and centuries-old traditions was overwhelming.

Climbing a short flight of steps, they found themselves in a large chamber from which corridors radiated in several directions. A small crowd was milling around, and people sat in expectant attitudes along wooden benches. On the right a reception desk was flanked by a stout policeman in full regalia, helmet and all.

Matthews walked up to the desk, and collected a form which he filled in and handed to the policeman. Nothing happened for some time. Then a uniformed official appeared, shouted a string of quite incomprehensible words, and gathered the forms from the policeman. He then vanished down one of the corridors.

"What on earth did he say?" hissed Dirk in the silence that had suddenly descended.

"He said that Mr. Jones, Lady Carruthers, and someone else whose name I couldn't catch, aren't in the House at the moment."

The message must have been generally understood, for groups of disgruntled constituents began to drift out of the chamber, foiled of their prey.

"Now we've got to wait," said Matthews, "but it shouldn't be long, as we're expected."

From time to time in the next ten minutes other names were called, and occasionally members arrived to collect their guests. Sometimes Matthews pointed out a notable of whom Dirk had never heard, though he did his best to disguise the fact.

Presently he noticed that the policeman was pointing them out to a tall young man who was very far from his conception of an elderly Irish baronet.

The young man came over to them.

"How do you do?" he said. "My name is Fox. Sir Michael is engaged for a few moments, so he asked me to look after you. Perhaps you'd care to listen to the debate until Sir Michael's free?"

"I'm sure we would," Matthews replied, a little too heartily. Dirk guessed that the experience was not particularly novel to him, but he was delighted at the chance of witnessing Parliament in action.

They followed their guide through interminable corridors and beneath numberless archways. Finally he handed them over to an ancient attendant who might very well have witnessed the signing of Magna Charta.

"He'll find you a good seat," promised Mr. Fox. "Sir Michael will be along for you in a few minutes."

They thanked him and followed the attendant up a winding stairway.

"Who was that?" asked Dirk.

"Robert Fox—Labour M.P. for Taunton," explained Matthews. "That's one thing about the House—everyone always helps everybody else. Parties don't matter as much as outsiders might think." He turned to the attendant.

"What's being debated now?"

"The Second Reading of the Soft Drinks (Control) Bill," said the ancient in a funereal voice.

"Oh, dear!" said Matthews. "Let's hope it *is* only for a few minutes!"

The benches high in the gallery gave them a good view of the debating chamber. Photographs had made his surroundings quite familiar to Dirk, but he had always pictured a scene of animation with members rising to cry "On a point of order!" or, better still, "Shame!" "Withdraw!" and other Parliamentary noises. Instead, he saw about thirty languid gentlemen draped along the benches while a junior minister read a not-very-enthralling schedule of prices and profits. While he watched, two members simultaneously decided they had had enough and, with little curtseys to the Speaker, hastily withdrew —no doubt, thought Dirk, in search of drinks that were not particularly soft.

His attention wandered from the scene below and he examined the great chamber around him. It seemed very well preserved for its age, and it was wonderful to think of the historic scenes it had witnessed down the centuries, right back to——

"Looks pretty good, doesn't it?" whispered Matthews. "It was only finished in 1950, you know."

Dirk came back to earth with a bump.

"Good heavens! I thought it was centuries old!"

"Oh no: Hitler wrote off the earlier chamber in the Blitz."

Dirk felt rather annoyed with himself for not remembering this, and turned his attention once more to the debate. There were now fifteen members present on the Government side, while the Conservative and Labour parties on the Opposition benches could only muster a baker's dozen between them.

The paneled door against which they were sitting opened abruptly, and a smiling round face beamed at them. Matthews shot to his feet as their host greeted them with many apologies. Out in the corridor, where voices could be raised again, introductions were effected and they followed Sir Michael through yet more passages to the restaurant. Dirk decided that he had never seen so many acres of wooden paneling in his life.

The old baronet must have been well over seventy, but he walked with a springy step and his complexion was almost cherubic. His tonsured pate made the resemblance to some medieval abbot so striking that Dirk felt he had just stepped into Glastonbury or Wells before the dissolution of the monasteries. Yet if he closed his eyes, Sir Michael's accent transported him instantly to metropolitan New York. The last time he had encountered a brogue like that, its owner had been handing him a ticket for passing a "Stop" sign.

They sat down to tea and Dirk carefully declined the offer of coffee. During the meal they discussed trivialities and avoided the object of the meeting. It was only broached when they had moved out on to the long terrace flanking the Thames which, Dirk could not help thinking, was a scene of much greater activity than the debating chamber itself. Little groups of people stood or sat around, talking briskly, and there was much coming and going of messengers. Sometimes the members would, *en masse*, disengage themselves apologetically from their guests and dash off to register their votes. During one of these lacunae, Matthews did his best to make Parliamentary procedure clear to Dirk.

"You'll realize," he said, "that most of the work is done in the committee rooms. Except during important debates, only the specialists or the members who are particularly interested are actually in the Chamber. The others are working on reports or seeing constituents in their little cubbyholes all over the building."

"Now, boys," boomed Sir Michael as he returned, having collected a tray of drinks on the way, "tell me about this scheme of yours for going to the Moon."

Matthews cleared his throat, and Dirk pictured his mind running rapidly through all the possible opening gambits.

"Well, Sir Michael," he began, "it's only a logical extension of what mankind's been doing since history began. For thousands of years the human race has been spreading over the world until the whole globe has been explored and colonized. The time's now come to make the next step and to cross space to the other planets. Humanity must always have new frontiers, new horizons. Otherwise it will sooner or later sink back into decadence. Interplanetary travel's the next stage in our development, and it will be wise to take it before it's forced upon us by shortage of raw materials or space. And there are also psychological reasons for space flight. Many years ago someone likened our little Earth to a goldfish bowl inside which the human mind couldn't keep circling forever with stagnation. The world was big enough for mankind in the days of the stagecoach and the sailing ship, but it's far too small now that we can round it in a couple of hours."

Matthews leaned back to watch the effect of his shock tactics. For a moment Sir Michael looked a little dazed: then he made a quick recovery and downed the remainder of his drink.

"It's all a little overwhelming," he said ruefully. "But what will you do when you get to the Moon, anyway?"

"You must realize," said Matthews, pressing on remorselessly, "that the Moon's only the beginning. Fifteen million square miles is quite a good beginning, to be sure, but we only look upon it as a stepping-stone to the planets. As you know, there's no free air or water there, so the first colonies will have to be totally enclosed. But the low gravity will make it easy to build very large structures and plans have been drawn up for whole cities under great transparent domes."

"Seems to me," said Sir Michael shrewdly, "that you're going to take your 'goldfish bowls' with you!"

Matthews nearly smiled.

"A good point," he conceded, "but probably the Moon will be mainly used by the astronomers and physicists for scientific research. It's enormously important to them, and whole new areas of knowledge will be opened up when they can build labs and observatories up there."

"And will that make the world a better or a happier place?"

"That, as always, depends on humanity. Knowledge is neutral, but one *must* possess it to do either good or ill."

Matthews waved his arm along the great river moving sluggishly past them between its crowded banks.

"Everything you can see, everything in our modern world, is possible because of the knowledge which men won in ancient times. And civilization isn't static: if it stands still, it will die."

There was silence for a while. Almost in spite of himself, Dirk felt deeply impressed. He wondered if he had been wrong in thinking that Matthews was merely an efficient salesman, propagating the ideals of others. Was he no more than a talented instrumentalist, performing a piece of music with complete technical skill but without any real feeling? He could not be sure. Matthews, extrovert though he was, concealed depths of reserve which Dirk could never plumb. In this, though in no other respect, he filled the specifications of that fabulous creature, the typical Englishman.

"I've had a good many letters," said Sir Michael presently, "from friends of mine in Ireland who don't like the idea at all and think we were never intended to leave the Earth. What am I to say to them?"

"Remind them of history," replied Matthews. "Tell them that we're explorers, and ask them not to forget that once upon a time *someone* had to discover Ireland!" He gave Dirk a glance as if to say: "Here it comes!"

"Imagine that it's five centuries ago, Sir Michael, and that my name's Christopher Columbus. You want to know why I'm anxious to sail westward across the Atlantic, and I've tried to give you my reasons. I don't know whether they've convinced you: you may not be particularly interested in opening up a new route to the Indies. But this is the important point—neither of us can imagine just how much this voyage is going to mean to the world. *Tell your friends, Sir Michael, to think what a difference it would have made to Ireland if America had never been discovered.* The Moon's a bigger place than North and South America combined—and it's only the first and smallest of the worlds we're going to reach."

The great reception hall was almost deserted when they said good-bye to Sir Michael. He still seemed a trifle dazed when they shook hands and parted.

"I hope that settles the Irish question for a while," said Matthews as they walked out of the building into the shadow of the Victoria Tower. "What did you think of the old boy?"

"He seemed a grand character. I'd give a lot to hear him explaining your ideas to his constituents."

"Yes," Matthews replied, "that should be rather entertaining."

They walked on for a couple of yards, past the main entrance and towards the bridge. Then Matthews said abruptly:

"What do *you* think of it all, anyway?"

Dirk hedged.

"I think I agree with you—logically," he said. "But somehow I can't feel about it the way you seem to do. Later, perhaps, I may—I just can't tell."

He looked at the great city around him, throbbing with life and commerce. It seemed as ageless and eternal as the hills: whatever the future brought, surely this could never pass away! Yet Matthews had been right, and he of all people should recognize it. Civilization could never stand still. Over the very ground on which he was walking, the mammoths had once come trampling through the rushes at the river's edge. They, and not the ape-men watching from their caves, had been the masters of this land. But the day of the ape had dawned at last; the forests and swamps had given way before the might of his machines. Dirk knew now that the story was merely beginning. Even at this moment, on far worlds beneath strange suns, Time and the Gods were preparing for Man the sites of cities yet to be.

EIGHT

Sir Robert Derwent, M.A., F.R.S., Director-General of Interplanetary, was a rather tough-looking character who invariably reminded people of the late Winston Churchill. The resemblance was somewhat spoiled by his addiction to pipes, of which, according to rumor, he possessed two varieties—"Normal" and "Emergency." The "Emergency" model was always kept fully fueled so that it could be brought into action at once when unwelcome visitors arrived. The secret mixture used for this purpose was believed to consist largely of sulphurated tea leaves.

Sir Robert was such a striking personality that a host of legends had grown up around him. Many of these had been concocted by his assistants, who would have gone through Hell for their chief—and frequently did, since his command of language was not that normally expected of an ex-Astronomer Royal. He was no respecter of persons or properties, and some of his retorts to famous but not excessively intelligent questioners had become historic. Even Royalty had been glad to disengage itself from his fire on one celebrated occasion. Yet despite all this façade, he was at heart a kindly and sensitive person. A good many people suspected this, but very few had ever been able to prove it to their satisfaction.

At the age of sixty, and three times a grandfather, Sir Robert appeared to be a rather well-preserved forty-five. Like his historic double, he attributed this to a careful neglect of all the elementary rules of health and a steady intake of nicotine. A brilliant reporter had once aptly called him "a scientific Francis Drake—one of the astronomical explorers of the Second Elizabethan Age."

There was nothing very Elizabethan about the Director-General as he sat reading the day's mail beneath a faint nimbus of tobacco smoke. He dealt with his correspondence at an astonishing rate, stacking the letters in small piles as he finished them. From time to time he filed a communication directly into the wastepaper basket, from which his staff would carefully retrieve it for inclusion in a voluminous folder with the elegant title "NUTS." About one per cent of Interplanetary's incoming mail came under this category.

He had just finished when the office door opened and Dr. Groves, Interplanetary's psychological adviser, came in with a file of reports. Sir Robert looked at him morosely.

"Well, you bird of ill-omen—what's all this fuss about young Hassell? I thought that everything was under control."

Groves looked worried as he laid down the folder.

"So did I, until a few weeks ago. Until then all five of the boys were shaping well and showing no signs of strain. Then we noticed that Vic was being worried by something, and I finally had it out with him yesterday."

"It's his wife, I suppose?"

"Yes. The whole thing's very unfortunate. Vic's just the sort of father who gives trouble at the best of times, and Maude Hassell doesn't know that he'll probably be on his way to the Moon when the boy arrives."

The D.-G. raised his eyebrows.

"You know it's a boy?"

"The Weismann-Mathers treatment is ninety-five per cent certain. Vic wanted a son—just in case he didn't get back."

"I see. How do you think Mrs. Hassell will react when she knows? Of course, it still isn't certain that Vic *is* going to be in the crew."

"I think she'll be all right. But Vic's the one who's worrying. How did you feel when *your* first kid arrived?"

Sir Robert grinned.

"That's digging into the past. As it happens, I was away myself—on an eclipse expedition. I very nearly smashed a coronograph, so I understand Vic's point of view. But it's a damned nuisance; you'll just have to reason with him. Tell him to have it out with his wife, but ask her not to say anything. Are there any other complications likely to arise?"

"Not that I can foresee. But you never can tell."

"No, you can't, can you?"

The Director-General's eyes strayed to the little motto in its frame at the back of his desk. Dr. Groves could not see them from where he sat, but he knew the lines by heart and they had often intrigued him:

> *"There is always a thing forgotten*
> *Whenever the world goes well."*

One day, he'd have to ask where that came from.

PART TWO

Two hundred and seventy miles above the Earth, "Beta" was making her third circuit of the globe. Skirting the atmosphere like a tiny satellite, she was completing one revolution every ninety minutes. Unless the pilot turned on her motors again, she would remain here forever, on the frontiers of space.

Yet, "Beta" was a creature of the upper atmosphere rather than the deeps of space. Like those fish which sometimes clamber onto the land, she was venturing outside her true element, and her great wings were now useless sheets of metal burning beneath the savage sun. Not until she returned to the air far beneath would they be of any service again.

Fixed upon "Beta's" back was a streamlined torpedo that might, at first glance, have been taken for another rocket. But there were no observation ports, no motor nozzles, no signs of landing gear. The sleek metal shape was almost featureless, like a giant bomb awaiting the moment of release. It was the first of the fuel containers for "Alpha," holding tons of liquid methane which would be pumped into the spaceship's tanks when it was ready to make its voyage.

"Beta" seemed to be hanging motionless against the ebon sky, while the Earth itself turned beneath her. The technicians aboard the ship, checking their instruments and relaying their findings to the control stations on the planet below, were in no particular hurry. It made little difference to them whether they circled the Earth once or a dozen times. They would stay in their orbit until they were satisfied with their tests—unless, as the chief engineer had remarked, they were forced down earlier by a shortage of cigarettes.

Presently, minute puffs of gas spurted along the line of contact between "Beta" and the fuel tank upon her back. The explosive bolts connecting them had been sheared: slowly, at the rate of a few feet a minute, the great tank began to drift away from the ship.

In the hull of "Beta" an airlock door opened and two men floated out in their unwieldy spacesuits. With short bursts of gas from tiny cylinders, they directed themselves towards the drifting fuel tank and began to inspect it carefully. One of them opened a little hatch and

43

started to take instrument readings, while the other began a survey of the hull with a portable leak detector.

Nothing else happened for nearly an hour, apart from occasional spurts of vapor from "Beta's" auxiliary steering jets. The pilot was turning her so that she pointed against her orbital motion, and was obviously taking his time over the maneuver. A distance of nearly a hundred feet now lay between "Beta" and the fuel tank she had carried up from Earth. It was hard to realize that during their slow separation the two bodies had almost circled the Earth.

The space-suited engineers had finished their task. Slowly they jetted back to the waiting ship and the airlock door closed again behind them. There was another long pause as the pilot waited for the exact moment to begin braking.

Quite suddenly, a stream of unbearable incandescence jetted from "Beta's" stern. The white-hot gases seemed to form a solid bar of light. To the men in the ship, normal weight would have returned again as the motors started to thrust. Every five seconds, "Beta" was losing a hundred miles an hour of her speed. She was breaking her orbit, and would soon be falling back to Earth.

The intolerable flame of the atomic rocket flickered and died. Once more the little controlling jets spurted vapor: the pilot was in a hurry now as he swung the ship round on her axis again. Out in space, one orientation was as good as another—but in a few minutes the ship would be entering the atmosphere and must be pointing in the direction of her motion.

It would always be a tense moment, waiting for that first contact. To the men in the ship, it came in the form of a gentle but irresistible tugging of their seat-straps. Slowly it increased, minute by minute, until presently there came the faintest whisper of sound through the insulation of the wall. They were trading altitude for speed—speed which they could only lose against air-resistance. If the rate of exchange was too great, the stubby wings would snap, the hull would turn to molten metal, and the ship would crash in meteoric ruin down through a hundred miles of sky.

The wings were biting again into the thin air streaming past them at eighteen thousand miles an hour. Although the control surfaces were still useless, the ship would soon be responding sluggishly to their commands. Even without the use of his engines, the pilot could choose a landing spot almost anywhere on Earth. He was flying a hypersonic glider whose speed had given it world-wide range.

Very slowly, the ship was settling down through the stratosphere, losing speed minute by minute. At little more than a thousand miles an hour, the air-scoops of the ramjets were opened and the atomic furnaces began to glow with deadly life. Streams of burning air were being blasted from the nozzles and in its wake the ship was leaving the familiar reddish-brown tinge of nitric oxides. It was riding the atmosphere again, safely under power, and could turn once more for home.

The final test was over. Almost three hundred miles above, exchanging night and day every forty minutes, the first fuel tank was spinning in its eternal orbit. In a few days its companions would be launched in the same path, by the same means. They would be lashed together, awaiting the moment when they would pour their contents into the empty tanks of "Alpha" and speed the spaceship on the journey to the Moon. . . .

ONE

As Matthews put it, the "Department of Negative Publicity" had gone into forward gear at last—and once started, it changed rapidly into top. The successful launching of the first fuel container, and the safe return of "Beta" showed that everything that could be checked was functioning perfectly. The now fully trained crew would be leaving for Australia in a few days, and the need for secrecy was past.

A hilarious morning was spent at Southbank as the Press reports of the first visit to the "Nursery" came in. The science editors of the great dailies had, as usual, produced reasonably accurate accounts: but some of the smaller papers, who had sent along sports reporters, dramatic critics, or anyone else who happened to be handy, had printed some truly marvelous stories. Matthews spent most of the day in a state of mingled mirth and mortification, launching a telephonic barrage in the general direction of Fleet Street. Dirk warned him that it would be wise to save most of his indignation for the arrival of the transatlantic Press reports.

Hassell, Leduc, Clinton, Richards and Taine promptly became the targets of almost unparalleled curiosity. Their life-stories (thoughtfully mimeographed well in advance by Public Relations) were promptly serialized in newspapers all over the world. Offers of matrimony poured in by every post, descending impartially upon the married and the unmarried men alike. Begging letters also arrived in hordes: as Richards remarked wryly: "Everyone except life-insurance agents wants to sell us *something*."

The affairs of Interplanetary were now moving towards their climax with the smoothness of a military operation. In a week, the crew and all the higher staff would be leaving for Australia. With them would go everyone else who could possibly think of a suitable excuse. During the next few days many preoccupied expressions were to be seen around the building. Junior clerks had a habit of suddenly discovering sick aunts in Sydney or impecunious cousins in Canberra who required their presence immediately.

The idea of the farewell party had, it seemed, originated in the Director-General's mind and had been enthusiastically taken up by McAndrews, who was annoyed at not having thought of it himself. All the Headquarters staff was to be invited, as well as large numbers of people from industry, the Press, the universities and the innumerable organizations with which Interplanetary had dealings. After much whittling of lists and a good deal of heartburning, just over seven hundred invitations had been sent out. Even the Chief Accountant, still boggling at the thought of a two-thousand-pound "hospitality" item, had been brought to heel by threats of exclusion.

There were a few who thought that these celebrations were premature and it would be better to wait until the "Prometheus" returned. To these critics it was pointed out that many of the workers on the project would not be returning to London after the launch, but would be going back to their own countries. This was the last opportunity of getting them all together. Pierre Leduc summed up the crew's attitude when he said: "If we come back, we'll have enough parties then to last us the rest of our lives. If we *don't*, then you ought to give us a good send-off."

The hotel selected for the Bacchanalia was one of the best in London, but not one so good that only a few of the executives and practically none of the scientists would feel at ease. Speeches, it had been solemnly promised, would be kept to a minimum to leave as much time as possible for the proper business. This suited Dirk, who had a hatred for orations but a considerable fondness for banquets and buffets.

He arrived ten minutes before the official time, and found Matthews pacing up and down the foyer, flanked by a couple of muscular waiters. He indicated them without a smile.

"My strong-arm men," he said. "Look carefully, and you can see the bulges in their hip-pockets. We expect lots of gate-crashers, particularly from the section of Fleet Street we haven't invited. I'm afraid you'll have to look after yourself tonight, but the chaps with 'Steward' on their lapels will tell you who's who if there's anyone you want to meet."

"That's all right," said Dirk, checking his hat and coat. "I hope you get time to have a snack now and then while you're holding the fort."

"My emergency reserves are well organized. You'll get your drinks, by the way, from the chaps labeled 'Fuel Technician.' We've called all the drinks after some rocket fuel or other, so no one will know what they've got until they drink it—if then. But I'll give you a tip."

"What's that?"

"*Lay off the hydrazine hydrate!*"

"Thanks for the warning," laughed Dirk. He was somewhat relieved to find, a few minutes later, that Matthews had been pulling his leg and that no such disguises had been employed.

The place filled rapidly in the next half-hour. Dirk did not know more than one person in twenty, and felt a little out in the cold. Consequently he kept somewhat nearer the bar than was altogether good for him. From time to time he nodded to acquaintances, but most of them were too fully engaged elsewhere to join him. He was rather glad when another equally unattached guest settled down beside him in search of company.

They got into conversation in a somewhat desultory manner, and after a while the talk came around, inevitably, to the approaching adventure.

"By the way," said the stranger, "I've not seen you around Interplanetary before. Have you been here long?"

"Only three weeks or so," said Dirk. "I'm on a special job for the University of Chicago."

"Indeed?"

Dirk felt talkative, and the other seemed to show a flattering interest in his affairs.

"I've got to write the official history of the first voyage and the events leading up to it. This trip is going to be one of the most important things that's ever happened, and it's necessary to have a complete record for the future."

"But surely there'll be thousands of technical reports and newspaper accounts?"

"Quite true: but you forget that they'll be written for contemporaries and will assume a background which may only be familiar to present-day readers. I have to try and stand outside of Time, as it were, and produce a record which can be read with full understanding ten thousand years from today."

"Phew! Some job!"

"Yes: it's only become possible recently through the new developments in the study of language and meaning, and the perfection of symbolic vocabularies. But I'm afraid I'm boring you."

To his annoyance, the other didn't contradict him.

"I suppose," said the stranger casually, "you've got to know the people round here pretty well. I mean, you're in rather a privileged position."

"That's true: they've looked after me excellently and helped me all they could."

"There goes young Hassell," said his companion. "He looks a bit worried, but so would I in his shoes. Have you got to know the crew at all well?"

"Not yet, though I hope to do so. I've spoken to Hassell and Leduc a couple of times, but that's all."

"Who do you think's going to be chosen for the trip?"

Dirk was about to give his not-very-well-informed views on this subject when he saw Matthews frantically signaling to him from the other side of the room. For a moment alarming possibilities of sartorial disaster raced through his mind. Then a slow suspicion dawned, and with a mumbled excuse he disengaged himself from his companion.

A few moments later, Matthews confirmed his fears.

"Mike Wilkins is one of the best—we used to work together on the *News*. But for goodness' sake be careful what you say to him. If you'd murdered your wife he'd get it out of you by asking leading questions about the weather."

"Still, I don't think there's much I could tell him that he doesn't know already."

"Don't you believe it. Before you know where you are, you'll be featured in the paper as 'an important official of Interplanetary' and I'll be sending out the usual ineffective disclaimers."

"I see. How many other reporters have we got among our guests?"

"About twelve were *invited*," said Matthews darkly. "I should just avoid all heart-to-heart talks with people you don't know. Excuse me now—I must go back on guard duty."

As far as he was concerned, thought Dirk, the party was hardly going with a swing. The Public Relations Department seemed to have an obsession about security, which Dirk considered they had pushed to extremes. However, he could understand Matthews's horror of unofficial interviews—he had seen some of their gruesome results.

For quite a time after this Dirk's attention was fully occupied by an astonishingly pretty girl who appeared to have arrived without an escort—a fact somewhat surprising in itself. He had just, after much vacillation, decided to step into the breach when it became all too obvious that the escort had merely been engaged on convoy duties elsewhere. Dirk hadn't missed his opportunity: he had never had one. He turned once more to philosophical musings.

His spirits, however, revived considerably during dinner. The meal itself was excellent and even the Director-General's speech (which set a limit for all the others) only lasted ten minutes. It was, as far as Dirk could remember, an extremely witty address full of private jokes which produced roars of laughter in some quarters and sickly smiles in others. Interplanetary had always been fond of laughing at itself in private, but only recently could it afford the luxury of doing so in public.

The remaining few orations were even shorter: several speakers would clearly have liked more time, but dared not take it. Finally McAndrews, who had acted throughout as a very efficient Master of Ceremonies, called a toast for the success of the "Prometheus" and her crew.

Afterwards there was much dancing to the gentle, nostalgic rhythms so popular in the late '70's. Dirk, who was a very bad dancer at the best of times, made several erratic circuits with Mrs. Matthews and the wives of other officials before an increasing lack of muscular co-ordination warned him off the field. He then sat watching the proceedings through a benevolent glow, thinking what nice people all his friends were and tut-tutting slightly when he noticed dancers who had obviously taken aboard just a little too much "fuel."

It must have been around midnight when he suddenly became aware that someone was speaking to him. (He hadn't been asleep, of course, but it was refreshing to close one's eyes now and then.) He turned sluggishly and found a tall, middle-aged man watching him with some amusement from the next chair. To Dirk's surprise, he was not in evening dress and did not seem to be worried by the fact.

"I saw your fraternity badge," said the other by way of introduction. "I'm Sigma Xi myself. Only got back from California this evening—too late for the dinner."

So that explained the dress, thought Dirk, feeling rather pleased with himself at so brilliant a piece of deduction. He shook hands, glad to meet a fellow Californian—though he couldn't catch the name. It seemed to be something like Mason, but it didn't really matter.

For some time they discussed American affairs and speculated on the Democrats' chances of returning to power. Dirk contended that the Liberals would once again hold the balance, and made some brilliant comments on the advantages and disadvantages of the three-party system. Strangely enough, his companion seemed unimpressed by his wit, and brought the conversation back to Interplanetary.

"You haven't been here very long, have you?" he queried. "How are you getting on?"

Dirk told him, at length. He explained his job, and enlarged lavishly upon its scope and importance. When he had finished his work, all subsequent eras and all possible planets would realize exactly what the conquest of space had meant to the age which had achieved it.

His friend seemed very interested, though there was a trace of amusement in his voice about which Dirk might have to reprimand him, gently but firmly.

"How have you got on in your contacts with the technical side?" he asked.

"To tell the truth," said Dirk sadly, "I've been intending to do something about this for the last week. But I'm rather scared of scientists, you know. Besides, there's Matthews. He's been very helpful, but he has his own ideas of what I should do and I'm anxious not to hurt his feelings."

That was a deplorably weak sort of statement, but there was a lot of truth in it. Matthews had organized everything a little too completely.

Thinking of Alfred brought back memories, and Dirk was filled with a sudden grave suspicion. He looked carefully at his companion, determined not to be caught again.

The fine profile and the wide, intelligent brow were reassuring, but Dirk was now too old a hand at the game to be deceived. Alfred, he thought, would be proud of the way he was evading definite answers to his companion's queries. It was rather a pity, of course, since the other was a fellow American and had come a long way in search of a "scoop"; still, his first loyalty now was with his hosts.

The other must have realized that he was getting nowhere, for presently he rose to his feet and gave Dirk a quizzical smile.

"I think," he said, as he took his leave, "that I may be able to put you in touch with the right people on the technical side. Ring me tomorrow at Extension 3—don't forget—3."

Then he was gone, leaving Dirk in a highly confused state of mind. His fears, it seemed, had been groundless: the fellow belonged to Interplanetary after all. Oh well, it couldn't be helped.

His next clear recollection was saying good-night to Matthews in the foyer. Alfred still seemed annoyingly bright and energetic, and very pleased with the success of the party—though it seemed that he had suffered from qualms from time to time.

"During that horn-pipe," he said, "I was quite certain that the floor was going to give way. Do you realize that would have delayed the conquest of space by at least half a century?"

Dirk did not feel particularly interested in such metaphysical speculations, but as he bade a sleepy good-night he suddenly remembered his unknown Californian.

"By the way," he said, "I got talking with another American—thought he was a journalist at first. He'd just arrived in town—you must have seen him—he wasn't wearing evening dress. Told me to ring him tomorrow at extension something-or-other. Know who he was?"

Matthews's eyes twinkled.

"You thought he was another journalist, did you? I hope you remembered my warning."

"Yes," said Dirk proudly. "I never told him a thing. Though it wouldn't have mattered, would it?"

Matthews pushed him into the cab and slammed the door. He leaned through the window for his parting words.

"No, it certainly wouldn't," he said. "That was only Professor Maxton, the Deputy Director-General. Go home and sleep it off!"

TWO

Dirk managed to arrive at the office in time for lunch—a meal which, he noticed, did not seem very popular. He had never seen so few customers in the canteen before.

When he rang up Extension 3 and introduced himself sheepishly, Professor Maxton seemed glad to hear him and invited him round at once. He found the Deputy D.-G. in the next office to Sir Robert Derwent, almost surrounded with packing cases—holding, he explained, special test gear which was to be flown to Australia at once. Their conversation was frequently interrupted by the Professor's orders and counter-orders to his perspiring assistants as they checked through their equipment.

"I'm sorry if I seemed a bit offhand last night," said Dirk apologetically. "The fact is, I wasn't quite myself."

"I gathered that," said Maxton dryly. "After all, you had several hours' start on me! Hi, you dope, don't carry that recorder upside down! Sorry, Alexson, I didn't mean you."

He paused for breath.

"This is an infernal business—you never know what you'll want and you can be pretty sure that in the end the most important stuff will get left behind."

"What's it all for?" asked Dirk, quite overcome by the arrays of glittering equipment and the sight of more radio tubes than he had ever seen before at any one time in his life.

"Post-mortem gear," said Maxton succinctly. "'Alpha's' main instrument readings are telemetered back to Earth. If anything goes wrong, at least we'll know what happened."

"This isn't very cheerful talk after last night's gaiety."

"No, but it's practical talk and may save millions of dollars, as well as a good many lives. I've heard all about your project in the States, and thought it was a very interesting idea. Who started it?"

"The Rockefeller Foundation—History and Records Division."

"I'm glad the historians have finally realized that science does play quite a part in shaping the world. When I was a kid their textbooks were nothing but limitary primers. Then the economic determinists held the field—until the neo-Freudians routed them with great slaughter. We've only just got that lot under control—so let's hope we're going to get a balanced view at last."

"That's exactly what I'm aiming at," said Dirk. "I realize that all sorts of motives must have inspired the man who founded Interplanetary. I want to unravel and analyze them as far as possible. On the factual side, I've been supplied with everything I want by Matthews."

"Matthews? Oh, the chap from Public Relations. They think they run the place—don't believe everything they tell you, especially about us."

Dirk laughed.

"I thought that Interplanetary was all one big, happy family!"

"On the whole we get along pretty well, especially at the top. At least, we present a united front to the outside world. As a class, I think scientists work together better than any other, especially when they have a common goal. But you always have clashing personalities, and there seems an inevitable rivalry between the technical and the non-technical grades. Sometimes it's just good-natured fun, but often there's a certain amount of bitterness behind it."

While Maxton was speaking, Dirk had been studying him carefully. His first impression had been confirmed. The D.D.-G. was not only a man of obvious brilliance, but one of wide culture and sympathies. Dirk wondered how he got on with his equally brilliant but ferociously forthright colleague, Sir Robert. Two such contrasting personalities would either work together very well—or not at all.

At the age of fifty, Professor Maxton was generally regarded as the world's leading atomic engineer. He had played a major part in the development of nuclear propulsion systems for aircraft, and the drive units of the "Prometheus" were based almost entirely on his designs. The fact that such a man, who could have demanded almost any price from industry, was willing to work here at a nominal salary, seemed to Dirk a very significant point.

Maxton called out to a fair-haired young man in the late twenties who was just passing.

"Come here a minute, Ray—I've got another job for you!"

The other approached with a rueful grin.

"I hope it's nothing tough. I've got a bit of a headache this morning."

The D.D.-G. grinned at Dirk but refrained, after an obvious struggle, from making any comment.

He introduced them briefly.

"Dr. Alexson—Ray Collins, my personal assistant. Ray's line is hyperdynamics—short, but only just, for hypersonic aerodynamics, in case you didn't know. Ray—Dr. Alexson's a history specialist, so I guess you wonder what he's doing here. He hopes to be the Gibbon of astronautics."

"Not the 'Decline and Fall of Interplanetary,' I hope! Pleased to meet you."

"I want you to help Dr. Alexson with any technical queries. I've only just rescued him from the clammy clutches of McAndrews's mob, so he'll probably have some pretty weird ideas about things."

He turned to survey the surrounding chaos, found that his assistants were undermining the precarious seat he had adopted, and shifted to another packing case.

"I'd better explain," he continued, "though you probably know it already, that our little technical empire has three main divisions. Ray here is one of the airborne experts; he's concerned with getting the ship safely through the atmosphere—in both directions—with the minimum of wear and tear. His section used to be looked down upon by the spacehounds, who regarded the atmosphere as just a nuisance. They've changed their tune now that we've shown them how to use the air as a free fuel supply—for the first part of the trip at least."

That was one of the hundred or so points that Dirk had never properly understood, and he made a mental note, putting it first on his list of questions.

"Then there are the astronomers and mathematicians, who form a tight little trade-union of their own—though they've suffered some pretty heavy infiltration from the electronics engineers with their calculating machines. They, of course, have to compute orbits and do our mathematical donkey-work, which is very extensive indeed. Sir Robert himself is in charge of their affairs.

"Finally there are the rocket engineers, bless 'em. You won't find many here, for they're nearly all in Australia.

"So that's the set-up, though I've neglected several groups like the communications and control people, and the medical experts. I'll turn you over to Ray now, and he'll look after you."

Dirk winced slightly at the phrase; he felt that rather too many people had been "looking after him." Collins led him to a small office not far away where they sat down and exchanged cigarettes. After puffing thoughtfully for some time, the aerodynamicist jerked his thumb towards the door and remarked:

"What do you think of the Chief?"

"I'm a bit biased, you know; we're from the same State. He seems a most remarkable man—cultured as well as technically brilliant. It's not a usual combination. And he's been very helpful."

Collins began to wax enthusiastic.

"That's perfectly true. He's the best chap you could possibly work for, and I don't think he has a single enemy. That's quite a contrast to Sir Robert, who has dozens among people who know him only slightly."

"I've met the Director-General only once. I didn't know quite what to make of him."

Collins laughed.

"It takes a long time to get used to the D.-G.—he certainly hasn't Professor Maxton's easy charm. If you do a job badly, the D.-G. will burn your ears off while the Prof. will give you a hurt look that makes you feel like a professional baby-poisoner. Both techniques work perfectly, and everyone's very fond of Sir Robert when they get to know him."

Dirk examined the room with more than casual interest. It was a typical small drafting room with a modern internally illuminated tracing table occupying one corner. The walls were covered with elaborate and obscure graphs, interspersed with photographs of rockets removing themselves spectacularly to distant parts. A place of honor was given to a magnificent view of the Earth from a height of at least a thousand miles. Dirk guessed it was a still from the film that Matthews had arranged for him to see. On Collins's desk was a photograph of quite a different sort—a portrait of a very pretty girl whom Dirk thought he had seen once or twice at lunch. Collins must have noticed his interest, but as he didn't elucidate Dirk guessed that he was still unmarried and, like himself, an optimistic bachelor.

"I suppose," the aerodynamicist said presently, "you've seen our film, 'The Road to Space'?"

"Yes, I thought it was very good."

"It saves a lot of talking and puts over the basic ideas pretty clearly. But of course it's rather out-of-date now, and I guess you're still very much in the dark about the latest developments—particularly the atomic drive in the 'Prometheus.'"

"That's true," said Dirk. "It's a complete mystery to me."

Collins gave a puzzled little grin.

"That baffles us," he complained. "From the technical point of view, it's far simpler than the internal combustion engine which everyone understands perfectly. But for some reason, people assume that an atomic drive *must* be incomprehensible, so they won't even make an effort to understand it."

"I'll make the effort," Dirk laughed. "It's up to you to do the rest. But please remember—I want to know only just enough to follow what's happening. I've no intention of setting myself up as a designer of spaceships!"

THREE

"I suppose I can assume," said Collins, a little doubtfully, "that you're quite happy about common-or-garden rockets and understand how they work in a vacuum?"

"I can see," replied Dirk, "that if you throw a lot of matter away from you at great speed, there's bound to be a recoil."

"Good. It's amazing how many people still seem to think that a rocket has to have 'something to push against,' as they invariably put it. You'll appreciate, then, that a rocket designer is always trying to get the maximum possible velocity—and a bit more—from the jet which drives his machine forward. Obviously, the speed of the exhaust determines the velocity which his rocket will attain.

"The old chemical rockets, like V.2, had jet speeds of one or two miles a second. With such performances, to carry a load of one ton to the Moon and back would have needed several *thousand* tons of fuel, which wasn't practicable. What everyone wanted was a weightless fuel supply. Atomic reactions, which are a million or more times as powerful as chemical ones, virtually gave us this. The energy released by the few pounds of matter in the first atomic bombs could have taken a thousand tons to the Moon—and back.

"But though the energy had been released, no one knew exactly how to use it for propulsion. That little problem has only just been solved, and it's taken thirty years to produce the very inefficient atomic rockets we have today.

"Look at the problem from this point of view. In the chemical rocket, we get our driving exhaust by burning a fuel and letting the hot gases acquire speed by expanding through a nozzle. In other words, we exchange heat for velocity—the hotter our combustion chamber, the faster the jet will leave it. We'd get the same result if we didn't actually burn the fuel at all, but heated the combustion chamber from some outside source. In other words, we could make a rocket by pumping any gas we liked—even air—into a heating unit, and then letting it expand through a nozzle. O.K.?"

"Yes, that's straightforward enough so far."

"Very well. Now as you know, you can get as much heat as you like out of an atomic pile by making it of richer and richer materials. If you overdo it, of course, the pile will melt down into a puddle of liquid uranium with carbon bobbing about on the surface. Long before that sort of thing happened, any sensible man would have got hull-down over the horizon."

"You mean it might go up like an atomic bomb?"

"No, it couldn't do that. But an unapproachable radioactive furnace could be just as nasty in its quiet way. However, don't look so alarmed—this couldn't happen if the most elementary precautions were taken.

"We had, then, to design some kind of atomic reactor which would heat a gas stream to a very high temperature indeed—at least 4,000 degrees Centigrade. Since all known metals melt a long way below this, the problem gave us a bit of a headache!

"The answer we produced is called the 'line-focused reactor.' It's a long, thin, plutonium pile, and gas is pumped in at one end and becomes heated as it travels through. The final result is a central core of intensely hot gas into which we can concentrate or focus the heat from the surrounding elements. In the middle the jet temperature is over 6,000 degrees—hotter than the sun—but where it touches the walls it's only a quarter of this.

"So far, I haven't said *what* gas we're going to use. I think you'll realize that the lighter it is—strictly speaking, the lower its molecular weight—the faster it will be moving when it comes out of the jet. Since hydrogen is the lightest of all elements, it would be the ideal fuel, with helium a fairly good runner-up. I ought to explain, by the way, that we still use the word 'fuel,' even though we don't actually burn it but simply use it as a working fluid."

"That's one thing that had me puzzled," confessed Dirk. "The old chemical rockets carried their own oxygen tanks, and it's a bit disconcerting to find that the present machines don't do anything of the sort."

Collins laughed.

"We could even use helium as a 'fuel,'" he said, "though that won't burn at all—or indeed take part in any chemical reaction.

"Now although hydrogen's the ideal working fluid, as I called it, it's impossible stuff to carry round. In the liquid state it boils at a fantastically low temperature, and it's so light that a spaceship would have to have fuel tanks the size of gasometers. So we carry it combined with carbon in the form of liquid methane—CH_4—which isn't hard to handle and has a reasonable density. In the reactor it breaks down to carbon and hydrogen. The carbon's a bit of a nuisance, and tends to clog the works, but it can't be helped. Every so often we get rid of it by turning off the main jet and flushing out the motor with a draft of oxygen. It makes quite a pretty firework display.

"That, then, is the principle of the spaceship's motors. They give exhaust speeds three times that of any chemical rocket, but even so, we still have to carry a tremendous amount of fuel. And there are all sorts of other problems I've not mentioned: shielding the crew from the pile radiations was the worst.

"'Alpha,' the upper component of the 'Prometheus,' weighs about three hundred tons of which two hundred and forty are fuel. If it starts from an orbit around the Earth, it can just make the landing on the Moon and return with a small reserve.

"It has, as you know, to be carried up to that orbit by 'Beta.' 'Beta' is a very heavy, super-high-speed flying-wing, also powered by atomic jets. She starts as a ramjet, using air as 'fuel,' and only switches over to her methane tanks when she leaves the top of the atmosphere. As you'll realize, not having to carry any fuel for the first stage of the journey helps things enormously.

"At take-off, the 'Prometheus' weighs five hundred tons, and is not only the fastest but the heaviest of all flying machines. To get it airborne, Westinghouse has built us a five-mile-long electric launching track out in the desert. It cost nearly as much as the ship itself, but of course it will be used over and over again.

"To sum up, then: we launch the two components together and they climb until the air's too thin to operate the ramjets any more. 'Beta' then switches over to her fuel tanks and reaches circular velocity at a height of about three hundred miles. 'Alpha,' of course, hasn't used any fuel at all—in fact, its tanks are almost empty when 'Beta' carries it up.

"Once the 'Prometheus' has homed on the fuel containers we've got circling up there, the two ships separate, 'Alpha' couples up to the tanks with pipe-lines and pumps the fuel aboard. We've already practiced this sort of thing and know it can be done. Orbital refueling, it's called, and it's really the key to the whole problem, because it lets us do the job in several stages. It would be quite impossible to build one huge spaceship that would make the journey to the Moon and back on a single load of fuel.

"Once 'Alpha's' tanked up, it runs its motors until it's built up the extra two miles a second to get out of its orbit and go to the Moon. It reaches the Moon after four days, stays there a week and then returns, getting back into the same orbit as before. The crew transfers to 'Beta,' which is still patiently circling with her very bored pilot (who won't get any of the publicity) and is brought down to Earth again. And that's all there is to it. What could be simpler?"

"You make me wonder," laughed Dirk, "why it hasn't been done years ago."

"That's the usual reaction," said Collins in mock disgust. "It's not easy for outsiders to realize the terrific problems that had to be overcome in almost every stage of the work. That's where the time and money went. It wouldn't have been possible, even now, without the world-wide research that's been going on for the last thirty years. Most of our job was collecting the results of other people's work and adapting them to our use."

"How much," said Dirk thoughtfully, "would you say the 'Prometheus' cost?"

"It's almost impossble to say. The research of the world's laboratories for two generations, right back to the 1920's, has gone into the machine. You should include the two billion dollars the atomic bomb project cost, the hundreds of millions of marks the Germans put into Peenemünde, and the scores of millions of pounds the British Government spent on the Australian range."

"I agree, but you must have some idea of the money that actually went into the 'Prometheus' itself."

"Well, even there we got quite priceless technical assistance—and equipment—for nothing. However, Professor Maxton once calculated that the ship's cost about ten million pounds in research and five millions in direct construction. That means, someone pointed out, that we're buying the Moon for a pound a square mile! It doesn't seem a lot, and of course the later ships will be a good deal cheaper. Incidentally, I believe we're almost recovering our expenses for the first trip on the film and radio rights! But who cares about the money, anyway?"

His eyes wandered towards that photograph of the distant Earth, and his voice became suddenly thoughtful.

"We're gaining the freedom of the whole Universe, and all that that implies. I don't think it can be valued in terms of pounds and dollars. In the long run, knowledge always pays for itself in hard cash —but it's still absolutely beyond price."

FOUR

Dirk's meeting with Professor Maxton and Raymond Collins marked an unconscious turning point in his thinking, and indeed in his way of life. He felt, perhaps wrongly, that he had now found the source of the ideas which McAndrews and Matthews had passed on to him at second hand.

No one could have been more unlike the coldly passionless scientist of fiction than the Deputy Director-General. He was not only a first-class engineer, but he was obviously fully aware of the implications of his work. It would be a fascinating study to discover the motives which had led him, and his colleagues, into this field. The quest for personal power did not seem a likely explanation in the cases that Dirk had met. He must guard against wishful thinking, but these men seemed to have a disinterested outlook which was very refreshing. Interplanetary was inspired by a missionary zeal which technical competence and a sense of humor had preserved from fanaticism.

Dirk was still only partly aware of the effects his new surroundings were having on his own character. He was losing much of his diffidence; the thought of meeting strangers, which not long ago had filled him with mild apprehension or at least with annoyance, no longer worried him at all. For the first time in his life, he was with men who were shaping the future and not merely interpreting the dead past. Though he was only an onlooker, he was beginning to share their emotions and to feel with their triumphs and defeats.

"I'm quite impressed," he wrote in his Journal that evening, "by Professor Maxton and his staff. They seem to have a much clearer and wider view of Interplanetary's aims than the non-technical people I've met. Matthews, for instance, is always talking about the scientific advances which will come when we reach the Moon. Perhaps because they take that sort of thing for granted, the scientists themselves seem more interested in the cultural and philosophical repercussions. But I mustn't generalize from a few cases which may not be typical.

"I feel that I've now a pretty clear view of the whole organization. It's now mostly a matter of filling in details, and I should be able to do that from my notes and the mass of photostats I've collected. I no longer have the impression of being a stranger watching some incomprehensible machine at work. In fact, I now feel that I'm almost a part of the organization—though I mustn't let myself get too involved. It's impossible to be neutral, but *some* detachment is necessary.

"Until now I've had various doubts and reservations concerning space flight. I felt, subconsciously, that it was too big a thing for man. Like Pascal, I was terrified by the silence and emptiness of infinite space. I see now that I was wrong.

"The mistake I made was the old one of clinging to the past. Today I met men who think as naturally in millions of miles as I do in thousands. Once there was a time when a thousand miles was a distance beyond all comprehension, yet now it is the space we cover between one meal and the next. That change of scale is about to occur again—and with unprecedented swiftness.

"The planets, I see now, are no further away than our minds will make them. It will take the 'Prometheus' a hundred hours to reach the Moon, and all the time she will be speaking to Earth and the eyes of the world will be upon her. How little a thing interplanetary travel seems if we match it against the weeks and the months and the years of the great voyages of the past!

"Everything is relative, and the time will surely come when our minds embrace the Solar System as now they do the Earth. Then, I suppose, when the scientists are looking thoughtfully towards the stars, many will cry: 'We don't want interstellar flight! The nine planets were good enough for our grandfathers and they're good enough for us!'"

Dirk laid his pen down with a smile and let his mind wander in the realms of fantasy. Would Man ever face that stupendous challenge and send his ships into the gulf between the stars? He remembered a phrase he had once read: "Interplanetary distances are a million times as great as those to which we are accustomed in everyday life, but interstellar distances are a million-fold greater still." His mind quailed before the thought, but still he clung to that phrase: *"Everything is relative."* In a few thousand years, Man had come from coracle to spaceship. What might he yet do in the eons that lay ahead?

FIVE

It would be false to suggest that the five men on whom the eyes of the world were now fixed regarded themselves as daring adventurers about to risk their lives in a stupendous scientific gamble. They were all practical, hardheaded technicians who had no intention of taking part in a gamble of any kind—at least, where the lives were concerned. There was a risk, of course, but one took risks when one caught the 8.10 to the City.

Each had reacted in his own way to the publicity of the past week. They had expected it, and they had been well prepared. Hassell and Leduc had been in the public eye before and knew how to enjoy the experience while avoiding its more annoying aspects. The other three members of the crew, having fame thrust suddenly upon them, showed a tendency to huddle together for mutual protection. This move was fatal, as it made them easy meat for reporters.

Clinton and Taine were still sufficiently unused to the experience of being interviewed to enjoy it, but their Canadian colleague Jimmy Richards hated it. His replies, none too helpful at the beginning, became progressively more and more brusque as time went by and he grew tired of answering the same questions *ad nauseam*. On one famous occasion, when harried by a particularly overbearing lady reporter, his behavior became somewhat less than gallant. According to the description later circulated by Leduc, the interview went something like this:

"Good morning, Mr. Richards. I wonder if you'd mind answering a few questions for the *West Kensington Clarion?*"

Richards (bored but still fairly affable): "Certainly, though I have to meet my wife in a few minutes."

"Have you been married long?"

"About twelve years."

"Oh: any children?"

"Two: both girls, if I remember correctly."

"Does your wife approve of your flying off from Earth like this?"

"She'd better."

(Pause, during which interviewer realizes that, for once, her ignorance of shorthand is going to be no handicap.)

"I suppose you have always felt an urge to go out to the stars, to—er—place the flag of humanity upon other worlds?"

"Nope. Never thought about it until a couple of years ago."

"Then how did you get chosen for this flight?"

"Because I'm the second best atomic engineer in the world."

"The first being?"

"Professor Maxton, who's too valuable to risk."

"Are you at all nervous?"

"Oh yes. I'm frightened of spiders, lumps of plutonium more than a foot across, and anything that makes noises in the night."

"I mean—are you nervous about this voyage?"

"I'm scared stiff. Look—you can see me trembling." (Demonstrates. Minor damage to furniture.)

"What do you expect to find on the Moon?"

"Lots of lava, and very little else."

(Interviewer wearing a hunted look, and now clearly preparing to disengage.)

"Do you expect to find any life on the Moon?"

"Very likely. As soon as we land, I expect there'll be a knock on the door and a voice will say: 'Would you mind answering a few questions for the *Selenites' Weekly?*'"

Not all interviews, of course, were anything like this flagrant example, and it is only fair to say that Richards swore the whole thing had been concocted by Leduc. Most of the reporters who covered Interplanetary's affairs were science graduates who had migrated into journalism. Theirs was a somewhat thankless task, since the newspaper world frequently regarded them as interlopers while the scientists looked upon them as apostates and backsliders.

Perhaps no single point had attracted more public interest than the fact that two of the crew would be reserves and would be fated to remain on Earth. For a time speculation about the ten possible combinations became so popular that the bookmakers began to take an interest in the subject. It was generally assumed that since Hassell and Leduc were both rocket pilots one but not both of them would be chosen. As this sort of discussion might have bad effects on the men themselves, the Director-General made it clear that no such argument was valid. Because of their training, *any* three men would form an efficient crew. He hinted, without making a definite promise, that the final choice might have to be made by ballot. No one, least of all the five men concerned, really believed this.

Hassell's preoccupation with his unborn son had now become common knowledge—which did not help matters. It had begun as a faint worry at the back of his mind which for a long time he had been able to keep under control. But as the weeks passed, it had come to trouble him more and more until his efficiency began to fall. When he realized this, it worried him still more and so the process had gathered momentum.

Since his fear was not a personal one, but concerned someone he loved, and since it had a logical foundation, there was little that psychologists could do about it. They could not suggest, to a man of his temperament and character, that he ask to be withdrawn from the expedition. They could only watch: and Hassell knew perfectly well that they were watching.

SIX

Dirk spent little time at Southbank during the days before the exodus. It was impossible to work there: those who were going to Australia were too busy packing and tidying up their affairs, while those who weren't seemed in a very unco-operative mood. The irrepressible Matthews had been one of the sacrifices: McAndrews was leaving him in charge. It was a very sensible arrangement, but the two men were no longer on speaking terms. Dirk was very glad to keep out of their way, especially as they had been a little upset over his desertion to the scientists.

He saw equally little of Maxton and Collins, as the technical department was in a state of organized uproar. It had apparently been decided that *everything* might be needed in Australia. Only Sir Robert Derwent seemed perfectly happy amid the disorder, and Dirk was somewhat astonished to receive a summons from him one morning. As it happened, it came on one of the few days when he was at Headquarters. It was his first meeting with the Director-General since their brief introduction on the day of his arrival.

He entered somewhat timidly, thinking of all the tales he had heard about Sir Robert. The D.-G. probably noticed and understood his diffidence, for there was a distinct twinkle in his eye as he shook hands and offered his visitor a seat.

The room was no larger than many other offices which Dirk had seen at Southbank, but its position at a corner of the building gave it an unrivaled view. One could see most of the Embankment from Charing Cross to London Bridge.

Sir Robert lost no time in getting to the point.

"Professor Maxton's been telling me about your job," he said. "I suppose you've got us all fluttering around in your killing-bottle, ready to be pinned down for posterity to examine?"

"I hope, Sir Robert," smiled Dirk, "that the final result won't be quite as static as that. I'm not here primarily as a recorder of facts, but of influences and motives."

The Director-General tapped thoughtfully on his desk, then remarked quietly: "And what motives, would you say, underlie our work?"

The question, through its very directness, took Dirk somewhat aback.

"They're very complex," he began defensively. "Provisionally, I'd say they fall into two classes—material and spiritual."

"I find it rather difficult," said the D.-G. mildly, "to picture a third category."

Dirk gave a slightly embarrassed smile.

"Perhaps I'm a little too comprehensive," he said. "What I mean is this: The first men seriously to advance the idea of interplanetary travel were visionaries in love with a dream. The fact that they were also technicians doesn't matter—they were, essentially, artists using their science to create something new. If space flight had been of no conceivable practical use, they would have wished to have achieved it just the same.

"Theirs was the spiritual motive, as I've called it. Perhaps 'intellectual' is a better word. You can't analyze it any further, because it represents a basic human impulse—that of curiosity. On the material side, you now have the vision of great new industries and engineering processes, and the desire of the billion-dollar communication companies to replace their myriads of surface transmitters by two or three stations out in space. This is the Wall Street side of the picture, which of course came a good deal later."

"And which motive," said Sir Robert, pressing on ruthlessly, "would you say is predominant here?"

Dirk was now beginning to feel completely at ease.

"Before I came to Southbank," he said, "I thought of Interplanetary—when I thought of it at all—as a group of technicians out for scientific dividends. That's what you pretend to be, and you deceive a lot of people. The description may apply to some of the middle grades of your organization—but it isn't true at the top."

Dirk drew back his bow, and took a long shot at that invisible target out there in the dark.

"*I think that Interplanetary is run—and always has been run—by visionaries, poets if you like, who also happen to be scientists. Sometimes the disguise isn't very good.*"

There was silence for a while. Then Sir Robert said, in a somewhat subdued voice, though with a trace of a chuckle:

"It's an accusation that's been thrown at us before. We've never denied it. Someone once said that all human activity was a form of play. We're not ashamed of wanting to play with spaceships."

"And in the course of your play," said Dirk, "you will change the world, and perhaps the Universe."

He looked at Sir Robert with new understanding. He no longer saw that determined, bull-dog head with its broad sweep of brow, for he had suddenly remembered Newton's description of himself as a small child picking up brightly colored pebbles on the shore of the ocean of knowledge.

Sir Robert Derwent, like all great scientists, was such a child. Dirk believed that, in the final analysis, he would have crossed space for no other reason than to watch the Earth turning from night to day above the glittering lunar peaks, or to see Saturn's rings, in all their unimaginable glory, bridging the sky of his nearest moon.

SEVEN

The knowledge that this was his last day in London filled Dirk with a sense of guilty regret. Regret, because he had seen practically nothing of the place; guilt, because he couldn't help feeling that this was partly his own fault. It was true that he had been furiously busy, but looking back on the past few weeks it was hard to believe that he'd found it impossible to visit the British Museum more than twice, or St. Paul's Cathedral even once. He did not know when he would see London again, for he would return direct to America.

It was a fair but rather cool day, with the usual possibility of rain later. There was no work he could do at his flat, for all his papers had been packed and even now were halfway round the world ahead of him. He had said good-bye to those members of Interplanetary's staff he would not see again: most of the others he would meet at London Airport early tomorrow morning. Matthews, who seemed to have grown quite attached to him, had become almost tearful, and even his sparring partners Sam and Bert had insisted on a little farewell celebration at the office. When he walked away from Southbank for the last time, Dirk realized with a pang that he was also saying good-bye to one of the happiest periods of his life. It had been happy because it had been full, because it had extended all his resources to the utmost—above all, because he had been among men whose lives had a purpose which they knew was greater than themselves.

Meanwhile, he had an empty day on his hands and did not know how to occupy it. In theory, such a situation was impossible; but it seemed to have happened now.

He went into the quiet square, wondering if he had been wise to leave his raincoat behind. It was only a few hundred yards to the Embassy, where he had a little business to conduct, but he was rash enough to take a short cut. As a result he promptly lost himself in the labyrinth of side streets and culs-de-sac which made London such a continual source of exasperating delight. Only a lucky glimpse of the Roosevelt Memorial finally gave him his bearings again.

A leisurely lunch with some of his Embassy acquaintances at their favorite club disposed of the earlier afternoon; then he was left to his own resources. He could go anywhere he pleased, could see the places which otherwise he might always be sorry to have missed. Yet a kind of restless lethargy made him feel unable to do anything but wander at random through the streets. The sun had finally secured its bridgehead, and the afternoon was warm and relaxing. It was pleasant to drift through the back streets and to come by chance upon buildings older than the United States—yet bearing such notices as: "Grosvenor Radio and Electronic Corporation," or "Provincial Airways, Ltd."

Late in the afternoon Dirk emerged into what, he concluded, must be Hyde Park. For a full hour he circulated under the trees, always keeping within sight of the adjoining roads. The Albert Memorial held him paralyzed with frank disbelief for many minutes, but he finally escaped from its hypnotic spell and decided to cut back across the Park to Marble Arch.

He had forgotten the impassioned oratory for which that spot was famous, and it was very entertaining to wander from one crowd to another, listening to the speakers and their critics. What, he wondered, had ever given people the idea that the British were reserved and undemonstrative?

He stood for some time enthralled by a duet between one orator and his heckler in which each maintained with equal passion that Karl Marx had—and had *not*—made a certain remark. What the remark was Dirk never discovered, and he began to suspect that the disputants themselves had long since forgotten it. From time to time helpful interjections were provided by the good-natured crowd, which obviously had no strong feelings on the subject but wanted to keep the pot boiling.

The next speaker was engaged in proving, apparently with the aid of Biblical texts, that Doomsday was at hand. He reminded Dirk of those apocalyptic prophets of the anxious year A.D. 999; would their successors, ten centuries later, still be predicting the Day of Wrath as the year 1999 drew to its close? He could hardly doubt it. In many ways human nature changed very little: the prophets would still be there, and there would still be some to believe them.

He moved on to the next group. A small but attentive audience was gathered around an elderly, white-haired man who was giving a lecture—a remarkably well-informed lecture—on philosophy. Not all the speakers, Dirk decided, were by any means cranks. This lecturer might have been a retired schoolmaster with such strong views on adult education that he felt himself impelled to hold forth in the marketplace to all who would listen.

His discourse was on Life, its origin and its destiny. His thoughts, like those of his listeners, were no doubt influenced by that winged thunderbolt lying in the desert on the far side of the world, for presently he began to speak of the astronomical stage upon which the strange drama of life was being played.

He painted a vivid picture of the sun and its circling planets, taking the thoughts of his listeners with him from world to world. He had a gift for picturesque phrases, and though Dirk was not sure that he confined himself to accepted scientific knowledge, the general impression he gave was accurate enough.

Tiny Mercury, blistering beneath its enormous sun, he pictured as a world of burning rocks washed by sluggish oceans of molten metal. Venus, Earth's sister planet, was forever hidden from us by those rolling clouds which had not parted once during the centuries in which men had gazed upon her. Beneath that blanket might be oceans and forests and the hum of strange life. Or there might be nothing but a barren wilderness swept by scorching winds.

He spoke of Mars; and one could see a ripple of increased attention spread through his audience. Forty million miles outward from the Sun, Nature had scored her second hit. Here again was life: we could see the changing colors which on our own world spoke of the passing seasons. Though Mars had little water, and his atmosphere was stratospherically thin, vegetation and perhaps animal life could exist there. Of intelligence, there was no conclusive evidence at all.

Beyond Mars the giant outer worlds lay in a frozen twilight which grew ever dimmer and colder as the Sun dwindled to a distant star. Jupiter and Saturn were crushed beneath atmospheres thousands of miles deep—atmospheres of methane and ammonia, torn by hurricanes which we could observe across half a billion miles or more of space. If there was life on those strange outer planets, and the still colder worlds beyond, it would be more weird than anything we could imagine. Only in the temperate zone of the Solar System, the narrow belt in which floated Venus, Earth and Mars, could there be life as we knew it.

Life as we knew it! And how little we knew! What right had *we* on our puny world to assume that it set the pattern for all the Universe? Could conceit go farther?

The Universe was not hostile to life, but merely indifferent. Its strangeness was an opportunity and a challenge—a challenge which intelligence would accept. Shaw had spoken the truth, half a century ago, when he put these words into the mouth of Lilith, who came before Adam and Eve:

"Of Life only there is no end; and though of its million starry mansions many are empty and many still unbuilt, and though its vast domain is as yet unbearably desert, my seed shall one day fill it and master it to its uttermost confines."

The clear, cultured voice died away, and Dirk became once more conscious of his surroundings. It had been a remarkable performance: he would like to know more about the speaker, who was now quietly dismantling his little platform and preparing to wheel it away in a dilapidated handcart. The crowd was dispersing around him, looking for fresh attractions. From time to time half-heard phrases borne down the wind told Dirk that the other speakers were still operating at full blast.

Dirk turned to leave, and as he did so caught sight of a face which he recognized. For a moment he was taken completely by surprise: the coincidence seemed too improbable to be true.

Standing in the crowd, only a few feet away from him, was Victor Hassell.

EIGHT

Maude Hassell had needed no elaborate explanations when her husband had said, rather abruptly, that he was "going for a stroll around the Park." She understood perfectly, and merely expressed a hope that he wouldn't be recognized, and would be back in time for tea. Both of these wishes were doomed to disappointment, as she was fairly sure they would be.

Victor Hassell had lived in London for almost half his life, but his earliest impressions of the city were still the most vivid and still held the strongest place in his affections. As a young engineering student he had lodged in the Paddington area and had walked to college every day across Hyde Park and Kensington Gardens. When he thought of London, he did not picture busy streets and world-famous buildings, but quiet avenues of trees and open fields, and the wide sands of Rotten Row along which the Sunday morning riders would still be cantering on their fine horses when humanity's first ships were turning homewards from the stars. And there was no need for him to remind Maude of their first encounter beside the Serpentine, only two years ago, but a lifetime away. From all these places he must now take his leave.

He spent a little time in South Kensington, wandering past the old colleges which formed so large a part of his memories. They had not changed: the students with their folders and T-squares and slide-rules were just the same. It was strange to think that almost a century ago the young H. G. Wells had been one of that eager, restless throng.

Acting upon impulse, Hassell walked into the Science Museum and came, as he had so often done before, to the replica of the Wright biplane. Thirty years earlier the original machine had been hanging here in the great gallery, but it had long since gone back to the United States and few now remembered Orville Wright's protracted battle with the Smithsonian Institution which had been the cause of its exile.

Seventy-five years—a long lifetime, no more—lay between the flimsy wooden framework that had skimmed a few yards across the ground at Kitty Hawk, and the great projectile that might soon be taking him to the Moon. And he did not doubt that in another lifetime, the "Prometheus" would look as quaint and as primitive as the little biplane suspended above his head.

Hassell came out into Exhibition Road to find the sun shining brightly. He might have stayed longer in the Science Museum, but a number of people had been staring at him a little too intently. His chances of remaining unrecognized were, he imagined, probably lower inside this building than almost anywhere on Earth.

He walked slowly across the Park along the paths he knew so well, pausing once or twice to admire views he might never see again. There was nothing morbid in his realization of this: indeed, he could appreciate with some detachment the increased intensity it gave to his emotions. Like most men, Victor Hassell was afraid of death; but there were occasions when it was a justifiable risk. That, at least, had been true when there was merely himself to consider. He only wished he could prove it was still true, but in that he had so far failed.

There was a bench not far from Marble Arch where he and Maude had often sat together in the days before their marriage. He had proposed to her here a good many times, and she had turned him down almost—but not quite—as frequently. He was glad to see that it was unoccupied at the moment, and he dropped into it with a little sigh of satisfaction.

His contentment was short-lived, for less than five minutes later he was joined by an elderly gentleman who settled himself down behind a pipe and the *Manchester Guardian*. (That anyone should wish to guard Manchester had always struck Hassell as baffling in the extreme.) He decided to move, after a sufficient interval, but before he could do this without obvious rudeness there was a further interruption. Two small boys who had been strolling along the pathway did a sudden turn to starboard and walked up to the bench. They looked at him steadily in the uninhibited way that some small boys have, then the elder said accusingly: "Hey, Mister, are you Vic Hassell?"

Hassell gave them a critical examination. They were clearly brothers, and as unattractive a pair as one would meet in a day's march. He shuddered slightly as he realized what a hazardous business parenthood was.

In normal circumstances, Hassell would have carefully confessed to the charge, since he had not forgotten many of his own schoolboy enthusiasms. He would probably have done so even now had he been approached more politely, but these urchins appeared to be playing truant from Dr. Fagin's Academy for Young Delinquents.

He looked at them fixedly and said, in his best Mayfair *circa* 1920 voice, "It's half-past three, and I *haven't* any change for a sixpence."

At this masterly *non sequitur* the younger boy turned to his brother and said heatedly: "Garn, George—I told you he weren't!"

The other slowly strangled him by twisting his tie and continued as if nothing had happened.

"You're Vic Hassell, the rocket bloke."

"Do I look like Mr. Hassell?" said Mr. Hassell in tones of indignant surprise.

"Yes."

"That's odd—no one's ever told me so."

This statement might be misleading, but it was the literal truth. The two boys looked at him thoughtfully: Junior had now been granted the luxury of respiration. Suddenly George appealed to the *Manchester Guardian*, though there was now a welcome note of uncertainty in his voice.

"He's kidding us, Mister, ain't he?"

A pair of spectacles reared themselves over the paper, and stared at them owlishly. Then they focused on Hassell, who began to feel uncomfortable. There was a long, brooding silence.

Then the stranger tapped his paper and said severely: "There's a photo of Mr. Hassell in here. The nose is quite different. Now please go away."

The paper barricade was re-erected. Hassell looked into the distance, ignoring his inquisitors, who continued to stare disbelievingly at him for another minute. Finally, to his relief, they began to move away, still arguing with each other.

Hassell was wondering if he should thank his unknown supporter when the other folded his newspaper and removed his glasses.

"You know," he said, with a slight cough, "there *is* a striking resemblance."

Hassell gave a shrug. He wondered if he should own up, but decided not to do so.

"To tell the truth," he said, "it has caused me some annoyance before."

The stranger looked at him thoughtfully, though his eyes had a misty, faraway look.

"They're leaving for Australia tomorrow, aren't they?" he said rhetorically. "I suppose they've got a fifty-fifty chance of coming back from the Moon?"

"I should say it's a lot better than that."

"Still, it *is* a chance, and I suppose at this very moment young Hassell's wondering if he'll ever see London again. It would be interesting to know what he's doing—you could learn a lot about him from that."

"I guess you could," said Hassell, shifting uncomfortably in his seat and wondering how he could get away. The stranger, however, seemed in a talkative mood.

"There's an editorial here," he said, waving his crumpled paper, "all about the implications of space flight and the effect it's going to have on everyday life. That sort of thing's all very well, but when are we going to *settle down*? Eh?"

"I don't quite follow you," said Hassell, not altogether truthfully.

"There's room for everyone on this world, and if we run it properly we'll not find a better, even if we go gallivanting right around the Universe."

"Perhaps," said Hassell mildly, "we'll only appreciate Earth when we have done just that."

"Humph! Then more fools us. Aren't we ever going to rest and have some peace?"

Hassell, who had met this argument before, gave a little smile.

"The dream of the Lotus Eaters," he said, "is a pleasant fantasy for the individual—but it would be death for the race."

Sir Robert Derwent had once made that remark, and it had become one of Hassell's favorite quotations.

"The Lotus Eaters? Let's see—what did Tennyson say about them —nobody reads him nowadays. 'There is sweet music here that softer falls . . .' No, it isn't that bit. Ah, I have it!

> *" 'Is there any peace*
> *In ever climbing up the climbing wave?"*

Well, young man, *is* there?"

"For some people—yes," said Hassell. "And perhaps when space flight arrives they'll all rush off to the planets and leave the Lotus Eaters to their dreams. That should satisfy everybody."

"And the meek shall inherit the Earth, eh?" said his companion, who seemed to have a very literary turn of mind.

"You could put it that way," smiled Hassell. He looked automatically at his watch, determined not to become involved in an argument which could have only one result.

"Dear me, I must be going. Thanks for the talk."

He rose to leave, thinking he'd preserved his incognito rather well. The stranger gave him a curious little smile and said quietly: "Good-bye." He waited until Hassell had gone twenty feet, then called after him in a louder voice: "And good luck—Ulysses!"

Hassell stopped dead, then swiveled round in his tracks—but the other was already walking briskly in the direction of Hyde Park Corner. He watched the tall, spare figure lose itself in the crowd; and only then did he say to himself explosively: "Well I'll be damned!"

Then he shrugged his shoulders and walked on towards Marble Arch, intending to listen once again to the soapbox orators who had given him so much amusement in his youth.

It did not take Dirk long to realize that the coincidence was hardly so surprising after all. Hassell, he remembered, lived in the West London area. What was more natural than that he, too, should be taking his last look at the city? It might well be his last in a far more final sense than Dirk's.

Their eyes met across the crowd. Hassell gave a little start of recognition, but Dirk did not suppose he would remember him by name. He pushed his way towards the young pilot and introduced himself somewhat awkwardly. Hassell would probably prefer to be left alone, but he could scarcely turn aside without speaking. Moreover, he had always wanted to meet the Englishman and this seemed far too good an opportunity to miss.

"Did you hear that last talk?" asked Dirk, by way of starting the conversation.

"Yes," replied Hassell. "I happened to be passing and overheard what the old chap was saying. I've often seen him here before; he's one of the saner specimens. It's rather a mixed bag, isn't it?" He laughed and waved in the general direction of the crowd.

"Very," said Dirk. "But I'm glad I've seen the place in action. It's quite an experience."

As he spoke, he studied Hassell carefully. It was not easy to judge his age, which might have been anything from twenty-five to thirty-five. He was slightly built, with clear-cut features and unruly brown hair. A scar from an early rocket crash ran diagonally across his left cheek, but was only visible now and then when the skin became taut.

"After listening to that talk," said Dirk, "I must say that the Universe doesn't sound a very attractive place. It's not surprising that a lot of people would prefer to stay at home."

Hassell laughed.

"It's funny you should say that; I've just been talking to an old fellow who was making the same point. He knew who I was, but pretended he didn't. The argument I brought forward was that there are two kinds of mind—the adventurous, inquisitive types and the stay-at-homes who're quite happy to sit in their own back-gardens. I think they're both necessary, and it's silly to pretend that one's right and the other isn't."

"I think I must be a hybrid," smiled Dirk. "I like to sit in my back-garden—but I also like the wanderers to drop in now and then to tell me what they've seen."

He broke off abruptly, then added: "What about sitting down for a drink somewhere?"

He felt tired and thirsty and so, for the same reason, did Hassell.

"Just for a moment, then," said Hassell. "I want to get back before five."

Dirk could understand this, though as it happened he knew nothing of the other's domestic preoccupations. He let Hassell navigate him to the lounge of the Cumberland, where they sat down thankfully behind a couple of large beers.

"I don't know," said Dirk with an apologetic cough, "if you've heard of my job."

"As a matter of fact I have," said Hassell with an engaging smile. "We were wondering when you were going to catch up with us. You're the expert on motives and influences, aren't you?"

Dirk was surprised, as well as a trifle embarrassed, to discover how far his fame had spread.

"Er—yes," he admitted. "Of course," he added hastily, "I'm not primarily concerned with individual cases, but it's very useful to me if I can find just how people got involved in astronautics in the first place."

He wondered if Hassell would take the bait. After a minute, he began to nibble and Dirk felt all the sensations of an angler watching his float twitching, at long last, on the surface of some placid lake.

"We've argued that often enough at the Nursery," said Hassell. "There's no simple answer. It depends on the individual."

Dirk generated an encouraging silence.

"Consider Taine, for example. He's the pure scientist, looking for knowledge and not much interested in the consequences. That's why, despite his brains, he'll always be a smaller man than the D.-G. Mind you—I'm not criticizing. One Sir Robert's probably quite enough for a single generation!

"Clinton and Richards are engineers and love machinery for its own sake, though they're much more human than Taine. I guess you've heard how Jimmy deals with reporters he doesn't like—I thought so! Clinton's a queer sort of fellow and you never know exactly what's going on in his mind. In their cases, however, they were chosen for the job—they didn't go after it.

"Now, Pierre's just about as different from the rest as he could be. He's the kind who likes adventure for itself—that's why he became a rocket pilot. It was his big mistake, though he didn't realize it at the time. There's nothing adventurous about rocket flying: either it goes according to plan—or else, *Bang!*"

He brought his fist down on the table, checking it in the last fraction of an inch so that the glasses scarcely rattled. The unconscious precision of the movement filled Dirk with admiration. He could not, however, let Hassell's remarks go unchallenged.

"I seem to remember," Dirk said, "a little contretemps of yours which must have given you a certain amount of—er—excitement."

Hassell smiled disparagingly.

"That sort of thing happens once in a thousand times. On the remaining nine hundred and ninety-nine occasions, the pilot's simply there because he weighs less than the automatic machinery that could do the same job."

He paused, looking over Dirk's shoulder, and a slow smile came across his face.

"Fame has its compensations," he murmured. "One of them is approaching right now."

A hotel dignitary was wheeling a little trolley towards them, wheeling it with the air of a high-priest bringing a sacrifice to the altar. He stopped at their table, and produced a bottle which, if Dirk could judge from its cobwebbed exterior, was considerably older than he himself.

"With the compliments of the management, sir," said the official, bowing towards Hassell, who made appreciative noises but looked a little alarmed at the attention now being concentrated on him from all sides.

Dirk knew nothing of wines, but he did not see how any skill in that complicated art could have made the smooth liquid slide more voluptuously down his throat. It was such a discreet, such a well-bred wine that they had no hesitation in toasting themselves, then Interplanetary, and then the "Prometheus." Their appreciation so delighted the management that another bottle would have been forthcoming immediately, but Hassell gracefully refused and explained that he was already very late, which was perfectly true.

They parted in a high good humor on the steps of the Underground, feeling that the afternoon had come to a brilliant *finale*. Not until Hassell had gone did Dirk realize that the young pilot had said nothing, absolutely nothing, about himself. Was it modesty—or merely lack of time? He had been surprisingly willing to discuss his colleagues; it seemed almost as if he was anxious to divert attention from himself.

Dirk stood worrying over this for a moment: then, whistling a little tune, he began to walk slowly homewards along Oxford Street. Behind him, the sun was going down upon his last evening in England.

PART THREE

For thirty years the world had been slowly growing used to the idea that, some day, men were going to reach the planets. The prophecies of the early pioneers of astronautics had come true so many times since the first rockets climbed through the stratosphere that few people disbelieved them now. That tiny crater near Aristarchus, and the television films of the other side of the Moon were achievements which could not be denied.

Yet there had been some who had deplored or even denounced them. To the man in the street, interplanetary flight was still a vast, somewhat terrifying possibility just below the horizon of everyday life. The general public, as yet, had no particular feelings about space flight except the vague realization that "Science" was going to bring it about in the indefinite future.

Two distinct types of mentality, however, had taken astronautics very seriously indeed, though for quite different reasons. The practically simultaneous impact of the long-range rocket and the atomic bomb upon the military mind had, in the 1950's, produced a crop of blood-curdling prophecies from the experts in mechanized murder. For some years there had been much talk of bases on the Moon or even—more appropriately—upon Mars. The United States Army's belated discovery, at the end of the Second World War, of Oberth's twenty-year-old plans for "space-stations" had revived ideas which it was a gross understatement to call "Wellsian."

In his classic book, Wege zur Raumschiffahrt, Oberth had discussed the building of great "space-mirrors" which could focus sunlight upon the Earth, either for peaceful purposes or for the incineration of enemy cities. Oberth himself never took this last idea very seriously, and must have been surprised at its solemn reception two decades later.

The fact that it would be very easy to bombard the Earth from the Moon, and very difficult to attack the Moon from the Earth, had made many uninhibited military experts declare that, for the sake of peace, their particular country must seize our satellite before any war-mongering rival could reach it. Such arguments were common in the decade following the release of atomic energy, and were a typical by-product of that era's political paranoia. They died, unlamented, as the world slowly returned to sanity and order.

A second and perhaps more important body of opinion, while admitting that interplanetary travel was possible, opposed it on mystical or religious grounds. The "theological opposition," as it was usually termed, believed that man would be disobeying some divine edict if he ventured away from his world. In the phrase of Interplanetary's earliest and most brilliant critic, the Oxford don C. S. Lewis, astronomical distances were "God's quarantine regulations." If man overcame them, he would be guilty of something not far removed from blasphemy.

Since these arguments were not founded on logic, they were quite irrefutable. From time to time Interplanetary had issued counterblasts, pointing out that the same objections might very well have been brought against all explorers who had ever lived. The astronomical distances which twentieth-century man could bridge in minutes with his radio waves were less of a barrier than the great oceans must have seemed to his Stone Age ancestors. No doubt in prehistoric times there were those who shook their heads and prophesied disaster when the young men of the tribe went in search of new lands in the terrifying, unknown world around them. Yet it was well that the search had been made before the glaciers came grinding down from the Pole.

One day the glaciers would return; and that was the least of the dooms that might descend upon the Earth before its course was run. Some of these could only be guessed, but one at least was almost certain in the ages ahead.

There comes a time in the life of every star when the delicate balance of its atomic furnaces must tilt, one way or the other. In the far future the descendants of Man might catch, from the safety of the outermost planets, a last glimpse of their birthplace as it sank into the fires of the detonating Sun.

One objection to space flight which these critics brought forward was, on the face of it, more convincing. Since Man, they argued, had caused so much misery upon his own world, could he be trusted to behave on others? Above all, would the miserable story of conquest and enslavement of one race by another be repeated again, endlessly and forever, as human culture spread from one world to the next?

Against this there could be no fully convincing answer: only a

*clash of rival faiths—the ancient conflict between pessimism and op-
timism, between those who believed in Man and those who did not.
But the astronomers had made one contribution to the debate by
pointing out the falseness of the historical analogy. Man, who had
been civilized only for a millionth of the life of his planet, was not
likely to encounter races on other worlds which would be primitive
enough for him to exploit or enslave. Any ships from Earth which set
out across space with thoughts of interplanetary empire might find
themselves, at the end of their voyage, with no greater hopes of conquest than a fleet of savage war-canoes drawing slowly into New
York harbor.*

*The announcement that the "Prometheus" might be launched
within a few weeks had revived all these speculations and many more.
Press and radio talked of little else, and for a while the astronomers
made a profitable business of writing guardedly optimistic articles
about the Solar System. A Gallup poll carried out in Great Britain
during this period showed that 41 per cent of the public thought
interplanetary travel was a good thing, 26 per cent were against it,
and 33 per cent had not made up their minds. These figures—particularly the 33 per cent—caused some despondency at Southbank and
resulted in many conferences in the Public Relations Department,
which was now busier than it had ever been before.*

*Interplanetary's usual trickle of visitors had grown to a mighty
flood bearing upon its bosom some very exotic characters. Matthews
had evolved a standard procedure for dealing with most of these.
The people who wanted to go on the first trip were offered a ride in
the Medical Section's giant centrifuge, which could produce accelera-
tions of ten gravities. Very few accepted this offer, and those who did,
when they had recovered, were then passed to the Dynamics Department, where the mathematicians administered the* coup de grâce *by
asking them unanswerable questions.*

*No one, however, had found an effective means of dealing with the
genuine cranks—though they could sometimes be neutralized by a
kind of mutual reaction. It was one of Matthews's unfulfilled ambi-
tions to be visited simultaneously by a flat-earther and one of those
still more eccentric people who are convinced that the world is on the
inside of a hollow sphere. This would, he was sure, result in a highly
entertaining debate.*

*Very little could be done about the psychic explorers (usually
middle-aged spinsters) who were already perfectly well acquainted
with the Solar System and all too anxious to impart their knowledge.*

Matthews had been optimistic enough to hope, now that the crossing of space was so close at hand, that they would not be so eager to have their ideas tested by reality. He was disappointed, and one unfortunate member of his staff was employed almost full time listening to these ladies give highly colored and mutually incompatible accounts of lunar affairs.

More serious and significant were the letters and comments in the great newspapers, many of which demanded official replies. A minor canon of the Church of England wrote a vigorous and much publicized letter to The London Times, denouncing Interplanetary and all its works. Sir Robert Derwent promptly went into action behind the scenes and, as he put it, "trumped the fellow with an archbishop." It was rumored that he had a cardinal and a rabbi in reserve if attacks came from other quarters.

No one was particularly surprised when a retired brigadier, who had apparently spent the last thirty years in suspended animation in the outskirts of Aldershot, wanted to know what steps were being taken to incorporate the Moon into the British Commonwealth. Simultaneously, a long-dormant major-general erupted in Atlanta and asked Congress to make the Moon the Fifty-first State. Similar demands were to be heard in almost every country in the world—with the possible exception of Switzerland and Luxembourg—while the international lawyers realized that a crisis of which they had long been warned was now almost upon them.

At this moment Sir Robert Derwent issued the famous manifesto which had been prepared many years ago against this very day.

"Within a few weeks," the message ran, "we hope to launch the first spaceship from the Earth. We do not know whether we shall succeed, but the power to reach the planets is now almost within our grasp. This generation stands upon the brink of the ocean of space, preparing for the greatest adventure in all history.

"There are some whose minds are so rooted in the past that they believe the political thinking of our ancestors can still be applied when we reach other worlds. They even talk of annexing the Moon in the name of this or that nation, forgetting that the crossing of space has required the united efforts of scientists from every country in the world.

"There are no nationalities beyond the stratosphere: any worlds we may reach will be the common heritage of all men—unless other forms of life have already claimed them for their own.

"We, who have striven to place humanity upon the road to the stars, make this solemn declaration, now and for the future:

"We will take no frontiers into space."

ONE

"I think it's hard lines on Alfred," remarked Dirk, "having to stay behind now that the fun's beginning."

McAndrews gave a noncommittal grunt.

"We couldn't both go," he said. "Headquarters is being decimated as it is. Too many people seem to think this is just a good excuse for a holiday."

Dirk forbore from comment, though sorely tempted. In any case, his own presence could not be regarded as strictly necessary. He conjured up a last sympathetic picture of poor Matthews, staring gloomily over the sluggish Thames, and turned his mind to happier things.

The Kentish coastline was still visible astern, for the liner had not yet gained its full height or speed. There was scarcely any sense of movement, but suddenly Dirk had an indefinable feeling of change. Others must have noticed it also for Leduc, who was sitting opposite, nodded with satisfaction.

"The ramjets are starting to fire," he said. "They'll be cutting the turbines now."

"That means," put in Hassell, "that we're doing over a thousand."

"Knots, miles or kilometers an hour, or rods, poles or perches per microsecond?" asked somebody.

"For heaven's sake," groaned one of the technicians, "don't start *that* argument again!"

"When do we arrive?" asked Dirk, who knew the answer perfectly well but was anxious to create a diversion.

"We touch down at Karachi in about six hours, get six hours' sleep, and should be in Australia twenty hours from now. Of course we have to add—or subtract—about half a day for time difference, but someone else can work that out."

"Bit of a come-down for you, Vic," Richards laughed at Hassell. "The last time you went round the world it took you ninety minutes!"

"One mustn't exaggerate," said Hassell. "I was way out, and it took a good hundred. Besides, it was a day and a half before I could get down again!"

"Speed's all very well," said Dirk philosophically, "but it gives one a false impression of the world. You get shot from one place to another in a few hours and forget that there's anything in between."

"I quite agree," put in Richards unexpectedly. "Travel quickly if you *must*, but otherwise you can't beat the good old sailing yacht. When I was a kid I spent most of my spare time cruising around the Great Lakes. Give me five miles an hour—or twenty-five thousand. I've no use for stagecoaches or aeroplanes or anything else in between."

The conversation then became technical, and degenerated into a wrangle over the relative merits of jets, athodyds and rockets. Someone pointed out that the airscrews could still be seen doing good work in the obscurer corners of China, but he was ruled out of order. After a few minutes of this, Dirk was glad when McAndrews challenged him to a game of chess on a miniature board.

He lost the first game over Southeastern Europe, and fell asleep before completing the second—probably through the action of some defense mechanism, as McAndrews was much the better player. He woke up over Iran, just in time to land and go to sleep again. It was therefore not surprising that when Dirk reached the Timor Sea, and readjusted his watch for Australian time, he was not quite sure whether he should be awake or not.

His companions, who had synchronized their sleep more efficiently, were in better shape and began to crowd to the observation ports as they neared the end of their journey. They had been crossing barren desert, with occasional fertile areas, for almost two hours when Leduc, who had been map-reading, suddenly cried out: "There it is—over on the left!"

Dirk followed his pointing finger. For a moment he saw nothing; then he made out, many miles away, the buildings of a compact little town. To one side of it was an airstrip, and beyond that, an almost invisible black line that stretched across the desert. It seemed to be an unusually straight railroad; then Dirk saw that it led from nowhere to nowhere. It began in the desert and ended in the desert. It was the first five miles of the road that would lead his companions to the Moon.

A few minutes later the great launching track was beneath them, and with a thrill of recognition Dirk saw the winged bullet of the "Prometheus" glistening on the airfield beside it. Everyone became suddenly silent, staring down at the tiny silver dart which meant so much to them but which only a few had ever seen save in drawings and photographs. Then it was hidden by a block of low buildings as the liner banked and they came in to land.

"So this is Luna City!" remarked someone without enthusiasm. "It looks like a deserted gold-rush town."

"Maybe it is," said Leduc. "They used to have gold mines in these parts, didn't they?"

"Surely you know," said McAndrews pompously, "that Luna City was built by the British Government around 1950 as a rocket research base. Originally it had an aborigine name—something to do with spears or arrows, I believe."

"I wonder what the aborigines think of these goings-on? There are still some of them out in the hills, aren't there?"

"Yes," said Richards, "they've got a reservation a few hundred miles away, well off the line of fire. They probably think we're crazy, and I guess they're right."

The truck which had collected the party at the airstrip came to a halt before a large office building.

"Leave your kit aboard," instructed the driver. "This is where you get your hotel reservations."

No one was much amused at the jest. Accommodation at Luna City consisted largely of Army huts, some of which were almost thirty years old. The more modern buildings would certainly be occupied by the permanent residents, and the visitors were full of gloomy forebodings.

Luna City, as it had been called for the last five years, had never quite lost its original military flavor. It was laid out like an Army camp, and though energetic amateur gardeners had done their best to brighten it up, their efforts had only served to emphasize the general drabness and uniformity.

The normal population of the settlement was about three thousand, of whom the majority were scientists or technicians. In the next few days there would be an influx limited only by the accommodation—and perhaps not even by that. One newsreel company had already sent in a consignment of tents, and its personnel were making anxious inquiries about Luna City's weather.

To his relief, Dirk found that the room allocated to him, though small, was clean and comfortable. About a dozen members of the administrative staff also occupied the block, while across the way Collins and the other scientists from Southbank formed a second colony. The Cockneys, as they christened themselves, quickly enlivened the place by such notices as "To the Underground" and "Line-up here for 25 bus."

The first day in Australia was, for the whole party, entirely occupied by the mechanics of getting settled and learning the geography of the "city." The little town had one great point in its favor—it was compact and the tall tower of the meteorological building served as a good landmark. The airstrip was about two miles away, and the head of the launching track another mile beyond that. Although everyone was eager to see the spaceship, the visit had to wait until the second day. In any case Dirk was far too busy during the first twelve hours frantically trying to locate his notes and records, which seemed to have gone astray somewhere between Calcutta and Darwin. He eventually found them at Technical Stores, which was on the point of consigning the lot back to England as they couldn't find his name on Interplanetary's establishment list.

At the end of the first exhausting day, Dirk nevertheless still had enough energy to record his impressions of the place.

"*Midnight*. Luna City, as Ray Collins puts it, looks like being 'good fun'—though I guess the fun would wear off after a month or so. The accommodation is quite reasonable, though the furniture is rather scanty and there's no running water in the block. I'll have to go half a mile to get a shower, but this is hardly 'roughing it'!

"McA. and some of his people are in this building. I'd rather have been with Collins's crowd across the way, but I can't very well ask to be transferred.

"Luna City reminds me of the Air Force bases I've seen in the war films. It has the same bleakly efficient appearance, the same atmosphere of restless energy. And like an air base, it exists for a machine —the spaceship instead of the bomber.

"From my window I can see, a quarter of a mile away, the dark shape of some office buildings which look very incongruous here in the desert under these strange brilliant stars. A few windows are still lit up, and one could imagine that the scientists are working feverishly against time to overcome some last-minute difficulty. But I happen to know that said scientists are making a devil of a noise in the next block, entertaining their friends. Probably the burner of midnight oil is some unfortunate accountant or storekeeper trying to balance his books.

"A long way off to the left, through a gap in the buildings, I can see a faint smear of light low down on the horizon. The 'Prometheus' is out there, lying under the floodlights. It's strange to think that she —or rather 'Beta'—has been up into space a dozen times or more on those fueling runs. Yet 'Beta' belongs to our planet, while 'Alpha,' which is still earthbound, will soon be up among the stars, never to touch the surface of this world again. We're all very eager to see the ship, and won't waste any time tomorrow in getting out to the launching site.

"*Later.* Ray hauled me out to meet his friends. I feel flattered, since I noticed McA. and Co. weren't invited. I can't remember the names of anyone I was introduced to, but it was good fun. And so to bed."

TWO

Even when first seen from ground level a mile away, the "Prometheus" was an impressive sight. She stood on her multiple undercarriage at the edge of the great concrete apron around the launcher, the scoops of her air-intakes gaping like hungry mouths. The smaller and lighter "Alpha" lay in its special cradle a few yards away, ready to be hoisted into position. Both machines were surrounded with cranes, tractors and various types of mobile equipment.

A rope barrier was slung round the site, and the truck halted at the opening in the cordon, beneath a large notice which read:

WARNING—RADIOACTIVE AREA!

No unauthorized persons allowed past
this point.
Visitors wishing to examine the ship,
contact Ext. 47 (Pub. Rel. IIa).

THIS IS FOR YOUR PROTECTION!

Dirk looked a little nervously at Collins as they gave their identities and were waved past the barrier.

"I'm not sure I altogether like this," he said.

"Oh," replied Collins cheerfully, "there's no need to worry, as long as you keep near me. We won't go near any dangerous areas. And I always carry one of these."

He pulled a small rectangular box out of his coat pocket. It appeared to be made of plastic and had a tiny loud-speaker set into one side.

"What is it?"

"Geiger alarm. Goes off like a siren if there's any dangerous activity around."

Dirk waved his hand towards the great machine looming ahead of them.

"Is it a spaceship or an atomic bomb?" he asked plaintively.

Collins laughed.

"If you got in the way of the jet, you'd never notice the difference."

They were now standing beneath the slim, pointed snout of "Beta" and her great wings, sweeping away from them on either side, made her look like a moth in repose. The dark caverns of the air-scoops looked ominous and menacing, and Dirk was puzzled by the strange fluted objects which protruded from them at various places. Collins noticed his curiosity.

"Shock diffusers," he explained. "It's quite impossible to get one kind of air-intake to operate over the whole speed range from five hundred miles an hour at sea level to eighteen thousand miles an hour at the top of the stratosphere. Those gadgets are adjustable and can be moved in and out. Even so the whole thing's shockingly inefficient and only the fact that we've unlimited power makes it possible at all. Let's see if we can get aboard."

Her stubby undercarriage made it easy to enter the machine through the airlock door in her side. The rear of the ship, Dirk noticed, had been carefully fenced off with great movable barriers so that no one could approach it. He commented on this to Collins.

"That part of 'Beta,'" said the aerodynamicist grimly, "is Strictly Out of Bounds until the year 2000 or so."

Dirk looked at him blankly.

"What do you mean?"

"Just that. Once the atomic drive's started to operate, and the piles get radioactive, nothing can ever go near them again. They won't be safe to touch for years."

Even Dirk, who was certainly no engineer, began to realize the practical difficulties this must involve.

"Then how the devil do you inspect the motors, or put things right when they've gone wrong? Don't tell me that your designs are so perfect that there aren't any breakdowns!"

Collins smiled.

"That's the biggest headache of atomic engineering. You'll have a chance to see how it's done later."

There was surprisingly little to see aboard "Beta," since most of the ship consisted of fuel tanks and motors, invisible and unapproachable behind their barriers of shielding. The long, thin cabin at the nose might have been the control room of any airliner, but was more elaborately appointed since the crew of pilot and maintenance engineer would be living aboard her for nearly three weeks. They would have a very boring time, and Dirk was not surprised to see that the ship's equipment included a microfilm library and projector. It would be unfortunate, to say the least, if the two men had incompatible personalities: but no doubt the psychologists had checked this point with meticulous care.

Partly because he understood so little of what he saw, and partly because he was more anxious to go aboard "Alpha," Dirk soon grew tired of examining the control room. He walked to the tiny, thick windows and looked at the view ahead.

"Beta" was pointing out across the desert, almost parallel with the launching track over which she would be racing in a few days' time. It was easy to imagine that, even now, she was waiting to leap into the sky and to climb towards the stratosphere with her precious burden. . . .

The floor suddenly trembled as the ship began to move. Dirk felt a cold hand clutch at his heart and he almost overbalanced, only saving himself by grabbing at a rail in front of him. Not until then did he see the little tractor fussing around the ship and realize he had made a fool of himself. He hoped that Ray hadn't noticed his behavior, for he must certainly have turned pretty green.

"O.K.," said Collins at last, having finished his careful inspection. "Now let's look at 'Alpha.'"

They climbed out of the machine, which had now been pushed farther back into its surrounding barriers.

"I guess they're doing something to the motors," said Collins. "They've made—let's see—fifteen runs now without any trouble. Which is quite a feather in Prof. Maxton's cap."

Dirk was still wondering how "they" were doing anything at all to those terrifying inaccessible engines, but another query had crossed his mind.

"Listen," he said, "there's one thing I've been meaning to have out with you for some time. What sex *is* the 'Prometheus'? Everyone seems to use he, she or it quite impartially. I don't expect scientists to understand grammar, but still—"

Collins chuckled.

"That's just the kind of point we *are* particular about," he said. "It's been laid down officially somewhere. Although 'Prometheus' is, of course, 'he,' we call the entire ship 'she,' as in nautical practice. 'Beta' is also 'she,' but 'Alpha,' the spaceship, is an 'it.' What could be simpler?"

"Quite a lot of things. However, I suppose it's O.K. as long as you're consistent. I'll jump on you when you aren't."

"Alpha" was an even more compact mass of motors and fuel tanks than the bigger ship. It had, of course, no fins or aerofoils of any kind, but there were signs that many oddly-shaped devices had been retracted into the hull. Dirk asked his friend about these.

"Those will be the radio antennae, periscopes, and outriggers for the steering jets," explained Collins. "Back at the rear you'll see where the big shock absorbers for the lunar landing have been retracted. When 'Alpha's' out in space they can all be extended and the crew can check 'em over to see if they're working properly. They can then stay out for good, since there's no air resistance for the rest of the voyage."

There was radiation screening around "Alpha's" rocket units, so it was impossible to get a complete view of the spaceship. It reminded Dirk of the fuselage of an old-fashioned airliner which had lost its wings or was yet to acquire them. In some ways "Alpha" strongly resembled a giant artillery shell, with an unexpected circlet of portholes near the nose. The cabin for the crew occupied less than a fifth of the rocket's length. Behind it were the multitudinous machines and controls which would be needed on the half-million-mile journey.

Collins roughly indicated the different sections of the machine.

"Just behind the cabin," he said, "we've put the airlock and the main controls which may have to be adjusted in flight. Then come the fuel tanks—six of them—and the refrigeration plant to keep the methane liquid. Next we have the pumps and turbines, and then the motor itself which extends halfway along the ship. There's a great wad of shielding around it, and the whole of the cabin is in the radiation shadow so that the crew gets the maximum protection. But the rest of the ship's 'hot,' though the fuel itself helps a good deal with the shielding."

The tiny airlock was just large enough to hold two people, and Collins went ahead to reconnoiter. He warned Dirk in advance that the cabin would probably be too full to admit visitors, but a moment later he emerged again and signaled for him to enter.

"Everyone except Jimmy Richards and Digger Clinton has gone over to the workshops," he said. "We're in luck—there's bags of room."

That, Dirk soon discovered, was a remarkable exaggeration. The cabin had been designed for three people living under zero gravity, when walls and floor were freely interchangeable and its whole volume could be used for any purpose. Now that the machine was lying horizontally on Earth, conditions were decidedly cramped.

Clinton, the Australian electronics specialist, was half buried in a vast wiring diagram which he had been forced to wrap around himself in order to get it into the cabin. He looked, Dirk thought, rather like a caterpillar spinning its cocoon. Richards seemed to be running through some tests on the controls.

"Don't look alarmed," he said as Dirk watched him anxiously. "We won't take off—there's nothing in the fuel tanks!"

"I'm getting rather a complex about this," Dirk confessed. "Next time I come aboard, I'd like to make sure that we're tied down to a nice, fat anchor."

"As some anchors go," laughed Richards, "it needn't be such a big one. 'Alpha' hasn't much thrust—about a hundred tons. But it can keep it up for a long time!"

"Only a hundred tons thrust? But she weighs three times that!"

Collins coughed delicately in the background.

"*It*, I thought we decided," he remarked. However, Richards seemed willing to adopt the new gender.

"Yes, but she's in free space when she starts, and when she takes off from the Moon her effective weight will be only about thirty-five tons. So everything's under control."

The layout of "Alpha's" cabin seemed to be the result of a pitched battle between science and surrealism. The design had been determined by the fact that for eight days the occupants would have no gravity at all, and would know nothing of "up" or "down"; while for a somewhat longer period, when the ship was standing on the Moon, there would be a low gravitational field along the axis of the machine.

As at the moment the center-line was horizontal, Dirk had a feeling that he should really be walking on the walls or roof.

Yet it was a moment he would remember all his life, this visit to the first of all spaceships. The little portholes through which he was now looking would, in a few days' time, be staring out across the lonely lunar plains; the sky above would not be blue, but black and studded with stars. If he closed his eyes, he could almost imagine he was on the Moon already, and that if he looked through the upper portholes he would see the Earth hanging in the heavens. Though he went over the ship several times again, Dirk was never able to recapture the emotions of this first visit.

There was a sudden scrambling noise in the airlock and Collins said hastily:

"We'd better get out before the rush starts and someone gets trampled to death. The boys are coming back."

He managed to hold off the boarding party long enough for them to make good their escape. Dirk saw that Hassell, Leduc, Taine and three other men were all preparing to enter the ship—several with large pieces of equipment—and his mind boggled as he tried to picture conditions within. He hoped that nothing or nobody got broken.

Down on the concrete apron he relaxed and stretched himself again. He glanced up at one of the portholes to see what was happening in the ship, but was hardly surprised to find his view effectively blocked. Someone was sitting on the window.

"Well," said Collins, offering him a welcome cigarette. "What do you think of our little toys?"

"I can see where all the money's gone," Dirk answered. "It seems an awful lot of machinery to take three men just across the road, as you put it."

"There's some more to see yet. Let's go over to the launcher."

The launching track was impressive by its very simplicity. Two sets of rails began in the concrete apron—and went straight out to disappear over the horizon. It was the finest example of perspective that Dirk had ever seen.

The catapult shuttle was a huge metal carriage with arms that would grasp the "Prometheus" until the ship had gained flying speed. It would be just too bad, Dirk thought, if they failed to release at the right time.

"Launching five hundred tons at as many m.p.h. must take quite a generating plant," he said to Collins. "Why doesn't the 'Prometheus' take off under her own power?"

"Because with that initial loading she stalls at four-fifty, and the ramjets don't operate until just above that. So we have to get up speed first. The energy for the launch comes from the main power station over there; that smaller building beside it houses a battery of flywheels which are brought up to speed just before the take-off. Then they're coupled directly to the generators."

"I see," said Dirk. "You wind up the elastic, and away she goes."

"That's the idea," Collins replied. "When 'Alpha's' launched, 'Beta' isn't overloaded any more, and can be brought in to land at a reasonable speed—less than two hundred and fifty miles an hour; which is easy to anyone who makes a hobby of flying two-hundred-ton gliders!"

THREE

The milling crowd in the little hangar became suddenly quiet as the Director-General climbed up onto the dais. He had spurned amplifiers, and his voice rang strongly between the metal walls. As he spoke, hundreds of stylos began to race over hundreds of pads.

"I'd like," Sir Robert began, "to have a few words with you now that everyone's here. We're particularly anxious to assist you in your job, and to give you every opportunity of reporting the take-off, which as you know is in five days' time.

"First of all, you'll realize that it's physically impossible to let everyone look over the ship. We've admitted as many as we could in the last week, but after tomorrow we can accept no more visitors aboard. The engineers will be making their final adjustments then—and I might also say that we've already had one or two cases of—ahem!—souvenir hunting.

"You've all had a chance of selecting observation sites along the launching track. There should be plenty of room for everyone in the first four kilometers. But remember—*no one must go past the red barrier at five kilometers*. That's where the jets start firing, and it's still slightly radioactive from previous launchings. When the blast opens up, it will spray fission products over a wide area. We'll give the all-clear as soon as it's safe for you to collect the automatic cameras you have mounted out there.

"A number of people have asked when the radiation shields are being taken away from the ships so that they can be seen properly. We'll be doing this tomorrow afternoon and you can come and watch then. Bring binoculars or telescopes if you want to look at the jet units—you won't be allowed closer than a hundred yards. And if anyone thinks this is a lot of nonsense, there are two people in hospital here who sneaked up to have a good look and now wish they hadn't.

"If for any reason there's a last-minute hold-up, launching will be delayed twelve hours, twenty-four hours, or, at the most, thirty-six hours. After that we'll have to wait for the next lunation—that is, for four weeks. It makes very little difference *when* we go to the Moon, as far as the ship is concerned, but we're anxious to land in daylight in the region we know best.

"The two components will separate about an hour after take-off. It should be possible to see 'Alpha's' blast if the rocket is above the horizon when it begins its powered orbit. We will be relaying any broadcast messages over the camp speaker system, and on our local wave-length.

"'Alpha' should be on its way to the Moon, in free fall, about ninety minutes after take-off. We expect the first broadcast about then. After that, there will be nothing much happening for three days, when the braking maneuvers begin, about thirty thousand miles from the Moon. If for any reason the fuel consumption has been too high, there will be no landing. The ship will be turned into an orbit around the Moon, at a height of a few hundred kilometers, and will circle it until the time for the precomputed return flight.

"Now, are there any questions?"

There was silence for a minute. Then someone from the back of the crowd called out:

"When do we know who's going to be in the crew, sir?"

The Director-General gave a worried little smile.

"Probably tomorrow. But please remember—this thing is much too big for personalities. It doesn't matter a damn *who* actually goes on the first flight. The journey itself is what counts."

"Can we talk to the crew when the ship's in space?"

"Yes, there will be limited opportunities for doing that. We hope to arrange a general broadcast once a day. And, of course, we'll be exchanging fixes and technical information continuously, so the ship will always be in contact with ground stations somewhere on Earth."

"What about the actual landing on the Moon—how's that being broadcast?"

"The crew will be much too busy to give running commentaries for our benefit. But the microphones will be live, so we'll have a good idea of what's happening. Also the observatories will be able to see the jet when it's firing. It will probably create quite a disturbance when it hits the Moon."

"What's the program after the landing, sir?"

"The crew will decide it in the light of circumstances. Before they leave the ship, they'll broadcast a description of everything they see, and the television camera will be set panning. So we should have some really good pictures—it's a full color system, by the way.

"That will take about an hour, and will give time for any dust and radiation products to disperse. Then two members of the crew will put on spacesuits and start exploring. They will radio back their impressions to the ship, and these will be relayed directly to Earth.

"We hope it will be possible to make a fair survey of a region about ten kilometers across, but we're taking no risks at all. Thanks to the television link, anything that's discovered can be shown immediately to us back on Earth. What we're particularly anxious to find, of course, are mineral deposits from which we can manufacture fuel on the Moon. We'll naturally be looking for signs of life as well, but no one will be more surprised than us if we find any."

"If you catch a Selenite," said someone facetiously, "will you bring him back for the zoo?"

"Certainly not!" said Sir Robert firmly, but with a twinkle in his eye. "If we start that sort of thing, we're likely to end up in zoos ourselves."

"When will the ship be coming back?" asked another voice.

"It will land in the early morning, and take off again in the late afternoon, lunar time. That means a stay of about eight of our days. The return trip lasts four and a half days, so the total absence will be sixteen to seventeen days.

"No more questions? Right, then I'll leave it at that. But there's one other thing. To make sure that everyone has a clear idea of the technical background, we've arranged three talks in the next few days. They'll be given by Taine, Richards and Clinton, and each will cover his special line of territory—but in non-technical language. I strongly advise you not to miss them. Thank you!"

The ending of the address could not have been more perfectly timed. As the Director-General stepped down from the dais, a sudden, tremendous thunder came rolling up across the desert, setting the steel hangar reverberating like a drum.

Three miles away, "Alpha" was testing its motors at perhaps a tenth of their full power. It was a sound that tore at the eardrums and set the teeth on edge; what it would be like at full thrust was beyond imagination.

Beyond imagination, and beyond knowledge, for no one would ever hear it. When "Alpha's" rockets fired again, the ship would be in the eternal silence between the worlds, where the explosion of an atomic bomb is as soundless as the clash of snowflakes beneath a winter moon.

FOUR

Professor Maxton looked rather tired as he arranged the maintenance sheets carefully on his desk in a neat pile. Everything had been checked; everything was working perfectly—almost too perfectly, it seemed. The motors would have their final inspection to-morrow; meanwhile the stores could be moved into the two ships. It was a pity, he meditated, that one had to leave a stand-by crew aboard the "Beta" while she circled the Earth. But it could not be avoided, since the instruments and the refrigeration plant for the fuel had to be looked after, and both machines would have to be fully maneuverable in order to make contact again. One school of thought considered that "Beta" should land and take off once more a fortnight later to meet the returning "Alpha." There had been much argument over this, but the orbital view had finally been accepted. It would be introducing fewer additional hazards to leave "Beta" where she was, already in position just outside the atmosphere.

The machines were ready; but what, thought Maxton, of the men? He wondered if the Director-General had yet made his decision, and abruptly decided to go to see him.

He was not surprised to find the chief psychologist already with Sir Robert. Dr. Groves gave him a friendly nod as he entered.

"Hello, Rupert. I suppose you're afraid I've called the whole thing off?"

"If you *did*," said Maxton grimly, "I think I'd get up a scratch crew from my staff and go myself. We'd probably manage pretty well, at that. But, seriously, how are the boys?"

"They're fine. It won't be easy to choose your three men—but I hope you can do it soon, as the waiting puts an unfair strain on them. There's no further reason for delay, is there?"

"No; they've all been reaction-tested on the controls and are fully familiar with the ship. We're all set to go."

"In that case," said the Director-General, "we'll settle it first thing tomorrow."

"How?"

"By ballot, as we promised. It's the only way to prevent bad feeling."

"I'm glad of that," said Maxton. He turned to the psychologist again.

"Are you *quite* sure about Hassell?"

"I was coming to him. He'll go all right, and he really wants to go. He's not worrying so much now that the last-minute excitement has got hold of him. But there's still one snag."

"What's that?"

"I think this is *very* unlikely, but suppose anything goes wrong at this end while he's on the Moon? The baby's due just around mid-voyage, you know."

"I see. If his wife died, to take the worst case, what effect would it have on him?"

"It isn't easy to answer that, as he'll already be under conditions quite unlike any which a human being has experienced before. He may take it calmly, or he may crack up. I think it's a vanishingly small risk, but it's there."

"We could, of course, lie to him," said Sir Robert thoughtfully, "but I've always been rather particular about ends and means. I'd hate to have a trick like that on my conscience."

There was silence for a few minutes. Then the Director-General continued:

"Well, thanks very much, Doctor. Rupert and I will talk it over. If we decide it's absolutely necessary, we might ask Hassell to step down."

The psychologist paused at the door.

"You *might*," he said, "but I'd hate to try it myself."

The night was ablaze with stars when Professor Maxton left the Director-General's office and walked wearily across to the living-quarters. It gave him a guilty feeling to realize that he didn't know the names of half the constellations he could see. One night he'd get Taine to identify them for him. But he would have to hurry; Taine might have only three more nights on Earth.

Over to the left he could see the crew's quarters, blazing with lights. He hesitated for a moment, then walked swiftly towards the low building.

The first room, Leduc's, was empty, though the lights were on and it had only just been vacated. Its occupant had already stamped his personality upon it and piles of books lay around the place—far more than there seemed any point in bringing on such a short visit. Maxton glanced at the titles—mostly French—and once or twice his eyebrows rose slightly. He filed away one or two words to await his next contact with a really comprehensive French dictionary.

A charming photograph of Pierre's two children, sitting happily in a model rocket, was in a place of honor upon the desk. A portrait of his very beautiful wife was standing on the dressing-table, but the effect of domesticity was somewhat spoiled by the half-dozen photographs of other young ladies pinned on the wall.

Maxton moved to the next room, which happened to be Taine's. Here he found Leduc and the young astronomer deeply engrossed in a game of chess. He watched their tactics critically for a time, with the usual result that they accused him of ruining their play. At this he challenged the winner; Leduc won and Maxton polished him off in about thirty moves.

"That," he said, as the board was put away, "should stop you getting overconfident. Dr. Groves says it's a common failing of yours."

"Has Dr. Groves said anything else?" asked Leduc with elaborate casualness.

"Well, I'm giving away no medical confidences when I say that you've all passed your tests and can go on to High School. So first thing tomorrow we're going to have a sweepstake to select the three guinea pigs."

Expressions of relief came over his listeners' faces. They had been almost promised, it was true, that the final choice would be by ballot but until now they had not been sure, and the feeling that they were all potential rivals had sometimes strained their relationships.

"Are the rest of the boys in?" asked Maxton. "I think I'll go and tell them."

"Jimmy's probably asleep," said Taine, "but Arnold and Vic are still awake."

"Good. Be seeing you in the morning."

Strange noises emerging from Richards's room showed that the Canadian was very much asleep. Maxton went on down the passage and knocked at Clinton's door.

The scene that confronted him almost took his breath away: it might have been a film set showing a mad scientist's laboratory. Lying on the floor in a tangle of radio tubes and wiring, Clinton seemed to be hypnotized by a cathode-ray oscilloscope, the screen of which was filled with fantastic geometrical figures, continually shifting and changing. In the background a radio was softly playing Rachmaninoff's rightly little-known Fourth Piano Concerto, and Maxton slowly realized that the figures on the screen were synchronized with the music.

He clambered onto the bed, which seemed the safest place to be, and watched until Clinton finally pried himself off the floor.

"Assuming that you know yourself," he said at last, "can you tell me what the heck you're trying to do?"

Clinton tiptoed gingerly over the confusion and sat down beside him.

"It's an idea I've been working on for some years," he explained apologetically.

"Well, I hope you remember what happened to the late Mr. Frankenstein."

Clinton, who was a serious individual, failed to respond.

"I call it a kaleidophone," he said. "The idea is that it will convert any rhythmical sound, such as music, into pleasing and symmetrical, but always changing, visual patterns."

"That would make an amusing toy. But would the average nursery run to that number of radio tubes?"

"It's *not* a toy," said Clinton, slightly hurt. "The television people, and the cartoon film industry, would find it very useful. It would be ideal for providing interludes during long musical broadcasts, which always get boring. In fact, I was hoping to make a bit of money out of it."

"My dear fellow," grinned Maxton, "if you're one of the first men to get to the Moon, I don't think you'll ever be in any real danger of starving in the gutter in your old age."

"No, I suppose not."

"The real reason why I dropped in was to tell you that we're having a ballot for the crew first thing tomorrow. Don't electrocute yourself before then. I'm going to see Hassell now—so good night."

Hassell was lying in bed reading when Professor Maxton knocked and entered.

"Hello, Prof," he said. "What are you doing around at this ungodly hour?"

Maxton came straight to the point.

"We're having the draw for the crew tomorrow morning. Thought you'd like to know."

Hassell was silent for a moment.

"That means," he said, in a slightly thick voice, "that we've all got through."

"Good heavens, Vic," protested Maxton heartily, "surely *you* never had any doubts!"

Hassell's eyes seemed to avoid him. They also avoided, Maxton noticed, the photograph of his wife on the dressing-table.

"As you all know," Hassell said presently, "I've been rather worried about—Maude."

"That's natural enough, but I gather that everything is O.K. What are you going to call the boy, by the way?"

"Victor William."

"Well, I guess that when he arrives Vic Junior will be about the most famous baby in the world. Too bad the television system's one-way. You'll have to wait until you get back before you can see him."

"When and if," muttered Hassell.

"Look here, Vic," said Maxton firmly. "You *do* want to go, don't you?"

Hassell looked up in half-ashamed defiance.

"Of course I do," he snapped.

"Very well then. You've got three chances in five of being chosen, like everyone else. But if you don't come out of the hat this time, then you'll be on the second trip, which in some ways will be even more important, since by then we'll be making our first attempt to establish a base. That's fair enough, isn't it?"

Hassell was silent for a moment. Then he said, somewhat despondently:

"The first voyage will be the one that History will remember. After that, they'll all merge together."

Now was the moment, Professor Maxton decided, to lose his temper. He could do this with great skill and accuracy when the occasion demanded it.

"Listen to me, Vic," he stormed. "What about the people who *built* the blasted ship? How do you think *we* like having to wait until the tenth or the twentieth or the hundredth crossing before we have our chance? And if you're such a damn fool as to want fame—then good God, man, have you forgotten—*someone's got to pilot the first ship to Mars!*"

The explosion died away. Then Hassell grinned across at him and gave him a little laugh.

"Can I take that as a promise, Prof?"

"It isn't mine to make, confound you."

"No, I don't suppose it is. But I see your argument—if I miss the boat this time I won't be too upset. Now I think I'll go to sleep."

FIVE

The spectacle of the Director-General carefully carrying a wastepaper basket into Professor Maxton's office might normally have caused some amusement, but everyone regarded him solemnly as he entered. There were no bowler hats, it seemed, in the whole of Luna City: the wastepaper basket would have to act as a less dignified substitute.

Apart from the five members of the crew, who were painstakingly showing their nonchalance in the background, the only other people in the room were Maxton, McAndrews, two members of the administrative staff—and Alexson. Dirk had no particular reason to be there but McAndrews had invited him in. The Director of Public Relations was always doing helpful things like this, but Dirk strongly suspected that he was trying to secure his foothold in the official history.

Professor Maxton picked up a dozen small strips of paper from his desk and flicked them between his fingers.

"Right—are we all ready?" he said. "Here's a slip for each of you to put your name on. If anyone's too nervous to write, he can make a cross and we'll get it witnessed."

This little sally did much to relieve the tension and there were some good-natured jibes as the slips were signed and handed back, already folded.

"Good; now I'll mix them up with the blanks—so. Who'd like to do the draw?"

There was a moment's hesitation. Then, acting on some unanimous impulse, the four other crew members pushed Hassell to the front. He looked rather sheepish as Professor Maxton held the basket out towards him.

"No cheating, Vic!" he said. "And only one at a time! Close your eyes and dip."

Hassell plunged his hand into the basket and pulled out one of the slips. He handed it to Sir Robert, who quickly unfolded it.

"Blank," he said.

There was a little sigh of annoyance—or relief?

Another slip. Again—

"Blank."

"Hey, is everyone using invisible ink?" asked Maxton. "Try again, Vic."

This time he was lucky.

"P. Leduc."

Pierre said something very quickly in French and looked extremely pleased with himself. Everyone congratulated him hastily and turned at once back to Hassell.

He immediately scored a second bull's-eye.

"J. Richards."

Tension was now at its highest. Looking carefully, Dirk saw that Hassell's hand was trembling very slightly as he pulled out the fifth strip.

"Blank."

"Here we go again!" groaned someone. He was right.

"Blank."

And yet a third time—

"Blank."

Someone who had forgotten to breathe lately gave a long, deep suspiration.

Hassell handed the eighth slip to the Director-General.

"Lewis Taine."

The tension broke. Everyone crowded around the three chosen men. For a moment Hassell stood perfectly still; then he turned towards the others. His face showed absolutely no emotion of any kind. Then Professor Maxton clapped him on the shoulder and said something that Dirk could not hear. Hassell's face relaxed and he answered with a wry smile. Dirk distinctly caught the word "Mars"; then, looking quite cheerful, Hassell joined the others in congratulating his friends.

"That'll do!" boomed the Director-General, grinning all over his face. "Come across to my office—I may have a few unopened bottles around the place."

The company trooped next door, only McAndrews excusing himself on the grounds that he had to get hold of the Press. For the next quarter of an hour several sedate toasts were drunk in some excellent Australian wines which the Director-General had obviously obtained for this occasion. Then the little party broke up with a general air of relieved satisfaction. Leduc, Richards and Taine were dragged off to face the cameras, while Hassell and Clinton remained for a while in conference with Sir Robert. No one ever knew exactly what he said to them, but they both seemed quite cheerful when they emerged.

When the little ceremony was over, Dirk attached himself to Professor Maxton, who also seemed very pleased with himself and was whistling tunelessly.

"I bet you're glad that's over," said Dirk.

"I certainly am. Now we all know where we stand."

They walked together for a few yards without saying anything. Then Dirk remarked, very innocently: "Have I ever told you about my particular hobby?"

Professor Maxton looked somewhat taken aback.

"No; what is it?"

Dirk gave an apologetic cough.

"I'm supposed to be quite a good amateur conjurer."

Professor Maxton stopped his whistling, very abruptly. A profound silence fell. Then Dirk said reassuringly: "There's no need to worry. I'm quite sure that no one else noticed anything—particularly Hassell."

"You," said Professor Maxton firmly, "are a confounded nuisance. I suppose you'll want to put him down in your infernal history?"

Dirk chuckled.

"Perhaps, though I'm not a gossip writer. I noticed that you only palmed Hassell's slip, so presumably the others *were* chosen by chance. Or had you already arranged what names the D.-G. would call out? Were all those blanks genuine, for instance?"

"You are a suspicious blighter! No, the others really were chosen by fair ballot."

"What do you think Hassell will do now?"

"He'll stay for the take-off, and still be home with time to spare."

"And Clinton—how will he take it?"

"He's a phlegmatic individual; it won't worry him. We're getting the pair of them working right away on the plans for the next trip. That should keep them from fretting and moping."

He turned anxiously to Dirk.

"You'll promise never to say anything about this?"

Dirk gave a grin.

"'Never' is a heck of a long time. Shall we settle for the year 2000?"

"Always thinking about posterity, aren't you? Very well then—the year 2000 it is. But on one condition!"

"What's that?"

"I'll expect a *de luxe*, autographed copy of your report to read through in my old age!"

SIX

Dirk was making a tentative draft of his preface when the telephone rang noisily. The fact that he had a telephone at all was somewhat surprising, for many much more important people lacked one and were always coming in to borrow his. But it had fallen out that way during the allocation of offices, and although he expected to lose it at any moment no one had yet arrived to remove the instrument.

"That you, Dirk? Ray Collins here. We've got the screens off the 'Prometheus' so you can see the whole ship at last. And you remember asking me how we serviced the motors?"

"Yes."

"Come along and you can watch. It's worth seeing."

Dirk sighed and put away his notes. One day he would really get started, and then the history would materialize at a terrific rate. He was not at all worried, for he now knew his methods of working. It was no good starting before he had marshaled all the facts, and as yet he had not finished indexing his notes and references.

It was a very cold day, and he wrapped himself up thoroughly as he walked towards "Oxford Circus." Most of Luna City's traffic converged upon this intersection, and he should be able to get a lift to the launching site. Transport was precious at the base and there was a continual battle between the various departments for the possession of the few available trucks and cars.

He stamped around in the cold for about ten minutes before a jeep loaded with journalists on the same mission came roaring by. It looked somewhat like a traveling optician's shop, since it bristled with cameras, telescopes and binoculars. Nevertheless Dirk managed to find room for himself among the window display.

The jeep swirled into the parking area and everyone clambered out, lugging their equipment. Dirk gave a hand to a very small reporter with a very large telescope and tripod—partly out of good nature but partly because he hoped he'd be able to have a look through it himself.

The two great ships now lay bare of all coverings and screens; for the first time one could fully appreciate their size and proportions. "Beta" might, at a casual glance, have been taken for a conventional airliner of fairly normal design. Dirk, who knew very little about aircraft, would not have given her a second glance had he seen her taking off from his local field.

"Alpha" no longer seemed quite so much like a giant shell. The spaceship's radio and navigational equipment had now been extended, and its lines were completely spoiled by a small forest of masts and outriggers of various kinds. Someone inside must have been operating the controls, for occasionally a mast would retract or extend itself farther.

Dirk followed the crowd around to the rear of the ship. A roughly triangular area had been roped off, so that the "Prometheus" was at one apex and they were at the base. The nearest they could get to the machine's driving units was about a hundred yards. Looking into those gaping nozzles, Dirk felt no particular desire to come any closer.

Cameras and binoculars were being brought into action, and presently Dirk managed to get his look through the telescope. The rocket motors seemed only a few yards away, but he could see nothing except a metal pit full of darkness and mystery. Out of that nozzle would soon be coming hundreds of tons of radioactive gas at fifteen thousand miles an hour. Beyond it, hidden in shadow, were the pile elements that no human being could ever again approach.

Someone was coming towards them through the forbidden area— but keeping very close to the rope barrier. As he approached Dirk saw that it was Dr. Collins. The engineer grinned at him and said: "Thought I'd find you here. We're just waiting for the servicing staff to arrive. That's a nice telescope you've got—can I have a look?"

"It isn't mine," explained Dirk. "It belongs to this gentleman here."

The little journalist would be delighted if the Professor cared to have a look—and still more so if he'd explain what there was to see, anyway.

Collins stared intently for some seconds. Then he straightened up and said: "I'm afraid there's not a lot to see at present—we should have a spotlight shining up the jet to illuminate the interior. But you'll be glad of that telescope in a minute."

He gave a wry little smile.

"It's rather a queer feeling, you know," he said to Dirk, "looking at a machine you've helped build yourself—and which you can never go near again without committing suicide."

While he spoke, an extraordinary vehicle was approaching across the concrete. It was a very large truck, not unlike those which television companies use for outside broadcasts, and it was towing a machine at which Dirk could only stare in baffled amazement. As it went past, he had a confused impression of jointed levers, small electric motors, chain drives and worm-wheels, and other devices he could not identify.

The two vehicles came to a halt just inside the danger area. A door opened in the big truck, and half a dozen men clambered out. They uncoupled the trailer, and began connecting it up to three large armored cables which they unwound from drums at the front of the van.

The strange machine suddenly came to life. It rolled forward on its little balloon tires, as though testing its mobility. The jointed levers began to flex and unflex, giving a weird impression of mechanical life. A moment later it started to roll purposefully towards the "Prometheus," the larger machine following behind it at the same speed.

Collins was grinning hugely at Dirk's amazement and the obvious surprise of the journalists around him.

"That's Tin Lizzie," he said, by way of introduction. "She's not really a true robot, as every movement she makes is controlled directly by the men in the van. It takes a crew of three to run her, and it's one of the most highly skilled jobs in the world."

Lizzie was now within a few yards of "Alpha's" jets, and after some precise footwork with her bogies she came to a gentle halt. A long, thin arm carrying several obscure pieces of machinery disappeared down that ominous tunnel.

"Remote servicing machinery," explained Collins to his interested audience, "has always been one of the most important side-lines of atomic engineering. It was first developed on a large scale for the Manhattan Project during the War. Since then it's become quite an industry in itself. Lizzie is just one of the more spectacular products. She could almost repair a watch—or at least an alarm clock!"

"Just how does the crew control her?" asked Dirk.

"There's a television camera on that arm, so they can see the work just as if they were watching it directly. All movements are carried out by servo motors controlled through those cables."

No one could see what Lizzie was now doing, and it was a long time before she slowly backed away from the rocket. She was carrying, Dirk saw, a curiously shaped bar about three feet long which she held firmly in her metal claws. The two vehicles withdrew three-quarters of the way to the barrier, and as they approached the journalists hastily retreated from that drab gray object in the robot's claws. Collins, however, stood his ground, so Dirk decided it must be safe to remain.

There was a sudden, raucous buzzing from the engineer's coat pocket, and Dirk jumped a foot in the air. Collins held up his hand and the robot came to a halt about forty feet away. Its controllers, Dirk guessed, must be watching them through the television eyes.

Collins waved his arms, and the bar slowly rotated in the robot's claws. The buzzing of the radiation alarm ceased abruptly and Dirk breathed again.

"There's usually some sort of beaming effect from an irregular object like that," explained Collins. "We're still in its radiation field, of course, but it's too weak to be dangerous."

He turned towards the telescope, which had been temporarily deserted by its owner.

"This is rather handy," he said. "I didn't intend to do a visual inspection myself, but this is too good a chance to miss—that is, if we can focus at this distance."

"Exactly what are you trying to do?" asked Dirk as his friend racked the eyepiece out to its fullest extent.

"That's one of the reactor elements from the pile," said Collins absently. "We want to check it for activity. H'm—it seems to be standing up to it all right. Like a peep?"

Dirk peered through the telescope. He could see a few square inches of what at first sight appeared to be metal; then he decided that it was some kind of ceramic coating. It was so close that he could distinctly make out the surface texture.

"What would happen," he said, "if you touched it?"

"You'd certainly get very bad delayed burns, gamma and neutron. If you stayed near it long enough, you'd die."

Dirk stared in fascinated horror at that innocent gray surface which seemed only a few inches away.

"I suppose," he said, "that the bits in an atomic bomb would look very much like this."

"Just as harmless, anyway," agreed Collins. "But there's no danger of an explosion here. The fissionable material we use is all denatured. If we went to a lot of trouble, we *could* get an explosion—but a very small one."

"What do you mean by that?" asked Dirk suspiciously.

"Oh, just a large bang," said Collins cheerfully. "I couldn't give the figures offhand, but it would probably be no better than a few hundred tons of dynamite. Nothing to worry about at all!"

SEVEN

The senior staff lounge always gave Dirk the impression of a slightly down-at-heel London club. The fact that he had never been in a London club—prosperous or otherwise—did nothing to shake this firm conviction.

Yet at any one time the British contingent in the lounge was likely to be in the minority, and almost every accent in the world could be heard here during the course of the day. It made no difference to the atmosphere of the place, which seemed to emanate from the very English barman and his two assistants. Despite all onslaughts, they had kept the Union Jack flying here in the social center of Luna City. Only once had they yielded any territory, and even then the enemy had been swiftly routed. Six months ago the Americans had imported a brand-new Coca-Cola machine, which for a while had gleamed resplendently against the somber wooden paneling. But not for long: there had been some hasty consultations and much midnight carpentry in the workshops. One morning when the thirsty clients arrived, they found that the chromium plating had disappeared, and that they must now obtain their drinks from what might have been one of the late Mr. Chippendale's minor masterpieces. The *status quo* had been restored, but as to how it had happened the barman confessed complete ignorance.

Dirk always called at least once a day to collect his mail and read the papers. In the evening the place usually became rather crowded and he preferred to stay in his room, but tonight Maxton and Collins had dragged him out of retirement. The conversation, as usual, was not very far from the enterprise at hand.

"I think I'll be going to Taine's lecture tomorrow," said Dirk. "He's talking about the Moon, isn't he?"

"Yes; I bet he'll be pretty cautious now that he knows he's going! He might have to eat his words if he's not careful."

"We've given him a perfectly free hand," explained Maxton. "He'll probably talk about long-term plans and the use of the Moon as a refueling base to reach the planets."

"That should be interesting. Richards and Clinton will both be talking about engineering, I suppose, and I've had quite enough of that."

"Thanks!" laughed Collins. "It's nice to know that our efforts are appreciated!"

"Do you know," said Dirk suddenly, "I've never even seen the Moon through a big telescope."

"We could fix that up any evening this week—say after tomorrow. The Moon's only a day old at the moment. There are several telescopes here that would give you a pretty good view."

"I wonder," said Dirk thoughtfully, "if we're going to find life—I mean intelligent life—anywhere in the solar system?"

There was a long pause. Then Maxton said abruptly: "I don't think so."

"Why not?"

"Look at it this way. It's taken us only ten thousand years to get away from stone axes to spaceships. That means that interplanetary

travel must come pretty early in the development of any culture—
that is, if it proceeds along technological lines at all."

"But it needn't," said Dirk. "And if you throw in prehistory, it's
taken us a million years to get to spaceships."

"That's still only a thousandth—or less—of the age of the solar system. If there was any civilization on Mars, it probably died before humanity emerged from the jungle. If it still flourished, it would have
visited us long ago."

"That's so plausible," replied Dirk, "that I'm sure it isn't true.
Moreover, you can find plenty of incidents which make it look as if
we *have* been visited in the past, by things or ships that didn't like
the look of us and sheered off again."

"Yes, I've read some of those accounts, and they're very interesting
too. But I'm a skeptic: if anything ever has visited Earth, which I
doubt, I'll be very surprised if it came from the other planets. Space
and time are so big that it just doesn't seem probable that we'll have
neighbors only across the road."

"That seems a pity," said Dirk. "I think the most exciting thing
about astronautics is the possibility it opens up of meeting other
types of minds. It won't make the human race seem quite so lonely."

"That's perfectly true; but perhaps it will be just as well if we can
spend the next few centuries quietly exploring the solar system by
ourselves. At the end of that time we'll have acquired a lot more wisdom—and I *mean* wisdom, not mere knowledge. Perhaps we'll be
ready then to make contact with other races. At the moment—well,
we're still only forty years from Hitler."

"Then how long do you think we'll have to wait," said Dirk, a little
discouraged, "before we have our first contact with another civilization?"

"Who can say? It may be as near in time as the Wright Brothers—
or as far away as the building of the pyramids. It may even, of course,
happen a week from tomorrow when the 'Prometheus' lands on the
Moon. But I'm darned sure it won't."

"Do you really think," asked Dirk, "that we'll ever get to the stars?"

Professor Maxton sat in silence for a moment, thoughtfully blowing
clouds of cigarette smoke.

"I think so. Some day," he said.

"How?" persisted Dirk.

"If we can get an atomic drive that's more than fifty per cent efficient, we can reach nearly the velocity of light—perhaps three-quarters

of it, at any rate. That means it's about five years traveling from star to star. A long time, but still possible even for us short-lived creatures. And one day, I hope, we'll live a lot longer than we do today. A *heck* of a lot longer."

Dirk had a sudden vision of the three of them from the point of view of an outside observer. He sometimes had these moments of objectivity, and they were valuable in preserving his sense of proportion. Here they were, two men in the thirties and one in the fifties, sitting in their armchairs around the low table carrying their drinks. They might have been businessmen discussing a deal, or resting after a round of golf. Their background was utterly commonplace; from time to time snatches of everyday conversation drifted across from other groups, and there was a faint "clicking" of table-tennis balls from the room next door.

Yes, they might have been discussing stocks and shares, or the new car, or the latest gossip. But instead, they were wondering how to reach the stars.

"Our present atomic drives," said Collins, "are about one hundredth of one per cent efficient. So it will be quite a while before we think of going to Alpha Centauri."

(*In the background a plaintive voice was saying: "Hey, George, what's happened to my gin and lime?"*)

"Another question," said Dirk. "Is it absolutely certain that we can't travel faster than light?"

"In this universe, yes. It's the limiting velocity for all material objects. A miserable six hundred million miles an hour!"

(*"Three bitters, please, George!"*)

"Still," said Maxton slowly and thoughtfully, "there may even be a way around that."

"What do you mean?" asked Dirk and Collins simultaneously.

"In *our* universe, two points may be light-years apart. But they might be almost touching in a higher space."

(*"Where's the* Times? *No, you ass, not the New York thing!"*)

"I draw the line at the fourth dimension," said Collins with a grin. "That's a bit too fantastic for me. I'm a practical engineer—I hope!"

(*In the table-tennis room next door, it sounded as if an absent-minded victor had just jumped the net to shake hands with his opponent.*)

"At the beginning of this century," Professor Maxton retorted, "practical engineers felt the same way about the theory of relativity.

But it caught up with them a generation later." He rested his elbows on the table and stared into the remote distance.

"What," he said slowly, "do you imagine the *next* hundred years will bring?"

EIGHT

The big nissen hut was supposed to be connected to the camp's heating system, but no one would have noticed it. Dirk, who had grown accustomed to life at Luna City, had wisely brought his overcoat with him. He felt sorry for the unfortunate members of the audience who had neglected this elementary precaution. By the end of the lecture, they would have a vivid impression of conditions on the outer planets. About two hundred people were already seated on the benches, and more were continually arriving, since it was still only five minutes after the time at which the lecture was supposed to start. In the middle of the room a couple of anxious electricians were making last-minute adjustments to an episcope. Half a dozen armchairs had been placed in front of the speaker's dais, and were the targets of many covetous eyes. As clearly as if they had been labeled, they proclaimed to the world: "Reserved for the Director-General."

A door at the back of the hut opened, and Sir Robert Derwent entered, followed by Taine, Professor Maxton, and several others whom Dirk did not recognize. All but Sir Robert sat down in the front row, leaving the center seat empty.

The shuffling and whispering ceased as the Director-General stepped onto the dais. He looked, Dirk thought, like some great impresario about to ring up the curtain. And so, in a sense, he was.

"Mr. Taine," said Sir Robert, "has kindly consented to give us a talk on the objects of our first expedition. As he was one of its planners, and as he will be taking part in it, I'm sure we'll hear his views with great interest. After he's talked about the Moon, I gather that Mr. Taine is going to—er—let his hair down and discuss the plans we have for the rest of the solar system. I believe he has it pretty well organized all the way out to Pluto. Mr. Taine." (Applause.)

As he climbed onto the platform, Dirk studied the astronomer carefully. He had paid little attention to him until now: indeed, apart from his chance meeting with Hassell he had had few opportunities of studying any of the crew.

Taine was a slightly plump young man who seemed scarcely in the middle twenties, though he was actually just under thirty. Astronautics, thought Dirk, certainly catches them young. No wonder that Richards, at thirty-five, was considered quite an old crock by his colleagues.

When he spoke, Taine's voice was dry and precise and his words carried clearly throughout the hut. He was a good speaker, but had an annoying habit of juggling with pieces of chalk—which he frequently missed.

"I needn't tell you very much about the Moon as a whole," he said, "since you've already read or heard quite enough about it in the past few weeks. But I'll discuss the place where we intend to land, and say what we hope to do when we get there.

"First of all, here's a view of the whole Moon. (Slide One, please.) Since it's full, and the sun is shining vertically on the center of the disk, everything looks flat and uninteresting. The dark area here at the bottom right is the Mare Imbrium, in which we'll be landing.

"Now this is the Moon when she's nine days old—which is how you'll see her from Earth when we arrive. As the sun's shining at an angle, you'll see that the mountains near the center show up very clearly—look at those long shadows they throw.

"Let's go closer and examine the Mare Imbrium in detail. The name, by the way, means 'Sea of Rains,' but of course it isn't a sea and it doesn't rain there or anywhere else on the Moon. The old astrologers called it that in the days before the invention of the telescope.

"You'll see from this close-up that the Mare is a fairly flat plain bounded at the top (that's the south, by the way) by this really magnificent range—the lunar Apennines. To the north we have this smaller range, the Alps. The scale here gives you an idea of the distances: that crater, for example, is about fifty miles across.

"This area is one of the most interesting ones on the Moon, and certainly has the finest scenery, but we can only explore a small region on our first visit. We shall land about here (next slide, please), and this is a drawing of the area under the greatest magnification we can use. It's as you'd see it with the naked eye from a distance of two hundred miles away in space.

"The exact spot for the landing will be decided during the approach. We'll be falling slowly for the last hundred miles and should have time to select a suitable area. Since we're coming down vertically on shock absorbers, and holding off against the rockets until the last moment, we need only a few square yards of reasonably horizontal surface. Some pessimist has suggested that we may descend on what turns out to be dry quicksand, but this doesn't seem at all likely.

"We will leave the ship in couples, roped together, while one remains aboard to relay messages back to Earth. Our spacesuits carry air for twelve hours, and will insulate us against the whole range of temperatures encountered on the Moon—that is, from boiling point to a couple of hundred degrees below zero, Fahrenheit. Since we'll be there during the daytime, we won't run into the low temperatures unless we stay in shadow for long periods.

"I can't hope to mention all the work we intend to do during our week on the Moon, so I'll merely touch on some of the highlights.

"First of all, we're taking some compact but very powerful telescopes and hope to get clearer views of the planets than have ever been possible before. This equipment, like much of our stores, will be left behind for future expeditions.

"We are bringing back thousands of geological—I should say 'selenological'—samples for analysis. We're looking for minerals containing hydrogen, since once we can establish a fuel extraction plant on the Moon, the cost of voyages will be cut to a tenth or even less. More important still, we can start thinking of trips to the other planets.

"We're also taking a good deal of radio gear. As you know, the Moon has enormous possibilities as a relay station and we hope to investigate some of these. In addition we shall be making all sorts of physical measurements which will be of the greatest scientific interest. One of the most important of these is the determination of the Moon's magnetic field in order to test Blackett's theory. And, of course, we hope to get a splendid collection of photographs and films.

"Sir Robert has promised you that I'm going to 'let my hair down.' Well, I don't know about that but you may be interested in what I, personally, think the lines of development will be in the next decade or so.

"First of all, we have to establish a semi-permanent base on the Moon. If we're lucky in our first choice, we may be able to build it where we make our initial landing. Otherwise we'll have to try again.

"Quite extensive plans have been drawn up for such a base. It would be self-contained as far as possible, and would grow its own food supplies under glass. The Moon, with its fourteen days of continuous sunlight, should be a horticulturist's paradise!

"As we learn more about the Moon's natural resources, the base will be expanded and developed. We expect mining operations at an early date—but they will be to provide materials for use on the Moon. It will be far too expensive to import any but very rare substances to Earth.

"At the present time, journeys to the Moon are extremely costly and difficult because we have to carry fuel for the return trip. When we can refuel on the Moon, we shall be able to use much smaller and more economical machines. And, as I remarked just now, we'll be able to go to the planets.

"It sounds paradoxical, but it's easier to make the forty-million-mile journey from a lunar base to Mars than it is to cross the quarter of a million miles between Earth and Moon. It takes much longer, of course—about two hundred and fifty days—but it doesn't take more fuel.

"The Moon, thanks to its low gravitational field, is the stepping-stone to the planets—the base for the exploration of the solar system. If everything goes smoothly, we should be making plans for reaching Mars and Venus about ten years from now.

"I don't propose to speculate about Venus, except to say that we'll almost certainly make a radar survey of her before we attempt a landing. It should be possible to get accurate radar maps of the hidden surface, unless her atmosphere is very odd indeed.

"The exploration of Mars will be very much like the exploration of the Moon in some respects. We may not need spacesuits to go around in, but we'll certainly need oxygen equipment. The Martian base will be up against the same problems as the Lunar one, though in a much less acute form. But it will have one disadvantage—it will be a long way from home and will have to rely much more on its own resources. The almost certain presence of some kind of life will also affect the settlement in ways we can't predict. If there *is* intelligence on Mars—which I doubt—then our plans may have to be changed completely; we may not be able to stay there at all. The possibilities as far as Mars is concerned are almost endless; that's why it's such an interesting place.

"Beyond Mars, the scale of the solar system opens out and we cannot do much exploring until we have faster ships. Even our 'Prometheus' could reach the outer planets, but she couldn't get back and the journey would take many years. However, by the end of the century, I believe we may be getting ready to go to Jupiter and, perhaps, Saturn. Very probably these expeditions will start from Mars.

"We cannot of course hope to *land* on those two planets: if they have solid surfaces at all, which is doubtful, they are thousands of miles down beneath an atmosphere we dare not enter. If there is any form of life inside those sub-arctic infernos, I don't see how we can ever contact it—or how it can ever know anything about us.

"The chief interest on Saturn and Jupiter lies in their systems of moons. Saturn has at least twelve, Jupiter at least fifteen. What's more, many of them are fair-sized worlds—bigger than our Moon. Titan, Saturn's largest satellite, is half as big as Earth, and it's known to have an atmosphere, though not a breathable one. They are all very cold indeed, but that is not a serious objection now that we can get unlimited quantities of heat from atomic reactions.

"The three outermost planets won't concern us for quite a long time to come—perhaps fifty years or more. We know very little about them at the moment, in any case.

"That's all I'm going to say now. I hope I've made it clear that the journey we're taking next week, though it seems so tremendous by our present standards, is really only the first step. It's exciting and interesting, but we must keep it in its true perspective. The Moon's a small world, and in some ways not a very promising one, but it will lead us eventually to eight other planets, some bigger than the Earth, and more than thirty moons of various sizes. The total area we're opening up for exploration in the next few decades is at least ten times that of the land surface of this planet. That should provide room for everybody.

"Thank you."

Taine stopped abruptly, without any rhetorical flourishes, like a broadcaster caught out by the studio clock. There was dead silence in the hut for perhaps half a minute as his audience came slowly back to earth. Then there was a polite trickle of applause, which slowly grew as more and more of Taine's listeners discovered that they were still standing on the solid ground.

The reporters, stamping their feet and trying to restore their circulation, began to file out into the open. Dirk wondered how many had realized, for the first time, that the Moon was not a goal but a beginning—the first step upon an infinite road. It was a road, he now believed, along which all races must travel in the end, lest they wither and die upon their little, lonely worlds.

For the first time one could now see the "Prometheus" as a whole. "Alpha" had at last been hoisted into position upon "Beta's" broad shoulders, giving her a somewhat ugly, hunchbacked appearance. Even Dirk, to whom all flying machines looked very much alike, could not now have confused the great ship with anything else that had ever ridden the skies.

He followed Collins up the ladder of the movable gantry for his last look at the interior of the spaceship. It was evening and there were few people about. Beyond the warning ropes some photographers were trying to get shots of the machine with the sun going down behind it. The "Prometheus" would make an impressive sight silhouetted against the fading glory of the western sky.

"Alpha's" cabin was as bright and tidy as an operating theater. Yet there were personal touches: here and there articles which obviously belonged to the crew had been stowed away in niches where they were firmly secured by elastic bands. Several pictures and photographs had been pasted against convenient walls, and over the pilot's desk a plastic frame carried a portrait of (so Dirk assumed) Leduc's wife. Charts and mathematical tables had been secured at strategic spots where they could be quickly consulted. Dirk suddenly remembered, for the first time in days, his visit to the training mock-up in England, where he had stood before this same array of instruments in a quiet London suburb. That seemed a lifetime ago, and more than half a world away.

Collins walked over to a tall locker and swung open the door.

"You haven't seen one of these before, have you?" he asked.

The three flaccid spacesuits hanging from their hooks looked like creatures of the deep sea, dredged up from the darkness into the light of day. The thick, flexible covering yielded easily at Dirk's touch, and he felt the presence of reinforcing metal hoops. Transparent helmets like large goldfish bowls were secured in recesses at the side of the locker.

"Just like diving suits, aren't they?" said Collins. "As a matter of fact, 'Alpha' is more like a submarine than anything else—though our design problems are a lot easier, as we haven't such pressures to contend with."

"I'd like to sit in the pilot's position," said Dirk abruptly. "Is it all right?"

"Yes, as long as you don't touch anything."

Collins watched with a slight smile as the other settled himself down in the seat. He knew the impulse, having yielded to it himself more often than once.

When the ship was under power, or standing vertically on the Moon, the seat would have swung forwards through a right angle from its present position. What was now the floor beneath Dirk's feet would then be the wall in front of him, and the periscope eyepiece which his boots now had to avoid would be conveniently placed for his use. Because of this rotation—so unfamiliar to the human mind—it was hard to capture the sensations which the ship's pilot would have when he occupied this seat.

Dirk rose and turned to go. He followed Collins in silence to the airlock, but paused for a moment at the thick oval door for a last look around the quiet cabin.

"Good-bye, little ship," he said in his mind. "Good-bye—and good luck!"

It was dark when they stepped out onto the gantry, and the floodlights spilled pools of brilliance upon the concrete below. A cold wind was blowing, and the night blazed with stars of which he would never know the names. Suddenly Collins, standing in the gloom beside him, caught his arm and pointed silently to the horizon.

Almost lost in the faint afterglow of the sunset, the two-day-old sickle of the New Moon was sliding down into the west. Clasped in its arms was the dimly luminous disk which still awaited the advent of day. Dirk tried to picture the great mountains and the wrinkled plains still waiting for the sun to rise upon them, yet already ablaze with the cold light of the almost full Earth.

Millions upon millions of times the Earth had waxed and waned above that silent land, and only shadows had ever moved upon its face. Since the dawn of terrestrial life, perhaps a dozen craters had crumbled and decayed, but it had known no other change than this. And now at last, after all these ages, its loneliness was coming to an end.

NINE

Two days before take-off, Luna City was probably one of the calmest and least agitated spots on Earth. All preparations had been completed except the final fueling and some last-minute tests. There was nothing to do except wait until the Moon moved to its appointed place.

In the great newspaper offices all over the planet, sub-editors were busily preparing their headlines, and writing possible alternative stories which could be quickly trimmed to fit all but the most stubborn facts. Perfect strangers in buses and trains were liable to swap astronomical knowledge at the slightest provocation. Only a very spectacular murder was likely to receive the attention it normally commanded.

In every continent, long-range radar sets were being tuned up to follow "Alpha" on its journey into space. The little radar beacon aboard the spaceship would enable its position to be checked at every moment of the voyage.

Fifty feet underground at Princeton University, one of the world's greatest electronic computers was standing by. Should it be necessary for any reason for the ship to change its orbit, or to delay its return, a new trajectory must be calculated through the shifting gravitational fields of Earth and Moon. An army of mathematicians would take months to do this; the Princeton calculator could produce the answer, already printed, in a few hours.

Every radio amateur in the world who could operate on the spaceship's frequency was giving his equipment a last-minute check. There would not be many who could both receive and interpret the hyperfrequency, pulse-modulated signals from the ship, but there would be a few. The watchdogs of the ether, the Communications Commissioners, were standing by to deal with any unauthorized transmitters which might try to break into the circuit.

On their mountain tops, the astronomers were preparing for their private race—the contest to see who would get the best and clearest photographs of the landing. "Alpha" was far too small to be seen when it reached the Moon—but the flare of the jets as they splashed across the lunar rocks should be visible at least a million miles away.

Meanwhile the three men who held the center of the world's stage gave interviews when they felt like it, slept long hours in their huts, or relaxed violently at table-tennis, which was about the only form of sport that Luna City provided. Leduc, who had a macabre sense of humor, amused himself by telling his friends the useless or insulting things he had left them in his will. Richards behaved as if nothing of the slightest importance had happened, and insisted on making elaborate social engagements for three weeks' time. Taine was seldom seen at all; it transpired later that he was busily writing a mathematical treatise which had very little to do with astronautics. It was, in fact, concerned with the total possible number of games of bridge, and the length of time it would take to play them all.

Very few people indeed knew that the meticulous Taine could, had he wished, have made much more money out of fifty-two pieces of card than he was ever likely to from astronomy. Not that he would do at all badly now, if he came back safely from the Moon. . . .

Sir Robert Derwent lay completely relaxed in his armchair, the room in darkness save for the pool of light from the reading lamp. He was almost sorry that the two or three days' margin for last-minute hold-ups had not been required. It was still a night and a day and a night again before the take-off—and there was nothing to do but wait.

The Director-General did not like waiting. It gave him time to think, and thought was the enemy of contentment. Now, in the quiet hours of the night, as the greatest moment of his life approached, he was revisiting the past in search of his youth.

The forty years of struggle, of success and heartbreak, still lay in the future. He was a boy again, at the very beginning of his university career, and the Second World War which had stolen six years of his life was still no more than a threatening cloud on the horizon. He was lying in a Shropshire wood on one of those spring mornings that had never come again, and the book he was reading was the one he still held in his hands. In faded ink upon the fly-leaf were the words, written in a curiously half-formed hand: "Robert A. Derwent. 22 June 1935."

The book was the same—but where, now, was the music of the singing words that once had set his heart on fire? He was too wise and too old; the tricks of alliteration and repetition could not deceive him now, and the emptiness of thought was all too clear. Yet ever and again there would come a faint echo from the past, and for a moment the blood would rush to his cheeks as it had done those forty years ago. Sometimes a single phrase would be enough:

> "*O Love's lute heard about the lands of Death!*"

Sometimes a couplet:

> "*Until God loosen over land and sea*
> *The thunder of the trumpets of the night.*"

The Director-General stared into space. He himself was loosening such a thunder as the world had never heard before. Upon the Indian Ocean the sailors would look up from their ships as those roaring motors stormed across the sky; the tea-planters of Ceylon would hear them, now faint and thin, going westwards into Africa. The Arabian oilfields would catch the last reverberations as they filtered down from the fringe of space.

Sir Robert turned the pages idly, halting wherever the flying words caught his mind.

> "*It is not much that a man can save*
> *On the sands of life, in the straits of time,*
> *Who swims in sight of the third great wave,*
> *That never a swimmer shall cross or climb.*"

What had he saved from Time? Far more, he knew, than most men. Yet he had been almost forty before he had found any aim in life. His love for mathematics had always been with him, but for long it had been a purposeless passion. Even now, it seemed that chance had made him what he was.

> "*There lived a singer in France of old*
> *By the tideless dolorous midland sea.*
> *In a land of sand and ruin and gold*
> *There shone one woman, and none but she.*"

The magic failed and faded. His mind went back to the war years, when he had fought in that silent battle of the laboratories. While men were dying on land and sea and air, he had been tracing the paths of electrons through interlocking magnetic fields. Nothing could have been more remotely academic; yet from the work in which he had shared had come the greatest tactical weapon of the war.

It had been a small step from radar to celestial mechanics, from electron orbits to the paths of planets round the sun. The techniques he had applied in the little world of the magnetron could be used again on the cosmic scale. Perhaps he had been lucky; after only ten years of work he had made his reputation through his attack on the three-body problem. Ten years later, somewhat to everyone's surprise —including his own—he had been Astronomer Royal.

> "*The pulse of war and passion of wonder,*
> *The heavens that murmur, the sounds that shine,*
> *The stars that sing and the loves that thunder,*
> *The music burning at heart like wine. . . .*"

He might have held that post efficiently and with success for the remainder of his life, but the *zeitgeist* of astronautics had been too strong for him. His mind had told him that the crossing of space was about to come, but how near it was he had not at first recognized. When that knowledge had finally dawned, he had known at last the purpose of his life, and the long years of toil had reaped their harvest.

> "*Ah, had I not taken my life up and given*
> *All that life gives and the years let go,*
> *The wine and honey, the balm and leaven,*
> *The dreams reared high and the hopes brought low?*"

He flicked the yellowing pages a dozen at a time, until his eyes caught the narrow columns of print for which he had been searching. Here at least the magic lingered; here nothing had altered, and the words still beat against his brain with the old, insistent rhythm. There had been a time when the verses, head to tail in an endless chain, had threaded their way through his mind for hour upon hour until the very words had lost their meaning:

> "*Then star nor sun shall waken,*
> *Nor any change of light:*
> *Nor sound of waters shaken,*
> *Nor any sound or sight:*
> *Nor wintry leaves nor vernal,*
> *Nor days nor things diurnal;*
> *Only the sleep eternal*
> *In an eternal night.*"

The eternal night would come, and too soon for Man's liking. But at least before they guttered and died, he would have known the stars; before it faded like a dream, the Universe would have yielded up its secrets to his mind. Or if not to his, then to the minds that would come after and would finish what he had now begun.

Sir Robert closed the slim volume and placed it back upon the shelf. His voyage into the past had ended in the future, and it was time to return.

Beside his bed, the telephone began to call for attention in angry, urgent bursts.

TEN

No one ever learned a great deal about Jefferson Wilkes, simply because there was very little indeed to know about him. He had been a junior accountant in a Pittsburgh factory for almost thirty years, during which time he had been promoted once. He did his work with a laborious thoroughness that was the despair of his employers. Like millions of his contemporaries, he had practically no understanding of the civilization in which he found himself. Twenty-five years ago he had married, and no one was surprised to discover that his wife had left him in a matter of months.

Not even his friends—though there was no evidence that he had ever possessed any—would have maintained that Jefferson Wilkes was a profound thinker. Yet there was one matter to which, after his fashion, he had given very serious thought.

The world would never know what had first turned the pathetic little mind of Jefferson Wilkes outwards towards the stars. It was more than probable that the motive had been a desire to escape from the drab reality of his everyday life. Whatever the reason, he had studied the writings of those who predicted the conquest of space. And he had decided that, at all costs, it must be stopped.

As far as could be gathered, Jefferson Wilkes believed that the attempt to enter space would bring down upon humanity some stupendous metaphysical doom. There was even evidence that he considered the Moon to be Hell, or at least Purgatory. Any premature arrival by mankind in those infernal regions would obviously have incalculable and—to say the least—unfortunate consequences.

To gain support for his ideas, Jefferson Wilkes did what thousands before him had done. He sought to convert others to his beliefs by forming an organization to which he gave the declamatory title:

"The Rockets Must Not Rise!" Since any doctrine, however fantastic, will gain some adherents, Wilkes eventually acquired a few score supporters among the obscurer religious sects that flourish exotically in the western United States. Very swiftly, however, the microscopic movement was rent by schism and counter-schism. At the end of it all, the Founder was left with shattered nerves and depleted finances. If one wishes to draw so fine a distinction, it may be said that he then became insane.

When the "Prometheus" was built, Wilkes decided that her departure could only be prevented by his own efforts. A few weeks before the take-off, he liquidated his meager assets and withdrew his remaining money from the bank. He found that he would still need one hundred and fifty-five dollars to take him to Australia.

The disappearance of Jefferson Wilkes surprised and pained his employers, but after a hasty inspection of his books they made no efforts to trace him. One does not call in the police when, after thirty years of faithful service, a member of the staff steals one hundred and fifty-five dollars from a safe containing several thousand.

Wilkes had no difficulty in reaching Luna City, and when he was there no one took any notice of him. Interplanetary's staff probably thought he was one of the hundreds of reporters around the base, while the reporters took him for a member of the staff. He was, in any case, the sort of man who could have walked straight into Buckingham Palace without attracting the slightest attention—and the sentries would have sworn that no one had entered.

What thoughts passed through the narrow gateway of Jefferson Wilkes's mind when he saw the "Prometheus" lying on her launching cradle, no one will ever know. Perhaps until that moment he had not realized the magnitude of the task he had set himself. He could have done great damage with a bomb—but though bombs may be come by in Pittsburgh as in all great cities, the ways of acquiring them are not common knowledge—particularly among respectable accountants.

From the rope barriers, whose purpose he could not fully comprehend, he had watched the stores being loaded and the engineers making their final tests. He had noticed that, when night came, the great ship was left unattended beneath the floodlights, and that even these were switched off in the small hours of the morning.

Would it not be far better, he thought, to let the ship leave Earth but to ensure that it would never return? A damaged ship could be repaired; one that vanished without explanation would be a far more effective deterrent—a warning that might be heeded.

Jefferson Wilkes's mind was innocent of science, but he knew that a spaceship must carry its own air-supply, and he knew that air was kept in cylinders. What would be simpler than to empty them so that the loss would not be discovered until too late? He did not wish to harm the crew, and was sincerely sorry that they would come to such an end, but he saw no alternative.

It would be tedious to enumerate the defects in Jefferson Wilkes's brilliant plan. The air-supply of the "Prometheus" was not even carried in cylinders, and had Wilkes managed to empty the liquid oxygen tanks he would have had some unpleasantly frigid surprises. The routine instrument check would, in any case, have told the crew exactly what had happened before take-off, and even without an oxygen reserve the air-conditioning plant could have maintained a breathable atmosphere for many hours. There would have been time to enter one of the emergency return orbits which could be quickly computed for just such a calamity.

Last, and far from least, Wilkes had to get aboard the ship. He did not doubt that this could be done, for the gantry was left in position every night, and he had studied it so carefully that he could climb it even in the dark. When the crowd had been surging around the head of the ship, he had mingled with it and had seen no sign of locks on that curious, inward-opening door.

He waited in an empty hangar at the edge of the field until the thin moon had set. It was very cold, and he had not been prepared for this since it was summertime in Pennsylvania. But his mission had made him resolute and when at last the blazing floodlights died he had started to cross that empty sea of concrete towards the black wings spread beneath the stars.

The rope barrier halted him and he ducked under it. A few minutes later his groping hands felt a metal framework in the darkness before him, and he made his way around the base of the gantry. He paused at the foot of the metal steps, listening into the night. The world was utterly silent; on the horizon he could see the glow of such lights as were still burning in Luna City. A few hundred yards away he could just make out the dim silhouettes of buildings and hangars, but they were dark and deserted. He began to climb the steps.

He paused again, listening, at the first platform twenty feet from the ground, and again he was reassured. His electric torch and the tools he thought he might need were heavy in his pockets; he felt a little proud of his foresight and the smoothness with which he had carried out his plan.

That was the last step: he was on the upper platform. He gripped his torch with one hand, and a moment later the walls of the spaceship were smooth and cold beneath his fingers.

Into the building of the "Prometheus" had gone millions of pounds and more millions still of dollars. The scientists who had obtained such sums from governments and great industrial undertakings were not exactly fools. To most men—though not to Jefferson Wilkes—it would have seemed improbable that the fruit of all their labors should be left unguarded and unprotected in the night.

Many years ago the planning staff had foreseen the possibility of sabotage by religious fanatics, and one of Interplanetary's most cherished files contained the threatening letters which these people had been illogical enough to write. All reasonable precautions had therefore been taken—and taken by experts, some of whom had themselves spent years during the War sabotaging Axis or Allied equipment.

Tonight the watchman in the concrete bunker at the edge of the macadam was a law student named Achmet Singh, who was earning a little money during his vacation in a way that suited him very well. He had only to be at his post eight hours a day, and the job gave him ample time for study. When Jefferson Wilkes came to the first rope barrier, Achmet Singh was fast asleep—as, surprisingly enough, he was quite expected to be. But five seconds later, he was wide awake.

Singh punched the alarm cut-off button, and moved swiftly across to the control panel, cursing fluently in three languages and four religions. This was the second time this had happened on his watch: before, a stray dog belonging to one of the staff had set off the alarms. The same thing had probably happened again.

He switched on the image converter, waiting impatiently for the few seconds it took the tubes to warm up. Then he grasped the projector controls and started to survey the ship.

To Achmet Singh, it seemed that a purple searchlight was shining across the concrete towards the launching platform. Through the beam of the searchlight, utterly unconscious of its presence, a man was cautiously feeling his way towards the "Prometheus." It was impossible not to laugh at his movements as he groped blindly along while all around him was bathed with light. Achmet Singh followed him steadily with the beam of the infra-red projector until he came to the gantry. The secondary alarms went into action then, and again Singh switched them off. He would not act, he decided, until he had learned the midnight prowler's motives.

When Jefferson Wilkes paused with some satisfaction on the first platform, Achmet Singh secured an excellent photograph which would be conclusive evidence in any court of law. He waited until Wilkes had reached the airlock itself; then he decided to act.

The blast of light which pinned Wilkes against the walls of the spaceship blinded him as effectively as the darkness through which he had been feeling his way. For a moment the shock was so paralyzing that he could not move. Then a great voice roared at him out of the night.

"What are you doing there? Come down at once!"

Automatically he began to stumble down the steps. He had reached the lower platform before his mind lost its paralysis and he looked desperately around for a means of escape. By shielding his eyes, he could now see a little; the fatal ring of floodlights around the "Prometheus" was only a hundred yards across and beyond it lay darkness and, perhaps, safety.

The voice called again from beyond the pool of light.

"Hurry up! Come this way—we've got you covered!"

The "we" was pure invention on the part of Singh, though it was true that reinforcements in the form of two annoyed and sleepy police sergeants were on the way.

Jefferson Wilkes finished his slow descent, and stood trembling with reaction on the concrete, steadying himself against the gantry. He remained almost motionless for half a minute: then, as Achmet Singh had anticipated, he suddenly bolted around the ship and disappeared. He would be running towards the desert, and could be rounded up easily enough, but it would save time if he could be scared back again. The watchman knocked down another loudspeaker switch.

When that same voice roared at him again out of the darkness ahead, where he had thought to find safety, the terrified little spirit of Jefferson Wilkes finally despaired. In unreasoning fear, like some wild animal he ran back to the ship and tried to hide himself in its shadow. Yet even now the impulse that had brought him round the world still drove him blindly on, though he was scarcely aware of his motives or his actions. He began to work his way along the base of the ship, always keeping in the shadows.

The great hollow shaft only a few feet above his head seemed to offer a second way into the machine—or, at least, a chance of hiding until he could escape. In ordinary times, he could never have made that climb over the smooth metal walls, but fear and determination gave him strength. Achmet Singh, looking into his television screen a hundred yards away, became suddenly ashen. He began to speak, quickly and urgently, into his microphone.

Jefferson Wilkes did not hear him; he scarcely noticed that the great voice from the night was no longer peremptory, but pleading. It meant nothing to him now; he was conscious only of the dark tunnel ahead. Holding his torch in one hand, he began to crawl along it.

The walls were made of some gray, rock-like material that was hard yet oddly warm to the touch. It seemed to Wilkes as if he was entering a cave with perfectly circular walls; after a few yards it widened and he could almost walk if he bent double. Around him now was a meaningless mosaic of metal bars and that strange gray rock—the most refractory of all ceramics—over which he had been crawling.

He could go no farther; the cave had suddenly divided into a series of branching passages too small for him to enter. Shining his torch along them he could see that the walls were pierced with jets and nozzles. He might have done some damage here, but they were all beyond his reach.

Jefferson Wilkes slumped down on the hard, unyielding floor. The torch fell from his nerveless fingers and the darkness enfolded him again. He was too exhausted for disappointment or regret. He did not notice, nor could he have understood, the faint unwavering glow that was burning in the walls around him.

A long time later, some noise in the external world drew his mind back from wherever it had fled. He sat up and stared around him, not knowing where he was or how he had come here. Far away he could see a faint circle of light, the mouth of this mysterious cavern. Beyond that opening were voices and the sounds of machines moving to and fro. He knew that they were hostile and that he must remain here where they could not find him.

It was not to be. A brilliant light passed like a rising sun across the mouth of his cave, then returned to shine full upon him. It was moving down the tunnel, and behind it was something strange and huge which his mind could not grasp.

He screamed in terror as those metal claws came full into the light and reached forward to grasp him. Then he was being dragged helplessly out into the open where his unknown enemies were waiting.

There was a confusion of light and noises all around him. A great machine that seemed to be alive was holding him in its metal arms and rolling away from a tremendous winged shape that should have aroused memories, but did not. Then he was lowered to the ground in a circle of waiting men.

He wondered why they did not come near, why they kept so far away and looked at him so strangely. He did not resist when long poles carrying shining instruments were waved around him as if exploring his body. Nothing mattered now; he felt only a dull sickness and an overwhelming desire for sleep.

Suddenly a wave of nausea swept over him and he crumpled to the ground. Impulsively, the men standing in that wide circle moved a pace towards him—and then drew back.

The twisted, infinitely pathetic figure lay like a broken doll beneath the glaring lights. There was no sound or movement anywhere; in the background, the great wings of the "Prometheus" brooded above their pools of shadow. Then the robot glided forward, trailing its armored cables across the concrete. Very gently, the metal arms reached down and the strange hands unfolded.

Jefferson Wilkes had reached the end of his journey.

ELEVEN

Dirk hoped that the crew had spent a better night than he had. He was still sleepy and confused, but he had a distinct impression of being awakened more than once by the sound of cars driven recklessly through the night. Perhaps there had been a fire somewhere, but he had heard no alarm.

He was shaving when McAndrews came into his room, obviously bursting with news. The Director of Public Relations looked as if he had been up half the night, which indeed was very nearly the case.

"Have you heard the news?" he said breathlessly.

"*What* news?" asked Dirk, switching off his shaver with some annoyance.

"There's been an attempt to sabotage the ship."

"What!"

"It happened about one o'clock this morning. The detectors spotted a man trying to get aboard 'Alpha.' When the watchman challenged him the damn fool tried to hide himself—in 'Beta's' exhaust!"

It was some seconds before the full meaning of the words dawned. Then Dirk remembered what Collins had told him when he had looked through the telescope into that deadly pit.

"What happened to him?" he said thickly.

"They called to him through loud-speakers, but he took no notice. So they had to get him out with the servicing robot. He was still alive, but too hot to go near. He died a couple of minutes later. The doctors say he probably never knew what had happened to him—you don't when you get a dose like that."

Feeling a little sick, Dirk slumped down on his bed.

"Did he do any damage?" he asked at length.

"We don't think so. He never got into the ship, and there was nothing he could do to the jet. They were afraid he might have left a bomb, but luckily he hadn't."

"He must have been crazy! Any idea who he was?"

"Probably a religious maniac of some kind. We get a lot of them after us. The police are trying to trace him from the contents of his pockets."

There was a gloomy pause before Dirk spoke again.

"Not a very good send-off for the 'Prometheus,' is it?"

McAndrews shrugged his shoulders, somewhat callously.

"I don't think anyone round here's likely to be superstitious! Are you coming out to watch the fueling? It's scheduled for two o'clock. I'll give you a lift down in the car."

Dirk was not enthusiastic.

"Thanks all the same," he said, "but I've got rather a lot to do. And anyway, there won't be much to see, will there? I mean, pumping a few hundred tons of fuel isn't going to be very exciting. I suppose it *could* be—but in that event I'd rather not be there!"

McAndrews seemed slightly annoyed, but Dirk couldn't help that. At the moment he felt singularly little desire to go near the "Prometheus" again. It was an irrational feeling, of course; for why should one blame the great ship if it protected itself against its enemies?

Throughout the day Dirk could hear the roar of helicopters arriving in a continual stream from the great Australian cities, while from time to time a transcontinental jet would come whistling down into the airport. Where these early arrivals expected to spend the night he could not imagine. It was none too warm in the centrally heated huts, and the news reporters unlucky enough to be under canvas had told terrible stories of hardship, many of which were very nearly true.

Late in the afternoon he met Collins and Maxton in the lounge and heard that the fueling had been carried out with no difficulty. As Collins said: "We have now only to light the blue touch-paper and retire."

"By the way," remarked Maxton, "didn't you say the other night that you'd never seen the Moon through a telescope? We're going over to the Observatory in a minute. Why not come along?"

"I'd love to—but don't say that *you've* never looked at her, either!"

Maxton grinned.

"That would be a 'very poor show,' as Ray would put it. I happen to know my way around the Moon quite well, but I doubt if more than half the people in Interplanetary have ever used a telescope. The D.-G.'s the best example of that. He spent ten years on astronomical research before he ever went near an observatory."

"Don't say I told you," said Collins with great seriousness, "but I've found that astronomers are divided into two species. The first is purely nocturnal and spends its working hours taking photos of objects so far away that they probably don't exist any more. They're not interested in the solar system, which they consider a very odd and almost inexcusable accident. During the daytime they may be found sleeping under large stones and in warm, dry places.

"Members of the second species work more normal hours and inhabit offices full of calculating machines and lady computers. This hinders them a lot; nevertheless they manage to produce reams of mathematics about the—probably non-existent—objects photographed by their colleagues, with whom they communicate through little notes left with the night-watchman.

"Both species have one thing in common. They are never known, except in moments of extreme mental aberration, actually to *look* through their telescopes. Still, they do get some very pretty photographs."

"I think," laughed Professor Maxton, "that the nocturnal species should be emerging any moment now. Let's go."

The "Observatory" at Luna City had been erected largely for the amusement of the technical staff, which included far more amateur astronomers than professionals. It consisted of a group of wooden huts which had been drastically modified to hold about a dozen instruments of all sizes from three to twelve inches' aperture. A twenty-inch reflector was now under construction, but would not be completed for some weeks.

The visitors had, it seemed, already discovered the Observatory and were making full use of it. Some scores of people were lining up hopefully in front of the various buildings, while the thwarted owners of the telescopes were giving them two-minute peeks accompanied by impromptu lectures. They had not bargained for this when they had gone out to have a look at the four-day-old Moon, and they had now given up all hope of having a view themselves.

"It's a pity they can't charge a pound a head," said Collins thoughtfully as he looked at the queue.

"Perhaps they are," answered Professor Maxton. "We might at least put up a collecting box for impecunious atomic engineers."

The dome of the twelve-inch reflector—the only instrument which was not privately owned and which actually belonged to Interplanetary—was closed and the building was locked. Professor Maxton drew out a bunch of master keys and tried them one by one until the door opened. The nearest in line immediately broke ranks and started to pour towards them.

"Sorry," shouted the Professor, as he slammed the door behind them, "it's out of order!"

"You mean it *will* be out of order," said Collins darkly. "Do you know how to use one of these things?"

"We should be able to figure it out," answered Maxton, with just a shade of uncertainty in his voice.

Dirk's very high opinion of the two scientists began to fall abruptly.

"Do you mean to tell me," he said, "that you're going to risk using an instrument as complicated and expensive as this without knowing anything about it? Why, it would be like someone who didn't know how to drive getting into an automobile and trying to start it!"

"Goodness gracious," protested Collins, though with a slight twinkle in his eye. "You don't think *this* thing is complicated, do you? Compare it with a bicycle, if you like—but not a car!"

"Very well," retorted Dirk, "just try and ride a bicycle without any practice beforehand!"

Collins merely laughed and continued his examination of the controls. For some time he and the Professor exchanged technical conversation which no longer impressed Dirk, since he could see that they knew very little more about the telescope than he did himself.

After some experimenting, the instrument was swung round to the Moon, now fairly low in the southwest. For a long time, it seemed to Dirk, he waited patiently in the background while the two engineers looked to their full. Finally he got fed up.

"You *did* invite me, you know," he remonstrated. "Or have you forgotten?"

"Sorry," apologized Collins, giving up his position with obvious reluctance. "Have a look now—focus up with this knob."

At first Dirk could see only a blinding whiteness with darker patches here and there. He slowly turned the focusing knob, and suddenly the picture became clear and sharp, like some brilliant etching.

He could see a good half of the crescent, the tips of the horns being out of the field. The edge of the Moon was a perfect arc of a circle, without any sign of unevenness. But the line dividing night and day was ragged, and broken in many places by mountains and uplands which threw long shadows across the plains below. There were few of the great craters he had expected to see, and he guessed that most of them must lie in the part of the disk that was still unlit.

He focused his attention upon a great oval plain bordered with mountains, which reminded him irresistibly of a dried-up ocean bed. It was, he supposed, one of the Moon's so-called seas, but it was easy to tell that there was no water anywhere in that calm, still landscape spread out beneath him. Every detail was sharp and brilliant, save when a ripple like a heat-haze made the whole picture tremble for a moment. The Moon was sinking into the horizon mists, and the image was being disturbed by its slanting, thousand-mile passage through the Earth's atmosphere.

At one point just inside the darkened area of the disk a group of brilliant lights shone like beacon fires blazing in the lunar night. They puzzled Dirk for a moment, until he realized that he was looking upon great mountain peaks which had caught the sun hours before the dawning light had struck into the lowlands around their bases.

He understood now why men had spent their lives watching the shadows come and go across the face of that strange world which seemed so near yet which, until his generation, had been the symbol of all that could never be attained. He realized that in a lifetime one could not exhaust its wonders; always there would be something fresh to see as the eye grew more skilled in tracing out that wealth of almost infinite detail.

Something was blocking his view and he looked up in annoyance. The Moon was descending below the level of the dome; he could lower the telescope no farther. Someone switched on the lights again and he saw that Collins and Maxton were grinning at him.

"I hope you've seen all you want to," said the Professor. "We had ten minutes apiece—*you* have been there for twenty-five and I'm darned glad the Moon set when it did!"

TWELVE

"Tomorrow we launch the 'Prometheus.' I say 'we,' because I find it no longer possible to stand aside and play the part of a disinterested spectator. No one on Earth can do that; the events of the next few hours will shape the lives of all men who will ever be born, down to the end of time.

"Someone once pictured humanity as a race of islanders who have not yet learned the art of making ships. Out across the ocean we can see other islands about which we have wondered and speculated since the beginning of history. Now, after a million years, we have made our first primitive canoe; tomorrow we will watch it sail through the coral reef and vanish over the horizon.

"This evening I saw, for the first time in my life, the Moon's glittering mountains and great dusky plains. The country over which Leduc and his companions will be walking in less than a week was still invisible, waiting for the sunrise which will not come for another three of our days. Yet its night must be brilliant beyond imagination, for the Earth will be more than half-full in its sky.

"I wonder how Leduc, Richards and Taine are spending their last night on Earth? They will, of course, have put all their affairs in order, and there'll be nothing left for them to do. Are they relaxing, listening to music, reading—or just sleeping?"

James Richards was doing none of these things. He was seated in the lounge with his friends, drinking very slowly and carefully, while he regaled them with entertaining stories of the tests he had been given by crazy psychologists trying to decide if he was normal, and if so, what could be done about it. The psychologists he was libeling formed the largest—and most appreciative—part of his audience. They let him talk until midnight; then they put him to bed. It took six of them to do it.

Pierre Leduc had spent the evening out at the ship, watching some fuel evaporation tests that were being carried out on "Alpha." There was very little point in his being present, but although gentle hints had been dropped from time to time, no one could get rid of him. Just before midnight the Director-General arrived, exploded good-naturedly and sent him back in his own car with strict orders to get some sleep. Whereupon Leduc spent the next two hours in bed reading *La Comédie Humaine.*

Only Lewis Taine—the precise, unemotional Taine—had used his last night on Earth in ways that might have been expected. He had sat for hours at his desk preparing drafts and destroying them one by one. Late in the evening he had finished; in careful long-hand he transcribed the letter which had cost him so much thought. Then he sealed it and attached a formal little note:

Dear Professor Maxton,

If I do not return, I should be obliged if you would arrange for this letter to be delivered.

Sincerely,
L. Taine.

Letter and note he placed in a large envelope which he addressed to Maxton. Then he picked up the bulky file of alternative flight orbits and began to make pencil notes in the margins.

He was himself again.

THIRTEEN

The message which Sir Robert had been expecting arrived soon after dawn by one of the high-speed mailplanes which, later in the day, would be carrying the films of the launching back to Europe. It was a brief official minute, signed only with a pair of initials which the whole world would have recognized even without the help of the words: "10, Downing Street" which ran along the head of the paper. Yet it was not entirely a formal document, for beneath the initials the same hand had written: "Good luck!"

When Professor Maxton arrived a few minutes later, Sir Robert handed him the paper without a word. The American read it slowly and gave a sigh of relief.

"Well, Bob," he said, "we've done our share. It's up to the politicians now—but we'll keep pushing them from behind."

"It's not been as difficult as I feared; the statesmen have learned to pay attention to us since Hiroshima."

"And when will the plan come up before the General Assembly?"

"In about a month, when the British and American governments will formally propose that 'all planets or celestial bodies unoccupied or unclaimed by non-human forms of life, etc. etc., be deemed international areas freely accessible to all peoples, and that no sovereign state be permitted to claim any such astronomical bodies for its exclusive occupation or development . . .' and so on."

"And what about the proposed Interplanetary Commission?"

"That will have to be discussed later. At the moment the important thing is to get agreement on the first stages. Now that our governments have formally adopted the plan—it will be on the radio by this afternoon—we can start lobbying like hell. You're best at this sort of thing—can you write a little speech on the lines of our first Manifesto —one that Leduc can broadcast from the Moon? Emphasize the astronomical viewpoint, and the stupidity of even attempting to carry nationalism into space. Think you can do it before take-off? Not that it matters if you can't, except that it may leak out too soon if we have to radio the script."

"O.K.—I'll get the rough draft checked over by the political experts, and then leave you to put in the adjectives as usual. But I don't think it will need any purple passages this time. As the first message to come from the Moon, it will have quite enough psychological punch by itself!"

Never before had any part of the Australian desert known such a population density. Special trains from Adelaide and Perth had been arriving throughout the night, and thousands of cars and private aircraft were parked on either side of the launching track. Jeeps were continually patroling up and down the kilometer-wide safety zones, shooing away too inquisitive visitors. No one at all was allowed past the five-kilometer mark, and at this point the canopy of circling air-craft also came to an abrupt end.

The "Prometheus" lay glittering in the low sunlight, throwing a fantastic shadow far across the desert. Until now she had seemed only a thing of metal, but at last she was alive and waiting to fulfill the dreams of her creators. The crew was already aboard when Dirk and his companions arrived. There had been a little ceremony for the benefit of the newsreels and television cameras, but no formal speeches. These could come, if they were needed, in three weeks' time.

In quiet, conversational tones the loud-speakers along the track were saying: "Instrument check completed: launching generators run-ning at half speed: one hour to go."

The words came rolling back across the desert, muffled by dis-tance, from the further speakers: "One hour to go—hour to go—go—go—go . . ." until they had died away into the northwest.

"I think we'd better get into position," said Professor Maxton. "It's going to take us some time to drive through this crowd. Take a good look at 'Alpha'—it's the last opportunity you'll have."

The announcer was speaking again, but this time his words were not intended for them. Dirk realized that he was overhearing part of a world-wide sequence of instructions.

"All sounding stations should be ready to fire. Sumatra, India, Iran —let us have your readings within the next fifteen minutes."

Many miles away in the desert, something went screaming up into the sky, leaving behind it a pure white vapor trail that might have been drawn with a ruler. While Dirk watched, the long milky column began to writhe and twist as the winds of the stratosphere dispersed it.

"Met rocket," said Collins, answering his unspoken question. "We've got a chain of them along the flight path, so we'll know pres-sures and temperatures all the way up to the top of the atmosphere. Just before the take-off, the pilot of 'Beta' will be warned if there's anything unusual ahead of him. That's one worry that Leduc won't have. There's no weather out in space!"

Across Asia, the slim rockets with their fifty kilograms of instru-ments were climbing through the stratosphere on their way to space. Their fuel had been exhausted in the first few seconds of flight, but their speed was great enough to carry them a hundred kilometers from the Earth. As they rose—some in sunlight, others still in darkness—

they sent back to the ground a continual stream of radio impulses, which would be caught and translated and passed on to Australia. Presently they would fall back to Earth, their parachutes would blossom, and most of them would be found and used again. Others, not so fortunate, would fall into the sea or, perhaps, end their days as tribal gods in the jungles of Borneo.

The three-mile drive along the crowded and very primitive road took them nearly twenty minutes, and more than once Professor Maxton had to make a detour into the no-man's-land which he himself had put out of bounds. The concentration of cars and spectators was greatest when they came to the five kilometer mark—and ended abruptly at a barrier of red-painted poles.

A small platform had been erected here from old packing cases, and this improvised stand was already occupied by Sir Robert Derwent and several of his staff. Also present, Dirk noticed with interest, were Hassell and Clinton. He wondered what thoughts were passing through their minds.

From time to time the Director-General made comments into a microphone, and there were one or two portable transmitters around. Dirk, who had vaguely expected to see batteries of instruments, was a little disappointed. He realized that all the technical operations were being carried out elsewhere, and this was merely an observation post.

"Twenty-five minutes to go," said the loud-speakers. "Launching generators will now run up to full operating speed. All radar-tracking stations and observatories in the main network should be standing by."

From the low platform, almost the whole of the launching track could be seen. To the right were the massed crowds and beyond them the low buildings of the airport. The "Prometheus" was clearly visible on the horizon, and from time to time the sunlight caught her sides so that they glittered like mirrors.

"Fifteen minutes to go."

Leduc and his companions would be lying in those curious seats, waiting for them to tilt under the first surge of acceleration. Yet it was strange to think that they would have nothing to do for almost an hour, when the separation of the ships would take place high above the Earth. All the initial responsibility lay upon the pilot of "Beta," who would get very little credit for his share in the proceedings—though in any case he was merely repeating what he had done a dozen times before.

"Ten minutes to go. All aircraft are reminded of their safety instructions."

The minutes were ticking past: an age was dying and a new one was being born. And suddenly the impersonal voice from the loudspeakers recalled to Dirk that morning, thirty-three years ago, when another group of scientists had stood waiting in another desert, preparing to unleash the energies that power the suns.

"Five minutes to go. All heavy electrical loads must be shed. Domestic circuits will be cut immediately."

A great silence had come over the crowd; all eyes were fixed upon those shining wings along the skyline. Somewhere close at hand a child, frightened by the stillness, began to cry.

"One minute to go. Warning rockets away."

There was a great "Swoosh!" from the empty desert over on the left, and a ragged line of crimson flares began to drift slowly down the sky. Some helicopters which had been edging forward minute by minute went hastily into reverse.

"Automatic take-off controller now in operation. Synchronized timing signal—*Now!*"

There was a "click" as the circuit was changed, and the faint rushing of long-distant static came from the speakers. Then there boomed over the desert a sound which, through its very familiarity, could not have been more unexpected.

In Westminster, halfway round the world, Big Ben was preparing to strike the hour.

Dirk glanced at Professor Maxton, and saw that he too was completely taken aback. But there was a faint smile on the Director-General's lips, and Dirk remembered that for a half a century Englishmen all over the world had waited beside their radios for that sound from the land which they might never see again. He had a sudden vision of other exiles, in the near or far future, listening upon strange planets to those same bells ringing out across the deeps of space. A booming silence seemed to fill the desert as the chimes of the last quarter died away, echoing in the distance from one loud-speaker to the next. Then the first stroke of the hour thundered over the desert, and over the waiting world. The speaker circuit was suddenly cut.

Yet nothing had changed: the "Prometheus" still lay brooding on the horizon like a great metal moth. Then Dirk saw that the space between her wings and the skyline was a little less than it had been, and a moment later he could tell quite clearly that the ship was expanding as it moved towards him. Faster and faster, in an absolute and uncanny silence, the "Prometheus" came racing down the track. It seemed only a moment before it was abreast of him, and for the very last time he could see "Alpha," smooth and pointed and glittering upon its back. As the ship rushed past to the left out into the empty desert, he could just hear the "swish!" of the air split by its passage. Even that was very faint, and the electric catapult made no sound at all. Then the "Prometheus" was shrinking silently into the distance.

Seconds later, that silence was shattered by a roar as of a thousand waterfalls plunging down the face of mile-high cliffs. The sky seemed to shake and tremble around them; the "Prometheus" itself had vanished from sight behind a cloud of whirling dust. In the heart of that cloud something was burning with an intolerable brilliance that the eye could not have borne for a moment without the intervening haze. The dust cloud thinned, and the thunder of the jets was softened by distance. Then Dirk could see that the fragment of sun he had been watching through half-shut eyes no longer followed the surface of the Earth, but was lifting, steadily and strongly, up from the horizon. The "Prometheus" was free from her launching cradle, was climbing on the world-wide circuit that would lead her into space.

The fierce white flare dwindled and shrank to nothingness against the empty sky. For a while the mutter of the departing jets rumbled around the heavens until it too was lost, drowned by the noise of circling aircraft.

Dirk scarcely noticed the shouting of the crowds as life returned to the desert behind him. Once again there had come into his mind the picture he was never wholly to forget—that image of the lonely island lost in a boundless and untraveled sea.

Boundless it was, infinite it might be—but it was untraveled no longer. Beyond the lagoon, past the friendly shelter of the coral reef, the first frail ship was sailing into the unknown perils and wonders of the open sea.

EPILOGUE

Dirk Alexson, sometime Professor of Social History at the University of Chicago, opened the bulky package on his desk with fingers that trembled slightly. For some minutes he struggled with the elaborate wrappings; then the book lay before him, clean and bright as it had left the printers three days ago.

He looked at it silently for a few moments, running his fingers over the binding. His eyes strayed to the shelf where its five companions rested. They had waited years, most of them, to be joined by this last volume.

Professor Alexson rose to his feet and walked over to the bookshelf, carrying the new arrival with him. A careful observer might have noticed something very odd about his walk: it had a curious springiness that one would not have expected from a man who was nearing sixty. He placed the book beside its five companions, and stood for a long time, completely motionless, staring at the little row of volumes.

The binding and lettering were well matched—he had been very particular about that—and the set was pleasing to the eye. Into those books had gone the greater part of his working life, and now that the task was ended he was well content. Yet it brought a great emptiness of spirit to realize that his work was done.

He took down the sixth volume again and walked back to his desk. He had not the heart to begin at once the search for the misprints, the infelicities which he knew must exist. In any case, they would be brought to his notice soon enough.

The binding protested stiffly as he opened the volume and glanced down the chapter headings, wincing slightly as he came to "Errata—Vols. I-V." Yet he had made few avoidable mistakes—and above all, he had made no enemies. At times in the last decade that had been none too easy. Some of the hundreds of men whose names were in the final index had not been flattered by his words, but no one had ever accused him of undue partiality. He did not believe that anyone could have guessed which of the men in the long and intricate story had been his personal friends.

He turned to the frontispiece—and his mind went back through more than twenty years. There lay the "Prometheus," waiting for the moment of her destiny. Somewhere in that crowd away to the left he himself was standing, a young man with his life's work still before him. And a young man, though he did not know it then, under sentence of death.

Professor Alexson walked over to the window of his study and stared out into the night. The view, as yet, was little obstructed by buildings, and he hoped it would remain that way, so that he could always watch the slow sunrise on the mountains fifteen miles beyond the city.

It was midnight, but the steady white radiance spilling down those tremendous slopes made the scene almost as bright as day. Above the mountains, the stars were shining with that unwavering light that still seemed strange to him. And higher still . . .

Professor Alexson threw back his head and stared through half-closed eyelids at the blinding white world on which he could never walk again. It was very brilliant tonight, for almost all the northern hemisphere was wreathed in dazzling clouds. Only Africa and the Mediterranean regions were unobscured. He remembered that it was winter beneath those clouds; though they looked so beautiful and so brilliant across a quarter of a million miles of space, they would seem a dull and somber gray to the sunless lands they covered.

Winter, summer, autumn, spring—they meant nothing here. He had taken leave of them all when he made his bargain. It was a hard bargain, but a fair one. He had parted from waves and clouds, from winds and rainbows, from blue skies and the long twilight of summer evenings. In exchange, he had received an indefinite stay of execution.

He remembered, across the years, those endless arguments with Maxton, Collins and the rest about the value of space flight to the human race. Some of their predictions had come true, others had not—but as far as he was concerned, they had proved their case up to the hilt. Matthews had been speaking the truth when he said, long ago, that the greatest benefits which the crossing of space would bring were those which could never have been guessed beforehand.

More than a decade ago the heart specialists had given him three years to live, but the great medical discoveries made at the lunar base had come just in time to save him. Under a sixth of a gravity, where a man weighed less than thirty pounds, a heart which would have failed on Earth could still beat strongly for years. There was even a possibility—almost terrifying in its social implications—that the span of human life might be greater on the Moon than upon the Earth.

Far sooner than anyone had dared to hope, astronautics had paid its greatest and most unexpected dividend. Here within the curve of the Apennines, in the first of all cities ever to be built outside the Earth, five thousand exiles were living useful and happy lives, safe from the deadly gravity of their own world. In time they would re-build all that they had left behind them; even now the avenue of cedars along Main Street was a brave symbol of the beauty that would be born in the years to come. Professor Alexson hoped he would live to see the building of the Park when the second and much larger Dome was constructed three miles away to the north.

All over the Moon, life was stirring again. It had flickered once, and died, a thousand million years ago; this time it would not fail, for it was part of a rising flood that in a few centuries would have surged to the outermost planets.

Professor Alexson ran his fingers, as he had so often done before, over the piece of Martian sandstone that Victor Hassell had given him years ago. One day, if he wished, he might go to that strange little world; there would soon be ships that could make the crossing in three weeks when the planet was at its nearest. He had changed worlds once; he might do so a second time if he ever became obsessed by the sight of the unattainable Earth.

Beneath its turban of cloud, Earth was taking leave of the twentieth century. In the shining cities, as midnight moved around the world, the crowds would be waiting for the first stroke of the hour which would sunder them forever from the old year and the old century.

Such a hundred years had never been before, and could scarcely come again. One by one the dams had burst, the last frontiers of the mind had been swept away. When the century dawned, Man had been preparing for the conquest of the air; when it died, he was gathering his strength upon Mars for the leap to the outer planets. Only Venus still held him at bay, for no ship had yet been built which could descend through the convection gales raging perpetually between the sunlit hemisphere and the darkness of the Night Side. From only five hundred miles away, the radar screens had shown the pattern of continents and seas beneath those racing clouds—and Venus, not Mars, had become the great enigma of the solar system.

As he saluted the dying century, Professor Alexson felt no regrets: the future was too full of wonder and promise. Once more the proud ships were sailing for unknown lands, bearing the seeds of new civilizations which in the ages to come would surpass the old. The rush to the new worlds would destroy the suffocating restraints which had poisoned almost half the century. The barriers had been broken, and men could turn their energies outwards to the stars instead of striving among themselves.

Out of the fears and miseries of the Second Dark Age, drawing free—oh, might it be forever!—from the shadows of Belsen and Hiroshima, the world was moving towards its most splendid sunrise. After five hundred years, the Renaissance had come again. The dawn that would burst above the Apennines at the end of the long lunar night would be no more brilliant than the age that had now been born.

Part II

ON THE LIGHT SIDE

Big Game Hunt

Although by general consent Harry Purvis stands unrivalled among the "White Hart" *clientele* as a purveyor of remarkable stories (some of which, we suspect, may be slightly exaggerated) it must not be thought that his position has never been challenged. There have even been occasions when he has gone into temporary eclipse. Since it is always entertaining to watch the discomfiture of an expert, I must confess that I take a certain glee in recalling how Professor Hinckelberg disposed of Harry on his own home ground.

Many visiting Americans pass through the "White Hart" in the course of the year. Like the residents, they are usually scientists or literary men, and some distinguished names have been recorded in the visitors' book that Drew keeps behind the bar. Sometimes the newcomers arrive under their own power, diffidently introducing themselves as soon as they have the opportunity. (There was the time when a shy Nobel Prize winner sat unrecognised in a corner for an hour before he plucked up enough courage to say who he was.) Others arrive with letters of introduction, and not a few are escorted in by regular customers and then thrown to the wolves.

Professor Hinckelberg glided up one night in a vast fish-tailed Cadillac he'd borrowed from the fleet in Grosvenor Square. Heaven only knows how he had managed to insinuate it through the side streets that lead to the "White Hart", but amazingly enough all the fenders seemed intact. He was a large lean man, with that Henry Ford-Wilbur Wright kind of face that usually goes with the slow, taciturn speech of the sun-tanned pioneer. It didn't in Professor Hinckelberg's case. He could talk like an L.P. record on a 78 turntable. In about ten seconds we'd discovered that he was a zoologist on leave of absence from a North Virginia college, that he was attached to the Office of Naval Research on some project to do with plankton, that he was tickled pink with London and even liked English beer, that he'd heard about us through a letter in *Science* but couldn't believe we were true, that Stevenson was O.K. but if the Democrats wanted to get back they'd better import Winston, that he'd like to know what the heck was wrong with all our telephone call boxes and could he retrieve the small fortune in coppers of which they had mulcted him, that there seemed to be a lot of empty glasses around and how about filling them up, boys?

On the whole the Professor's shock-tactics were well received, but when he made a momentary pause for breath I thought to myself "Harry'd better look out. This guy can talk rings round him." I glanced at Purvis, who was only a few feet away from me, and saw that his lips were pursed into a slight frown. I sat back luxuriously and awaited results.

As it was a fairly busy evening, it was quite sometime before Professor Hinckelberg had been introduced to everybody. Harry, usually so forward at meeting celebrities, seemed to be keeping out of the way. But eventually he was cornered by Arthur Vincent, who acts as informal club secretary and makes sure that everyone signs the visitors' book.

"I'm sure you and Harry will have a lot to talk about," said Arthur, in a burst of innocent enthusiasm. "You're both scientists, aren't you? And Harry's had some most extraordinary things happen to him.

Tell the Professor about the time you found that U 235 in your letter-box. . . ."

"I don't think," said Harry, a trifle too hastily, "that Professor—ah —Hinckelberg wants to listen to my little adventure. I'm sure he must have a lot to tell *us*."

I've puzzled my head about that reply a good deal since then. It wasn't in character. Usually, with an opening like this, Purvis was up and away. Perhaps he was sizing up the enemy, waiting for the Professor to make the first mistake, and then swooping in to the kill. If that was the explanation, he'd misjudged his man. He never had a chance, for Professor Hinckelberg made a jet-assisted take-off and was immediately in full flight.

"Odd you should mention that," he said. "I've just been dealing with a most remarkable case. It's one of these things that can't be written up as a proper scientific paper, and this seems a good time to get it off my chest. I can't often do that, because of this darned se-curity—but so far no one's gotten round to classifying Dr. Grinnell's experiments, so I'll talk about them while I can."

Grinnell, it seemed was one of the many scientists trying to in-terpret the behaviour of the nervous system in terms of electrical circuits. He had started, as Grey Walter, Shannon and others had done, by making models that could reproduce the simpler actions of living creatures. His greatest success in this direction had been a me-chanical cat that could chase mice and could land on its feet when dropped from a height. Very quickly, however, he had branched off in another direction owing to his discovery of what he called "neural in-duction." This was, to simplify it greatly, nothing less than a method of actually *controlling* the behaviour of animals.

It had been known for many years that all the processes that take place in the mind are accompanied by the production of minute elec-tric currents, and for a long time it has been possible to record these complex fluctuations—though their exact interpretation is still un-known. Grinnell had not attempted the intricate task of analysis; what he had done was a good deal simpler, though its achievement was still complicated enough. He had attached his recording device to various animals, and thus been able to build up a small library, if one could call it that, of electrical impulses associated with their be-haviour. One pattern of voltage might correspond to a movement to the right, another with travelling in a circle, another with complete stillness, and so on. That was an interesting enough achievement, but Grinnell had not stopped there. By "playing back" the impulses he had recorded, he could compel his subjects to repeat their previous actions—whether they wanted to or not.

That such a thing might be possible in theory almost any neurologist would admit, but few would have believed that it could be done in practice owing to the enormous complexity of the nervous system. And it was true that Grinnell's first experiments were carried out on very low forms of life, with relatively simple responses.

"I saw only one of his experiments," said Hinckelberg. "There was a large slug crawling on a horizontal piece of glass, and half a dozen tiny wires led from it to a control panel which Grinnell was operating. There were two dials—that was all—and by suitable adjustments he could make the slug move in any direction. To a layman, it would have seemed a trivial experiment, but I realised that it might have tremendous implications. I remember telling Grinnell that I hoped his device could never be applied to human beings. I'd been reading Orwell's '1984' and I could just imagine what Big Brother would do with a gadget like this.

"Then, being a busy man, I forgot all about the matter for a year. By the end of that time, it seems, Grinnell had improved his apparatus considerably and had worked up to more complicated organisms, though for technical reasons he had restricted himself to invertebrates. He had now built up a substantial store of 'orders' which he could then play back to his subjects. You might think it surprising that such diverse creatures as worms, snails, insects, crustaceans and so on would be able to respond to the same electrical commands, but apparently that was the case.

"If it had not been for Dr. Jackson, Grinnell would probably have stayed working away in the lab for the rest of his life, moving steadily up the animal kingdom. Jackson was a very remarkable man—I'm sure you must have seen some of his films. In many circles he was regarded as a publicity-hunter rather than a real scientist, and academic circles were suspicious of him because he had far too many interests. He'd led expeditions into the Gobi Desert, up the Amazon, and had even made one raid on the Antarctic. From each of these trips he had returned with a best-selling book and a few miles of Kodachrome. And despite reports to the contrary, I believe he *had* obtained some valuable scientific results, even if they were slightly incidental.

"I don't know how Jackson got to hear of Grinnell's work, or how he talked the other man into co-operating. He could be very persuasive, and probably dangled vast appropriations before Grinnell's eyes—for he was the sort of man who could get the ear of the trustees. Whatever happened, from that moment Grinnell became mysteriously secretive. All we knew was that he was building a much larger version of his apparatus, incorporating all the latest refinements. When challenged, he would squirm nervously and say 'We're going big game hunting.'

"The preparations took another year, and I expect that Jackson—who was always a hustler—must have been mighty impatient by the end of that time. But at last everything was ready. Grinnell and all his mysterious boxes vanished in the general direction of Africa.

"*That* was Jackson's work. I suppose he didn't want any premature publicity, which was understandable enough when you consider the somewhat fantastic nature of the expedition. According to the hints with which he had—as we later discovered—carefully misled us all, he hoped to get some really remarkable pictures of animals in their wild state, using Grinnell's apparatus. I found this rather hard to swallow, unless Grinnell had somehow succeeded in linking his device to a radio transmitter. It didn't seem likely that he'd be able to attach his wires and electrodes to a charging elephant. . . .

"They'd thought of that, of course, and the answer seems obvious now. Sea water is a good conductor. They weren't going to Africa at all, but were heading out into the Atlantic. But they hadn't lied to us. They were after big game, all right. The biggest game there is. . . .

"We'd never have known what happened if their radio operator hadn't been chattering to an amateur friend over in the States. From his commentary it's possible to guess the sequence of events. Jackson's ship—it was only a small yacht, bought up cheaply and converted for the expedition—was lying-to not far from the Equator off the west coast of Africa, and over the deepest part of the Atlantic. Grinnell was angling: his electrodes had been lowered into the abyss, while Jackson waited impatiently with his camera.

"They waited a week before they had a catch. By that time, tempers must have been rather frayed. Then, one afternoon on a perfectly calm day, Grinnell's meters started to jump. Something was caught in the sphere of influence of the electrodes.

"Slowly, they drew up the cable. Until now, the rest of the crew must have thought them mad, but everyone must have shared their excitement as the catch rose up through all those thousands of feet of darkness until it broke surface. Who can blame the radio operator if, despite Jackson's orders, he felt an urgent need to talk things over with a friend back on the safety of dry land?

"I won't attempt to describe what they saw, because a master has done it before me. Soon after the report came in, I turned up my copy of 'Moby Dick' and re-read the passage; I can still quote it from memory and don't suppose I'll ever forget it. This is how it goes, more or less:

"'A vast pulpy mass, furlongs in length, of a glancing cream-colour, lay floating on the water, innumerable long arms radiating from its centre, curling and twisting like a nest of anacondas, as if blindly to catch at any hapless object within reach.'

"Yes: Grinnell and Jackson had been after the largest and most mysterious of all living creatures—the giant squid. Largest? Almost certainly: *Bathyteuthis* may grow up to a hundred feet long. He's not as heavy as the sperm whales who dine upon him, but he's a match for them in length.

"So here they were, with this monstrous beast that no human being had ever before seen under such ideal conditions. It seems that Grinnell was calmly putting it through its paces while Jackson ecstatically shot off yards of film. There was no danger, though it was twice the size of their boat. To Grinnell, it was just another mollusc that he could control like a puppet by means of his knobs and dials. When he had finished, he would let it return to its normal depths and it could swim away again, though it would probably have a bit of a hangover.

"What one wouldn't give to get hold of that film! Altogether apart from its scientific interest, it would be worth a fortune in Hollywood. You must admit that Jackson knew what he was doing: he'd seen the limitations of Grinnell's apparatus and put it to its most effective use. What happened next was not his fault."

Professor Hinckelberg sighed and took a deep draught of beer, as if to gather strength for the finale of his tale.

"No, if anyone is to blame it's Grinnell. Or, I should say, it *was* Grinnell, poor chap. Perhaps he was so excited that he overlooked a precaution he would undoubtedly have taken in the lab. How otherwise can you account for the fact that he didn't have a spare fuse handy when the one in the power supply blew out?

"And you can't really blame *Bathyteuthis*, either. Wouldn't *you* have been a little annoyed to be pushed about like this? And when the orders suddenly ceased and you were your own master again, you'd take steps to see it remained that way. I sometimes wonder, though, if Jackson stayed filming to the very end. . . ."

"Did I ever tell you," said Harry Purvis modestly, "about the time I prevented the evacuation of southern England?"

"You did not," said Charles Willis, "or if you did, I slept through it."

"Well, then," continued Harry, when enough people had gathered round him to make a respectable audience. "It happened two years ago at the Atomic Energy Research Establishment near Clobham. You all know the place, of course. But I don't think I've mentioned that I worked there for a while, on a special job I can't talk about."

"*That* makes a nice change," said John Wyndham, without the slightest effect.

"It was on a Saturday afternoon," Harry began. "A beautiful day in late spring. There were about six of us scientists in the bar of the

'Black Swan', and the windows were open so that we could see down the slopes of Clobham Hill and out across the country to Upchester, about thirty miles away. It was so clear, in fact, that we could pick out the twin spires of Upchester Cathedral on the horizon. You couldn't have asked for a more peaceful day.

"The staff from the Establishment got on pretty well with the locals, though at first they weren't at all happy about having us on their doorsteps. Apart from the nature of our work, they'd believed that scientists were a race apart, with no human interests. When we'd beaten them up at darts a couple of times, and bought a few drinks, they changed their minds. But there was still a certain amount of half-serious leg-pulling, and we were always being asked what we were going to blow up next.

"On this afternoon there should have been several more of us present, but there'd been a rush job in the Radioisotopes Division and so we were below strength. Stanley Chambers, the landlord, commented on the absence of some familiar faces.

"'What's happened to all your pals today?' he asked my boss, Dr. French.

"'They're busy at the works,' French replied—we always called the Establishment 'the Works', as that made it seem more homely and less terrifying. 'We had to get some stuff out in a hurry. They'll be along later.'

"'One day,' said Stan severely, 'you and your friends are going to let out something you won't be able to bottle up again. And *then* where will we all be?'

"'Half-way to the Moon,' said Dr. French. I'm afraid it was rather an irresponsible sort of remark, but silly questions like this always made him lose patience.

"Stan Chambers looked over his shoulder as if he was judging how much of the hill stood between him and Clobham. I guessed he was calculating if he'd have time to reach the cellar—or whether it was worth trying anyway.

"'About these—isotopes—you keep sending to the hospitals,' said a thoughtful voice. 'I was at St. Thomas' last week, and saw them moving some around in a lead safe that must have weighed a ton. It gave me the creeps, wondering what would happen if someone forgot to handle it properly.'

"'We calculated the other day,' said Dr. French, obviously still annoyed at the interruption to his darts, 'that there was enough uranium in Clobham to boil the North Sea.'

"Now that was a silly thing to say: and it wasn't true, either. But I couldn't very well reprimand my own boss, could I?

"The man who'd been asking these questions was sitting in the alcove by the window, and I noticed that he was looking down the road with an anxious expression.

" 'The stuff leaves your place on trucks, doesn't it?' he asked, rather urgently.

" 'Yes: a lot of isotopes are short-lived, and so they've got to be delivered immediately.'

" 'Well, there's a truck in trouble down the hill. Would it be one of yours?'

"The dart-board was forgotten in the general rush to the window. When I managed to get a good look, I could see a large truck, loaded with packing cases, careering down the hill about a quarter of a mile away. From time to time it bounced off one of the hedges: it was obvious that the brakes had failed and the driver had lost control. Luckily there was no on-coming traffic, or a nasty accident would have been inevitable. As it was, one looked probable.

"Then the truck came to a bend in the road, left the pavement, and tore through the hedge. It rocked along with diminishing speed for fifty yards, jolting violently over the rough ground. It had almost come to rest when it encountered a ditch and, very sedately, canted over on to one side. A few seconds later the sound of splintering wood reached us as the packing cases slid off to the ground.

" 'That's that,' said someone with a sigh of relief. 'He did the right thing, aiming for the hedge. I guess he'll be shaken up, but he won't be hurt.'

"And then we saw a most perplexing sight. The door of the cab opened, and the driver scrambled out. Even from this distance, it was clear that he was highly agitated—though, in the circumstances, that was natural enough. But he did not, as one would have expected, sit down to recover his wits. On the contrary: he promptly took to his heels and ran across the field as if all the demons of hell were after him.

"We watched open-mouthed, and with rising apprehension, as he dwindled down the hill. There was an ominous silence in the bar, except for the ticking of the clock that Stan always kept exactly ten minutes fast. Then someone said 'D'you think we'd better stay? I mean—it's only half a mile. . . .'

"There was an uncertain movement away from the window. Then Dr. French gave a nervous little laugh.

" 'We don't know if it *is* one of our trucks,' he said. 'And anyway, I was pulling your legs just now. It's completely impossible for any of this stuff to explode. He's just afraid his tank's going to catch fire.'

" 'Oh yes?' said Stan. 'Then why's he still running? He's half-way down the hill now.'

" 'I know!' suggested Charlie Evan, from the Instruments Section. 'He's carrying explosives, and is afraid they're going to go up.'

"I had to scotch that one. 'There's no sign of a fire, so what's he worried about now? And if he *was* carrying explosives, he'd have a red flag or something.'

" 'Hang on a minute,' said Stan. 'I'll go and get my glasses.'

"No one moved until he came back: no one, that is, except the tiny figure far down the hill-side, which had now vanished into the woods without slackening its speed.

"Stan stared through the binoculars for an eternity. At last he lowered them with a grunt of disappointment.

" 'Can't see much,' he said. 'The truck's tipped over in the wrong direction. Those crates are all over the place—some of them have busted open. See if you can make anything of it.'

"French had a long stare, then handed the glasses to me. They were a very old-fashioned model, and didn't help much. For a moment it seemed to me that there was a curious haziness about some of the boxes—but that didn't make sense. I put it down to the poor condition of the lenses.

"And there, I think, the whole business would have fizzled out if those cyclists hadn't appeared. They were puffing up the hill on a tandem, and when they came to the fresh gap in the hedge they promptly dismounted to see what was going on. The truck was visible from the road and they approached it hand in hand, the girl obviously hanging back, the man telling her not to be nervous. We could imagine their conversation: it was a most touching spectacle.

"It didn't last long. They got to within a few yards of the truck—and then departed at high speed in opposite directions. Neither looked back to observe the other's progress; and they were running, I noticed, in a most peculiar fashion.

"Stan, who'd retrieved his glasses, put them down with a shaky hand.

" 'Get out the cars!' he said.

" 'But—' began Dr. French.

"Stan silenced him with a glare. 'You damned scientists!' he said, as he slammed and locked the till (even at a moment like this, he remembered his duty) 'I knew you'd do it sooner or later.'

"Then he was gone, and most of his cronies with him. They didn't stop to offer us a lift.

" 'This is perfectly ridiculous!' said French. 'Before we know where we are, those fools will have started a panic and there'll be hell to pay.'

"I knew what he meant. Someone would tell the police: cars would be diverted away from Clobham: the telephone lines would be blocked with calls—it would be like the Orson Welles 'War of the Worlds' scare back in 1938. Perhaps you think I'm exaggerating, but you can never underestimate the power of panic. And people were scared, remember, of our place, and were half-expecting something like this to happen.

"What's more, I don't mind telling you that by this time we weren't any too happy ourselves. We were simply unable to imagine what was going on down there by the wrecked truck, and there's nothing a scientist hates more than being completely baffled.

"Meanwhile I'd grabbed Stan's discarded binoculars and had been studying the wreck very carefully. As I looked, a theory began to evolve in my mind. There *was* some—aura—about those boxes. I stared until my eyes began to smart, and then said to Dr. French: 'I think I know what it is. Suppose you ring up Clobham Post Office and try to intercept Stan, or at least to stop him spreading rumours if he's already got there. Say that everything's under control—there's nothing to worry about. While you're doing that, I'm going to walk down to the truck and test my theory.'

"I'm sorry to say that no one offered to follow me. Though I started down the road confidently enough, after a while I began to be a little less sure of myself. I remembered an incident that's always struck me as one of history's most ironic jokes, and began to wonder if something of the same sort might not be happening now. There was once a volcanic island in the Far East, with a population of about 50,000. No one worried about the volcano, which had been quiet for a hundred years. Then, one day, eruptions started. At first they were minor, but they grew more intense hour by hour. The people started to panic, and tried to crowd aboard the few boats in harbour so that they could reach the mainland.

"But the island was ruled by a military commandant who was determined to keep order at all costs. He sent out proclamations saying that there was no danger, and he got his troops to occupy the ships so that there would be no loss of life as people attempted to leave in overloaded boats. Such was the force of his personality, and the example of his courage, that he calmed the multitude, and those who had been trying to get away crept shame-faced back to their homes, where they sat waiting for conditions to return to normal.

"So when the volcano blew up a couple of hours later, taking the whole island with it, there weren't any survivors at all. . . .

"As I got near the truck, I began to see myself in the role of that misguided commandant. After all, there are some times when it is brave to stay and face danger, and others when the most sensible thing to do is to take to the hills. But it was too late to turn back now, and I was fairly sure of my theory."

"I know," said George Whiteley, who always liked to spoil Harry's stories if he could. "It was gas."

Harry didn't seem at all perturbed at losing his climax.

"Ingenious of you to suggest it. That's just what I did think, which shows that we can all be stupid at times.

"I'd got to within fifty feet of the truck when I stopped dead, and though it was a warm day a most unpleasant chill began to spread out from the small of my back. For I could see something that blew my gas theory to blazes and left nothing at all in its place.

"A black, crawling mass was writhing over the surface of one of the packing cases. For a moment I tried to pretend to myself that it was some dark liquid oozing from a broken container. But one rather well-known characteristic of liquids is that they can't defy gravity. This thing was doing just that: and it was also quite obviously alive. From where I was standing, it looked like the pseudopod of some giant amoeba as it changed its shape and thickness, and wavered to and fro over the side of the broken crate.

"Quite a few fantasies that would have done credit to Edgar Allan Poe flitted through my mind in those few seconds. Then I remembered my duty as a citizen and my pride as a scientist: I started to walk forward again, though in no great haste.

"I remember sniffing cautiously, as if I still had gas on the mind.

Yet it was my ears, not my nose, that gave me the answer, as the sound from that sinister, seething mass built up around me. It was a sound I'd heard a million times before, but never as loud as this. And I sat down—not too close—and laughed and laughed and laughed. Then I got up and walked back to the pub.

" 'Well,' said Dr. French eagerly, 'what is it? We've got Stan on the line—caught him at the crossroads. But he won't come back until we can tell him what's happening.'

" 'Tell Stan,' I said, 'to rustle up the local apiarist, and bring him along at the same time. There's a big job for him here.'

" 'The local *what?*' said French. Then his jaw dropped. 'My God! You don't mean. . . .'

" 'Precisely,' I answered, walking behind the bar to see if Stan had any interesting bottles hidden away. 'They're settling down now, but I guess they're still pretty annoyed. I didn't stop to count, but there must be half a million bees down there trying to get back into their busted hives.' "

The Ultimate Melody

Have you ever noticed that, when there are twenty or thirty people talking together in a room, there are occasional moments when everyone becomes suddenly silent, so that for a second there's a sudden, vibrating emptiness that seems to swallow up all sound? I don't know how it affects other people, but when it happens it makes me feel cold all over. Of course, the whole thing's merely caused by the laws of probability, but somehow it seems more than a mere coinciding of conversational pauses. It's almost as if everybody is listening for something—they don't know what. At such moments I say to myself:

> But at my back I always hear
> Time's wingéd chariot hurrying near. . . .

That's how *I* feel about it, however cheerful the company in which it happens. Yes, even if it's in the "White Hart."

It was like that one Wednesday evening when the place wasn't quite as crowded as usual. The Silence came, as unexpectedly as it always does. Then, probably in a deliberate attempt to break that unsettling feeling of suspense, Charlie Willis started whistling the latest hit tune. I don't even remember what it was. I only remember that it triggered off one of Harry Purvis' most disturbing stories.

"Charlie," he began, quietly enough. "That darn tune's driving me mad. I've heard it every time I've switched on the radio for the last week."

There was a sniff from John Christopher.

"You ought to stay tuned to the Third Programme. Then you'd be safe."

"Some of us," retorted Harry, "don't care for an exclusive diet of Elizabethan madrigals. But don't let's quarrel about *that*, for heaven's sake. Has it ever occurred to you that there's something rather—*fundamental*—about hit tunes?"

"What do you mean?"

"Well, they come along out of nowhere, and then for weeks everybody's humming them, just as Charlie did then. The good ones grab hold of you so thoroughly that you just can't get them out of your head—they go round and round for days. And then, suddenly, they've vanished again."

"I know what you mean," said Art Vincent. "There are some melodies that you can take or leave, but others stick like treacle, whether you want them or not."

"Precisely. I got saddled that way for a whole week with the big theme from the finale of Sibelius Two—even went to sleep with it running round inside my head. Then there's that 'Third Man' piece—da di da di *daa*, di da, di *daa* . . . look what *that* did to everybody."

Harry had to pause for a moment until his audience had stopped zithering. When the last "Plonk!" had died away he continued:

"Precisely! You all felt the same way. Now what *is* there about these tunes that has this effect? Some of them are great music—others just banal, but they've obviously got *something* in common."

"Go on," said Charlie. "We're waiting."

"I don't know what the answer is," replied Harry. "And what's more, I don't want to. For I know a man who found out."

Automatically, someone handed him a beer, so that the tenor of his tale would not be disturbed. It always annoyed a lot of people when he had to stop in mid-flight for a refill.

"I don't know why it is," said Harry Purvis, "that most scientists are interested in music, but it's an undeniable fact. I've known several large labs that had their own amateur symphony orchestras—some of them quite good, too. As far as the mathematicians are concerned, one can think of obvious reasons for this fondness: music, particularly classical music, has a form which is almost mathematical. And then, of course, there's the underlying theory—harmonic relations, wave analysis, frequency distribution, and so on. It's a fascinating study in itself, and one that appeals strongly to the scientific mind. Moreover, it doesn't—as some people might think—preclude a purely aesthetic appreciation of music for its own sake.

"However, I must confess that Gilbert Lister's interest in music was purely cerebral. He was, primarily, a physiologist, specialising in the study of the brain. So when I said that his interest was cerebral, I meant it quite literally. 'Alexander's Ragtime Band' and the Choral Symphony were all the same to him. He wasn't concerned with the sounds themselves, but only what happened when they got past the ears and started doing things to the brain.

"In an audience as well educated as this," said Harry, with an emphasis that made it sound positively insulting, "there will be no one who's unaware of the fact that much of the brain's activity is electrical. There are, in fact, steady pulsing rhythms going on all the time, and they can be detected and analysed by modern instruments. This was Gilbert Lister's line of territory. He could stick electrodes on your scalp and his amplifiers would draw your brainwaves on yards of tape. Then he could examine them and tell you all sorts of interesting things about yourself. Ultimately, he claimed, it would be possible to identify anyone from their encephalogram—to use the correct term— more positively than by fingerprints. A man might get a surgeon to change his skin, but if we ever got to the stage when surgery could change your brain—well, you'd have turned into somebody else, anyway, so the system still wouldn't have failed.

"It was while he was studying the alpha, beta and other rhythms in the brain that Gilbert got interested in music. He was sure that there must be some connexion between musical and mental rhythms. He'd play music at various tempos to his subjects and see what effect it had on their normal brain frequencies. As you might expect, it had a lot, and the discoveries he made led Gilbert on into more philosophical fields.

"I only had one good talk with him about his theories. It was not that he was at all secretive—I've never met a scientist who was, come to think of it—but he didn't like to talk about his work until he knew where it was leading. However, what he told me was enough to prove that he'd opened up a very interesting line of territory, and thereafter I made rather a point of cultivating him. My firm supplied some of his equipment, but I wasn't averse to picking up a little profit on the side. It occurred to me that *if* Gilbert's ideas worked out, he'd need a business manager before you could whistle the opening bar of the Fifth Symphony. . . .

"For what Gilbert was trying to do was to lay a scientific foundation for the theory of hit tunes. Of course, he didn't think of it that way: he regarded it as a pure research project, and didn't look any further ahead than a paper in the *Proceedings of the Physical Society*. But I spotted its financial implications at once. They were quite breath-taking.

"Gilbert was sure that a great melody, or a hit tune, made its impression on the mind because in some way it fitted in with the fundamental electrical rhythms going on in the brain. One analogy he used was 'It's like a Yale key going into a lock—the two patterns have got to fit before anything happens.'

"He tackled the problem from two angles. In the first place, he took hundreds of the really famous tunes in classical and popular music and analysed their structure—their morphology, as he put it. This was done automatically, in a big harmonic analyser that sorted out all the frequencies. Of course, there was a lot more to it than this, but I'm sure you've got the basic idea.

"At the same time, he tried to see how the resulting patterns of waves agreed with the natural electrical vibrations of the brain. Because it was Gilbert's theory—and this is where we get into rather deep philosophical waters—that all existing tunes were merely crude approximations to one fundamental melody. Musicians had been groping for it down the centuries, but they didn't know what they were doing, because they were ignorant of the relation between music and mind. Now that this had been unravelled, it should be possible to discover the Ultimate Melody."

"Huh!" said John Christopher. "It's only a rehash of Plato's theory of ideals. You know—all the objects of our material world are merely crude copies of the ideal chair or table or what-have-you. So your friend was after the ideal melody. And did he find it?"

"I'll tell you," continued Harry imperturbably. "It took Gilbert about a year to complete his analysis, and then he started on the synthesis. To put it crudely, he built a machine that would automatically construct patterns of sound according to the laws that he'd uncovered. He had banks of oscillators and mixers—in fact, he modified an ordinary electronic organ for this part of the apparatus—which were controlled by his composing machine. In the rather childish way that scientists like to name their offspring, Gilbert had called this device Ludwig.

"Maybe it helps to understand how Ludwig operated if you think of him as a kind of kaleidoscope, working with sound rather than light. But he was a kaleidoscope set to obey certain laws, and those laws—so Gilbert believed—were based on the fundamental structure of the human mind. If he could get the adjustments correct, Ludwig would be bound, sooner or later, to arrive at the Ultimate Melody as he searched through all the possible patterns of music.

"I had one opportunity of hearing Ludwig at work, and it was uncanny. The equipment was the usual nondescript mess of electronics which one meets in any lab: it might have been a mock-up of a new computer, a radar gunsight, a traffic control system, or a ham radio. It was very hard to believe that, if it worked, it would put every composer in the world out of business. Or would it? Perhaps not: Ludwig might be able to deliver the raw material, but surely it would still have to be orchestrated.

"Then the sound started to come from the speaker. At first it seemed to me that I was listening to the five-finger exercises of an accurate but completely uninspired pupil. Most of the themes were quite banal: the machine would play one, then ring the changes on it bar after bar until it had exhausted all the possibilities before going on to the next. Occasionally a quite striking phrase would come up, but on the whole I was not at all impressed.

"However, Gilbert explained that this was only a trial run and that the main circuits had not yet been set up. When they were, Ludwig would be far more selective: at the moment, he was playing everything that came along—he had no sense of discrimination. When he had acquired that, *then* the possibilities were limitless.

"That was the last time I ever saw Gilbert Lister. I had arranged to meet him at the lab about a week later, when he expected to have made substantial progress. As it happened, I was about an hour late for my appointment. And that was very lucky for me. . . .

"When I got there, they had just taken Gilbert away. His lab assistant, an old man who'd been with him for years, was sitting distraught and disconsolate among the tangled wiring of Ludwig. It took me a long time to discover what had happened, and longer still to work out the explanation.

"There was no doubt of one thing. Ludwig had finally worked. The assistant had gone off to lunch while Gilbert was making the final adjustments, and when he came back an hour later the laboratory was pulsing with one long and very complex melodic phrase. Either the machine had stopped automatically at that point, or Gilbert had switched it over to REPEAT. At any rate, he had been listening, for several hundred times at least, to that same melody. When his assistant found him, he seemed to be in a trance. His eyes were open yet unseeing, his limbs rigid. Even when Ludwig was switched off, it made no difference. Gilbert was beyond help.

"What had happened? Well, I suppose we should have thought of it, but it's so easy to be wise after the event. It's just as I said at the beginning. If a composer, working merely by rule of thumb, can produce a melody which can dominate your mind for days on end, imagine the effect of the Ultimate Melody for which Gilbert was searching! Supposing it existed—and I'm not admitting that it does—it would form an endless ring in the memory circuits of the mind. It would go round and round forever, obliterating all other thoughts. All the cloying melodies of the past would be mere ephemerae compared to it. Once it had keyed into the brain, and distorted the circling waveforms which are the physical manifestations of consciousness itself—that would be the end. And that is what happened to Gilbert.

"They've tried shock therapy—everything. But it's no good; the pattern has been set, and it can't be broken. He's lost all consciousness of the outer world, and has to be fed intravenously. He never moves or reacts to external stimuli, but sometimes, they tell me, he twitches in a peculiar way as if he is beating time. . . .

"I'm afraid there's no hope for him. Yet I'm not sure if his fate is a horrible one, or whether he should be envied. Perhaps, in a sense, he's found the ultimate reality that philosophers like Plato are always talking about. I really don't know. And sometimes I find myself wondering just what that infernal melody *was* like, and almost wishing that I'd been able to hear it perhaps once. There might have been some way of doing it in safety: remember how Ulysses listened to the song of the sirens and got away with it . . . ? But there'll never be a chance now, of course."

"I was waiting for this," said Charles Willis nastily. "I suppose the apparatus blew up, or something, so that as usual there's no way of checking your story."

Harry gave him his best more-in-sorrow-than-in-anger look.

"The apparatus was quite undamaged," he said severely. "What happened next was one of those completely maddening things for which I shall never stop blaming myself. You see, I'd been too interested in Gilbert's experiment to look after my firm's business in the way that I should. I'm afraid he'd fallen badly behind with his payments, and when the Accounts Department discovered what had happened to him they acted quickly. I was only off for a couple of days on another job, and when I got back, do you know what had happened? They'd pushed through a court order, and had seized all their property. Of course that had meant dismantling Ludwig: when I saw him next he was just a pile of useless junk. And all because of a few pounds! It made me weep."

"I'm sure of it," said Eric Maine. "But you've forgotten Loose End Number Two. *What about Gilbert's assistant?* He went into the lab while the gadget was going full blast. Why didn't it get him, too? You've slipped up here, Harry."

H. Purvis, Esquire, paused only to drain the last drops from his glass and to hand it silently across to Drew.

"Really!" he said. "Is this a cross-examination? I didn't mention the point because it was rather trivial. But it explains why I was never able to get the slightest inkling of the nature of that melody. You see, Gilbert's assistant was a first-rate lab technician, but he'd never been able to help much with the adjustments to Ludwig. For he was one of those people who are completely tone-deaf. To him, the Ultimate Melody meant no more than a couple of cats on a garden wall."

Nobody asked any more questions: we all, I think, felt the desire to commune with our thoughts. There was a long, brooding silence before the "White Hart" resumed its usual activities. And even then, I noticed, it was every bit of ten minutes before Charlie started whistling "La Ronde" again.

Moving Spirit

We were discussing a sensational trial at the Old Bailey when Harry Purvis, whose talent for twisting the conversation to his own ends is really unbelievable, remarked casually: "I was once an expert witness in a rather interesting case."

"Only a *witness?*" said Drew, as he deftly filled two glasses of Bass at once.

"Yes—but it was a rather close thing. It was in the early part of the war, about the time we were expecting the invasion. That's why you never heard about it at the time."

"What makes you assume," said Charles Willis suspiciously, "that we never did hear of it?"

It was one of the few times I'd ever seen Harry caught trying to cover up his tracks. "Qui s'excuse s'accuse," I thought to myself, and waited to see what evading action he'd take.

"It was such a peculiar case," he replied with dignity, "that I'm sure you'd have reminded me of it if you ever saw the reports. My name was featured quite prominently. It all happened in an out-of-the-way part of Cornwall, and it concerned the best example of that rare species, the genuine mad scientist, that I've ever met."

Perhaps that wasn't really a fair description, Purvis amended hastily. Homer Ferguson was eccentric and had little foibles like keeping a pet boa constrictor to catch the mice, and never wearing shoes around the house. But he was so rich that no one noticed things like this.

Homer was also a competent scientist. Many years ago he had graduated from Edinburgh University, but having plenty of money he had never done a stroke of real work in his life. Instead, he pottered round the old vicarage he'd bought not far from Newquay and amused himself building gadgets. In the last forty years he'd invented television, ball-point pens, jet propulsion, and a few other trifles. However, as he had never bothered to take out any patents, other people had got the credit. This didn't worry him in the least as he was of a singularly generous disposition, except with money.

It seemed that, in some complicated way, Purvis was one of his few living relatives. Consequently when Harry received a telegram one day requesting his assistance at once, he knew better than to refuse. No one knew exactly how much money Homer had, or what he intended to do with it. Harry thought he had as good a chance as anyone, and he didn't intend to jeopardize it. At some inconvenience he made the journey down to Cornwall and turned up at the rectory.

He saw what was wrong as soon as he entered the grounds. Uncle Homer (he wasn't really an uncle, but he'd been called that as long as Harry could remember) had a shed beside the main building which he used for his experiments. That shed was now minus roof and windows, and a sickly odor hovered around it. There had obviously been an explosion, and Harry wondered, in a disinterested sort of way, if Uncle had been badly injured and wanted advice on drawing up a new will.

He ceased day-dreaming when the old man, looking the picture of health (apart from some sticking plaster on his face), opened the door for him.

"Good of you to come so quickly," he boomed. He seemed genuinely pleased to see Harry. Then his face clouded over. "Fact is, my boy, I'm in a bit of a jam and I want you to help. My case comes up before the local Bench tomorrow."

This was a considerable shock. Homer had been as law-abiding a citizen as any motorist in petrol-rationed Britain could be expected to be. And if it was the usual black-market business, Harry didn't see how he could be expected to help.

"Sorry to hear about this, Uncle. What's the trouble?"

"It's a long story. Come into the library and we'll talk it over."

Homer Ferguson's library occupied the entire west wing of the somewhat decrepit building. Harry believed that bats nested in the rafters, but had never been able to prove it. When Homer had cleared a table by the simple expedient of tilting all the books off onto the floor, he whistled three times, a voice-operated relay tripped somewhere, and a gloomy Cornish voice drifted out of a concealed loudspeaker.

"Yes, Mr. Ferguson?"

"Maida, send across a bottle of the new whiskey."

There was no reply except an audible sniff. But a moment later there came a creaking and clanking, and a couple of square feet of library shelving slid aside to reveal a conveyor belt.

"I can't get Maida to come into the library," complained Homer, lifting out a loaded tray. "She's afraid of Boanerges, though he's perfectly harmless."

Harry found it hard not to feel some sympathy for the invisible Maida. All six feet of Boanerges was draped over the case holding the "Encyclopaedia Britannica", and a bulge amidships indicated that he had dined recently.

"What do you think of the whiskey?" asked Homer when Harry had sampled some and started to gasp for breath.

"It's—well, I don't know what to say. It's—phew—rather strong. I never thought—"

"Oh, don't take any notice of the label on the bottle. *This* brand never saw Scotland. And that's what all the trouble's about. I made it right here on the premises."

"Uncle!"

"Yes, I know it's against the law, and all that sort of nonsense. But you can't get any good whiskey these days—it all goes for export. It seemed to me that I was being patriotic making my own, so that there was more left over for the dollar drive. But the Excise people don't see it that way."

"I think you'd better let me have the whole story," said Harry. He was gloomily sure that there was nothing he could do to get his uncle out of this scrape.

Homer had always been fond of the bottle, and wartime shortages had hit him badly. He was also, as has been hinted, disinclined to give away money, and for a long time he had resented the fact that he had to pay a tax of several hundred percent on a bottle of whiskey. When he couldn't get his own supply any more, he had decided it was time to act.

The district he was living in probably had a good deal to do with his decision. For some centuries, the Customs and Excise had waged a never-ending battle with the Cornish fisherfolk. It was rumored that the last incumbent of the old vicarage had possessed the finest cellar in the district next to that of the Bishop himself—and had never paid a penny in duty on it. So Uncle Homer merely felt he was carrying on an old and noble tradition.

There was little doubt, moreover, that the spirit of pure scientific enquiry also inspired him. He felt sure that this business about being aged in the wood for seven years was all rubbish, and was confident that he could do a better job with ultrasonics and ultraviolet rays.

The experiment went well for a few weeks. But late one evening there was one of those unfortunate accidents that will happen even in the best-conducted laboratories, and before Uncle knew what had happened, he was draped over a beam, while the grounds of the vicarage were littered with pieces of copper tubing.

Even then it would not have mattered much had not the local Home Guard been practicing in the neighborhood. As soon as they heard the explosion, they immediately went into action, Sten guns at the ready. Had the invasion started? If so, they'd soon fix it.

They were a little disappointed to discover that it was only Uncle, but as they were used to his experiments they weren't in the least surprised at what had happened. Unfortunately for Uncle, the Lieutenant in charge of the squad happened to be the local exciseman, and the combined evidence of his nose and his eyes told him the story in a flash.

"So tomorrow," said Uncle Homer, looking rather like a small boy who had been caught stealing candy, "I have to go up before the Bench, charged with possessing an illegal still."

"I should have thought," replied Harry, "that was a matter for the Assizes, not the local magistrates."

"We do things our own way here," answered Homer, with more than a touch of pride. Harry was soon to discover how true this was.

They got little sleep that night, as Homer outlined his defence, overcame Harry's objections, and hastily assembled the apparatus he intended to produce in court.

"A Bench like this," he explained, "is always impressed by experts. If we dared, I'd like to say you were someone from the War Office, but they could check up on that. So we'll just tell them the truth—about your qualifications, that is."

"Thank you," said Harry. "And suppose my college finds out what I'm doing?"

"Well, you won't claim to be acting for anyone except yourself. The whole thing is a private venture."

"I'll say it is," said Harry.

The next morning they loaded their gear into Homer's ancient Austin, and drove into the village. The Bench was sitting in one of the classrooms of the local school, and Harry felt that time had rolled back a few years and he was about to have an unpleasant interview with his old headmaster.

"We're in luck," whispered Homer, as they were ushered into their cramped seats. "Major Fotheringham is in the Chair. He's a good friend of mine."

That would help a lot, Harry agreed. But there were two other justices on the Bench as well, and one friend in court would hardly be sufficient. Eloquence, not influence, was the only thing that could save the day.

The courtroom was crowded, and Harry found it surprising that so many people had managed to get away from work long enough to watch the case. Then he realized the local interest that it would have aroused, in view of the fact that—in normal times, at least—smuggling was a major industry in these parts. He was not sure whether that would mean a sympathetic audience. The natives might well regard Homer's form of private enterprise as unfair competition. On the other hand, they probably approved on general principles with anything that put the excisemen's noses out of joint.

The charge was read by the Clerk of the Court, and the somewhat damning evidence produced. Pieces of copper tubing were solemnly inspected by the justices, each of whom in turn looked severely at Uncle Homer. Harry began to see his hypothetical inheritance becoming even more doubtful.

When the case for the prosecution was completed, Major Fotheringham turned to Homer.

"This appears to be a serious matter, Mr. Ferguson. I hope you have a satisfactory explanation."

"I have, your Honor," replied the defendant in a tone that practically reeked of injured innocence. It was amusing to see His Honor's look of relief, and the momentary frown, quickly replaced by calm confidence, that passed across the face of H. M. Customs and Excise.

"Do you wish to have a legal representative? I notice that you have not brought one with you."

"It won't be necessary. The whole case is founded on such a trivial misunderstanding that it can be cleared up without complications like that. I don't wish to incur the prosecution in unnecessary costs."

This frontal onslaught brought a murmur from the body of the court, and a flush to the cheeks of the Customs man. For the first time he began to look a little unsure of himself. If Ferguson thought the Crown would be paying costs, he must have a pretty good case. Of course, he might only be bluffing. . . .

Homer waited until the mild stir had died away before creating a considerably greater one.

"I have called a scientific expert to explain what happened at the vicarage," he said. "And owing to the nature of the evidence, I must ask, for security reasons, that the rest of the proceedings be *in camera.*"

"You want me to clear the court?" said the Chairman incredulously.

"I am afraid so, sir. My colleague, Doctor Purvis, feels that the fewer people concerned in this case, the better. When you have heard the evidence, I think you will agree with him. If I might say so, it is a great pity that it has already attracted so much publicity. I am afraid it may bring certain—ah—confidential matters to the wrong ears."

Homer glared at the Customs officer, who fidgeted uncomfortably in his seat.

"Oh, very well," said Major Fotheringham. "This is all very irregular, but we live in irregular times. Mr. Clerk, clear the court."

After some grumbling and confusion, and an overruled protest from the prosecution, the order was carried out. Then, under the interested gaze of the dozen people left in the room, Harry Purvis uncovered the apparatus he had unloaded from the Baby Austin.

After his qualifications had been presented to the court, he took the witness stand.

"I wish to explain, your Honor," he began, "that I have been engaged on explosives research, and that is why I happen to be acquainted with the defendant's work." The opening part of this statement was perfectly true. It was about the last thing said that day that was.

"You mean—bombs and so forth?"

"Precisely, but on a fundamental level. We are always looking for new and better types of explosives, as you can imagine. Moreover, we in government research and the academic world are continually on the lookout for good ideas from outside sources. And quite recently, Unc—er, Mr. Ferguson, wrote to us with a most interesting suggestion for a completely new type of explosive. The interesting thing about it was that it employed *non-explosive* materials such as sugar, starch and so on."

"Eh?" said the Chairman. "A non-explosive explosive? That's impossible."

Harry smiled sweetly.

"I know, sir—that is one's immediate reaction. But like most great ideas, this has the simplicity of genius. I am afraid, however, that I shall have to do a little explaining to make my point."

The Bench looked very attentive, and also a little alarmed. Harry surmised that it had probably encountered expert witnesses before. He walked over to a table that had been set up in the middle of the courtroom, and which was now covered with flasks, piping, and bottles of liquids.

"I hope, Mr. Purvis," said the Chairman nervously, "that you're not going to do anything dangerous."

"Of course not, sir. I merely wish to demonstrate some basic scientific principles. Once again, I wish to stress the importance of keeping this between these four walls." He paused solemnly and everyone looked duly impressed.

"Mr. Ferguson," he began, "is proposing to tap one of the fundamental forces of nature. It is a force on which every living thing depends—a force, gentlemen, which keeps *you* alive, even though you may never have heard of it."

He moved over to the table and took up his position beside the flasks and bottles.

"Have you ever stopped to consider," he said, "how the sap manages to reach the highest leaf of a tall tree? It takes a lot of force to pump water a hundred—sometimes over three hundred—feet from the ground. Where does that force come from? I'll show you, with this practical example.

"Here I have a strong container, divided into two parts by a porous membrane. On one side of the membrane is pure water—on the other, a concentrated solution of sugar and other chemicals which I do not propose to specify. Under these conditions, a pressure is set up, known as *osmotic* pressure. The pure water tries to pass through the membrane, as if to dilute the solution on the other side. I've now sealed the container, and you'll notice the pressure gauge here on the right—see how the pointer's going up. That's osmotic pressure for you. This same force acts through the cell walls in our bodies, causing fluid movement. It drives the sap up the trunk of trees, from the roots to the topmost branches. It's a universal force, and a powerful one. To Mr. Ferguson must go the credit of first attempting to harness it."

Harry paused impressively and looked round the court.

"Mr. Ferguson," he said, "was attempting to develop the Osmotic Bomb."

It took some time for this to sink in. Then Major Fotheringham leaned forward and said in a hushed voice: "Are we to presume that he had succeeded in manufacturing this bomb, and that it exploded in his workshop?"

"Precisely, your Honor. It is a pleasure—an unusual pleasure, I might say—to present a case to so perspicacious a court. Mr. Ferguson had succeeded, and he was preparing to report his method to us when, owing to an unfortunate oversight, a safety device attached to the bomb failed to operate. The results, you all know. I think you will need no further evidence of the power of this weapon—and you will realize its importance when I point out that the solutions it contains are all extremely common chemicals."

Major Fotheringham, looking a little puzzled, turned to the prosecution lawyer.

"Mr. Whiting," he said, "have you any questions to ask the witness?"

"I certainly have, your Honor. I've never heard such a ridiculous—"

"You will please confine yourself to questions of fact."

"Very good, your Honor. May I ask the witness how he accounts

he large quantity of alcohol vapor immediately after the explo-
1?"

"I rather doubt if the inspector's nose was capable of accurate
quantitative analysis. But admittedly there was some alcohol vapor
released. The solution used in the bomb contained about 25 percent.
By employing dilute alcohol, the mobility of the inorganic ions is
restricted and the osmotic pressure raised—a desirable effect, of
course."

That should hold them for a while, thought Harry. He was right.
It was a good couple of minutes before the second question. Then
the prosecution's spokesman waved one of the pieces of copper tubing in the air.

"What function did these carry out?" he said, in as nasty a tone of
voice as he could manage. Harry affected not to notice the sneer.

"Manometer tubing for the pressure gauges," he replied promptly.

The Bench, it was clear, was already far out of its depth. This was
just where Harry wanted it to be. But the prosecution still had one
card up its sleeve. There was a furtive whispering between the exciseman and his legal eagle. Harry looked nervously at Uncle Homer, who
shrugged his shoulders with a "Don't ask *me!*" gesture.

"I have some additional evidence I wish to present to the court,"
said the Customs lawyer briskly, as a bulky brown paper parcel was
hoisted onto the table.

"Is this in order, your Honor?" protested Harry. "All evidence
against my—ah—colleague should already have been presented."

"I withdraw my statement," the lawyer interjected swiftly. "Let us
say that this is not evidence for *this* case, but material for later proceedings." He paused ominously to let that sink in. "Nevertheless, if
Mr. Ferguson can give a satisfactory answer to our questions now,
this whole business can be cleared up right away." It was obvious
that the last thing the speaker expected—or hoped for—was such a
satisfactory explanation.

He unwrapped the brown paper, and there were three bottles of a
famous brand of whiskey.

"Uh-huh," said Uncle Homer. "I was wondering—"

"Mr. Ferguson," said the Chairman of the Bench. "There is no need
for you to make any statement unless you wish."

Harry Purvis shot Major Fotheringham a grateful glance. He
guessed what had happened. The prosecution had, when prowling
through the ruins of Uncle's laboratory, acquired some bottles of his

home-brew. Their action was probably illegal, since they would not have had a search-warrant—hence the reluctance in producing the evidence. The case had seemed sufficiently clear-cut without it.

It certainly appeared pretty clear-cut now. . . .

"These bottles," said the representative of the Crown, "do not contain the brand advertised on the label. They have obviously been used as convenient receptacles for the defendant's—shall we say—chemical solutions." He gave Harry Purvis an unsympathetic glance. "We have had these solutions analysed, with most interesting results. Apart from an abnormally high alcohol concentration, the contents of these bottles are virtually indistinguishable from—"

He never had time to finish his unsolicited and certainly unwanted testimonial to Uncle Homer's skill. For at that moment, Harry Purvis became aware of an ominous whistling sound. At first he thought it was a falling bomb—but that seemed unlikely, as there had been no air raid warning. Then he realized that the whistling came from close at hand; from the courtroom table, in fact. . . .

"Take cover!" he yelled.

The court went into recess with a speed never matched in the annals of British law. The three justices disappeared behind the dais; those in the body of the room burrowed into the floor or sheltered under desks. For a protracted, anguished moment nothing happened, and Harry wondered if he had given a false alarm. Then there was a dull, peculiarly muffled explosion, a great tinkling of glass—and a smell like a blitzed brewery. Slowly, the court emerged from shelter.

The Osmotic Bomb had proved its power. More important still, it had destroyed the evidence for the prosecution.

The Bench was none too happy about dismissing the case; it felt, with good reason, that its dignity had been assailed. Moreover, each one of the justices would have to do some fast talking when he got home: the mist of alcohol had penetrated everything. Though the Clerk of the Court rushed round opening windows (none of which, oddly enough, had been broken) the fumes seemed reluctant to disperse. Harry Purvis, as he removed pieces of bottle-glass from his hair, wondered if there would be some intoxicated pupils in class tomorrow.

Major Fotheringham, however, was undoubtedly a real sport, and as they filed out of the devastated courtroom, Harry heard him say to his Uncle: "Look here, Ferguson—it'll be ages before we can get those Molotov Cocktails we've been promised by the War Office. What about making some of these bombs of yours for the Home

Guard? If they don't knock out a tank, at least they'll make the crew drunk and incapable."

"I'll certainly think about it, Major," replied Uncle Homer, who still seemed a little dazed by the turn of events.

He recovered somewhat as they drove back to the vicarage along the narrow, winding lanes with their high walls of unmortared stone.

"I hope, Uncle," remarked Harry, when they had reached a relatively straight stretch and it seemed safe to talk to the driver, "that you don't intend to rebuild that still. They'll be watching you like hawks and you won't get away with it again."

"Very well," said Uncle, a little sulkily. "Confound these brakes! I had them fixed only just before the war!"

"Hey!" cried Harry. "Watch out!"

It was too late. They had come to a cross-roads at which a brand-new HALT sign had been erected. Uncle braked hard, but for a moment nothing happened. Then the wheels on the left seized up, while those on the right continued gaily spinning. The car did a hair-pin bend, luckily without turning over, and ended in the ditch pointing in the direction from which it had come.

Harry looked reproachfully at his Uncle. He was about to frame a suitable reprimand when a motor-cycle came out of the side-turning and drew up to them.

It was not going to be their lucky day, after all. The village police-sergeant had been lurking in ambush, waiting to catch motorists at the new sign. He parked his machine by the roadside and leaned in through the window of the Austin.

"You all right, Mr. Ferguson?" he said. Then his nose wrinkled up, and he looked like Jove about to deliver a thunderbolt. "This won't do," he said. "I'll have to put you on a charge. Driving under the influence is a *very* serious business."

"But I've not touched a drop all day!" protested Uncle, waving an alcohol-sodden sleeve under the sergeant's twitching nose.

"Do you expect me to believe *that*?" snorted the irate policeman, pulling out his note-book. "I'm afraid you'll have to come to the station with me. Is your friend sober enough to drive?"

Harry Purvis didn't answer for a moment. He was too busy beating his head against the dash-board.

"Well," we asked Harry. "What did they do to your Uncle?"

"Oh, he got fined five pounds and had his license endorsed for drunken driving. Major Fotheringham wasn't in the Chair, unfortunately, when the case came up, but the other two justices were still on the Bench. I guess they felt that even if he was innocent this time, there was a limit to everything."

"And did you ever get any of his money?"

"No fear! He was very grateful, of course, and he's told me that I'm mentioned in his will. But when I saw him last, what do you think he was doing? He was searching for the Elixir of Life."

Harry sighed at the overwhelming injustice of things.

"Sometimes," he said gloomily, "I'm afraid he's found it. The doctors say he's the healthiest seventy-year-old they've ever seen. So all I got out of the whole affair was some interesting memories and a hangover."

"A hangover?" asked Charlie Willis.

"Yes," replied Harry, a faraway look in his eye. "You see, the exciseman hadn't seized *all* the evidence. We had to—ah—destroy the rest. It took us the best part of a week. We invented all sorts of things during that time—but we never discovered what they were."

The Man Who Ploughed the Sea

The adventures of Harry Purvis have a kind of mad logic that makes them convincing by their very improbability. As his complicated but neatly dove-tailed stories emerge, one becomes lost in a sort of baffled wonder. Surely, you say to yourself, no one would have the nerve to make *that* up—such absurdities only occur in real life, not in fiction. And so criticism is disarmed, or at any rate discomfitted, until Drew shouts "Time, gentlemen, *pleeze!*" and throws us all out into the cold hard world.

Consider, for example, the unlikely chain of events which involved Harry in the following adventure. If he'd wanted to invent the whole thing, surely he could have managed it a lot more simply. There was not the slightest need, from the artistic point of view, to have started at Boston to make an appointment off the coast of Florida. . . .

Harry seems to have spent a good deal of time in the United States, and to have quite as many friends there as he has in England. Sometimes he brings them to the "White Hart," and sometimes they leave again under their own power. Often, however, they succumb to the illusion that beer which is tepid is also innocuous. (I am being unjust to Drew: his beer is *not* tepid. And if you insist, he will give you, for no extra charge, a piece of ice every bit as large as a postage-stamp.)

This particular saga of Harry's began, as I have indicated, at Boston, Mass. He was staying as a house-guest of a successful New England lawyer when one morning his host said, in the casual way Americans have: "Let's go down to my place in Florida. I want to get some sun."

"Fine," said Harry, who'd never been to Florida. Thirty minutes later, to his considerable surprise, he found himself moving south in a red Jaguar saloon at a formidable speed.

The drive in itself was an epic worthy of a complete story. From Boston to Miami is a little matter of 1,568 miles—a figure which, according to Harry, is now engraved on his heart. They covered the distance in 30 hours, frequently to the sound of ever-receding police sirens as frustrated squad-cars dwindled astern. From time to time considerations of tactics involved them in evasive manoeuvres and they had to shoot off into secondary roads. The Jaguar's radio tuned in to all the police frequencies, so they always had plenty of warning if an interception was being arranged. Once or twice they just managed to reach a state line in time, and Harry couldn't help wondering what his host's clients would have thought had they known the strength of the psychological urge which was obviously getting him away from them. He also wondered if he was going to see anything of Florida at all, or whether they would continue at this velocity down US 1 until they shot into the ocean at Key West.

They finally came to a halt sixty miles south of Miami, down on the Keys—that long, thin line of island hooked on to the lower end of Florida. The Jaguar angled suddenly off the road and weaved a way through a rough track cut in the mangroves. The road ended in a wide clearing at the edge of the sea, complete with dock, 35 foot cabin cruiser, swimming pool, and modern ranch-type house. It was quite a nice little hide-away, and Harry estimated that it must have cost the best part of a hundred thousand dollars.

He didn't see much of the place until the next day, as he collapsed straight into bed. After what seemed far too short a time, he was awakened by a sound like a boiler factory in action. He showered and dressed in slow motion, and was reasonably back to normal by the time he had left his room. There seemed to be no one in the house, so he went outside to explore.

By this time he had learned not to be surprised at anything, so he barely raised his eyebrows when he found his host working down at the dock, straightening out the rudder on a tiny and obviously home-made submarine. The little craft was about twenty feet long, had a conning tower with large observation windows, and bore the name "Pompano" stencilled on her prow.

After some reflection, Harry decided that there was nothing really very unusual about all this. About five million visitors come to Florida every year, most of them determined to get on or into the sea. His host happened to be one of those fortunate enough to indulge in his hobby in a big way.

Harry looked at the "Pompano" for some time, and then a disturbing thought struck him. "George," he said, "do you expect me to go down in *that* thing?"

"Why, sure," answered George, giving a final bash at the rudder. "What are you worried about? I've taken her out lots of times—she's safe as houses. We won't be going deeper than twenty feet."

"There are circumstances," retorted Harry, "when I should find a mere six feet of water more than adequate. And didn't I mention my claustrophobia? It always comes on badly at this time of year."

"Nonsense!" said George. "You'll forget all about that when we're out on the reef." He stood back and surveyed his handiwork, then said with a sigh of satisfaction, "Looks O.K. now. Let's have some breakfast."

During the next thirty minutes, Harry learned a good deal about the "Pompano." George had designed and built her himself, and her powerful little Diesel could drive her at five knots when she was fully submerged. Both crew and engine breathed through a snorkel tube, so there was no need to bother about electric motors and an independent air supply. The length of the snorkel limited dives to twenty-five feet, but in these shallow waters this was no great handicap.

"I've put a lot of novel ideas into her," said George enthusiastically. "Those windows, for instance—look at their size. They'll give you a perfect view, yet they're quite safe. I use the old Aqualung principle to keep the air-pressure in the 'Pompano' exactly the same as the water-pressure outside, so there's no strain on the hull or the ports."

"And what happens," asked Harry, "if you get stuck on the bottom?"

"I open the door and get out, of course. There are a couple of spare Aqualungs in the cabin, as well as a life-raft with a waterproof radio, so that we can always yell for help if we get in trouble. Don't worry— I've thought of everything."

"Famous last words," muttered Harry. But he decided that after the ride down from Boston he undoubtedly had a charmed life: the sea was probably a safer place than US 1 with George at the wheel.

He made himself thoroughly familiar with the escape arrangements before they set out, and was fairly happy when he saw how well designed and constructed the little craft appeared to be. The fact that a lawyer had produced such a neat piece of marine engineering in his spare time was not in the least unusual. Harry had long ago discovered that a considerable number of Americans put quite as much effort into their hobbies as into their professions.

They chugged out of the little harbour, keeping to the marked channel until they were well clear of the coast. The sea was calm and as the shore receded the water became steadily more and more transparent. They were leaving behind the fog of pulverized coral which clouded the coastal waters, where the waves were incessantly tearing at the land. After thirty minutes they had come to the reef, visible below them as a kind of patchwork quilt above which multicolored fish pirouetted to and fro. George closed the hatches, opened the valve of the buoyancy tanks, and said gaily, "Here we go!"

The wrinkled silk veil lifted, crept past the window, distorting all vision for a moment—and then they were through, no longer aliens looking into the world of waters, but denizens of that world themselves. They were floating above a valley carpeted with white sand, and surrounded by low hills of coral. The valley itself was barren but the hills around it were alive with things that grew, things that crawled and things that swam. Fish as dazzling as neon signs wandered lazily among the animals that looked like trees. It seemed not only a breathtakingly lovely but also a peaceful world. There was no haste, no sign of the struggle for existence. Harry knew very well that this was an illusion, but during all the time they were submerged he never saw one fish attack another. He mentioned this to George, who commented: "Yes, that's a funny thing about fish. They seem to have definite feeding times. You can see barracuda swimming around and if the dinner gong hasn't gone the other fish won't take any notice of them."

A ray, looking like some fantastic black butterfly, flapped its way across the sand, balancing itself with its long, whiplike tail. The sensitive feelers of a crayfish waved cautiously from a crack in the coral; the exploring gestures reminded Harry of a soldier testing for snipers with his hat on a stick. There was so much life, of so many kinds, crammed in this single spot that it would take years of study to recognize it all.

The "Pompano" cruised very slowly along the valley, while George gave a running commentary.

"I used to do this sort of thing with the Aqualung," he said, "but then I decided how nice it would be to sit in comfort and have an engine to push me around. Then I could stay out all day, take a meal along, use my cameras and not give a damn if a shark was sneaking up on me. There goes a tang—did you ever see such a brilliant blue in your life? Besides, I could show my friends around down here while still being able to talk to them. That's one big handicap with ordinary diving gear—you're deaf and dumb and have to talk in signs. Look at those angelfish—one day I'm going to fix up a net to catch some of them. See the way they vanish when they're edge-on! Another reason why I built the 'Pompano' was so that I could look for wrecks. There are hundreds in this area—it's an absolute graveyard. The 'Santa Margarita' is only about fifty miles from here, in Biscayne Bay. She went down in 1595 with seven million dollars of bullion aboard. And there's a little matter of sixty-five million off Long Cay, where fourteen galleons sank in 1715. The trouble is, of course, that most of these wrecks have been smashed up and overgrown with coral, so it wouldn't do you a lot of good even if you did locate them. But it's fun to try."

By this time Harry had begun to appreciate his friend's psychology. He could think of few better ways of escaping from a New England law practice. George was a repressed romantic—and not such a repressed one, either, now that he came to think of it.

They cruised along happily for a couple of hours, keeping in water that was never more than forty feet deep. Once they grounded on a dazzling stretch of broken coral, and took time off for liverwurst sandwiches and glasses of beer. "I drank some ginger beer down here once," said George. "When I came up the gas inside me expanded and it was a very odd sort of feeling. Must try it with champagne some day."

Harry was just wondering what to do with the empties when the "Pompano" seemed to go into eclipse as a dark shadow drifted overhead. Looking up through the observation window, he saw that a ship was moving slowly past twenty feet above their heads. There was no danger of a collision, as they had pulled down their snort for just this reason and were subsisting for the moment on their capital as far as air was concerned. Harry had never seen a ship from underneath and began to add another novel experience to the many he had acquired today.

He was quite proud of the fact that, despite his ignorance of matters nautical, he was just as quick as George at spotting what was wrong with the vessel sailing overhead. Instead of the normal shaft and screw, this ship had a long tunnel running the length of its keel. As it passed above them, the "Pompano" was rocked by the sudden rush of water.

"I'll be damned!" said George, grabbing the controls. "That looks like some kind of jet propulsion system. It's about time somebody tried one out. Let's have a look."

He pushed up the periscope, and discovered that the ship slowly cruising past them was the "Valency" of New Orleans. "That's a funny name," he said. "What does it mean?"

"I would say," answered Harry, "that it means the owner is a chemist—except for the fact that no chemist would ever make enough money to buy a ship like that."

"I'm going to follow her," decided George. "She's only making five knots, and I'd like to see how that dingus works."

He elevated the snort, got the Diesel running, and started in pursuit. After a brief chase, the "Pompano" drew within fifty feet of the "Valency," and Harry felt rather like a submarine commander about to launch a torpedo. They couldn't miss from this distance.

In fact, they nearly made a direct hit. For the "Valency" suddenly slowed to a halt, and before George realized what had happened, he was alongside her. "No signals!" he complained, without much logic. A minute later, it was clear that the manoeuvre was no accident. A lasso dropped neatly over the "Pompano's" snorkel and they were efficiently gaffed. There was nothing to do but emerge, rather sheepishly, and make the best of it.

Fortunately, their captors were reasonable men and could recognize the truth when they heard it. Fifteen minutes after coming aboard the "Valency," George and Harry were sitting on the bridge while a uniformed steward brought them highballs and they listened attentively to the theories of Dr. Gilbert Romano.

They were still both a little overawed at being in Dr. Romano's presence: it was rather like meeting a live Rockefeller or a reigning duPont. The Doctor was a phenomenon virtually unknown in Europe and unusual even in the United States—the big scientist who had become a bigger businessman. He was now in his late seventies and had just been retired—after a considerable tussle—from the chairmanship of the vast chemical engineering firm he had founded.

It is rather amusing, Harry told us, to notice the subtle social distinctions which differences in wealth can produce even in the most democratic country. By Harry's standards, George was a very rich man: his income was around a hundred thousand dollars a year. But Dr. Romano was in another price range altogether, and had to be treated accordingly with a kind of friendly respect which had nothing to do with obsequiousness. On his side, the Doctor was perfectly free and easy; there was nothing about him that gave any impression of wealth, if one ignored such trivia as hundred-and-fifty-foot ocean-going yachts.

The fact that George was on first-name terms with most of the Doctor's business acquaintances helped to break the ice and to establish the purity of their motives. Harry spent a boring half-hour while business deals ranging over half the United States were discussed in terms of what Bill So-and-so did in Pittsburgh, who Joe Somebody Else ran into at the Bankers' Club in Houston, how Clyde Thingummy happened to be playing golf at Augusta while Ike was there. It was a glimpse of a mysterious world where immense power was wielded by men who all seemed to have gone to the same colleges, or who at any rate belonged to the same clubs. Harry soon became aware of the fact that George was not merely paying court to Dr. Romano because that was the polite thing to do. George was too shrewd a lawyer to miss this chance of building up some good-will, and appeared to have forgotten all about the original purpose of their expedition.

Harry had to wait for a suitable gap in the conversation before he could raise the subject which really interested him. When it dawned on Dr. Romano that he was talking to another scientist, he promptly abandoned finance and George was the one who was left out in the cold.

The thing that puzzled Harry was why a distinguished chemist should be interested in marine propulsion. Being a man of direct action, he challenged the Doctor on this point. For a moment the scientist appeared a little embarrassed and Harry was about to apologize for his inquisitiveness—a feat that would have required real effort on his part. But before he could do this, Dr. Romano had excused himself and disappeared into the bridge.

He came back five minutes later with a rather satisfied expression, and continued as if nothing had happened.

"A very natural question, Mr. Purvis," he chuckled. "I'd have asked it myself. But do you really expect me to tell you?"

"Er—it was just a vague sort of hope," confessed Harry.

"Then I'm going to surprise you—surprise you twice, in fact. I'm going to answer you, and I'm going to show you that I'm *not* passionately interested in marine propulsion. Those bulges on the bottom of my ship which you were inspecting with such great interest do contain the screws, but they also contain a good deal else as well.

"Let me give you," continued Dr. Romano, now obviously warming up to his subject, "a few elementary statistics about the ocean. We can see a lot of it from here—quite a few square miles. Did you know that every cubic mile of sea-water contains a hundred and fifty *million* tons of minerals."

"Frankly, no," said George. "It's an impressive thought."

"It's impressed me for a long time," said the Doctor. "Here we go grubbing about in the earth for our metals and chemicals, while every element that exists can be found in sea-water. The ocean, in fact, is a kind of universal mine which can never be exhausted. We may plunder the land, but we'll never empty the sea.

"Men have already started to mine the sea, you know. Dow Chemicals have been taking out bromine for years: every cubic mile contains about three hundred thousand tons. More recently, we've started to do something about the five million tons of magnesium per cubic mile. But that sort of thing is merely a beginning.

"The great practical problem is that most of the elements present in sea-water are in such low concentrations. The first seven elements make up about 99 percent of the total, and it's the remaining one percent that contains all the useful metals except magnesium.

"All my life I've wondered how we could do something about this, and the answer came during the war. I don't know if you're familiar with the techniques used in the atomic energy field to remove minute quantities of isotopes from solutions: some of those methods are still pretty much under wraps."

"Are you talking about ion-exchange resins?" hazarded Harry.

"Well—something similar. My firm developed several of these techniques on A.E.C. contracts, and I realized at once that they would have wider applications. I put some of my bright young men to work and they have made what we call a 'molecular sieve'. That's a mighty descriptive expression: in its way, the thing *is* a sieve, and we can set it to select anything we like. It depends on very advanced wave-mechanical theories for its operation, but what it actually does is absurdly simple. We can choose any component of sea-water we like, and get the sieve to take it out. With several units, working in series, we can take out one element after another. The efficiency's quite high, and the power consumption negligible."

"I know!" yelped George. "You're extracting gold from sea-water!"

"Huh!" snorted Dr. Romano in tolerant disgust. "I've got better things to do with my time. Too much damn gold around, anyhow. I'm after the commercially useful metals—the ones our civilisation is going to be desperately short of in another couple of generations. And as a matter of fact, even with my sieve it wouldn't be worth going after gold. There are only about fifty pounds of the stuff in every cubic mile."

"What about uranium?" asked Harry. "Or is that scarcer still?"

"I rather wish you hadn't asked that question," replied Dr. Romano with a cheerfulness that belied the remark. "But since you can look it up in any library, there's no harm in telling you that uranium's two hundred times *more* common than gold. About seven tons in every cubic mile—a figure which is, shall we say, distinctly interesting. So why bother about gold?"

"Why indeed?" echoed George.

"To continue," said Dr. Romano, duly continuing, "even with the molecular sieve, we've still got the problem of processing enormous volumes of sea-water. There are a number of ways one could tackle this: you could build giant pumping stations, for example. But I've always been keen on killing two birds with one stone, and the other day I did a little calculation that gave the most surprising result. I found that every time the 'Queen Mary' crosses the Atlantic, her screws chew up about a tenth of a cubic mile of water. Fifteen million tons of minerals, in other words. Or to take the case you indiscreetly mentioned—almost a ton of uranium on every Atlantic crossing. Quite a thought, isn't it?

"So it seemed to me that all we need do to create a very useful mobile extraction plant was to put the screws of any vessel inside a tube which would compel the slip-stream to pass through one of my sieves. Of course, there's a certain loss of propulsive power, but our experimental unit works very well. We can't go quite as fast as we did, but the further we cruise the more money we make from our mining operations. Don't you think the shipping companies will find that very attractive? But of course that's merely incidental. I look forward to the building of floating extraction plants that will cruise round and round in the ocean until they've filled their hoppers with anything you care to name. When that day comes, we'll be able to stop tearing up the land and all our material shortages will be over. Everything goes back to the sea in the long run anyway, and once we've unlocked that treasure-chest, we'll be all set for eternity."

For a moment there was silence on deck, save for the faint clink of ice in the tumblers, while Dr. Romano's guests contemplated this dazzling prospect. Then Harry was struck by a sudden thought.

"This is quite one of the most important inventions I've ever heard of," he said. "That's why I find it rather odd that you should have confided in us so fully. After all, we're perfect strangers, and for all you know might be spying on you."

The old scientist chortled gaily.

"Don't worry about *that*, my boy," he reassured Harry. "I've already been on to Washington and had my friends check up on you."

Harry blinked for a minute, then realized how it had been done. He remembered Dr. Romano's brief disappearance, and could picture what had happened. There would have been a radio call to Washington, some senator would have got on to the Embassy, the Ministry of Supply representative would have done his bit—and in five minutes the Doctor would have got the answer he wanted. Yes, Americans were very efficient—those who could afford to be.

It was about this time that Harry became aware of the fact that they were no longer alone. A much larger and more impressive yacht than the "Valency" was heading towards them, and in a few minutes he was able to read the name "Sea Spray". Such a name, he thought, was more appropriate to billowing sails than throbbing Diesels, but there was no doubt that the "Spray" was a very pretty creature indeed.

He could understand the looks of undisguised covetousness that both George and Dr. Romano now plainly bore.

The sea was so calm that the two yachts were able to come alongside each other, and as soon as they had made contact a sunburned, energetic man in the late forties vaulted over onto the deck of the "Valency". He strode up to Dr. Romano, shook his hand vigorously, said, "Well, you old rascal, what are you up to?" and then looked enquiringly at the rest of the company. The Doctor carried out the introductions: it seemed that they had been boarded by Professor Scott McKenzie, who'd been sailing *his* yacht down from Key Largo.

"Oh no!" cried Harry to himself. "This is *too* much! One millionaire scientist per day is all I can stand."

But there was no getting away from it. True, McKenzie was very seldom seen in the academic cloisters, but he was a genuine Professor none the less, holding the chair of geophysics at some Texas college. Ninety percent of his time, however, he spent working for the big oil companies and running a consulting firm of his own. It rather looked as if he had made his torsion balances and seismographs pay quite well for themselves. In fact, though he was a much younger man than Dr. Romano, he had even more money owing to being in a more rapidly expanding industry. Harry gathered that the peculiar tax laws of the Sovereign State of Texas also had something to do with it. . . .

It seemed an unlikely coincidence that these two scientific tycoons should have met by chance, and Harry waited to see what skullduggery was afoot. For a while the conversation was confined to generalities, but it was obvious that Professor McKenzie was extremely inquisitive about the Doctor's other two guests. Not long after they had been introduced, he made some excuse to hop back to his own ship and Harry moaned inwardly. If the Embassy got two separate enquiries about him in the space of half an hour, they'd wonder what he'd been up to. It might even make the F.B.I. suspicious, and then how would he get those promised twenty-four pairs of nylons out of the country?

Harry found it quite fascinating to study the relation between the two scientists. They were like a couple of fighting cocks circling for position. Romano treated the younger man with a downright rudeness which, Harry suspected, concealed a grudging admiration. It was clear that Dr. Romano was an almost fanatical conservationist, and regarded the activities of McKenzie and his employers with the greatest disapproval. "You're a gang of robbers," he said once. "You're seeing how quickly you can loot this planet of its resources, and you don't give a damn about the next generation."

"And what," answered McKenzie, not very originally, "has the next generation ever done for us?"

The sparring continued for the best part of an hour, and much of what went on was completely over Harry's head. He wondered why he and George were being allowed to sit in on all this, and after a while he began to appreciate Dr. Romano's technique. He was an opportunist of genius: he was glad to keep them round, now that they had turned up, just to worry Professor McKenzie and to make him wonder what other deals were afoot.

He let the molecular sieve leak out bit by bit, as if it wasn't *really* important and he was only mentioning it in passing. Professor McKenzie, however, latched on to it at once, and the more evasive Romano became, the more insistent was his adversary. It was obvious that he was being deliberately coy, and that though Professor McKenzie knew this perfectly well, he couldn't help playing the older scientist's game.

Dr. Romano had been discussing the device in a peculiarly oblique fashion, as if it were a future project rather than an existing fact. He outlined its staggering possibilities, and explained how it would make all existing forms of mining obsolete, besides removing forever the danger of world metal shortages.

"If it's so good," exclaimed McKenzie presently, "why haven't you made the thing?"

"What do you think I'm doing out here in the Gulf Stream?" retorted the Doctor. "Take a look at this."

He opened a locker beneath the sonar set, and pulled out a small metal bar which he tossed to McKenzie. It looked like lead, and was obviously extremely heavy. The Professor hefted it in his hand and said at once: "Uranium. Do you mean to say. . . ."

"Yes—every gram. And there's plenty more where that came from." He turned to Harry's friend and said: "George—what about taking the Professor down in your submarine to have a look at the works? He won't see much, but it'll show him we're in business."

McKenzie was still so thoughtful that he took a little thing like a private submarine in his stride. He returned to the surface fifteen minutes later, having seen just enough to whet his appetite.

"The first thing I want to know," he said to Romano, "is why you're showing this to *me!* It's about the biggest thing that ever happened—why isn't your own firm handling it?"

Romano gave a little snort of disgust.

"You know I've had a row with the Board," he said. "Anyway, that lot of old dead-beats couldn't handle anything as big as this. I hate to admit it, but you Texas pirates are the boys for the job."

"This is a private venture of yours?"

"Yes: the company knows nothing about it, and I've sunk half a million of my own money into it. It's been a kind of hobby of mine. I felt someone had to undo the damage that was going on, the rape of the continents by people like—"

"All right—we've heard that before. Yet you propose giving it to us?"

"Who said anything about giving?"

There was a pregnant silence. Then McKenzie said cautiously; "Of course, there's no need to tell you that we'll be interested—very interested. If you'll let us have the figures on efficiency, extraction rates, and all the other relevant statistics—no need to tell us the actual technical details if you don't want to—then we'll be able to talk business. I can't really speak for my associates but I'm sure that they can raise enough cover to make any deal—"

"Scott," said Romano—and his voice now held a note of tiredness that for the first time reflected his age—"I'm not interested in doing a deal with your partners. I haven't time to haggle with the boys in the front room and their lawyers and their lawyers' lawyers. Fifty years I've been doing that sort of thing, and believe me, I'm tired. This is *my* development. It was done with *my* money, and all the equipment is in *my* ship. I want to do a personal deal, direct with you. You can handle it from then on."

McKenzie blinked.

"I couldn't swing anything as big as this," he protested. "Sure, I appreciate the offer, but if this does what you say, it's worth billions. And I'm just a poor but honest millionaire."

"Money I'm no longer interested in. What would I do with it at my time of life? No, Scott, there's just one thing I want now—and I want it right away, this minute. Give me the 'Sea Spray', and you can have my process."

"You're crazy! Why, even with inflation, you could build the 'Spray' for inside a million. And your process must be worth—"

"I'm not arguing, Scott. What you say is true, but I'm an old man in a hurry, and it would take me a year to get a ship like yours built. I've wanted her ever since you showed her to me back at Miami. My proposal is that you take over the 'Valency', with all her lab equipment and records. It will only take an hour to swap our personal effects—we've a lawyer here who can make it all legal. And then I'm heading out into the Caribbean, down through the islands, and across the Pacific."

"You've got it all worked out?" said McKenzie in awed wonder.

"Yes. You can take it or leave it."

"I never heard such a crazy deal in my life," said McKenzie, somewhat petulantly. "Of course I'll take it. I know a stubborn old mule when I see one."

The next hour was one of frantic activity. Sweating crew-members rushed back and forth with suitcases and bundles, while Dr. Romano sat happily in the midst of the turmoil he had created, a blissful smile upon his wrinkled old face. George and Professor McKenzie went into a legal huddle, and emerged with a document which Dr. Romano signed with hardly a glance.

Unexpected things began to emerge from the "Sea Spray", such as a beautiful mutation mink and a beautiful non-mutation blonde.

"Hello, Sylvia," said Dr. Romano politely. "I'm afraid you'll find the quarters here a little more cramped. The Professor never mentioned you were aboard. Never mind—we won't mention it either. Not actually in the contract, but a gentleman's agreement, shall we say? It would be such a pity to upset Mrs. McKenzie."

"I don't know *what* you mean!" pouted Sylvia. "Someone has to do all the Professor's typing."

"And you do it damn badly, my dear," said McKenzie, assisting her over the rail with true Southern gallantry. Harry couldn't help admiring his composure in such an embarrassing situation—he was by no means sure that he would have managed as well. But he wished he had the opportunity to find out.

At last the chaos subsided, the stream of boxes and bundles subsided to a trickle. Dr. Romano shook hands with everybody, thanked George and Harry for their assistance, strode to the bridge of the "Sea Spray", and ten minutes later, was half-way to the horizon.

Harry was wondering if it wasn't about time for them to take their departure as well—they had never got round to explaining to Professor McKenzie what they were doing here in the first place—when the radio-telephone started calling. Dr. Romano was on the line.

"Forgotten his tooth-brush, I suppose," said George. It was not quite as trivial as that. Fortunately, the loudspeaker was switched on. Eavesdropping was practically forced upon them and required none of the effort that makes it so embarrassing to a gentleman.

"Look here, Scott," said Dr. Romano, "I think I owe you some sort of explanation."

"If you've gypped me, I'll have you for every cent—"

"Oh, it's not like that. But I did rather pressurize you, though everything I said was perfectly true. Don't get too annoyed with me— you've got a bargain. It'll be a long time, though, before it makes you any money, and you'll have to sink a few millions of your own into it first. You see, the efficiency has to be increased by about three orders of magnitude before it will be a commercial proposition: that bar of uranium cost me a couple of thousand dollars. Now don't blow your top—it *can* be done—I'm certain of that. Dr. Kendall is the man to get: he did all the basic work—hire him away from my people however much it costs you. You're a stubborn cuss and I know you'll finish the job now it's on your hands. That's why I wanted you to have it. Poetic justice, too—you'll be able to repay some of the damage you've done to the land. Too bad it'll make you a billionaire, but that can't be helped.

"Wait a minute—don't cut in on me. I'd have finished the job myself if I had the time, but it'll take at least three more years. And the doctors say I've only got six months: I wasn't kidding when I said I was in a hurry. I'm glad I clinched the deal without having to tell you that, but believe me I'd have used it as a weapon if I had to. Just one thing more—when you do get the process working, name it after me, will you? That's all—it's no use calling me back. I won't answer—and I know you can't catch me."

Professor McKenzie didn't turn a hair.

"I thought it was something like that," he said to no one in particular. Then he sat down, produced an elaborate pocket slide-rule, and became oblivious to the world. He scarcely looked up when George and Harry, feeling very much outclassed, made their polite departure and silently snorkeled away.

"Like so many things that happen these days," concluded Harry Purvis, "I still don't know the final outcome of this meeting. I rather imagine that Professor McKenzie has run into some snags, or we'd have heard rumors about the process by now. But I've not the slightest doubt that sooner or later it'll be perfected, so get ready to sell your mining shares. . . .

"As for Dr. Romano, he wasn't kidding, though his doctors were a little out in their estimates. He lasted a full year, and I guess the 'Sea Spray' helped a lot. They buried him in mid-Pacific, and it's just occurred to me that the old boy would have appreciated that. I told you what a fanatical conservationist he was, and it's a piquant thought that even now some of his atoms may be going through his own molecular sieve. . . .

"I notice some incredulous looks, but it's a fact. If you took a tumbler of water, poured it into the ocean, mixed well, then filled the glass from the sea, there'd still be some scores of molecules of water from the original sample in the tumbler. So—" he gave a gruesome little chuckle—"it's only a matter of time before not only Dr. Romano, but all of us, make some contribution to the sieve. And with that thought, gentlemen, I bid you all a very pleasant good-night."

One of the things that makes Harry Purvis' tales so infernally convincing is their detailed verisimilitude. Consider, for instance, this example. I've checked the places and information as thoroughly as I can—I had to, in order to write up this account—and everything fits into place. How do you explain that unless—but judge for yourself . . .

"I've often noticed," Harry began, "how tantalizing little snippets of information appear in the Press and then, sometimes years later, one comes across their sequels. I've just had a beautiful example. In the spring of 1954—I've looked up the date—it was April 19—an iceberg was reported off the coast of Florida. I remember spotting this news item and thinking it highly peculiar. The Gulf Stream, you know, is born in the Straits of Florida, and I didn't see *how* an iceberg could get that far south before it melted. But I forgot about the whole business almost immediately, thinking it was just another of those tall stories which the papers like to print when there isn't any real news.

"And then, about a week ago, I met a friend who'd been a Commander in the U.S. Navy, and he told me the whole astonishing tale. It's such a remarkable story that I think it ought to be better known, though I'm sure that a lot of people simply won't believe it.

"Any of you who are familiar with domestic American affairs may know that Florida's claim to be the Sunshine State is strongly disputed by some of the other forty-seven members of the Union. I don't suppose New York or Maine or Connecticut are very serious contenders, but the State of California regards the Florida claim as an almost personal affront, and is always doing its best to refute it. The Floridians hit back by pointing to the famous Los Angeles smogs, then the Californians say, with careful anxiety, 'Isn't it about time you had another hurricane?' and the Floridians reply, 'You can count on us when you want any earthquake relief.' So it goes on, and this is where my friend Commander Dawson came into the picture.

"The Commander had been in submarines, but was now retired. He'd been working as technical advisor on a film about the exploits of the submarine service when he was approached one day with a very peculiar proposition. I won't say that the California Chamber of Commerce was behind it, as that might be libel. You can make your own guesses . . .

"Anyway, the idea was a typical Hollywood conception. So I thought at first, until I remembered that dear old Lord Dunsany had used a similar theme in one of his short stories. Maybe the Californian sponsor was a Jorkens fan, just as I am.

"The scheme was delightful in its boldness and simplicity. Commander Dawson was offered a substantial sum of money to pilot an artificial iceberg to Florida, with a bonus if he could contrive to strand it on Miami Beach at the height of the season.

"I need hardly say that the Commander accepted with alacrity: he came from Kansas himself, so could view the whole thing dispassionately as a purely commercial proposition. He got together some of his old crew, swore them to secrecy, and after much waiting in Washington corridors managed to obtain temporary loan of an obsolete submarine. Then he went to a big air-conditioning company, convinced them of his credit and his sanity, and got the icemaking plant installed in a big blister on the sub's deck.

"It would take an impossible amount of power to make a solid iceberg, even a small one, so a compromise was necessary. There would be an outer coating of ice a couple of feet thick, but Frigid Freda, as she was christened, was to be hollow. She would look quite impressive from outside, but would be a typical Hollywood stage set when one got behind the scenes. However, nobody would see her inner secrets except the Commander and his men. She would be set adrift when the prevailing winds and currents were in the right direction, and would last long enough to cause the calculated alarm and despondency.

"Of course, there were endless practical problems to be solved. It would take several days of steady freezing to create Freda, and she must be launched as near her objective as possible. That meant that the submarine—which we'll call the *Marlin*—would have to use a base not too far from Miami.

"The Florida Keys were considered but at once rejected. There was no privacy down there any more; the fishermen now outnumbered the mosquitoes and a submarine would be spotted almost instantly. Even if the *Marlin* pretended she was merely smuggling, she wouldn't be able to get away with it. So that plan was out.

"There was another problem that the Commander had to consider. The coastal waters round Florida are extremely shallow, and though Freda's draught would only be a couple of feet, everybody knew that an honest-to-goodness iceberg was nearly all below the waterline. It wouldn't be very realistic to have an impressive-looking berg sailing through two feet of water. That would give the show away at once.

"I don't know exactly how the Commander overcame these technical problems, but I gather that he carried out several tests in the Atlantic, far from any shipping routes. The iceberg reported in the news was one of his early productions. Incidentally, neither Freda nor her brethren would have been a danger to shipping—being hollow, they would have broken up on impact.

Finally, all the preparations were complete. The *Marlin* lay out in the Atlantic, some distance north of Miami, with her ice-manufacturing equipment going full blast. It was a beautiful clear night, with a crescent moon sinking in the west. The *Marlin* had no navigation lights, but Commander Dawson was keeping a very strict watch for other ships. On a night like this, he'd be able to avoid them without being spotted himself.

"Freda was still in an embryonic stage. I gather that the technique used was to inflate a large plastic bag with super-cooled air, and spray water over it until a crust of ice formed. The bag could be removed when the ice was thick enough to stand up under its own weight. Ice is not a very good structural material, but there was no need for Freda to be very big. Even a small iceberg would be as disconcerting to the Florida Chamber of Commerce as a small baby to an unmarried lady.

"Commander Dawson was in the conning tower, watching his crew working with their sprays of ice-cold water and jets of freezing air. They were now quite skilled at this unusual occupation, and delighted in little artistic touches. However, the Commander had had to put a stop to attempts to reproduce Marilyn Monroe in ice—though he filed the idea for future reference.

"Just after midnight he was startled by a flash of light in the northern sky, and turned in time to see a red glow die away on the horizon.

"'There's a plane down skipper!' shouted one of the lookouts. 'I just saw it crash!' Without hesitation, the Commander shouted down to the engine room and set course to the north. He'd got an accurate fix on the glow, and judged that it couldn't be more than a few miles away. The presence of Freda, covering most of the stern of his vessel, would not affect his speed appreciably, and in any case there was no way of getting rid of her quickly. He stopped the freezers to give more power to the main diesels, and shot ahead at full speed.

"About thirty minutes later the lookout, using powerful night-glasses, spotted something lying in the water. 'It's still afloat,' he said. 'Some kind of airplane all right—but I can't see any sign of life. And I think the wings have come off.'

"He had scarcely finished speaking when there was an urgent report from another watcher.

"'Look, skipper—thirty degrees to starboard! What's that?'

"Commander Dawson swung around and whipped up his glasses. He saw, just visible above the water, a small oval object spinning rapidly on its axis.

"'Uh-huh,' he said, 'I'm afraid we've got company. That's a radar scanner—there's another sub here.' Then he brightened considerably. 'Maybe we can keep out of this after all,' he remarked to his second in command. 'We'll watch to see that they start rescue operations, then sneak away.'

" 'We may have to submerge and abandon Freda. Remember they'll have spotted us by now on their radar. Better slacken speed and behave more like a real iceberg.'

"Dawson nodded and gave the order. This was getting complicated, and anything might happen in the next few minutes. The other sub would have observed the *Marlin* merely as a blip on its radar screen, but as soon as it upped periscope its commander would start investigating. Then the fat would be in the fire . . .

"Dawson analyzed the tactical situation. The best move, he decided, was to employ his unusual camouflage to the full. He gave the order to swing the *Marlin* around so that her stern pointed towards the still submerged stranger. When the other sub surfaced, her commander would be most surprised to see an iceberg, but Dawson hoped he would be too busy with rescue operations to bother about Freda.

"He pointed his glasses towards the crashed plane—and then had his second shock. It was a very peculiar type of aircraft indeed—and there was something wrong—

" 'Of course!' said Dawson to his Number One. 'We should have thought of this—that thing isn't an airplane at all. It's a missile from the range over at Cocoa—look, you can see the floatation bags. They must have inflated on impact, and that sub was waiting out here to take it back.'

"He'd remembered that there was a big missile launching range over on the east coast of Florida, at a place with the unlikely name of Cocoa on the still more improbable Banana River. Well, at least there was nobody in danger, and if the *Marlin* sat tight there was a sporting chance that they'd be none the worse for this diversion.

"Their engines were just turning over, so that they had enough control to keep hiding behind their camouflage. Freda was quite large enough to conceal their conning tower, and from a distance, even in better light than this, the *Marlin* would be totally invisible. There was one horrid possibility, though. The other sub might start shelling them on general principles, as a menace to navigation. No: it would just report them by radio to the coast-guards, which would be a nuisance but would not interfere with their plans.

" 'Here she comes!' said Number One. 'What class is she?'

"They both stared through their glasses as the submarine, water pouring from its sides, emerged from the faintly phosphorescent ocean. The moon had now almost set, and it was difficult to make out any details. The radar scanner, Dawson was glad to see, had stopped its rotation and was pointing at the crashed missile. There was something odd about the design of that conning tower, though . . .

"Then Dawson swallowed hard, lifted the mike to his mouth, and whispered to his crew in the bowels of the *Marlin:* 'Does anyone down there speak Russian . . . ?'

"There was a long silence, but presently the engineer officer climbed up into the conning tower.

" 'I know a bit, skipper,' he said. 'My grandparents came from the Ukraine. What's the trouble?'

" 'Take a look at this,' said Dawson grimly. 'There's an interesting piece of poaching going on here. I think we ought to stop it . . .' "

Harry Purvis has a most annoying habit of breaking off just when a story reaches its climax, and ordering another beer—or, more usually, getting someone else to buy him one. I've watched him do this so often that now I can tell just when the climax is coming by the level in his glass. We had to wait, with what patience we could, while he refueled.

"When you think about it," he said thoughtfully, "it was jolly hard luck on the commander of that Russian submarine. I imagine they shot him when he got back to Vladivostock, or wherever he came from. For what court of inquiry would have believed his story? If he was fool enough to tell the truth, he'd have said 'We were just off the Florida coast when an iceberg shouted at us in Russian, "Excuse me— I think that's *our* property!" ' Since there would be a couple of MVD men aboard the ship, the poor guy would have had to make up *some* kind of story, but whatever he said wouldn't be very convincing . . .

"As Dawson had calculated, the Russian sub simply ran for it as soon as it knew it had been spotted. And remembering that he was an officer on the reserve, and that his duty to his country was more important than his contractual obligations to any single state, the commander of the *Marlin* really had no choice in his subsequent actions. He picked up the missile, defrosted Freda, and set course for Cocoa—first sending a radio message that caused a great flurry in the Navy Department and started destroyers racing out into the Atlantic. Perhaps Inquisitive Ivan never got back to Vladivostock after all. . . .

"The subsequent explanations were a little embarrassing, but I gather that the rescued missile was so important that no one asked too many questions about the *Marlin*'s private war. The attack on Miami Beach had to be called off, however, at least until the next season. It's satisfactory to relate that even the sponsors of the project, though they had sunk a lot of money into it, weren't too disappointed. They each have a certificate signed by the Chief of Naval Operations, thanking them for valuable but unspecified services to their country. These cause such envy and mystification to all their Los Angeles friends that they wouldn't part with them for anything . . .

"Yet I don't want you to think that nothing more will ever come of the whole project; you ought to know American publicity men better than that. Freda may be in suspended animation, but one day she'll be revived. All the plans are ready, down to such little details as the accidental presence of a Hollywood film unit on Miami Beach when Freda comes sailing in from the Atlantic.

"So this is one of those stories I can't round off to a nice, neat ending. The preliminary skirmishes have taken place, but the main engagement is still to come. And this is the thing I often wonder about —*what will Florida do to the Californians when it discovers what's going on?* Any suggestions, anybody?"

What Goes Up

One of the reasons why I am never too specific about the exact location of the "White Hart" is frankly, because we want to keep it to ourselves. This is not merely a dog-in-the-manger attitude: we have to do it in pure self-protection. As soon as it gets around that scientists, editors and science-fiction writers are forgathering at some locality, the weirdest collection of visitors is likely to turn up. Peculiar people with new theories of the universe, characters who have been "cleared" by Dianetics (God knows what they were like before), intense ladies who are liable to go all clairvoyant after the fourth gin—these are the less exotic specimens. Worst of all, however, are the Flying Sorcerers: no cure short of mayhem has yet been discovered for them.

It was a black day when one of the leading exponents of the Flying

Saucer religion discovered our hideout and fell upon us with shrill cries of delight. Here, he obviously told himself, was fertile ground for his missionary activities. People who were already interested in spaceflight, and even wrote books and stories about its imminent achievement, would be a pushover. He opened his little black bag and produced the latest pile of sauceriana.

It was quite a collection. There were some interesting photographs of flying saucers made by an amateur astronomer who lives right beside Greenwich Observatory, and whose busy camera has recorded such a remarkable variety of spaceships, in all shapes and sizes, that one wonders what the professionals next door are doing for their salaries. Then there was a long statement from a gentleman in Texas who had just had a casual chat with the occupants of a saucer making a wayside halt on route to Venus. Language, it seemed, had presented no difficulties: it had taken about ten minutes of arm-waving to get from "Me—Man. This—Earth" to highly esoteric information about the use of the fourth dimension in space-travel.

The masterpiece, however, was an excited letter from a character in South Dakota who had actually been offered a lift in a flying saucer, and had been taken for a spin round the Moon. He explained at some length how the saucer travelled by hauling itself along magnetic lines of force, rather like a spider going up its thread.

It was at this point that Harry Purvis rebelled. He had been listening with a professional pride to tales which even he would never have dared to spin, for he was an expert at detecting the yield-point of his audience's credulity. At the mention of lines of magnetic force, however, his scientific training overcame his frank admiration of these latter-day Munchausens, and he gave a snort of disgust.

"That's a lot of nonsense," he said. "I can prove it to you—magnetism's my speciality."

"Last week," said Drew sweetly, as he filled two glasses of ale at once, "you said that crystal structure was your speciality."

Harry gave him a superior smile.

"I'm a *general* specialist," he said loftily. "To get back to where I was before that interruption, the point I want to make is that there's no such thing as a line of magnetic force. It's a mathematical fiction— exactly on a par with lines of longitude or latitude. Now if anyone said they'd invented a machine that worked by pulling itself along parallels of latitude, everybody would know that they were talking drivel. But because few people know much about magnetism, and it sounds rather mysterious, crackpots like this guy in South Dakota can get away with the tripe we've just been hearing."

There's one charming characteristic about the "White Hart"—we may fight among each other, but we show an impressive solidarity in times of crisis. Everyone felt that something had to be done about our unwelcome visitor: for one thing, he was interfering with the serious business of drinking. Fanaticism of any kind casts a gloom over the most festive assembly, and several of the regulars had shown signs of leaving despite the fact that it was still two hours to closing time.

So when Harry Purvis followed up his attack by concocting the most outrageous story that even he had ever presented in the "White Hart", no one interrupted him or tried to expose the weak points in his narrative. We knew that Harry was acting for us all—he was fighting fire with fire, as it were. And we knew that he wasn't expecting us to believe him (if indeed he ever did) so we just sat back and enjoyed ourselves.

"If you want to know how to propel spaceships," began Harry, "and mark you, I'm not saying anything one way or the other about the existence of flying saucers—then you must forget magnetism. You must go straight to gravity—that's the basic force of the universe, after all. But it's going to be a tricky force to handle, and if you don't believe me just listen to what happened only last year to a scientist down in Australia. I shouldn't really tell you this, I suppose, because I'm not sure of its security classification, but if there's any trouble I'll swear that I never said a word.

"The Aussies, as you may know, have always been pretty hot on scientific research, and they had one team working on fast reactors— those house-broken atomic bombs which are so much more compact than the old uranium piles. The head of the group was a bright but rather impetuous young nuclear physicist I'll call Dr. Cavor. That, of course, wasn't his real name, but it's a very appropriate one. You'll all recollect, I'm sure, the scientist Cavor in Wells' FIRST MEN IN THE MOON, and the wonderful gravity-screening material Cavorite he discovered?

"I'm afraid dear old Wells didn't go into the question of Cavorite very thoroughly. As he put it, it was opaque to gravity just as a sheet of metal is opaque to light. Anything placed above a horizontal sheet of cavorite, therefore, became weightless and floated up into space.

"Well, it isn't as simple as that. Weight represents energy—an enormous amount of it—which can't just be destroyed without any fuss.

You'd have to put a terrific amount of work into even a small object in order to make it weightless. Antigravity screens of the Cavorite type, therefore, are quite impossible—they're in the same class as perpetual motion."

"Three of my friends have made perpetual motion machines," began our unwanted visitor rather stuffily. Harry didn't let him get any further: he just steamed on and ignored the interruption.

"Now our Australian Dr. Cavor wasn't searching for antigravity, or anything like it. In pure science, you can be pretty sure that nothing fundamental is ever discovered by anyone who's actually looking for it—that's half the fun of the game. Dr. Cavor was interested in producing atomic power: what he found was antigravity. And it was quite some time before he realised that was what he'd discovered.

"What happened, I gather, was this: The reactor was of a novel and rather daring design, and there was quite a possibility that it might blow up when the last pieces of fissile material were inserted. So it was assembled by remote control in one of Australia's numerous convenient deserts, all the final operations being observed through TV sets.

"Well, there was no explosion—which would have caused a nasty radio-active mess and wasted a lot of money, but wouldn't have damaged anything except a lot of reputations. What actually happened was much more unexpected, and much more difficult to explain.

"When the last piece of enriched uranium was inserted, the control rods pulled out, and the reactor brought up to criticality—everything went dead. The meters in the remote control room, two miles from the reactor, all dropped back to zero. The TV screen went blank. Cavor and his colleagues waited for the bang, but there wasn't one. They looked at each other for a moment with many wild surmises: then, without a word, they climbed up out of the buried control chamber.

"The reactor building was completely unchanged: it sat out there in the desert, a commonplace cube of brick holding a million pounds worth of fissile material and several years of careful design and development. Cavor wasted no time: he grabbed the jeep, switched on a portable Geiger counter, and hurried off to see what had happened.

"He recovered consciousness in hospital a couple of hours later. There was little wrong with him apart from a bad headache, which was nothing to the one his experiment was going to give him during the next few days. It seemed that when he got to within twenty feet of the reactor, his jeep had hit something with a terrific crash. Cavor had got tangled in the steering wheel and had a nice collection of bruises: the Geiger counter, oddly enough, was quite undamaged and was still clucking away quietly to itself, detecting no more than the normal cosmic-ray background.

"Seen from a distance, it had looked a perfectly normal sort of accident, that might have been caused by the jeep going into a rut. But Cavor hadn't been driving all that fast, luckily for him, and anyway there was no rut at the scene of the crash. What the jeep had run into was something quite impossible. It was an invisible wall, apparently the lower rim of a hemispherical dome, which entirely surrounded the reactor. Stones thrown up in the air slid back to the ground along the surface of this dome, and it also extended underground as far as digging could be carried out. It seemed as if the reactor was at the exact center of an impenetrable, spherical shell.

"Of course, this was marvellous news and Cavor was out of bed in no time, scattering nurses in all directions. He had no idea what had happened, but it was a lot more exciting than the humdrum piece of nuclear engineering that had started the whole business.

"By now you're probably all wondering what the devil a sphere of force—as you science-fiction writers would call it—has to do with antigravity. So I'll jump several days and give you the answers that Cavor and his team discovered only after much hard work and the consumption of many gallons of that potent Australian beer.

"The reactor, when it had been energised, had somehow produced an antigravity field. All the matter inside a twenty-foot-radius sphere had been made weightless, and the enormous amount of energy needed to do this had been extracted, in some utterly mysterious manner, from the uranium in the pile. Calculations showed that the amount of energy in the reactor was just sufficient to do the job. Presumably the sphere of force would have been larger still if there had been more ergs available in the power-source.

"I can hear someone just waiting to ask a question, so I'll anticipate them. Why didn't this weightless sphere of earth and air float up into space? Well, the earth was held together by its cohesion, anyway, so there was no reason why it should go wandering off. As for the air, that was forced to stay inside the zone of zero-gravity for a most surprising and subtle reason which leads me to the crux of this whole peculiar business.

"Better fasten your seat-belts for the next bit: we've got a bumpy passage ahead. Those of you who know something about potential theory won't have any trouble, and I'll do my best to make it as easy as I can for the rest.

"People who talk glibly about antigravity seldom stop to consider its implications, so let's look at a few fundamentals. As I've already said, weight implies energy—lots of it. That energy is entirely due to Earth's gravity field. *If you remove an object's weight*, that's precisely equivalent to taking it clear outside Earth's gravity. And any rocket engineer will tell you how much energy *that* requires."

Harry turned to me and said: "There's an analogy I'd like to borrow from one of your books, Arthur, that puts across the point I'm trying to make. You know—comparing the fight against Earth's gravity to climbing out of a deep pit."

"You're welcome," I said. "I pinched it from Doc Richardson, anyway."

"Oh," replied Harry. "I thought it was too good to be original. Well, here we go. If you hang on to this really very simple idea, you'll be O.K. To take an object clear away from the Earth requires as much work as lifting it *four thousand miles* against the steady drag of normal gravity. Now the matter inside Cavor's zone of force was still on the Earth's surface, but it was weightless. From the energy point of view, therefore, it was outside the Earth's gravity field. It was inaccessible as if it was on top of a four thousand mile high mountain.

"Cavor could stand outside the antigravity zone and look into it from a point a few inches away. To cross those few inches, he would have to do as much work as if he climbed Everest seven hundred times. It wasn't surprising that the jeep stopped in a hurry. No material object had stopped it, but from the point of view of dynamics it had run smack into a cliff four thousand miles high . . .

"I can see some blank looks that are not entirely due to the lateness of the hour. Never mind: if you don't get all this, just take my word for it. It won't spoil your appreciation of what follows—at least, I hope not.

"Cavor had realised at once that he had made one of the most important discoveries of the age, though it was some time before he worked out just what was going on. The final clue to the anti-gravitational nature of the field came when they shot a rifle bullet into it and observed the trajectory with a high-speed camera. Ingenious, don't you think?

"The next problem was to experiment with the field's generator and to find just what had happened inside the reactor when it had been switched on. This was a problem indeed. The reactor was there in plain sight, twenty feet away. But to reach it would require slightly more energy than going to the Moon . . .

"Cavor was not disheartened by this, nor by the inexplicable failure of the reactor to respond to any of its remote controls. He theorised that it had been completely drained of energy, if one can use a rather misleading term, and that little if any power was needed to maintain the antigravity field once it had been set up. This was one of the many things that could only be determined by examination on the spot. So by hook or by crook, Dr. Cavor would have to go there.

"His first idea was to use an electrically-driven trolley, supplied with power through cables which it dragged behind it as it advanced into the field. A hundred horsepower generator, running continuously for seventeen hours, would supply enough energy to take a man of average weight on the perilous twenty-foot journey. A velocity of slightly over a foot an hour did not seem much to boast about, until you remembered that advancing one foot into the antigravity field was equivalent to a two hundred mile vertical climb.

"The theory was sound, but in practice the electric trolley wouldn't work. It started to push its way into the field, but began to skid after it had traversed half an inch. The reason was obvious when one started to think about it. Though the power was there, the traction wasn't. No wheeled vehicle could climb a gradient of two hundred miles per foot.

"This minor setback did not discourage Dr. Cavor. The answer, he realised at once, was to produce the traction at a point outside the field. When you wanted to lift a load vertically, you didn't use a cart: you used a jack or an hydraulic ram.

"The result of this argument was one of the oddest vehicles ever built. A small but comfortable cage, containing sufficient provisions to last a man for several days, was mounted at the end of a twenty-foot-long horizontal girder. The whole device was supported off the ground by balloon tires, and the theory was that the cage could be pushed right into the center of the field by a machine which would remain outside its influence. After some thought, it was decided that the best prime-mover would be the common or garden bulldozer.

"A test was made with some rabbits in the passenger compartment —and I can't help thinking that there was an interesting psychological point here. The experimenters were trying to get it both ways: as scientists they'd be pleased if their subjects got back alive, and as Australians they'd be just as happy if they got back dead. But perhaps I'm being a little too fanciful . . . (You know, of course, how Australians feel about rabbits.)

"The bulldozer chugged away hour after hour, forcing the weight of the girder and its insignificant payload up the enormous gradient. It was an uncanny sight—all this energy being expended to move a couple of rabbits twenty feet across a perfectly horizontal plain. The subjects of the experiment could be observed throughout the operation: they seemed to be perfectly happy and quite unaware of their historic rôle.

"The passenger compartment reached the centre of the field, was held there for an hour, and then the girder was slowly backed out again. The rabbits were alive, in good health, and to nobody's particular surprise there were now six of them.

"Dr. Cavor, naturally, insisted on being the first human being to venture into a zero-gravity field. He loaded up the compartment with torsion balances, radiation detectors, and periscopes so that he could look into the reactor when he finally got to it. Then he gave the signal, the bulldozer started chugging, and the strange journey began.

"There was, naturally, telephone communications from the passenger compartment to the outside world. Ordinary sound waves couldn't cross the barrier, for reasons which were still a little obscure, but radio and telephone both worked without difficulty. Cavor kept up a running commentary as he was edged forward into the field, describing his own reactions and relaying instrument readings to his colleagues.

"The first thing that happened to him, though he had expected it, was nevertheless rather unsettling. During the first few inches of his advance, as he moved through the fringe of the field, the direction of the vertical seemed to swing around. 'Up' was no longer toward the sky: it was now in the direction of the reactor hut. To Cavor, it felt as if he was being pushed up the face of a vertical cliff, with the reactor twenty feet above him. For the first time, his eyes and his ordinary human senses told him the same story as his scientific training. He could *see* that the centre of the field was, gravity-wise, higher than the place from which he had come. However, imagination still boggled at the thought of all the energy it would need to climb that innocent-looking twenty feet, and the hundreds of gallons of diesel fuel that must be burned to get him there.

"There was nothing else of interest to report on the journey itself, and at last, twenty hours after he had started, Cavor arrived at his destination. The wall of the reactor hut was right beside him, though to him it seemed not a wall but an unsupported floor sticking out at right angles from the cliff up which he had risen. The entrance was just above his head, like a trapdoor through which he would have to climb. This would present no great difficulty, for Dr. Cavor was an energetic young man, extremely eager to find just how he had created this miracle.

"Slightly too eager, in fact. For as he tried to work his way into the door, he slipped and fell off the platform that had carried him there.

"That was the last anyone ever saw of him—but it wasn't the last they heard of him. Oh dear no! He made a very big noise indeed . . .

"You'll see why when you consider the situation in which this unfortunate scientist now found himself. Hundreds of kilowatt-hours of energy had been pushed into him—enough to lift him to the Moon and beyond. All that work had been needed to take him to a point of zero gravitational potential. As soon as he lost his means of support, that energy began to reappear. To get back to our earlier and very picturesque analogy—the poor doctor had slipped off the edge of the four-thousand-mile-high mountain he had ascended.

"He fell back the twenty feet that had taken almost a day to climb. 'Ah, what a fall was there, my countrymen!' It was precisely equivalent, in terms of energy, to a free drop from the remotest stars down to the surface of the Earth. And you all know how much velocity an object acquires in *that* fall. It's the same velocity that's needed to get it there in the first place—the famous velocity of escape. Seven miles a second, or twenty-five thousand miles an hour.

"That's what Dr. Cavor was doing by the time he got back to his starting point. Or to be more accurate, that's the speed he involuntarily tried to reach. As soon as he passed Mach 1 or 2, however, air-resistance began to have its little say. Dr. Cavor's funeral pyre was the finest, and indeed, the only, meteor display ever to take place entirely at sea level. . . .

"I'm sorry that this story hasn't got a happy ending. In fact, it hasn't got an ending at all, because that sphere of zero gravitational potential is still sitting there in the Australian desert, apparently doing nothing at all but in fact producing ever-increasing amounts of frustration in scientific and official circles. I don't see *how* the authorities can hope to keep it secret much longer. Sometimes I think how odd it is that the world's tallest mountain is in Australia—and that though it's four thousand miles high the airliners often fly right over it without knowing it's there."

You will hardly be surprised to hear that H. Purvis finished his narration at this point: even he could hardly take it much further, and no-one wanted him to. We were all, including his most tenacious critics, lost in admiring awe. I have since detected six fallacies of a fundamental nature in his description of Dr. Cavor's Frankensteinian fate, but at the time they never even occurred to me. (And I don't propose to reveal them now. They will be left, as the mathematics text-books put it, as an exercise for the reader.) What had earned our undying gratitude, however, was the fact that at some slight sacrifice of truth he had managed to keep Flying Saucers from invading the "White Hart." It was almost closing time, and too late for our visitor to make a counter attack.

That is why the sequel seems a little unfair. A month later, some-one brought a very odd publication to one of our meetings. It was nicely printed and laid out with professional skill, the misuse of which was sad to behold. The thing was called FLYING SAUCER REVELATIONS—and there on the front page was a full and de-tailed account of the story Purvis had told us. It was printed abso-lutely straight—and what was much worse than that, from poor Harry's point of view, was that it was attributed to him by name.

Since then he has had 4,375 letters on the subject, most of them from California. Twenty-four called him a liar; 4,205 believed him absolutely. (The remaining ones he couldn't decipher and their con-tents still remain a matter of speculation.)

I'm afraid he's never quite got over it, and I sometimes think he's going to spend the rest of his life trying to stop people believing the one story he never expected to be taken seriously.

There may be a moral here. For the life of me I can't find it.

Trouble with the Natives

The flying saucer came down vertically through the clouds, braked to a halt about fifty feet from the ground, and settled with a considerable bump on a patch of heather-strewn moorland.

"That," said Captain Wyxtpthll, "was a lousy landing." He did not, of course, use precisely these words. To human ears his remarks would have sounded rather like the clucking of an angry hen. Master Pilot Krtclugg unwound three of his tentacles from the control panel, stretched all four of his legs, and relaxed comfortably.

"Not my fault the automatics have packed up again," he grumbled. "But what do you expect with a ship that should have been scrapped five thousand years ago? If those cheese-paring form-fillers back at Base Planet——"

"Oh, all right! We're down in one piece, which is more than I expected. Tell Crysteel and Danstor to come in here. I want a word with them before they go."

Crysteel and Danstor were, very obviously, of a different species from the rest of the crew. They had only one pair of legs and arms, no eyes at the back of the head, and other physical deficiencies which their colleagues did their best to overlook. These very defects, however, had made them the obvious choice for this particular mission, for it had needed only a minimum of disguise to let them pass as human beings under all but the closest scrutiny.

"Now you're perfectly sure," said the Captain, "that you understand your instructions?"

"Of course," said Crysteel, slightly huffed. "This isn't the first time I've made contact with a primitive race. My training in anthropology——"

"Good. And the language?"

"Well, that's Danstor's business, but I can speak it reasonably fluently now. It's a very simple language, and after all we've been studying their radio programs for a couple of years."

"Any other points before you go?"

"Er—there's just one matter." Crysteel hesitated slightly. "It's quite obvious from their broadcasts that the social system is very primitive, and that crime and lawlessness are widespread. Many of the wealthier citizens have to use what are called 'detectives' or 'special agents' to protect their lives and property. Now we know it's against regulations, but we were wondering . . ."

"What?"

"Well, we'd feel much safer if we could take a couple of Mark III disrupters with us."

"Not on your life! I'd be court-martialed if they heard about it at the Base. Suppose you killed some of the natives—then I'd have the Bureau of Interstellar Politics, the Aborigines Conservancy Board, and half a dozen others after me."

"There'd be just as much trouble if *we* got killed," Crysteel pointed out with considerable emotion. "After all, you're responsible for our safety. Remember that radio play I was telling you about? It described a typical household, but there were two murders in the first half hour!"

"Oh, very well. But only a Mark II—we don't want you to do too much damage if there *is* trouble."

"Thanks a lot; that's a great relief. I'll report every thirty minutes as arranged. We shouldn't be gone more than a couple of hours."

Captain Wyxtpthll watched them disappear over the brow of the hill. He sighed deeply.

"Why," he said, "of all the people in the ship did it have to be *those* two?"

"It couldn't be helped," answered the pilot. "All these primitive races are terrified of anything strange. If they saw *us* coming, there'd be general panic and before we knew where we were the bombs would be falling on top of us. You just can't rush these things."

Captain Wyxtpthll was absentmindedly making a cat's cradle out of his tentacles in the way he did when he was worried.

"Of course," he said, "if they don't come back I can always go away and report the place dangerous." He brightened considerably. "Yes, that would save a lot of trouble."

"And waste all the months we've spent studying it?" said the pilot, scandalized. "They won't be wasted," replied the captain, unraveling himself with a flick that no human eye could have followed. "Our report will be useful for the next survey ship. I'll suggest that we make another visit in—oh, let's say five thousand years. By then the place may be civilized—though frankly, I doubt it."

Samuel Higginsbotham was settling down to a snack of cheese and cider when he saw the two figures approaching along the lane. He wiped his mouth with the back of his hand, put the bottle carefully down beside his hedge-trimming tools, and stared with mild surprise at the couple as they came into range.

"Mornin'," he said cheerfully between mouthfuls of cheese.

The strangers paused. One was surreptitiously ruffling through a small book which, if Sam only knew, was packed with such common phrases and expressions as: "Before the weather forecast, here is a gale warning," "Stick 'em up—I've got you covered!", and "Calling all cars!" Danstor, who had no needs for these aids to memory, replied promptly enough.

"Good morning, my man," he said in his best B.B.C. accent. "Could you direct us to the nearest hamlet, village, small town or other such civilized community?"

"Eh?" said Sam. He peered suspiciously at the strangers, aware for the first time that there was something very odd about their clothes. One did not, he realized dimly, normally wear a roll-top sweater with a smart pin-striped suit of the pattern fancied by city gents. And the fellow who was still fussing with the little book was actually wearing full evening dress which would have been faultless but for the lurid green and red tie, the hob-nailed boots and the cloth cap. Crysteel and Danstor had done their best, but they had seen too many television plays. When one considers that they had no other source of information, their sartorial aberrations were at least understandable.

Sam scratched his head. Furriners, I suppose, he told himself. Not even the townsfolk got themselves up like this.

He pointed down the road and gave them explicit directions in an accent so broad that no one residing outside the range of the B.B.C.'s West Regional transmitter could have understood more than one word in three. Crysteel and Danstor, whose home planet was so far away that Marconi's first signals couldn't possibly have reached it yet, did even worse than this. But they managed to get the general idea and retired in good order, both wondering if their knowledge of English was as good as they had believed.

So came and passed, quite uneventfully and without record in the history books, the first meeting between humanity and beings from Outside.

"I suppose," said Danstor thoughtfully, but without much conviction, "that he wouldn't have done? It would have saved us a lot of trouble."

"I'm afraid not. Judging by his clothes, and the work he was obviously engaged upon, he could not have been a very intelligent or valuable citizen. I doubt if he could even have understood who we were."

"Here's another one!" said Danstor, pointing ahead.

"Don't make sudden movements that might cause alarm. Just walk along naturally, and let him speak first."

The man ahead strode purposefully toward them, showed not the slightest signs of recognition, and before they had recovered was already disappearing into the distance.

"Well!" said Danstor.

"It doesn't matter," replied Crysteel philosophically. "He probably wouldn't have been any use either."

"That's no excuse for bad manners!"

They gazed with some indignation at the retreating back of Professor Fitzsimmons as, wearing his oldest hiking outfit and engrossed in a difficult piece of atomic theory, he dwindled down the lane. For the first time, Crysteel began to suspect uneasily that it might not be as simple to make contact as he had optimistically believed.

Little Milton was a typical English village, nestling at the foot of the hills whose higher slopes now concealed so portentous a secret. There were very few people about on this summer morning, for the men were already at work and the womenfolk were still tidying up after the exhausting task of getting their lords and masters safely out of the way. Consequently Crysteel and Danstor had almost reached the center of the village before their first encounter, which happened to be with the village postman, cycling back to the office after completing his rounds. He was in a very bad temper, having had to deliver a penny postcard to Dodgson's farm, a couple of miles off his normal route. In addition, the weekly parcel of laundry which Gunner Evans sent home to his doting mother had been a lot heavier than usual, as well it might, since it contained four tins of bully beef pinched from the cookhouse.

"Excuse me," said Danstor politely.

"Can't stop," said the postman, in no mood for casual conversation. "Got another round to do." Then he was gone.

"This is really the limit!" protested Danstor. "Are they *all* going to be like this?"

"You've simply got to be patient," said Crysteel. "Remember their customs are quite different from ours; it may take some time to gain their confidence. I've had this sort of trouble with primitive races before. Every anthropologist has to get used to it."

"Hmm," said Danstor. "I suggest that we call at some of their houses. Then they won't be able to run away."

"Very well," agreed Crysteel doubtfully. "But avoid anything that looks like a religious shrine, otherwise we may get into trouble."

Old Widow Tomkins' council-house could hardly have been mistaken, even by the most inexperienced of explorers, for such an object. The old lady was agreeably excited to see two gentlemen standing on her doorstep, and noticed nothing at all odd about their clothes. Visions of unexpected legacies, of newspaper reporters asking about her 100th birthday (she was really only 95, but had managed to keep it dark) flashed through her mind. She picked up the slate she kept hanging by the door and went gaily forth to greet her visitors.

"You'll have to write it down," she simpered, holding out the slate. "I've been deaf this last twenty years."

Crysteel and Danstor looked at each other in dismay. This was a completely unexpected snag, for the only written characters they had ever seen were television program announcements, and they had never fully deciphered those. But Danstor, who had an almost photographic memory, rose to the occasion. Holding the chalk very awkwardly, he wrote a sentence which, he had reason to believe, was in common use during such breakdowns in communication.

As her mysterious visitors walked sadly away, old Mrs. Tomkins stared in baffled bewilderment at the marks on her slate. It was some time before she deciphered the characters—Danstor had made several mistakes—and even then she was little the wiser.

TRANSMISSIONS WILL BE RESUMED AS
SOON AS POSSIBLE.

It was the best that Danstor could do; but the old lady never did get to the bottom of it.

They were little luckier at the next house they tried. The door was answered by a young lady whose vocabulary consisted largely of giggles, and who eventually broke down completely and slammed the door in their faces. As they listened to the muffled, hysterical laughter, Crysteel and Danstor began to suspect, with sinking hearts, that their disguise as normal human beings was not as effective as they had intended.

At Number 3, on the other hand, Mrs. Smith was only too willing to talk—at 120 words to the minute in an accent as impenetrable as Sam Higginsbotham's. Danstor made his apologies as soon as he could get a word in edgeways, and moved on.

"Doesn't *anyone* talk as they do on the radio?" he lamented. "How do they understand their own programs if they all speak like this?"

"I think we must have landed in the wrong place," said Crysteel, even his optimism beginning to fail. It sagged still further when he had been mistaken, in swift succession, for a Gallup Poll investigator, the prospective Conservative candidate, a vacuum-cleaner salesman, and a dealer from the local black market.

At the sixth or seventh attempt they ran out of housewives. The door was opened by a gangling youth who clutched in one clammy paw an object which at once hypnotized the visitors. It was a magazine whose cover displayed a giant rocket climbing upward from a crater-studded planet which, whatever it might be, was obviously not the Earth. Across the background were the words: "Staggering Stories of Pseudo-Science. Price 25 cents."

Crysteel looked at Danstor with a "Do you think what I think?" expression which the other returned. Here at last, surely, was someone who could understand them. His spirits mounting, Danstor addressed the youngster.

"I think you can help us," he said politely. "We find it very difficult to make ourselves understood here. You see, we've just landed on this planet from space and we want to get in touch with your government."

"Oh," said Jimmy Williams, not yet fully returned to Earth from his vicarious adventures among the outer moons of Saturn. "Where's your spaceship?"

"It's up in the hills; we didn't want to frighten anyone."

"Is it a rocket?"

"Good gracious no. They've been obsolete for thousands of years."

"Then how does it work? Does it use atomic power?"

"I suppose so," said Danstor, who was pretty shaky on physics. "Is there any other kind of power?"

"This is getting us nowhere," said Crysteel, impatient for once. "We've got to ask *him* questions. Try and find where there are some officials we can meet."

Before Danstor could answer, a stentorian voice came from inside the house.

"Jimmy! Who's there?"

"Two . . . men," said Jimmy, a little doubtfully. "At least, they look like men. They've come from Mars. I always said that was going to happen."

There was the sound of ponderous movements, and a lady of elephantine bulk and ferocious mien appeared from the gloom. She glared at the strangers, looked at the magazine Jimmy was carrying, and summed up the situation.

"You ought to be ashamed of yourselves!" she cried, rounding on Crysteel and Danstor. "It's bad enough having a good-for-nothing son in the house who wastes all his time reading this rubbish, without grown men coming along putting more ideas into his head. Men from Mars, indeed! I suppose you've come in one of those flying saucers!"

"But I never mentioned Mars," protested Danstor feebly.

Slam! From behind the door came the sound of violent altercation, the unmistakable noise of tearing paper, and a wail of anguish. And that was that.

"Well," said Danstor at last. "What do we try next? And why did he say we came from Mars? That isn't even the nearest planet, if I remember correctly."

"I don't know," said Crysteel. "But I suppose it's natural for them to assume that we come from some close planet. They're going to have a shock when they find the truth. Mars, indeed! That's even worse than here, from the reports I've seen." He was obviously beginning to lose some of his scientific detachment.

"Let's leave the houses for a while," said Danstor. "There must be some more people outside."

This statement proved to be perfectly true, for they had not gone much further before they found themselves surrounded by small boys making incomprehensible but obviously rude remarks.

"Should we try and placate them with gifts?" said Danstor anxiously. "That usually works among more backward races."

"Well, have you brought any?"

"No, I thought you——"

Before Danstor could finish, their tormentors took to their heels and disappeared down a side street. Coming along the road was a majestic figure in a blue uniform.

Crysteel's eyes lit up.

"A policeman!" he said. "Probably going to investigate a murder somewhere. But perhaps he'll spare us a minute," he added, not very hopefully.

P. C. Hinks eyed the strangers with some astonishment, but managed to keep his feelings out of his voice.

"Hello, gents. Looking for anything?"

"As a matter of fact, yes," said Danstor in his friendliest and most soothing tone of voice. "Perhaps you can help us. You see, we've just landed on this planet and want to make contact with the authorities."

"Eh?" said P. C. Hinks startled. There was a long pause—though not too long, for P. C. Hinks was a bright young man who had no intention of remaining a village constable all his life. "So you've just landed, have you? In a spaceship, I suppose?"

"That's right," said Danstor, immensely relieved at the absence of the incredulity, or even violence, which such announcements all too often provoked on the more primitive planets.

"Well, well!" said P. C. Hinks, in tones which he hoped would inspire confidence and feelings of amity. (Not that it mattered much if they both became violent—they seemed a pretty skinny pair.) "Just tell me what you want, and I'll see what we can do about it."

"I'm so glad," said Danstor. "You see, we've landed in this rather remote spot because we don't want to create a panic. It would be best to keep our presence known to as few people as possible until we have contacted your government."

"I quite understand," replied P. C. Hinks, glancing round hastily to see if there was anyone through whom he could send a message to his sergeant. "And what do you propose to do then?"

"I'm afraid I can't discuss our long-term policy with regard to Earth," said Danstor cagily. "All I can say is that this section of the Universe is being surveyed and opened up for development, and we're quite sure we can help you in many ways."

"That's very nice of you," said P. C. Hinks heartily. "I think the best thing is for you to come along to the station with me so that we can put through a call to the Prime Minister."

"Thank you very much," said Danstor, full of gratitude. They walked trustingly beside P. C. Hinks, despite his slight tendency to keep behind them, until they reached the village police station.

"This way, gents," said P. C. Hinks, politely ushering them into a room which was really rather poorly lit and not at all well furnished, even by the somewhat primitive standards they had expected. Before they could fully take in their surroundings, there was a "click" and they found themselves separated from their guide by a large door composed entirely of iron bars.

"Now don't worry," said P. C. Hinks. "Everything will be quite all right. I'll be back in a minute."

Crysteel and Danstor gazed at each other with a surmise that rapidly deepened to a dreadful certainty.

"We're locked in!"

"This is a prison!"

"Now what are we going to do?"

"I don't know if you chaps understand English," said a languid voice from the gloom, "but you might let a fellow sleep in peace."

For the first time, the two prisoners saw that they were not alone. Lying on a bed in the corner of the cell was a somewhat dilapidated young man, who gazed at them blearily out of one resentful eye.

"My goodness!" said Danstor nervously. "Do you suppose he's a dangerous criminal?"

"He doesn't look very dangerous at the moment," said Crysteel, with more accuracy than he guessed.

"What are *you* in for, anyway?" asked the stranger, sitting up unsteadily. "You look as if you've been to a fancy-dress party. Oh, my poor head!" He collapsed again into the prone position.

"Fancy locking up anyone as ill as this!" said Danstor, who was a kind-hearted individual. Then he continued, in English, "I don't know why we're here. We just told the policeman who we were and where we came from, and this is what's happened."

"Well, who are you?"

"We've just landed——"

"Oh, there's no point in going through all that again," interrupted Crysteel. "We'll never get anyone to believe us."

"Hey!" said the stranger, sitting up once more. "What language is that you're speaking? I know a few, but I've never heard anything like that."

"Oh, all right," Crysteel said to Danstor. "You might as well tell him. There's nothing else to do until that policeman comes back anyway."

At this moment, P. C. Hinks was engaged in earnest conversation with the superintendent of the local mental home, who insisted stoutly that all his patients were present. However, a careful check was promised and he'd call back later.

Wondering if the whole thing was a practical joke, P. C. Hinks put the receiver down and quietly made his way to the cells. The three prisoners seemed to be engaged in friendly conversation, so he tip-toed away again. It would do them all good to have a chance to cool down. He rubbed his eye tenderly as he remembered what a battle it had been to get Mr. Graham into the cell during the small hours of the morning.

That young man was now reasonably sober after the night's celebrations, which he did not in the least regret. (It was, after all, quite an occasion when your degree came through and you found you'd got Honors when you'd barely expected a Pass.) But he began to fear that he was still under the influence as Danstor unfolded his tale and waited, not expecting to be believed.

In these circumstances, thought Graham, the best thing to do was to behave as matter-of-factly as possible until the hallucinations got fed up and went away.

"If you really have a spaceship in the hills," he remarked, "surely you can get in touch with it and ask someone to come and rescue you?"

"We want to handle this ourselves," said Crysteel with dignity. "Besides, you don't know our captain."

They sounded very convincing, thought Graham. The whole story hung together remarkably well. And yet . . .

"It's a bit hard for me to believe that you can build interstellar spaceships, but can't get out of a miserable village police station."

Danstor looked at Crysteel, who shuffled uncomfortably.

"We could get out easily enough," said the anthropologist. "But we don't want to use violent means unless it's absolutely essential. You've no idea of the trouble it causes, and the reports we might have to fill in. Besides, if we do get out, I suppose your Flying Squad would catch us before we got back to the ship."

"Not in Little Milton," grinned Graham. "Especially if we could get across to the 'White Hart' without being stopped. My car is over there."

"Oh," said Danstor, his spirits suddenly reviving. He turned to his companion and a lively discussion followed. Then, very gingerly, he produced a small black cylinder from an inner pocket, handling it with much the same confidence as a nervous spinster holding a loaded gun for the first time. Simultaneously, Crysteel retired with some speed to the far corner of the cell.

It was at this precise moment that Graham knew, with a sudden icy certainty, that he was stone-sober and that the story he had been listening to was nothing less than the truth.

There was no fuss or bother, no flurry of electric sparks or colored rays—but a section of the wall three feet across dissolved quietly and collapsed into a little pyramid of sand. The sunlight came streaming into the cell as, with a great sigh of relief, Danstor put his mysterious weapon away.

"Well, come on," he urged Graham. "We're waiting for you."

There were no signs of pursuit, for P. C. Hinks was still arguing on the phone, and it would be some minutes yet before that bright young man returned to the cells and received the biggest shock of his official career. No one at the "White Hart" was particularly surprised to see Graham again; they all knew where and how he had spent the night, and expressed hope that the local Bench would deal leniently with him when his case came up.

With grave misgivings, Crysteel and Danstor climbed into the back of the incredibly ramshackle Bentley which Graham affectionately addressed as "Rose." But there was nothing wrong with the engine under the rusty bonnet, and soon they were roaring out of Little Milton at fifty miles an hour. It was a striking demonstration of the relativity of speed, for Crysteel and Danstor, who had spent the last few years traveling tranquilly through space at several million miles a second, had never been so scared in their lives. When Crysteel had recovered his breath he pulled out his little portable transmitter and called the ship.

"We're on the way back," he shouted above the roar of the wind. "We've got a fairly intelligent human being with us. Expect us in— whoops!—I'm sorry—we just went over a bridge—about ten minutes. What was that? No, of course not. We didn't have the slightest trouble. Everything went perfectly smoothly. *Good-by.*"

Graham looked back only once to see how his passengers were faring. The sight was rather unsettling, for their ears and hair (which had not been glued on very firmly) had blown away and their real selves were beginning to emerge. Graham began to suspect, with some discomfort, that his new acquaintances also lacked noses. Oh well, one could grow used to anything with practice. He was going to have plenty of that in the years ahead.

The rest, of course, you all know; but the full story of the first landing on Earth, and of the peculiar circumstances under which Ambassador Graham became humanity's representative to the universe at large, has never before been recounted. We extracted the main details, with a good deal of persuasion, from Crysteel and Danstor themselves, while we were working in the Department of Extraterrestrial affairs.

It was understandable, in view of their success on Earth, that they should have been selected by their superiors to make the first contact with our mysterious and secretive neighbors, the Martians. It is also understandable, in the light of the above evidence, that Crysteel and Danstor were so reluctant to embark on this later mission, and we are not really very surprised that nothing has ever been heard of them since.

Part III

ON THE SERIOUS SIDE

A Walk in the Dark

Robert Armstrong had walked just over two miles, as far as he could judge, when his torch failed. He stood still for a moment, unable to believe that such a misfortune could really have befallen him. Then, half maddened with rage, he hurled the useless instrument away. It landed somewhere in the darkness, disturbing the silence of this little world. A metallic echo came ringing back from the low hills: then all was quiet again.

This, thought Armstrong, was the ultimate misfortune. Nothing more could happen to him now. He was even able to laugh bitterly at his luck, and resolved never again to imagine that the fickle goddess had ever favored him. Who would have believed that the only tractor at Camp IV would have broken down when he was just setting off for Port Sanderson? He recalled the frenzied repair work, the relief when the second start had been made—and the final debacle when the caterpillar track had jammed.

It was no use then regretting the lateness of his departure: he could not have foreseen these accidents, and it was still a good four hours before the "Canopus" took off. He *had* to catch her, whatever happened; no other ship would be touching at this world for another month.

Apart from the urgency of his business, four more weeks on this out-of-the-way planet were unthinkable.

There had been only one thing to do. It was lucky that Port Sanderson was little more than six miles from the camp—not a great distance, even on foot. He had had to leave all his equipment behind, but it could follow on the next ship and he could manage without it. The road was poor, merely stamped out of the rock by one of the Board's hundred-ton crushers, but there was no fear of going astray.

Even now, he was in no real danger, though he might well be too late to catch the ship. Progress would be slow, for he dare not risk losing the road in this region of canyons and enigmatic tunnels that had never been explored. It was, of course, pitch-dark. Here at the edge of the Galaxy the stars were so few and scattered that their light was negligible. The strange crimson sun of this lonely world would not rise for many hours, and although five of the little moons were in the sky they could barely be seen by the unaided eye. Not one of them could even cast a shadow.

Armstrong was not the man to bewail his luck for long. He began to walk slowly along the road, feeling its texture with his feet. It was, he knew, fairly straight except where it wound through Carver's Pass. He wished he had a stick or something to probe the way before him, but he would have to rely for guidance on the feel of the ground.

It was terribly slow at first, until he gained confidence. He had never known how difficult it was to walk in a straight line. Although the feeble stars gave him his bearings, again and again he found himself stumbling among the virgin rocks at the edge of the crude roadway. He was traveling in long zigzags that took him to alternate sides of the road. Then he would stub his toes against the bare rock and grope his way back on to the hard-packed surface once again.

Presently it settled down to a routine. It was impossible to estimate his speed; he could only struggle along and hope for the best. There were four miles to go—four miles and as many hours. It should be easy enough, unless he lost his way. But he dared not think of that.

Once he had mastered the technique he could afford the luxury of thought. He could not pretend that he was enjoying the experience, but he had been in much worse positions before. As long as he remained on the road, he was perfectly safe. He had been hoping that as his eyes became adapted to the starlight he would be able to see the way, but he now knew that the whole journey would be blind. The discovery gave him a vivid sense of his remoteness from the heart of the Galaxy. On a night as clear as this, the skies of almost any other planet would have been blazing with stars. Here at this outpost of the Universe the sky held perhaps a hundred faintly gleaming points of light, as useless as the five ridiculous moons on which no one had ever bothered to land.

A slight change in the road interrupted his thoughts. Was there a curve here, or had he veered off to the right again? He moved very slowly along the invisible and ill-defined border. Yes, there was no mistake: the road was bending to the left. He tried to remember its appearance in the daytime, but he had only seen it once before. Did this mean that he was nearing the Pass? He hoped so, for the journey would then be half completed.

He peered ahead into the blackness, but the ragged line of the horizon told him nothing. Presently he found that the road had straightened itself again and his spirits sank. The entrance to the Pass must still be some way ahead: there were at least four miles to go.

Four miles—how ridiculous the distance seemed! How long would it take the "Canopus" to travel four miles? He doubted if man could measure so short an interval of time. And how many trillions of miles had he, Robert Armstrong, traveled in his life? It must have reached a staggering total by now, for in the last twenty years he had scarcely stayed more than a month at a time on any single world. This very year, he had twice made the crossing of the Galaxy, and that was a notable journey even in these days of the phantom drive.

He tripped over a loose stone, and the jolt brought him back to reality. It was no use, here, thinking of ships that could eat up the light-years. He was facing nature, with no weapons but his own strength and skill.

It was strange that it took him so long to identify the real cause of his uneasiness. The last four weeks had been very full, and the rush of his departure, coupled with the annoyance and anxiety caused by the tractor's breakdowns, had driven everything else from his mind. Moreover, he had always prided himself on his hard-headedness and lack of imagination. Until now, he had forgotten all about that first evening at the Base, when the crews had regaled him with the usual tall yarns concocted for the benefit of newcomers.

It was then that the old Base clerk had told the story of his walk by night from Port Sanderson to the camp, and of what had trailed him through Carver's Pass, keeping always beyond the limit of his torchlight. Armstrong, who had heard such tales on a score of worlds, had paid it little attention at the time. This planet, after all, was known to be uninhabited. But logic could not dispose of the matter as easily as that. Suppose, after all, there was some truth in the old man's fantastic tale . . . ?

It was not a pleasant thought, and Armstrong did not intend to brood upon it. But he knew that if he dismissed it out of hand it would continue to prey on his mind. The only way to conquer imaginary fears was to face them boldly; he would have to do that now.

His strongest argument was the complete barrenness of this world and its utter desolation, though against that one could set many counter-arguments, as indeed the old clerk had done. Man had only lived on this planet for twenty years, and much of it was still unexplored. No one could deny that the tunnels out in the wasteland were rather puzzling, but everyone believed them to be volcanic vents. Though, of course, life often crept into such places. With a shudder he remembered the giant polyps that had snared the first explorers of Vargon III.

It was all very inconclusive. Suppose, for the sake of argument, one granted the existence of life here. What of that?

The vast majority of life forms in the Universe were completely indifferent to man. Some, of course, like the gas-beings of Alcoran or the roving wave-lattices of Shandaloon, could not even detect him but passed through or around him as if he did not exist. Others were merely inquisitive, some embarrassingly friendly. There were few indeed that would attack unless provoked.

Nevertheless, it was a grim picture that the old stores clerk had painted. Back in the warm, well-lighted smoking-room, with the drinks going around, it had been easy enough to laugh at it. But here in the darkness, miles from any human settlement, it was very different.

It was almost a relief when he stumbled off the road again and had to grope with his hands until he found it once more. This seemed a very rough patch, and the road was scarcely distinguishable from the rocks around. In a few minutes, however, he was safely on his way again.

It was unpleasant to see how quickly his thoughts returned to the same disquieting subject. Clearly it was worrying him more than he cared to admit.

He drew consolation from one fact: it had been quite obvious that no one at the base had believed the old fellow's story. Their questions and banter had proved that. At the time, he had laughed as loudly as any of them. After all, what *was* the evidence? A dim shape, just seen in the darkness, that might well have been an oddly formed rock. And the curious clicking noise that had so impressed the old man—anyone could imagine such sounds at night if they were sufficiently overwrought. If it had been hostile, why hadn't the creature come any closer? "Because it was afraid of my light," the old chap had said. Well, that was plausible enough: it would explain why nothing had ever been seen in the daylight. Such a creature might live underground, only emerging at night—damn it, why was he taking the old idiot's ravings so seriously! Armstrong got control of his thoughts again. If he went on this way, he told himself angrily, he would soon be seeing and hearing a whole menagerie of monsters.

There was, of course, one factor that disposed of the ridiculous story at once. It was really very simple; he felt sorry he hadn't thought of it before. *What would such a creature live on?* There was not even a trace of vegetation on the whole of the planet. He laughed to think that the bogy could be disposed of so easily—and in the same instant felt annoyed with himself for not laughing aloud. If he was so sure of his reasoning, why not whistle, or sing, or do anything to keep up his spirits? He put the question fairly to himself as a test of his manhood. Half-ashamed, he had to admit that he was still afraid—afraid because "there *might* be something in it, after all." But at least his analysis had done him some good.

It would have been better if he had left it there, and remained half-convinced by his argument. But a part of his mind was still busily trying to break down his careful reasoning. It succeeded only too well, and when he remembered the plant-beings of Xantil Major the shock was so unpleasant that he stopped dead in his tracks.

Now the plant-beings of Xantil were not in any way horrible. They were in fact extremely beautiful creatures. But what made them appear so distressing now was the knowledge that they could live for indefinite periods with no food whatsoever. All the energy they needed for their strange lives they extracted from cosmic radiation—and that was almost as intense here as anywhere else in the universe.

He had scarcely thought of one example before others crowded into his mind and he remembered the life form on Trantor Beta, which was the only one known capable of directly utilizing atomic energy. That too had lived on an utterly barren world, very much like this . . .

Armstrong's mind was rapidly splitting into two distinct portions, each trying to convince the other and neither wholly succeeding. He did not realize how far his morale had gone until he found himself holding his breath lest it conceal any sound from the darkness about him. Angrily, he cleared his mind of the rubbish that had been gathering there and turned once more to the immediate problem.

There was no doubt that the road was slowly rising, and the silhouette of the horizon seemed much highei in the sky. The road began to twist, and suddenly he was aware of great rocks on either side of him. Soon only a narrow ribbon of sky was still visible, and the darkness became, if possible, even more intense.

Somehow, he felt safer with the rock walls surrounding him: it meant that he was protected except in two directions. Also, the road had been levelled more carefully and it was easy to keep it. Best of all, he knew now that the journey was more than half completed.

For a moment his spirits began to rise. Then, with maddening perversity, his mind went back into the old grooves again. He remembered that it was on the far side of Carver's Pass that the old clerk's adventure had taken place—if it had ever happened at all.

In half a mile, he would be out in the open again, out of the protection of these sheltering rocks. The thought seemed doubly horrible now and he already felt a sense of nakedness. He could be attacked from any direction, and he would be utterly helpless . . .

Until now, he had still retained some self-control. Very resolutely he had kept his mind away from the one fact that gave some color to the old man's tale—the single piece of evidence that had stopped the banter in the crowded room back at the camp and brought a sudden hush upon the company. Now, as Armstrong's will weakened, he recalled again the words that had struck a momentary chill even in the warm comfort of the base building.

The little clerk had been very insistent on one point. He had never heard any sound of pursuit from the dim shape sensed, rather than seen, at the limit of his light. There was no scuffling of claws or hoofs on rock, nor even the clatter of displaced stones. It was as if, so the old man had declared in that solemn manner of his, "as if the thing that was following could see perfectly in the darkness, and had many small legs or pads so that it could move swiftly and easily over the rock—like a giant caterpillar or one of the carpet-things of Kralkor II."

Yet, although there had been no noise of pursuit, there had been one sound that the old man had caught several times. It was so unusual that its very strangeness made it doubly ominous. It was a faint but horribly persistent *clicking*.

The old fellow had been able to describe it very vividly—much too vividly for Armstrong's liking now.

"Have you ever listened to a large insect crunching its prey?" he said. "Well, it was just like that. I imagine that a crab makes exactly the same noise with its claws when it clashes them together. It was a—what's the word?—a *chitinous* sound."

At this point, Armstrong remembered laughing loudly. (Strange, how it was all coming back to him now.) But no one else had laughed, though they had been quick to do so earlier. Sensing the change of tone, he had sobered at once and asked the old man to continue his story. How he wished now that he had stifled his curiosity!

It had been quickly told. The next day, a party of skeptical technicians had gone into the no-man's land beyond Carver's Pass. They were not skeptical enough to leave their guns behind, but they had no cause to use them for they found no trace of any living thing. There were the inevitable pits and tunnels, glistening holes down which the light of the torches rebounded endlessly until it was lost in the distance—but the planet was riddled with them.

Though the party found no sign of life, it discovered one thing it did not like at all. Out in the barren and unexplored land beyond the Pass they had come upon an even larger tunnel than the rest. Near the mouth of that tunnel was a massive rock, half embedded in the ground. And the sides of that rock had been worn away *as if it had been used as an enormous whetstone.*

No less than five of those present had seen this disturbing rock. None of them could explain it satisfactorily as a natural formation, but they still refused to accept the old man's story. Armstrong had asked them if they had ever put it to the test. There had been an uncomfortable silence. Then big Andrew Hargraves had said: "Hell, who'd walk out to the Pass at night just for fun!" and had left it at that. Indeed, there was no other record of anyone walking from Port Sanderson to the camp by night, or for that matter by day. During the hours of light, no unprotected human being could live in the open beneath the rays of the enormous, lurid sun that seemed to fill half the sky. And no one would walk six miles, wearing radiation armor, if the tractor was available.

Armstrong felt that he was leaving the Pass. The rocks on either side were falling away, and the road was no longer as firm and well packed as it had been. He was coming out into the open plain once more, and somewhere not far away in the darkness was that enigmatic pillar that might have been used for sharpening monstrous fangs or claws. It was not a reassuring thought, but he could not get it out of his mind.

Feeling distinctly worried now, Armstrong made a great effort to pull himself together. He would try to be rational again; he would think of business, the work he had done at the camp—anything but this infernal place. For a while, he succeeded quite well. But presently, with a maddening persistence, every train of thought came back to the same point. He could not get out of his mind the picture of that inexplicable rock and its appalling possibilities. Over and over again he found himself wondering how far away it was, whether he had already passed it, and whether it was on his right or his left. . . .

The ground was quite flat again, and the road drove on straight as an arrow. There was one gleam of consolation: Port Sanderson could not be much more than two miles away. Armstrong had no idea how long he had been on the road. Unfortunately his watch was not illuminated and he could only guess at the passage of time. With any luck, the "Canopus" should not take off for another two hours at least. But he could not be sure, and now another fear began to enter his mind—the dread that he might see a vast constellation of lights rising swiftly into the sky ahead, and know that all this agony of mind had been in vain.

He was not zigzagging so badly now, and seemed to be able to anticipate the edge of the road before stumbling off it. It was probable, he cheered himself by thinking, that he was traveling almost as fast as if he had a light. If all went well, he might be nearing Port Sanderson in thirty minutes—a ridiculously small space of time. How he would laugh at his fears when he strolled into his already reserved stateroom in the "Canopus," and felt that peculiar quiver as the phantom drive hurled the great ship far out of this system, back to the clustered star-clouds near the center of the Galaxy—back toward Earth itself, which he had not seen for so many years. One day, he told himself, he really must visit Earth again. All his life he had been making the promise, but always there had been the same answer— lack of time. Strange, wasn't it, that such a tiny planet should have played so enormous a part in the development of the Universe, should even have come to dominate worlds far wiser and more intelligent than itself!

Armstrong's thoughts were harmless again, and he felt calmer. The knowledge that he was nearing Port Sanderson was immensely reassuring, and he deliberately kept his mind on familiar, unimportant matters. Carver's Pass was already far behind, and with it that thing he no longer intended to recall. One day, if he ever returned to this world, he would visit the Pass in the daytime and laugh at his fears. In twenty minutes now, they would have joined the nightmares of his childhood.

It was almost a shock, though one of the most pleasant he had ever known, when he saw the lights of Port Sanderson come up over the horizon. The curvature of this little world was very deceptive: it did not seem right that a planet with a gravity almost as great as Earth's should have a horizon so close at hand. One day, someone would have to discover what lay at this world's core to give it so great a density. Perhaps the many tunnels would help—it was an unfortunate turn of thought, but the nearness of his goal had robbed it of terror now. Indeed, the thought that he might really be in danger seemed to give his adventure a certain piquancy and heightened interest. Nothing could happen to him now, with ten minutes to go and the lights of the Port already in sight.

A few minutes later, his feelings changed abruptly when he came to the sudden bend in the road. He had forgotten the chasm that caused his detour, and added half a mile to the journey. Well, what of it? he thought stubbornly. An extra half-mile would make no difference now—another ten minutes, at the most.

It was very disappointing when the lights of the city vanished. Armstrong had not remembered the hill which the road was skirting; perhaps it was only a low ridge, scarcely noticeable in the daytime. But by hiding the lights of the Port it had taken away his chief talisman and left him again at the mercy of his fears.

Very unreasonably, his intelligence told him, he began to think how horrible it would be if anything happened now, so near the end of the journey. He kept the worst of his fears at bay for a while, hoping desperately that the lights of the city would soon reappear. But as the minutes dragged on, he realized that the ridge must be longer than he imagined. He tried to cheer himself by the thought that the city would be all the nearer when he saw it again, but somehow logic seemed to have failed him now. For presently he found himself doing something he had not stooped to, even out in the waste by Carver's Pass.

He stopped, turned slowly round, and with bated breath listened until his lungs were nearly bursting.

The silence was uncanny, considering how near he must be to the Port. There was certainly no sound from behind him. Of course there wouldn't be, he told himself angrily. But he was immensely relieved. The thought of that faint and insistent clicking had been haunting him for the last hour.

So friendly and familiar was the noise that did reach him at last that the anticlimax almost made him laugh aloud. Drifting through the still air from a source clearly not more than a mile away came the sound of a landing-field tractor, perhaps one of the machines loading the "Canopus" itself. In a matter of seconds, thought Armstrong, he would be around this ridge with the Port only a few hundred yards ahead. The journey was nearly ended. In a few moments, this evil plain would be no more than a fading nightmare.

It seemed terribly unfair: so little time, such a small fraction of a human life, was all he needed now. But the gods have always been unfair to man, and now they were enjoying their little jest. For there could be no mistaking the rattle of monstrous claws in the darkness *ahead of him.*

The Forgotten Enemy

The thick furs thudded softly to the ground as Professor Millward jerked himself upright on the narrow bed. This time, he was sure, it had been no dream; the freezing air that rasped against his lungs still seemed to echo with the sound that had come crashing out of the night.

He gathered the furs around his shoulders and listened intently. All was quiet again: from the narrow windows on the western walls long shafts of moonlight played upon the endless rows of books, as they played upon the dead city beneath. The world was utterly still; even in the old days the city would have been silent on such a night, and it was doubly silent now.

With weary resolution Professor Millward shuffled out of bed, and doled a few lumps of coke into the glowing brazier. Then he made his way slowly toward the nearest window, pausing now and then to rest his hand lovingly on the volumes he had guarded all these years.

He shielded his eyes from the brilliant moonlight and peered out into the night. The sky was cloudless: the sound he had heard had not been thunder, whatever it might have been. It had come from the north, and even as he waited it came again.

Distance had softened it, distance and the bulk of the hills that lay beyond London. It did not race across the sky with the wantonness of thunder, but seemed to come from a single point far to the north. It was like no natural sound that he had ever heard, and for a moment he dared to hope again.

Only Man, he was sure, could have made such a sound. Perhaps the dream that had kept him here among these treasures of civilization for more than twenty years would soon be a dream no longer. Men were returning to England, blasting their way through the ice and snow with the weapons that science had given them before the coming of the Dust. It was strange that they should come by land, and from the north, but he thrust aside any thoughts that would quench the newly kindled flame of hope.

Three hundred feet below, the broken sea of snow-covered roofs lay bathed in the bitter moonlight. Miles away the tall stacks of Battersea Power Station glimmered like thin white ghosts against the night sky. Now that the dome of St. Paul's had collapsed beneath the weight of snow, they alone challenged his supremacy.

Professor Millward walked slowly back along the bookshelves, thinking over the plan that had formed in his mind. Twenty years ago he had watched the last helicopters climbing heavily out of Regent's Park, the rotors churning the ceaselessly falling snow. Even then, when the silence had closed around him, he could not bring himself to believe that the North had been abandoned forever. Yet already he had waited a whole generation, among the books to which he had dedicated his life.

In those early days he had sometimes heard, over the radio which was his only contact with the South, of the struggle to colonize the now-temperate lands of the Equator. He did not know the outcome of that far-off battle, fought with desperate skill in the dying jungles and across deserts that had already felt the first touch of snow. Perhaps it had failed; the radio had been silent now for fifteen years or more. Yet if men and machines were indeed returning from the north

—of all directions—he might again be able to hear their voices as they spoke to one another and to the lands from which they had come.

Professor Millward left the University building perhaps a dozen times a year, and then only through sheer necessity. Over the past two decades he had collected everything he needed from the shops in the Bloomsbury area, for in the final exodus vast supplies of stocks had been left behind through lack of transport. In many ways, indeed, his life could be called luxurious: no professor of English literature had ever been clothed in such garments as those he had taken from an Oxford Street furrier's.

The sun was blazing from a cloudless sky as he shouldered his pack and unlocked the massive gates. Even ten years ago packs of starving dogs had hunted in this area, and though he had seen none for years he was still cautious and always carried a revolver when he went into the open.

The sunlight was so brilliant that the reflected glare hurt his eyes; but it was almost wholly lacking in heat. Although the belt of cosmic dust through which the Solar System was now passing had made little visible difference to the sun's brightness, it had robbed it of all strength. No one knew whether the world would swim out into the warmth again in ten or a thousand years, and civilization had fled southward in search of lands where the word "summer" was not an empty mockery.

The latest drifts had packed hard and Professor Millward had little difficulty in making the journey to Tottenham Court Road. Sometimes it had taken him hours of floundering through the snow, and one year he had been sealed in his great concrete watchtower for nine months.

He kept away from the houses with their dangerous burdens of snow and their Damoclean icicles, and went north until he came to the shop he was seeking. The words above the shattered windows were still bright: "Jenkins & Sons. Radio and Electrical. Television A Specialty."

Some snow had drifted through a broken section of roofing, but the little upstairs room had not altered since his last visit a dozen years ago. The all-wave radio still stood on the table, and empty tins scattered on the floor spoke mutely of the lonely hours he had spent here before all hope had died. He wondered if he must go through the same ordeal again.

Professor Millward brushed the snow from the copy of *The Ama-*

teur Radio Handbook for 1965, which had taught him what little he knew about wireless. The test-meters and batteries were still lying in their half-remembered places, and to his relief some of the batteries still held their charge. He searched through the stock until he had built up the necessary power supplies, and checked the radio as well as he could. Then he was ready.

It was a pity that he could never send the manufacturers the testimonial they deserved. The faint "hiss" from the speaker brought back memories of the B.B.C., of the nine o'clock news and symphony concerts, of all the things he had taken for granted in a world that was gone like a dream. With scarcely controlled impatience he ran across the wave-bands, but everywhere there was nothing save that omnipresent hiss. That was disappointing, but no more: he remembered that the real test would come at night. In the meantime he would forage among the surrounding shops for anything that might be useful.

It was dusk when he returned to the little room. A hundred miles above his head, tenuous and invisible, the Heaviside Layer would be expanding outward toward the stars as the sun went down. So it had done every evening for millions of years, and for half a century only, Man had used it for his own purposes, to reflect around the world his messages of hate or peace, to echo with trivialities or to sound with music once called immortal.

Slowly, with infinite patience, Professor Millward began to traverse the shortwave bands that a generation ago had been a babel of shouting voices and stabbing morse. Even as he listened, the faint hope he had dared to cherish began to fade within him. The city itself was no more silent than the once-crowded oceans of ether. Only the faint crackle of thunderstorms half the world away broke the intolerable stillness. Man had abandoned his latest conquest.

Soon after midnight the batteries faded out. Professor Millward did not have the heart to search for more, but curled up in his furs and fell into a troubled sleep. He got what consolation he could from the thought that if he had not proved his theory, he had not disproved it either.

The heatless sunlight was flooding the lonely white road when he began the homeward journey. He was very tired, for he had slept little and his sleep had been broken by the recurring fantasy of rescue.

The silence was suddenly broken by the distant thunder that came rolling over the white roofs. It came—there could be no doubt now

—from beyond the northern hills that had once been London's playground. From the buildings on either side little avalanches of snow went swishing out into the wide street; then the silence returned.

Professor Millward stood motionless, weighing, considering, analyzing. The sound had been too long-drawn to be an ordinary explosion—he was dreaming again—it was nothing less than the distant thunder of an atomic bomb, burning and blasting away the snow a million tons at a time. His hopes revived, and the disappointments of the night began to fade.

That momentary pause almost cost him his life. Out of a side-street something huge and white moved suddenly into his field of vision. For a moment his mind refused to accept the reality of what he saw; then the paralysis left him and he fumbled desperately for his futile revolver. Padding toward him across the snow, swinging its head from side to side with a hypnotic, serpentine motion, was a huge polar bear.

He dropped his belongings and ran, floundering over the snow toward the nearest buildings. Providentially the Underground entrance was only fifty feet away. The steel grille was closed, but he remembered breaking the lock many years ago. The temptation to look back was almost intolerable, for he could hear nothing to tell how near his pursuer was. For one frightful moment the iron lattice resisted his numbed fingers. Then it yielded reluctantly and he forced his way through the narrow opening.

Out of his childhood there came a sudden, incongruous memory of an albino ferret he had once seen weaving its body ceaselessly across the wire netting of its cage. There was the same reptile grace in the monstrous shape, almost twice as high as a man, that reared itself in baffled fury against the grille. The metal bowed but did not yield beneath the pressure; then the bear dropped to the ground, grunted softly and padded away. It slashed once or twice at the fallen haversack, scattering a few tins of food into the snow, and vanished as silently as it had come.

A very shaken Professor Millward reached the University three hours later, after moving in short bounds from one refuge to the next. After all these years he was no longer alone in the city. He wondered if there were other visitors, and that same night he knew the answer. Just before dawn he heard, quite distinctly, the cry of a wolf from somewhere in the direction of Hyde Park.

By the end of the week he knew that the animals of the North were on the move. Once he saw a reindeer running southward, pursued by a pack of silent wolves, and sometimes in the night there were sounds of deadly conflict. He was amazed that so much life still existed in the white wilderness between London and the Pole. Now something was driving it southward, and the knowledge brought him a mounting excitement. He did not believe that these fierce survivors would flee from anything save Man.

The strain of waiting was beginning to affect Professor Millward's mind, and for hours he would sit in the cold sunlight, his furs wrapped around him, dreaming of rescue and thinking of the way in which men might be returning to England. Perhaps an expedition had come from North America across the Atlantic ice. It might have been years upon its way. But why had it come so far north? His favorite theory was that the Atlantic ice-packs were not safe enough for heavy traffic further to the south.

One thing, however, he could not explain to his satisfaction. There had been no air reconnaissance; it was hard to believe that the art of flight had been lost so soon.

Sometimes he would walk along the ranks of books, whispering now and then to a well-loved volume. There were books here that he had not dared to open for years, they reminded him so poignantly of the past. But now, as the days grew longer and brighter, he would sometimes take down a volume of poetry and re-read his old favorites. Then he would go to the tall windows and shout the magic words over the rooftops, as if they would break the spell that had gripped the world.

It was warmer now, as if the ghosts of lost summers had returned to haunt the land. For whole days the temperature rose above freezing, while in many places flowers were breaking through the snow. Whatever was approaching from the north was nearer, and several times a day that enigmatic roar would go thundering over the city, sending the snow sliding upon a thousand roofs. There were strange, grinding undertones that Professor Millward found baffling and even ominous. At times it was almost as if he were listening to the clash of mighty armies, and sometimes a mad but dreadful thought came into his mind and would not be dismissed. Often he would wake in the night and imagine he heard the sound of mountains moving to the sea.

So the summer wore away, and as the sound of that distant battle drew steadily nearer Professor Millward was the prey of ever more violently alternating hopes and fears. Although he saw no more wolves or bears—they seemed to have fled southward—he did not risk leaving the safety of his fortress. Every morning he would climb to the highest window of the tower and search the northern horizon with field-glasses. But all he ever saw was the stubborn retreat of the snows above Hampstead, as they fought their bitter rearguard action against the sun.

His vigil ended with the last days of the brief summer. The grinding thunder in the night had been nearer than ever before, but there was still nothing to hint at its real distance from the city. Professor Millward felt no premonition as he climbed to the narrow window and raised his binoculars to the northern sky.

As a watcher from the walls of some threatened fortress might have seen the first sunlight glinting on the spears of an advancing army, so in that moment Professor Millward knew the truth. The air was crystal-clear, and the hills were sharp and brilliant against the cold blue of the sky. They had lost almost all their snow. Once he would have rejoiced at that, but it meant nothing now.

Overnight, the enemy he had forgotten had conquered the last defenses and was preparing for the final onslaught. As he saw that deadly glitter along the crest of the doomed hills, Professor Millward understood at last the sound he had heard advancing for so many months. It was little wonder he had dreamed of mountains on the march.

Out of the North, their ancient home, returning in triumph to the lands they had once possessed, the glaciers had come again.

The Parasite

"There is nothing you can do," said Connolly, "nothing at all. Why did you have to follow me?" He was standing with his back to Pearson, staring out across the calm blue water that led to Italy. On the left, behind the anchored fishing fleet, the sun was setting in Mediterranean splendor, incarnadining land and sky. But neither man was even remotely aware of the beauty all around.

Pearson rose to his feet, and came forward out of the little café's shadowed porch, into the slanting sunlight. He joined Connolly by the cliff wall, but was careful not to come too close to him. Even in normal times Connolly disliked being touched. His obsession, whatever it might be, would make him doubly sensitive now.

"Listen, Roy," Pearson began urgently. "We've been friends for twenty years, and you ought to know I wouldn't let you down this time. Besides——"

"I know. You promised Ruth."

"And why not? After all, she is your wife. She has a right to know what's happened." He paused, choosing his words carefully. "She's worried, Roy. Much more worried than if it was only another woman." He nearly added the word "again," but decided against it.

Connolly stubbed out his cigarette on the flat-topped granite wall, then flicked the white cylinder out over the sea, so that it fell twisting and turning toward the waters a hundred feet below. He turned to face his friend.

"I'm sorry, Jack," he said, and for a moment there was a glimpse of the familiar personality which, Pearson knew, must be trapped somewhere within the stranger standing at his side. "I know you're trying to be helpful, and I appreciate it. But I wish you hadn't followed me. You'll only make matters worse."

"Convince me of that, and I'll go away."

Connolly sighed.

"I could no more convince you than that psychiatrist you persuaded me to see. Poor Curtis! He was such a well-meaning fellow. Give him my apologies, will you?"

"I'm not a psychiatrist, and I'm not trying to cure you—whatever that means. If you like it the way you are, that's your affair. But I think you ought to let us know what's happened, so that we can make plans accordingly."

"To get me certified?"

Pearson shrugged his shoulders. He wondered if Connolly could see through his feigned indifference to the real concern he was trying to hide. Now that all other approaches seemed to have failed, the "frankly-I-don't-care" attitude was the only one left open to him.

"I wasn't thinking of that. There are a few practical details to worry about. Do you want to stay here indefinitely? You can't live without money, even on Syrene."

"I can stay at Clifford Rawnsley's villa as long as I like. He was a friend of my father's you know. It's empty at the moment except for the servants, and they don't bother me."

Connolly turned away from the parapet on which he was resting.

"I'm going up the hill before it's dark," he said. The words were abrupt, but Pearson knew that he was not being dismissed. He could follow if he pleased, and the knowledge brought him the first satisfaction he had felt since locating Connolly. It was a small triumph, but he needed it.

They did not speak during the climb; indeed, Pearson scarcely had the breath to do so. Connolly set off at a reckless pace, as if deliberately attempting to exhaust himself. The island fell away beneath them, the white villas gleamed like ghosts in the shadowed valleys, the little fishing boats, their day's work done, lay at rest in the harbor. And all around was the darkling sea.

When Pearson caught up with his friend, Connolly was sitting in front of the shrine which the devout islanders had built on Syrene's highest point. In the daytime, there would be tourists here, photographing each other or gaping at the much-advertised beauty spread beneath them, but the place was deserted now.

Connolly was breathing heavily from his exertions, yet his features were relaxed and for the moment he seemed almost at peace. The shadow that lay across his mind had lifted, and he turned to Pearson with a smile that echoed his old, infectious grin.

"He hates exercise, Jack. It always scares him away."

"And who is he?" said Pearson. "Remember, you haven't introduced us yet."

Connolly smiled at his friend's attempted humor; then his face suddenly became grave.

"Tell me, Jack," he began. "Would you say I have an overdeveloped imagination?"

"No: you're about average. You're certainly less imaginative than I am."

Connolly nodded slowly.

"That's true enough, Jack, and it should help you to believe me. Because I'm certain I could never have invented the creature who's haunting me. He really exists. I'm not suffering from paranoiac hallucinations, or whatever Dr. Curtis would call them.

"You remember Maude White? It all began with her. I met her at one of David Trescott's parties, about six weeks ago. I'd just quarreled with Ruth and was rather fed up. We were both pretty tight, and as I was staying in town she came back to the flat with me."

Pearson smiled inwardly. Poor Roy! It was always the same pattern, though he never seemed to realize it. Each affair was different to him, but to no one else. The eternal Don Juan, always seeking—always disappointed, because what he sought could be found only in the cradle or the grave, but never between the two.

"I guess you'll laugh at what knocked me out—it seems so trivial, though it frightened me more than anything that's ever happened in my life. I simply went over to the cocktail cabinet and poured out the drinks, as I've done a hundred times before. It wasn't until I'd handed one to Maude that I realized I'd filled *three* glasses. The act was so perfectly natural that at first I didn't recognize what it meant. Then I looked wildly around the room to see where the other man was—even then I knew, somehow, that it wasn't a man. But, of course, he wasn't there. He was nowhere at all in the outside world: he was hiding deep down inside my own brain. . . ."

The night was very still, the only sound a thin ribbon of music winding up to the stars from some café in the village below. The light of the rising moon sparkled on the sea; overhead, the arms of the crucifix were silhouetted against the darkness. A brilliant beacon on the frontiers of twilight, Venus was following the sun into the west.

Pearson waited, letting Connolly take his time. He seemed lucid and rational enough, however strange the story he was telling. His face was quite calm in the moonlight, though it might be the calmness that comes after acceptance of defeat.

"The next thing I remember is lying in bed while Maude sponged my face. She was pretty frightened: I'd passed out and cut my forehead badly as I fell. There was a lot of blood around the place, but that didn't matter. The thing that really scared me was the thought that I'd gone crazy. That seems funny, now that I'm much more scared of being sane.

"*He* was still there when I woke up; he's been there ever since. Somehow I got rid of Maude—it wasn't easy—and tried to work out what had happened. Tell me, Jack, do you believe in telepathy?"

The abrupt challenge caught Pearson off his guard.

"I've never given it much thought, but the evidence seems rather convincing. Do you suggest that someone else is reading your mind?"

"It's not as simple as that. What I'm telling you now I've discovered slowly—usually when I've been dreaming or slightly drunk. You may say that invalidates the evidence, but I don't think so. At first it was the only way I could break through the barrier that separates me from Omega—I'll tell you later why I've called him that. But now there aren't any obstacles: I know he's there all the time, waiting for me to let down my guard. Night and day, drunk or sober, I'm conscious of his presence. At times like this he's quiescent, watching me out of the corner of his eye. My only hope is that he'll grow tired of waiting, and go in search of some other victim."

Connolly's voice, calm until now, suddenly came near to breaking.

"Try and imagine the horror of that discovery: the effect of learning that every act, every thought or desire that flitted through your mind was being watched and shared by another being. It meant, of course, the end of all normal life for me. I had to leave Ruth and I couldn't tell her why. Then, to make matters worse, Maude came chasing after me. She wouldn't leave me alone, and bombarded me with letters and phone calls. It was hell. I couldn't fight both of them, so I ran away. And I thought that on Syrene, of all places, he would find enough to interest him without bothering me."

"Now I understand," said Pearson softly. "So *that's* what he's after. A kind of telepathic Peeping Tom—no longer content with mere watching. . . ."

"I suppose you're humoring me," said Connolly, without resentment. "But I don't mind, and you've summed it up pretty accurately, as you usually do. It was quite a while before I realized what his game was. Once the first shock had worn off, I tried to analyze the position logically. I thought backward from that first moment of recognition, and in the end I knew that it wasn't a sudden invasion of my mind. He'd been with me for years, so well hidden that I'd never guessed it. I expect you'll laugh at this, knowing me as you do. But I've never been altogether at ease with a woman, even when I've been making love to her, and now I know the reason. Omega has always been there, sharing my emotions, gloating over the passions he can no longer experience in his body.

"The only way I kept any control was by fighting back, trying to come to grips with him and to understand what he was. And in the end I succeeded. He's a long way away and there must be some limit to his powers. Perhaps that first contact was an accident, though I'm not sure.

"What I've told you already, Jack, must be hard enough for you to believe, but it's nothing to what I've got to say now. Yet remember—you agreed that I'm not an imaginative man, and see if you can find a flaw anywhere in this story.

"I don't know if you've read any of the evidence suggesting that telepathy is somehow independent of time. I *know* that it is. Omega doesn't belong to our age: he's somewhere in the future, immensely far ahead of us. For a while I thought he must be one of the last men —that's why I gave him his name. But now I'm not sure; perhaps he belongs to an age when there are a myriad different races of man, scattered all over the universe—some still ascending, others sinking into decay. His people, wherever and whenever they may be, have reached the heights and fallen from them into the depths the beasts can never know. There's a sense of evil about him, Jack—the real evil that most of us never meet in all our lives. Yet sometimes I feel almost sorry for him, because I know what has made him the thing he is.

"Have you ever wondered, Jack, what the human race will do when science has discovered everything, when there are no more worlds to be explored, when all the stars have given up their secrets? Omega is one of the answers. I hope he's not the only one, for if so everything we've striven for is in vain. I hope that he and his race are an isolated cancer in a still healthy universe, but I can never be sure.

"They have pampered their bodies until they are useless, and too late they have discovered their mistake. Perhaps they have thought, as some men have thought, that they could live by intellect alone. And perhaps they are immortal, and that must be their real damnation. Through the ages their minds have been corroding in their feeble bodies, seeking some release from their intolerable boredom. They have found it at last in the only way they can, by sending back their minds to an earlier, more virile age, and becoming parasites on the emotions of others.

"I wonder how many of them there are? Perhaps they explain all cases of what used to be called possession. How they must have ransacked the past to assuage their hunger! Can't you picture them, flocking like carrion crows around the decaying Roman Empire, jostling one another for the minds of Nero and Caligula and Tiberius? Perhaps Omega failed to get those richer prizes. Or perhaps he hasn't much choice and must take whatever mind he can contact in any age, transferring from that to the next whenever he has the chance.

"It was only slowly, of course, that I worked all this out. I think it adds to his enjoyment to know that I'm aware of his presence. I think he's deliberately helping—breaking down his side of the barrier. For in the end, I was able to see him."

Connolly broke off. Looking around, Pearson saw that they were no longer alone on the hilltop. A young couple, hand in hand, were coming up the road toward the crucifix. Each had the physical beauty so common and so cheap among the islanders. They were oblivious to the night around them and to any spectators, and went past without the least sign of recognition. There was a bitter smile on Connolly's lips as he watched them go.

"I suppose I should be ashamed of this, but I was wishing then that he'd leave me and go after that boy. But he won't; though I've refused to play his game any more, he's staying to see what happens."

"You were going to tell me what he's like," said Pearson, annoyed at the interruption. Connolly lit a cigarette and inhaled deeply before replying.

"Can you imagine a room without walls? He's in a kind of hollow, egg-shaped space—surrounded by blue mist that always seems to be twisting and turning, but never changes its position. There's no entrance or exit—and no gravity, unless he's learned to defy it. Because he floats in the center, and around him is a circle of short, fluted cylinders, turning slowly in the air. I think they must be machines of some kind, obeying his will. And once there was a large oval hanging beside him, with perfectly human, beautifully formed arms coming from it. It could only have been a robot, yet those hands and fingers seemed alive. They were feeding and massaging him, treating him like a baby. It was horrible. . . .

"Have you ever seen a lemur or a spectral tarsier? He's rather like that—a nightmare travesty of mankind, with huge malevolent eyes. And this is strange—it's not the way one had imagined evolution going—he's covered with a fine layer of fur, as blue as the room in which he lives. Every time I've seen him he's been in the same position, half curled up like a sleeping baby. I think his legs have completely atrophied; perhaps his arms as well. Only his brain is still active, hunting up and down the ages for its prey.

"And now you know why there was nothing you or anyone else could do. Your psychiatrists might cure me if I was insane, but the science that can deal with Omega hasn't been invented yet."

Connolly paused, then smiled wryly.

"Just because I'm sane, I realize that you can't be expected to believe me. So there's no common ground on which we can meet."

Pearson rose from the boulder on which he had been sitting, and shivered slightly. The night was becoming cold, but that was nothing to the feeling of inner helplessness that had overwhelmed him as Connolly spoke.

"I'll be frank, Roy," he began slowly. "Of course I don't believe you. But insofar as you believe in Omega yourself, he's real to you, and I'll accept him on that basis and fight him with you."

"It may be a dangerous game. How do we know what he can do when he's cornered?"

"I'll take that chance," Pearson replied, beginning to walk down the hill. Connolly followed him without argument. "Meanwhile, just what do you propose to do yourself?"

"Relax. Avoid emotion. Above all, keep away from women—Ruth, Maude, and the rest of them. That's been the hardest job. It isn't easy to break the habits of a lifetime."

"I can well believe that," replied Pearson, a little dryly. "How successful have you been so far?"

"Completely. You see, his own eagerness defeats his purpose, by filling me with a kind of nausea and self-loathing whenever I think of sex. Lord, to think that I've laughed at the prudes all my life, yet now I've become one myself!"

There, thought Pearson in a sudden flash of insight, was the answer. He would never have believed it, but Connolly's past had finally caught up with him. Omega was nothing more than a symbol of conscience, a personification of guilt. When Connolly realized this, he would cease to be haunted. As for the remarkably detailed nature of the hallucination, that was yet another example of the tricks the human mind can play in its efforts to deceive itself. There must be some reason why the obsession had taken this form, but that was of minor importance.

Pearson explained this to Connolly at some length as they approached the village. The other listened so patiently that Pearson had an uncomfortable feeling that he was the one who was being humored, but he continued grimly to the end. When he had finished, Connolly gave a short, mirthless laugh.

"Your story's as logical as mine, but neither of us can convince the other. If you're right, then in time I may return to 'normal.' I can't disprove the possibility; I simply don't believe it. You can't imagine how real Omega is to me. He's more real than you are: if I close my eyes you're gone, but he's still there. I wish I knew what he was waiting for! I've left my old life behind; *he* knows I won't go back to it while he's there. So what's he got to gain by hanging on?" He turned to Pearson with a feverish eagerness. "That's what really frightens me, Jack. He must know what my future is—all my life must be like a book he can dip into where he pleases. So there must still be some experience ahead of me that he's waiting to savor. Sometimes—sometimes I wonder if it's my death."

They were now among the houses at the outskirts of the village, and ahead of them the nightlife of Syrene was getting into its stride.

Now that they were no longer alone, there came a subtle change in Connolly's attitude. On the hilltop he had been, if not his normal self, at least friendly and prepared to talk. But now the sight of the happy, carefree crowds ahead seemed to make him withdraw into himself. He lagged behind as Pearson advanced and presently refused to come any further.

"What's the matter?" asked Pearson. "Surely you'll come down to the hotel and have dinner with me?"

Connolly shook his head.

"I can't," he said. "I'd meet too many people."

It was an astonishing remark from a man who had always delighted in crowds and parties. It showed, as nothing else had done, how much Connolly had changed. Before Pearson could think of a suitable reply, the other had turned on his heels and made off up a side-street. Hurt and annoyed, Pearson started to pursue him, then decided that it was useless.

That night he sent a long telegram to Ruth, giving what reassurance he could. Then, tired out, he went to bed.

Yet for an hour he was unable to sleep. His body was exhausted, but his brain was still active. He lay watching the patch of moonlight move across the pattern on the wall, marking the passage of time as inexorably as it must still do in the distant age that Connolly had glimpsed. Of course, that was pure fantasy—yet against his will Pearson was growing to accept Omega as a real and living threat. And in a sense Omega *was* real—as real as those other mental abstractions, the Ego and the Subconscious Mind.

Pearson wondered if Connolly had been wise to come back to Syrene. In times of emotional crisis—there had been others, though none so important as this—Connolly's reaction was always the same. He would return again to the lovely island where his charming, feckless parents had borne him and where he had spent his youth. He was seeking now, Pearson knew well enough, the contentment he had known only for one period of his life, and which he had sought so vainly in the arms of Ruth and all those others who had been unable to resist him.

Pearson was not attempting to criticize his unhappy friend. He never passed judgments; he merely observed with a bright-eyed, sympathetic interest that was hardly tolerance, since tolerance implied the relaxation of standards which he had never possessed. . . .

After a restless night, Pearson finally dropped into a sleep so sound that he awoke an hour later than usual. He had breakfast in his room, then went down to the reception desk to see if there was any reply from Ruth. Someone else had arrived in the night: two traveling cases, obviously English, were stacked in a corner of the hall, waiting for the porter to move them. Idly curious, Pearson glanced at the labels to see who his compatriot might be. Then he stiffened, looked hastily around, and hurried across to the receptionist.

"This Englishwoman," he said anxiously. "When did she arrive?"

"An hour ago, Signor, on the morning boat."

"Is she in now?"

The receptionist looked a little undecided, then capitulated gracefully.

"No, Signor. She was in a great hurry, and asked me where she could find Mr. Connolly. So I told her. I hope it was all right."

Pearson cursed under his breath. It was an incredible stroke of bad luck, something he would never have dreamed of guarding against. Maude White was a woman of even greater determination than Connolly had hinted. Somehow she had discovered where he had fled, and pride or desire or both had driven her to follow. That she had come to this hotel was not surprising; it was an almost inevitable choice for English visitors to Syrene.

As he climbed the road to the villa, Pearson fought against an increasing sense of futility and uselessness. He had no idea what he should do when he met Connolly and Maude. He merely felt a vague yet urgent impulse to be helpful. If he could catch Maude before she reached the villa, he might be able to convince her that Connolly was a sick man and that her intervention could only do harm. Yet was this true? It was perfectly possible that a touching reconciliation had already taken place, and that neither party had the least desire to see him.

They were talking together on the beautifully laid-out lawn in front of the villa when Pearson turned through the gates and paused for breath. Connolly was resting on a wrought-iron seat beneath a palm tree, while Maude was pacing up and down a few yards away. She was speaking swiftly; Pearson could not hear her words, but from the intonation of her voice she was obviously pleading with Connolly. It was an embarrassing situation. While Pearson was still wondering whether to go forward, Connolly looked up and caught sight of him. His face was a completely expressionless mask; it showed neither welcome nor resentment.

At the interruption, Maude spun round to see who the intruder was, and for the first time Pearson glimpsed her face. She was a beautiful woman, but despair and anger had so twisted her features that she looked like a figure from some Greek tragedy. She was suffering not only the bitterness of being scorned, but the agony of not knowing why.

Pearson's arrival must have acted as a trigger to her pent-up emotions. She suddenly whirled away from him and turned toward Connolly, who continued to watch her with lack-lustre eyes. For a moment Pearson could not see what she was doing; then he cried in horror: "Look out, Roy!"

Connolly moved with surprising speed, as if he had suddenly emerged from a trance. He caught Maude's wrist, there was a brief struggle, and then he was backing away from her, looking with fascination at something in the palm of his hand. The woman stood motionless, paralyzed with fear and shame, knuckles pressed against her mouth.

Connolly gripped the pistol with his right hand and stroked it lovingly with his left. There was a low moan from Maude.

"I only meant to frighten you, Roy! I swear it!"

"That's all right, my dear," said Connolly softly. "I believe you. There's nothing to worry about." His voice was perfectly natural. He turned toward Pearson, and gave him his old, boyish smile.

"So *this* is what he was waiting for, Jack," he said. "I'm not going to disappoint him."

"No!" gasped Pearson, white with terror. "Don't, Roy, for God's sake!"

But Connolly was beyond the reach of his friend's entreaties as he turned the pistol to his head. In that same moment Pearson knew at last, with an awful clarity, that Omega was real and that Omega would now be seeking for a new abode.

He never saw the flash of the gun or heard the feeble but adequate explosion. The world he knew had faded from his sight, and around him now were the fixed yet crawling mists of the blue room. Staring from its center—as they had stared down the ages at how many others? —were two vast and lidless eyes. They were satiated for the moment, but for the moment only.

For three hundred years, while its fame spread across the world, the little town had stood here at the river's bend. Time and change had touched it lightly; it had heard from afar both the coming of the Armada and the fall of the Third Reich, and all Man's wars had passed it by.

Now it was gone, as though it had never been. In a moment of time the toil and treasure of centuries had been swept away. The vanished streets could still be traced as faint marks in the vitrified ground, but of the houses, nothing remained. Steel and concrete, plaster and ancient oak—it had mattered little at the end. In the moment of death they had stood together, transfixed by the glare of the detonating bomb. Then, even before they could flash into fire, the blast waves had reached them and they had ceased to be. Mile upon mile the ravening hemisphere of flame had expanded over the level farmlands, and from its heart had risen the twisting totem-pole that had haunted the minds of men for so long, and to such little purpose.

The rocket had been a stray, one of the last ever to be fired. It was hard to say for what target it had been intended. Certainly not London, for London was no longer a military objective. London, indeed, was no longer anything at all. Long ago the men whose duty it was had calculated that three of the hydrogen bombs would be sufficient for that rather small target. In sending twenty, they had been perhaps a little overzealous.

This was not one of the twenty that had done their work so well. Both its destination and its origin were unknown: whether it had come across the lonely Arctic wastes or far above the waters of the Atlantic, no one could tell and there were few now who cared. Once there had been men who had known such things, who had watched from afar the flight of the great projectiles and had sent their own missiles to meet them. Often that appointment had been kept, high above the Earth where the sky was black and sun and stars shared the heavens together. Then there had bloomed for a moment that indescribable flame, sending out into space a message that in centuries to come other eyes than Man's would see and understand.

But that had been days ago, at the beginning of the War. The defenders had long since been brushed aside, as they had known they must be. They had held on to life long enough to discharge their duty; too late, the enemy had learned his mistake. He would launch no further rockets; those still falling he had dispatched hours ago on secret trajectories that had taken them far out into space. They were returning now unguided and inert, waiting in vain for the signals that should lead them to their destinies. One by one they were falling at random upon a world which they could harm no more.

The river had already overflowed its banks; somewhere down its course the land had twisted beneath that colossal hammer-blow and the way to the sea was no longer open. Dust was still falling in a fine rain, as it would do for days as Man's cities and treasures returned to the world that had given them birth. But the sky was no longer wholly darkened, and in the west the sun was settling through banks of angry cloud.

A church had stood here by the river's edge, and though no trace of the building remained, the gravestones that the years had gathered round it still marked its place. Now the stone slabs lay in parallel rows, snapped off at their bases and pointing mutely along the line of the blast. Some were half flattened into the ground, others had been cracked and blistered by terrific heat, but many still bore the messages they had carried down the centuries in vain.

The light died in the west and the unnatural crimson faded from the sky. Yet still the graven words could be clearly read, lit by a steady, unwavering radiance, too faint to be seen by day but strong enough to banish night. The land was burning: for miles the glow of its radioactivity was reflected from the clouds. Through the glimmering landscape wound the dark ribbon of the steadily widening river, and as the waters submerged the land that deadly glow continued unchanging in the depths. In a generation, perhaps, it would have faded from sight, but a hundred years might pass before life could safely come this way again.

Timidly the waters touched the worn gravestone that for more than three hundred years had lain before the vanished altar. The church that had sheltered it so long had given it some protection at the last, and only a slight discoloration of the rock told of the fires that had passed this way. In the corpse-light of the dying land, the archaic words could still be traced as the water rose around them, breaking at last in tiny ripples across the stone. Line by line the epitaph upon which so many millions had gazed slipped beneath the conquering waters. For a little while the letters could still be faintly seen; then they were gone forever.

> Good frend for Iesvs sake forbeare,
> To digg the dvst encloased heare
> Blest be ye man yt spares thes stones,
> And cvrst be he yt moves my bones.

Undisturbed through all eternity the poet could sleep in safety now: in the silence and darkness above his head, the Avon was seeking its new outlet to the sea.

The Possessed

And now the sun ahead was so close that the hurricane of radiation was forcing the Swarm back into the dark night of space. Soon it would be able to come no closer; the gales of light on which it rode from star to star could not be faced so near their source. Unless it encountered a planet very soon, and could fall down into the peace and safety of its shadow, this sun must be abandoned as had so many before.

Six cold outer worlds had already been searched and discarded. Either they were frozen beyond all hope of organic life, or else they harbored entities of types that were useless to the Swarm. If it was to survive, it must find hosts not too unlike those it had left on its doomed and distant home. Millions of years ago the Swarm had begun its journey, swept starward by the fires of its own exploding sun. Yet even now the memory of its lost birthplace was still sharp and clear, an ache that would never die.

There was a planet ahead, swinging its cone of shadow through the flame-swept night. The senses that the Swarm had developed upon its long journey reached out toward the approaching world, reached out and found it good.

The merciless buffeting of radiation ceased as the black disc of the planet eclipsed the sun. Falling freely under gravity, the Swarm dropped swiftly until it hit the outer fringe of the atmosphere. The first time it had made planetfall it had almost met its doom, but now it contracted its tenuous substance with the unthinking skill of long practice, until it formed a tiny, close-knit sphere. Slowly its velocity slackened, until at last it was floating motionless between earth and sky.

For many years it rode the winds of the stratosphere from Pole to Pole, or let the soundless fusillades of dawn blast it westward from the rising sun. Everywhere it found life, but nowhere intelligence. There were things that crawled and flew and leaped, but there were no things that talked or built. Ten million years hence there might be creatures here with minds that the Swarm could possess and guide for its own purposes; there was no sign of them now. It could not guess which of the countless life-forms on this planet would be the heir to the future, and without such a host it was helpless—a mere pattern of electric charges, a matrix of order and self-awareness in a universe of chaos. By its own resources the Swarm had no control over matter, yet once it had lodged in the mind of a sentient race there was nothing that lay beyond its powers.

It was not the first time, and it would not be the last, that the planet had been surveyed by a visitant from space—though never by one in such peculiar and urgent need. The Swarm was faced with a tormenting dilemma. It could begin its weary travels once more, hoping that ultimately it might find the conditions it sought, or it could wait here on this world, biding its time until a race had arisen which would fit its purpose.

It moved like mist through the shadows, letting the vagrant winds take it where they willed. The clumsy, ill-formed reptiles of this young world never saw its passing, but it observed them, recording, analyzing, trying to extrapolate into the future. There was so little to choose between all these creatures; not one showed even the first faint glimmerings of conscious mind. Yet if it left this world in search of another, it might roam the universe in vain until the end of time.

At last it made its decision. By its very nature, it could choose both alternatives. The greater part of the Swarm would continue its travels among the stars, but a portion of it would remain on this world, like a seed planted in the hope of future harvest.

It began to spin upon its axis, its tenuous body flattening into a disc. Now it was wavering at the frontiers of visibility—it was a pale ghost, a faint will-of-the-wisp that suddenly fissured into two unequal fragments. The spinning slowly died away: the Swarm had become two, each an entity with all the memories of the original, and all its desires and needs.

There was a last exchange of thoughts between parent and child who were also identical twins. If all went well with them both, they would meet again in the far future here at this valley in the mountains. The one who was staying would return to this point at regular intervals down the ages; the one who continued the search would send back an emissary if ever a better world was found. And then they would be united again, no longer homeless exiles vainly wandering among the indifferent stars.

The light of dawn was spilling over the raw, new mountains when the parent swarm rose up to meet the sun. At the edge of the atmosphere the gales of radiation caught it and swept it unresisting out beyond the planets, to start again upon the endless search.

The one that was left began its almost equally hopeless task. It needed an animal that was not so rare that disease or accident could make it extinct, nor so tiny that it could never acquire any power over the physical world. And it must breed rapidly, so that its evolution could be directed and controlled as swiftly as possible.

The search was long and the choice difficult, but at last the Swarm selected its host. Like rain sinking into thirsty soil, it entered the bodies of certain small lizards and began to direct their destiny.

It was an immense task, even for a being which could never know death. Generation after generation of the lizards was swept into the past before there came the slightest improvement in the race. And always, at the appointed time, the Swarm returned to its rendezvous among the mountains. Always it returned in vain: there was no messenger from the stars, bringing news of better fortune elsewhere.

The centuries lengthened into millennia, the millennia into eons. By the standards of geological time, the lizards were now changing rapidly. Presently they were lizards no more, but warm-blooded, fur-covered creatures that brought forth their young alive. They were still small and feeble, and their minds were rudimentary, but they contained the seeds of future greatness.

Yet not only the living creatures were altering as the ages slowly passed. Continents were being rent asunder, mountains being worn down by the weight of the unwearying rain. Through all these changes, the Swarm kept to its purpose; and always, at the appointed times, it went to the meeting place that had been chosen so long ago, waited patiently for a while, and came away. Perhaps the parent swarm was still searching or perhaps—it was a hard and terrible thought to grasp—some unknown fate had overtaken it and it had gone the way of the race it had once ruled. There was nothing to do but to wait and see if the stubborn life-stuff of this planet could be forced along the path to intelligence.

And so the eons passed. . . .

Somewhere in the labyrinth of evolution the Swarm made its fatal mistake and took the wrong turning. A hundred million years had gone since it came to Earth, and it was very weary. It could not die, but it could degenerate. The memories of its ancient home and of its destiny were fading: its intelligence was waning even while its hosts climbed the long slope that would lead to self-awareness.

By a cosmic irony, in giving the impetus which would one day bring intelligence to this world, the Swarm had exhausted itself. It had reached the last stage of parasitism; no longer could it exist apart from its hosts. Never again could it ride free above the world, driven by wind and sun. To make the pilgrimage to the ancient rendezvous, it must travel slowly and painfully in a thousand little bodies. Yet it continued the immemorial custom, driven on by the desire for reunion which burned all the more fiercely now that it knew the bitterness of failure. Only if the parent swarm returned and reabsorbed it could it ever know new life and vigor.

The glaciers came and went; by a miracle the little beasts that now housed the waning alien intelligence escaped the clutching fingers of the ice. The oceans overwhelmed the land, and still the race survived. It even multiplied, but it could do no more. This world would never be its heritage, for far away in the heart of another continent a certain monkey had come down from the trees and was looking at the stars with the first glimmerings of curiosity.

The mind of the Swarm was dispersing, scattering among a million tiny bodies, no longer able to unite and assert its will. It had lost all cohesion; its memories were fading. In a million years, at most, they would all be gone.

Only one thing remained—the blind urge which still, at intervals which by some strange aberration were becoming ever shorter, drove it to seek its consummation in a valley that long ago had ceased to exist.

Quietly riding the lane of moonlight, the pleasure steamer passed the island with its winking beacon and entered the fjord. It was a calm and lovely night, with Venus sinking in the west out beyond the Faroes, and the lights of the harbor reflected with scarcely a tremor in the still waters far ahead.

Nils and Christina were utterly content. Standing side by side against the boat rail, their fingers locked together, they watched the wooded slopes drift silently by. The tall trees were motionless in the moonlight, their leaves unruffled by even the merest breath of wind, their slender trunks rising whitely from pools of shadow. The whole world was asleep; only the moving ship dared to break the spell that had bewitched the night.

Then suddenly, Christina gave a little gasp and Nils felt her fingers tighten convulsively on his. He followed her gaze: she was staring out across the water, looking toward the silent sentinels of the forest.

"What is it, darling?" he asked anxiously.

"Look!" she replied, in a whisper Nils could scarcely hear. "There— under the pines!"

Nils stared, and as he did so the beauty of the night ebbed slowly away and ancestral terrors came crawling back from exile. For beneath the trees the land was alive: a dappled brown tide was moving down the slopes of the hill and merging into the dark waters. Here was an open patch on which the moonlight fell unbroken by shadow. It was changing even as he watched: the surface of the land seemed to be rippling downward like a slow waterfall seeking union with the sea.

And then Nils laughed and the world was sane once more. Christina looked at him, puzzled but reassured.

"Don't you remember?" he chuckled. "We read all about it in the paper this morning. They do this every few years, and always at night. It's been going on for days."

He was teasing her, sweeping away the tension of the last few minutes. Christina looked back at him, and a slow smile lit up her face.

"Of course!" she said. "How stupid of me!" Then she turned once more toward the land and her expression became sad, for she was very tender-hearted.

"Poor little things!" she sighed. "I wonder why they do it?"

Nils shrugged his shoulders indifferently.

"No one knows," he answered. "It's just one of those mysteries. I shouldn't think about it if it worries you. Look—we'll soon be in harbor!"

They turned toward the beckoning lights where their future lay, and Christina glanced back only once toward the tragic, mindless tide that was still flowing beneath the moon.

Obeying an urge whose meaning they had never known, the doomed legions of the lemmings were finding oblivion beneath the waves.

The Awakening

Marlan was bored, with the ultimate boredom that only Utopia can supply. He stood before the great window and stared down at the scudding clouds, driven by the gale that was racing past the foothills of the city. Sometimes, through a rent in the billowing white blanket, he could catch a glimpse of lakes and forests and the winding ribbon of the river that flowed through the empty land he now so seldom troubled to visit. Twenty miles away to the west, rainbow-hued in the sunlight, the upper peaks of the artificial mountain that was City Nine floated above the clouds, a dream island adrift in the cold wastes of the stratosphere. Marlan wondered how many of its inhabitants were staring listlessly across at him, equally dissatisfied with life.

There was, of course, one way of escape, and many had chosen it.

But that was so obvious, and Marlan avoided the obvious above all things. Besides, while there was still a chance that life might yet hold some new experience, he would not pass through the door that led to oblivion.

Out of the mist that lay beneath him, something bright and flaming burst through the clouds and dwindled swiftly toward the deep blue of the zenith. With lack-lustre eyes, Marlan watched the ascending ship: once—how long ago!—the sight would have lifted his heart. Once he too had gone on such journeys, following the road along which Man had found his greatest adventures. But now on the twelve planets and the fifty moons there was nothing one could not find on Earth. Perhaps, if only the stars could have been reached, humanity might have avoided the cul-de-sac in which it was now trapped; there would still have remained endless vistas of exploration and discovery. But the spirit of mankind had quailed before the awful immensities of interstellar space. Man had reached the planets while he was still young, but the stars had remained forever beyond his grasp.

And yet—Marlan stiffened at the thought and stared along the twisting vapor-trail that marked the path of the departed ship—if Space had defeated him, there was still another conquest to be attempted. For a long time he stood in silent thought, while, far beneath, the storm's ragged hem slowly unveiled the buttresses and ramparts of the city, and below those, the forgotten fields and forests which had once been Man's only home.

The idea appealed to Sandrak's scientific ingenuity; it presented him with interesting technical problems which would keep him occupied for a year or two. That would give Marlan ample time to wind up his affairs, or, if necessary, to change his mind.

If Marlan felt any last-minute hesitations, he was too proud to show it as he said good-by to his friends. They had watched his plans with morbid curiosity, convinced that he was indulging in some unusually elaborate form of euthanasia. As the door of the little spaceship closed behind Marlan, they walked slowly away to resume the pattern of their aimless lives; and Roweena wept, but not for long.

While Marlan made his final preparations, the ship climbed on its automatic course, gaining speed until the Earth was a silver crescent, then a fading star lost against the greater glory of the sun. Rising upward from the plane in which the planets move, the ship drove steadily toward the stars until the sun itself had become no more than a blazing point of light. Then Marlan checked his outward speed, swinging the ship round into an orbit that made it the outermost of all the sun's children. Nothing would ever disturb it here; it would circle the sun for eternity, unless by some inconceivable chance it was captured by a wandering comet.

For the last time Marlan checked the instruments that Sandrak had built. Then he went to the innermost chamber and sealed the heavy metal door. When he opened it again, it would be to learn the secret of human destiny.

His mind was empty of all emotion as he lay on the thickly padded couch and waited for the machines to do their duty. He never heard the first whisper of gas through the vents; but consciousness went out like an ebbing tide.

Presently the air crept hissing from the little chamber, and its store of heat drained outward into the ultimate cold of space. Change and decay could never enter here; Marlan lay in a tomb that would outlast any that man had ever built on Earth, and might indeed outlast the Earth itself. Yet it was more than a tomb, for the machines it carried were biding their time, and every hundred years a circuit opened and closed, counting the centuries.

So Marlan slept, in the cold twilight beyond Pluto. He knew nothing of the life that ebbed and flowed upon Earth and its sister planets while the centuries lengthened into millennia, the millennia into eons. On the world that had once been Marlan's home, the mountains crumbled and were swept into the sea; the ice crawled down from the Poles as it had done so many times before and would do many times again. On the ocean beds the mountains of the future were built layer by layer from the falling silt, and presently rose into the light of day, and in a little while followed the forgotten Alps and Himalayas to their graves.

The sun had changed very little, all things considered, when the patient mechanisms of Marlan's ship reawakened from their long sleep. The air hissed back into the chamber, the temperature slowly climbed from the verge of absolute zero to a level at which life might start again. Gently, the handling machines began the delicate series of tasks which should revitalize their master.

Yet he did not stir. During the long ages that had passed since Marlan began his sleep, something had failed among the circuits that should have awakened him. Indeed, the marvel was that so much had functioned correctly; for Marlan still eluded Death, though his servants would never recall him from his slumbers.

And now the wonderful ship remembered the commands it had been given so long ago. For a little while, as its multitudinous mechanisms slowly warmed to life, it floated inert with the feeble sunlight glinting on its walls. Then, ever more swiftly, it began to retrace the path along which it had traveled when the world was young. It did not check its speed until it was once more among the inner planets, its metal hull warming beneath the rays of the ancient unwearying sun. Here it began its search, in the temperate zone where the Earth had once circled; and here it presently found a planet it did not recognize.

The size was correct, but all else was wrong. Where were the seas that once had been Earth's greatest glory? Not even their empty beds were left: the dust of vanished continents had clogged them long ago. And where, above all, was the Moon? Somewhere in the forgotten past it had crept earthward and met its doom, for the planet was now girdled, as once only Saturn had been, by a vast, thin halo of circling dust.

For a while the robot controls searched through their electronic memories as the ship considered the situation. Then it made its decision, if a machine could have shrugged its shoulders, it would have done so. Choosing a landing place at random, it fell gently down through the thin air and came to rest on a flat plain of eroded sandstone. It had brought Marlan home; there was nothing more that it could do. If there was still life on the Earth, sooner or later it would find him.

And here, indeed, those who were now masters of Earth presently came upon Marlan's ship. Their memories were long, and the tarnished metal ovoid lying upon the sandstone was not wholly strange to them. They conferred among each other with as much excitement as their natures allowed and, using their own strange tools, began to break through the stubborn walls until they reached the chamber where Marlan slept.

In their way, they were very wise, for they could understand the purpose of Marlan's machines and could tell where they had failed in their duty. In a little while the scientists had made what repairs were necessary, though they were none too hopeful of success. The best that they could expect was that Marlan's mind might be brought, if only for a little while, back to the borders of consciousness before Time exacted its long-deferred revenge.

The light came creeping back into Marlan's brain with the slowness of a winter dawn. For ages he lay on the frontiers of self-awareness, knowing that he existed but not knowing who he was or whence he had come. Then fragments of memory returned, and fitted one by one into the intricate jigsaw of personality, until at last Marlan knew that he was—Marlan. Despite his weakness, the knowledge of success brought him a deep and burning sense of satisfaction. The curiosity that had driven him down the ages when his fellows had chosen the blissful sleep of euthanasia would soon be rewarded: he would know what manner of men had inherited the earth.

Strength returned. He opened his eyes. The light was gentle, and did not dazzle him, but for a moment all was blurred and misty. Then he saw figures looming dimly above him, and was filled with a sense of dreamlike wonder, for he remembered that he should have been alone on his return to life, with only his machines to tend him.

And now the scene came swiftly into focus, and staring back at him, showing neither enmity nor friendship, neither excitement nor indifference, were the fathomless eyes of the Watchers. The thin, grotesquely articulated figures stood around him in a close-packed circle, looking down at him across a gulf which neither his mind nor theirs could ever span.

Other men would have felt terror, but Marlan only smiled, a little sadly, as he closed his eyes forever. His questing spirit had reached its goal; he had no more riddles to ask of Time. For in the last moment of his life, as he saw those waiting round him, he knew that the ancient war between Man and insect had long ago been ended, and that Man was not the victor.

Exile of the Eons

Already the mountains were trembling with the thunder that only man can make. But here the war seemed very far away, for the full moon hung over The Himalayas and the blinding furies of the battle were still hidden below the edge of the world. Not for long would they remain. The Master knew that the last remnants of his fleet were being hurled from the sky as the circle of death closed swiftly on his stronghold.

In a few hours at the most, the Master and his dreams of empire would have vanished into the past. Nations would still curse his name, but they would no longer fear it. Later, even the hatred would be gone and he would mean no more to the world than Hitler or Napoleon or Genghis Khan. Like them he would be a blurred figure far down the infinite corridor of time, dwindling toward oblivion.

Far to the south, a mountain was suddenly edged with violet flame. Ages later, the balcony on which the Master stood shuddered beneath the impact of the ground wave racing through the rocks below. Later still, the air brought the echo to a mammoth concussion. Surely they could not be so close already! The Master hoped it was no more than a stray torpedo that had swept through the contracting battle line. If it were not, time was even shorter than he feared.

The Chief of Staff walked out from the shadows and joined him by the rail. The Marshal's hard face—the second most hated in all the world—was lined and beaded with sweat. He had not slept for many days and his once gaudy uniform hung limply upon him. Yet his eyes, though unutterably weary, were still resolute even in defeat. He stood in silence, awaiting his last orders. Nothing else was left for him to do.

Thirty miles away, the eternal snow-plume of Everest flamed a lurid red, reflecting the glare of some colossal fire below the horizon. Still the Master neither moved nor gave any sign. Not until a salvo of torpedoes passed high overhead with a demon wail did he turn and, with one backward glance at the world he would see no more, descend into the depths.

The lift dropped a thousand feet and the sound of battle died away. As he stepped out of the shaft, the Master paused for a moment to press a hidden switch. The Marshal smiled when he heard the crash of falling rock far above, and knew that pursuit and escape were equally impossible.

As of old, the handful of generals sprang to their feet when the Master entered the room. He walked to his place in silence, steeling himself for the last and hardest speech he would ever have to make. Burning into his soul he could feel the eyes of the men he had led to ruin. Behind and beyond them he could see the squadrons, the divisions, the armies whose blood was on his hands. And more terrible still were the silent specters of the nations that now could never be born.

At last he began to speak. The hypnosis of his voice was as powerful as ever, and after a few words he became once more the perfect, implacable machine whose destiny was destruction.

"This, gentlemen, is the last of all our meetings. There are no more plans to make, no more maps to study. Somewhere above our heads the fleet we built with such pride and care is fighting to the end. In a few minutes, not one of all those thousands of machines will be left in the sky.

"I know that for all of us here surrender is unthinkable, even if it were possible, so in this room you will shortly have to die. You have served our cause and deserved better, but it was not to be. Yet I do not wish you to think that we have wholly failed. In the past, as you saw many times, my plans were always ready for everything that might arise, no matter how improbable. You should not, therefore, be surprised to learn that I was prepared even for defeat."

Still the same superb orator, he paused for effect, noting with satisfaction the ripple of interest, the sudden alertness on the tired faces of his listeners.

"My secret is safe enough with you," he continued, "for the enemy will never find this place. The entrance is already blocked by many hundreds of feet of rock."

Still there was no movement. Only the Director of Propaganda turned suddenly white, and swiftly recovered—but not swiftly enough to escape the Master's eye. The Master smiled inwardly at this belated confirmation of an old doubt. It mattered little now; true and false, they would all die together.

All but one.

"Two years ago," he went on, "when we lost the battle of Antarctica, I knew that we could no longer be certain of victory. So I made my preparations for this day. The enemy has already sworn to kill me. I could not remain in hiding anywhere on the Earth, still less hope to rebuild our fortunes.

"But there is another way, though a desperate one.

"Five years ago, one of our scientists perfected the technique of suspended animation. He found that by relatively simple means all life processes could be arrested for an indefinite time. I am going to use this discovery to escape from the present into a future which will have forgotten me. There I can begin the struggle again, with the help of certain devices that might yet have won this war had we been granted more time.

"Good-by, gentlemen. And once again, my thanks for your help and my regrets at your ill fortune."

He saluted, turned on his heel, and was gone. The metal door thudded decisively behind him. There was a frozen silence; then the Director of Propaganda rushed to the exit, only to recoil with a startled cry. The steel door was already too hot to touch. It had been welded immovably into the wall.

The Minister for War was the first to draw his automatic.

The Master was in no great hurry now. On leaving the council room he had thrown the secret switch of the welding circuit. The same action had opened a panel in the wall of the corridor, revealing a small circular passage sloping steadily upward. He began to walk slowly along it.

Every few hundred feet the tunnel angled sharply, though still continuing the upward climb. At each turning the Master stopped to throw a switch, and there was the thunder of falling rock as a section of corridor collapsed.

Five times the passageway changed its course before it ended in a spherical, metal-walled room. Multiple doors closed softly on rubber seatings, and the last section of tunnel crashed behind. The Master would not be disturbed by his enemies, nor by his friends.

He looked swiftly around the room to satisfy himself that all was ready. Then he walked to a simple control board and threw, one after another, a set of tiny switches. They had to carry little current—but they had been built to last. So had everything in that strange room. Even the walls were made of metals far less ephemeral than steel.

Pumps started to whine, drawing the air from the chamber and replacing it with sterile nitrogen. Moving more swiftly now, the Master went to the padded couch and lay down. He thought he could feel himself bathed by the bacteria-destroying rays from the lamps above his head, but that of course was fancy. From a recess beneath the couch he drew a hypodermic and injected a milky fluid into his arm.

Then he relaxed and waited.

It was already very cold. Soon the refrigerators would bring the temperature down far below freezing, and would hold it there for many hours. Then it would rise to normal, but by that time the process would be completed, all bacteria would be dead and the Master could sleep, unchanged, forever.

He had planned to wait a hundred years. More than that he dared not delay, for when he awoke he would have to master all the changes in science and society that the passing years had wrought. Even a century might have altered the face of a civilization beyond his understanding, but that was a risk he would have to take. Less than a century would not be safe, for the world would still be full of bitter memories.

Sealed in a vacuum beneath the couch were the electronic counters operated by thermocouples hundreds of feet above, on the eastern face of the mountain where no snow could ever cling. Every day the rising sun would operate them and the counters would add one unit to their store. So the coming of dawn would be noted in the darkness where the Master slept.

When any one of the counters reached the total of thirty-six thousand, a switch would close and oxygen would flow back into the chamber. The temperature would rise, and the automatic hypodermic strapped to the Master's arm would inject the calculated amount of fluid. He would awaken. Then he would press the button which would blast away the mountainside and give him free passage to the outer world.

Everything had been considered. There could be no failure. All the machinery had been triplicated and was as perfect as science could contrive.

The Master's last thought as consciousness ebbed was not of his past life, nor of the mother whose hopes he had betrayed. Unbidden and unwelcome, there came into his mind the words of an ancient poet:

To sleep, perchance to dream . . .

No, he would not, he dared not dream. He would only sleep . . . sleep . . . sleep . . .

Twenty miles away, the battle was coming to its end. Not a dozen of the Master's ships were left, fighting hopelessly against overwhelming fire. The action would have ended long ago had the attackers not been ordered to risk no ships in unnecessary adventures. The decision was to be left to the long-range artillery. So the great destroyers, the airborne battleships of this age, lay with their fighter screens in the shelter of the mountains, pouring salvo after salvo into the doomed formations.

Aboard the flagship, a young Hindu gunnery officer set vernier dials with infinite care and gently pressed a pedal with his foot. There was the faintest of shocks as the dirigible torpedoes left their cradles and hurled themselves at the enemy. The young Indian sat waiting tensely as the chronometer ticked off the seconds. This, he thought, was probably the last salvo he would ever fire. Somehow he felt none of the elation he had expected; indeed, he was surprised to discover a kind of impersonal sympathy for his doomed opponents, whose lives were now ebbing with every passing second.

Far away a sphere of violet fire blossomed above the mountains, among the darting specks that were enemy ships. The gunner leaned forward tensely and counted. One-two-three-four-five times came that peculiar explosion. Then the sky cleared. The struggling specks were gone.

In his log, the gunner noted briefly: "0124 hrs. Salvo No. 12 fired. Five torps exploded among enemy ships, which were destroyed. One torp failed to detonate."

He signed the entry with a flourish and laid down his pen. For a while he sat staring at the log's familiar brown cover, with the cigarette burns at the edges and the inevitable stained rings where cups and glasses had been carelessly set down. Idly he thumbed through the leaves, noting once again the handwriting of his many predecessors. And as he had done so often before, he turned to a familiar page where a man who had once been his friend had begun to sign his name but had never lived to complete it.

With a sigh, he closed the book and locked it away. The war was over.

Far away among the mountains, the torpedo that had failed to explode was still gaining speed under the drive of its rockets. Now it was a scarcely visible line of light, racing between the walls of a lonely valley. Already the snows that had been disturbed by the scream of its passage were beginning to rumble down the mountain slopes.

There was no escape from the valley: it was blocked by a sheer wall a thousand feet high. Here the torpedo that had missed its mark found a greater one. The Master's tomb was too deep in the mountain even to be shaken by the explosion but the hundreds of tons of falling rock swept away three tiny instruments and their connections, and a future that might have been went with them into oblivion.

The first rays of the rising sun would still fall on the shattered face of the mountain, but the counters that were waiting for the thirty-six thousandth dawn would still be waiting when dawns and sunsets were no more.

In the silence of the tomb that was not quite a tomb, the Master knew nothing of this. And he slumbered on, until the century was far behind—very far indeed.

After what by some standards would have been a little while, the earth's crust decided it had borne the weight of The Himalayas for long enough. Slowly the mountains dropped, tilting the southern plains of India toward the sky. And presently the plateau of Ceylon was the highest point on the surface of the globe, and the ocean about Everest was five and a half miles deep. Yet the Master's slumber was still dreamless and undisturbed.

Slowly, patiently, the silt drifted down through the towering ocean heights onto the wreck of The Himalayas. The blanket that would one day be chalk began to thicken at the rate of an inch or two every century. If one had returned some time later, one might have found that the sea bed was no longer five miles down, or even four, or three. Then the land tilted again, and a mighty range of limestone mountains towered where once had been the oceans of Tibet. But the Master knew nothing of this, nor was his sleep troubled when it happened again and again and yet again.

Now the rain and the rivers were washing away the chalk and carrying it out to the strange new oceans, and the surface was moving down toward the hidden tomb. Slowly the miles of rock were winnowed away until at last the sphere which housed the Master's body returned to the light of day—though to a day much longer, and much dimmer, than it had been when the Master closed his eyes.

Little did the Master dream of the races that had flowered and died since that early morning of the world when he went to his long sleep. Very far away was that morning now, and the shadows were lengthening to the east; the sun was dying and the world was very old. But still the children of Adam ruled its seas and skies, and filled with their tears and laughter the plains and the valleys and the woods that were older than the shifting hills.

The Master's dreamless sleep was more than half ended when Trevindor the Philosopher was born, between the fall of the Ninety-seventh Dynasty and the rise of the Fifth Galactic Empire. He was born on a world very far from Earth. Few were the men who now set foot on the ancient home of their race, so distant from the throbbing heart of the Universe.

They brought Trevindor to Earth when his brief clash with the Empire had come to its inevitable end. Here he was tried by the men whose ideals he had challenged, and here it was that they pondered long over the manner of his necessary fate.

The case was unique. The gentle, philosophic culture that now ruled the Galaxy had never before met with opposition, even on the level of pure intellect, and the polite but implacable conflict of wills had left it severely shaken. It was typical of the Council's members that, when a decision had proved impossible, they had appealed to Trevindor himself for help.

In the whitely gleaming Hall of Justice, that had not been entered for nigh on a million years, Trevindor stood proudly facing the men who had proved stronger than he. In silence he listened to their request; then he paused in reflection. His judges waited patiently until at last he spoke.

"You suggest that I should promise not to defy you again," he began, "but I shall make no promise that I may be unable to keep. Our views are too divergent and sooner or later we should clash again.

"There was a time when your choice would have been easy. You could have exiled me, or put me to death. But today—where among all the worlds of the Universe is there one planet where you could hide me if I did not choose to stay? Remember, I have many disciples scattered the length and breadth of the Galaxy.

"There remains the other alternative. I shall bear you no malice if you revive the ancient custom of execution to meet my case."

There was a murmur of annoyance from the Council, and the President replied sharply, his color heightening.

"That remark is in questionable taste. We asked for serious suggestions, not reminders—even if intended humorously—of the barbaric customs of our remote ancestors."

Trevindor accepted the rebuke with a bow. "I was merely mentioning all the possibilities. There are two others that have occurred to me. It would be a simple matter to change my mind pattern to your way of thinking so that no future disagreement can arise."

"We have already considered that. We were forced to reject it, attractive though it is, for the destruction of your personality would be equivalent to murder. There are only fifteen more powerful intellects than yours in the Universe, and we have no right to tamper with it. And your final suggestion?"

"Though you cannot exile me in space, there is still one alternative. The river of Time stretches ahead of us as far as our thoughts can go. Send me down that stream to an age when you are certain this civilization will have passed. That I know you can do with the aid of the Roston time-field."

There was a long pause. In silence the members of the Council were passing their decisions to the complex analysis machine which would weigh them one against the other and arrive at the verdict. At length the President spoke.

"It is agreed. We will send you to an age when the sun is still warm enough for life to exist on the Earth, but so remote that any trace of our civilization is unlikely to survive. We will also provide you with everything necessary for your safety and reasonable comfort. You may leave us now. We will call for you again as soon as all arrangements have been made."

Trevindor bowed, and left the marble hall. No guards followed him. There was nowhere he could flee, even if he wished, in this Universe which the great Galactic liners could span in a single day.

For the first and the last time, Trevindor stood on the shore of what had once been the Pacific, listening to the wind sighing through the leaves of what had once been palms. The few stars of the nearly empty region of space through which the sun was now passing shone with a steady light through the dry air of the aging world. Trevindor wondered bleakly if they would still be shining when he looked again upon the sky, in a future so distant that the sun itself would be sinking to its death.

There was a tinkle from the tiny communicator band upon his wrist. So, the time had come. He turned his back upon the ocean and walked resolutely to meet his fate. Before he had gone a dozen steps, the time-field had seized him and his thoughts froze in an instant that would remain unchanged while the oceans shrank and vanished, the Galactic Empire passed away, and the great star clusters crumbled into nothingness.

But, to Trevindor, no time elapsed at all. He only knew that at one step there had been moist sand beneath his feet, and at the next hard, baked rock. The palms had vanished, the murmur of the sea was stilled. It needed only a glance to show that even the memory of the sea had long since faded from this parched and dying world. To the far horizon, a great desert of red sandstone stretched unbroken and unrelieved by any growing thing. Overhead, the orange disk of a strangely altered sun glowered from a sky so black that many stars were clearly visible.

Yet, it seemed, there was still life on this ancient world. To the north—if that were still the north—the somber light glinted upon some metallic structure. It was a few hundred yards away, and as Trevindor started to walk toward it he was conscious of a curious lightness, as if gravity itself had weakened.

He had not gone far before he saw that he was approaching a low metal building which seemed to have been set down on the plain rather than constructed there, for it tilted slightly with the slope of the land. Trevindor wondered at his incredible good fortune at finding civilization so easily. Another dozen steps, and he realized that not chance but design had so conveniently placed this building here, and that it was as much a stranger to this world as he himself.

There was no hope at all that anyone would come to meet him as he walked toward it.

The metal plaque above the door added little to what he had already surmised. Still new and untarnished as if it had just been engraved—as indeed, in a sense, it had—the lettering brought a message at once of hope and of bitterness.

To Trevindor, the greetings of the Council.

This building, which we have sent after you through the timefield, will supply all your needs for an indefinite period.

We do not know if civilization will still exist in the age in which you find yourself. Man may now be extinct, since the chromosome K Star K will have become dominant and the race may have mutated into something no longer human. That is for you to discover.

You are now in the twilight of the Earth and it is our hope that you are not alone. But if it is your destiny to be the last living creature on this once lovely world, remember that the choice was yours. Farewell.

Twice Trevindor read the message, recognizing with an ache the closing words which could only have been written by his friend, the poet Cintillarne. An overwhelming sense of loneliness and isolation came flooding into his soul. He sat down upon a shelf of rock and buried his face in his hands.

A long time later, he arose to enter the building. He felt more than grateful to the long-dead Council which had treated him so chivalrously. The technical achievement of sending an entire building through time was one he had believed beyond the resources of his age. A sudden thought struck him and he glanced again at the engraved lettering, noticing for the first time the date it bore. It was five thousand years later than the time when he had faced his peers in the Hall of Justice.

Fifty centuries had passed before his judges could redeem their promise to a man as good as dead. Whatever the faults of the Council, its integrity was of an order beyond the comprehension of an earlier age.

Many days passed before Trevindor left the building again. Nothing had been overlooked: even his beloved thought records were there. He could continue to study the nature of reality and to construct philosophies until the end of the Universe, barren though that occupation would be if his were the only mind left on Earth. There was little danger, he thought wryly, that his speculations concerning the purpose of human existence would once again bring him into conflict with society.

Not until he had investigated the building thoroughly did Trevindor turn his attention once more to the outer world. The supreme problem was that of contacting civilization, should such still exist. He had been provided with a powerful receiver, and for hours he wandered up and down the spectrum in the hope of discovering a station. The far-off crackle of static came from the instrument and once there was a burst of what might have been speech in a tongue that was certainly not human. But nothing else rewarded his search. The ether, which had been man's faithful servant for so many ages, was silent at last.

The little automatic flyer was Trevindor's sole remaining hope. He had what was left of eternity before him, and Earth was a small planet. In a few years at the most, he could have explored it all.

So the months passed while the exile began his methodical exploration of the world, returning ever and again to his home in the desert of red sandstone.

Everywhere he found the same picture of desolation and ruin. How long ago the seas had vanished he could not even guess, but in their dying they had left endless wastes of salt, encrusting both plains and mountains with a blanket of dirty gray.

Trevindor felt glad that he had not been born on Earth and so had never known it in the glory of its youth. Stranger though he was, the loneliness and desolation of the world chilled his heart; had he lived here before, its sadness would have been unbearable.

Thousands of square miles of desert passed beneath Trevindor's fleeting ship as he searched the world from pole to pole. Only once did he find any sign that Earth had ever known civilization. In a deep valley near the equator he discovered the ruins of a small city of strange white stone and stranger architecture. The buildings were perfectly preserved, though half buried by the drifting sand, and for a moment Trevindor felt a surge of somber joy at the knowledge that man had, after all, left some traces of his handiwork on the world that had been his first home.

The emotion was short-lived. The buildings were stranger than Trevindor had realized, for no man could ever have entered them. Their only openings were wide, horizontal slots close to the ground; there were no windows of any kind. Trevindor's mind reeled as he tried to imagine the creatures that must have occupied them. In spite of his growing loneliness, he felt glad that the dwellers in this inhuman city had passed away so long before his time. He did not linger here, for the bitter night was almost upon him and the valley filled him with an oppression that was not entirely rational.

And once, he actually discovered life. He was cruising over the bed of one of the lost oceans when a flash of color caught his eye. Upon a knoll which the drifting sand had not yet buried was a thin, wiry covering of grass. That was all, but the sight brought tears to his eyes.

He grounded the machine and stepped out, treading warily lest he destroy even one of the struggling blades. Tenderly he ran his hands over the threadbare carpet which was all the life that Earth now knew. Before he left, he sprinkled the spot with as much water as he could spare. It was a futile gesture, but one which made him feel happier.

The search was now nearly completed. Trevindor had long ago given up all hope, but his indomitable spirit still drove him on across the face of the world. He could not rest until he had proved what as yet he only feared. And thus it was that he came at last to the Master's tomb as it lay gleaming dully in the sunlight from which it had been banished so unthinkably long.

The Master's mind awoke before his body. As he lay powerless, unable even to lift his eyelids, memory came flooding back. The hundred years were safely behind him. His gamble, the most desperate that any man had ever made, had succeeded! An immense weariness came over him and for a while consciousness faded once more.

Presently the mists cleared again and he felt stronger, though still too weak to move. He lay in the darkness gathering his strength together. What sort of a world, he wondered, would he find when he stepped forth from the mountainside into the light of day? Would he be able to put his plans into—? What was that? A spasm of sheer terror shook the very foundations of his mind. Something was moving beside him, here in the tomb where nothing should be stirring but himself.

Then, calm and clear, a thought rang through his mind and quelled in an instant the fears that had threatened to overturn it.

"Do not be alarmed. I have come to help you. You are safe, and everything will be well."

The Master was too stunned to make any reply, but his subconscious must have formulated some sort of answer, for the thought came again.

"That is good. I am Trevindor, like yourself an exile in this world. Do not move, but tell me how you came here and what is your race, for I have seen none like it."

And now fear and caution were creeping back into the Master's mind. What manner of creature was this that could read his thoughts, and what was it doing in his secret sphere? Again that clear, cold thought echoed through his brain like the tolling of a bell.

"Once more I tell you that you have nothing to fear. Why are you alarmed because I can see into your mind? Surely there is nothing strange in that."

"Nothing strange!" cried the Master. "Who are you—what are you, for God's sake?"

"A man like yourself. But your race must be primitive indeed if the reading of thoughts is foreign to you."

A terrible suspicion began to dawn in the Master's brain. The answer came even before he consciously framed the question.

"You have slept infinitely longer than a hundred years. The world you knew has ceased to be for longer than you can imagine."

The Master heard no more. Once again the darkness swept over him and he sank down into unconsciousness.

In silence Trevindor stood by the couch on which the Master lay. He was filled with an elation which for the moment outweighed any disappointment he might feel. At least, he would no longer have to face the future alone. All the terror of the Earth's loneliness, that was weighing so heavily upon his soul, had vanished in a moment. *No longer alone* . . . no longer alone!

The Master was beginning to stir once more, and into Trevindor's mind crept broken fragments of thought. Pictures of the world the

Master had known began to form. At first Trevindor could make nothing of them; then, suddenly, the jumbled shards fell into place. A wave of horror swept over him at the appalling vista of nation battling against nation, of cities flaming to destruction. What kind of world was this? Could man have sunk so low from the peaceful age Trevindor had known? There had been legends of such things, from times incredibly remote, but man had left them with his childhood. Surely they could never have returned!

The broken thoughts were more vivid now, and even more horrible. It was truly a nightmare age from which this other exile had come— no wonder that he had fled from it!

Suddenly the truth began to dawn in the mind of Trevindor as, sick at heart, he watched the ghastly patterns passing through the Master's brain. This was no exile seeking refuge from an age of horror. This was the very creator of that horror, who had embarked on the river of time with one purpose alone—to spread contagion down to later years.

Passions that Trevindor had never imagined began to parade themselves before his eyes: ambition, the lust for power, cruelty, intolerance, hatred. He tried to close his mind, but found he had lost the power to do so. With a cry of anguish, Trevindor rushed out into the silent desert.

It was night, and very still, for the Earth was now too weary even for winds to blow. The darkness hid everything, but Trevindor knew that it could not hide the thoughts of that other mind with which he now must share the world. Once he had been alone, and he had imagined nothing more dreadful. But now he knew that there were things more fearful even than solitude.

The stillness of the night, and the glory of the stars that had once been his friends, brought calm to the soul of Trevindor. Slowly he turned and retraced his footsteps, walking heavily, for he was about to perform a deed that no man of his kind had ever done before.

The Master was erect when Trevindor re-entered the sphere. Perhaps some hint of the other's purpose dawned upon his mind, for he was very pale. Steadfastly, Trevindor forced himself to look once more into the Master's brain. His mind recoiled at the chaos of conflicting emotions, now shot through with sickening flashes of fear. Out of the maelstrom one coherent thought came timidly quavering.

"What are you going to do? Why do you look at me like that?"

Trevindor made no reply, holding his mind aloof from contamination while he marshaled his resolution and all his strength.

The tumult in the Master's mind was rising to crescendo. For a moment his mounting terror brought something akin to pity to the gentle spirit of Trevindor, and his will faltered. But then there came again the picture of those ruined and burning cities.

With all the power of his intellect, backed by thousands of centuries of mental evolution, he struck at the man before him. Into the Master's mind, obliterating all else, flooded the single thought of—death.

For a moment the Master stood motionless, his eyes staring wildly. His breath froze as his lungs ceased their work; in his veins the pulsing blood, which had been stilled for so long, now congealed forever.

Without a sound, the Master toppled and lay still.

Very slowly Trevindor turned and walked out into the night. Like a shroud the silence and loneliness of the world descended upon him. The sand, thwarted so long, began to drift through the open portals of the Master's tomb.

Second Dawn

"Here they come," said Eris, rising to his forefeet and turning to look down the long valley. For a moment the pain and bitterness had left his thoughts, so that even Jeryl, whose mind was more closely tuned to his than to any other, could scarcely detect it. There was even an undertone of softness that recalled poignantly the Eris she had known in the days before the War—the old Eris who now seemed almost as remote and as lost as if he were lying with all the others out there on the plain.

A dark tide was flowing up the valley, advancing with a curious, hesitant motion, making odd pauses and little bounds forward. It was flanked with gold—the thin line of the Atheleni guards, so terrifyingly few compared with the black mass of the prisoners. But they were enough: indeed, they were only needed to guide that aimless river on its faltering way. Yet at the sight of so many thousands of the enemy, Jeryl found herself trembling and instinctively moved toward her mate, silver pelt resting against gold. Eris gave no sign that he had understood or even noticed the action.

The fear vanished as Jeryl saw how slowly the dark flood was moving forward. She had been told what to expect, but the reality was even worse than she had imagined. As the prisoners came nearer, all the hate and bitterness ebbed from her mind, to be replaced by a sick compassion. No one of her race need evermore fear the aimless, idiot horde that was being shepherded through the pass into the valley it would never leave again.

The guards were doing little more than urge the prisoners on with meaningless but encouraging cries, like nurses calling to infants too young to sense their thoughts. Strain as she might, Jeryl could detect no vestige of reason in any of those thousands of minds passing so near at hand. That brought home to her, more vividly than could anything else, the magnitude of the victory—and of the defeat. Her mind was sensitive enough to detect the first faint thoughts of children, hovering on the verge of consciousness. The defeated enemy had become not even children, but babies with the bodies of adults.

The tide was passing within a few feet of them now. For the first time, Jeryl realized how much larger than her own people the Mithraneans were, and how beautifully the light of the twin suns gleamed on the dark satin of their bodies. Once a magnificent specimen, towering a full head above Eris, broke loose from the main body and came blundering toward them, halting a few paces away. Then it crouched down like a lost and frightened child, the splendid head moving uncertainly from side to side as if seeking it knew not what. For a moment the great, empty eyes fell full upon Jeryl's face. She was as beautiful, she knew, to the Mithraneans as to her own race—but there was no flicker of emotion on the blank features, and no pause in the aimless movement of the questing head. Then an exasperated guard drove the prisoner back to his fellows.

"Come away," Jeryl pleaded. "I don't want to see any more. Why did you ever bring me here?" The last thought was heavy with reproach.

Eris began to move away over the grassy slopes in great bounds that she could not hope to match, but as he went his mind threw its message back to hers. His thoughts were still gentle, though the pain beneath them was too deep to be concealed.

"I wanted everyone—even you—to see what we had to do to win the War. Then, perhaps, we will have no more in our lifetimes."

He was waiting for her on the brow of the hill, undistressed by the mad violence of his climb. The stream of prisoners was now too far below for them to see the details of its painful progress. Jeryl crouched down beside Eris and began to browse on the sparse vegetation that had been exiled from the fertile valley. She was slowly beginning to recover from the shock.

"But what will happen to them?" she asked presently, still haunted by the memory of that splendid, mindless giant going into a captivity it could never understand.

"They can be taught how to eat," said Eris. "There is food in the valley for half a year, and then we'll move them on. It will be a heavy strain on our own resources, but we're under a moral obligation—and we've put it in the peace treaty."

"They can never be cured?"

"No. Their minds have been totally destroyed. They'll be like that until they die."

There was a long silence. Jeryl let her gaze wander across the hills, falling in gentle undulations to the edge of the ocean. She could just make out, beyond a gap in the hills, the distant lines of blue that marked the sea—the mysterious, impassable sea. Its blue would soon be deepening into darkness, for the fierce white sun was setting and presently there would only be the red disk—hundreds of times larger but giving far less light—of its pale companion.

"I suppose we had to do it," Jeryl said at last. She was thinking almost to herself, but she let enough of her thoughts escape for Eris to overhear.

"You've seen them," he answered briefly. "They were bigger and stronger than we. Though we outnumbered them, it was a stalemate: in the end, I think they would have won. By doing what we did, we saved thousands from death—or mutilation."

The bitterness came back into his thoughts, and Jeryl dared not look at him. He had screened the depths of his mind, but she knew that he was thinking of the shattered ivory stump upon his forehead. The War had been fought, except at the very end, with two weapons only—the razor-sharp hoofs of the little, almost useless fore-paws, and the unicorn-like horns. With one of these, Eris could never fight again, and from the loss stemmed much of the embittered harshness that sometimes made him hurt even those who loved him.

Eris was waiting for someone, though who it was Jeryl could not guess. She knew better than to interrupt his thoughts while he was in his present mood, and so remained silently beside him, her shadow merging with his as it stretched far along the hilltop.

Jeryl and Eris came of a race which, in Nature's lottery, had been luckier than most—and yet had missed one of the greatest prizes of all. They had powerful bodies and powerful minds, and they lived in a world which was both temperate and fertile. By human standards, they would have seemed strange but by no means repulsive. Their sleek, fur-covered bodies tapered to a single giant rear-limb that could send them leaping over the ground in thirty-foot bounds. The two fore-limbs were much smaller, and served merely for support and steadying. They ended in pointed hoofs that could be deadly in combat, but had no other useful purpose.

Both the Atheleni and their cousins, the Mithraneans, possessed mental powers that had enabled them to develop a very advanced mathematics and philosophy: but over the physical world they had no control at all. Houses, tools, clothes—indeed, artifacts of any kind—were utterly unknown to them. To races which possessed hands, tentacles, or other means of manipulation, their culture would have seemed incredibly limited: yet such is the adaptability of the mind, and the power of the commonplace, that they seldom realized their handicaps and could imagine no other way of life. It was natural to wander in great herds over the fertile plains, pausing where food was plentiful and moving on again when it was exhausted. This nomadic life had given them enough leisure for philosophy and even for certain arts. Their telepathic powers had not yet robbed them of their voices and they had developed a complex vocal music and an even more complex choreography. But they took the greatest pride of all in the range of their thoughts: for thousands of generations they had sent their minds roving through the misty infinities of metaphysics. Of *physics*, and indeed of all the sciences of matter, they knew nothing—not even that they existed.

"Someone's coming," said Jeryl suddenly. "Who is it?"

Eris did not bother to look, but there was a sense of strain in his reply.

"It's Aretenon. I agreed to meet him here."

"I'm so glad. You were such good friends once—it upset me when you quarreled."

Eris pawed fretfully at the turf, as he did when he was embarrassed or annoyed.

"I lost my temper with him when he left me during the fifth battle of the Plain. Of course I didn't know then why he had to go."

Jeryl's eyes widened in sudden amazement and understanding.

"You mean—he had something to do with the Madness, and the way the War ended?"

"Yes. There were very few people who knew more about the mind than he did. I don't know what part he played, but it must have been an important one. I don't suppose he'll ever be able to tell us much about it."

Still a considerable distance below them, Aretenon was zigzagging up the hillside in great leaps. A little later he had reached them, and instinctively bent his head to touch horns with Eris in the universal gesture of greeting. Then he stopped, horribly embarrassed, and there was an awkward pause until Jeryl came to the rescue with some conventional remarks.

When Eris spoke, Jeryl was relieved to sense his obvious pleasure at meeting his friend again, for the first time since their angry parting at the height of the War. It had been longer still since her last meeting with Aretenon, and she was surprised to see how much he had changed. He was considerably younger than Eris—but no one would have guessed it now. Some of his once-golden pelt was turning black with age, and with a flash of his old humor Eris remarked that soon no one would be able to tell him from a Mithranean.

Aretenon smiled.

"That would have been useful in the last few weeks. I've just come through their country, helping to round up the wanderers. We weren't very popular, as you might expect. If they'd known who I was, I don't suppose I'd have got back alive—armistice or no armistice."

"You weren't actually in charge of the Madness, were you?" asked Jeryl, unable to control her curiosity.

She had a momentary impression of thick, defensive mists forming around Aretenon's mind, shielding all his thoughts from the outer world. Then the reply came, curiously muffled, and with a sense of distance that was very rare in telepathic contact.

"No: I wasn't in supreme charge. But there were only two others between myself and—the top."

"Of course," said Eris, rather petulantly, "I'm only an ordinary soldier and don't understand these things. But I'd like to know just how you did it. Naturally," he added, "neither Jeryl nor myself would talk to anyone else."

Again that veil seemed to descend over Aretenon's thoughts. Then it lifted, ever so slightly.

"There's very little I'm allowed to tell. As you know, Eris, I was always interested in the mind and its workings. Do you remember the games we used to play, when I tried to uncover your thoughts, and you did your best to stop me? And how I sometimes made you carry out acts against your will?"

"I still think," said Eris, "that you couldn't have done that to a stranger, and that I was really unconsciously co-operating."

"That was true then—but it isn't any longer. The proof lies down there in the valley." He gestured toward the last stragglers who were being rounded up by the guards. The dark tide had almost passed, and soon the entrance to the valley would be closed.

"When I grew older," continued Aretenon, "I spent more and more of my time probing into the ways of the mind, and trying to discover why some of us can share our thoughts so easily, while others can never do so but must remain always isolated and alone, forced to communicate by sounds or gestures. And I became fascinated by those rare minds that are completely deranged, so that those who possess them seem less than children.

"I had to abandon these studies when the War began. Then, as you know, they called for me one day during the fifth battle. Even now, I'm not quite sure who was responsible for that. I was taken to a place a long way from here, where I found a little group of thinkers, many of whom I already knew.

"The plan was simple—and tremendous. From the dawn of our race we've known that two or three minds, linked together, could be used to control another mind, *if it were willing*, in the way that I used to control yours. We've employed this power for healing since ancient times. Now we planned to use it for destruction.

"There were two main difficulties. One was bound up with that curious limitation of our normal telepathic powers—the fact that, except in rare cases, we can only have contact over a distance *with someone we already know*, and can communicate with strangers only when we are actually in their presence.

"The second, and greater problem, was that the massed power of many minds would be needed, and never before had it been possible to link together more than two or three. How we succeeded is our main secret: like all such things, it seems easy now it has been done. And once we had started, it was simpler than we had expected. Two minds are more than twice as powerful as one, and three are much more than thrice as powerful as a single will. The exact mathematical relationship is an interesting one. You know how very rapidly the number of ways a group of objects may be arranged increases with the size of the group? Well, a similar relationship holds in this case.

"So in the end we had our Composite Mind. At first it was unstable, and we could hold it together for only a few seconds. It's still a tremendous strain on our mental resources, and even now we can only do it for—well, for long enough.

"All these experiments, of course, were carried out in great secrecy. If we could do this, so could the Mithraneans, for their minds are as good as ours. We had a number of their prisoners, and we used them as subjects."

For a moment the veil that hid Aretenon's inner thoughts seemed to tremble and dissolve: then he regained control.

"That was the worst part. It was bad enough to send madness into a far land, but it was infinitely worse when you could watch with your own eyes the effects of what you did.

"When we had perfected our technique, we made the first long-distance test. Our victim was someone so well-known to one of our prisoners—whose mind we had taken over—that we could identify him completely and thus the distance between us was no objection. The experiment worked, but of course no one suspected that we were responsible.

"We did not operate again until we were certain that our attack would be so overwhelming that it would end the War. From the minds of our prisoners we had identified about a score of Mithraneans—their friends and kindred—in such detail that we could pick them out and destroy them. As each mind fell beneath our attack, it gave up to us the knowledge of others, and so our power increased. We could have done far more damage than we did, for we took only the males."

"Was that," asked Jeryl bitterly, "so very merciful?"

"Perhaps not: but it should be remembered to our credit. We stopped as soon as the enemy sued for peace, and, as we alone knew what had happened, we went into their country to undo what damage we could. It was little enough."

There was a long silence. The valley was deserted now, and the white sun had set. A cold wind was blowing over the hills, passing, where none could follow it, out across the empty and untraveled sea. Then Eris spoke his thoughts almost whispering to Aretenon's mind.

"You did not come to tell me this, did you? There is something more." It was a statement rather than a query.

"Yes," replied Aretenon. "I have a message for you—one that will surprise you a good deal. It's from Therodimus."

"Therodimus! I thought—"

"You thought he was dead, or worse still, a traitor. He's neither, although he's lived in enemy territory for the last twenty years. The Mithraneans treated him as we did, and gave him everything he needed. They recognized his mind for what it was, and even during the War no one touched him. Now he wants to see you again."

Whatever emotions Eris was feeling at this news of his old teacher, he gave no sign of them. Perhaps he was recalling his youth, remembering now that Therodimus had played a greater part in the shaping of his mind than had any other single influence. But his thoughts were barred to Aretenon and even to Jeryl.

"What's he been doing all this time?" Eris asked at length. "And why does he want to see me now?"

"It's a long and complicated story," said Aretenon, "but Therodimus has made a discovery quite as remarkable as ours, and one that may have even greater consequences."

"Discovery? What sort of discovery?"

Aretenon paused, looking thoughtfully along the valley. The guards were returning, leaving behind only the few who would be needed to deal with any wandering prisoners.

"You know as much of our history as I do, Eris," he began. "It took, we believe, something like a million generations for us to reach our present level of development—and that's a tremendous length of time! Almost all the progress we've made has been due to our telepathic powers: without them we'd be little different from all those other animals that show such puzzling resemblances to us. We're very proud of our philosophy and our mathematics, of our music and dancing—but have you ever thought, Eris, that there might be other lines of cultural development which we've never even dreamed of? *That there might be other forces in the Universe besides mental ones?*"

"I don't know what you mean," said Eris flatly.

"It's hard to explain, and I won't try—except to say this. Do you realize just how pitiably feeble is our control over the external world, and how useless these limbs of ours really are? No—you can't, for you won't have seen what I have. But perhaps this will make you understand."

The pattern of Aretenon's thoughts modulated suddenly into a minor key.

"I remember once coming upon a bank of beautiful and curiously complicated flowers. I wanted to see what they were like inside, so I tried to open one, steadying it between my hoofs and picking it apart with my teeth. I tried again and again—and failed. In the end, half mad with rage, I trampled all those flowers into the dirt."

Jeryl could detect the perplexity in Eris's mind, but she could see that he was interested and curious to know more.

"I have had that sort of feeling, too," he admitted. "But what can one do about it? And after all, is it really important? There are a good many things in this universe which are not exactly as we should like them."

Aretenon smiled.

"That's true enough. But Therodimus has found out how to do something about it. Will you come and see him?"

"It must be a long journey."

"About twenty days from here, and we have to go across a river."

Jeryl felt Eris give a little shudder. The Atheleni hated water, for the excellent and sufficient reason that they were too heavy-boned to swim, and promptly drowned if they fell into it.

"It's in enemy territory: they won't like me."

"They respect you, and it might be a good idea for you to go—a friendly gesture, as it were."

"But I'm wanted here."

"You can take my word that nothing you do here is as important as the message Therodimus has for you—and for the whole world."

Eris veiled his thoughts for a moment, then uncovered them briefly.

"I'll think about it," he said.

It was surprising how little Aretenon managed to say on the many days of the journey. From time to time Eris would challenge the defenses of his mind with half-playful thrusts, but always they were parried with an effortless skill. About the ultimate weapon that had ended the War he would say nothing, but Eris knew that those who had wielded it had not yet disbanded and were still at their secret hiding place. Yet though he would not talk about the past, Aretenon often spoke of the future, and with the urgent anxiety of one who had helped to shape it and was not sure if he had acted aright. Like many others of his race, he was haunted by what he had done, and the sense of guilt sometimes overwhelmed him. Often he made remarks which puzzled Eris at the time, but which he was to remember more and more vividly in the years ahead.

"We've come to a turning-point in our history, Eris. The powers we've uncovered will soon be shared by the Mithraneans, and another war will mean destruction for us both. All my life I've worked to increase our knowledge of the mind, but now I wonder if I've brought something into the world that is too powerful, and too dangerous, for us to handle. Yet it's too late, now, to retrace our footsteps: sooner or later our culture was bound to come to this point, and to discover what we have found.

"It's a terrible dilemma: and there's only one solution. We cannot go back, and if we go forward we may meet disaster. So we must change the very nature of our civilization, and break completely with the million generations behind us. You can't imagine how that could be done: nor could I, until I met Therodimus and he told me of his dream.

"The mind is a wonderful thing, Eris—but by itself it is helpless in the universe of matter. We know now how to multiply the power of our brains by an enormous factor: we can solve, perhaps, the great problems of mathematics that have baffled us for ages. But neither our unaided minds, nor the group-mind we've now created, can alter in the slightest the one fact that all through history has brought us and the Mithraneans into conflict—the fact that the food supply is fixed, and our populations are not."

Jeryl would watch them, taking little part in their thoughts, as they argued these matters. Most of their discussions took place while they were browsing, for like all active ruminants they had to spend a considerable part of each day searching for food. Fortunately the land through which they were passing was extremely fertile—indeed, its fertility had been one of the causes of the War. Eris, Jeryl was glad to see, was becoming something of his old self again. The feeling of frustrated bitterness that had filled his mind for so many months had not lifted, but it was no longer as all-pervading as it had been.

They left the open plain on the twenty-second day of their journey. For a long time they had been traveling through Mithranean territory, but those few of their ex-enemies they had seen had been inquisitive rather than hostile. Now the grasslands were coming to an end, and the forest with all its primeval terrors lay ahead.

"Only one carnivore lives in this region," Aretenon reassured them, "and it's no match for the three of us. We'll be past the trees in a day and a night."

"A night—in the forest!" gasped Jeryl, half petrified with terror at the very thought.

Aretenon was obviously a little ashamed of himself.

"I didn't like to mention it before," he apologized, "but there's really no danger. I've done it by myself, several times. After all, none of the great flesh-eaters of ancient times still exists—and it won't be really dark, even in the woods. The red sun will still be up."

Jeryl was still trembling slightly. She came of a race which, for thousands of generations, had lived on the high hills and the open plains, relying on speed to escape from danger. The thought of going among trees—and in the dim red twilight while the primary sun was down—filled her with panic. And of the three of them, only Aretenon possessed a horn with which to fight. (It was nothing like so long or sharp, thought Jeryl, as Eris's had been.)

She was still not at all happy even when they had spent a completely uneventful day moving through the woods. The only animals they saw were tiny, long-tailed creatures that ran up and down the tree-trunks with amazing speed, gibbering with anger as the intruders passed. It was entertaining to watch them, but Jeryl did not think that the forest would be quite so amusing in the night.

Her fears were well founded. When the fierce white sun passed below the trees, and the crimson shadows of the red giant lay everywhere, a change seemed to come over the world. A sudden silence swept across the forest—a silence abruptly broken by a very distant wail toward which the three of them turned instinctively, ancestral warnings shrieking in their minds.

"What was that?" gasped Jeryl.

Aretenon was breathing swiftly, but his reply was calm enough.

"Never mind," he said. "It was a long way off. I don't know what it was."

And Jeryl knew that he was lying.

They took turns keeping guard, and the long night wore slowly away. From time to time Jeryl would awaken from troubled dreams into the nightmare reality of the strange, distorted trees gathered threateningly around her. Once, when she was on guard, she heard the sound of a heavy body moving through the woods very far away —but it came no nearer and she did not disturb the others. So at last the longed-for brilliance of the white sun began to flood the sky, and the day had come again.

Aretenon, Jeryl thought, was probably more relieved than he pretended to be. He was almost boyish as he frisked around in the morning sunlight, snatching an occasional mouthful of foliage from an overhanging branch.

"We've only half a day to go now," he said cheerfully. "We'll be out of the forest by noon."

There was a mischievous undertone to his thoughts that puzzled Jeryl. It seemed as if Aretenon was keeping still another secret from them, and Jeryl wondered what further obstacles they would have to overcome. By midday she knew, for their way was barred by a great river flowing slowly past them as if in no haste to meet the sea.

Eris looked at it with some annoyance, measuring it with a practiced eye.

"It's much too deep to ford here. We'll have to go a long way upstream before we can cross."

Aretenon smiled.

"On the contrary," he said cheerfully, "we're going *downstream*."

Eris and Jeryl looked at him in amazement.

"Are you mad?" Eris cried.

"You'll soon see. We've not far to go now—you've come all this way, so you might as well trust me for the rest of the journey."

The river slowly widened and deepened. If it had been impassable before, it was doubly so now. Sometimes, Eris knew, one came upon a steam across which a tree had fallen, so that one could walk over on the trunk—though it was a risky thing to do. But this river was the width of many trees, and was growing no narrower.

"We're nearly there," said Aretenon at last. "I recognize the place. Someone should be coming out of those woods at any moment." He gestured with his horn to the trees on the far side of the river, and almost as he did so three figures came bounding out onto the bank. Two of them, Jeryl saw, were Atheleni: the third was a Mithranean.

They were now nearing a great tree, standing by the water's edge, but Jeryl had paid it little attention: she was too interested in the figures on the distant bank, wondering what they were going to do next. So when Eris's amazement exploded like a thunderclap in the depths of her own mind, she was too confused for a moment to realize its cause. Then she turned toward the tree, and saw what Eris had seen.

To some minds and some races, few things could have been more natural or more commonplace than a thick rope tied round a tree trunk, and floating out across the waters of a river to another tree on the far bank. Yet it filled both Jeryl and Eris with the terror of the unknown, and for one awful moment Jeryl thought that a gigantic snake was emerging from the water. Then she saw that it was not alive, but her fear remained. For it was the first artificial object that she had ever seen.

"Don't worry about *what* it is, or how it was put there," counseled Aretenon. "It's going to carry you across, and that's all that matters for the moment. Look—there's someone coming over now!"

One of the figures on the far bank had lowered itself into the water, and was working its way with its fore-limbs along the rope. As it came nearer—it was the Mithranean, and a female—Jeryl saw that it was carrying a second and much smaller rope looped round the upper part of its body.

With the skill of long practice, the stranger made her way across the floating cable, and emerged dripping from the river. She seemed to know Aretenon, but Jeryl could not intercept their thoughts.

"I can go across without any help," said Aretenon, "but I'll show you the easy way."

He slipped the loop over his shoulder and, dropping into the water, hooked his fore-limbs over the fixed cable. A moment later he was being dragged across at a great speed by the two others on the far bank where, after much trepidation, Eris and Jeryl presently joined him.

It was not the sort of bridge one would expect from a race which could quite easily have dealt with the mathematics of a reinforced concrete arch—if the possibility of such an object had ever occurred to it. But it served its purpose, and once it had been made, they could use it readily enough.

Once it had been made. But—who had made it?

When their dripping guides had rejoined them, Aretenon gave his friends a warning.

"I'm afraid you're going to have a good many shocks while you're here. You'll see some very strange sights, but when you understand them, they'll cease to puzzle you in the slightest. In fact, you will soon come to take them for granted."

One of the strangers, whose thoughts neither Eris nor Jeryl could intercept, was giving him a message.

"Therodimus is waiting for us," said Aretenon. "He's very anxious to see you."

"I've been trying to contact him," complained Eris. "But I've not succeeded."

Aretenon seemed a little troubled.

"You'll find he's changed," he said. "After all, you've not seen each other for many years. It may be some time before you can make full contact again."

Their road was a winding one through the forest, and from time to time curiously narrow paths branched off in various directions. Therodimus, thought Eris, must have changed indeed for him to have taken up permanent residence among trees. Presently the track opened out into a large, semicircular clearing with a low white cliff lying along its diameter. At the foot of the cliff were several dark holes of varying sizes—obviously the openings of caves.

It was the first time that either Eris or Jeryl had ever entered a cave, and they did not greatly look forward to the experience. They were relieved when Aretenon told them to wait just outside the opening, and went on alone toward the puzzling yellow light that glowed in the depths. A moment later, dim memories began to pulse in Eris's mind, and he knew that his old teacher was coming, even though he could no longer fully share his thoughts.

Something stirred in the gloom, and then Therodimus came out into the sunlight. At the sight of him, Jeryl screamed once and buried her head in Eris's mane, but Eris stood firm, though he was trembling as he had never done before battle. For Therodimus blazed with a magnificence that none of his race had ever known since history began. Around his neck hung a band of glittering objects that caught and refracted the sunlight in myriad colors, while covering his body was a sheet of some thick, many-hued material that rustled softly as he walked. And his horn was no longer the yellow of ivory: some magic had changed it to the most wonderful purple that Jeryl had ever seen.

Therodimus stood motionless for a moment, savoring their amazement to the full. Then his rich laugh echoed in their minds, and he reared up upon his hind-limb. The colored garment fell whispering to the ground, and at a toss of his head the glittering necklace arched like a rainbow into a corner of the cave. But the purple horn remained unchanged.

It seemed to Eris that he stood at the brink of a great chasm, with Therodimus beckoning to him on the far side. Their thoughts struggled to form a bridge, but could make no contact. Between them was the gulf of half a lifetime and many battles, of myriad unshared experiences—Therodimus' years in this strange land, his own mating with Jeryl and the memory of their lost children. Though they stood face to face, a few feet only between them, their thoughts could never meet again.

Then Aretenon, with all the power and authority of his unsurpassed skill, did something to his mind that Eris was never quite able to recall. He only knew that the years seemed to have rolled back, that he was once more the eager, anxious pupil—and that he could speak to Therodimus again.

It was strange to sleep underground, but less unpleasant than spending the night amid the unknown terrors of the forest. As she watched the crimson shadows deepening beyond the entrance to the little cave, Jeryl tried to collect her scattered thoughts. She had understood only a small part of what had passed between Eris and Therodimus, but she knew that something incredible was taking place. The evidence of her eyes was enough to prove that: today she had seen things for which there were no words in her language.

She had heard things, too. As they had passed one of the cave-mouths, there had come from it a rhythmic, "whirring" sound, unlike that made by any animal she knew. It had continued steadily without pause or break as long as she could hear it, and even now its unhurried rhythm had not left her mind. Aretenon, she believed, had also noticed it, though without any surprise: Eris had been too engrossed with Therodimus.

The old philosopher had told them very little, preferring, as he said, to show them his empire when they had had a good night's rest. Nearly all their talk had been concerned with the events of their own land during the last few years, and Jeryl found it somewhat boring. Only one thing had interested her, and she had eyes for little else. That was the wonderful chain of colored crystals that Therodimus had worn around his neck. What it was, or how it had been created, she could not imagine: but she coveted it. As she fell asleep, she found herself thinking idly, but more than half seriously, of the sensation it would cause if she returned to her people with such a marvel gleaming against her own pelt. It would look so much better there than upon old Therodimus.

Aretenon and Therodimus met them at the cave soon after dawn. The philosopher had discarded his regalia—which he had obviously worn only to impress his guests—and his horn had returned to its normal yellow. That was one thing Jeryl thought she could understand, for she had come across fruits whose juices could cause such color changes.

Therodimus settled himself at the mouth of the cave. He began his narration without preliminaries, and Eris guessed that he must have told it many times before to earlier visitors.

"I came to this place, Eris, about five years after leaving our country. As you know, I was always interested in strange lands, and from the Mithraneans I'd heard rumors that intrigued me very much. How I traced them to their source is a long story that doesn't matter now. I crossed the river far upstream one summer, when the water was very low. There's only one place where it can be done, and then only in the driest years. Higher still the river loses itself in the mountains, and I don't think there's any way through them. So this is virtually an island—almost completely cut off from Mithranean territory.

"It's an island, but it's not uninhabited. The people who live here are called the Phileni, and they have a very remarkable culture—one entirely different from our own. Some of the products of that culture you've already seen.

"As you know, there are many different races on our world, and quite a few of them have some sort of intelligence. But there is a great gulf between us and all other creatures. As far as we know, we are the only beings capable of abstract thought and complex logical processes.

"The Phileni are a much younger race than ours, and they are intermediate between us and the other animals. They've lived here on this rather large island for several thousand generations—but their rate of development has been many, many times swifter than ours. They neither possess nor understand our telepathic powers, but they have something else which we may well envy—something which is responsible for the whole of their civilization and its incredibly rapid progress."

Therodimus paused, then rose slowly to his feet.

"Follow me," he said. "I'll take you to see the Phileni."

He led them back to the caves from which they had come the night before, pausing at the entrance from which Jeryl had heard that strange, rhythmic whirring. It was clearer and louder now, and she saw Eris start as though he had noticed it for the first time. Then Therodimus uttered a high-pitched whistle, and at once the whirring slackened, falling octave by octave until it had ebbed into silence. A moment later something came toward them out of the semigloom.

It was a little creature, scarcely half their height, and it did not hop, but walked upon two jointed limbs that seemed very thin and feeble. Its large spherical head was dominated by three huge eyes, set far apart and capable of independent movement. With the best will in the world, Jeryl did not think it was very attractive.

Then Therodimus uttered another whistle, and the creature raised its fore-limbs toward them.

"Look closely," said Therodimus, very gently, "and you will see the answer to many of your questions."

For the first time, Jeryl saw that the creature's fore-limbs did not end in hoofs, or indeed after the fashion of any animal with which she was acquainted. Instead, they divided into at least a dozen thin, flexible tentacles and two hooked claws.

"Go toward it, Jeryl," commanded Therodimus. "It has something for you."

Hesitantly, Jeryl moved forward. She noticed that the creature's body was crossed with bands of some dark material, to which were attached unidentifiable objects. It dropped a fore-limb to one of these, and a cover opened to reveal a cavity, inside which something glittered. Then the little tentacles were clutching that marvelous crystal necklace, and with a movement so swift and dexterous that Jeryl could scarcely follow it, the Phileni moved forward and clasped it round her neck.

Therodimus brushed aside her confusion and gratitude, but his shrewd old mind was well pleased. Jeryl would be his ally now in whatever he planned to do. But Eris's emotions might not be so easily swayed, and in this matter mere logic was not enough. His old pupil had changed so much, had been so deeply wounded by the past, that Therodimus could not be certain of success. Yet he had a plan that could turn even these difficulties to his advantage.

He gave another whistle, and the Phileni made a curious waving gesture with its hands and disappeared into the cave. A moment later that strange whirring ascended once more from the silence, but Jeryl's curiosity was now quite overshadowed by her delight in her new possession.

"We'll go through the woods," said Therodimus, "to the nearest settlement—it's only a little way from here. The Phileni don't live in the open, as we do. In fact, they differ from us in almost every conceivable way. I'm even afraid," he added ruefully, "that they're much better natured than we are, and I believe that one day they'll be more intelligent. But first of all, let me tell you what I've learned about them, so that you can understand what I'm planning to do."

The mental evolution of any race is conditioned, even dominated, by physical factors which that race almost invariably takes for granted as part of the natural order of things. The wonderfully sensitive hands of the Phileni had enabled them to find by experiment and trial facts which had taken the planet's only other intelligent species a thousand times as long to discover by pure deduction. Quite early in their history, the Phileni had invented simple tools. From these they had proceeded to fabrics, pottery, and the use of fire. When Therodimus had discovered them, they had already invented the lathe and the potter's wheel, and were about to move into their first Metal Age— with all that that implied.

On the purely intellectual plane, their progress had been less rapid. They were clever and skillful, but they had a dislike of abstract thought and their mathematics was purely empirical. They knew, for example, that a triangle with sides in the ratio three-four-five was right-angled, but had not suspected that this was only a special case of a much more general law. Their knowledge was full of such yawning gaps which, despite the help of Therodimus and his several-score disciples, they seemed in no great hurry to fill.

Therodimus they worshipped as a god, and for two whole generations of their short-lived race they had obeyed him in everything, giving him all the products of their skill that he needed, and making at his suggestion the new tools and devices that had occurred to him. The partnership had been incredibly fertile, for it was as if both races had suddenly been released from their shackles. Great manual skill and great intellectual powers had fused in a fruitful union probably unique in all the universe—and progress that would normally have taken millennia had been achieved in less than a decade.

As Aretenon had promised them, though Eris and Jeryl saw many marvels, they came across nothing that they could not understand once they had watched the little Phileni craftsmen at work and had seen with what magic their hands shaped natural materials into lovely or useful forms. Even their tiny towns and primitive farms soon lost their wonder and became part of the accepted order of things.

Therodimus let them look their fill, until they had seen every aspect of this strangely sophisticated Stone Age culture. Because they knew no different, they found nothing incongruous in the sight of a Phileni potter—who could scarcely count beyond ten—shaping a series of complex algebraic surfaces under the guidance of a young Mithranean mathematician. Like all his race, Eris possessed tremendous powers of mental visualization, but he realized how much easier geometry would be if one could actually *see* the shapes one was considering. From this beginning (though he could not guess it) would one day evolve the idea of a written language.

Jeryl was fascinated above all things by the sight of the little Phileni women weaving fabrics upon their primitive looms. She could sit for hours watching the flying shuttles and wishing that she could use them. Once one had seen it done, it seemed so simple and obvious— and so utterly beyond the power of the clumsy, useless limbs of her own people.

They grew very fond of the Phileni, who seemed eager to please and were pathetically proud of all their manual skills. In these new and novel surroundings, meeting fresh wonders every day, Eris seemed to be recovering from some of the scars which the War had left upon his mind. Jeryl knew, however, that there was still much damage to be undone. Sometimes, before he could hide them, she would come across raw, angry wounds in the depths of Eris's mind, and she feared that many of them—like the broken stump of his horn —would never heal. Eris had hated the War, and the manner of its ending still oppressed him. Beyond this, Jeryl knew, he was haunted by the fear that it might come again.

These troubles she often discussed with Therodimus, of whom she had now grown very fond. She still did not fully understand why he had brought them here, or what he and his followers were planning to do. Therodimus was in no hurry to explain his actions, for he wished Jeryl and Eris to draw their own conclusions as far as possible. But at last, five days after their arrival, he called them to his cave.

"You've now seen," he began, "most of the things we have to show you here. You know what the Phileni can do, and perhaps you have thought how much our own lives will be enriched once we can use the products of their skill. That was my first thought when I came here, all those years ago.

"It was an obvious and rather naïve idea, but it led to a much greater one. As I grew to know the Phileni, and found how swiftly their minds had advanced in so short a time, I realized what a fearful disadvantage our own race had always labored under. I began to wonder how much further forward *we* would have been had we the Phileni's control over the physical world. It is not a question of mere convenience, or the ability to make beautiful things like that necklace of yours, Jeryl, but something much more profound. It is the difference between ignorance and knowledge, between weakness and power.

"We have developed our minds, and our minds alone, until we can go no further. As Aretenon has told you, we have now come to a danger that threatens our entire race. We are under the shadow of the irresistible weapon against which there can be no defense.

"The solution is, quite literally, in the hands of the Phileni. We must use their skills to reshape our world, and so remove the cause of all our wars. We must go back to the beginning and re-lay the foundations of our culture. It won't be *our* culture alone, though, for we shall share it with the Phileni. They will be the hands—we the brains. Oh, I have dreamed of the world that may come, ages ahead, when even the marvels you see around you now will be considered childish toys! But not many are philosophers, and I need an argument more substantial than dreams. That final argument I believe I may have found, though I cannot yet be certain.

"I have asked you here, Eris, partly because I wanted to renew our old friendship, and partly because your word will now have far greater influence than mine. You are a hero among your own people, and the Mithraneans also will listen to you. I want you to return, taking with you some of the Phileni and their products. Show them to your people, and ask them to send their young men here to help us with our work."

There was a pause during which Jeryl could gather no hints of Eris's thoughts. Then he replied hesitantly:

"But I still don't understand. These things that the Phileni make are very pretty, and some of them may be useful to us. But how can they change us as profoundly as you seem to think?"

Therodimus sighed. Eris could not see past the present into the future that was yet to be. He had not caught, as Therodimus had done, the promise that lay beyond the busy hands and tools of the Phileni—the first faint intimations of the Machine. Perhaps he would never understand: but he could still be convinced.

Veiling his deeper thoughts, Therodimus continued:

"Perhaps some of these things are toys, Eris—but they may be more powerful than you think. Jeryl, I know, would be loath to part with hers . . . and perhaps I can find one that would convince you."

Eris was skeptical, and Jeryl could see that he was in one of his darker moods.

"I doubt it very much," he said.

"Well, I can try." Therodimus gave a whistle, and one of the Phileni came running up. There was a short exchange of conversation.

"Would you come with me, Eris? It will take some time."

Eris followed him, the others, at Therodimus' request, remaining behind. They left the large cave and went toward the row of smaller ones which the Phileni used for their various trades.

The strange whirring was sounding loudly in Eris's ears, but for a moment he could not see its cause, the light of the crude-oil lamps being too faint for his eyes. Then he made out one of the Phileni bending over a wooden table upon which something was spinning rapidly, driven by a belt from a treadle operated by another of the little creatures. He had seen the potters using a similar device, but this was different. It was shaping wood, not clay, and the potter's fingers had been replaced by a sharp metal blade from which long, thin shavings were curling out in fascinating spirals. With their huge eyes, the Phileni, who disliked full sunlight, could see perfectly in the gloom, but it was some time before Eris could discover just what was happening. Then, suddenly, he understood.

"Aretenon," said Jeryl when the others had left them, "why should the Phileni do all these things for us? Surely they're quite happy as they are?"

The question, Aretenon thought, was typical of Jeryl and would never have been asked by Eris.

"They will do anything that Therodimus says," he answered, "but even apart from that there's so much we can give them as well. When we turn our minds to their problems, we can see how to solve them in ways that would never have occurred to them. They're very eager to learn, and already we must have advanced their culture by hundreds of generations. Also, they're physically very feeble. Although we don't possess their dexterity, our strength makes possible tasks they could never attempt."

They had wandered to the edge of the river, and stood for a moment watching the unhurried waters moving down to the sea. Then Jeryl turned to go upstream, but Aretenon stopped her.

"Therodimus doesn't want us to go that way, yet," he explained. "It's just another of his little secrets. He never likes to reveal his plans until they're ready."

Slightly piqued, and distinctly curious, Jeryl obediently turned back. She would, of course, come this way again as soon as there was no one else about.

It was very peaceful here in the warm sunlight, among the pools of heat trapped by the trees. Jeryl had almost lost her fear of the forest, though she knew she would never be quite happy there.

Aretenon seemed very abstracted, and Jeryl knew that he wished to say something and was marshaling his thoughts. Presently he began to speak, with the freedom that is possible only between two people who are fond of each other but have no emotional ties.

"It is very hard, Jeryl," he began, "to turn one's back on the work of a lifetime. Once I had hoped that the great new forces we have discovered could be safely used, but now I know that is impossible, at least for many ages. Therodimus was right—we can go no further with our minds alone. Our culture has been hopelessly one-sided, though through no fault of ours. We cannot solve the fundamental problem of peace and war without a command over the physical world such as the Phileni possess—and which we hope to borrow from them.

"Perhaps there will be other great adventures here for our minds, to make us forget what we will have to abandon. We shall be able to learn something from Nature at last. What is the difference between fire and water, between wood and stone? What are the suns, and what are those millions of faint lights we see in the sky when both the suns are down? Perhaps the answers to all these questions may lie at the end of the new road along which we must travel."

He paused.

"New knowledge—new wisdom—in realms we have never dreamed of before. It may lure us away from the dangers we have encountered: for certainly nothing we can learn from Nature will ever be as great a threat as the peril we have uncovered in our own minds."

The flow of Aretenon's thoughts was suddenly interrupted. Then he said: "I think that Eris wants to see you."

Jeryl wondered why Eris had not sent the message to her: she wondered, too, at the undertone of amusement—or was it something else? —in Aretenon's mind.

There was no sign of Eris as they approached the caves, but he was waiting for them and came bounding out into the sunlight before they could reach the entrance. Then Jeryl gave an involuntary cry, and retreated a pace or two as her mate came toward her.

For Eris was whole again. Gone was the shattered stump on his forehead: it had been replaced by a new, gleaming horn no less splendid than the one that he had lost.

In a belated gesture of greeting, Eris touched horns with Aretenon. Then he was gone into the forest in great joyous leaps—but not before his mind had met Jeryl's as it had seldom done since the days before the War.

"Let him go," said Therodimus softly. "He would rather be alone. When he returns I think you will find him—different." He gave a little laugh. "The Phileni are clever, are they not? Now, perhaps, Eris will be more appreciative of their 'toys.'"

"I know I am impatient," said Therodimus, "but I am old now, and I want to see the changes begin in my own lifetime. That is why I am starting so many schemes in the hope that some at least will succeed. But this is the one, above all, in which I have put most faith."

For a moment he lost himself in his thoughts. Not one in a hundred of his own race could fully share his dream. Even Eris, though he now believed in it, did so with his heart rather than his mind. Perhaps Aretenon—the brilliant and subtle Aretenon, so desperately anxious to neutralize the powers he had brought into the world— might have glimpsed the reality. But his was of all minds the most impenetrable, save when he wished otherwise.

"You know as well as I do," continued Therodimus, as they walked upstream, "that our wars have only one cause—Food. We and the Mithraneans are trapped on this continent of ours with its limited resources, which we can do nothing to increase. Ahead of us we have always the nightmare of starvation, and for all our vaunted intelligence there has been nothing we can do about it. Oh yes, we have scraped some laborious irrigation ditches with our fore-hoofs, but how slight their help has been!

"The Phileni have discovered how to grow crops that increase the fertility of the ground many-fold. I believe that we can do the same— once we have adapted their tools for our own use. That is our first and most important task, but it is not the one on which I have set my heart. The final solution to our problem, Eris, *must be the discovery of new, virgin lands into which our people can migrate.*"

He smiled at the other's amazement.

"No, don't think I'm mad. Such lands do exist, I'm sure of it. Once I stood at the edge of the ocean and watched a great flight of birds coming inland from far out at sea. I have seen them flying outward, too, so purposefully that I was certain they were going to some other country. And I have followed them with my thoughts."

"Even if your theory is true, which it probably is," said Eris, "what use is it to us?" He gestured to the river flowing beside them. "We drown in the water, and you cannot build a rope to support us—" His thoughts suddenly faded out into a jumbled chaos of ideas.

Therodimus smiled.

"So you have guessed what I hope to do. Well, now you can see if you are right."

They had come to a level stretch of bank, upon which a group of Phileni were busily at work, under the supervision of some of Therodimus' assistants. Lying at the water's edge was a strange object which, Eris realized, was made of many tree-trunks joined together by ropes.

They watched in fascination as the orderly tumult reached its climax. There was a great pulling and pushing, and the raft moved ponderously into the water with a mighty splash. The spray had scarcely ceased to fall when a young Mithranean leaped from the bank and began to dance gleefully upon the logs, which were now tugging at the moorings as if eager to break away and follow the river down to the sea. A moment later he had been joined by others, rejoicing in their mastery of a new element. The little Phileni, unable to make the leap, stood watching patiently on the bank while their masters enjoyed themselves.

There was an exhilaration about the scene that no one could miss, though perhaps few of those present realized that they were at a turning point in history. Only Therodimus stood a little apart from the rest, lost in his own thoughts. This primitive raft, he knew, was merely a beginning. It must be tested upon the river, then along the shores of the ocean. The work would take years, and he was never likely to see the first voyagers returning from those fabulous lands whose existence was still no more than a guess. But what had been begun, others would finish.

Overhead, a flight of birds was passing across the forest. Therodimus watched them go, envying their freedom to move at will over land and sea. He had begun the conquest of the water for his race, but that the skies might one day be theirs also was beyond even his imagination.

Aretenon, Jeryl, and the rest of the expedition had already crossed the river when Eris said good-bye to Therodimus. This time they had crossed without a drop of water touching their bodies, for the raft had come downstream and was performing valuable duties as a ferry. A new and much improved model was already under construction, as it was painfully obvious that the prototype was not exactly seaworthy. These initial difficulties would be quickly overcome by designers who, even if they were forced to work with Stone Age tools, could handle with ease the mathematics of metacenters, buoyancies, and advanced hydrodynamics.

"Your task won't be a simple one," said Therodimus, "for you cannot show your people all the things you have seen here. At first you must be content to sow the seed, to arouse interest and curiosity—particularly among the young, who will come here to learn more. Perhaps you will meet opposition: I expect so. But every time you return to us, we shall have new things to show you to strengthen your arguments."

They touched horns: then Eris was gone, taking with him the knowledge that was to change the world—so slowly at first, then ever more swiftly. Once the barriers were down, once the Mithraneans and the Atheleni had been given the simple tools which they could fasten to their fore-limbs and use unaided, progress would be swift. But for the present they must rely on the Phileni for everything: and there were so few of them.

Therodimus was well content. Only in one respect was he disappointed, for he had hoped that Eris, who had always been his favorite, might also be his successor. The Eris who was now returning to his own people was no longer self-obsessed or embittered, for he had a mission and hope for the future. But he lacked the keen, far-ranging vision that was needed here: it would be Aretenon who must continue what he had begun. Still, that could not be helped, and there was no need yet to think of such matters. Therodimus was very old, but he knew that he would be meeting Eris many times again here by the river at the entrance to his land.

The ferry was gone now, and though he had expected it, Eris stopped, amazed at the great span of the bridge, swaying slightly in the breeze. Its execution did not quite match its design—a good deal of mathematics had gone into its parabolic suspension—but it was still the first great engineering feat in history. Constructed entirely of wood and rope though it was, it forecast the shape of the metal giants to come.

Eris paused in the middle. He could see smoke rising from the shipyards facing the ocean, and thought he could just glimpse the masts of some of the new vessels that were being built for coastal trade. It was hard to believe that when he had first crossed this river he had been dragged over, dangling from a rope.

Aretenon was waiting for them on the far bank. He moved rather slowly now, but his eyes were still bright with the old, eager intelligence. He greeted Eris warmly.

"I'm glad you could come now. You're just in time."

That, Eris knew, could mean only one thing.

"The ships are back?"

"Almost: they were sighted an hour ago, out on the horizon. They should be here at any moment, and then we shall know the truth at last, after all these years. If only—"

His thoughts faded out, but Eris could continue them. They had come to the great pyramid of stones beneath which Therodimus lay —Therodimus, whose brain was behind everything they saw, but who could never learn now if his most cherished dream was true or not.

There was a storm coming up from the ocean, and they hurried along the new road that skirted the river's edge. Small boats of a kind that Eris had not seen before went past them occasionally, operated by Atheleni or Mithraneans with wooden paddles strapped to their fore-limbs. It always gave Eris great pleasure to see such new conquests, such new liberations of his people from their age-old chains. Yet sometimes they reminded him of children who had suddenly been let loose into a wonderful new world, full of exciting and interesting things that must be done, whether they were likely to be useful or not. However, anything that promised to make his race into better sailors was more than useful. In the last decade Eris had discovered that pure intelligence was sometimes not enough: there were skills that could not be acquired by any amount of mental effort. Though his people had largely overcome their fear of water, they were still quite incompetent on the ocean, and the Phileni had therefore become the first navigators of the world.

Jeryl looked nervously around her as the first peal of thunder came rolling in from the sea. She was still wearing the necklace that Therodimus had given her so long ago: but it was by no means the only ornament she carried now.

"I hope the ships will be safe," she said anxiously.

"There's not much wind, and they will have ridden out much worse storms than this," Aretenon reassured her, as they entered his cave. Eris and Jeryl looked round with eager interest to see what new wonders the Phileni had made during their absence: but if there were any they had been hidden away, as usual, until Aretenon was ready to show them. He was still rather childishly fond of such little surprises and mysteries.

There was an air of absent-mindedness about the meeting that would have puzzled an onlooker ignorant of its cause. As Eris talked of all the changes in the outer world, of the success of the new Phileni settlements, and of the steady growth of agriculture among his people, Aretenon listened with only half his mind. His thoughts, and those of his friends, were far out at sea, meeting the on-coming ships, which might be bringing the greatest news their world had ever received.

As Eris finished his report, Aretenon rose to his feet and began to move restlessly around the chamber.

"You have done better than we dared to hope at the beginning. At least there has been no war for a generation, and our food supply is ahead of the population for the first time in history—thanks to our new agricultural techniques."

Aretenon glanced at the furnishings of his chamber, recalling with an effort the fact that in his own youth almost everything he saw would have appeared impossible or even meaningless to him. Not even the simplest of tools had existed then, at least in the knowledge of his people. Now there were ships and bridges and houses—and these were only the beginning.

"I am well satisfied," he said. "We have, as we planned, diverted the whole stream of our culture, turning it away from the dangers that lay ahead. The powers that made the Madness possible will soon be forgotten: only a handful of us still know of them, and we will take our secrets with us. Perhaps when our descendants rediscover them they will be wise enough to use them properly. But we have uncovered so many new wonders that it may be a thousand generations before we turn again to look into our own minds and to tamper with the forces locked within them."

The mouth of the cave was illuminated by a sudden flash of lightning. The storm was coming nearer, though it was still some miles away. Rain was beginning to fall in large, angry drops from the leaden sky.

"While we're waiting for the ships," said Aretenon rather abruptly, "come into the next cave and see some of the new things we have to show you since your last visit."

It was a strange collection. Side by side on the same bench were tools and inventions which in other cultures had been separated by thousands of years of time. The Stone Age was past: bronze and iron had come, and already the first crude scientific instruments had been built for experiments that were driving back the frontiers of the unknown. A primitive retort spoke of the beginnings of chemistry, and by its side were the first lenses that the world had seen—waiting to reveal the unsuspected universes of the infinitely small and the infinitely great.

The storm was upon them as Aretenon's description of these new wonders drew to a close. From time to time he had glanced nervously at the mouth of the cave, as if awaiting a messenger from the harbor, but they had remained undisturbed save by the occasional crash of thunder.

"I've shown you everything of importance," he said, "but here's something that may amuse you while we're waiting. As I said, we've sent expeditions everywhere to collect and classify all the rocks they can, in the hope of finding useful minerals. One of them brought back this."

He extinguished the lights and the cave became completely dark.

"It will be some time before your eyes grow sensitive enough to see it," Aretenon warned. "Just look over there in that corner."

Eris strained his eyes into the darkness. At first he could see nothing: then, slowly, a glimmering blue light became faintly visible. It was so vague and diffuse that he could not focus his eyes upon it, and he automatically moved forward.

"I shouldn't go too near," advised Aretenon. "It seems to be a perfectly ordinary mineral, but the Phileni who found it and carried it here got some very strange burns from handling it. Yet it's quite cold to the touch. One day we'll learn its secret: but I don't suppose it's anything at all important."

A vast curtain of sheet-lightning split the sky, and for a moment the reflected glare lighted up the cave, pinning weird shadows against the walls. At the same moment one of the Phileni staggered into the entrance and called something to Aretenon in his thin, reedy voice. He gave a great shout of triumph, as one of his ancestors might have done on some ancient battlefield: then his thoughts came crashing into Eris's mind.

"Land! They've found land—a whole new continent waiting for us!"

Eris felt the sense of triumph and victory well up within him like water bursting from a spring. Clear ahead now into the future lay the new, the glorious road along which their children would travel, mastering the world and all its secrets as they went. The vision of Therodimus was at last sharp and brilliant before his eyes.

He felt for the mind of Jeryl, so that she could share his joy—and found that it was closed to him. Leaning toward her in the darkness, he could sense that she was still staring into the depths of the cave, as if she had never heard the wonderful news, and could not tear her eyes away from the enigmatic glow.

Out of the night came the roar of the belated thunder as it raced across the sky. Eris felt Jeryl tremble beside him, and sent out his thoughts to comfort her.

"Don't let the thunder frighten you," he said gently. "What is there to fear now?"

"I do not know," replied Jeryl. "I am frightened—but not of the thunder. Oh, Eris, it is a wonderful thing we have done, and I wish that Therodimus could be here to see it. But where will it lead in the end—this new road of ours?"

Out of the past, the words that Aretenon had once spoken had risen up to haunt her. She remembered their walk by the river, long ago, when he had talked of his hopes and had asked: "Certainly nothing we can learn from Nature will ever be as great a threat as the peril we have uncovered in our own minds." Now the words seemed to mock her and to cast a shadow over the golden future: but why, she could not say.

Alone, perhaps, of all the races in the Universe, her people had reached the second crossroads—and had never passed the first. Now they must go along the road that they had missed, and must face the challenge at its end—the challenge from which, this time, they could not escape.

In the darkness, the faint glow of dying atoms burned unwavering in the rock. It would still be burning there, scarcely dimmed, when Jeryl and Eris had been dust for centuries. It would be only a little fainter when the civilization they were building had at last unlocked its secrets.

Part IV

THE SANDS OF MARS

ONE

"So this is the first time you've been upstairs?" said the pilot, leaning back idly in his seat so that it rocked to and fro in the gimbals. He clasped his hands behind his neck in a nonchalant manner that did nothing to reassure his passenger.

"Yes," said Martin Gibson, never taking his eyes from the chronometer as it ticked away the seconds.

"I thought so. You never got it quite right in your stories—all that nonsense about fainting under the acceleration. Why must people write such stuff? It's bad for business."

"I'm sorry," Gibson replied. "But I think you must be referring to my earlier stories. Space-travel hadn't got started then, and I had to use my imagination."

"Maybe," said the pilot grudgingly. (He wasn't paying the slightest attention to the instruments, and take-off was only two minutes away.) "It must be funny, I suppose, for this to be happening to you, after writing about it so often."

The adjective, thought Gibson, was hardly the one he would have used himself, but he saw the other's point of view. Dozens of his heroes—and villains—had gazed hypnotised at remorseless second-hands, waiting for the rockets to hurl them into infinity. And now—as it always did if one waited long enough—the reality had caught up with the fiction. The same moment lay only ninety seconds in his own future. Yes, it *was* funny, a beautiful case of poetic justice.

The pilot glanced at him, read his feelings, and grinned cheerfully. "Don't let your own stories scare you. Why, I once took off standing up, just for a bet, though it was a damn silly thing to do."

"I'm not scared," Gibson replied with unnecessary emphasis.

"Hmmm," said the pilot, condescending to glance at the clock. The second-hand had one more circuit to go. "Then I shouldn't hold on to the seat like that. It's only beryl-manganese; you might bend it."

Sheepishly, Gibson relaxed. He knew that he was building up synthetic responses to the situation, but they seemed none the less real for all that.

"Of course," said the pilot, still at ease but now, Gibson noticed, keeping his eyes fixed on the instrument panel, "it wouldn't be very comfortable if it lasted more than a few minutes—ah, there go the fuel pumps. Don't worry when the vertical starts doing funny things, but let the seat swing where it likes. Shut your eyes if that helps at all. (Hear the igniter jets start then?) We take about ten seconds to build up to full thrust—there's really nothing to it, apart from the noise. You just have to put up with that. I SAID, YOU JUST HAVE TO PUT UP WITH THAT!"

But Martin Gibson was doing nothing of the sort. He had already slipped gracefully into unconsciousness at an acceleration that had not yet exceeded that of a high-speed elevator.

He revived a few minutes and a thousand kilometres* later, feeling quite ashamed of himself. A beam of sunlight was shining full on his face, and he realised that the protective shutter on the outer hull must have slid aside. Although brilliant, the light was not as intoler-

---

* The metric system is used throughout this account of space-travel. This decimal system is based upon the metre equalling 39.37 inches. Thus a kilometre would be slightly over one-half mile (0.62 mi.).

ably fierce as he would have expected; then he saw that only a fraction of the full intensity was filtering through the deeply tinted glass.

He looked at the pilot, hunched over his instrument board and busily writing up the log. Everything was very quiet, but from time to time there would come curiously muffled reports—almost miniature explosions—that Gibson found disconcerting. He coughed gently to announce his return to consciousness, and asked the pilot what they were.

"Thermal contraction in the motors," he replied briefly. "They've been running round five thousand degrees and cool mighty fast. You feeling all right now?"

"I'm fine," Gibson answered, and meant it. "Shall I get up?"

Psychologically, he had hit the bottom and bounced back. It was a very unstable position, though he did not realise it.

"If you like," said the pilot doubtfully. "But be careful—hang on to something solid."

Gibson felt a wonderful sense of exhilaration. The moment he had waited for all his life had come. He was in space! It was too bad that he'd missed the take-off, but he'd gloss that part over when he wrote it up.

From a thousand kilometres away, Earth was still very large—and something of a disappointment. The reason was quickly obvious. He had seen so many hundreds of rocket photographs and films that the surprise had been spoilt; he knew exactly what to expect. There were the inevitable moving bands of cloud on their slow march round the world. At the centre of the disc, the divisions between land and sea were sharply defined, and an infinite amount of minute detail was visible, but towards the horizon everything was lost in the thickening haze. Even in the cone of clear vision vertically beneath him, most of the features were unrecognisable and therefore meaningless. No doubt a meteorologist would have gone into transports of delight at the animated weather-map displayed below—but most of the meteorologists were up in the space stations, anyway, where they had an even better view. Gibson soon grew tired of searching for cities and other works of man. It was chastening to think that all the thousands of years of human civilisation had produced no appreciable change in the panorama below.

Then Gibson began to look for the stars, and met his second disappointment. They were there, hundreds of them, but pale and wan, mere ghosts of the blinding myriads he had expected to find. The dark glass of the port was to blame; in subduing the sun, it had robbed the stars of all their glory.

Gibson felt a vague annoyance. Only one thing had turned out quite as expected. The sensation of floating in mid-air, of being able to propel oneself from wall to wall at the touch of a finger, was just as delightful as he had hoped—though the quarters were too cramped for any ambitious experiments. Weightlessness was an enchanting, a fairy-like state, now that there were drugs to immobilise the balance organs and space-sickness was a thing of the past. He was glad of that. How his heroes had suffered! (His heroines too, presumably, but one never mentioned that.) He remembered Robin Blake's first flight, in the original version of "Martian Dust." When he'd written that, he had been heavily under the influence of D. H. Lawrence. (It would be interesting, one day, to make a list of the authors who *hadn't* influenced him at one time or another.)

There was no doubt that Lawrence was magnificent at describing physical sensations, and quite deliberately Gibson had set out to defeat him on his own ground. He had devoted a whole chapter to space-sickness, describing every symptom from the queasy premonitions that could sometimes be willed aside, the subterranean upheavals that even the most optimistic could no longer ignore, the volcanic cataclysms of the final stages, and the ultimate, merciful exhaustion.

The chapter had been a masterpiece of stark realism. It was too bad that his publishers, with an eye on a squeamish "Book of the Month" Club, had insisted on removing it. He had put a lot of work into that chapter; while he was writing it, he had really *lived* those sensations. Even now—

"It's very puzzling," said the M.O. thoughtfully as the now quiescent author was propelled through the airlock. "He's passed his medical tests O.K., and of course he'll have had the usual injections before leaving Earth. It must be psychosomatic."

"I don't care what it is," complained the pilot bitterly, as he followed the cortege into the heart of Space Station One. "All I want to know is—who's going to clean up my ship?"

No one seemed inclined to answer this heart-felt question, least of all Martin Gibson, who was only vaguely conscious of white walls drifting by his field of vision. Then, slowly, there was a sensation of increasing weight, and a warm, caressing glow began to steal through his limbs. Presently he became fully aware of his surroundings. He was in a hospital ward, and a battery of infrared lamps was bathing him with a glorious, enervating warmth, that sank through his flesh to the very bones.

"Well?" said the medical officer presently.

Gibson grinned feebly.

"I'm sorry about this. Is it going to happen again?"

"I don't know how it happened the first time. It's very unusual; the drugs we have now are supposed to be infallible."

"I think it was my own fault," said Gibson apologetically. "You see, I've got a rather powerful imagination, and I started thinking about the symptoms of space-sickness—in quite an objective sort of way, of course—but before I knew what had happened——"

"Well, just stop it!" ordered the doctor sharply. "Or we'll have to send you right back to Earth. You can't do this sort of thing if you're going to Mars. There wouldn't be much left of you after three months."

A shudder passed through Gibson's tortured frame. But he was rapidly recovering, and already the nightmare of the last hour was fading into the past.

"I'll be O.K.," he said. "Let me out of this muffle-furnace before I cook."

A little unsteadily, he got to his feet. It seemed strange, here in space, to have normal weight again. Then he remembered that Station One was spinning on its axis, and the living quarters were built around the outer walls so that centrifugal force could give the illusion of gravity.

The great adventure, he thought ruefully, hadn't started at all well. But he was determined not to be sent home in disgrace. It was not merely a question of his own pride: the effect on his public and his reputation would be deplorable. He winced as he visualised the headlines: "GIBSON GROUNDED! SPACE-SICKNESS ROUTS AUTHOR-ASTRONAUT." Even the staid literary weeklies would pull his leg, and as for "Time" —no, it was unthinkable!

"It's lucky," said the M.O., "that we've got twelve hours before the ship leaves. I'll take you into the zero-gravity section and see how you manage there, before I give you a clean bill of health."

Gibson also thought that was a good idea. He had always regarded himself as fairly fit, and until now it had never seriously occurred to him that this journey might be not merely uncomfortable but actually dangerous. You could laugh at space-sickness—when you'd never experienced it yourself. Afterwards, it seemed a very different matter.

The Inner Station—"Space Station One," as it was usually called—was just over two thousand kilometres from Earth, circling the planet every two hours. It had been Man's first stepping-stone to the stars, and though it was no longer technically necessary for spaceflight, its presence had a profound effect on the economics of interplanetary travel. All journeys to the Moon or the planets started from here; the unwieldy atomic ships floated alongside this outpost of Earth while the cargoes from the parent world were loaded into their holds. A ferry service of chemically fuelled rockets linked the station to the planet beneath, for by law no atomic drive unit was allowed to operate within a thousand kilometres of the Earth's surface. Even this safety margin was felt by many to be inadequate, for the radioactive blast of a nuclear propulsion unit could cover that distance in less than a minute.

Space Station One had grown with the passing years, by a process of accretion, until its original designers would never have recognised it. Around the central spherical core had accumulated observatories, communications labs with fantastic aerial systems, and mazes of scientific equipment which only a specialist could identify. But despite all these additions, the main function of the artificial moon was still that of refuelling the little ships with which Man was challenging the immense loneliness of the Solar System.

"Quite sure you're feeling O.K. now?" asked the doctor as Gibson experimented with his feet.

"I think so," he replied, unwilling to commit himself.

"Then come along to the reception room and we'll get you a drink —a nice hot drink," he added, to prevent any misunderstanding. "You can sit there and read the paper for half an hour before we decide what to do with you."

It seemed to Gibson that anticlimax was being piled on anticlimax. He was two thousand kilometres from Earth, with the stars all around him; yet here he was forced to sit sipping sweet tea—tea!—in what might have been an ordinary dentist's waiting-room. There were no windows, presumably because the sight of the rapidly revolving heavens might have undone the good work of the medical staff. The only way of passing the time was to skim through piles of magazines which he'd already seen, and which were difficult to handle as they were ultra-lightweight editions apparently printed on cigarette paper. Fortunately he found a very old copy of "Argosy" containing a story he had written so long ago that he had completely forgotten the ending, and this kept him happy until the doctor returned.

"Your pulse seems normal," said the M.O. grudgingly. "We'll take you along to the zero-gravity chamber. Just follow me and don't be surprised at anything that happens."

With this cryptic remark he led Gibson out into a wide, brightly lit corridor that seemed to curve upwards in both directions away from the point at which he was standing. Gibson had no time to examine this phenomenon, for the doctor slid open a side door and started up a flight of metal stairs. Gibson followed automatically for a few paces, then realised just what lay ahead of him and stopped with an involuntary cry of amazement.

Immediately beneath his feet, the slope of the stairway was a reasonable forty-five degrees, but it rapidly became steeper until only a dozen metres ahead the steps were rising vertically. Thereafter—and it was a sight that might have unnerved anyone coming across it for the first time—the increase of gradient continued remorselessly until the steps began to overhang and at last passed out of sight above and *behind* him.

Hearing his exclamation, the doctor looked back and gave a reassuring laugh.

"You mustn't always believe your eyes," he said. "Come along and see how easy it is."

Reluctantly Gibson followed, and as he did so he became aware that two very peculiar things were happening. In the first place, he was gradually becoming lighter; in the second, despite the obvious steepening of the stairway, the slope beneath his feet remained at a constant forty-five degrees. The vertical direction itself, in fact, was slowly tilting as he moved forward, so that despite its increasing curvature the gradient of the stairway never altered.

It did not take Gibson long to arrive at the explanation. All the apparent gravity was due to the centrifugal force produced as the station spun slowly on its axis, and as he approached the centre the force was diminishing to zero. The stairway itself was winding in towards the axis along some sort of spiral—once he'd have known its mathematical name—so that despite the radial gravity field the slope underfoot remained constant. It was the sort of thing that people who lived in space stations must get accustomed to quickly enough; presumably when they returned to Earth the sight of a normal stairway would be equally unsettling.

At the end of the stairs there was no longer any real sense of "up" or "down." They were in a long cylindrical room, criss-crossed with ropes but otherwise empty, and at its far end a shaft of sunlight came blasting through an observation port. As Gibson watched, the beam moved steadily across the metal walls like a questing searchlight, was momentarily eclipsed, then blazed out again from another window. It was the first indication Gibson's senses had given him of the fact that the station was really spinning on its axis, and he timed the rotation roughly by noting how long the sunlight took to return to its original position. The "day" of this little artificial world was less than ten seconds; that was sufficient to give a sensation of normal gravity at its outer walls.

Gibson felt rather like a spider in its web as he followed the doctor hand-over-hand along the guide ropes, towing himself effortlessly through the air until they came to the observation post. They were, he saw, at the end of a sort of chimney jutting out along the axis of the station, so that they were well clear of its equipment and apparatus and had an almost unrestricted view of the stars.

"I'll leave you here for a while," said the doctor. "There's plenty to look at, and you should be quite happy. If not—well, remember there's normal gravity at the bottom of those stairs!"

Yes, thought Gibson; *and* a return trip to Earth by the next rocket as well. But he was determined to pass the test and to get a clean bill of health.

It was quite impossible to realise that the space station itself was rotating, and not the framework of sun and stars: to believe otherwise required an act of faith, a conscious effort of will. The stars were moving so quickly that only the brighter ones were clearly visible and the sun, when Gibson allowed himself to glance at it out of the corner of his eye, was a golden comet that crossed the sky every five seconds. With this fantastic speeding up of the natural order of events, it was easy to see how ancient man had refused to believe that his own solid earth was rotating, and had attributed all movement to the turning celestial sphere.

Partly occulted by the bulk of the station, the Earth was a great crescent spanning half the sky. It was slowly waxing as the station raced along on its globe-encircling orbit; in some forty minutes it would be full, and an hour after that would be totally invisible, a black shield eclipsing the sun while the station passed through its cone of shadow. The Earth would go through all its phases—from new to full and back again—in just two hours. The sense of time became distorted as one thought of these things; the familiar divisions of day and night, of months and seasons, had no meaning here.

About a kilometre from the station, moving with it in its orbit but not at the moment connected to it in any way, were the three spaceships that happened to be "in dock" at the moment. One was the tiny arrowhead of the rocket that had brought him, at such expense and such discomfort, up from Earth an hour ago. The second was a lunar-bound freighter of, he guessed, about a thousand tons gross. And the third, of course, was the *Ares*, almost dazzling in the splendour of her new aluminium paint.

Gibson had never become reconciled to the loss of the sleek, streamlined spaceships which had been the dream of the early twentieth century. The glittering dumb-bell hanging against the stars was not *his* idea of a space-liner; though the world had accepted it, he had not. Of course, he knew the familiar arguments—there was no need for streamlining in a ship that never entered an atmosphere, and therefore the design was dictated purely by structural and power-plant considerations. Since the violently radioactive drive-unit had to be as far away from the crew quarters as possible, the double-sphere and long connecting tube was the simplest solution.

It was also, Gibson thought, the ugliest; but that hardly mattered since the *Ares* would spend practically all her life in deep space where the only spectators were the stars. Presumably she was already fuelled and merely waiting for the precisely calculated moment when her motors would burst into life, and she would pull away out of the orbit in which she was circling and had hitherto spent all her existence, to swing into the long hyperbola that led to Mars.

When that happened, he would be aboard, launched at last upon the adventure he had never really believed would come to him.

TWO

The captain's office aboard the *Ares* was not designed to hold more than three men when gravity was acting, but there was plenty of room for six while the ship was in a free orbit and one could stand on walls or ceiling according to taste. All except one of the group clustered at surrealist angles around Captain Norden had been in space before and knew what was expected of them, but this was no ordinary briefing. The maiden flight of a new spaceship is always an occasion and the *Ares* was the first of her line—the first, indeed, of all spaceships ever to be built primarily for passengers and not for freight. When she was fully commissioned, she would carry a crew of thirty and a hundred and fifty passengers in somewhat spartan comfort. On her first voyage, however, the proportions were almost reversed and at the moment her crew of six was waiting for the single passenger to come aboard.

"I'm still not quite clear," said Owen Bradley, the electronics officer, "what we are supposed to do with the fellow when we've got him. Whose bright idea was this, anyway?"

"I was coming to that," said Captain Norden, running his hands over where his magnificent blond hair had been only a few days before. (Spaceships seldom carry professional barbers, and though there are always plenty of eager amateurs one prefers to put off the evil day as long as possible.) "You all know of Mr. Gibson, of course."

This remark produced a chorus of replies, not all of them respectful.

"I think his stories stink," said Dr. Scott. "The later ones, anyway. 'Martian Dust' wasn't bad, but of course it's completely dated now."

"Nonsense!" snorted astrogator Mackay. "The last stories are much the best, now that Gibson's got interested in fundamentals and has cut out the blood and thunder."

This outburst from the mild little Scot was most uncharacteristic. Before anyone else could join in, Captain Norden interrupted.

"We're not here to discuss literary criticism, if you don't mind. There'll be plenty of time for that later. But there are one or two points the Corporation wants me to make clear before we begin. Mr. Gibson is a very important man—a distinguished guest—and he's been invited to come on this trip so that he can write a book about it later. It's not just a publicity stunt." ("Of course not!" interjected Bradley, with heavy sarcasm.) "But naturally the Corporation hopes that future clients won't be—er discouraged by what they read. Apart from that, we *are* making history; our maiden voyage ought to be recorded properly. So try and behave like gentlemen for a while; Gibson's book will probably sell half a million copies, and your future reputations may depend on your behaviour these next three months!"

"That sounds dangerously like blackmail to me," said Bradley.

"Take it that way if you please," continued Norden cheerfully. "Of course, I'll explain to Gibson that he can't expect the service that will be provided later when we've got stewards and cooks and Lord knows what. He'll understand that, and won't expect breakfast in bed every morning."

"Will he help with the washing-up?" asked someone with a practical turn of mind.

Before Norden could deal with this problem in social etiquette a sudden buzzing came from the communications panel, and a voice began to call from the speaker grille.

"Station One calling *Ares*—your passenger's coming over."

Norden flipped a switch and replied, "O.K.—we're ready." Then he turned to the crew.

"With all these hair-cuts around, the poor chap will think it's graduation day at Alcatraz. Go and meet him, Jimmy, and help him through the airlock when the tender couples up."

Martin Gibson was still feeling somewhat exhilarated at having surmounted his first major obstacle—the M.O. at Space Station One. The loss of gravity on leaving the station and crossing to the *Ares* in the tiny, compressed-air driven tender had scarcely bothered him at all, but the sight that met his eyes when he entered Captain Norden's cabin caused him a momentary relapse. Even when there was no gravity, one liked to pretend that *some* direction was "down," and it seemed natural to assume that the surface on which chairs and table were bolted was the floor. Unfortunately the majority decision seemed otherwise, for two members of the crew were hanging like stalactites from the "ceiling," while two more were relaxed at quite arbitrary angles in mid-air. Only the Captain was, according to Gibson's ideas, the right way up. To make matters worse, their shaven heads gave these normally quite presentable men a faintly sinister appearance, so that the whole tableau looked like a family reunion at Castle Dracula.

There was a brief pause while the crew analysed Gibson. They all recognised the novelist at once; his face had been familiar to the public ever since his first best-seller, *Thunder in the Dawn*, had appeared nearly twenty years ago. He was a chubby yet sharp-featured little man, still on the right side of forty-five, and when he spoke his voice was surprisingly deep and resonant.

"This," said Captain Norden, working round the cabin from left to right, "is my engineer, Lieutenant Hilton. This is Dr. Mackay, our navigator—only a Ph.D., not a *real* doctor, like Dr. Scott here. Lieutenant Bradley is Electronics Officer, and Jimmy Spencer, who met you at the airlock, is our supernumerary and hopes to be Captain when he grows up."

Gibson looked round the little group with some surprise. There were so few of them—five men and a boy! His face must have revealed his thoughts, for Captain Norden laughed and continued.

"Not many of us, are there? But you must remember that this ship is almost automatic—and besides, nothing ever happens in space. When we start the regular passenger run, there'll be a crew of thirty. On this trip, we're making up the weight in cargo, so we're really travelling as a fast freighter."

Gibson looked carefully at the men who would be his only companions for the next three months. His first reaction (he always distrusted first reactions, but was at pains to note them) was one of astonishment that they seemed so ordinary—when one made allowance for such superficial matters as their odd attitudes and temporary baldness. There was no way of guessing that they belonged to a profession more romantic than any that the world had known since the last cowboys traded in their broncos for helicopters.

At a signal which Gibson did not intercept, the others took their leave by launching themselves with fascinatingly effortless precision through the open doorway. Captain Norden settled down in his seat again and offered Gibson a cigarette. The author accepted it doubtfully.

"You don't mind smoking?" he asked. "Doesn't it waste oxygen?"

"There'd be a mutiny," laughed Norden, "if I had to ban smoking for three months. In any case, the oxygen consumption's negligible."

Captain Norden, thought Gibson a little ruefully, was not fitting at all well into the expected pattern. The skipper of a space-liner, according to the best—or at least the most popular—literary tradition, should be a grizzled, keen-eyed veteran who had spent half his life in the ether and could navigate across the Solar System by the seat of his pants, thanks to his uncanny knowledge of the space-ways. He must also be a martinet; when he gave orders, his officers must jump to attention (not an easy thing under zero gravity), salute smartly, and depart at the double.

Instead, the captain of the *Ares* was certainly less than forty, and might have been taken for a successful business executive. As for being a martinet—so far Gibson had detected no signs of discipline whatsoever. This impression, he realised later, was not strictly accurate. The only discipline aboard the *Ares* was entirely self-imposed; that was the only form possible among the type of men who composed her crew.

"So you've never been in space before," said Norden, looking thoughtfully at his passenger.

"I'm afraid not. I made several attempts to get on the lunar run, but it's absolutely impossible unless you're on official business. It's a pity that space-travel's still so infernally expensive."

Norden smiled.

"We hope the *Ares* will do something to change that. I must say," he added, "that you seem to have managed to write quite a lot about the subject with ah—the minimum of practical experience."

"Oh, that!" said Gibson airily, with what he hoped was a light laugh. "It's a common delusion that authors must have experienced everything they describe in their books. I read all I could about space-travel when I was younger and did my best to get the local colour right. Don't forget that all my interplanetary novels were written in the early days—I've hardly touched the subject in the last few years. It's rather surprising that people still associate my name with it."

Norden wondered how much of this modesty was assumed. Gibson must know perfectly well that it was his space-travel novels that had made him famous—and had prompted the Corporation to invite him on this trip. The whole situation, Norden realised, had some highly entertaining possibilities. But they would have to wait; in the meantime he must explain to this landlubber the routine of life aboard the private world of the *Ares*.

"We keep normal Earth-time—Greenwich Meridian—aboard the ship and everything shuts down at 'night.' There are no watches, as there used to be in the old days; the instruments can take over when we're sleeping, so we aren't on continuous duty. That's one reason why we can manage with such a small crew. On this trip, as there's plenty of space, we've all got separate cabins. Yours is a regular passenger stateroom; the only one that's fitted up, as it happens. I think you'll find it comfortable. Is all your cargo aboard? How much did they let you take?"

"A hundred kilos. It's in the airlock."

"A hundred kilos?" Norden managed to repress his amazement.

The fellow must be emigrating—taking all his family heirlooms with him. Norden had the true astronaut's horror of surplus mass, and did not doubt that Gibson was carrying a lot of unnecessary rubbish. However, if the Corporation had O.K.'d it, and the authorised load wasn't exceeded, he had nothing to complain about.

"I'll get Jimmy to take you to your room. He's our odd-job man for this trip, working his passage and learning something about space-flight. Most of us start that way, signing up for the lunar run during college vacations. Jimmy's quite a bright lad—he's already got his Bachelor's degree."

By now Gibson was beginning to take it quite for granted that the cabin-boy would be a college graduate. He followed Jimmy—who seemed somewhat overawed by his presence—to the passengers' quarters.

The stateroom was small, but beautifully planned and designed in excellent taste. Ingenious lighting and mirror-faced walls made it seem much larger than it really was, and the pivoted bed could be reversed during the "day" to act as a table. There were very few reminders of the absence of gravity; everything had been done to make the traveller feel at home.

For the next hour Gibson sorted out his belongings and experimented with the room's gadgets and controls. The device that pleased him most was a shaving mirror which, when a button was pressed, transformed itself into a porthole looking out on the stars. He wondered just how it was done.

At last everything was stowed away where he could find it; there was absolutely nothing else for him to do. He lay down on the bed and buckled the elastic belts around his chest and thighs. The illusion of weight was not very convincing, but it was better than nothing and did give some sense of a vertical direction.

Lying at peace in the bright little room that would be his world for the next hundred days, he could forget the disappointments and petty annoyances that had marred his departure from Earth. There was nothing to worry about now; for the first time in almost as long as he could remember, he had given his future entirely into the keeping of others. Engagements, lecture appointments, deadlines—all these things he had left behind on Earth. The sense of blissful relaxation was too good to last, but he would let his mind savour it while he could.

A series of apologetic knocks on the cabin door roused Gibson from sleep an indeterminate time later. For a moment he did not realise where he was; then full consciousness came back; he unclipped the retaining straps and thrust himself off the bed. As his movements were still poorly co-ordinated he had to make a carom off the nominal ceiling before reaching the door.

Jimmy Spencer stood there, slightly out of breath.

"Captain's compliments, sir, and would you like to come and see the take-off?"

"I certainly would," said Gibson. "Wait until I get my camera."

He reappeared a moment later carrying a brand-new Leica XXA, at which Jimmy stared with undisguised envy, and festooned with auxiliary lenses and exposure meters. Despite these handicaps, they quickly reached the observation gallery, which ran like a circular belt around the body of the *Ares*.

For the first time Gibson saw the stars in their full glory, no longer dimmed either by atmosphere or by darkened glass, for he was on the night side of the ship and the sun-filters had been drawn aside. The *Ares*, unlike the space-station, was not turning on her axis but was held in the rigid reference system of her gyroscopes so that the stars were fixed and motionless in her skies.

As he gazed on the glory he had so often, and so vainly, tried to describe in his books, Gibson found it very hard to analyse his emotions—and he hated to waste an emotion that might profitably be employed in print. Oddly enough neither the brightness nor the sheer numbers of the stars made the greatest impression on his mind. He had seen skies little inferior to this from the tops of mountains on Earth, or from the observation decks of stratoliners; but never before had he felt so vividly the sense that the stars were all around him, down to the horizon he no longer possessed, and even below, under his very feet.

Space Station One was a complicated, brightly polished toy floating in nothingness a few metres beyond the port. There was no way in which its distance or size could be judged, for there was nothing familiar about its shape, and the sense of perspective seemed to have failed. Earth and Sun were both invisible, hidden behind the body of the ship.

Startlingly close, a disembodied voice came suddenly from a hidden speaker.

"One hundred seconds to firing. Please take your positions."

Gibson automatically tensed himself and turned to Jimmy for advice. Before he could frame any questions, his guide said hastily, "I must get back on duty," and disappeared in a graceful power-dive, leaving Gibson alone with his thoughts.

The next minute and a half passed with remarkable slowness, punctuated though it was with frequent time-checks from the speakers. Gibson wondered who the announcer was; it did not sound like Norden's voice, and probably it was merely a recording, operated by the automatic circuit which must now have taken over control of the ship.

"Twenty seconds to go. Thrust will take about ten seconds to build up."

"Ten seconds to go."

"Five seconds, four, three, two, one——"

Very gently, something took hold of Gibson and slid him down the curving side of the porthole-studded wall on to what had suddenly become the floor. It was hard to realise that up and down had returned once more, harder still to connect their reappearance with that distant, attenuated thunder that had broken in upon the silence of the ship. Far away in the second sphere that was the other half of the *Ares*, in that mysterious, forbidden world of dying atoms and automatic machines which no man could ever enter and live, the forces that powered the stars themselves were being unleashed. Yet there was none of that sense of mounting, pitiless acceleration that always accompanies the take-off of a chemically propelled rocket. The *Ares* had unlimited space in which to manœuvre; she could take as long as she pleased to break free from her present orbit and crawl slowly out into the transfer hyperbola that would lead her to Mars. In any case, the utmost power of the atomic drive could move her two-thousand-ton mass with an acceleration of only a tenth of a gravity; at the moment it was throttled back to less than half of this small value.

It did not take Gibson long to re-orientate himself. The ship's acceleration was so low—it gave him, he calculated, an effective weight of less than four kilogrammes—that his movements were still practically unrestricted. Space Station One had not moved from its apparent position, and he had to wait almost a minute before he could detect that the *Ares* was, in fact, slowly drawing away from it. Then he belatedly remembered his camera, and began to record the departure. When he had finally settled (he hoped) the tricky problem of the right exposure to give a small, brilliantly lit object against a jet-black background, the station was already appreciably more distant. In less than ten minutes, it had dwindled to a distant point of light that was hard to distinguish from the stars.

When Space Station One had vanished completely, Gibson went round to the day side of the ship to take some photographs of the receding Earth. It was a huge, thin crescent when he first saw it, far too large for the eye to take in at a single glance. As he watched, he could see that it was slowly waxing, for the *Ares* must make at least one more circuit before she could break away and spiral out towards Mars. It would be a good hour before the Earth was appreciably smaller and in that time it would pass again from new to full.

Well, this is it, thought Gibson. Down there is all my past life, and the lives of all my ancestors back to the first blob of jelly in the first primeval sea. No colonist or explorer setting sail from his native land ever left so much behind as I am leaving now. Down beneath those clouds lies the whole of human history; soon I shall be able to eclipse with my little finger what was, until a lifetime ago, all of Man's dominion and everything that his art had saved from time.

This inexorable drawing away from the known into the unknown had almost the finality of death. Thus must the naked soul, leaving all its treasures behind it, go out at last into the darkness and the night.

Gibson was still watching at the observation post when, more than an hour later, the *Ares* finally reached escape velocity and was free from Earth. There was no way of telling that this moment had come and passed, for Earth still dominated the sky and the motors still maintained their muffled, distant thunder. Another ten hours of continuous operation would be needed before they had completed their task and could be closed down for the rest of the voyage.

Gibson was sleeping when that moment came. The sudden silence, the complete loss of even the slight gravity the ship had enjoyed these last few hours, brought him back to a twilight sense of awareness. He looked dreamily around the darkened room until his eye found the little pattern of stars framed in the porthole. They were, of course, utterly motionless. It was impossible to believe that the *Ares* was now racing out from the Earth's orbit at a speed so great that even the Sun could never hold her back.

Sleepily, he tightened the fastenings of his bedclothes to prevent himself drifting out into the room. It would be nearly a hundred days before he had any sense of weight again.

THREE

The same pattern of stars filled the porthole when a series of bell-like notes tolling from the ship's public address system woke Gibson from a comparatively dreamless sleep. He dressed in some haste and hurried out to the observation deck, wondering what had happened to Earth overnight.

It is very disconcerting, at least to an inhabitant of Earth, to see two moons in the sky at once. But there they were, side by side, both in their first quarter, and one about twice as large as the other. It was several seconds before Gibson realised that he was looking at Moon and Earth together—and several seconds more before he finally grasped the fact that the smaller and more distant crescent was his own world.

The *Ares* was not, unfortunately, passing very close to the Moon, but even so it was more than ten times as large as Gibson had ever seen it from the Earth. The interlocking chains of crater-rings were clearly visible along the ragged line separating day from night, and the still unilluminated disc could be faintly seen by the reflected earthlight falling upon it. And surely— Gibson bent suddenly forward, wondering if his eyes had tricked him. Yet there was no doubt of it: down in the midst of that cold and faintly gleaming land, waiting for the dawn that was still many days away, minute sparks of light were burning like fireflies in the dusk. They had not been there fifty years ago; they were the lights of the first lunar cities, telling the stars that life had come at last to the Moon after a billion years of waiting.

A discreet cough from nowhere in particular interrupted Gibson's reverie. Then a slightly overamplified voice remarked in a conversational tone:

"If Mr. Gibson will kindly come to the mess-room, he will find some tepid coffee and a few flakes of cereal still left on the table."

He glanced hurriedly at his watch. He had completely forgotten about breakfast—an unprecedented phenomenon. No doubt someone had gone to look for him in his cabin and, failing to find him there, was paging him through the ship's public address system.

When he burst apologetically into the mess-room he found the crew engaged in technical controversy concerning the merits of various types of spaceships.

While he ate, Gibson watched the little group of arguing men, fixing them in his mind and noting their behaviour and characteristics. Norden's introduction had merely served to give them labels; as yet they were not definite personalities to him. It was curious to think that before the voyage had ended, he would probably know every one of them better than most of his acquaintances back on Earth. There could be no secrets and no masks aboard the tiny world of the *Ares*.

At the moment, Dr. Scott was talking. (Later, Gibson would realise that there was nothing very unusual about this.) He seemed a somewhat excitable character, inclined to lay down the law at a moment's provocation on subjects about which he could not possibly be qualified to speak. His most successful interrupter was Bradley, the electronics and communications expert—a dryly cynical person who seemed to take a sardonic pleasure in verbal sabotage. From time to time he would throw a small bombshell into the conversation which would halt Scott for a moment, though never for long. Mackay, the little Scots mathematician, also entered the battle from time to time, speaking rather quickly in a precise, almost pedantic fashion. He would, Gibson thought, have been more at home in a university common-room than on a spaceship.

Captain Norden appeared to be acting as a not entirely disinterested umpire, supporting first one side and then the other in an effort to prevent any conclusive victory. Young Spencer was already at work, and Hilton, the only remaining member of the crew, had taken no part in the discussion. The engineer was sitting quietly watching the others with a detached amusement, and his face was hauntingly familiar to Gibson. Where had they met before? Why, of course— what a fool he was not to have realised it!—this was *the* Hilton. Gibson swung round in his chair so that he could see the other more clearly. His half-finished meal was forgotten as he looked with awe and envy at the man who had brought the *Arcturus* back to Mars after the greatest adventure in the history of spaceflight. Only six men had ever reached Saturn; and only three of them were still alive. Hilton had stood, with his lost companions, on those far-off moons whose very names were magic—Titan, Encladus, Tethys, Rhea, Dione . . . He had seen the incomparable splendour of the great rings spanning the sky in symmetry that seemed too perfect for nature's contriving. He had been into that Ultima Thule in which circled the cold outer giants of the Sun's scattered family, and he had returned again to the light and warmth of the inner worlds. "Yes," thought Gibson, "there are a good many things I want to talk to you about before this trip's over."

The discussion group was breaking up as the various officers drifted—literally—away to their posts, but Gibson's thoughts were still circling Saturn as Captain Norden came across to him and broke into his reverie.

"I don't know what sort of schedule you've planned," he said, "but I suppose you'd like to look over our ship. After all, that's what usually happens around this stage in one of your stories."

Gibson smiled, somewhat mechanically. He feared it was going to be some time before he lived down his past.

"I'm afraid you're quite right there. It's the easiest way, of course, of letting the reader know how things work, and sketching in the *locale* of the plot. Luckily it's not so important now that everyone knows exactly what a spaceship is like inside. One can take the technical details for granted, and get on with the story. But when I started writing about astronautics, back in the '60's, one had to hold up the plot for thousands of words to explain how the spacesuits worked, how the atomic drive operated, and clear up anything else that might come into the story."

"Then I can take it," said Norden, with the most disarming of smiles, "that there's not a great deal we can teach you about the *Ares*."

Gibson managed to summon up a blush.

"I'd appreciate it very much if you'd show me round—whether you do it according to the standard literary pattern or not."

"Very well," grinned Norden. "We'll start at the control room. Come along."

For the next two hours they floated along the labyrinth of corridors that crossed and criss-crossed like arteries in the spherical body of the *Ares*. Soon, Gibson knew, the interior of the ship would be so familiar to him that he could find his way blindfold from one end to the other; but he had already lost his way once and would do so again before he had learned his way around.

As the ship was spherical, it had been divided into zones of latitude like the Earth. The resulting nomenclature was very useful, since it at once gave a mental picture of the liner's geography. To go "North" meant that one was heading for the control cabin and the crew's quarters. A trip to the Equator suggested that one was visiting either the great dining-hall, occupying most of the central plane of the ship, or the observation gallery which completely encircled the liner. The Southern hemisphere was almost entirely fuel tank, with a few storage holds and miscellaneous machinery. Now that the *Ares* was no longer using her motors, she had been swung round in space so that the Northern Hemisphere was in perpetual sunlight and the "uninhabited" Southern one in darkness. At the South Pole itself was a small metal door bearing a set of impressive official seals and the notice: "To be Opened only under the Express Orders of the Captain or his Deputy." Behind it lay the long, narrow tube connecting the main body of the ship with the smaller sphere, a hundred metres away, which held the power plant and drive units. Gibson wondered what was the point of having a door at all if no one could ever go through it; then he remembered that there must be some provision to enable the servicing robots of the Atomic Energy Commission to reach their work.

Strangely enough, Gibson received one of his strongest impressions not from the scientific and technical wonders of the ship, which he had expected to see in any case, but from the empty passenger quarters—a honeycomb of closely packed cells that occupied most of the North Temperate Zone. The impression was rather a disagreeable one. A house so new that no one has ever lived in it can be more lonely than an old, deserted ruin that has once known life and may still be peopled by ghosts. The sense of desolate emptiness was very strong here in the echoing, brightly lit corridors which would one day be crowded with life, but which now lay bleak and lonely in the sunlight piped through the walls—a sunlight much bluer than on Earth and therefore hard and cold.

Gibson was quite exhausted, mentally and physically, when he got back to his room. Norden had been an altogether too conscientious guide, and Gibson suspected that he had been getting some of his own back, and thoroughly enjoying it. He wondered exactly what his companions thought of his literary activities; probably he would not be left in ignorance for long.

He was lying in his bunk, sorting out his impressions, when there came a modest knock on the door.

"Damn," said Gibson, quietly. "Who's that?" he continued, a little louder.

"It's Jim—Spencer, Mr. Gibson. I've got a radiogram for you."

Young Jimmy floated into the room, bearing an envelope with the Signals Officer's stamp. It was sealed, but Gibson surmised that he was the only person on the ship who didn't know its contents. He had a shrewd idea of what they would be, and groaned inwardly. There was really no way of escape from Earth; it could catch you wherever you went.

The message was brief and contained only one redundant word:

NEW YORKER, REVUE DES QUATRE MONDES, LIFE INTERPLANETARY WANT FIVE THOUSAND WORDS EACH. PLEASE RADIO BY NEXT SUNDAY. LOVE. RUTH.

Gibson sighed. He had left Earth in such a rush that there had been no time for a final consultation with his agent, Ruth Goldstein, apart from a hurried phone-call half-way around the world. But he'd told her quite clearly that he wanted to be left alone for a fortnight. It never made any difference, of course. Ruth always went happily ahead, confident that he would deliver the goods on time. Well, for once he wouldn't be bullied and she could darned well wait; he'd earned this holiday.

He grabbed his scribbling pad and, while Jimmy gazed ostentatiously elsewhere, wrote quickly:

SORRY. EXCLUSIVE RIGHTS ALREADY PROMISED TO SOUTH ALABAMA PIG KEEPER AND POULTRY FANCIER. WILL SEND DETAILS ANY MONTH NOW. WHEN ARE YOU GOING TO POISON HARRY? LOVE. MART.

Harry was the literary, as opposed to the business, half of Goldstein and Co. He had been happily married to Ruth for over twenty years, during the last fifteen of which Gibson had never ceased to remind them both that they were getting in a rut and needed a change and that the whole thing couldn't possibly last much longer.

Goggling slightly, Jimmy Spencer disappeared with this unusual message, leaving Gibson alone with his thoughts. Of course, he would have to start work some time, but meanwhile his typewriter was buried down in the hold where he couldn't see it. He had even felt like attaching one of those "NOT WANTED IN SPACE—MAY BE STOWED IN VACUUM" labels, but had manfully resisted the temptation. Like most writers who had never had to rely solely on their literary earnings, Gibson hated *starting* to write. Once he had begun, it was different . . . sometimes.

His holiday lasted a full week. At the end of that time, Earth was merely the most brilliant of the stars and would soon be lost in the glare of the Sun. It was hard to believe that he had ever known any life but that of the little, self-contained universe that was the *Ares*. And its crew no longer consisted of Norden, Hilton, Mackay, Bradley, and Scott—but of John, Fred, Angus, Owen, and Bob.

He had grown to know them all, though Hilton and Bradley had a curious reserve that he had been unable to penetrate. Each man was a definite and sharply contrasted character; almost the only thing they had in common was intelligence. Gibson doubted if any of them had an I.Q. of less than 120, and he sometimes wriggled with embarrassment as he remembered the crews he had imagined for some of his fictional spaceships. He recalled Master Pilot Graham, from "Five Moons Too Many"—still one of his favourite characters. Graham had been tough (had he not once survived half a minute in vacuum before being able to get to his spacesuit?) and he regularly disposed of a bottle of whisky a day. He was a distinct contrast to Dr. Angus Mackay, Ph.D. (Astron.), F.R.A.S., who was now sitting quietly in a corner reading a much annotated copy of "The Canterbury Tales" and taking an occasional squirt from a bulbful of milk.

The mistake that Gibson had made, along with so many other writers back in the '50's and '60's, was the assumption that there would be no fundamental difference between ships of space and ships of the sea—or between the men who manned them. There were parallels, it was true, but they were far outnumbered by the contrasts. The reason was purely technical, and should have been foreseen, but the popular writers of the mid-century had taken the lazy course and had tried to use the traditions of Herman Melville and Frank Dana in a medium for which they were grotesquely unfitted.

A ship of space was much more like a stratosphere liner than anything that had ever moved on the face of the ocean, and the technical training of its crew was at much higher level even than that required in aviation. A man like Norden had spent five years at college, three years in space, and another two back at college on advanced astronautical theory before qualifying for his present position.

Gibson was having a quiet game of darts with Dr. Scott when the first excitement of the voyage burst unexpectedly upon them. There are not many games of skill that can be played in space; for a long time cards and chess had been the classical stand-bys, until some ingenious Englishman had decided that a flight of darts would perform very well in the absence of gravity. The distance between thrower and board had been increased to ten metres, but otherwise the game still obeyed the rules that had been formulated over the centuries amid an atmosphere of beer and tobacco smoke in English pubs.

Gibson had been delighted to find that he was quite good at the game. He almost always managed to beat Scott, despite—or because of—the other's elaborate technique. This consisted of placing the "arrow" carefully in mid-air, and then going back a couple of metres to squint along it before smacking it smartly on its way.

Scott was optimistically aiming for a treble twenty when Bradley drifted into the room bearing a signals form in his hand.

"Don't look now," he said in his soft, carefully modulated voice, "but we're being followed."

Everyone gaped at him as he relaxed in the doorway. Mackay was the first to recover.

"Please elucidate," he said primly.

"There's a Mark III carrier missile coming after us hell for leather. It's just been launched from the Outer Station and should pass us in four days. They want me to catch it with our radio control as it goes by, but with the dispersion it will have at this range that's asking a lot. I doubt if it will go within a hundred thousand kilometres of us."

"What's it in aid of? Someone left their toothbrush behind?"

"It seems to be carrying urgent medical supplies. Here, Doc, you have a look."

Dr. Scott examined the message carefully.

"This *is* interesting. They think they've got an antidote for Martian fever. It's a serum of some kind; the Pasteur Institute's made it. They must be pretty sure of the stuff if they've gone to all this trouble to catch us."

"What, for heaven's sake, is a Mark III missile—not to mention Martian fever?" exploded Gibson at last.

Dr. Scott answered before anyone else could get a word in.

"Martian fever isn't really a Martian disease. It seems to be caused by a terrestrial organism that we carried there and which liked the new climate more than the old one. It has the same sort of effect as malaria: people aren't often killed by it, but its economic effects are very serious. In any one year the percentage of man-hours lost——"

"Thank you very much. I remember all about it now. And the missile?"

Hilton slid smoothly into the conversation.

"That's simply a little automatic rocket with radio control and a very high terminal speed. It's used to carry cargoes between the space-stations, or to chase after spaceships when they've left anything behind. When it gets into radio range it will pick up our transmitter and home on to us. Hey, Bob," he said suddenly, turning to Scott, "why haven't they sent it direct to Mars? It could get there long before we do."

"Because its little passengers wouldn't like it. I'll have to fix up some cultures for them to live in, and look after them like a nursemaid. Not my usual line of business, but I think I can remember some of the stuff I did at St. Thomas's."

"Wouldn't it be appropriate," said Mackay with one of his rare attempts at humour, "if someone went and painted the Red Cross outside?"

Gibson was thinking deeply.

"I was under the impression," he said after a pause, "that life on Mars was very healthy, both physically and psychologically."

"You mustn't believe all you read in books," drawled Bradley. "Why anyone should ever want to go to Mars I can't imagine. It's flat, it's cold, and it's full of miserable half-starved plants looking like something out of Edgar Allan Poe. We've sunk millions into the place and haven't got a penny back. Anyone who goes there of his own free will should have his head examined. Meaning no offence, of course."

Gibson only smiled amicably. He had learned to discount Bradley's cynicism by about ninety per cent; but he was never quite sure how far the other was only *pretending* to be insulting. For once, however, Captain Norden asserted his authority; not merely to stop Bradley from getting away with it, but to prevent such alarm and despondency from spreading into print. He gave his electronics officer an angry glare.

"I ought to tell you, Martin," he said, "that although Mr. Bradley doesn't like Mars, he takes an equally poor view of Earth and Venus. So don't let his opinions depress you."

"I won't," laughed Gibson. "But there's one thing I'd like to ask."

"What's that?" said Norden anxiously.

"Does Mr. Bradley take as 'poor a view,' as you put it, of Mr. Bradley as he does of everything else?"

"Oddly enough, he does," admitted Norden. "That shows that one at least of his judgments is accurate."

"*Touché*," murmured Bradley, for once at a loss. "I will retire in high dudgeon and compose a suitable reply. Meanwhile, Mac, will you get the missile's co-ordinates and let me know when it should come into range?"

"All right," said Mackay absently. He was deep in Chaucer again.

FOUR

During the next few days Gibson was too busy with his own affairs to take much part in the somewhat limited social life of the *Ares*. His conscience had smitten him, as it always did when he rested for more than a week, and he was hard at work again.

The typewriter had been disentangled from his belongings and now occupied the place of honour in the little cabin. Sheets of manuscript lay everywhere—Gibson was an untidy worker—and had to be prevented from escaping by elastic bands. There had been a lot of trouble with the flimsy carbon paper, which had a habit of getting into the airflow and glueing itself against the ventilator, but Gibson had now mastered the minor techniques of life under zero gravity. It was amazing how quickly one learned them, and how soon they became a part of everyday life.

Gibson had found it very hard to get his impressions of space down on paper; one could not very well say "space is awfully big" and leave it at that. The take-off from Earth had taxed his skill to the utmost. He had not actually lied, but anyone who read his dramatic description of the Earth falling away beneath the blast of the rocket would certainly never get the impression that the writer had then been in a state of blissful unconsciousness, swiftly followed by a state of far from blissful consciousness.

As soon as he had produced a couple of articles which would keep Ruth happy for a while (she had meanwhile sent three further radiograms of increasing asperity) he went Northwards to the Signals Office. Bradley received the sheets of MSS. with marked lack of enthusiasm.

"I suppose this is going to happen every day from now on," he said glumly.

"I hope so—but I'm afraid not. It depends on my inspiration."

"There's a split infinitive right here on the top of page 2."

"Excellent; nothing like 'em."

"You've put 'centrifugal' on page 3 where you mean 'centripetal.'"

"Since I get paid by the word, don't you think it's generous of me to use such long ones?"

"There are two successive sentences on page 4 beginning with 'And.'"

"Look here, are you going to send the damned stuff, or do I have to do it myself?"

Bradley grinned.

"I'd like to see you try. Seriously, though, I should have warned you to use a black ribbon. Contrast isn't so good with blue, and though the facsimile sender will be able to handle it all right at this range, when we get further away from Earth it's important to have a nice, clean signal."

As he spoke, Bradley was slipping the quarto sheets into the tray of the automatic transmitter. Gibson watched, fascinated, as they disappeared one by one into the maw of the machine and emerged five seconds later into the wire collecting-basket. It was strange to think that his words were now racing out through space in a continuous stream, getting a million kilometres further away every three seconds.

He was just collecting his MSS. sheets again when a buzzer sounded somewhere in the jungle of dials, switches and meter panels that covered practically the entire wall of the little office. Bradley shot across to one of his receivers and proceeded to do incomprehensible things with great rapidity. A piercing whistle started to come from a loudspeaker.

"The carrier's in range at last," said Bradley, "but it's a long way off—at a guess I'd say it will miss us by a hundred thousand kilometres."

"What can we do about that?"

"Very little. I've got our own beacon switched on, and if it picks up our signals it will home on to us automatically and navigate itself to within a few kilometres of us."

"And if it *doesn't* pick us up?"

"Then it will just go shooting on out of the Solar System. It's travelling fast enough to escape from the Sun; so are we, for that matter."

"That's a cheerful thought. How long would it take us?"

"To do what?"

"To leave the system."

"A couple of years, perhaps. Better ask Mackay. I don't know *all* the answers—I'm not like one of the characters in your books!"

"You may be one yet," said Gibson darkly, and withdrew.

The approach of the missile had added an unexpected—and welcome—element of excitement to life aboard the *Ares*. Once the first fine careless rapture had worn off, space-travel could become exceedingly monotonous. It would be different in future days, when the liner was crowded with life, but there were times when her present loneliness could be very depressing.

The missile sweepstake had been organised by Dr. Scott, but the prizes were held firmly by Captain Norden. Some calculations of Mackay's indicated that the projectile would miss the *Ares* by a hundred and twenty-five thousand kilometres, with an uncertainty of plus or minus thirty thousand. Most of the bets had been placed near the most probable value, but some pessimists, mistrusting Mackay completely, had gone out to a quarter of a million kilometres. The bets weren't in cash, but in far more useful commodities such as cigarettes, candies, and other luxuries. Since the crew's personal weight allowance was strictly limited, these were far more valuable than pieces of paper with marks on them. Mackay had even thrown a half-bottle of whisky into the pool, and had thereby staked a claim to a volume of space about twenty thousand kilometres across. He never drank the stuff himself, he explained, but was taking some to a compatriot on Mars, who couldn't get the genuine article and was unable to afford the passage back to Scotland. No one believed him, which, as the story was more or less true, was a little unfair.

"Jimmy!"

"Yes, Captain Norden."

"Have you finished checking the oxygen gauges?"

"Yes, sir. All O.K."

"What about that automatic recording gear those physicists have put in the hold? Does it look as if it's still working?"

"Well, it's making the same sort of noises as it did when we started."

"Good. You've cleaned up that mess in the kitchen where Mr. Hilton let the milk boil over?"

"Yes, Captain."

"Then you've really finished everything?"

"I suppose so, but I was hoping——"

"That's fine. I've got a rather interesting job for you—something quite out of the usual run of things. Mr. Gibson wants to start polishing up his astronautics. Of course, any of us could tell him all he wants to know, but—er—you're the last one to come from college and maybe you could put things across better. You've not forgotten the beginner's difficulties—*we'd* tend to take too much for granted. It won't take much of your time—just go along when he asks and deal with his questions. I'm sure you can manage."

Exit Jimmy, glumly.

"Come in," said Gibson, without bothering to look up from his typewriter. The door opened behind him and Jimmy Spencer came floating into the room.

"Here's the book, Mr. Gibson. I think it will give you everything you want. It's Richardson's 'Elements of Astronautics,' special light-weight edition."

He laid the volume in front of Gibson, who turned over the thin sheets with an interest that rapidly evaporated as he saw how quickly the proportion of words per page diminished. He finally gave up half-way through the book after coming across a page where the only sentence was "Substituting for the value of perihelion distance from Equation 15.3, we obtain . . ." All else was mathematics.

"Are you *quite* sure this is the most elementary book in the ship?" he asked doubtfully, not wishing to disappoint Jimmy. He had been a little surprised when Spencer had been appointed as his unofficial tutor, but had been shrewd enough to guess the reason. Whenever there was a job that no one else wanted to do, it had a curious ten-dency to devolve upon Jimmy.

"Oh yes, it really *is* elementary. It manages without vector notation and doesn't touch perturbation theory. You should see some of the books Mackay has in his room. Each equation takes a couple of pages of print."

"Well, thanks anyway. I'll give you a shout when I get stuck. It's about twenty years since I did any maths, though I used to be quite hot at it once. Let me know when you want the book back."

"There's no hurry, Mr. Gibson. I don't very often use it now I've got on to the advanced stuff."

"Oh, before you go, maybe you can answer a point that's just cropped up. A lot of people are still worried about meteors, it seems, and I've been asked to give the latest information on the subject. Just how dangerous are they?"

Jimmy pondered for a moment.

"I could tell you, roughly," he said, "but if I were you I'd see Mr. Mackay. He's got tables giving the exact figures."

"Right, I'll do that."

Gibson could quite easily have rung Mackay but any excuse to leave his work was too good to be missed. He found the little astrogator playing tunes on the big electronic calculating machine.

"Meteors?" said Mackay. "Ah, yes, a very interesting subject. I'm afraid, though, that a great deal of highly misleading information has been published about them. It wasn't so long ago that people believed a spaceship would be riddled as soon as it left atmosphere."

"Some of them still do," replied Gibson. "At least, they think that large-scale passenger travel won't be safe."

Mackay gave a snort of disgust.

"Meteors are considerably less dangerous than lightning and the biggest normal one is a lot smaller than a pea."

"But, after all, one ship has been damaged by them!"

"You mean the *Star Queen?* One serious accident in the last five years is quite a satisfactory record. No ship has ever actually been *lost* through meteors."

"What about the *Pallas?*"

"No one knows what happened to her. That's only the popular theory. It's not at all popular among the experts."

"So I can tell the public to forget all about the matter?"

"Yes. Of course, there *is* the question of dust. . . ."

"Dust?"

"Well, if by meteors you mean fairly large particles, from a couple of millimetres upwards, you needn't worry. But dust is a nuisance, particularly on space-stations. Every few years someone has to go over the skin to locate the punctures. They're usually far too small to be visible to the eye, but a bit of dust moving at fifty kilometres a second can get through a surprising thickness of metal."

This sounded faintly alarming to Gibson, and Mackay hastened to reassure him.

"There really isn't the slightest need to worry," he repeated. "There's always a certain hull leakage taking place; the air supply simply takes it in its stride."

However busy Gibson might be, or pretend to be, he always found time to wander restlessly around the echoing labyrinths of the ship, or to sit looking at the stars from the equatorial observation gallery.

He had formed a habit of going there during the daily concert. At 15.00 hours precisely the ship's public address system would burst into life and for an hour the music of Earth would whisper or roar through the empty passageways of the *Ares*. Every day a different person would choose the programmes, so one never knew what was coming —though after a while it was easy to guess the identity of the arranger. Norden played light classics and opera; Hilton practically nothing but Beethoven and Tschaikovsky. They were regarded as hopeless low-brows by Mackay and Bradley, who indulged in astringent chamber music and atonal cacophonies of which no one else could make head or tail, or indeed particularly desired to. The ship's micro-library of books and music was so extensive that it would outlast a lifetime in space. It held, in fact, the equivalent of a quarter of a million books and some thousands of orchestral works, all recorded in electronic patterns, awaiting the orders that would bring them into life.

Gibson was sitting in the observation gallery, trying to see how many of the Pleiades he could resolve with the naked eye, when a small projectile whispered past his ear and attached itself with a "thwack!" to the glass of the port, where it hung vibrating like an arrow. At first sight, indeed, this seemed exactly what it was and for a moment Gibson wondered if the Cherokee were on the warpath again. Then he saw that a large rubber sucker had replaced the head, while from the base, just behind the feathers, a long, thin thread trailed away into the distance. At the end of the thread was Dr. Robert Scott, M.D., hauling himself briskly along like an energetic spider.

Gibson was still composing some suitably pungent remark when, as usual, the doctor got there first.

"Don't you think it's cute?" he said. "It's got a range of twenty metres—only weighs half a kilo, and I'm going to patent it as soon as I get back to Earth."

"Why?" said Gibson, in tones of resignation.

"Good gracious, can't you see? Suppose you want to get from one place to another inside a space-station where there's no rotational gravity. All you've got to do is to fire it at any flat surface near your destination, and reel in the cord. It gives you a perfect anchor until you release the sucker."

"And just what's wrong with the usual way of getting around?"

"When you've been in space as long as *I* have," said Scott smugly, "you'll know what's wrong. There are plenty of handholds for you to grab in a ship like this. But suppose you want to go over to a blank wall at the other side of a room, and you launch yourself through the air from wherever you're standing. What happens? Well, you've got to break your fall somehow, usually with your hands, unless you can twist round on the way. Incidentally, do you know the commonest complaint a spaceship M.O. has to deal with? It's sprained wrists, and *that's* why. Anyway, even when you get to your target you'll bounce back unless you can grab hold of something. You might even get stranded in mid-air. I did that once in Space Station Three, in one of the big hangars. The nearest wall was fifteen metres away and I couldn't reach it."

"Couldn't you spit your way towards it?" said Gibson solemnly. "I thought that was the approved way out of the difficulty."

"You try it some day and see how far it gets you. Anyway, it's not hygienic. Do you know what I had to do? It was most embarrassing. I was only wearing shorts and vest, as usual, and I calculated that they had about a hundredth of my mass. If I could throw them away at thirty metres a second, I could reach the wall in about a minute."

"And did you?"

"Yes. But the Director was showing his wife round the Station that afternoon, so now you know why I'm reduced to earning my living on an old hulk like this, working my way from port to port when I'm not running a shady surgery down by the docks."

"I think you've missed your vocation," said Gibson admiringly. "You should be in my line of business."

"I don't think you believe me," complained Scott bitterly.

"That's putting it mildly. Let's look at your toy."

Scott handed it over. It was a modified air pistol, with a spring-loaded reel of nylon thread attached to the butt.

"It looks like——"

"If you say it's like a ray-gun I'll certify you as infectious. Three people have made that crack already."

"Then it's a good job you interrupted me," said Gibson, handing the weapon back to the proud inventor. "By the way, how's Owen getting on? Has he contacted that missile yet?"

"No, and it doesn't look as if he's going to. Mac says it will pass about a hundred and forty-five thousand kilometres away—certainly out of range. It's a damn shame; there's not another ship going to Mars for months, which is why they were so anxious to catch us."

"Owen's a queer bird, isn't he?" said Gibson with some inconsequence.

"Oh, he's not so bad when you get to know him. It's quite untrue what they say about him poisoning his wife. She drank herself to death of her own free will," replied Scott with relish.

Owen Bradley, Ph.D., M.I.E.E., M.I.R.E., was very annoyed with life. Like every man aboard the *Ares*, he took his job with a passionate seriousness, however much he might pretend to joke about it. For the last twelve hours he had scarcely left the communications cabin, hoping that the continuous carrier wave from the missile would break into the modulation that would tell him it was receiving his signals and would begin to steer itself towards the *Ares*. But it was completely indifferent, and he had no right to expect otherwise. The little auxiliary beacon which was intended to call such projectiles had a reliable range of only twenty thousand kilometres; though that was ample for all normal purposes, it was quite inadequate now.

Bradley dialled the astrogation office on the ship's intercom, and Mackay answered almost at once.

"What's the latest, Mac?"

"It won't come much closer. I've just reduced the last bearing and smoothed out the errors. It's now a hundred and fifty thousand kilometres away, travelling on an almost parallel course. Nearest point will be a hundred and forty-four thousand, in about three hours. So I've lost the sweep—and I suppose we lose the missile."

"Looks like it, I'm afraid," grunted Bradley, "but we'll see. I'm going down to the workshop."

"Whatever for?"

"To make a one-man rocket and go after the blasted thing, of course. That wouldn't take more than half an hour in one of Martin's stories. Come down and help me."

Mackay was nearer the ship's equator than Bradley; consequently he had reached the workshop at the South Pole first and was waiting in mild perplexity when Bradley arrived, festooned with lengths of coaxial cable he had collected from stores. He outlined his plan briefly.

"I should have done this before, but it will make rather a mess and I'm one of those people who always go on hoping till the last moment. The trouble with our beacon is that it radiates in all directions —it has to, of course, since we never know where a carrier's coming from. I'm going to build a beam array and squirt *all* the power I've got after our runaway."

He produced a rough sketch of a simple Yagi aerial and explained it swiftly to Mackay.

"This dipole's the actual radiator—the others are directors and reflectors. Antique, but it's easy to make and it should do the job. Call Hilton if you want any help. How long will it take?"

Mackay, who for a man of his tastes and interests had a positively atavistic skill with his hands, glanced at the drawings and the little pile of materials Bradley had gathered.

"About an hour," he said, already at work. "Where are you going now?"

"I've got to go out on the hull and disconnect the plumbing from the beacon transmitter. Bring the array round to the airlock when you're ready, will you?"

Mackay knew little about radio, but he understood clearly enough what Bradley was trying to do. At the moment the tiny beacon on the *Ares* was broadcasting its power over the entire sphere of space. Bradley was about to disconnect it from its present aerial system and aim its whole output accurately towards the fleeing projectile, thus increasing its range many-fold.

It was about an hour later that Gibson met Mackay hurrying through the ship behind a flimsy structure of parallel wires, spaced apart by plastic rods. He gaped at it in amazement as he followed Mackay to the lock, where Bradley was already waiting impatiently in his cumbersome spacesuit, the helmet open beside him.

"What's the nearest star to the missile?" Bradley asked.

Mackay thought rapidly.

"It's nowhere near the ecliptic now," he mused. "The last figures I got were—let's see—declination fifteen something north, right ascension about fourteen hours. I suppose that will be—I never can remember these things!—somewhere in Böotes. Oh yes—it won't be far from Arcturus: not more than ten degrees away, I'd say at a guess. I'll work out the exact figures in a minute."

"That's good enough to start with. I'll swing the beam around, anyway. Who's in the Signals Cabin now?"

"The Skipper and Fred. I've rung them up and they're listening to the monitor. I'll keep in touch with you through the hull transmitter."

Bradley snapped the helmet shut and disappeared through the airlock. Gibson watched him go with some envy. He had always wanted to wear a spacesuit, but though he had raised the matter on several occasions Norden had told him it was strictly against the rules.

Spacesuits were very complex mechanisms and he might make a mistake in one—and then there would be hell to pay and perhaps a funeral to be arranged under rather novel circumstances.

Bradley wasted no time admiring the stars once he had launched himself through the outer door. He jetted slowly over the gleaming expanse of hull with his reaction units until he came to the section of plating he had already removed. Underneath it a network of cables and wires lay nakedly exposed to the blinding sunlight, and one of the cables had already been cut. He made a quick temporary connection, shaking his head sadly at the horrible mis-match that would certainly reflect half the power right back to the transmitter. Then he found Arcturus and aimed the beam towards it. After waving it around hopefully for a while, he switched on his suit radio.

"Any luck?" he asked anxiously.

Mackay's despondent voice came through the loudspeaker.

"Nothing at all. I'll switch you through to communications."

Norden confirmed the news.

"The signal's still coming in, but it hasn't acknowledged us yet."

Bradley was taken aback. He had been quite sure that this would do the trick; at the very least, he must have increased the beacon's range by a factor of ten in this one direction. He waved the beam around for a few more minutes, then gave it up. Already he could visualise the little missile with its strange but precious cargo slipping silently out of his grasp, out towards the unknown limits of the Solar System—and beyond.

He called Mackay again.

"Listen, Mac," he said urgently, "I want you to check those co-ordinates again and then come out here and have a shot yourself. I'm going in to doctor the transmitter."

When Mackay had relieved him, Bradley hurried back to his cabin. He found Gibson and the rest of the crew gathered glumly round the monitor receiver from which the unbroken whistle from the distant, and now receding, missile was coming with a maddening indifference.

There were very few traces of his normally languid, almost feline movements as Bradley pulled out circuit diagrams by the dozen and tore into the communications rack. It took him only a moment to run a pair of wires into the heart of the beacon transmitter. As he worked, he fired a series of questions at Hilton.

"You know something about these carrier missiles. How long must it receive our signal to give it time to home accurately on to us?"

"That depends, of course, on its relative speed and several other factors. In this case, since it's a low-acceleration job, a good ten minutes, I should say."

"And then it doesn't matter even if our beacon fails?"

"No. As soon as the carrier's vectored itself towards you, you can go off the air again. Of course, you'll have to send it another signal when it passes right by you, but that should be easy."

"How long will it take to get here if I *do* catch it?"

"A couple of days, maybe less. What are you trying out now?"

"The power amplifiers of this transmitter run at seven hundred and fifty volts. I'm taking a thousand-volt line from another supply, that's all. It will be a short life and a merry one, but we'll double or treble the output while the tubes last."

He switched on the intercom and called Mackay, who, not knowing the transmitter had been switched off for some time, was still carefully holding the array lined up on Arcturus, like an armour-plated William Tell aiming a crossbow.

"Hello, Mac, you all set?"

"I am practically ossified," said Mackay with dignity. "How much longer——"

"We're just starting now. Here goes."

Bradley threw the switch. Gibson, who had been expecting sparks to start flying, was disappointed. Everything seemed exactly as before; but Bradley, who knew better, looked at his meters and bit his lips savagely.

It would take radio waves only half a second to bridge the gap to that tiny, far-off rocket with its wonderful automatic mechanisms that must remain forever lifeless unless this signal could reach them. The half-second passed, and the next. There had been time for the reply, but still that maddening heterodyne whistle came unbroken from the speaker. Then, suddenly, it stopped. For an age there was absolute silence. A hundred and fifty thousand kilometres away, the robot was investigating this new phenomenon. It took perhaps five seconds to make up its mind—and the carrier wave broke through again, but now modulated into an endless string of "beep-beep-beeps."

Bradley checked the enthusiasm in the cabin.

"We're not out of the wood yet," he said. "Remember it's got to hold our signal for ten minutes before it can complete its course alterations." He looked anxiously at his meters and wondered how long it would be before the output tubes gave up the unequal battle.

They lasted seven minutes, but Bradley had spares ready and was on the air again in twenty seconds. The replacements were still operating when the missile carrier wave changed its modulation once more, and with a sigh of relief Bradley shut down the maltreated beacon.

"You can come indoors now, Mac," he called into the microphone. "We made it."

"Thank heavens for that. I've nearly got sunstroke, as well as calcification of the joints, doing this Cupid's bow act out here."

"When you've finished celebrating," complained Gibson, who had been an interested but baffled spectator, "perhaps you'll tell me in a few short, well-chosen phrases just how you managed to pull this particular rabbit out of the hat."

"By beaming our beacon signal and then overloading the transmitter, of course."

"Yes, I know that. What I don't understand is why you've switched it off again."

"The controlling gear in the missile has done its job," explained Bradley, with the air of a professor of philosophy talking to a mentally retarded child. "That first signal indicated that it had detected our wave; we knew then that it was automatically vectoring on to us. That took it several minutes, and when it had finished it shut off its motors and sent us the second signal. It's still at almost the same distance, of course, but it's heading towards us now and should be passing in a couple of days. I'll have the beacon running again then. That will bring it to within a kilometre or less."

There was a gentle cough at the back of the room.

"I hate to remind you, sir . . ." began Jimmy.

Norden laughed.

"O.K.—I'll pay up. Here are the keys—locker 26. What are you going to do with that bottle of whisky?"

"I was thinking of selling it back to Dr. Mackay."

"Surely," said Scott, looking severely at Jimmy, "this moment demands a general celebration, at which a toast . . ."

But Jimmy didn't stop to hear the rest. He had fled to collect his loot.

FIVE

"An hour ago we had only one passenger," said Dr. Scott, nursing the long metal case delicately through the airlock. "Now we've got several billion."

"How do you think they've stood the journey?" asked Gibson.

"The thermostats seemed to be working well, so they should be all right. I'll transfer them to the cultures I've got ready, and then they should be quite happy until we get to Mars, gorging themselves to their little hearts' content."

Gibson moved over to the nearest observation post. He could see the stubby, white-painted shape of the missile lying alongside the airlock, with the slack mooring cables drifting away from it like the tentacles of some deep-sea creature. When the rocket had been brought almost to rest a few kilometres away by its automatic radio equipment, its final capture had been achieved by much less sophisticated techniques. Hilton and Bradley had gone out with cables and lassoed the missile as it slowly drifted by. Then the electric winches on the *Ares* had hauled it in.

"What's going to happen to the carrier now?" Gibson asked Captain Norden, who was also watching the proceedings.

"We'll salvage the drive and control assembly and leave the carcase in space. It wouldn't be worth the fuel to carry it all back to Mars. So until we start accelerating again, we'll have a little moon of our own."

"Like the dog in Jules Verne's story."

"What, 'From the Earth to the Moon'? I've never read it. At least, I tried once, but couldn't be bothered. That's the trouble with all those old stories. Nothing is deader than yesterday's science-fiction—and Verne belongs to the day before yesterday."

Gibson felt it necessary to defend his profession.

"So you don't consider that science-fiction can ever have any permanent literary value?"

"I don't think so. It may sometimes have a *social* value when it's written, but to the next generation it must always seem quaint and archaic. Just look what happened, for example, to the space-travel story."

"Go on. Don't mind my feelings—as if you would."

Norden was clearly warming to the subject, a fact which did not surprise Gibson in the least. If one of his companions had suddenly been revealed as an expert on reafforestation, Sanskrit, or bimetallism, Gibson would now have taken it in his stride. In any case, he knew that science-fiction was widely—sometimes hilariously—popular among professional astronauts.

"Very well," said Norden. "Let's see what happened there. Up to 1960—maybe 1970—people were still writing stories about the first journey to the Moon. They're all quite unreadable now. When the Moon was reached, it was safe to write about Mars and Venus for another few years. Now *those* stories are dead too; no one would read them except to get a laugh. I suppose the outer planets will be a good investment for another generation; but the interplanetary romances our grandfathers knew really came to an end in the late 1970's."

"But the theme of space-travel is still as popular as ever."

"Yes, but it's no longer science-fiction. It's either purely factual—the sort of thing you are beaming back to Earth now—or else it's pure fantasy. The stories have to go right outside the Solar System and so they might just as well be fairy tales. Which is all that most of them are."

Norden had been speaking with great seriousness, but there was a mischievous twinkle in his eye.

"I contest your argument on two points," said Gibson. "First of all people—lots of people—still read Wells' yarns, though they're a century old. And, to come from the sublime to the ridiculous, they still read *my* early books, like 'Martian Dust,' although facts have caught up with them and left them a long way in the rear."

"Wells wrote literature," answered Norden, "but even so, I think I can prove my point. Which of his stories are most popular? Why, the straight novels like 'Kipps' and 'Mr. Polly.' When the fantasies are read at all, it's in spite of their hopelessly dated prophecies, not because of them. Only 'The Time Machine' is still at all popular, simply because it's set so far in the future that it's not outmoded—and because it contains Wells' best writing."

There was a slight pause. Gibson wondered if Norden was going to take up his second point. Finally he said:

"When did you write 'Martian Dust'?"

Gibson did some rapid mental arithmetic.

"In '73 or '74."

"I didn't know it was as early as that. But that's part of the explanation. Space-travel was just about to begin then, and everybody knew it. You had already begun to make a name with conventional fiction, and 'Martian Dust' caught the rising tide very nicely."

"That only explains why it sold *then*. It doesn't answer my other point. It's still quite popular, and I believe the Martian colony has taken several copies, despite the fact that it describes a Mars that never existed outside my imagination."

"I attribute that to the unscrupulous advertising of your publisher, the careful way you've managed to keep in the public eye, and—just possibly—to the fact that it was the best thing you ever wrote. Moreover, as Mac would say, it managed to capture the *Zeitgeist* of the '70's, and that gives it a curiosity value now."

"Hmm," said Gibson, thinking matters over.

He remained silent for a moment; then his face creased into a smile and he began to laugh.

"Well, share the joke. What's so funny?"

"Our earlier conversation. I was just wondering what H. G. Wells would have thought if he'd known that one day a couple of men would be discussing his stories, half-way between Earth and Mars."

"Don't exaggerate," grinned Norden. "We're only a third of the way so far."

It was long after midnight when Gibson suddenly awoke from a dreamless sleep. Something had disturbed him—some noise like a distant explosion, far away in the bowels of the ship. He sat up in the darkness, tensing against the broad elastic bands that held him to his bed. Only a glimmer of starlight came from the porthole-mirror, for his cabin was on the night side of the liner. He listened, mouth half opened, checking his breath to catch the faintest murmur of sound.

There were many voices in the *Ares* at night, and Gibson knew them all. The ship was alive, and silence would have meant the death of all aboard her. Infinitely reassuring was the unresting, unhurried suspiration of the air-pumps, driving the man-made trade winds of this tiny planet. Against that faint but continuous background were other intermittent noises: the occasional "whirr" of hidden motors carrying out some mysterious and automatic task, the "tick," every thirty seconds precisely, of the electric clock, and sometimes the sound of water racing through the pressurised plumbing system. Certainly none of these could have roused him, for they were as familiar as the beating of his own heart.

Still only half awake, Gibson went to the cabin door and listened for a while in the corridor. Everything was perfectly normal; he knew that he must be the only man awake. For a moment he wondered if he should call Norden, then thought better of it. He might only have been dreaming, or the noise might have been produced by some equipment that had not gone into action before.

He was already back in bed when a thought suddenly occurred to him. Had the noise, after all, been so far away? That was merely his first impression; it might have been quite near. Anyway, he was tired, and it didn't matter. Gibson had a complete and touching faith in the ship's instrumentation. If anything had really gone wrong, the automatic alarms would have alerted everyone. They had been tested several times on the voyage, and were enough to awaken the dead. He could go to sleep, confident that they were watching over him with unresting vigilance.

He was perfectly correct, though he was never to know it; and by the morning he had forgotten the whole affair.

The camera swept out of the stricken council chamber, following the funeral cortege up the endlessly twining stairs, out on to the windy battlements above the sea. The music sobbed into silence; for a moment, the lonely figures with their tragic burden were silhouetted against the setting sun, motionless upon the ramparts of Elsinore. "Goodnight, sweet prince . . ." The play was ended.

The lights in the tiny theatre came on abruptly, and the State of Denmark was four centuries and fifty million kilometres away. Reluctantly, Gibson brought his mind back to the present, tearing himself free from the magic that had held him captive. What, he wondered, would Shakespeare have made of this interpretation, already a lifetime old, yet as untouched by time as the still older splendours of the immortal poetry? And what, above all would he have made of this fantastic theatre, with its latticework of seats floating precariously in mid-air with the flimsiest of supports?

"It's rather a pity," said Dr. Scott, as the audience of six drifted out into the corridor, "that we'll never have as fine a collection of films with us on our later runs. This batch is for the Central Martian Library, and we won't be able to hang on to it."

"What's the next programme going to be?" asked Gibson.

"We haven't decided. It may be a current musical, or we may carry on with the classics and screen 'Gone With the Wind.'"

"My grandfather used to rave about that; I'd like to see it now we have the chance," said Jimmy Spencer eagerly.

"Very well," replied Scott. "I'll put the matter to the Entertainments Committee and see if it can be arranged." Since this Committee consisted of Scott and no one else, these negotiations would presumably be successful.

Norden, who had remained sunk in thought since the end of the film, came up behind Gibson and gave a nervous little cough.

"By the way, Martin," he said. "You remember you were badgering me to let you go out in a spacesuit?"

"Yes. You said it was strictly against the rules."

Norden seemed embarrassed, which was somewhat unlike him.

"Well, it *is* in a way, but this isn't a normal trip and you aren't technically a passenger. I think we can manage it after all."

Gibson was delighted. He had always wondered what it was like to wear a spacesuit, and to stand in nothingness with the stars all around one. It never even occurred to him to ask Norden why he had changed his mind, and for this Norden was very thankful.

The plot had been brewing for about a week. Every morning a little ritual took place in Norden's room when Hilton arrived with the daily maintenance schedules, summarising the ship's performance and the behaviour of all its multitudinous machines during the past twenty-four hours. Usually there was nothing of any importance, and Norden signed the reports and filed them away with the log book. Variety was the last thing he wanted here, but sometimes he got it.

"Listen, Johnnie," said Hilton (he was the only one who called Norden by his first name; to the rest of the crew he was always "Skipper"). "It's quite definite now about our air-pressure. The drop's practically constant; in about ten days we'll be outside tolerance limits."

"Confound it! That means we'll have to do something. I was hoping it wouldn't matter till we dock."

"I'm afraid we can't wait until then; the records have to be turned over to the Space Safety Commission when we get home, and some nervous old woman is sure to start yelling if pressure drops below limits."

"Where do you think the trouble is?"

"In the hull, almost certainly."

"That pet leak of yours up round the North Pole?"

"I doubt it; this is too sudden. I think we've been holed again."

Norden looked mildly annoyed. Punctures due to meteoric dust happened two or three times a year on a ship of this size. One usually let them accumulate until they were worth bothering about, but this one seemed a little too big to be ignored.

"How long will it take to find the leak?"

"That's the trouble," said Hilton in tones of some disgust. "We've only one leak detector, and fifty thousand square metres of hull. It may take a couple of days to go over it. Now if it had only been a nice big hole, the automatic bulkheads would have gone into operation and located it for us."

"I'm mighty glad they didn't!" grinned Norden. "That would have taken some explaining away!"

Jimmy Spencer, who as usual got the job that no one else wanted to do, found the puncture three days later, after only a dozen circuits of the ship. The blurred little crater was scarcely visible to the eye, but the supersensitive leak detector had registered the fact that the vacuum near this part of the hull was not as perfect as it should have been. Jimmy had marked the place with chalk and gone thankfully back into the airlock.

Norden dug out the ship's plans and located the approximate position from Jimmy's report. Then he whistled softly and his eyebrows climbed towards the ceiling.

"Jimmy," he said, "does Mr. Gibson know what you've been up to?"

"No," said Jimmy. "I've not missed giving him his astronautics classes, though it's been quite a job to manage it as well as——"

"All right, all right! You don't think anyone else would have told him about the leak?"

"I don't know, but I think he'd have mentioned it if they had."

"Well, listen carefully. This blasted puncture is smack in the middle of his cabin wall, and if you breathe a word about it to him, I'll skin you. Understand?"

"Yes," gulped Jimmy, and fled precipitately.

"Now what?" said Hilton, in tones of resignation.

"We've got to get Martin out of the way on some pretext and plug the hole as quickly as we can."

"It's funny he never noticed the impact. It would have made quite a din."

"He was probably out at the time. *I'm* surprised he never noticed the air current; it must be fairly considerable."

"Probably masked by the normal circulation. But anyway, why all the fuss? Why not come clean about it and explain what's happened to Martin? There's no need for all this melodrama."

"Oh, isn't there? Suppose Martin tells his public that a 12th magnitude meteor has holed the ship—and then goes on to say that this sort of thing happens every other voyage? How many of his readers will understand not only that it's no real danger, but that we don't usually bother to do anything even when it does happen? I'll tell you what the popular reaction would be: 'If it was a little one, it might just as well be a big 'un.' The public's never trusted statistics. And can't you see the headlines: '*Ares* Holed by Meteor!' That *would* be bad for trade!"

"Then why not simply tell Martin and ask him to keep quiet?"

"It wouldn't be fair on the poor chap. He's had no news to hang his articles on to for weeks. It would be kinder to say nothing."

"O.K.," sighed Hilton. "It's your idea. Don't blame me if it backfires."

"It won't. I think I've got a watertight plan."

"I don't give a damn if it's watertight. Is it airtight?"

All his life Gibson had been fascinated by gadgets, and the space-suit was yet another to add to the collection of mechanisms he had investigated and mastered. Bradley had been detailed to make sure that he understood the drill correctly, to take him out into space, and to see that he didn't get lost.

Gibson had forgotten that the suits on the *Ares* had no legs, and that one simply sat inside them. That was sensible enough, since they were built for use under zero gravity, and not for walking on airless planets. The absence of flexible leg-joints greatly simplified the designs of the suits, which were nothing more than perspex-topped cylinders sprouting articulated arms at their upper ends. Along the sides were mysterious flutings and bulges concerned with the air conditioning, radio, heat regulators, and the low-powered propulsion system. There was considerable freedom of movement inside them: one could withdraw one's arms to get at the internal controls, and even take a meal without too many acrobatics.

Bradley had spent almost an hour in the airlock, making certain that Gibson understood all the main controls and catechising him on their operation. Gibson appreciated his thoroughness, but began to get a little impatient when the lesson showed no sign of ending. He eventually mutinied when Bradley started to explain the suit's primitive sanitary arrangements.

"Hang it all!" he protested, "we aren't going to be outside *that* long!"

Bradley grinned.

"You'd be surprised," he said darkly, "just how many people make that mistake."

He opened a compartment in the airlock wall and took out two spools of line, for all the world like fishermen's reels. They locked firmly into mountings on the suits so that they could not be accidentally dislodged.

"Number One safety precaution," he said. "Always have a lifeline anchoring you to the ship. Rules are made to be broken—but not this one. To make doubly sure, I'll tie your suit to mine with another ten metres of cord. Now we're ready to ascend the Matterhorn."

The outer door slid aside. Gibson felt the last trace of air tugging at him as it escaped. The feeble impulse set him moving towards the exit, and he drifted slowly out into the stars.

The slowness of motion and the utter silence combined to make the moment deeply impressive. The *Ares* was receding behind him with a terrifying inevitability. He was plunging into space—real space at last—his only link with safety that tenuous thread unreeling at his side. Yet the experience, though so novel, awoke faint echoes of familiarity in his mind.

His brain must have been working with unusual swiftness, for he recalled the parallel almost immediately. This was like the moment in his childhood—a moment, he could have sworn until now, forgotten beyond recall—when he had been taught to swim by being dropped into ten metres of water. Once again he was plunging headlong into a new and unknown element.

The friction of the reel had checked his momentum when the cord attaching him to Bradley gave a jerk. He had almost forgotten his companion, who was now blasting away from the ship with the little gas jets at the base of his suit, towing Gibson behind him.

Gibson was quite startled when the other's voice, echoing metallically from the speaker in his suit, shattered the silence.

"Don't use your jets unless I tell you. We don't want to build up too much speed, and we must be careful not to get our lines tangled."

"All right," said Gibson, vaguely annoyed at the intrusion into his privacy. He looked back at the ship. It was already several hundred metres away, and shrinking rapidly.

"How much line have we got?" he asked anxiously. There was no reply, and he had a moment of mild panic before remembering to press the "TRANSMIT" switch.

"About a kilometre," Bradley answered when he repeated the question. "That's enough to make one feel nice and lonely."

"Suppose it broke?" asked Gibson, only half joking.

"It won't. It could support your full weight, back on Earth. Even if it did, we could get back perfectly easily with our jets."

"And if they ran out?"

"This is a very cheerful conversation. I can't imagine that happening except through gross carelessness or about three simultaneous mechanical failures. Remember, there's a spare propulsion unit for just such emergencies—*and* you've got warning indicators in the suit which let you know well before the main tank's empty."

"But just *supposing*," insisted Gibson.

"In that case the only thing to do would be to switch on the suit's S.O.S. beacon and wait until someone came out to haul you back. I doubt if they'd hurry, in such circumstances. Anyone who got himself in a mess like that wouldn't receive much sympathy."

There was a sudden jerk; they had come to the end of the line. Bradley killed the rebound with his jets.

"We're a long way from home now," he said quietly.

It took Gibson several seconds to locate the *Ares*. They were on the night side of the ship so that it was almost wholly in shadow; the two spheres were thin, distant crescents that might easily have been taken for Earth and Moon, seen from perhaps a million kilometres away. There was no real sense of contact: the ship was too small and frail a thing to be regarded as a sanctuary any more. Gibson was alone with the stars at last.

He was always grateful that Bradley left him in silence and did not intrude upon his thoughts. Perhaps the other was equally overwhelmed by the splendid solemnity of the moment. The stars were so brilliant and so numerous that at first Gibson could not locate even the most familiar constellations. Then he found Mars, the brightest object in the sky next to the Sun itself, and so determined the plane of the ecliptic. Very gently, with cautious bursts from his gas jets, he swung the suit round so that his head pointed roughly towards the

Pole Star. He was "the right way up" again, and the star patterns were recognisable once more.

Slowly he made his way along the Zodiac, wondering how many other men in history had so far shared this experience. (Soon, of course, it would be common enough, and the magic would be dimmed by familiarity.) Presently he found Jupiter, and later Saturn—or so he imagined. The planets could no longer be distinguished from the stars by the steady, unwinking light that was such a useful, though sometimes treacherous, guide to amateur astronomers. Gibson did not search for Earth or Venus, for the glare of the sun would have dazzled him in a moment if he had turned his eyes in that direction.

A pale band of light welding the two hemispheres of the sky together, the whole ring of the Milky Way was visible. Gibson could see quite clearly the vents and tears along its edge, where entire continents of stars seemed trying to break away and go voyaging alone into the abyss. In the Southern Hemisphere, the black chasm of the Coal Sack gaped like a tunnel drilled through the stars into another universe.

The thought made Gibson turn towards Andromeda. There lay the great Nebula—a ghostly lens of light. He could cover it with his thumbnail, yet it was a whole galaxy as vast as the sky-spanning ring of stars in whose heart he was floating now. That misty spectre was a million times further away than the stars—and *they* were a million times more distant than the planets. How pitiful were all men's voyagings and adventures when seen against this background!

Gibson was looking for Alpha Centauri, among the unknown constellations of the Southern Hemisphere, when he caught sight of something which, for a moment, his mind failed to identify. At an immense distance, a white rectangular object was floating against the stars. That, at least, was Gibson's first impression; then he realised that his sense of perspective was at fault and that, in fact, he was really seeing something quite small, only a few metres away. Even then it was some time before he recognised this interplanetary wanderer for what it was—a perfectly ordinary sheet of quarto manuscript paper, very slowly revolving in space. Nothing could have been more commonplace—or more unexpected here.

Gibson stared at the apparition for some time before he convinced himself that it was no illusion. Then he switched on his transmitter and spoke to Bradley.

The other was not in the least surprised.

"There's nothing very remarkable about that," he replied, rather impatiently. "We've been throwing out waste every day for weeks, and as we haven't any acceleration some of it may still be hanging round. As soon as we start braking, of course, we'll drop back from it and all our junk will go shooting out of the Solar System."

How perfectly obvious, thought Gibson, feeling a little foolish, for nothing is more disconcerting than a mystery which suddenly evaporates. It was probably a rough draft of one of his own articles. If it had been a little closer, it would be amusing to retrieve it as a souvenir, and to see what effects its stay in space had produced. Unfortunately it was just out of reach, and there was no way of capturing it without slipping the cord that linked him with the *Ares*.

When he had been dead for ages, that piece of paper would still be carrying its message out among the stars; and what it was, he would never know.

Norden met them when they returned to the airlock. He seemed rather pleased with himself, though Gibson was in no condition to notice such details. He was still lost among the stars and it would be some time before he returned to normal—before his typewriter began to patter softly as he tried to recapture his emotions.

"You managed the job in time?" asked Bradley, when Gibson was out of hearing.

"Yes, with fifteen minutes to spare. We shut off the ventilators and found the leak right away with the good old smoky-candle technique. A blind rivet and a spot of quick-drying paint did the rest; we can plug the outer hull when we're in dock, if it's worth it. Mac did a pretty neat job—he's wasting his talents as a navigator."

SIX

For Martin Gibson, the voyage was running smoothly and pleasantly enough. As he always did, he had now managed to organise his surroundings (by which he meant not only his material environment but also the human beings who shared it with him) to his maximum comfort. He had done a satisfactory amount of writing, some of it quite good and most of it passable, though he would not get properly into his stride until he had reached Mars.

The flight was now entering upon its closing weeks, and there was an inevitable sense of anticlimax and slackening interest, which would last until they entered the orbit of Mars. Nothing would happen until then; for the time being all the excitements of the voyage were over.

The last high-light, for Gibson, had been the morning when he finally lost the Earth. Day by day it had come closer to the vast pearly wings of the corona, as though about to immolate all its millions in the funeral pyre of the Sun. One evening it had still been visible through the telescope—a tiny spark glittering bravely against the splendour that was soon to overwhelm it. Gibson had thought it might still be visible in the morning, but overnight some colossal explosion had thrown the corona half a million kilometres further into space, and Earth was lost against that incandescent curtain. It would be a week before it reappeared, and by then Gibson's world would have changed more than he would have believed possible in so short a time.

If anyone had asked Jimmy Spencer just what he thought of Gibson, that young man would have given rather different replies at various stages of the voyage. At first he had been quite overawed by his distinguished shipmate, but that stage had worn off very quickly. To do Gibson credit, he was completely free from snobbery, and he never made unreasonable use of his privileged position on board the *Ares*. Thus from Jimmy's point of view he was more approachable than the rest of the liner's inhabitants—all of whom were in some degree his superior officers.

When Gibson had started taking a serious interest in astronautics, Jimmy had seen him at close quarters once or twice a week and had made several efforts to weigh him up. This had not been at all easy, for Gibson never seemed to be the same person for very long. There were times when he was considerate and thoughtful and generally good company. Yet there were other occasions when he was so grumpy and morose that he easily qualified as the person on the *Ares* most to be avoided.

What Gibson thought of *him* Jimmy wasn't at all sure. He sometimes had an uncomfortable feeling that the author regarded him purely as raw material that might or might not be of value some day. Most people who knew Gibson slightly had that impression, and most of them were right. Yet as he had never tried to pump Jimmy directly, there seemed no real grounds for these suspicions.

Another puzzling thing about Gibson was his technical background. When Jimmy had started his evening classes, as everyone called them, he had assumed that Gibson was merely anxious to avoid glaring errors in the material he radioed back to Earth, and had no very deep interest in astronautics for its own sake. It soon became clear that this was far from being the case. Gibson had an almost pathetic anxiety to master quite abstruse branches of the science, and to demand mathematical proofs, some of which Jimmy was hard put to provide. The older man must once have had a good deal of technical knowledge, fragments of which still remained with him. How he had acquired it he never explained; nor did he give any reason for his almost obsessive attempts, doomed though they were to repeated failures, to come to grips with scientific ideas far too advanced for him. Gibson's disappointment after these failures was so obvious that Jimmy found himself very sorry for him—except on those occasions when his pupil became bad-tempered and showed a tendency to blame his instructor. Then there would be a brief exchange of discourtesies, Jimmy would pack up his books, and the lesson would not be resumed until Gibson had apologised.

Sometimes, on the other hand, Gibson took these setbacks with humorous resignation and simply changed the subject. He would then talk about his experiences in the strange literary jungle in which he lived—a world of weird and often carnivorous beasts whose behaviour Jimmy found quite fascinating. Gibson was a good raconteur, with a fine flair for purveying scandal and undermining reputations. He seemed to do this without any malice, and some of the stories he told Jimmy about the distinguished figures of the day quite shocked that somewhat strait-laced youth. The curious fact was that the people whom Gibson so readily dissected often seemed to be his closest friends. This was something that Jimmy found very hard to understand.

Yet despite all these warnings Jimmy talked readily enough when the time came. One of their lessons had grounded on a reef of integrodifferential equations and there was nothing to do but abandon ship. Gibson was in one of his amiable moods, and as he closed his books with a sigh he turned to Jimmy and remarked casually:

"You've never told me anything about yourself, Jimmy. What part of England do you come from, anyway?"

"Cambridge—at least, that's where I was born."

"I used to know it quite well, twenty years ago. But you don't live there now?"

"No; when I was about six, my people moved to Leeds. I've been there ever since."

"What made you take up astronautics?"

"It's rather hard to say. I was always interested in science, and of course spaceflight was the coming thing when I was growing up. So I suppose it was just natural. If I'd been born fifty years before, I guess I'd have gone into aeronautics."

"So you're interested in spaceflight purely as a technical problem, and not as—shall we say—something that might revolutionise human thought, open up new planets, and all that sort of thing?"

Jimmy grinned.

"I suppose that's true enough. Of course, I *am* interested in these ideas, but it's the technical side that really fascinates me. Even if there was nothing on the planets, I'd still want to know how to reach them."

Gibson shook his head in mock distress.

"You're going to grow up into one of those cold-blooded scientists who know everything about nothing. Another good man wasted!"

"I'm glad you think it *will* be a waste," said Jimmy with some spirit. "Anyway, why are you so interested in science?"

Gibson laughed, but there was a trace of annoyance in his voice as he replied:

"I'm only interested in science as a means, not as an end in itself."

That, Jimmy was sure, was quite untrue. But something warned him not to pursue the matter any further, and before he could reply Gibson was questioning him again.

It was all done in such a friendly spirit of apparently genuine interest that Jimmy couldn't avoid feeling flattered, couldn't help talking freely and easily. Somehow it didn't matter if Gibson was indeed studying him as disinterestedly and as clinically as a biologist watching the reactions of one of his laboratory animals. Jimmy felt like talking, and he preferred to give Gibson's motives the benefit of the doubt.

He talked of his childhood and early life, and presently Gibson understood the occasional clouds that sometimes seemed to overlie the lad's normally cheerful disposition. It was an old story—one of the oldest. Jimmy's mother had died when he was a little more than a baby, and his father had left him in the charge of a married sister. Jimmy's aunt had been kind to him, but he had never felt at home among his cousins, had always been an outsider. Nor had his father been a great deal of help, for he was seldom in England, and had died when Jimmy was about ten years old. He appeared to have left very little impression on his son, who, strangely enough, seemed to have clearer memories of the mother whom he could scarcely have known.

Once the barriers were down, Jimmy talked without reticence, as if glad to unburden his mind. Sometimes Gibson asked questions to prompt him, but the questions grew further and further apart and presently came no more.

"I don't think my parents were really very much in love," said Jimmy. "From what Aunt Ellen told me, it was all rather a mistake. There was another man first, but that fell through. My father was the next best thing. Oh, I know this sounds rather heartless, but please remember it all happened such a long time ago, and doesn't mean much to me now."

"I understand," said Gibson quietly; and it seemed as if he really did. "Tell me more about your mother."

"Her father—my granddad, that is—was one of the professors at the university. I think mother spent all her life in Cambridge. When she was old enough she went to college for her degree—she was studying history. Oh, all this can't possibly interest you!"

"It really does," said Gibson earnestly. "Go on."

So Jimmy talked. Everything he told must have been learned from hearsay, but the picture he gave Gibson was surprisingly clear and detailed. His listener guessed that Aunt Ellen must have been very talkative, and Jimmy a very attentive small boy.

It was one of those innumerable college romances that briefly flower and wither during that handful of years which seems a microcosm of life itself. But this one had been more serious than most. During her last term Jimmy's mother—he still hadn't told Gibson her name—had fallen in love with a young engineering student who was half-way through his college career. It had been a whirlwind romance, and the match was an ideal one despite the fact that the girl was several years older than the boy. Indeed, it had almost reached the stage of an engagement when—Jimmy wasn't quite sure what had happened. The young man had been taken seriously ill, or had had a nervous breakdown, and had never come back to Cambridge.

"My mother never really got over it," said Jimmy, with a grave assumption of wisdom which somehow did not seem completely incongruous. "But another student was very much in love with her, and so she married him. I sometimes feel rather sorry for my father, for he must have known all about the other affair. I never saw much of him because—why, Mr. Gibson, don't you feel well?"

Gibson forced a smile.

"It's nothing—just a touch of space—sickness. I get it now and then—it will pass in a minute."

He only wished that the words were true. All these weeks, in total ignorance and believing himself secure against all the shocks of time and chance, he had been steering a collision course with Fate. And now the moment of impact had come; the twenty years that lay behind had vanished like a dream, and he was face to face once more with the ghosts of his own forgotten past.

"There's something wrong with Martin," said Bradley, signing the signals log with a flourish. "It can't be any news he's had from Earth —I've read it all. Do you suppose he's getting homesick?"

"He's left it a little late in the day, if that's the explanation," replied Norden. "After all, we'll be on Mars in a fortnight. But you do rather fancy yourself as an amateur psychologist, don't you?"

"Well, who doesn't?"

"*I* don't for one," began Norden pontifically. "Prying into other people's affairs isn't one of my——"

An anticipatory gleam in Bradley's eyes warned him just in time, and to the other's evident disappointment he checked himself in midsentence. Martin Gibson, complete with notebook and looking like a cub reporter attending his first press conference, had hurried into the office.

"Well, Owen, what was it you wanted to show me?" he asked eagerly.

Bradley moved to the main communication rack.

"It isn't really very impressive," he said, "but it means that we've passed another milestone and always gives me a bit of a kick. Listen to this."

He pressed the speaker switch and slowly brought up the volume control. The room was flooded with the hiss and crackle of radio noise, like the sound of a thousand frying pans at the point of imminent ignition. It was a sound that Gibson had heard often enough in the signals cabin and, for all its unvarying monotony, it never failed to fill him with a sense of wonder. He was listening, he knew, to the voices of the stars and nebulae, to radiations that had set out upon their journey before the birth of Man. And buried far down in the depths of that crackling, whispering chaos there might be—there *must* be—the sounds of alien civilisations talking to one another in the deeps of space. But, alas, their voices were lost beyond recall in the welter of cosmic interference which Nature herself had made.

This, however, was certainly not what Bradley had called him to hear. Very delicately, the signals officer made some vernier adjustments, frowning a little as he did so.

"I had it on the nose a minute ago—hope it hasn't drifted off—ah, here it is!"

At first Gibson could detect no alteration in the barrage of noise. Then he noticed that Bradley was silently marking time with his hand —rather quickly, at the rate of some two beats every second. With this to guide him, Gibson presently detected the infinitely faint undulating whistle that was breaking through the cosmic storm.

"What is it?" he asked, already half guessing the answer.

"It's the radio beacon on Deimos. There's one on Phobos as well, but it's not so powerful and we can't pick it up yet. When we get nearer Mars, we'll be able to fix ourselves within a few hundred kilometres by using them. We're at ten times the usable range now, but it's nice to know."

Yes, thought Gibson, it is nice to know. Of course, these radio aids weren't essential when one could see one's destination all the time, but they simplified some of the navigational problems. As he listened with half-closed eyes to that faint pulsing, sometimes almost drowned by the cosmic barrage, he knew how the mariners of old must have felt when they caught the first glimpse of the harbour lights from far out at sea.

"I think that's enough," said Bradley, switching off the speaker and restoring silence. "Anyway, it should give you something new to write about—things have been pretty quiet lately, haven't they?"

He was watching Gibson intently as he said this, but the author never responded. He merely jotted a few words in his notebook, thanked Bradley with absent-minded and unaccustomed politeness, and departed to his cabin.

"You're quite right," said Norden when he had gone. "Something's certainly happened to Martin. I'd better have a word with Doc."

"I shouldn't bother," replied Bradley. "Whatever it is, I don't think it's anything you can handle with pills. Better leave Martin to work it out his own way."

"Maybe you're right," said Norden grudgingly. "But I hope he doesn't take too long over it!"

He had now taken almost a week. The initial shock of discovering that Jimmy Spencer was Kathleen Morgan's son had already worn off, but the secondary effects were beginning to make themselves felt. Among these was a feeling of resentment that anything like this should have happened to *him*. It was such an outrageous violation of the laws of probability—the sort of thing that would never have happened in one of Gibson's own novels. But life was so inartistic and there was really nothing one could do about it.

This mood of childish petulance was now passing, to be replaced by a deeper sense of discomfort. All the emotions he had thought safely buried beneath twenty years of feverish activity were now rising to the surface again, like deep-sea creatures slain in some submarine eruption. On Earth, he could have escaped by losing himself once more in the crowd, but here he was trapped, with nowhere to flee.

It was useless to pretend that nothing had really changed, to say: "Of course I knew that Kathleen and Gerald had a son: what difference does that make now?" It made a great deal of difference. Every time he saw Jimmy he would be reminded of the past and—what was worse—of the future that might have been. The most urgent problem now was to face the facts squarely, and to come to grips with the new situation. Gibson knew well enough that there was only one way in which this could be done, and the opportunity would arise soon enough.

Jimmy had been down to the Southern Hemisphere and was making his way along the equatorial observation deck when he saw Gibson sitting at one of the windows, staring out into space. For a moment he thought the other had not seen him, and had decided not to intrude upon his thoughts when Gibson called out: "Hello, Jimmy. Have you got a moment to spare?"

As it happened, Jimmy was rather busy. But he knew that there had been something wrong with Gibson, and realised that the older man needed his presence. So he came and sat on the bench recessed into the observation port, and presently he knew as much of the truth as Gibson thought good for either of them.

"I'm going to tell you something, Jimmy," Gibson began, "which is known to only a handful of people. Don't interrupt me and don't ask any questions—not until I've finished, at any rate.

"When I was rather younger than you, I wanted to be an engineer. I was quite a bright kid in those days and had no difficulty in getting into college through the usual examinations. As I wasn't sure what I intended to do, I took the five-year course in general engineering physics, which was quite a new thing in those days. In my first year I did fairly well—well enough to encourage me to work harder next time. In my second year I did—not brilliantly, but a lot better than average. And in the third year I fell in love. It wasn't exactly for the first time, but I knew it was the real thing at last.

"Now falling in love while you're at college may or may not be a good thing for you; it all depends on circumstances. If it's only a mild flirtation, it probably doesn't matter one way or the other. But if it's really serious, there are two possibilities.

"It may act as a stimulus—it may make you determined to do your best, to show that you're better than the other fellows. On the other hand, you may get so emotionally involved in the affair that nothing else seems to matter, and your studies go to pieces. That is what happened in my case."

Gibson fell into a brooding silence, and Jimmy stole a glance at him as he sat in the darkness a few feet away. They were on the night side of the ship, and the corridor lights had been dimmed so that the stars could be seen in their unchallenged glory. The constellation of Leo was directly ahead, and there in its heart was the brilliant ruby gem that was their goal. Next to the Sun itself, Mars was by far the brightest of all celestial bodies, and already its disc was just visible to the naked eye. The brilliant crimson light playing full on his face gave Gibson a healthy, even a cheerful appearance quite out of keeping with his feelings.

Was it true, Gibson wondered, that one never really forgot anything? It seemed now as if it might be. He could still see, as clearly as he had twenty years ago, that message pinned on the faculty noticeboard: "The Dean of Engineering wishes to see M. Gibson in his office at 3.00." He had had to wait, of course, until 3.15, and that hadn't helped. Nor would it have been so bad if the Dean had been sarcastic, or icily aloof, or even if he had lost his temper. Gibson could still picture that inhumanly tidy room, with its neat files and careful rows of books, could remember the Dean's secretary padding away on her typewriter in the corner, pretending not to listen.

(Perhaps, now he came to think of it, she wasn't pretending after all. The experience wouldn't have been so novel to her as it was to him.)

Gibson had liked and respected the Dean, for all the old man's finicky ways and meticulous pedantry, and now he had let him down, which made his failure doubly hard to bear. The Dean had rubbed it in with his "more in sorrow than in anger" technique, which had been more effective than he knew or intended. He had given Gibson another chance, but he was never to take it.

What made matters worse, though he was ashamed to admit the fact, was that Kathleen had done fairly well in her own exams. When his results had been published, Gibson had avoided her for several days, and when they met again he had already identified her with the cause of his failure. He could see this so clearly now that it no longer hurt. Had he really been in love if he was prepared to sacrifice Kathleen for the sake of his own self-respect? For that is what it came to; he had tried to shift the blame on to her.

The rest was inevitable. That quarrel on their last long cycle ride together into the country, and their returns by separate routes. The letters that hadn't been opened—above all, the letters that hadn't been written. Their unsuccessful attempt to meet, if only to say goodbye, on his last day in Cambridge. But even this had fallen through; the message hadn't reached Kathleen in time, and though he had waited until the last minute she had never come. The crowded train, packed with cheering students, had drawn noisily out of the station, leaving Cambridge and Kathleen behind. He had never seen either again.

There was no need to tell Jimmy about the dark months that had followed. He need never know what was meant by the simple words: "I had a breakdown and was advised not to return to college." Dr. Evans had made a pretty good job of patching him up, and he'd always be grateful for that. It was Evans who'd persuaded him to take up writing during his convalescence, with results that had surprised them both. (How many people knew that his first novel had been dedicated to his psychoanalyst? Well, if Rachmaninoff could do the same thing with the C Minor Concerto, why shouldn't he?)

Evans had given him a new personality and a vocation through which he could win back his self-confidence. But he couldn't restore the future that had been lost. All his life Gibson would envy the men who had finished what he had only begun—the men who could put after their names the degrees and qualifications he would never possess, and who would find their life's work in fields of which he could be only a spectator.

If the trouble had lain no deeper than this, it might not have mattered greatly. But in salvaging his pride by throwing the blame on to Kathleen he had warped his whole life. She, and through her all women, had become identified with failure and disgrace. Apart from a few attachments which had not been taken very seriously by either partner, Gibson had never fallen in love again, and now he realised that he never would. Knowing the cause of his complaint had helped him not in the least to find a cure.

None of these things, of course, need be mentioned to Jimmy. It was sufficient to give the bare facts, and to leave Jimmy to guess what he could. One day, perhaps, he might tell him more, but that depended on many things.

When Gibson had finished, he was surprised to find how nervously he was waiting for Jimmy's reactions. He felt himself wondering if the boy had read between the lines and apportioned blame where it was due, whether he would be sympathetic, angry—or merely embarrassed. It had suddenly become of the utmost importance to win Jimmy's respect and friendship, more important than anything that had happened to Gibson for a very long time. Only thus could he satisfy his conscience and quieten those accusing voices from the past.

He could not see Jimmy's face, for the other was in shadow and it seemed an age before he broke the silence.

"Why have you told me this?" he asked quietly. His voice was completely neutral—free both from sympathy or reproach.

Gibson hesitated before answering. The pause was natural enough, for, even to himself, he could hardly have explained all his motives.

"I just *had* to tell you," he said earnestly. "I couldn't have been happy until I'd done so. And besides—I felt I might be able to help, somehow."

Again that nerve-racking silence. Then Jimmy rose slowly to his feet.

"I'll have to think about what you've told me," he said, his voice still almost emotionless. "I don't know what to say now."

Then he was gone. He left Gibson in a state of extreme uncertainty and confusion, wondering whether he had made a fool of himself or not. Jimmy's self-control, his failure to react, had thrown him off balance and left him completely at a loss. Only of one thing was he certain: in telling the facts, he had already done a great deal to relieve his mind.

But there was still much that he had not told Jimmy; indeed there was still much that he did not know himself.

SEVEN

"This is completely crazy!" stormed Norden, looking like a berserk Viking chief. "There must be *some* explanation! Good heavens, there aren't any proper docking facilities on Deimos—how do they expect us to unload? I'm going to call the Chief Executive and raise hell!"

"I shouldn't if I were you," drawled Bradley. "Did you notice the signature? This isn't an instruction from Earth, routed through Mars. It originated in the C.E.'s office. The old man may be a Tartar, but he doesn't do things unless he's got a good reason."

"Name just one!"

Bradley shrugged his shoulders.

"I don't have to run Mars, so how would I know? We'll find out soon enough." He gave a malicious little chuckle. "I wonder how Mac is going to take it? He'll have to recompute our approach orbit."

Norden leaned across the control panel and threw a switch.

"Hello, Mac—Skipper here. You receiving me?"

There was a short pause; then Hilton's voice came from the speaker.

"Mac's not here at the moment. Any message?"

"All right—you can break it to him. We've had orders from Mars to re-route the ship. They've diverted us from Phobos—no reason given at all. Tell Mac to calculate an orbit to Deimos, and to let me have it as soon as he can."

"I don't understand it. Why, Deimos is just a lot of mountains with no——"

"Yes—we've been through all that! Maybe we'll know the answer when we get there. Tell Mac to contact me as soon as he can, will you?"

Dr. Scott broke the news to Gibson while the author was putting the final touches to one of his weekly articles.

"Heard the latest?" he exclaimed breathlessly. "We've been diverted to Deimos. Skipper's mad as hell—it may make us a day late."

"Does anyone know why?"

"No; it's a complete mystery. We've asked, but Mars won't tell."

Gibson scratched his head, examining and rejecting half a dozen ideas. He knew that Phobos, the inner moon, had been used as a base ever since the first expedition had reached Mars. Only 6,000 kilometres from the surface of the planet, and with a gravity less than a thousandth of Earth's, it was ideal for this purpose.

The *Ares* was due to dock in less than a week, and already Mars was a small disc showing numerous surface markings even to the naked eye. Gibson had borrowed a large Mercator projection of the planet and had begun to learn the names of its chief features—names that had been given, most of them, more than a century ago by astronomers who had certainly never dreamed that men would one day use them as part of their normal lives. How poetical those old mapmakers had been when they had ransacked mythology! Even to look at those words on the map was to set the blood pounding in the veins—Deucalion, Elysium, Eumenides, Arcadia, Atlantis, Utopia, Eos. . . . Gibson could sit for hours, fondling those wonderful names with his tongue, feeling as if in truth Keats' charm'd magic casements were opening before him. But there were no seas, perilous or otherwise, on Mars—though many of its lands were sufficiently forlorn.

The path of the *Ares* was now cutting steeply across the planet's orbit, and in a few days the motors would be checking the ship's outward speed. The change of velocity needed to deflect the voyage orbit from Phobos to Deimos was trivial, though it had involved Mackay in several hours of computing.

Every meal was devoted to discussing one thing—the crew's plans when Mars was reached. Gibson's could be summed up in one phrase —to see as much as possible. It was, perhaps, a little optimistic to imagine that one could get to know a whole planet in two months, despite Bradley's repeated assurances that two days was quite long enough for Mars.

The excitement of the voyage's approaching end had, to some extent, taken Gibson's mind away from his personal problems. He met Jimmy perhaps half a dozen times a day at meals and during accidental encounters, but they had not reopened their earlier conversation. For a while Gibson suspected that Jimmy was deliberately avoiding him, but he soon realised that this was not altogether the case. Like the rest of the crew, Jimmy was very busy preparing for the end of the voyage. Norden was determined to have the ship in perfect condition when she docked, and a vast amount of checking and servicing was in progress.

Yet despite this activity, Jimmy had given a good deal of thought to what Gibson had told him. At first he had felt bitter and angry towards the man who had been responsible, however unintentionally, for his mother's unhappiness. But after a while, he began to see Gibson's point of view and understood a little of the other's feelings. Jimmy was shrewd enough to guess that Gibson had not only left a good deal untold, but had put his own case as favourably as possible. Even allowing for this, however, it was obvious that Gibson genuinely regretted the past, and was anxious to undo whatever damage he could, even though he was a generation late.

It was strange to feel the sensation of returning weight and to hear the distant roar of the motors once again as the *Ares* reduced her speed to match the far smaller velocity of Mars. The manoeuvring and the final delicate course-corrections took more than twenty-four hours. When it was over, Mars was a dozen times as large as the full moon from Earth, with Phobos and Deimos visible as tiny stars whose movements could be clearly seen after a few minutes of observation.

Gibson had never really realised how red the great deserts were. But the simple word "red" conveyed no idea of the variety of colour on that slowly expanding disc. Some regions were almost scarlet, others yellow-brown, while perhaps the commonest hue was what could best be described as powdered brick.

It was late spring in the southern hemisphere, and the polar cap had dwindled to a few glittering specks of whiteness where the snow still lingered stubbornly on higher ground. The broad belt of vegetation between pole and desert was for the greater part a pale bluish-green, but every imaginable shade of colour could be found somewhere on that mottled disc.

The *Ares* was swimming into the orbit of Deimos at a relative speed of less than a thousand kilometres an hour. Ahead of the ship, the tiny moon was already showing a visible disc, and as the hours passed it grew until, from a few hundred kilometres away, it looked as large as Mars. But what a contrast it presented! Here were no rich reds and greens, only a dark chaos of jumbled rocks, of mountains which jutted up towards the stars at all angles in this world of practically zero gravity.

Slowly the cruel rocks slid closer and swept past them, as the *Ares* cautiously felt her way down towards the radio beacon which Gibson had heard calling days before. Presently he saw, on an almost level area a few kilometres below, the first signs that man had ever visited this barren world. Two rows of vertical pillars jutted up from the ground, and between them was slung a network of cables. Almost imperceptibly the *Ares* sank towards Deimos; the main rockets had long since been silenced, for the small auxiliary jets had no difficulty in handling the ship's effective weight of a few hundred kilogrammes.

It was impossible to tell the moment of contact; only the sudden silence when the jets were cut off told Gibson that the journey was over, and the *Ares* was now resting in the cradle that had been prepared for her. He was still, of course, twenty thousand kilometres from Mars and would not actually reach the planet itself for another day, in one of the little rockets that was already climbing up to meet them. But as far as the *Ares* was concerned, the voyage was ended.

The tiny cabin that had been his home for so many weeks would soon know him no more.

He left the observation deck and hurried up to the control room, which he had deliberately avoided during the last busy hours. It was no longer so easy to move around inside the *Ares*, for the minute gravitational field of Deimos was just sufficient to upset his instinctive movements and he had to make a conscious allowance for it. He wondered just what it would be like to experience a *real* gravitational field again. It was hard to believe that only three months ago the idea of having no gravity at all had seemed very strange and unsettling, yet now he had come to regard it as normal. How adaptable the human body was!

The entire crew was sitting round the chart table, looking very smug and self-satisfied.

"You're just in time, Martin," said Norden cheerfully. "We're going to have a little celebration. Go and get your camera and take our pictures while we toast the old crate's health."

"Don't drink it all before I come back!" warned Gibson, and departed in search of his Leica. When he re-entered, Dr. Scott was attempting an interesting experiment.

"I'm fed up with squirting my beer out of a bulb," he explained.

"I want to pour it properly into a glass now we've got the chance again. Let's see how long it takes."

"It'll be flat before it gets there," warned Mackay. "Let's see—*g*'s about half a centimetre a second squared, you're pouring from a height of . . ." He retired into a brown study.

But the experiment was already in progress. Scott was holding the punctured beer-tin about a foot above his glass—and, for the first time in three months, the word "above" had some meaning, even if very little. For, with incredible slowness, the amber liquid oozed out of the tin—so slowly that one might have taken it for syrup. A thin column extended downwards, moving almost imperceptibly at first, but then slowly accelerating. It seemed an age before the glass was reached; then a great cheer went up as contact was made and the level of the liquid began to creep upwards.

". . . I calculate it should take a hundred and twenty seconds to get there," Mackay's voice was heard to announce above the din.

"Then you'd better calculate again," retorted Scott. "That's two minutes, and it's already there!"

"Eh?" said Mackay, startled, and obviously realising for the first time that the experiment was over. He rapidly rechecked his calculations and suddenly brightened at discovering a misplaced decimal point.

"Silly of me! I never was any good at mental arithmetic. I meant twelve seconds, of course."

"And that's the man who got us to Mars!" said someone in shocked amazement. "I'm going to walk back!"

Nobody seemed inclined to repeat Scott's experiment, which, though interesting, was felt to have little practical value. Very soon large amounts of liquid were being squirted out of bulbs in the "normal" manner, and the party began to get steadily more cheerful. Dr. Scott recited the whole of that saga of the spaceways—and a prodigious feat of memory it was—which paying passengers seldom encounter and which begins:

"It was the spaceship *Venus* . . ."

Gibson followed for some time the adventures of this all too appropriately named craft and its ingenious though single-minded crew. Then the atmosphere began to get too close for him and he left to clear his head. Almost automatically, he made his way back to his favourite viewpoint on the observation deck.

He had to anchor himself in it, lest the tiny but persistent pull of Deimos dislodge him. Mars, more than half full and slowly waxing, lay dead ahead. Down there the preparations to greet them would already be under way, and even at this moment the little rockets would be climbing invisibly towards Deimos to ferry them down. Fourteen thousand kilometres below, but still six thousand kilometres above Mars, Phobos was transiting the unlighted face of the planet, shining brilliantly against its star-eclipsing crescent. Just what *was* happening on that little moon, Gibson wondered half-heartedly. Oh, well, he'd find out soon enough. Meanwhile he'd polish up his aerography. Let's see—there was the double fork of the Sinus Meridiani (very convenient, that, smack on the equator and in zero longitude) and over to the east was the Syrtis Major. Working from these two obvious landmarks he could fill in the finer detail. Margaritifer Sinus was showing up nicely today, but there was a lot of cloud over Xanthe, and——

"Mr. Gibson!"

He looked round, startled.

"Why, Jimmy—you had enough too?"

Jimmy was looking rather hot and flushed—obviously another seeker after fresh air. He wavered, a little unsteadily, into the observation seat and for a moment stared silently at Mars as if he'd never seen it before. Then he shook his head disapprovingly.

"It's awfully big," he announced to no one in particular.

"It isn't as big as Earth," Gibson protested. "And in any case your criticism's completely meaningless, unless you state what standards you're applying. Just what size do you think Mars should be, anyway?"

This obviously hadn't occurred to Jimmy and he pondered it deeply for some time.

"I don't know," he said sadly. "But it's still too big. *Everything's* too big."

This conversation was going to get nowhere, Gibson decided. He would have to change the subject.

"What are you going to do when you get down to Mars? You've got a couple of months to play with before the *Ares* goes home."

"Well, I suppose I'll wander round Port Lowell and go out and look at the deserts. I'd like to do a bit of exploring if I can manage it."

Gibson thought this quite an interesting idea, but he knew that to explore Mars on any useful scale was not an easy undertaking and required a good deal of equipment, as well as experienced guides. It was hardly likely that Jimmy could attach himself to one of the scientific parties which left the settlements from time to time.

"I've an idea," he said. "They're supposed to show me everything I want to see. Maybe I can organise some trips out into Hellas or Hesperia, where no one's been yet. Would you like to come? We might meet some Martians!"

That, of course, had been the stock joke about Mars ever since the first ships had returned with the disappointing news that there weren't any Martians after all. Quite a number of people still hoped, against all evidence, that there might be intelligent life somewhere in the many unexplored regions of the planet.

"Yes," said Jimmy, "that would be a great idea. No one can stop me, anyway—my time's my own as soon as we get to Mars. It says so in the contract."

He spoke this rather belligerently, as if for the information of any superior officers who might be listening, and Gibson thought it wisest to remain silent.

The silence lasted for some minutes. Then Jimmy began, very slowly, to drift out of the observation port and to slide down the sloping walls of the ship. Gibson caught him before he had travelled very far and fastened two of the elastic hand-holds to his clothing—on the principle that Jimmy could sleep here just as comfortably as anywhere else. He was certainly much too tired to carry him to his bunk.

Is it true that we only look our true selves when we are asleep? wondered Gibson. Jimmy seemed very peaceful and contented now that he was completely relaxed—although perhaps the ruby light from the great planet above gave him his appearance of well-being. Gibson hoped it was not all illusion. The fact that Jimmy had at last deliberately sought him out was significant. True, Jimmy was not altogether himself, and he might have forgotten the whole incident by morning. But Gibson did not think so. Jimmy had decided, perhaps not yet consciously, to give him another chance.

He was on probation.

Gibson awoke the next day with a most infernal din ringing in his ears. It sounded as if the *Ares* was falling to pieces around him, and he hastily dressed and hurried out into the corridor. The first person he met was Mackay, who didn't stop to explain but shouted after him as he went by. "The rockets are here! The first one's going down in two hours. Better hurry—you're supposed to be on it!"

Gibson scratched his head a little sheepishly.

"Someone ought to have told me," he grumbled. Then he remembered that someone had, so he'd only himself to blame. He hurried back to his cabin and began to throw his property into suitcases. From time to time the *Ares* gave a distinct shudder around him, and he wondered just what was going on.

Norden, looking rather harassed, met him at the airlock. Dr. Scott, also dressed for departure, was with him. He was carrying, with extreme care, a bulky metal case.

"Hope you two have a nice trip down," said Norden. "We'll be seeing you in a couple of days, when we've got the cargo out. So until then—oh, I almost forgot! I'm supposed to get you to sign this."

"What is it?" asked Gibson suspiciously. "I never sign anything until my agent's vetted it."

"Read it and see," grinned Norden. "It's quite an historic document."

The parchment which Norden had handed him bore these words:

THIS IS TO CERTIFY THAT MARTIN M. GIBSON, AUTHOR, WAS THE FIRST PASSENGER TO TRAVEL IN THE LINER ARES, OF EARTH, ON HER MAIDEN VOYAGE FROM EARTH TO MARS.

Then followed the date, and space for the signatures of Gibson and the rest of the crew. Gibson wrote his autograph with a flourish.

"I suppose this will end up in the museum of Astronautics, when they decide where they're going to build it," he remarked.

"So will the *Ares,* I expect," said Scott.

"That's a fine thing to say at the end of her first trip!" protested Norden. "But I guess you're right. Well, I must be off. The others are outside in their suits—shout to them as you go across. See you on Mars!"

For the second time, Gibson climbed into a spacesuit, now feeling quite a veteran at this sort of thing.

"Of course, you'll understand," explained Scott, "that when the service is properly organised the passengers will go across to the ferry through a connecting tube. That will cut out all this business."

"They'll miss a lot of fun," Gibson replied as he quickly checked the gauges on the little panel beneath his chin.

The outer door opened before them, and they jetted themselves slowly out across the surface of Deimos. The *Ares*, supported in the cradle of ropes (which must have been hastily prepared within the last week) looked as if a wrecking party had been at work on her. Gibson understood now the cause of the bangings and thumpings that had awakened him. Most of the plating from the southern hemisphere had been removed to get at the hold, and the space-suited members of the crew were bringing out the cargo, which was now being piled on the rocks around the ship. It looked, Gibson thought, a very haphazard sort of operation. He hoped that no one would accidentally give his luggage a push which would send it off irretrievably into space, to become a third and still tinier satellite of Mars.

Lying fifty metres from the *Ares*, and quite dwarfed by her bulk, were the two winged rockets that had come up from Mars during the night. One was already having cargo ferried into it; the other, a much smaller vessel, was obviously intended for passengers only. As Gibson slowly and cautiously followed Scott towards it, he switched over to the general wavelength of his suit and called good-bye to his crew-mates. Their envious replies came back promptly, interspersed with much puffing and blowing—for the loads they were shifting, though practically weightless, possessed their normal inertia and so were just as hard to set moving as on Earth.

"That's right!" came Bradley's voice. "Leave us to do all the work!"

"You've one compensation," laughed Gibson. "You must be the highest-paid stevedores in the Solar System!" He could sympathise with Bradley's point of view; this was not the sort of work for which the highly trained technicians of the *Ares* had signed on. But the mysterious diversion of the ship from the tiny though well-equipped port on Phobos had made such improvisations unavoidable.

One couldn't very well make individual good-byes on open circuit with half a dozen people listening, and in any case Gibson would be seeing everyone again in a few days. He would like to have had an extra word with Jimmy, but that would have to wait.

It was quite an experience seeing a new human face again. The rocket pilot came into the airlock to help them with their suits, which were gently deposited back on Deimos for future use simply by opening the outer door again and letting the air current do the rest. Then he led them into the tiny cabin and told them to relax in the padded seats.

"Since you've had no gravity for a couple of months," he said, "I'm taking you down as gently as I can. I won't use more than a normal Earth gravity—but even that may make you feel as if you weigh a ton. Ready?"

"Yes," said Gibson, trying valiantly to forget his last experience of this nature.

There was a gentle, far-away roar and something thrust him firmly down into the depths of his seat. The crags and mountains of Deimos sank swiftly behind; he caught a last glimpse of the *Ares*—a bright silver dumb-bell against that nightmare jumble of rocks.

Only a second's burst of power had liberated them from the tiny moon; they were now floating round Mars in a free orbit. For several minutes the pilot studied his instruments, receiving radio checks from the planet beneath, and swinging the ship round its gyros. Then he punched the firing key again, and the rockets thundered for a few seconds more. The ship had broken free from the orbit of Deimos, and was falling towards Mars. The whole operation was an exact replica, in miniature, of a true interplanetary voyage. Only the times and durations were changed; it would take them three hours, not months, to reach their goal, and they had only thousands instead of millions of kilometres to travel.

"Well," said the pilot, locking his controls and swinging round in his seat. "Had a good trip?"

"Quite pleasant, thanks," said Gibson. "Not much excitement, of course. Everything went very smoothly."

"How's Mars these days?" asked Scott.

"Oh, just the same as usual. All work and not much play. The big thing at the moment is the new dome we're building at Lowell. Three hundred metres clear span—you'll be able to think you're back on Earth. We're wondering if we can arrange clouds and rain inside it."

"What's all this Phobos business?" said Gibson, with a nose for news. "It caused us a lot of trouble."

"Oh, I don't think it's anything important. No one seems to know exactly, but there are quite a lot of people up there building a big lab. My guess is that Phobos is going to be a pure research station, and they don't want liners coming and going—and messing up their instruments with just about every form of radiation known to science."

Gibson felt disappointed at the collapse of several interesting theories. Perhaps if he had not been so intent on the approaching planet he might have considered this explanation a little more critically, but for the moment it satisfied him and he gave the matter no further thought.

When Mars seemed in no great hurry to come closer, Gibson decided to learn all he could about the practical details of life on the planet, now that he had a genuine colonist to question. He had a morbid fear of making a fool of himself, either by ignorance or tactlessness, and for the next couple of hours the pilot was kept busy alternating between Gibson and his instruments.

Mars was less than a thousand kilometres away when Gibson released his victim and devoted his whole attention to the expanding landscape beneath. They were passing swiftly over the equator, coming down into the outer fringes of the planet's extremely deep yet very tenuous atmosphere. Presently—and it was impossible to tell when the moment arrived—Mars ceased to be a planet floating in space, and became instead a landscape far below. Deserts and oases fled beneath; the Syrtis Major came and passed before Gibson had time to recognise it. They were fifty kilometres up when there came the first hint that the air was thickening around them. A faint and distant sighing, seeming to come from nowhere, began to fill the cabin. The thin air was tugging at their hurtling projectile with feeble fingers, but its strength would grow swiftly—too swiftly, if their navigation had been at fault. Gibson could feel the deceleration mounting as the ship slackened its speed; the whistle of air was now so loud, even through the insulation of the walls, that normal speech would have been difficult.

This seemed to last for a very long time, though it could only have been a few minutes. At last the wail of the wind died slowly away. The rocket had shed all its surplus speed against air resistance; the refractory material of its nose and knife-edged wings would be swiftly cooling from cherry-red. No longer a spaceship now, but simply a high-speed glider, the little ship was racing across the desert at less than a thousand kilometres an hour, riding down the radio beam into Port Lowell.

Gibson first glimpsed the settlement as a tiny white patch on the horizon, against the dark background of the Aurorae Sinus. The pilot swung the ship round in a great whistling arc to the south, losing altitude and shedding his surplus speed. As the rocket banked, Gibson had a momentary picture of half a dozen large, circular domes, clustered closely together. Then the ground was rushing up to meet him, there was a series of gentle bumps, and the machine rolled slowly to a standstill.

He was on Mars. He had reached what to ancient man had been a moving red light among the stars, what to the men of only a century ago had been a mysterious and utterly unattainable world—and what was now the frontier of the human race.

"There's quite a reception committee," remarked the pilot. "All the transport fleet's come out to see us. I didn't know they had so many vehicles serviceable!"

Two small, squat machines with very wide balloon tires had come racing up to meet them. Each had a pressurised driving cab, large enough to hold two people, but a dozen passengers had managed to crowd on to the little vehicles by grabbing convenient hand-holds. Behind them came two large half-tracked buses, also full of spectators. Gibson had not expected quite such a crowd, and began to compose a short speech.

"I don't suppose you know how to use these things yet," said the pilot, producing two breathing masks. "But you've only got to wear them for a minute while you get over to the Fleas." (The *what*? thought Gibson. Oh, of course, those little vehicles would be the famous Martian "Sand Fleas," the planet's universal transports.) "I'll fix them on for you. Oxygen O.K.? Right—here we go. It may feel a bit queer at first."

The air slowly hissed from the cabin until the pressure inside and out had been equalised. Gibson felt his exposed skin tingling uncomfortably; the atmosphere around him was now thinner than above the peak of Everest. It had taken three months of slow acclimatisation on the *Ares*, and all the resources of modern medical science, to enable him to step out on to the surface of Mars with no more protection than a simple oxygen mask.

It was flattering that so many people had come to meet him. Of course, it wasn't often that Mars could expect so distinguished a visitor, but he knew that the busy little colony had no time for ceremonial.

Dr. Scott emerged beside him, still carrying the large metal case he had nursed so carefully through the whole of the trip. At his appearance a group of the colonists came rushing forward, completely ignored Gibson, and crowded round Scott. Gibson could hear their voices, so distorted in this thin air as to be almost incomprehensible.

"Glad to see you again, Doc! Here—let us carry it!"

"We've got everything ready, and there are ten cases waiting in hospital now. We should know how good it is in a week."

"Come on—get into the bus and talk later!"

Before Gibson had realised what was happening, Scott and his impedimenta had been swept away. There was a shrill whine of a powerful motor and the bus tore off towards Port Lowell, leaving Gibson feeling as foolish as he had ever been in his life.

He had completely forgotten the serum. To Mars, its arrival was of infinitely greater importance than a visit by any novelist, however distinguished he might be on his own planet. It was a lesson he would not forget in a hurry.

Luckily, he had not been completely deserted—the Sand Fleas were still left. One of the passengers disembarked and hurried up to him.

"Mr. Gibson? I'm Westerman of the 'Times'—the 'Martian Times,' that is. Very pleased to meet you. This is——"

"Henderson, in charge of port facilities," interrupted a tall, hatchet-faced man, obviously annoyed that the other had got in first. "I've seen that your luggage will be collected. Jump aboard."

It was quite obvious that Westerman would have much preferred Gibson as his own passenger, but he was forced to submit with as good grace as he could manage. Gibson climbed into Henderson's Flea through the flexible plastic bag that was the vehicle's simple but effective airlock, and the other joined him a minute later in the driving cab. It was a relief to discard the breathing mask; the few minutes he had spent in the open had been quite a strain. He also felt very heavy and sluggish—the exact reverse of the sensation one would have expected on reaching Mars. But for three months he had known no gravity at all, and it would take him some time to grow accustomed to even a third of his terrestrial weight.

The vehicle began to race across the landing strip towards the domes of the Port, a couple of kilometres away. For the first time, Gibson noticed that all around him was the brilliant mottled green of the hardy plants that were the commonest life-form on Mars. Overhead the sky was no longer jet black, but a deep and glorious blue. The sun was not far from the zenith, and its rays struck with surprising warmth through the plastic dome of the cabin.

Gibson peered at the dark vault of the sky, trying to locate the tiny moon on which his companions were still at work. Henderson noticed his gaze, took one hand off the steering wheel, and pointed close to the Sun.

"There she is," he said.

Gibson shielded his eyes and stared into the sky. Then he saw, hanging like a distant electric arc against the blue, a brilliant star a little westwards of the Sun. It was far too small even for Deimos, but it was a moment before Gibson realised that his companion had mistaken the object of his search.

That steady, unwinking light, burning so unexpectedly in the daylight sky, was now, and would remain for many weeks, the morning star of Mars. But it was better known as Earth.

EIGHT

"Sorry to have kept you waiting," said Mayor Whittaker, "but you know the way it is—the Chief's been in conference for the last hour. I've only just been able to get hold of him myself to tell him you're here. This way—we'll take the short cut through Records."

It might have been an ordinary office on Earth. The door said, simply enough: "Chief Executive." There was no name; it wasn't necessary. Everyone in the Solar System knew who ran Mars—indeed, it was difficult to think of the planet without thinking of Warren Hadfield at the same time.

Gibson was surprised, when he rose from his desk, to see that the Chief Executive was a good deal shorter than he had imagined. He must have judged the man by his works, and had never guessed that he could give him a couple of inches in height. But the thin, wiry frame and sensitive, rather birdlike head were exactly as he had expected.

The interview began with Gibson somewhat on the defensive, for so much depended on his making a good impression. His way would be infinitely easier if he had the Chief on his side. In fact, if he made an enemy of Hadfield he might just as well go home right away.

"I hope Whittaker's been looking after you," said the Chief when the initial courtesies had been exchanged. "You'll realise that I couldn't see you before—I've only just got back from an inspection. How are you settling down here?"

"Quite well," smiled Gibson. "I'm afraid I've broken a few things by leaving them in mid-air, but I'm getting used to living with gravity again."

"And what do you think of our little city?"

"It's a remarkable achievement. I don't know how you managed to do so much in the time."

Hadfield was eyeing him narrowly.

"Be perfectly frank. It's smaller than you expected, isn't it?"

Gibson hesitated.

"Well, I suppose it is—but then I'm used to the standards of London and New York. After all, two thousand people would only make a large village back on Earth. Such a lot of Port Lowell's underground, too, and that makes a difference."

The Chief Executive seemed neither annoyed nor surprised.

"Everyone has a disappointment when they see Mars' largest city," he said. "Still, it's going to be a lot bigger in another week, when the new dome goes up. Tell me—just what are your plans now you've got here? I suppose you know I wasn't very much in favour of this visit in the first place."

"I gathered that on Earth," said Gibson, a little taken aback. He had yet to discover that frankness was one of the Chief Executive's major virtues; it was not one that endeared him to many people. "I suppose you were afraid I'd get in the way."

"Yes. But now you're here, we'll do the best for you. I hope you'll do the same for us."

"In what way?" asked Gibson, stiffening defensively.

Hadfield leaned across the table and clasped his hands together with an almost feverish intensity.

"We're at war, Mr. Gibson. We're at war with Mars and all the forces it can bring against us—cold, lack of water, lack of air. And we're at war with Earth. It's a paper war, true, but it's got its victories and defeats. I'm fighting a campaign at the end of a supply line that's never less than fifty million kilometres long. The most urgent goods take at least five months to reach me—and I only get them if Earth decides I can't manage any other way.

"I suppose you realise what I'm fighting for—my primary objective, that is? It's self-sufficiency. Remember that the first expeditions had to bring *everything* with them. Well, we can provide all the basic necessities of life now, from our own resources. Our workshops can make almost anything that isn't too complicated—but it's all a question of manpower. There are some very specialised goods that simply have to be made on Earth, and until our population's at least ten times as big we can't do much about it. Everyone on Mars is an expert at something—but there are more skilled trades back on Earth than there are people on this planet, and it's no use arguing with arithmetic.

"You see those graphs over there? I started keeping them five years ago. They show our production index for various key materials. We've reached the self-sufficiency level—that horizontal red line—for about half of them. I hope that in another five years there will be very few things we'll have to import from Earth. Even now our greatest need is manpower, and that's where you may be able to help us."

Gibson looked a little uncomfortable.

"I can't make any promises. Please remember that I'm here purely as a reporter. Emotionally, I'm on your side, but I've got to describe the facts as I see them."

"I appreciate that. But facts aren't everything. What I hope you'll explain to Earth is the things we hope to do, just as much as the things we've done. They're even more important—but we can achieve them only if Earth gives us its support. Not all your predecessors have realised that."

That was perfectly true, thought Gibson. He remembered a critical series of articles in the "Daily Telegraph" about a year before. The facts had been quite accurate, but a similar account of the first settlers' achievements after five years' colonisation of North America would probably have been just as discouraging.

"I think I can see both sides of the question," said Gibson. "You've got to realise that from the point of view of Earth, Mars is a long way away, costs a lot of money, and doesn't offer anything in return. The first glamour of interplanetary exploration has worn off. Now people are asking, 'What do we get out of it?' So far the answer's been, 'Very little.' I'm convinced that your work is important, but in my case it's an act of faith rather than a matter of logic. The average man back on Earth probably thinks the millions you're spending here could be better used improving his own planet—when he thinks of it at all, that is."

"I understand your difficulty; it's a common one. And it isn't easy to answer. Let me put it this way. I suppose most intelligent people would admit the value of a scientific base on Mars, devoted to pure research and investigation?"

"Undoubtedly."

"But they can't see the purpose of building up a self-contained culture, which may eventually become an independent civilisation?"

"That's the trouble, precisely. They don't believe it's possible—or, granted the possibility, don't think it's worth while. You'll often see articles pointing out that Mars will always be a drag on the home planet, because of the tremendous natural difficulties under which you're labouring."

"What about the analogy between Mars and the American colonies?"

"It can't be pressed too far. After all, men could breathe the air and find food to eat when they got to America!"

"That's true, but though the problem of colonising Mars is so much more difficult, we've got enormously greater powers at our control. Given time and material, we can make this a world as good to live on as Earth. Even now, you won't find many of our people who want to go back. They know the importance of what they're doing. Earth may not need Mars yet, but one day it will."

"I wish I could believe that," said Gibson, a little unhappily. He pointed to the rich green tide of vegetation that lapped, like a hungry sea, against the almost invisible dome of the city, at the great plain that hurried so swiftly over the edge of the curiously close horizon, and at the scarlet hills within whose arms the city lay. "Mars is an interesting world, even a beautiful one. But it can never be like Earth."

"Why should it be? And what do you mean by 'Earth,' anyway? Do you mean the South American pampas, the vineyards of France, the coral islands of the Pacific, the Siberian steppes? 'Earth' is every one of those! Wherever men can live, that will be home to someone, some day. And sooner or later men will be able to live on Mars without all this." He waved towards the dome which floated above the city and gave it life.

"Do you really think," protested Gibson, "that men can ever adapt themselves to the atmosphere outside? They won't be men any longer if they do!"

For a moment the Chief Executive did not reply. Then he remarked quietly: "I said nothing about men adapting themselves to Mars. Have you ever considered the possibility of Mars meeting us half-way?"

He left Gibson just sufficient time to absorb the words; then, before his visitor could frame the questions that were leaping to his mind, Hadfield rose to his feet.

"Well, I hope Whittaker looks after you and shows you everything you want to see. You'll understand that the transport situation's rather tight, but we'll get you to all the outposts if you give us time to make the arrangements. Let me know if there's any difficulty."

The dismissal was polite and, at least for the time being, final. The busiest man on Mars had given Gibson a generous portion of his time, and his questions would have to wait until the next opportunity.

"What do you think of the Chief, now you've met him?" said Mayor Whittaker when Gibson had returned to the outer office.

"He was very pleasant and helpful," replied Gibson cautiously. "Quite an enthusiast about Mars, isn't he?"

Whittaker pursed his lips.

"I'm not sure that's the right word. I think he regards Mars as an enemy to be beaten. So do we all, of course, but the Chief's got better reasons than most. You'd heard about his wife, hadn't you?"

"No."

"She was one of the first people to die of Martian fever, two years after they came here."

"Oh," said Gibson slowly. "I see. I suppose that's one reason why there's been such an effort to find a cure."

"Yes; the Chief's very much set on it. Besides, it's such a drain on our resources. We can't afford to be sick here!"

That last remark, thought Gibson as he crossed Broadway (so called because it was all of fifteen metres wide), almost summed up the position of the colony. He had still not quite recovered from his initial disappointment at finding how small Port Lowell was, and how deficient in all the luxuries to which he was accustomed on Earth. With its rows of uniform metal houses and few public buildings it was more of a military camp than a city, though the inhabitants had done their best to brighten it up with terrestrial flowers. Some of these had grown to impressive sizes under the low gravity, and Oxford Circus was now ablaze with sunflowers thrice the height of a man. Though they were getting rather a nuisance no one had the heart to suggest their removal; if they continued at their present rate of growth it would soon take a skilled lumberjack to fell them without endangering the port hospital.

Gibson continued thoughtfully up Broadway until he came to Marble Arch, at the meeting point of Domes One and Two. It was also, as he had quickly found, a meeting point in many other ways. Here, strategically placed near the multiple airlocks, was "George's," the only bar on Mars.

"Morning, Mr. Gibson," said George. "Hope the Chief was in a good temper."

As he had left the administration building less than ten minutes ago, Gibson thought this was pretty quick work. He was soon to find that news travelled very rapidly in Port Lowell, and most of it seemed to be routed through George.

George was an interesting character. Since tavern keepers were regarded as only relatively, and not absolutely, essential for the well-being of the Port, he had two official professions. On Earth he had been a well-known stage entertainer, but the unreasonable demands of the three or four wives he had acquired in a rush of youthful enthusiasm had made him decide to emigrate. He was now in charge of the Port's little theatre and seemed to be perfectly contented with life. Being in the middle forties, he was one of the oldest men on Mars.

"We've got a show on next week," he remarked, when he had served Gibson. "One or two quite good turns. Hope you'll be coming along."

"Certainly," said Gibson. "I'll look forward to it. How often do you have this sort of thing?"

"About once a month. We have film shows three times a week, so we don't really do too badly."

"I'm glad Port Lowell has some night-life."

"You'd be surprised. Still, I'd better not tell you about that or you'll be writing it all up in the papers."

"I don't write for *that* sort of newspaper," retorted Gibson, sipping thoughtfully at the local brew. It wasn't at all bad when you got used to it, though of course it was completely synthetic—the joint offspring of hydroponic farm and chemical laboratory.

The bar was quite deserted, for at this time of day everyone in Port Lowell would be hard at work. Gibson pulled out his notebook and began to make careful entries, whistling a little tune as he did so. It was an annoying habit, of which he was quite unconscious, and George counterattacked by turning up the bar radio.

For once it was a live programme, beamed to Mars from somewhere on the night side of Earth, punched across space by heaven-knows-how-many megawatts, then picked up and rebroadcast by the station on the low hills to the south of the city. Reception was good, apart from a trace of solar noise—static from that infinitely greater transmitter against whose background Earth was broadcasting. Gibson wondered if it was really worth all this trouble to send the voice of a somewhat mediocre soprano and a light orchestra from world to world. But half Mars was probably listening with varying degrees of sentimentality and homesickness—both of which would be indignantly denied.

Gibson finished the list of several score questions he had to ask someone. He still felt rather like a new boy at his first school; everything was so strange, nothing could be taken for granted. It was hard to believe that twenty metres on the other side of that transparent bubble lay a sudden death by suffocation. Somehow this feeling had never worried him on the *Ares*; after all, space was like that. But it seemed all wrong here, where one could look out across that brilliant green plain, now a battlefield on which the hardy Martian plants fought their annual struggle for existence—a struggle which would end in death for victors and vanquished alike with the coming of winter.

Suddenly Gibson felt an almost overwhelming desire to leave the narrow streets and go out beneath the open sky. For almost the first time, he found himself really missing Earth, the planet he had thought had so little more to offer him. Like Falstaff, he felt like babbling of green fields—with the added irony that green fields were all around him, tantalisingly visible yet barred from him by the laws of nature.

"George," said Gibson abruptly, "I've been here awhile and I haven't been outside yet. I'm not supposed to without someone to look after me. You won't have any customers for an hour or so. Be a sport and take me out through the airlock—just for ten minutes."

No doubt, thought Gibson a little sheepishly, George considered this a pretty crazy request. He was quite wrong; it had happened so often before that George took it very much for granted. After all, his job was attending to the whims of his customers, and most of the new boys seemed to feel this way after their first few days under the dome. George shrugged his shoulders philosophically, wondering if he should apply for additional credits as Port psycho-therapist, and disappeared into his inner sanctum. He came back a moment later, carrying a couple of breathing masks and their auxiliary equipment.

"We won't want the whole works on a nice day like this," he said, while Gibson clumsily adjusted his gear. "Make sure that sponge rubber fits snugly around your neck. All right—let's go. But only ten minutes, mind!"

Gibson followed eagerly, like a sheepdog behind its master, until they came to the dome exit. There were two locks here, a large one, wide open, leading into Dome Two, and a smaller one which led out on to the open landscape. It was simply a metal tube, about three metres in diameter, leading through the glass-brick wall which anchored the flexible plastic envelope of the dome to the ground.

There were four separate doors, none of which could be opened unless the remaining three were closed. Gibson fully approved of these precautions, but it seemed a long time before the last of the doors swung inwards from its seals and that vivid green plain lay open before him. His exposed skin was tingling under the reduced pressure, but the thin air was reasonably warm and he soon felt quite comfortable. Completely ignoring George, he ploughed his way briskly through the low, closely packed vegetation, wondering as he did why it clustered so thickly round the dome. Perhaps it was attracted by the warmth or the slow seepage of oxygen from the city.

He stopped after a few hundred metres, feeling at last clear of that oppressive canopy and once more under the open sky of heaven. The fact that his head, at least, was still totally enclosed somehow didn't seem to matter. He bent down and examined the plants among which he was standing knee-deep.

He had, of course, seen photographs of Martian plants many times before. They were not really very exciting, and he was not enough of a botanist to appreciate their peculiarities. Indeed if he had met such plants in some out-of-the-way part of Earth he would hardly have looked at them twice. None were higher than his waist, and those around him now seemed to be made of sheets of brilliant green parchment, very thin but very tough, designed to catch as much sunlight as possible without losing precious water. These ragged sheets were spread like little sails in the sun, whose progress across the sky they would follow until they dipped westwards at dusk. Gibson wished there were some flowers to add a touch of contrasting colour to the vivid emerald, but there were no flowers on Mars. Perhaps there had been, once, when the air was thick enough to support insects, but now most of the Martian plant-life was self-fertilised.

George caught up with him and stood regarding the natives with a morose indifference. Gibson wondered if he was annoyed at being so summarily dragged out of doors, but his qualms of conscience were unjustified. George was simply brooding over his next production, wondering whether to risk a Noel Coward play after the disaster that had resulted the last time his company had tried its hand with period pieces. Suddenly he snapped out of his reverie and said to Gibson, his voice thin but clearly audible over this short distance: "This is rather amusing. Just stand still for a minute and watch that plant in your shadow."

Gibson obeyed this peculiar instruction. For a moment nothing happened. Then he saw that, very slowly, the parchment sheets were folding in on one another. The whole process was over in about three minutes; at the end of that time the plant had become a little ball of green paper, tightly crumpled together and only a fraction of its previous size.

George chuckled.

"It thinks night's fallen," he said, "and doesn't want to be caught napping when the sun's gone. If you move away, it will think things over for half an hour before it risks opening shop again. You could probably give it a nervous breakdown if you kept this up all day."

"Are these plants any use?" said Gibson. "I mean, can they be eaten, or do they contain any valuable chemicals?"

"They certainly can't be eaten—they're not poisonous but they'd make you feel mighty unhappy. You see they're not really like plants on Earth at all. That green is just a coincidence. It isn't—what do you call the stuff——"

"Chlorophyll?"

"Yes. They don't depend on the air as our plants do; everything they need they get from the ground. In fact they can grow in a complete vacuum, like the plants on the Moon, if they've got suitable soil and enough sunlight."

Quite a triumph of evolution, thought Gibson. But to what purpose? he wondered. Why had life clung so tenaciously to this little world, despite the worst that nature could do? Perhaps the Chief Executive had obtained some of his own optimism from these tough and resolute plants.

"Hey!" said George. "It's time to go back."

Gibson followed meekly enough. He no longer felt weighed down by that claustrophobic oppression which was, he knew, partly due to the inevitable reaction at finding Mars something of an anticlimax. Those who had come here for a definite job, and hadn't been given time to brood, would probably by-pass this stage altogether. But he had been turned loose to collect his impressions, and so far his chief one was a feeling of helplessness as he compared what man had so far achieved on Mars with the problems still to be faced. Why, even now three-quarters of the planet was still unexplored! That was some measure of what remained to be done.

The first few days at Port Lowell had been busy and exciting enough. It had been a Sunday when he had arrived and Mayor Whittaker had been sufficiently free from the cares of office to show him round the city personally, once he had been installed in one of the four suites of the Grand Martian Hotel. (The other three had not yet been finished.) They had started at Dome One, the first to be built, and the Mayor had proudly traced the growth of his city from a group of pressurised huts only ten years ago. It was amusing—and rather touching—to see how the colonists had used wherever possible the names of familiar streets and squares from their own far-away cities. There was also a scientific system of numbering the streets in Port Lowell, but nobody ever used it.

Most of the living houses were uniform metal structures, two stories high, with rounded corners and rather small windows. They held two families and were none too large, since the birth-rate of Port Lowell was the highest in the known universe. This, of course, was hardly surprising since almost the entire population lay between the ages of twenty and thirty, with a few of the senior administrative staff creeping up into the forties. Every house had a curious porch which puzzled Gibson until he realised that it was designed to act as an airlock in an emergency.

Whittaker had taken him first to the administrative centre, the tallest building in the city. If one stood on its roof, one could almost reach up and touch the dome floating above. There was nothing very exciting about Admin. It might have been any office building on Earth, with its rows of desks and typewriters and filing cabinets.

Main Air was much more interesting. This, truly, was the heart of Port Lowell; if it ever ceased to function, the city and all those it held would soon be dead. Gibson had been somewhat vague about the manner in which the settlement obtained its oxygen. At one time he had been under the impression that it was extracted from the surrounding air, having forgotten that even such scanty atmosphere as Mars possessed contained less than one per cent of the gas.

Mayor Whittaker had pointed to the great heap of red sand that had been bulldozed in from outside the dome. Everyone called it "sand," but it had little resemblance to the familiar sand of Earth.

A complex mixture of metallic oxides, it was nothing less than the debris of a world that had rusted to death.

"All the oxygen we need's in these ores," said Whittaker, kicking at the caked powder. "And just about every metal you can think of. We've had one or two strokes of luck on Mars: this is the biggest."

He bent down and picked up a lump more solid than the rest.

"I'm not much of a geologist," he said, "but look at this. Pretty, isn't it? Mostly iron oxide, they tell me. Iron isn't much use, of course, but the other metals are. About the only one we can't get easily direct from the sand is magnesium. The best source of that's the old sea bed; there are some salt flats a hundred metres thick out in Xanthe and we just go and collect when we need it."

They walked into the low, brightly lit building, towards which a continual flow of sand was moving on a conveyor belt. There was not really a great deal to see, and though the engineer in charge was only too anxious to explain just what was happening, Gibson was content merely to learn that the ores were cracked in electric furnaces, the oxygen drawn off, purified and compressed, and the various metallic messes sent on for more complicated operations. A good deal of water was also produced here—almost enough for the settlement's needs, though other sources were available as well.

"Of course," said Mayor Whittaker, "in addition to storing the oxygen we've got to keep the air pressure at the correct value and to get rid of the CO_2. You realise, don't you, that the dome's kept up purely by the internal pressure and hasn't any other support at all?"

"Yes," said Gibson. "I suppose if that fell off the whole thing would collapse like a deflated balloon."

"Exactly. We keep 150 millimetres pressure in summer, a little more in winter. That gives almost the same oxygen pressure as in Earth's atmosphere. And we remove the CO_2 simply by letting plants do the trick. We imported enough for this job, since the Martian plants don't go in for photosynthesis."

"Hence the hypertrophied sunflowers in Oxford Circus, I suppose."

"Well, those are intended to be more ornamental than functional. I'm afraid they're getting a bit of a nuisance; I'll have to stop them from spraying seeds all over the city, or whatever it is that sunflowers do. Now let's walk over and look at the farm."

The name was a singularly misleading one for the big food-production plant filling Dome Three. The air was quite humid here, and the sunlight was augmented by batteries of fluorescent tubes so that growth could continue day and night. Gibson knew very little about hydroponic farming and so was not really impressed by the figures which Mayor Whittaker proudly poured into his ear. He could, however, appreciate that one of the greatest problems was meat production, and admired the ingenuity which had partly overcome this by extensive tissue-culture in great vats of nutrient fluid.

"It's better than nothing," said the Mayor a little wistfully. "But what I wouldn't give for a genuine lamb-chop! The trouble with natural meat production is that it takes up so much space and we simply can't afford it. However, when the new dome's up we're going to start a little farm with a few sheep and cows. The kids will love it—they've never seen any animals, of course."

This was not quite true, as Gibson was soon to discover: Mayor Whittaker had momentarily overlooked two of Port Lowell's best-known residents.

By the end of the tour Gibson began to suffer from slight mental indigestion. The mechanics of life in the city were so complicated, and Mayor Whittaker tried to show him *everything*. He was quite thankful when the trip was over and they returned to the Mayor's home for dinner.

"I think that's enough for one day," said Whittaker, "but I wanted to show you round because we'll all be busy tomorrow and I won't be able to spare much time. The Chief's away, you know, and won't be back until Thursday, so I've got to look after everything."

"Where's he gone?" asked Gibson, out of politeness rather than real interest.

"Oh, up to Phobos," Whittaker replied, with the briefest possible hesitation. "As soon as he gets back he'll be glad to see you."

The conversation had then been interrupted by the arrival of Mrs. Whittaker and family, and for the rest of the evening Gibson was compelled to talk about Earth. It was his first, but not by any means his last, experience of the insatiable interest which the colonists had in the home planet. They seldom admitted it openly, pretending to a stubborn indifference about the "old world" and its affairs. But their questions, and above all their rapid reactions to terrestrial criticisms and comments, belied this completely.

It was strange to talk to children who had never known Earth, who had been born and had spent all their short lives under the shelter of the great domes. What, Gibson wondered, did Earth mean to them? Was it any more real than the fabulous lands of fairy tales? All they knew of the world from which their parents had emigrated was at second hand, derived from books and pictures. As far as their own senses were concerned, Earth was just another star.

They had never known the coming of the seasons. Outside the dome, it was true, they could watch the long winter spread death over the land as the Sun descended in the northern sky, could see the strange plants wither and perish, to make way for the next generation when spring returned. But no hint of this came through the protecting barriers of the city. The engineers at the power plant simply threw in more heater circuits and laughed at the worst that Mars could do.

Yet these children, despite their completely artificial environment, seemed happy and well, and quite unconscious of all the things which they had missed. Gibson wondered just what their reactions would be if they ever came to Earth. It would be a very interesting experiment, but so far none of the children born on Mars were old enough to leave their parents.

The lights of the city were going down when Gibson left the Mayor's home after his first day on Mars. He said very little as Whittaker walked back with him to the hotel, for his mind was too full of jumbled impressions. In the morning he would start to sort them out, but at the moment his chief feeling was that the greatest city on Mars was nothing more than an over-mechanised village.

Gibson had not yet mastered the intricacies of the Martian calendar, but he knew that the week-days were the same as on Earth and that Monday followed Sunday in the usual way. (The months also had the same names, but were fifty to sixty days in length.) When he left the hotel at what he thought was a reasonable hour, the city appeared quite deserted. There were none of the gossiping groups of people who had watched his progress with such interest on the previous day. Everyone was at work in office, factory, or lab, and Gibson felt rather like a drone who had strayed into a particularly busy hive.

He found Mayor Whittaker beleaguered by secretaries and talking into two telephones at once. Not having the heart to intrude, Gibson tiptoed away and started a tour of exploration himself. There was not, after all, any great danger of becoming lost. The maximum distance he would travel in a straight line was less than half a kilometre. It was not the kind of exploration of Mars he had ever imagined in any of his books. . . .

So he had passed his first few days in Port Lowell wandering round and asking questions during working hours, spending the evenings with the families of Mayor Whittaker or other members of the senior staff. Already he felt as if he had lived here for years. There was nothing new to be seen; he had met everyone of importance, up to and including the Chief Executive himself.

But he knew he was still a stranger: he had really seen less than a thousand millionth of the whole surface of Mars. Beyond the shelter of the dome, beyond the crimson hills, over the edge of the emerald plain—all the rest of this world was mystery.

NINE

"Well, it's certainly nice to see you all again," said Gibson, carrying the drinks carefully across from the bar. "Now I suppose you're going to paint Port Lowell red. I presume the first move will be to contact the local girl friends?"

"That's never very easy," said Norden. "They *will* get married between trips, and you've got to be tactful. By the way, George, what's happened to Miss Margaret Mackinnon?"

"You mean Mrs. Henry Lewis," said George. "Such a fine baby boy, too."

"Has she called it John?" asked Bradley, not particularly *sotto voce*.

"Oh, well," sighed Norden, "I hope she's saved me some of the wedding cake. Here's to you, Martin."

"And to the *Ares*," said Gibson clinking glasses. "I hope you've put her together again. She looked in a pretty bad way the last time I saw her."

Norden chuckled.

"Oh, that! No, we'll leave all the plating off until we reload. The rain isn't likely to get in!"

"What do you think of Mars, Jimmy?" asked Gibson. "You're the only other new boy here besides myself."

"I haven't seen much of it yet," Jimmy replied cautiously. "Everything seems rather small, though."

Gibson spluttered violently and had to be patted on the back.

"I remember your saying just the opposite when we were on Deimos. But I guess you've forgotten it. You were slightly drunk at the time."

"I've never been drunk," said Jimmy indignantly.

"Then I compliment you on a first-rate imitation: it deceived me completely. But I'm interested in what you say, because that's exactly how I felt after the first couple of days, as soon as I'd seen all there was to look at inside the dome. There's only one cure—you have to go outside and stretch your legs. I've had a couple of short walks around, but now I've managed to grab a Sand Flea from Transport. I'm going to gallop up into the hills tomorrow. Like to come?"

Jimmy's eyes glistened.

"Thanks very much—I'd love to."

"Hey, what about us?" protested Norden.

"You've done it before," said Gibson. "But there'll be one spare seat, so you can toss for it. We've got to take an official driver; they won't let us go out by ourselves with one of their precious vehicles, and I suppose you can hardly blame them."

Mackay won the toss, whereupon the others immediately explained that they didn't really want to go anyway.

"Well, that settles that," said Gibson. "Meet me at Transport Section, Dome Four, at 10 tomorrow. Now I must be off. I've got three articles to write—or at any rate one article with three different titles."

The explorers met promptly on time, carrying the full protective equipment which they had been issued on arrival but so far had found no occasion to use. This comprised the headpiece, oxygen cylinders, and air purifier—all that was necessary out of doors on Mars on a warm day—and the heat-insulating suit with its compact power cells. This could keep one warm and comfortable even when the temperature outside was more than a hundred below. It would not be needed on this trip, unless an accident to the Flea left them stranded a long way away from home.

The driver was a tough young geologist who claimed to have spent as much time outside Port Lowell as in it. He looked extremely competent and resourceful, and Gibson felt no qualms at handing his valuable person into his keeping.

"Do these machines ever break down outside?" he asked as they climbed into the Flea.

"Not very often. They've got a terrific safety factor and there's really very little to go wrong. Of course, sometimes a careless driver gets stuck, but you can usually haul yourself out of anything with the winch. There have only been a couple of cases of people having to walk home in the last month."

"I trust we won't make a third," said Mackay, as the vehicle rolled into the lock.

"I shouldn't worry about that," laughed the driver, waiting for the outer door to open. "We won't be going far from base, so we can always get back even if the worst comes to the worst."

With a surge of power, they shot through the lock and out of the city. A narrow road had been cut through the low, vivid vegetation—a road which circled the port and from which other highways radiated to the nearby mines, to the radio station and observatory on the hills, and to the landing ground on which even now the *Ares'* freight was being unloaded as the rockets ferried it down from Deimos.

"Well," said the driver, halting at the first junction. "It's all yours. Which way do we go?"

Gibson was struggling with a map three sizes too big for the cabin. Their guide looked at it with scorn.

"I don't know where you got hold of *that*," he said. "I suppose Admin gave it to you. It's completely out of date, anyway. If you'll tell me where you want to go I can take you there without bothering about that thing."

"Very well," Gibson replied meekly. "I suggest we climb up into the hills and get a good look round. Let's go to the Observatory."

The Flea leapt forward along the narrow road and the brilliant green around them merged into a featureless blur.

"How fast can these things go?" asked Gibson, when he had climbed out of Mackay's lap.

"Oh, at least a hundred on a good road. But as there aren't any good roads on Mars, we have to take it easy. I'm doing sixty now. On rough ground you'll be lucky to average half that."

"And what about range?" said Gibson, obviously still a little nervous.

"A good thousand kilometres on one charge, even allowing pretty generously for heating, cooking, and the rest. For really long trips we tow a trailer with spare power cells. The record's about five thousand kilometres; I've done three before now, prospecting out in Argyre. When you're doing that sort of thing, you arrange to get supplies dropped from the air."

Though they had now been travelling for no more than a couple of minutes, Port Lowell was already falling below the horizon. The steep curvature of Mars made it very difficult to judge distances, and the fact that the domes were now half concealed by the curve of the planet made one imagine that they were much larger objects at a far greater distance than they really were.

Soon afterwards, they began to reappear as the Flea started climbing towards higher ground. The hills above Port Lowell were less than a kilometre high, but they formed a useful break for the cold winter winds from the south, and gave vantage points for radio station and observatory.

They reached the radio station half an hour after leaving the city. Feeling it was time to do some walking, they adjusted their masks and dismounted from the Flea, taking turns to go through the tiny collapsible airlock.

The view was not really very impressive. To the north, the domes of Port Lowell floated like bubbles on an emerald sea. Over to the west Gibson could just catch a glimpse of crimson from the desert which encircled the entire planet. As the crest of the hills still lay a little above him, he could not see southwards, but he knew that the green band of vegetation stretched for several hundred kilometres until it petered out into the Mare Erythraeum. There were hardly any plants here on the hilltop, and he presumed that this was due to the absence of moisture.

He walked over to the radio station. It was quite automatic, so there was no one he could buttonhole in the usual way, but he knew enough about the subject to guess what was going on. The giant parabolic reflector lay almost on its back, pointing a little east of the zenith—pointing to Earth, sixty million kilometres Sunwards. Along its invisible beam were coming and going the messages that linked these two worlds together. Perhaps at this very moment one of his own articles was flying Earthwards—or one of Ruth Goldstein's directives was winging its way towards him.

Mackay's voice, distorted and feeble in this thin air, made him turn round.

"Someone's coming in to land down there—over on the right."

With some difficulty, Gibson spotted the tiny arrowhead of the rocket moving swiftly across the sky, racing in on a free glide just as he had done a week before. It banked over the city and was lost behind the domes as it touched down on the landing strip. Gibson hoped it was bringing in the remainder of his luggage, which seemed to have taken a long time to catch up with him.

The Observatory was about five kilometres further south, just over the brow of the hills, where the lights of Port Lowell would not interfere with its work. Gibson had half expected to see the gleaming domes which on Earth were the trade-marks of the astronomers, but instead the only dome was the small plastic bubble of the living quarters. The instruments themselves were in the open, though there was provision for covering them up in the very rare event of bad weather.

Everything appeared to be completely deserted as the Flea approached. They halted beside the largest instrument—a reflector with a mirror which, Gibson guessed, was less than a metre across. It was an astonishingly small instrument for the chief observatory on Mars. There were two small refractors, and a complicated horizontal affair which Mackay said was a mirror-transit—whatever that might be. And this, apart from the pressurised dome, seemed to be about all.

There was obviously someone at home, for a small Sand Flea was parked outside the building.

"They're quite a sociable crowd," said the driver as he brought the vehicle to a halt. "It's a pretty dull life up here and they're always glad to see people. And there'll be room inside the dome for us to stretch our legs and have dinner in comfort."

"Surely we can't expect them to provide a meal for us," protested Gibson, who had a dislike of incurring obligations he couldn't readily discharge. The driver looked genuinely surprised; then he laughed heartily.

"This isn't Earth, you know. On Mars, everyone helps everyone else—we have to, or we'd never get anywhere. But I've brought our provisions along—all I want to use is their stove. If you'd ever tried to cook a meal inside a Sand Flea with four aboard you'd know why."

As predicted, the two astronomers on duty greeted them warmly, and the little plastic bubble's air-conditioning plant was soon dealing with the odours of cookery. While this was going on, Mackay had grabbed the senior member of the staff and started a technical discussion about the Observatory's work. Most of it was quite over Gibson's head, but he tried to gather what he could from the conversation.

Most of the work done here was, it seemed, positional astronomy—the dull but essential business of finding longitudes and latitudes, providing time signals and linking radio fixes with the main Martian grid. Very little observational work was done at all; the huge instruments on Earth's moon had taken *that* over long ago, and these small telescopes, with the additional handicap of an atmosphere above them, could not hope to compete. The parallaxes of a few nearer stars had been measured, but the very slight increase of accuracy provided by the wider orbit of Mars made it hardly worth while.

As he ate his dinner—finding to his surprise that his appetite was better than at any time since reaching Mars—Gibson felt a glow of satisfaction at having done a little to brighten the dull lives of these devoted men. Because he had never met enough of them to shatter the illusion, Gibson had an altogether disproportionate respect for astronomers, whom he regarded as leading lives of monkish dedication on their remote mountain eyries. Even his first encounter with the excellent cocktail bar on Mount Palomar had not destroyed this simple faith.

After the meal, at which everyone helped so conscientiously with the washing-up that it took twice as long as necessary, the visitors were invited to have a look through the large reflector. Since it was early afternoon, Gibson did not imagine that there would be a great deal to see; but this was an oversight on his part.

For a moment the picture was blurred, and he adjusted the focussing screw with clumsy fingers. It was not easy to observe with the special eyepiece needed when one was wearing a breathing mask, but after a while Gibson got the knack of it.

Hanging in the field of view, against the almost black sky near the zenith, was a beautiful pearly crescent like a three-day-old moon. Some markings were just visible on the illuminated portion, but though Gibson strained his eyes to the utmost he could not identify them. Too much of the planet was in darkness for him to see any of the major continents.

Not far away floated an identically shaped but much smaller and fainter crescent, and Gibson could distinctly see some of the familiar craters along its edge. They formed a beautiful couple, the twin planets Earth and Moon, but somehow they seemed too remote and ethereal to give him any feeling of homesickness or regret for all that he had left behind.

One of the astronomers was speaking, his helmet held close to Gibson's.

"When it's dark you can see the lights of the cities down there on the night side. New York and London are easy. The prettiest sight, though, is the reflections of the Sun off the sea. You get it near the edge of the disc when there's no cloud about—a sort of brilliant, shimmering star. It isn't visible now because it's mostly land on the crescent portion."

Before leaving the Observatory, they had a look at Deimos, which was rising in its leisurely fashion in the east. Under the highest power of the telescope the rugged little moon seemed only a few kilometres away, and to his surprise Gibson could see the *Ares* quite clearly as two gleaming dots close together. He also wanted to look at Phobos, but the inner moon had not yet risen.

When there was nothing more to be seen, they bade farewell to the two astronomers, who waved back rather glumly as the Flea drove off along the brow of the hill. The driver explained that he wanted to make a private detour to pick up some rock specimens, and as to Gibson one part of Mars was very much like another he raised no objection.

There was no real road over the hills, but ages ago all irregularities had been worn away so that the ground was perfectly smooth. Here and there a few stubborn boulders still jutted above the surface, displaying a fantastic riot of colour and shape, but these obstacles were easily avoided. Once or twice they passed small trees—if one could call them that—of a type which Gibson had never seen before. They looked rather like pieces of coral, completely stiff and petrified. According to their driver they were immensely old, for though they were certainly alive no one had yet been able to measure their rate of growth. The smallest value which could be derived for their age was fifty thousand years, and their method of reproduction was a complete mystery.

Towards mid-afternoon they came to a low but beautifully coloured cliff—"Rainbow Ridge," the geologist called it—which reminded Gibson irresistibly of the more flamboyant Arizona canyons, though on a much smaller scale. They got out of the Sand Flea and, while the driver chipped off his samples, Gibson happily shot off half a reel of the new Multichrome film he had brought with him for just such occasions. If it could bring out all those colours perfectly it must be as good as the makers claimed, but unfortunately he'd have to wait until he got back to Earth before it could be developed. No one on Mars knew anything about it.

"Well," said the driver, "I suppose it's time we started for home if we want to get back for tea. We can drive back the way we came, and keep to the high ground, or we can go round behind the hills. Any preferences?"

"Why not drive down into the plain? That would be the most direct route," said Mackay, who was now getting a little bored.

"And the slowest—you can't drive at any speed through those overgrown cabbages."

"I always hate retracing my steps," said Gibson. "Let's go round the hills and see what we can find there."

The driver grinned.

"Don't raise any false hopes. It's much the same on both sides. Here we go!"

The Flea bounced forward and Rainbow Ridge soon disappeared behind them. They were now winding their way through completely barren country, and even the petrified trees had vanished. Sometimes Gibson saw a patch of green which he thought was vegetation, but as they approached it invariably turned into another mineral outcrop. This region was fantastically beautiful, a geologist's paradise, and Gibson hoped that it would never be ravaged by mining operations. It was certainly one of the show places of Mars.

They had been driving for half an hour when the hills sloped down into a long, winding valley which was unmistakably an ancient watercourse. Perhaps fifty million years ago, the driver told them, a great river had flowed this way to lose its waters in the Mare Erythraeum—one of the few Martian "seas" to be correctly, if somewhat belatedly, named. They stopped the Flea and gazed down the empty river bed with mingled feelings. Gibson tried to picture this scene as it must have appeared in those remote days, when the great reptiles ruled the Earth and Man was still a dream of the distant future. The red cliffs would scarcely have changed in all that time, but between them the river would have made its unhurried way to the sea, flowing slowly under the weak gravity. It was a scene that might almost have belonged to Earth; and had it ever been witnessed by intelligent eyes? No one knew. Perhaps there had indeed been Martians in those days, but time had buried them completely.

The ancient river had left a legacy, for there was still moisture along the lower reaches of the valley. A narrow band of vegetation had come thrusting up from Erythraeum, its brilliant green contrasting vividly with the crimson of the cliffs. The plants were those which Gibson had already met on the other side of the hills, but here and there were strangers. They were tall enough to be called trees, but they had no leaves—only thin, whip-like branches which continually trembled despite the stillness of the air. Gibson thought they were some of the most sinister things he had ever seen—just the sort of ominous plant that would suddenly flick out its tentacles at an unsuspecting passer-by. In fact, as he was perfectly well aware, they were as harmless as everything else on Mars.

They had zigzagged down into the valley and were climbing the other slope when the driver suddenly brought the Flea to a halt.

"Hello!" he said. "This is odd. I didn't know there was any traffic in these parts."

For a moment Gibson, who was not really as observant as he liked to think, was at a loss. Then he noticed a faint track running along the valley at right angles to their present path.

"There have been some heavy vehicles here," said the driver. "I'm sure this track didn't exist the last time I came this way—let's see, about a year ago. And there haven't been any expeditions into Erythraeum in that time."

"Where does it lead?" asked Gibson.

"Well, if you go up the valley and over the top you'll be back in Port Lowell; that was what I intended to do. The other direction only leads out into the Mare."

"We've got time—let's go along it a little way."

Willingly enough, the driver swung the Flea around and headed down the valley. From time to time the track vanished as they went over smooth, open rock, but it always reappeared again. At last, however, they lost it completely.

The driver stopped the Flea.

"I know what's happened," he said. "There's only one way it could have gone. Did you notice that pass about a kilometre back? Ten to one it leads up there."

"And where would that take anyone?"

"That's the funny thing—it's a complete cul-de-sac. There's a nice little amphitheatre about two kilometres across, but you can't get out of it anywhere except the way you came in. I spent a couple of hours there once when we did the first survey of this region. It's quite a pretty little place, sheltered and with some water in the Spring."

"A good hide-out for smugglers," laughed Gibson.

The driver grinned.

"That's an idea. Maybe there's a gang bringing in contraband beefsteaks from Earth. I'd settle for one a week to keep my mouth shut."

The narrow pass had obviously once contained a tributary of the main river, and the going was a good deal rougher than in the main valley. They had not driven very far before it became quite clear that they were on the right track.

"There's been some blasting here," said the driver. "This bit of road didn't exist when I came this way. I had to make a detour up that slope, and nearly had to abandon the Flea."

"What do you think's going on?" asked Gibson, now getting quite excited.

"Oh, there are several research projects that are so specialised that one doesn't hear a lot about them. Some things can't be done near the city, you know. They may be building a magnetic observatory here—there's been some talk of that. The generators at Port Lowell would be pretty well shielded by the hills. But I don't think that's the explanation, for I'd have heard—Good Lord!"

They had suddenly emerged from the pass, and before them lay an almost perfect oval of green, flanked by the low, ochre hills. Once this might have been a lovely mountain lake; it was still a solace to the eye weary of lifeless, multicoloured rock. But for the moment Gibson scarcely noticed the brilliant carpet of vegetation; he was too astonished by the cluster of domes, like a miniature of Port Lowell itself, grouped at the edge of the little plain.

They drove in silence along the road that had been cut through the living green carpet. No one was moving outside the domes, but a large transporter vehicle, several times the size of the Sand Flea, showed that someone was certainly at home.

"This is quite a set-up," remarked the driver as he adjusted his mask. "There must be a pretty good reason for spending all this money. Just wait here while I go over and talk to them."

They watched him disappear into the airlock of the larger dome. It seemed to his impatient passengers that he was gone rather a long time. Then they saw the outer door open again and he walked slowly back towards them.

"Well?" asked Gibson eagerly as the driver climbed back into the cab. "What did they have to say?"

There was a slight pause; then the driver started the engine and the Sand Flea began to move off.

"I say—what about this famous Martian hospitality? Aren't we invited in?" cried Mackay.

The driver seemed embarrassed. He looked, Gibson thought, exactly like a man who had just discovered he's made a fool of himself. He cleared his throat nervously.

"It's a plant research station," he said, choosing his words with obvious care. "It's not been going for very long, which is why I hadn't heard of it before. We can't go inside because the whole place is sterile and they don't want spores brought in—we'd have to change all our clothes and have a bath of disinfectant."

"I see," said Gibson. Something told him it was no use asking any further questions. He knew, beyond all possibility of error, that his guide had told him only part of the truth—and the least important part at that. For the first time the little discrepancies and doubts that Gibson had hitherto ignored or forgotten began to crystallise in his mind. It had started even before he reached Mars, with the diversion of the *Ares* from Phobos. And now he had stumbled upon this hidden research station. It had been as big a surprise to their experienced guide as to them, but he was attempting to cover up his accidental indiscretion.

There was something going on. What it was, Gibson could not imagine. It must be big, for it concerned not only Mars but Phobos. It was something unknown to most of the colonists, yet something they would co-operate in keeping secret when they encountered it.

Mars was hiding something; and it could only be hiding it from Earth.

TEN

The Grand Martian Hotel now had no less than two residents, a state of affairs which imposed a severe strain on its temporary staff. The rest of his shipmates had made private arrangements for their accommodation in Port Lowell, but as he knew no one in the city Jimmy had decided to accept official hospitality. Gibson wondered if this was going to be a success; he did not wish to throw too great a strain on their still somewhat provisional friendship, and if Jimmy saw too much of him the results might be disastrous. He remembered an epigram which his best enemy had once concocted: "Martin's one of the nicest fellows you could meet, as long as you don't do it too often." There was enough truth in this to make it sting, and he had no wish to put it to the test again.

His life in the Port had now settled down to a fairly steady routine. In the morning he would work, putting on paper his impressions of

Mars—rather a presumptuous thing to do when he considered just how much of the planet he had so far seen. The afternoon was reserved for tours of inspection and interviews with the city's inhabitants. Sometimes Jimmy went with him on these trips, and once the whole of the *Ares* crew came along to the hospital to see how Dr. Scott and his colleagues were progressing with their battle against Martian fever. It was still too early to draw any conclusions, but Scott seemed fairly optimistic. "What we'd like to have," he said rubbing his hands ghoulishly, "is a really good epidemic so that we could test the stuff properly. We haven't enough cases at the moment."

Jimmy had two reasons for accompanying Gibson on his tours of the city. In the first place, the older man could go almost anywhere he pleased and so could get into all the interesting places which might otherwise be out of bounds. The second reason was a purely personal one—his increasing interest in the curious character of Martin Gibson.

Though they had now been thrown so closely together, they had never reopened their earlier conversation. Jimmy knew that Gibson was anxious to be friends and to make some recompense for whatever had happened in the past. He was quite capable of accepting this offer on a purely impersonal basis, for he realised well enough that Gibson could be extremely useful to him in his career. Like most ambitious young men, Jimmy had a streak of coldly calculating self-interest in his make-up, and Gibson would have been slightly dismayed at some of the appraisals which Jimmy had made of the advantages to be obtained from his patronage.

It would, however, be quite unfair to Jimmy to suggest that these material considerations were uppermost in his mind. There were times when he sensed Gibson's inner loneliness—the loneliness of the bachelor facing the approach of middle age. Perhaps Jimmy also realised—though not consciously as yet—that to Gibson he was beginning to represent the son he had never had. It was not a rôle that Jimmy was by any means sure he wanted, yet there were often times when he felt sorry for Gibson and would have been glad to please him. It is, after all, very difficult not to feel a certain affection towards someone who likes you.

The accident that introduced a new and quite unexpected element into Jimmy's life was really very trivial. He had been out alone one afternoon and, feeling thirsty, had dropped into the small café opposite the Administration building. Unfortunately he had not chosen his time well, for while he was quietly sipping a cup of tea which had never been within millions of kilometres of Ceylon, the place was suddenly invaded. It was the twenty-minute afternoon break when all work stopped on Mars—a rule which the Chief Executive had enforced in the interests of efficiency, though everyone would have much preferred to do without it and leave work twenty minutes earlier instead.

Jimmy was rapidly surrounded by an army of young women, who eyed him with alarming candour and a complete lack of diffidence. Although half a dozen men had been swept in on the flood, they crowded round one table for mutual protection, and judging by their intense expressions, continued to battle mentally with the files they had left on their desks. Jimmy decided to finish his drink as quickly as he could and get out.

A rather tough-looking woman in her late thirties—probably a senior secretary—was sitting opposite him, talking to a much younger girl on his side of the table. It was quite a squeeze to get past, and as Jimmy pushed into the crowd swirling through the narrow gangway, he tripped over an outstretched foot. He grabbed the table as he fell and managed to avoid complete disaster, but only at the cost of catching his elbow a sickening crack on the glass top. Forgetting in his agony that he was no longer back in the *Ares*, he relieved his feelings with a few well-chosen words. Then, blushing furiously, he recovered and bolted to freedom. He caught a glimpse of the elder woman trying hard not to laugh, and the younger one not even attempting such self-control.

And then, though it seemed inconceivable in retrospect, he forgot all about them both.

It was Gibson who quite accidentally provided the second stimulus. They were talking about the swift growth of the city during the last few years, and wondering if it would continue in the future. Gibson had remarked on the abnormal age distribution caused by the fact that no one under twenty-one had been allowed to emigrate to Mars, so that there was a complete gap between the ages of ten and twenty-one—a gap which, of course, the high birth-rate of the colony would soon fill. Jimmy had been listening half-heartedly when one of Gibson's remarks made him suddenly look up.

"That's funny," he said. "Yesterday I saw a girl who couldn't have been more than eighteen."

And then he stopped. For, like a delayed-action bomb, the mem-

ory of that girl's laughing face as he had stumbled from the café suddenly exploded in his mind.

He never heard Gibson tell him that he must have been mistaken.
He only knew that, whoever she was and wherever she had come
from, he had to see her again.

In a place the size of Port Lowell, it was only a matter of time
before one met everybody: the laws of chance would see to that.
Jimmy, however, had no intention of waiting until these doubtful
allies arranged a second encounter. The following day, just before
the afternoon break, he was drinking tea at the same table in the
little café.

This not very subtle move had caused him some mental anguish.
In the first case, it might seem altogether too obvious. Yet why
shouldn't he have tea here when most of Admin did the same? A
second and weightier objection was the memory of the previous day's
debacle. But Jimmy remembered an apt quotation about faint hearts
and fair ladies.

His qualms were unnecessary. Though he waited until the café had
emptied again, there was no sign of the girl or her companion. They
must have gone somewhere else.

It was an annoying but only temporary setback to so resourceful a
young man as Jimmy. Almost certainly she worked in the Admin
building, and there were innumerable excuses for visiting that. He
could think up enquiries about his pay, though these would hardly
get him into the depths of the filing system or the stenographer's
office, where she probably worked.

It would be best simply to keep an eye on the building when the
staff arrived and left, though how this could be done unobtrusively
was a considerable problem. Before he had made any attempt to
solve it, Fate stepped in again, heavily disguised as Martin Gibson,
slightly short of breath.

"I've been looking everywhere for you, Jimmy. Better hurry up and
get dressed. You know there's a show tonight? Well, we've all been
invited to have dinner with the Chief before going. That's in two
hours."

"What does one wear for formal dinners on Mars?" asked Jimmy.

"Black shorts and white tie, I think," said Gibson, a little doubtfully. "Or is it the other way round? Anyway, they'll tell us at the
hotel. I hope they can find something that fits me."

They did, but only just. Evening dress on Mars, where in the heat and air-conditioned cities all clothes were kept to a minimum, consisted simply of a white silk shirt with two rows of pearl buttons, a black bow tie, and black satin shorts with a belt of wide aluminium links on an elastic backing. It was smarter than might have been expected, but when fitted out Gibson felt something midway between a Boy Scout and Little Lord Fauntleroy. Norden and Hilton, on the other hand, carried it off quite well, Mackay and Scott were less successful, and Bradley obviously didn't give a damn.

The Chief's residence was the largest private house on Mars, though on Earth it would have been a very modest affair. They assembled in the lounge for a chat and sherry—real sherry—before the meal. Mayor Whittaker, being Hadfield's second-in-command, had also been invited, and as he listened to them talking to Norden, Gibson understood for the first time with what respect and admiration the colonists regarded the men who provided their sole link with Earth. Hadfield was holding forth at some length about the *Ares*, waxing quite lyrical over her speed and payload, and the effects these would have on the economy of Mars.

"Before we go in," said the Chief, when they had finished the sherry, "I'd like you to meet my daughter. She's just seeing to the arrangements—excuse me a moment while I fetch her."

He was gone only a few seconds.

"This is Irene," he said, in a voice that tried not to be proud but failed completely. One by one he introduced her to his guests, coming to Jimmy last.

Irene looked at him and smiled sweetly.

"I think we've met before," she said.

Jimmy's colour heightened, but he held his ground and smiled back.

"So we have," he replied.

It was really very foolish of him not to have guessed. If he had even started to think properly he would have known who she must have been. On Mars, the only man who could break the rules was the one who enforced them. Jimmy remembered hearing that the Chief had a daughter, but he had never connected the facts together. It all fell into place now: when Hadfield and his wife came to Mars they had brought their only child with them as part of the contract. No one else had ever been allowed to do so.

The meal was an excellent one, but it was largely wasted on Jimmy. He had not exactly lost his appetite—that would have been unthinkable—but he ate with a distracted air. As he was seated near the end of the table, he could see Irene only by dint of craning his neck in a most ungentlemanly fashion. He was very glad when the meal was over and they adjourned for coffee.

The other two members of the Chief Executive's household were waiting for the guests. Already occupying the best seats, a pair of beautiful Siamese cats regarded the visitors with fathomless eyes. They were introduced as Topaz and Turquoise, and Gibson, who loved cats, immediately started to try and make friends with them.

"Are you fond of cats?" Irene asked Jimmy.

"Rather," said Jimmy, who loathed them. "How long have they been here?"

"Oh, about a year. Just fancy—they're the only animals on Mars! I wonder if they appreciate it?"

"I'm sure Mars does. Don't they get spoiled?"

"They're too independent. I don't think they really care for any-one—not even Daddy, though he likes to pretend they do."

With great subtlety—though to any spectator it would have been fairly obvious that Irene was always one jump ahead of him—Jimmy brought the conversation round to more personal matters. He discovered that she worked in the accounting section, but knew a good deal of everything that went on in Administration, where she one day hoped to hold a responsible executive post. Jimmy guessed that her father's position had been, if anything, a slight handicap to her. Though it must have made life easier in some ways, in others it would be a definite disadvantage, as Port Lowell was fiercely democratic.

It was very hard to keep Irene on the subject of Mars. She was much more anxious to hear about Earth, the planet which she had left when a child and so must have, in her mind, a dream-like unreality. Jimmy did his best to answer her questions, quite content to talk about any-thing which held her interest. He spoke of Earth's great cities, its mountains and seas, its blue skies and scudding clouds, its rivers and rainbows—all the things which Mars had lost. And as he talked, he fell deeper and deeper beneath the spell of Irene's laughing eyes. That was the only word to describe them: she always seemed to be on the point of sharing some secret joke.

Was she still laughing at him? Jimmy wasn't sure—and he didn't mind. What rubbish it was, he thought, to imagine that one became tongue-tied on these occasions! He had never been more fluent in his life. . . .

He was suddenly aware that a great silence had fallen. Everyone was looking at him and Irene.

"Humph!" said the Chief Executive. "If you two have quite finished, we'd better get a move on. The show starts in ten minutes."

Most of Port Lowell seemed to have squeezed into the little theatre by the time they arrived. Mayor Whittaker, who had hurried ahead to check the arrangements, met them at the door and shepherded them into their seats, a reserved block occupying most of the front row. Gibson, Hadfield, and Irene were in the centre, flanked by Norden and Hilton—much to Jimmy's chagrin. He had no alternative but to look at the show.

Like all such amateur performances, it was good in parts. The musical items were excellent and there was one mezzo-soprano who was up to the best professional standards of Earth. Gibson was not surprised when he saw against her name on the programme: "Late of the Royal Covent Garden Opera."

A dramatic interlude then followed, the distressed heroine and old-time villain hamming it for all they were worth. The audience loved it, cheering and booing the appropriate characters and shouting gratuitous advice.

Next came one of the most astonishing ventriloquist acts that Gibson had ever seen. It was nearly over before he realised—only a minute before the performer revealed it deliberately—that there was a radio receiver inside the doll and an accomplice off-stage.

The next item appeared to be a skit on life in the city, and was so full of local allusions that Gibson understood only part of it. However, the antics of the main character—a harassed official obviously modelled on Mayor Whittaker—drew roars of laughter. These increased still further when he began to be pestered by a fantastic person who was continually asking ridiculous questions, noting the answers in a little book (which he was always losing), and photographing everything in sight.

It was several minutes before Gibson realised just what was going on. For a moment he turned a deep red; then he realised that there was only one thing he could do. He would have to laugh louder than anyone else.

The proceedings ended with community singing, a form of entertainment which Gibson did not normally go out of his way to seek —rather the reverse, in fact. But he found it more enjoyable than he had expected, and as he joined in the last choruses a sudden wave of emotion swept over him, causing his voice to peter out into nothingness. For a moment he sat, the only silent man in all that crowd, wondering what had happened to him.

The faces around provided the answer. Here were men and women united in a single task, driving towards a common goal, each knowing that their work was vital to the community. They had a sense of fulfilment which very few could know on Earth, where all the frontiers had long ago been reached. It was a sense heightened and made more personal by the fact that Port Lowell was still so small that everyone knew everybody else.

Of course, it was too good to last. As the colony grew, the spirit of these pioneering days would fade. Everything would become too big and too well organised; the development of the planet would be just another job of work. But for the present it was a wonderful sensation, which a man would be lucky indeed to experience even once in his lifetime. Gibson knew it was felt by all those around him, yet he could not share it. He was an outsider: that was the rôle he had always preferred to play—and now he had played it long enough. If it was not too late, he wanted to join in the game.

That was the moment, if indeed there was such a single point in time, when Martin Gibson changed his allegiance from Earth to Mars. No one ever knew. Even those beside him, if they noticed anything at all, were aware only that for a few seconds he had stopped singing, but had now joined in the chorus again with redoubled vigour.

In twos and threes, laughing, talking and singing, the audience slowly dissolved into the night. Gibson and his friends started back towards the hotel, having said good-bye to the Chief and Mayor Whittaker. The two men who virtually ran Mars watched them disappear down the narrow streets; then Hadfield turned to his daughter and remarked quietly: "Run along home now, dear—Mr. Whittaker and I are going for a little walk. I'll be back in half an hour."

They waited, answering good-nights from time to time, until the tiny square was deserted. Mayor Whittaker, who guessed what was coming, fidgeted slightly.

"Remind me to congratulate George on tonight's show," said Hadfield.

"Yes," Whittaker replied. "I loved the skit on our mutual headache,

Gibson. I suppose you want to conduct a post-mortem on his latest exploit?"

The Chief was slightly taken aback by this direct approach.

"It's rather too late now—and there's no real evidence that any real harm was done. I'm just wondering how to prevent future accidents."

"It was hardly the driver's fault. He didn't know about the Project and it was pure bad luck that he stumbled on it."

"Do you think Gibson suspects anything?"

"Frankly, I don't know. He's pretty shrewd."

"Of all the times to send a reporter here! I did everything I could to keep him away, heaven knows!"

"He's bound to find out that something's happening before he's here much longer. I think there's only one solution."

"What's that?"

"We'll just have to tell him. Perhaps not everything, but enough."

They walked in silence for a few yards. Then Hadfield remarked:

"That's pretty drastic. You're assuming he can be trusted completely."

"I've seen a good deal of him these last weeks. Fundamentally, he's on our side. You see, we're doing the sort of things he's been writing about all his life, though he can't quite believe it yet. What would be fatal would be to let him go back to Earth, suspecting something but now knowing what."

There was another long silence. They reached the limit of the dome and stared across the glimmering Martian landscape, dimly lit by the radiance spilling out from the city.

"I'll have to think it over," said Hadfield, turning to retrace his footsteps. "Of course, a lot depends on how quickly things move."

"Any hints yet?"

"No, confound them. You never can pin scientists down to a date."

A young couple, arms twined together, strolled past them obliviously. Whittaker chuckled.

"That reminds me. Irene seems to have taken quite a fancy to that youngster—what's his name—Spencer."

"Oh, I don't know. It's a change to see a fresh face around. And space travel is so much more romantic than the work we do here."

"All the nice girls love a sailor, eh? Well, don't say I didn't warn you!"

That something had happened to Jimmy was soon perfectly obvious to Gibson, and it took him no more than two guesses to arrive at the correct answer. He quite approved of the lad's choice: Irene seemed a very nice child, from what little he had seen of her. She was rather unsophisticated, but this was not necessarily a handicap. Much more important was the fact that she had a gay and cheerful disposition, though once or twice Gibson had caught her in a mood of wistfulness that was very attractive. She was also extremely pretty; Gibson was now old enough to realise that this was not all-important, though Jimmy might have different views on the subject.

At first, he decided to say nothing about the matter until Jimmy raised it himself. In all probability, the boy was still under the impression that no one had noticed anything in the least unusual. Gibson's self-control gave way, however, when Jimmy announced his intention of taking a temporary job in Port Lowell. There was nothing odd about this; indeed, it was a common practice among visiting space-crews, who soon got bored if they had nothing to do between trips. The work they chose was invariably technical and related in some way to their professional activities; Mackay, for example, was running evening classes in mathematics, while poor Dr. Scott had had no holiday at all, but had gone straight to the hospital immediately on reaching Port Lowell.

But Jimmy, it seemed, wanted a change. They were short of staff in the accounting section, and he thought his knowledge of mathematics might help. He put up an astonishingly convincing argument, to which Gibson listened with genuine pleasure.

"My dear Jimmy," he said, when it was finished. "Why tell *me* all this? There's nothing to stop your going right ahead if you want to."

"I know," said Jimmy, "but you see a lot of Mayor Whittaker and it might save trouble if you had a word with him."

"I'll speak to the Chief if you like."

"Oh no, I shouldn't——" Jimmy began. Then he tried to retrieve his blunder. "It isn't worth bothering him about such details."

"Look here, Jimmy," said Gibson with great firmness. "Why not come clean? Is this your idea, or did Irene put you up to it?"

It was worth travelling all the way to Mars to see Jimmy's expression. He looked rather like a fish that had been breathing air for some time and had only just realised it.

"Oh," he said at last, "I didn't know you knew. You won't tell anyone, will you?"

Gibson was just about to remark that this would be quite unnecessary, but there was something in Jimmy's eyes that made him abandon all attempts at humour. The wheel had come full circle; he was back again in that twenty-year-old-buried spring. He knew exactly what Jimmy was feeling now, and knew also that nothing which the future could bring to him would ever match the emotions he was discovering, still as new and fresh as on the first morning of the world. He might fall in love again in later days, but the memory of Irene would shape and colour all his life—just as Irene herself must be the memory of some ideal he had brought with him into this universe.

"I'll do what I can," said Gibson gently, and meant it with all his heart. Though history might repeat itself, it never did so exactly, and one generation could learn from the errors of the last. Some things were beyond planning or foresight, but he would do all he could to help; and this time, perhaps, the outcome might be different.

ELEVEN

The amber light was on. Gibson took a last sip of water, cleared his throat gently, and checked that the papers of his script were in the right order. No matter how many times he broadcast, his throat always felt this initial tightness. In the control room, the programme engineer held up her thumb; the amber changed abruptly to red.

"Hello, Earth. This is Martin Gibson speaking to you from Port Lowell, Mars. It's a great day for us here. This morning the new dome was inflated and now the city's increased its size by almost a half. I don't know if I can convey any impression of what a triumph this means, what a feeling of victory it gives to us here in the battle against Mars. But I'll try.

"You all know that it's impossible to breathe the Martian atmosphere—it's far too thin and contains practically no oxygen. Port Lowell, our biggest city, is built under six domes of transparent plastic held up by the pressure of the air inside—air which we can breathe comfortably though it's still much less dense than yours.

"For the last year a seventh dome has been under construction, a dome twice as big as any of the others. I'll describe it as it was yesterday, when I went inside before the inflation started.

"Imagine a great circular space half a kilometre across, surrounded by a thick wall of glass bricks twice as high as a man. Through this wall lead the passages to the other domes, and the exits direct on to the brilliant green Martian landscape all around us. These passages are simply metal tubes with great doors which close automatically if air escapes from any of the domes. On Mars, we don't believe in putting all our eggs in one basket!

"When I entered Dome Seven yesterday, all this great circular space was covered with a thin transparent sheet fastened to the surrounding wall, and lying limp on the ground in huge folds beneath which we had to force our way. If you can imagine being inside a deflated balloon you'll know exactly how I felt. The envelope of the dome is a very strong plastic, almost perfectly transparent and quite flexible—a kind of thick cellophane.

"Of course, I had to wear my breathing mask, for though we were sealed off from the outside there was still practically no air in the dome. It was being pumped in as rapidly as possible, and you could see the great sheets of plastic straining sluggishly as the pressure mounted.

"This went on all through the night. The first thing this morning I went into the dome again, and found that the envelope had now blown itself into a big bubble at the centre, though round the edges it was still lying flat. That huge bubble—it was about a hundred metres across—kept trying to move around like a living creature, and all the time it grew.

"About the middle of the morning it had grown so much that we could see the complete dome taking shape; the envelope had lifted away from the ground everywhere. Pumping was stopped for a while to test for leaks, then resumed again around midday. By now the sun was helping too, warming up the air and making it expand.

"Three hours ago the first stage of the inflation was finished. We took off our masks and let out a great cheer. The air still wasn't really thick enough for comfort, but it was breathable and the engineers could work inside without bothering about masks any more. They'll spend the next few days checking the great envelope for stresses, and looking for leaks. There are bound to be some, of course, but as long as the air loss doesn't exceed a certain value it won't matter.

"So now we feel we've pushed our frontier on Mars back a little further. Soon the new buildings will be going up under Dome Seven, and we're making plans for a small park and even a lake—the only one on Mars, that will be, for free water can't exist here in the open for any length of time.

"Of course, this is only a beginning, and one day it will seem a very small achievement; but it's a great step forward in our battle—it represents the conquest of another slice of Mars. And it means living space for another thousand people. Are you listening, Earth? Good night."

The red light faded. For a moment Gibson sat staring at the microphone, musing on the fact that his first words, though travelling at the speed of light, would only now be reaching Earth. Then he gathered up his papers and walked through the padded doors into the control room.

The engineer held up a telephone for him. "A call's just come through for you, Mr. Gibson," she said. "Someone's been pretty quick off the mark!"

"They certainly have," he replied with a grin. "Hello, Gibson here."

"This is Hadfield. Congratulations. I've just been listening—it went out over our local station, you know."

"I'm glad you liked it."

Hadfield chuckled.

"You've probably guessed that I've read most of your earlier scripts. It's been quite interesting to watch the change of attitude."

"What change?"

"When you started, we were 'they.' Now we're 'we.' Not very well put, perhaps, but I think my point's clear."

He gave Gibson no time to answer this, but continued without a break.

"I really rang up about this. I've been able to fix your trip to Skia at last. We've got a passenger jet going over there on Wednesday, with room for three aboard. Whittaker will give you the details. Good-bye."

The phone clicked into silence. Very thoughtfully, but not a little pleased, Gibson replaced it on the stand. What the Chief had said was true enough. He had been here for almost a month, and in that time his outlook towards Mars had changed completely. The first schoolboy excitement had lasted no more than a few days; the subsequent disillusionment only a little longer. Now he knew enough to regard the colony with a tempered enthusiasm not wholly based on logic. He was afraid to analyse it, lest it disappear completely. Some part of it, he knew, came from his growing respect for the people around him—his admiration for the keen-eyed competence, the readiness to take well-calculated risks, which had enabled them not merely to survive on this heartbreakingly hostile world, but to lay the foundations of the first extra-terrestrial culture. More than ever before, he felt a longing to identify himself with their work, wherever it might lead.

Meanwhile, his first real chance of seeing Mars on the large scale had arrived. On Wednesday he would be taking off for Port Schiaparelli, the planet's second city, ten thousand kilometres to the east in Trivium Charontis. The trip had been planned a fortnight ago, but every time something had turned up to postpone it. He would have to tell Jimmy and Hilton to get ready—they had been the lucky ones in the draw. Perhaps Jimmy might not be quite so eager to go now as he had been once. No doubt he was now anxiously counting the days left to him on Mars, and would resent anything that took him away from Irene. But if he turned down *this* chance, Gibson would have no sympathy for him at all.

"Neat job, isn't she?" said the pilot proudly. "There are only six like her on Mars. It's quite a trick designing a jet that can fly in this atmosphere, even with the low gravity to help you."

Gibson did not know enough about aerodynamics to appreciate the finer points of the aircraft, though he could see that the wing area was abnormally large. The four jet units were neatly buried just outboard of the fuselage, only the slightest of bulges betraying their position. If he had met such a machine on a terrestrial airfield Gibson would not have given it a second thought, though the sturdy tractor undercarriage might have surprised him. This machine was built to fly fast and far—and to land on any surface which was approximately flat.

He climbed in after Jimmy and Hilton and settled himself as comfortably as he could in the rather restricted space. Most of the cabin was taken up by large packing cases securely strapped in position— urgent freight for Skia, he supposed. It hadn't left a great deal of space for the passengers.

The motors accelerated swiftly until their thin whines hovered at the edge of hearing. There was the familiar pause while the pilot checked his instruments and controls; then the jets opened full out and the runway began to slide beneath them. A few seconds later there came the sudden reassuring surge of power as the take-off rockets fired and lifted them effortlessly up into the sky. The aircraft climbed steadily into the south, then swung round to starboard in a great curve that took it over the city.

The aircraft levelled out on an easterly course and the great island of Aurorae Sinus sank over the edge of the planet. Apart from a few oases, the open desert now lay ahead for thousands of kilometres.

The pilot switched his controls to automatic and came amidships to talk to his passengers.

"We'll be at Charontis in about four hours," he said. "I'm afraid there isn't much to look at on the way, though you'll see some fine colour effects when we go over Euphrates. After that it's more or less uniform desert until we hit the Syrtis Major."

Gibson did some rapid mental arithmetic.

"Let's see—we're flying east and we started rather late—it'll be dark when we get there."

"Don't worry about that—we'll pick up the Charontis beacon when we're a couple of hundred kilometres away. Mars is so small that you don't often do a long-distance trip in daylight all the way."

"How long have you been on Mars?" asked Gibson, who had now ceased taking photos through the observation ports.

"Oh, five years."

"Flying all the time?"

"Most of it."

"Wouldn't you prefer being in spaceships?"

"Not likely. No excitement in it—just floating around in nothing for months." He grinned at Hilton, who smiled amiably but showed no inclination to argue.

"Just what do you mean by 'excitement'?" said Gibson anxiously.

"Well, you've got some scenery to look at, you're not away from home for very long, and there's always the chance you may find something new. I've done half a dozen trips over the poles, you know—most of them in summer, but I went across the Mare Boreum last winter. A hundred and fifty degrees below outside! That's the record so far for Mars."

"I can beat that pretty easily," said Hilton. "At night it reaches two hundred below on Titan." It was the first time Gibson had ever heard him refer to the Saturnian expedition.

"By the way, Fred," he asked, "is this rumour true?"

"What rumour?"

"*You* know—that you're going to have another shot at Saturn."

Hilton shrugged his shoulders.

"It isn't decided—there are a lot of difficulties. But I think it will come off; it would be a pity to miss the chance. You see, if we can leave next year we can go past Jupiter on the way, and have our first really good look at him. Mac's worked out a very interesting orbit for us. We go rather close to Jupiter—right inside *all* the satellites—and let his gravitational field swing us round so that we head out in the right direction for Saturn. It'll need rather accurate navigation to give us just the orbit we want, but it can be done."

"Then what's holding it up?"

"Money, as usual. The trip will last two and a half years and will cost about fifty million. Mars can't afford it—it would mean doubling the usual deficit! At the moment we're trying to get Earth to foot the bill."

"It would come to that anyway in the long run," said Gibson. "But give me all the facts when we get home and I'll write a blistering *exposé* about cheeseparing terrestrial politicians. You mustn't underestimate the power of the press."

The talk then drifted from planet to planet, until Gibson suddenly remembered that he was wasting a magnificent chance of seeing Mars at first hand. Obtaining permission to occupy the pilot's seat—after promising not to touch anything—he went forward and settled himself comfortably behind the controls.

Five kilometres below, the coloured desert was streaking past him to the west. They were flying at what, on Earth, would have been a very low altitude, for the thinness of the Martian air made it essential to keep as near the surface as safety allowed. Gibson had never before received such an impression of sheer speed, for though he had flown in much faster machines on Earth, that had always been at heights where the ground was invisible. The nearness of the horizon added to the effect, for an object which appeared over the edge of the planet would be passing beneath a few minutes later.

From time to time the pilot came forward to check the course, though it was a pure formality, as there was nothing he need do until the voyage was nearly over. At mid-point some coffee and light refreshments were produced, and Gibson rejoined his companions in the cabin. Hilton and the pilot were now arguing briskly about Venus

—quite a sore point with the Martian colonists, who regarded that peculiar planet as a complete waste of time.

The sun was now very low in the west and even the stunted Martian hills threw long shadows across the desert. Down there the temperature was already below freezing point, and falling fast. The few hardy plants that had survived in this almost barren waste would have folded their leaves tightly together, conserving warmth and energy against the rigours of the night.

Gibson yawned and stretched himself. The swiftly unfolding landscape had an almost hypnotic effect and it was difficult to keep awake. He decided to catch some sleep in the ninety or so minutes that were left of the voyage.

Some change in the failing light must have woken him. For a moment it was impossible to believe that he was not still dreaming; he could only sit and stare, paralysed with sheer astonishment. No longer was he looking out across a flat, almost featureless landscape meeting the deep blue of the sky at the far horizon. Desert and horizon had both vanished; in their place towered a range of crimson mountains, reaching north and south as far as the eye could follow. The last rays of the setting sun caught their peaks and bequeathed to them its dying glory; already the foothills were lost in the night that was sweeping onwards to the west.

For long seconds the splendour of the scene robbed it of all reality and hence all menace. Then Gibson awoke from his trance, realising in one dreadful instant that they were flying far too low to clear those Himalayan peaks.

The sense of utter panic lasted only a moment—to be followed at once by a far deeper terror. Gibson had remembered now what the first shock had banished from his mind—the simple fact he should have thought of from the beginning.

There were no mountains on Mars.

Hadfield was dictating an urgent memorandum to the Interplanetary Development Board when the news came through. Port Schiaparelli had waited the regulation fifteen minutes after the aircraft's expected time of arrival, and Port Lowell Control had stood by for another ten before sending out the "Overdue" signal. One precious aircraft from the tiny Martian fleet was already standing by to search the line of flight as soon as dawn came. The high speed and low altitude essential for flight would make such a search very difficult, but when Phobos rose the telescopes up there could join in with far greater prospects of success.

The news reached Earth an hour later, at a time when there was nothing much else to occupy press or radio. Gibson would have been well satisfied by the resultant publicity: everywhere people began reading his last articles with a morbid interest. Ruth Goldstein knew nothing about it until an editor she was dealing with arrived waving the evening paper. She immediately sold the second reprint rights of Gibson's latest series for half as much again as her victim had intended to pay, then retired to her private room and wept copiously for a full minute. Both these events would have pleased Gibson enormously.

In a score of newspaper offices, the copy culled from the morgue began to be set up in type so that no time would be wasted. And in London a publisher who had paid Gibson a rather large advance began to feel very unhappy indeed.

Gibson's shout was still echoing through the cabin when the pilot reached the controls. Then he was flung to the floor as the machine turned over in an almost vertical bank in a desperate attempt to swing round to the north. When Gibson could climb to his feet again, he caught a glimpse of a strangely blurred orange cliff sweeping down upon them from only kilometres away. Even in that moment of panic, he could see that there was something very curious about that swiftly approaching barrier, and suddenly the truth dawned upon him at last. This was no mountain range, but something that might be no less deadly. They were running into a wind-borne wall of sand reaching from the desert almost to the edge of the stratosphere.

The hurricane hit them a second later. Something slapped the machine violently from side to side, and through the insulation of the hull came an angry whistling roar that was the most terrifying sound Gibson had ever heard in his life. Night had come instantly upon them and they were flying helplessly through a howling darkness.

It was all over in five minutes, but it seemed a lifetime. Their sheer speed had saved them, for the ship had cut through the heart of the hurricane like a projectile. There was a sudden burst of deep ruby twilight, the ship ceased to be pounded by a million sledge-hammers, and a ringing silence seemed to fill the little cabin. Through the rear observation port Gibson caught a last glimpse of the storm as it moved westwards, tearing up the desert in its wake.

His legs feeling like jellies, Gibson tottered thankfully into his seat and breathed an enormous sigh of relief. For a moment he wondered if they had been thrown badly off course, then realised that this scarcely mattered considering the navigational aids they carried.

It was only then, when his ears had ceased to be deafened by the storm, that Gibson had his second shock. The motors had stopped.

The little cabin was very tense and still. Then the pilot called out over his shoulder: "Get your masks on! The hull may crack when we come down." His fingers feeling very clumsy, Gibson dragged his breathing equipment from under the seat and adjusted it over his head. When he had finished, the ground already seemed very close, though it was hard to judge distances in the failing twilight.

A low hill swept by and was gone into the darkness. The ship banked violently to avoid another, then gave a sudden spasmodic jerk as it touched ground and bounced. A moment later it made contact again and Gibson tensed himself for the inevitable crash.

It was an age before he dared relax, still unable to believe that they were safely down. Then Hilton stretched himself in his seat, removed his mask, and called out to the pilot: "That was a very nice landing, Skipper. Now how far have we got to walk?"

For a moment there was no reply. Then the pilot called, in a rather strained voice: "Can anyone light me a cigarette? I've got the twitch."

"Here you are," said Hilton, going forward. "Let's have the cabin lights on now, shall we?"

The warm, comfortable glow did much to raise their spirits by banishing the Martian night, which now lay all around. Everyone began to feel ridiculously cheerful and there was much laughing at quite feeble jokes. The reaction had set in: they were so delighted at still being alive that the thousand kilometres separating them from the nearest base scarcely seemed to matter.

"That was quite a storm," said Gibson. "Does this sort of thing happen very often on Mars? And why didn't we get any warning?"

The pilot, now that he had got over his initial shock, was doing some quick thinking, the inevitable court of enquiry obviously looming large in his mind. Even on auto-pilot, he *should* have gone forward more often. . . .

"I've never seen one like it before," he said, "though I've done at least fifty trips between Lowell and Skia. The trouble is that we don't know anything about Martian meteorology, even now. And there are only half a dozen met stations on the planet—not enough to give us an accurate picture."

"What about Phobos? Couldn't they have seen what was happening and warned us?"

The pilot grabbed his almanac and ruffled rapidly through the pages.

"Phobos hasn't risen yet," he said after a brief calculation. "I guess the storm blew up suddenly out of Hades—appropriate name, isn't it? and has probably collapsed again now. I don't suppose it went anywhere near Charontis, so *they* couldn't have warned us either. It was just one of those accidents that's nobody's fault."

This thought seemed to cheer him considerably, but Gibson found it hard to be so philosophical.

"Meanwhile," he retorted, "we're stuck in the middle of nowhere. How long will it take them to find us? Or is there any chance of repairing the ship?"

"Not a hope of that; the jets are ruined. They were made to work on air, not sand, you know!"

"Well, can we radio Skia?"

"Not now we're on the ground. But when Phobos rises in—let's see—an hour's time, we'll be able to call the observatory and they can relay us on. That's the way we've got to do all our long-distance stuff here, you know. The ionosphere's too feeble to bounce signals round the way you do on Earth. Anyway, I'll go and check that the radio is O.K."

He went forward and started tinkering with the ship's transmitter, while Hilton busied himself checking the heaters and cabin air pressure, leaving the two remaining passengers looking at each other a little thoughtfully.

"This is a fine kettle of fish!" exploded Gibson, half in anger and half in amusement. "I've come safely from Earth to Mars—more than fifty million kilometres—and as soon as I set foot inside a miserable aeroplane *this* is what happens! I'll stick to spaceships in future."

Jimmy grinned. "It'll give us something to tell the others when we get back, won't it? Maybe we'll be able to do some real exploring at last." He peered through the windows, cupping his hands over his eyes to keep out the cabin light. The surrounding landscape was now in complete darkness, apart from the illumination from the ship.

"There seem to be hills all round us; we were lucky to get down in one piece. Good Lord—there's a cliff here on this side—another few metres and we'd have gone smack into it!"

"Any idea where we are?" Gibson called to the pilot. This tactless remark earned him a very stony stare.

"About 120 east, 20 north. The storm can't have thrown us very far off course."

"Then we're somewhere in the Aetheria," said Gibson, bending over the maps. "Yes—there's a hilly region marked here. Not much information about it."

"It's the first time anyone's ever landed here—that's why. This part of Mars is almost unexplored; it's been thoroughly mapped from the air, but that's all."

Gibson was amused to see how Jimmy brightened at this news. There was certainly something exciting about being in a region where no human foot had ever trodden before.

"I hate to cast a gloom over the proceedings," remarked Hilton, in a tone of voice hinting that this was exactly what he was going to do, "but I'm not at all sure you'll be able to radio Phobos even when it does rise."

"What!" yelped the pilot. "The set's O.K.—I've just tested it."

"Yes—but have you noticed where we are? We can't even *see* Phobos. That cliff's due south of us and blocks the view completely. That means that they won't be able to pick up our microwave signals. What's even worse, they won't be able to locate us in their telescopes."

There was a shocked silence.

"*Now* what do we do?" asked Gibson. He had a horrible vision of a thousand-kilometre trek across the desert to Charontis, but dismissed it from his mind at once. They couldn't possibly carry the oxygen for the trip, still less the food and equipment necessary. And no one could spend the night unprotected on the surface of Mars, even here near the Equator.

"We'll just have to signal in some other way," said Hilton calmly. "In the morning we'll climb those hills and have a look round. Meanwhile I suggest we take it easy." He yawned and stretched himself, filling the cabin from ceiling to floor. "We've got no immediate worries; there's air for several days, and power in the batteries to keep us warm almost indefinitely. We may get a bit hungry if we're here more than a week, but I don't think that's at all likely to happen."

By a kind of unspoken mutual consent, Hilton had taken control. Perhaps he was not even consciously aware of the fact, but he was now the leader of the little party. The pilot had delegated his own authority without a second thought.

"Phobos rises in an hour, you said?" asked Hilton.

"Yes."

"When does it transit? I can never remember what this crazy little moon of yours gets up to."

"Well, it rises in the west and sets in the east about four hours later."

"So it'll be due south around midnight?"

"That's right. Oh Lord—that means we won't be able to see it anyway. It'll be eclipsed for at least an hour!"

"*What* a moon!" snorted Gibson. "When you want it most badly, you can't even see the blasted thing!"

"That doesn't matter," said Hilton calmly. "We'll know just where it is, and it won't do any harm to try the radio then. That's all we can do tonight. Has anyone got a pack of cards? No? Then what about entertaining us, Martin, with some of your stories?"

It was a rash remark, and Gibson seized his chance immediately.

"I wouldn't dream of doing that," he said. "*You're* the one who has the stories to tell."

Hilton stiffened, and for a moment Gibson wondered if he had offended him. He knew that Hilton seldom talked about the Saturnian expedition, but this was too good an opportunity to miss. The chance would never come again, and, as is true of all great adventures, its telling would do their morale good. Perhaps Hilton realised this too, for presently he relaxed and smiled.

"You've got me nicely cornered, haven't you, Martin? Well, I'll talk —but on one condition."

"What's that?"

"No direct quotes, please!"

"As if I would!"

"And when you *do* write it up, let me see the manuscript first."

"Of course."

This was better than Gibson had dared to hope. He had no immediate intention of writing about Hilton's adventures, but it was nice to know that he could do so if he wished. The possibility that he might never have the chance simply did not cross his mind.

Outside the walls of the ship, the fierce Martian night reigned supreme—a night studded with needle-sharp, unwinking stars. The pale light of Deimos made the surrounding landscape dimly visible, as if lit with a cold phosphorescence. Out of the east Jupiter, the brightest object in the sky, was rising in his glory. But the thoughts of the four men in the crashed aircraft were six hundred million kilometres still further from the sun.

It still puzzled many people—the curious fact that man had visited Saturn but not Jupiter, so much closer at hand. But in space-travel, sheer distance is of no importance, and Saturn had been reached because of a single astonishing stroke of luck that still seemed too good to be true. Orbiting Saturn was Titan, the largest satellite in the Solar System—about twice the size of Earth's moon. As far back as 1944 it had been discovered that Titan possessed an atmosphere. It was not an atmosphere one could breathe: it was immensely more valuable than that. For it was an atmosphere of methane, one of the ideal propellants for atomic rockets.

This had given rise to a situation unique in the history of spaceflight. For the first time, an expedition could be sent to a strange world with the virtual certainty that refuelling would be possible on arrival.

The *Arcturus* and her crew of six had been launched in space from the orbit of Mars. She had reached the Saturnian systems only nine months later, with just enough fuel to land safely on Titan. Then the pumps had been started, and the great tanks replenished from the countless trillions of tons of methane that were there for the taking. Refuelling on Titan whenever necessary, the *Arcturus* had visited every one of Saturn's fifteen known moons, and had even skirted the great ring system itself. In a few months, more was learned about Saturn than in all the previous centuries of telescopic examination.

There had been a price to pay. Two of the crew had died of radiation sickness after emergency repairs to one of the atomic motors. They had been buried on Dione, the fourth moon. And the leader of the expedition, Captain Envers, had been killed by an avalanche of frozen air on Titan; his body had never been found. Hilton had assumed command, and had brought the *Arcturus* safely back to Mars a year later, with only two men to help him.

All these bare facts Gibson knew well enough. He could still remember listening to those radio messages that had come trickling back through space, relayed from world to world. But it was a different thing altogether to hear Hilton telling the story in his quiet, curiously impersonal manner, as if he had been a spectator rather than a participant.

He spoke of Titan and its smaller brethren, the little moons which, circling Saturn, made the planet almost a scale model of the Solar System. He described how at last they had landed on the innermost moon of all, Mimas, only half as far from Saturn as the Moon is from the Earth.

"We came down in a wide valley between a couple of mountains, where we were sure the ground would be pretty solid. We weren't going to make the mistake we did on Rhea! It was a good landing, and we climbed into our suits to go outside. It's funny how impatient you always are to do that, no matter how many times you've set down on a new world.

"Of course, Mimas hasn't much gravity—only a hundredth of Earth's. That was enough to keep us from jumping off into space. I liked it that way; you knew you'd always come down safely again if you waited long enough.

"It was early in the morning when we landed. Mimas has a day a bit shorter than Earth's—it goes round Saturn in twenty-two hours, and as it keeps the same face towards the planet its day and month are the same length—just as they are on the Moon. We'd come down in the northern hemisphere, not far from the Equator, and most of Saturn was above the horizon. It looked quite weird—a huge crescent horn sticking up into the sky, like some impossibly bent mountain thousands of miles high.

"Of course you've all seen the films we made—especially the speeded-up colour one showing a complete cycle of Saturn's phases. But I don't think they can give you much idea of what it was like to live with that enormous thing always there in the sky. It was so big, you see, that one couldn't take it in in a single view. If you stood facing it and held your arms wide open, you could just imagine your finger tips touching the opposite ends of the rings. We couldn't see the rings themselves very well, because they were almost edge-on, but you could always tell they were there by the wide, dusky band of shadow they cast on the planet.

"None of us ever got tired of watching it. It's spinning so fast, you know—the pattern was always changing. The cloud formations, if that's what they were, used to whip round from one side of the disc to the other in a few hours, changing continually as they moved. And there were the most wonderful colours—greens and browns and yellows chiefly. Now and then there'd be great, slow eruptions, and something as big as Earth would rise up out of the depths and spread itself sluggishly in a huge stain half-way round the planet.

"You could never take your eyes off it for long. Even when it was new and so completely invisible, you could still tell it was there because of the great hole in the stars. And here's a funny thing which I haven't reported because I was never quite sure of it. Once or twice, when we were in the planet's shadow and its disc should have been completely dark, I thought I saw a faint phosphorescent glow coming from the night side. It didn't last long—if it really happened at all. Perhaps it was some kind of chemical reaction going on down there in that spinning cauldron.

"Are you surprised that I want to go to Saturn again? What I'd like to do is to get *really* close this time—and by that I mean within a thousand kilometres. It should be quite safe and wouldn't take much power. All you need do is to go into a parabolic orbit and let yourself fall in like a comet going round the Sun. Of course, you'd only spend a few minutes actually close to Saturn, but you could get a lot of records in that time.

"And I want to land on Mimas again, and see that great shining crescent reaching half-way up the sky. It'll be worth the journey, just to watch Saturn waxing and waning, and to see the storms chasing themselves round his Equator. Yes—it would be worth it, even if *I* didn't get back this time."

There were no mock heroics in this closing remark. It was merely a simple statement of fact, and Hilton's listeners believed him completely. While the spell lasted, every one of them would be willing to strike the same bargain.

Gibson ended the long silence by going to the cabin window and peering out into the night.

"Can we have the lights off?" he called. Complete darkness fell as the pilot obeyed his request. The others joined him at the window.

"Look," said Gibson. "Up there—you can just see it if you crane your neck."

The cliff against which they were lying was no longer a wall of absolute and unrelieved darkness. On its very topmost peaks a new light was playing, spilling over the broken crags and filtering down into the valley. Phobos had leapt out of the west and was climbing on its meteoric rise towards the south, racing backwards across the sky.

Minute by minute the light grew stronger, and presently the pilot began to send out his signals. He had barely begun when the pale moonlight was snuffed out so suddenly that Gibson gave a cry of astonishment. Phobos had gone hurtling into the shadow of Mars, and though it was still rising it would cease to shine for almost an hour. There was no way of telling whether or not it would peep over the edge of the great cliff and so be in the right position to receive their signals.

They did not give up hope for almost two hours. Suddenly the light reappeared on the peaks, but shining now from the east. Phobos had emerged from its eclipse, and was now dropping down towards the horizon which it would reach in little more than an hour. The pilot switched off his transmitter in disgust.

"It's no good," he said. "We'll have to try something else."

"I know!" Gibson exclaimed excitedly. "Can't we carry the transmitter up the top of the hill?"

"I'd thought of that, but it would be the devil's own job to get it out without proper tools. The whole thing—aerials and all—is built into the hull."

"There's nothing more we can do tonight, anyway," said Hilton. "I suggest we all get some sleep before dawn. Good night, everybody."

It was excellent advice, but not easy to follow. Gibson's mind was still racing ahead, making plans for the morrow. Not until Phobos had at last plunged down into the east, and its light had ceased to play mockingly on the cliff above them, did he finally pass into a fitful slumber.

Even then he dreamed that he was trying to fix a belt-drive from the motors to the tractor undercarriage so that they could taxi the last thousand kilometres to Port Schiaparelli. . . .

TWELVE

When Gibson woke it was long after dawn. The sun was invisible behind the cliffs, but its rays reflected from the scarlet crags above them flooded the cabin with an unearthly, even a sinister light. He stretched himself stiffly; these seats had not been designed to sleep in, and he had spent an uncomfortable night.

He looked round for his companions—and realised that Hilton and the pilot had gone. Jimmy was still fast asleep; the others must have awakened first and gone out to explore. Gibson felt a vague annoyance at being left behind, but knew that he would have been still more annoyed if they had interrupted his slumbers.

There was a short message from Hilton pinned prominently on the wall. It said simply: "Went outside at 6.30. Will be gone about an hour. We'll be hungry when we get back. Fred."

The hint could hardly be ignored. Besides, Gibson felt hungry himself. He rummaged through the emergency food pack which the aircraft carried for such accidents, wondering as he did so just how long it would have to last them. His attempts to brew a hot drink in the tiny pressure-boiler aroused Jimmy, who looked somewhat sheepish when he realised he was the last to wake.

"Had a good sleep?" asked Gibson, as he searched round for the cups.

"Awful," said Jimmy, running his hands through his hair. "I feel I haven't slept for a week. Where are the others?"

His question was promptly answered by the sounds of someone entering the airlock. A moment later Hilton appeared, followed by the pilot. They divested themselves of masks and heating equipment —it was still around freezing point outside—and advanced eagerly on the pieces of chocolate and compressed meat which Gibson had portioned out with impeccable fairness.

"Well," said Gibson anxiously, "what's the verdict?"

"I can tell you one thing right away," said Hilton between mouthfuls. "We're damn lucky to be alive."

"I know that."

"You don't know the half of it—you haven't seen just where we landed. We came down parallel to this cliff for almost a kilometre before we stopped. If we'd swerved a couple of degrees to starboard —bang! When we touched down we did swing inwards a bit, but not enough to do any damage.

"We're in a long valley, running east and west. It looks like a geological fault rather than an old river bed, though that was my first guess. The cliff opposite us is a good hundred metres high, and practically vertical—in fact, it's got a bit of overhang near the top. Maybe it can be climbed farther along, but we didn't try. There's no need to, anyway—if we want Phobos to see us we've only got to walk a little way to the north, until the cliff doesn't block the view. In fact, I think that may be the answer—if we can push this ship out into the open. It'll mean we can use the radio, and will give the telescopes and air search a better chance of spotting us."

"How much does this thing weigh?" said Gibson doubtfully.

"About thirty tons with full load. There's a lot of stuff we can take out, of course."

"No there isn't!" said the pilot. "That would mean letting down our pressure, and we can't afford to waste air."

"Oh Lord, I'd forgotten that. Still, the ground's fairly smooth and the undercart's perfectly O.K."

Gibson made noises indicating extreme doubt. Even under a third of Earth's gravity, moving the aircraft was not going to be an easy proposition.

For the next few minutes his attention was diverted to the coffee, which he had tried to pour out before it had cooled sufficiently.

Releasing the pressure on the boiler immediately filled the room with steam, so that for a moment it looked as if everyone was going to inhale their liquid refreshment. Making hot drinks on Mars was always a nuisance, since water under normal pressure boiled at around sixty degrees Centigrade, and cooks who forgot this elementary fact usually met with disaster.

The dull but nourishing meal was finished in silence, as the castaways pondered their pet plans for rescue. They were not really worried; they knew that an intensive search would now be in progress, and it could only be a matter of time before they were located. But that time could be reduced to a few hours if they could get some kind of signal to Phobos.

After breakfast they tried to move the ship. By dint of much pushing and pulling they managed to shift it a good five metres. Then the caterpillar tracks sank into soft ground, and as far as their combined efforts were concerned the machine might have been completely bogged. They retired, panting, into the cabin to discuss the next move.

"Have we anything white which we could spread out over a large area?" asked Gibson.

This excellent idea came to nothing when an intensive search of the cabin revealed six handkerchiefs and a few pieces of grimy rag. It was agreed that, even under the most favourable conditions, these would not be visible from Phobos.

"There's only one thing for it," said Hilton. "We'll have to rip out the landing lights, run them out on a cable until they're clear of the cliff, and aim them at Phobos. I didn't want to do this if it could be avoided; it might make a mess of the wing and it's a pity to break up a good aeroplane."

By his glum expression, it was obvious that the pilot agreed with these sentiments.

Jimmy was suddenly struck with an idea.

"Why not fix up a heliograph?" he asked. "If we flashed a mirror on Phobos they ought to be able to see that."

"Across six thousand kilometres?" said Gibson doubtfully.

"Why not? They've got telescopes that magnify more than a thousand up there. Couldn't you see a mirror flashing in the sun if it was only six kilometres away?"

"I'm sure there's something wrong with that calculation, though I don't know what," said Gibson. "Things never work out as simply as that. But I agree with the general idea. Now who's got a mirror?"

After a quarter hour's search, Jimmy's scheme had to be abandoned. There simply was no such thing as a mirror on the ship.

"We could cut out a piece of the wing and polish that up," said Hilton thoughtfully. "That would be almost as good."

"This magnesium alloy won't take much of a polish," said the pilot, still determined to defend his machine to the last.

Gibson suddenly shot to his feet.

"Will someone kick me three times round the cabin?" he announced to the assembly.

"With pleasure," grinned Hilton, "but tell us why."

Without answering, Gibson went to the rear of the ship and began rummaging among his luggage, keeping his back to the interested spectators. It took him only a moment to find what he wanted; then he swung quickly round.

"Here's the answer," he said triumphantly.

A flash of intolerable light suddenly filled the cabin, flooding every corner with a harsh brilliance and throwing distorted shadows on the wall. It was as if lightning had struck the ship, and for several minutes everyone was half-blinded, still carrying on their retinas a frozen picture of the cabin as seen in that moment of searing incandescence.

"I'm sorry," said Gibson contritely. "I've never used it at full power indoors before—that was intended for night work in the open."

"Phew!" said Hilton, rubbing his eyes. "I thought you'd let off an atomic bomb. Must you scare everyone to death when you photograph them?"

"It's only like *this* for normal indoor use," said Gibson, demonstrating. Everyone flinched again, but this time the flash seemed scarcely noticeable. "It's a special job I had made for me before I left Earth. I wanted to be quite sure I could do colour photography at night if I wanted to. So far I haven't had a real chance of using it."

"Let's have a look at the thing," said Hilton.

Gibson handed over the flash-gun and explained its operation.

"It's built round a super-capacity condenser. There's enough for about a hundred flashes on one charge, and it's practically full."

"A hundred of the high-powered flashes?"

"Yes; it'll do a couple of thousand of the normal ones."

"Then there's enough electrical energy to make a good bomb in that condenser. I hope it doesn't spring a leak."

Hilton was examining the little gas-discharge tube, only the size of a marble, at the centre of the small reflector.

"Can we focus this thing to get a good beam?" he asked.

"There's a catch behind the reflector—that's the idea. It's rather a broad beam, but it'll help."

Hilton looked very pleased.

"They ought to see this thing on Phobos, even in broad daylight, if they're watching this part with a good telescope. We mustn't waste flashes, though."

"Phobos is well up now, isn't it?" asked Gibson. "I'm going out to have a shot right away."

He got to his feet and began to adjust his breathing equipment.

"Don't use more than ten flashes," warned Hilton. "We want to save them for night. And stand in any shadow you can find."

"Can I go out too?" asked Jimmy.

"All right," said Hilton. "But keep together and don't go wandering off to explore. I'm going to stay here and see if there's anything we can do with the landing lights."

The fact that they now had a definite plan of action had raised their spirits considerably. Clutching his camera and the precious flash-gun closely to his chest, Gibson bounded across the valley like a young gazelle. It was a curious fact that on Mars one quickly adjusted one's muscular efforts to the lower gravity, and so normally used strides no greater than on Earth. But the reserve of power was available, when necessity or high spirits demanded it.

They soon left the shadow of the cliff, and had a clear view of the open sky. Phobos was already high in the west, a little half-moon which would rapidly narrow to a thin crescent as it raced towards the south. Gibson regarded it thoughtfully, wondering if at this very moment someone might be watching this part of Mars. It seemed highly probable, for the approximate position of their crash would be known. He felt an irrational impulse to dance around and wave his arms—even to shout: "Here we are—can't you see us?"

What would this region look like in the telescopes which were, he hoped, now sweeping Aetheria? They would show the mottled green of the vegetation through which he was trudging, and the great cliff would be clearly visible as a red band casting a broad shadow over the valley when the sun was low. There would be scarcely any shadow now, for it was only a few hours from noon. The best thing to do, Gibson decided, was to get in the middle of the darkest area of vegetation he could find.

About a kilometre from the crashed ship the ground sloped down slightly, and here, in the lowest part of the valley, was a wide brownish belt which seemed to be covered with tall weeds. Gibson headed for this, Jimmy following close behind.

They found themselves among slender, leathery plants of a type they had never seen before. The leaves rose vertically out of the ground in long, thin streamers, and were covered with numberless pods which looked as if they might contain seeds. The flat sides were all turned towards the Sun, and Gibson was interested to note that while the sunlit sides of the leaves were black, the shadowed parts were a greyish white. It was a simple but effective trick to reduce loss of heat.

Without wasting time to botanise, Gibson pushed his way into the centre of the little forest. The plants were not crowded too closely together, and it was fairly easy to force a passage through them. When he had gone far enough he raised his flash-gun and squinted along it at Phobos.

The satellite was now a thin crescent not far from the Sun, and Gibson felt extremely foolish aiming his flash into the full glare of the summer sky. But the time was really well chosen, for it would be dark on the side of Phobos towards them and the telescopes there would be observing under favourable conditions.

He let off his ten shots in five pairs, spaced well apart. This seemed

the most economical way of doing it while still making sure that the
signals would look obviously artificial.

"That'll do for today," said Gibson. "We'll save the rest of our
ammunition until after dark. Now let's have a look at these plants.
Do you know what they remind me of?"

"Overgrown seaweed," replied Jimmy promptly.

"Right first time. I wonder what's in those pods? Have you got a
knife on you—thanks."

Gibson began carving at the nearest frond until he had punctured
one of the little black balloons. It apparently held gas, and under
considerable pressure, for a faint hiss could be heard as the knife
penetrated.

"What queer stuff!" said Gibson. "Let's take some back with us."

Not without difficulty, he hacked off one of the long black fronds
near the roots. A dark brown fluid began to ooze out of the severed
end, releasing tiny bubbles of gas as it did so. With this souvenir
hanging over his shoulder, Gibson began to make his way back to
the ship.

He did not know that he was carrying with him the future of a
world.

They had gone only a few paces when they encountered a denser
patch and had to make a detour. With the sun as a guide there was
no danger of becoming lost, especially in such a small region, and
they had made no attempt to retrace their footsteps exactly. Gibson
was leading the way, and finding it somewhat heavy going. He was
just wondering whether to swallow his pride and change places with
Jimmy when he was relieved to come across a narrow, winding track
leading more or less in the right direction.

To any observer, it would have been an interesting demonstration
of the slowness of some mental processes. For both Gibson and
Jimmy had walked a good six paces before they remembered the
simple but shattering truth that footpaths do not, usually, make
themselves.

"It's about time our two explorers came back, isn't it?" said the
pilot as he helped Hilton detach the floodlights from the underside
of the aircraft's wing. This had proved, after all, to be a fairly straightforward job, and Hilton hoped to find enough wiring inside the machine to run the lights far enough away from the cliff to be visible
from Phobos when it rose again. They would not have the brilliance

of Gibson's flash, but their steady beams would give them a better chance of being detected.

"How long have they been gone now?" said Hilton.

"About forty minutes. I hope they've had the sense not to get lost."

"Gibson's too careful to go wandering off. I wouldn't trust young Jimmy by himself, though—he'd want to start looking for Martians!"

"Oh, here they are. They seem to be in a bit of a hurry."

Two tiny figures had emerged from the middle distance and were bounding across the valley. Their haste was so obvious that the watchers downed tools and observed their approach with rising curiosity.

The fact that Gibson and Jimmy had returned so promptly represented a triumph of caution and self-control. For a long moment of incredulous astonishment they had stood staring at that pathway through the thin brown plants. On Earth, nothing could have been more commonplace; it was just the sort of track that cattle make across a hill, or wild animals through a forest. Its very familiarity had at first prevented them from noticing it, and even when they had forced their minds to accept its presence, they still kept trying to explain it away.

Gibson had spoken first, in a very subdued voice—almost as if he was afraid of being overheard.

"It's a path all right, Jimmy. But what could have made it, for heaven's sake? No one's ever been here before."

"It must have been some kind of animal."

"A fairly large one, too."

"Perhaps as big as a horse."

"Or a tiger."

The last remark produced an uneasy silence. Then Jimmy said: "Well, if it comes to a fight, that flash of yours should scare anything."

"Only if it had eyes," said Gibson. "Suppose it had some other sense?"

It was obvious that Jimmy was trying to think of good reasons for pressing ahead.

"I'm sure we could run faster, and jump higher, than anything else on Mars."

Gibson liked to believe that his decision was based on prudence rather than cowardice.

"We're not taking any risks," he said firmly. "We're going straight back to tell the others. *Then* we'll think about having a look round."

Jimmy had sense enough not to grumble, but he kept looking back wistfully as they returned to the ship. Whatever faults he might have, lack of courage was not among them.

It took some time to convince the others that they were not attempting a rather poor practical joke. After all, everyone knew why there couldn't be animal life on Mars. It was a question of metabolism: animals burned fuel so much faster than plants, and therefore could not exist in this thin, practically inert atmosphere. The biologists had been quick to point this out as soon as conditions on the surface of Mars had been accurately determined, and for the last ten years the question of animal life on the planet had been regarded as settled—except by incurable romantics.

"Even if you saw what you think," said Hilton, "there must be some natural explanation."

"Come and see for yourself," retorted Gibson. "I tell you it was a well-worn track."

"Oh, I'm coming," said Hilton.

"So am I," said the pilot.

"Wait a minute! We can't all go. At least one of us has got to stay behind."

For a moment Gibson felt like volunteering. Then he realised that he would never forgive himself if he did.

"*I* found the track," he said firmly.

"Looks as if I've got a mutiny on my hands," remarked Hilton. "Anyone got some money? Odd man out of you three stays behind."

"It's a wild goose chase, anyway," said the pilot, when he produced the only head. "I'll expect you home in an hour. If you take any longer I'll want you to bring back a genuine Martian princess, *à la* Edgar Rice Burroughs."

Hilton, despite his scepticism, was taking the matter more seriously.

"There'll be three of us," he said, "so it should be all right even if we do meet anything unfriendly. But just in case *none* of us come back, you've to sit right here and not go looking for us. Understand?"

"Very well. I'll sit tight."

The trio set off across the valley towards the little forest, Gibson leading the way. After reaching the tall thin fronds of "seaweed," they had no difficulty in finding the track again. Hilton stared at it in silence for a good minute, while Gibson and Jimmy regarded him with "I told you so" expressions. Then he remarked: "Let's have your flash-gun, Martin. I'm going first."

It would have been silly to argue. Hilton was taller, stronger, and more alert. Gibson handed over his weapon without a word.

There can be no weirder sensation than that of walking along a narrow track between high leafy walls, knowing that at any moment you may come face to face with a totally unknown and perhaps unfriendly creature. Gibson tried to remind himself that animals which had never before encountered man were seldom hostile—though there were enough exceptions to this rule to make life interesting.

They had gone about half-way through the forest when the track branched into two. Hilton took the turn to the right, but soon discovered that this was a *cul-de-sac*. It led to a clearing about twenty metres across, in which all the plants had been cut—or eaten—to within a short distance of the ground, leaving only the stumps showing. These were already beginning to sprout again, and it was obvious that this patch had been deserted for some time by whatever creatures had come here.

"Herbivores," whispered Gibson.

"And fairly intelligent," said Hilton. "See the way they've left the roots to come up again? Let's go back along the other branch."

They came across the second clearing five minutes later. It was a good deal larger than the first, and it was not empty.

Hilton tightened his grip on the flash-gun, and in a single smooth, well-practised movement Gibson swung his camera into position and began to take the most famous photographs ever made on Mars. Then they all relaxed, and stood waiting for the Martians to notice them.

In that moment centuries of fantasy and legend were swept away. All Man's dreams of neighbours not unlike himself vanished into limbo. With them, unlamented, went Wells' tentacled monstrosities and the other legions of crawling, nightmare horrors. And there vanished also the myth of coldly inhuman intelligences which might look down dispassionately on Man from their fabulous heights of wisdom—and might brush him aside with no more malice than he himself might destroy a creeping insect.

There were ten of the creatures in the glade, and they were all too busy eating to take any notice of the intruders. In appearance they resembled very plump kangaroos, their almost spherical bodies balanced on two large, slender hindlimbs. They were hairless, and their skin had a curious waxy sheen like polished leather. Two thin forearms, which seemed to be completely flexible, sprouted from the upper part of the body and ended in tiny hands like the claws of a bird —too small and feeble, one would have thought, to have been of much practical use. Their heads were set directly on the trunk with no suspicion of a neck, and bore two large pale eyes with wide pupils. There were no nostrils—only a very odd triangular mouth with three stubby bills which were making short work of the foliage. A pair of large, almost transparent ears hung limply from the head, twitching occasionally and sometimes folding themselves into trumpets which looked as if they might be extremely efficient sound detectors, even in this thin atmosphere.

The largest of the beasts was about as tall as Hilton, but all the others were considerably smaller. One baby, less than a metre high, could only be described by the overworked adjective "cute." It was hopping excitedly about in an effort to reach the more succulent leaves, and from time to time emitted thin, piping cries which were irresistibly pathetic.

"How intelligent would you say they are?" whispered Gibson at last.

"It's hard to say. Notice how they're careful not to destroy the plants they eat? Of course, that may be pure instinct—like bees knowing how to build their hives."

"They move very slowly, don't they? I wonder if they're warm-blooded."

"I don't see why they should have blood at all. Their metabolism must be pretty weird for them to survive in this climate."

"It's about time they took some notice of us."

"The big fellow knows we're here. I've caught him looking at us out of the corner of his eye. Do you notice the way his ears keep pointing towards us?"

"Let's go out into the open."

Hilton thought this over.

"I don't see how they can do us much harm, even if they want to. Those little hands look rather feeble—but I suppose those three-sided beaks could do some damage. We'll go forward, very slowly, for six paces. If they come at us, I'll give them a flash with the gun while you make a bolt for it. I'm sure we can outrun them easily. They certainly don't look built for speed."

Moving with a slowness which they hoped would appear reassuring rather than stealthy, they walked forward into the glade. There was now no doubt that the Martians saw them; half a dozen pairs of great, calm eyes stared at them, then looked away as their owners got on with the more important business of eating.

"They don't even seem to be inquisitive," said Gibson, somewhat disappointed. "Are we as uninteresting as all this?"

"Hello—Junior's spotted us! What's he up to?"

The smallest Martian had stopped eating and was staring at the intruders with an expression that might have meant anything from rank disbelief to hopeful anticipation of another meal. It gave a couple of shrill squeaks which were answered by a noncommittal "honk" from one of the adults. Then it began to hop towards the interested spectators.

It halted a couple of paces away, showing not the slightest signs of fear or caution.

"How do you do?" said Hilton solemnly. "Let me introduce us. On my right, James Spencer; on my left, Martin Gibson. But I'm afraid I didn't quite catch your name."

"Squeak," said the small Martian.

"Well, Squeak, what can we do for you?"

The little creature put out an exploring hand and tugged at Hilton's clothing. Then it hopped towards Gibson, who had been busily photographing this exchange of courtesies. Once again it put forward an enquiring paw, and Gibson moved the camera round out of harm's way. He held out his hand, and the little fingers closed round it with surprising strength.

"Friendly little chap, isn't he?" said Gibson, having disentangled himself with difficulty. "At least he's not as stuck-up as his relatives."

The adults had so far taken not the slightest notice of the proceedings. They were still munching placidly at the other side of the glade.

"I wish we had something to give him, but I don't suppose he could eat any of our food. Lend me your knife, Jimmy. I'll cut down a bit of seaweed for him, just to prove that we're friends."

This gift was gratefully received and promptly eaten, and the small hands reached out for more.

"You seem to have made a hit, Martin," said Hilton.

"I'm afraid it's cupboard love," sighed Gibson. "Hey, leave my camera alone—you can't eat that!"

"I say," said Hilton suddenly. "There's something odd here. What colour would you say this little chap is?"

"Why, brown in the front and—oh, a dirty grey at the back."

"Well, just walk to the other side of him and offer another bit of food."

Gibson obliged, Squeak rotating on his haunches so that he could grab the new morsel. And as he did so, an extraordinary thing happened.

The brown covering on the front of his body slowly faded, and in less than a minute had become a dingy grey. At the same time, exactly the reverse happened on the creature's back, until the interchange was complete.

"Good Lord!" said Gibson. "It's just like a chameleon. What do you think the idea is? Protective coloration?"

"No, it's cleverer than that. Look at those others over there. You see, they're always brown—or nearly black—on the side towards the sun. It's simply a scheme to catch as much heat as possible, and avoid re-radiating it. The plants do just the same—I wonder who thought of it first? It wouldn't be any use on an animal that had to move quickly, but some of those big chaps haven't changed position in the last five minutes."

Gibson promptly set to work photographing this peculiar phenomenon—not a very difficult feat to do, as wherever he moved Squeak always turned hopefully towards him and sat waiting patiently. When he had finished, Hilton remarked:

"I hate to break up this touching scene, but we said we'd be back in an hour."

"We needn't all go. Be a good chap, Jimmy—run back and say that we're all right."

But Jimmy was staring at the sky—the first to realise that for the last five minutes an aircraft had been circling high over the valley.

Their united cheer disturbed even the placidly browsing Martians, who looked round disapprovingly. It scared Squeak so much that he shot backwards in one tremendous hop, but soon got over his fright and came forward again.

"See you later!" called Gibson over his shoulder as they hurried out of the glade. The natives took not the slightest notice.

They were half-way out of the little forest when Gibson suddenly became aware of the fact that he was being followed. He stopped and looked back. Making heavy weather, but still hopping along gamely behind him, was Squeak.

"Shoo!" said Gibson, flapping his arms around like a distraught scarecrow. "Go back to mother! I haven't got anything for you."

It was not the slightest use, and his pause had merely enabled Squeak to catch up with him. The others were already out of sight, unaware that Gibson had dropped back. They therefore missed a very interesting cameo as Gibson tried, without hurting Squeak's feelings, to disengage himself from his new-found friend.

He gave up the direct approach after five minutes, and tried guile. Fortunately he had failed to return Jimmy's knife, and after much panting and hacking managed to collect a small pile of "seaweed" which he laid in front of Squeak. This, he hoped, would keep him busy for quite a while.

He had just finished this when Hilton and Jimmy came hurrying back to find what had happened to him.

"O.K.—I'm coming along now," he said. "I had to get rid of Squeak somehow. *That'll* stop him following."

The pilot in the crashed aircraft had been getting anxious, for the hour was nearly up and there was still no sign of his companions. By climbing on to the top of the fuselage he could see half-way across the valley, and to the dark area of vegetation into which they had disappeared. He was examining this when the rescue aircraft came driving out of the east and began to circle the valley.

When he was sure it had spotted him he turned his attention to the ground again. He was just in time to see a group of figures emerging into the open plain—and a moment later he rubbed his eyes in rank disbelief.

Three people had gone into the forest; but four were coming out. And the fourth looked a very odd sort of person indeed.

THIRTEEN

After what was later to be christened the most successful crash in the history of Martian exploration, the visit to Trivium Charontis and Port Schiaparelli was, inevitably, something of an anticlimax. Indeed, Gibson had wished to postpone it altogether and to

return to Port Lowell immediately with his prize. He had soon abandoned all attempts to jettison Squeak, and as everyone in the colony
would be on tenterhooks to see a real, live Martian it had been decided to fly the little creature back with them.

But Port Lowell would not let them return; indeed, it was ten days
before they saw the capital again. Under the great domes, one of the
decisive battles for the possession of the planet was now being
fought. It was a battle which Gibson knew of only through the radio
reports—a silent but deadly battle which he was thankful to have
missed.

The epidemic which Dr. Scott had asked for had arrived. At its
peak, a tenth of the city's population was sick with Martian fever. But
the serum from Earth broke the attack, and the battle was won with
only three fatal casualties. It was the last time that the fever ever
threatened the colony.

Taking Squeak to Port Schiaparelli involved considerable difficulties, for it meant flying large quantities of his staple diet ahead of
him. At first it was doubted if he could live in the oxygenated atmosphere of the domes, but it was soon discovered that this did not
worry him in the least—though it reduced his appetite considerably.
The explanation of this fortunate accident was not discovered until a
good deal later. What never was discovered at all was the reason for
Squeak's attachment to Gibson. Someone suggested, rather unkindly,
that it was because they were approximately the same shape.

Before they continued their journey, Gibson and his colleagues,
with the pilot of the rescue plane and the repair crew who arrived
later, made several visits to the little family of Martians. They discovered only the one group, and Gibson wondered if these were the
last specimens left on the planet. This, as it later turned out, was
not the case.

The rescue plane had been searching along the track of their flight
when it had received a radio message from Phobos reporting brilliant
flashes in Aetheria. (Just how those flashes had been made had puzzled everyone considerably until Gibson, with justifiable pride, gave
the explanation.) When they discovered it would take only a few
hours to replace the jet units on their plane, they had decided to wait
while the repairs were carried out and to use the time studying the
Martians in their natural haunts. It was then that Gibson first suspected the secret of their existence.

In the remote past they had probably been oxygen breathers, and their life processes still depended on the element. They could not obtain it direct from the soil, where it lay in such countless trillions of tons; but the plants they ate could do so. Gibson quickly found that the numerous "pods" in the seaweed-like fronds contained oxygen under quite high pressure. By slowing down their metabolism, the Martians had managed to evolve a balance—almost a symbiosis—with the plants which provided them, literally, with food and air. It was a precarious balance which, one would have thought, might have been upset at any time by some natural catastrophe. But conditions on Mars had long ago reached stability, and the balance would be maintained for ages yet—unless Man disturbed it.

The repairs took a little longer than expected, and they did not reach Port Schiaparelli until three days after leaving Port Lowell. The second city of Mars held less than a thousand people, living under two domes on a long, narrow plateau. This had been the site of the original landing on Mars, and so the position of the city was really an historical accident. Not until some years later, when the planet's resources began to be better known, was it decided to move the colony's centre of gravity to Lowell and not to expand Schiaparelli any further.

The little city was in many respects an exact replica of its larger and more modern rival. Its specialty was light engineering, geological— or rather aerological—research, and the exploration of the surrounding regions. The fact that Gibson and his colleagues had accidentally stumbled on the greatest discovery so far made on Mars, less than an hour's flight from the city, was thus the cause of some heartburning.

The visit must have had a demoralising effect on all normal activity in Port Schiaparelli, for wherever Gibson went everything stopped while crowds gathered around Squeak. A favourite occupation was to lure him into a field of uniform illumination and to watch him turn black all over, as he blissfully tried to extract the maximum advantage from this state of affairs. It was in Schiaparelli that someone hit on the deplorable scheme of projecting simple pictures on to Squeak, and photographing the result before it faded. One day Gibson was very annoyed to come across a photo of his pet bearing a crude but recognisable caricature of a well-known television star.

On the whole, their stay in Port Schiaparelli was not a very happy one. After the first three days they had seen everything worth seeing, and the few trips they were able to make into the surrounding countryside did not provide much of interest. Jimmy was continually worrying about Irene, and putting through expensive calls to Port Lowell. Gibson was impatient to get back to the big city which, not so long ago, he had called an overgrown village. Only Hilton, who seemed to possess unlimited reserves of patience, took life easily and relaxed while the others fussed around him.

There was one excitement during their stay in the city. Gibson had often wondered, a little apprehensively, what would happen if the pressurising dome ever failed. He received the answer—or as much of it as he had any desire for—one quiet afternoon when he was interviewing the city's chief engineer in his office. Squeak had been with them, propped up on his large, flexible lower limbs like some improbable nursery doll.

As the interview progressed, Gibson became aware that his victim was showing more than the usual signs of restiveness. His mind was obviously very far away, and he seemed to be waiting for something to happen. Suddenly, without warning, the whole building trembled slightly as if hit by an earthquake. Two more shocks, equally spaced, came in quick succession. From a loudspeaker on the wall a voice called urgently: "Blow-out! Practice only! You have ten seconds to reach shelter! Blow-out! Practice only!"

Gibson had jumped out of his chair, but immediately realised there was nothing he need do. From far away there came a sound of slamming doors—then silence. The engineer got to his feet and walked over to the window, overlooking the city's only main street.

"Everyone seems to have got to cover," he said. "Of course, it isn't possible to make these tests a complete surprise. There's one a month, and we have to tell people what day it will be because they might think it was the real thing."

"Just what are we all supposed to do?" asked Gibson, who had been told at least twice but had become a little rusty on the subject.

"As soon as you hear the signal—that's the three ground explosions —you've got to get under cover. If you're indoors you have to grab your breathing mask to rescue anyone who can't make it. You see, if pressure goes every house becomes a self-contained unit with enough air for several hours."

"And anyone out in the open?"

"It would take a few seconds for the pressure to go right down, and as every building has its own airlock it should always be possible to reach shelter in time. Even if you collapsed in the open, you'd probably be all right if you were rescued inside two minutes—unless you'd got a bad heart. And no one comes to Mars if he's got a bad heart."

"Well, I hope you never have to put this theory into practice!"

"So do we! But on Mars one has to be prepared for anything. Ah, there goes the All Clear."

The speaker had burst into life again.

"Exercise over. Will all those who failed to reach shelter in the regulation time please inform Admin in the usual way? End of message."

"Will they?" asked Gibson. "I should have thought they'd keep quiet."

The engineer laughed.

"That depends. They probably will if it was their own fault. But it's the best way of showing up weak points in our defences. Someone will come and say: 'Look here—I was cleaning one of the ore furnaces when the alarm went; it took me two minutes to get out of the blinking thing. What am *I* supposed to do if there's a real blow-out?' Then we've got to think of an answer, if we can."

Gibson looked enviously at Squeak, who seemed to be asleep, though an occasional twitch of the great translucent ears showed that he was taking some interest in the conversation.

"It would be nice if we could be like him and didn't have to bother about air-pressure. Then we could really do something with Mars."

"I wonder!" said the engineer thoughtfully. "What have *they* done except survive? It's always fatal to adapt oneself to one's surroundings. The thing to do is to alter your surroundings to suit you."

The words were almost an echo of the remark that Hadfield had made at their first meeting. Gibson was to remember them often in the years to come.

Their return to Port Lowell was almost a victory parade. The capital was in a mood of elation over the defeat of the epidemic, and it was now anxiously waiting to see Gibson and his prize. The scientists had prepared quite a reception for Squeak, the zoologists in particular being busily at work explaining away their early explanations for the absence of animal life on Mars.

Gibson had handed his pet over to the experts only when they had solemnly assured him that no thought of dissection had ever for a moment entered their minds. Then, full of ideas, he had hurried to see the Chief.

Hadfield had greeted him warmly. There was, Gibson was interested to note, a distinct change in the Chief's attitude towards him. At first it had been—well, not unfriendly, but at least somewhat reserved. He had not attempted to conceal the fact that he considered Gibson's presence on Mars something of a nuisance—another burden to add to those he already carried. This attitude had slowly changed until it was now obvious that the Chief Executive no longer regarded him as an unmitigated calamity.

"You've added some interesting citizens to my little empire," Hadfield said with a smile. "I've just had a look at your engaging pet. He's already bitten the Chief Medical Officer."

"I hope they're treating him properly," said Gibson anxiously.

"Who—the C.M.O.?"

"No—Squeak, of course. What I'm wondering is whether there are any other forms of animal life we haven't discovered yet—perhaps more intelligent."

"In other words, are these the only genuine Martians?"

"Yes."

"It'll be years before we know for certain, but I rather expect they are. The conditions which make it possible for them to survive don't occur in many places on the planet."

"That was one thing I wanted to talk to you about." Gibson reached into his pocket and brought out a frond of the brown "seaweed." He punctured one of the fronds, and there was the faint hiss of escaping gas.

"If this stuff is cultivated properly, it may solve the oxygen problem in the cities and do away with all our present complicated machinery. With enough sand for it to feed on, it would give you all the oxygen you need."

"Go on," said Hadfield noncommittally.

"Of course, you'd have to do some selective breeding to get the variety that gave most oxygen," continued Gibson, warming to his subject.

"Naturally," replied Hadfield.

Gibson looked at his listener with a sudden suspicion, aware that there was something odd about his attitude. A faint smile was playing about Hadfield's lips.

"I don't think you're taking me seriously!" Gibson protested bitterly.

Hadfield sat up with a start.

"On the contrary!" he retorted. "I'm taking you much more seriously than you imagine." He toyed with his paperweight, then apparently came to a decision. Abruptly he leaned towards his desk microphone and pressed a switch.

"Get me a Sand Flea and a driver," he said. "I want them at Lock One West in thirty minutes."

He turned to Gibson.

"Can you be ready by then?"

"What—yes, I suppose so. I've only got to get my breathing gear from the hotel."

"Good—see you in half an hour."

Gibson was there ten minutes early, his brain in a whirl. Transport had managed to produce a vehicle in time, and the Chief was punctual as ever. He gave the driver instructions which Gibson was unable to catch, and the Flea jerked out of the dome on to the road circling the city.

"I'm doing something rather rash, Gibson," said Hadfield as the brilliant green landscape flowed past them. "Will you give me your word that you'll say nothing of this until I authorise you?"

"Why, certainly," said Gibson, startled.

"I'm trusting you because I believe you're on our side, and haven't been as big a nuisance as I expected."

"Thank you," said Gibson dryly.

"*And* because of what you've just taught us about our own planet. I think we owe you something in return."

The Flea had swung round to the south, following the track that led up into the hills. And, quite suddenly, Gibson realised where they were going.

"Were you very upset when you heard that we'd crashed?" asked Jimmy anxiously.

"Of course I was," said Irene. "Terribly upset. I couldn't sleep for worrying about you."

"Now it's all over, though, don't you think it was worth it?"

"I suppose so, but somehow it keeps reminding me that in a month you'll be gone again. Oh, Jimmy, what shall we do then?"

Deep despair settled upon the two lovers. All Jimmy's present satisfaction vanished into gloom. There was no escaping from this inevitable fact. The *Ares* would be leaving Deimos in less than four weeks, and it might be years before he could return to Mars. It was a prospect too terrible for words.

"I can't possibly stay on Mars, even if they'd let me," said Jimmy. "I can't earn a living until I'm qualified, and I've still got two years' post-graduate work *and* a trip to Venus to do! There's only one thing for it!"

Irene's eyes brightened; then she relapsed into gloom.

"Oh, we've been through that before. I'm sure Daddy wouldn't agree."

"Well, it won't do any harm to try. I'll get Martin to tackle him."

"Mr. Gibson? Do you think he would?"

"I know he will, if I ask him. And he'll make it sound convincing."

"I don't see why he should bother."

"Oh, he likes me," said Jimmy with easy self-assurance. "I'm sure he'll agree with us. It's not right that you should stick here on Mars and never see anything of Earth. Paris—New York—London—why, you haven't lived until you've visited them. Do you know what I think?"

"What?"

"Your father's being selfish in keeping you here."

Irene pouted a little. She was very fond of her father and her first impulse was to defend him vigorously. But she was now torn between two loyalties, though in the long run there was no doubt which would win.

"Of course," said Jimmy, realising that he might have gone too far, "I'm sure he really means to do the best for you, but he's got so many things to worry about. He's probably forgotten what Earth is like and doesn't realise what you're losing! No, you must get away before it's too late."

Irene still looked uncertain. Then her sense of humour, so much more acute than Jimmy's, came to the rescue.

"I'm quite sure that if we were on Earth, and you had to go back to Mars, you'd be able to prove just as easily that I ought to follow you there!"

Jimmy looked a little hurt, then realised that Irene wasn't really laughing at him.

"All right," he said. "That's settled. I'll talk to Martin as soon as I see him—and ask him to tackle your Dad. So let's forget all about it until then, shall we?"

They did, very nearly.

———

The little amphitheatre in the hills above Port Lowell was just as Gibson had remembered it, except that the green of its lush vegetation had darkened a little, as if it had already received the first warning of the still far-distant autumn. The Sand Flea drove up to the largest of the four small domes, and they walked over to the airlock.

"When I was here before," said Gibson dryly, "I was told we'd have to be disinfected before we could enter."

"A slight exaggeration to discourage unwanted visitors," said Hadfield, unabashed. The outer door had opened at his signal, and they quickly stripped off their breathing apparatus. "We used to take such precautions, but they're no longer necessary."

The inner door slid aside and they stepped through into the dome. A man wearing the white smock of the scientific worker—the *clean* white smock of the very senior scientific worker—was waiting for them.

"Hello, Baines," said Hadfield. "Gibson—this is Professor Baines. I expect you've heard of each other."

They shook hands. Baines, Gibson knew, was one of the world's greatest experts on plant genetics. He had read a year or two ago that he had gone to Mars to study its flora.

"So you're the chap who's just discovered *Oxyfera*," said Baines dreamily. He was a large, rugged man with an absentminded air which contrasted strangely with his massive frame and determined features.

"Is that what you call it?" asked Gibson. "Well, I *thought* I'd discovered it. But I'm beginning to have doubts."

"You certainly discovered something quite as important," Hadfield reassured him. "But Baines isn't interested in animals, so it's no good talking to him about your Martian friends."

They were walking between low temporary walls which, Gibson saw, partitioned the dome into numerous rooms and corridors. The whole place looked as if it had been built in a great hurry; they came across beautiful scientific apparatus supported on rough packing cases, and everywhere there was an atmosphere of hectic improvisation. Yet, curiously enough, very few people were at work. Gibson obtained the impression that whatever task had been going on here was now completed and that only a skeleton staff was left.

Baines led them to an airlock connecting with one of the other domes, and as they waited for the last door to open he remarked quietly: "This may hurt your eyes a bit." With this warning, Gibson put up his hand as a shield.

His first impression was one of light and heat. It was almost as if he had moved from Pole to Tropics in a single step. Overhead, batteries of powerful lamps were blasting the hemispherical chamber with light. There was something heavy and oppressive about the air that was not only due to the heat, and he wondered what sort of atmosphere he was breathing.

This dome was not divided up by partitions; it was simply a large, circular space laid out into neat plots on which grew all the Martian plants which Gibson had ever seen, and many more besides. About a quarter of the area was covered by tall brown fronds which Gibson recognised at once.

"So you've known about them all the time?" he said, neither surprised nor particularly disappointed. (Hadfield was quite right: the Martians were *much* more important.)

"Yes," said Hadfield. "They were discovered about two years ago and aren't very rare along the equatorial belt. They only grow where there's plenty of sunlight, and your little crop was the farthest north they've ever been found."

"It takes a great deal of energy to split the oxygen out of the sand," explained Baines. "We've been helping them here with these lights, and trying some experiments of our own. Come and look at the result."

Gibson walked over to the plot, keeping carefully to the narrow path. These plants weren't, after all, exactly the same as those he had discovered, though they had obviously descended from the same stock. The most surprising difference was the complete absence of gas-pods, their place having been taken by myriads of minute pores.

"This is the important point," said Hadfield. "We've bred a variety which releases its oxygen directly into the air, because it doesn't need to store it any more. As long as it's got plenty of light and heat, it can extract all it needs from the sand and will throw off the surplus. *All the oxygen you're breathing now comes from these plants*—there's no other source in this dome."

"I see," said Gibson slowly. "So you'd already thought of my idea—and gone a good deal further. But I still don't understand the need for all this secrecy."

"What secrecy?" said Hadfield with an air of injured innocence.

"Really!" protested Gibson. "You've just asked me not to say anything about this place."

"Oh, that's because there will be an official announcement in a few days, and we haven't wanted to raise false hopes. But there hasn't been any real secrecy."

Gibson brooded over this remark all the way back to Port Lowell. Hadfield had told him a good deal, but had he told him everything? Where—if at all—did Phobos come into the picture? Gibson wondered if his supicions about the inner moon were completely unfounded; it could obviously have no connection with this particular project. He felt like trying to force Hadfield's hand by a direct question, but thought better of it. He might only make himself look a fool if he did.

The domes of Port Lowell were climbing up over the steeply convex horizon when Gibson broached the subject that had been worrying him for the past fortnight.

"The *Ares* is going back to Earth in three weeks, isn't she?" he remarked to Hadfield. The other merely nodded; the question was obviously a purely rhetorical one for Gibson knew the answer as well as anybody.

"I've been thinking," said Gibson slowly, "that I'd like to stay on Mars a bit longer. Maybe until next year."

"Oh," said Hadfield. The exclamation revealed neither congratulation nor disapproval, and Gibson felt a little piqued that his shattering announcement had fallen flat. "What about your work?" continued the Chief.

"All that can be done just as easily here as on Earth."

"I suppose you realise," said Hadfield, "that if you stay here you'll have to take up some useful profession." He smiled a little wryly. "That wasn't very tactful, was it? What I mean is that you'll have to do something to help run the colony. Have you any particular ideas in this line?"

This was a little more encouraging; at least it meant that Hadfield had not dismissed the suggestion at once. But it was a point that Gibson had overlooked in his first rush of enthusiasm.

"I wasn't thinking of making a permanent home here," he said a little lamely. "But I want to spend some time studying the Martians, and I'd like to see if I can find any more of them. Besides, I don't want to leave Mars just when things are getting interesting."

"What do you mean?" said Hadfield swiftly.

"Why—these oxygen plants, and getting Dome Seven into operation. I want to see what comes of all this in the next few months."

Hadfield looked thoughtfully at his passenger. He was less surprised than Gibson might have imagined, for he had seen this sort of thing happen before. He had even wondered if it was going to happen to Gibson, and was by no means displeased at the turn of events.

The explanation was really very simple. Gibson was happier now than he had ever been on Earth; he had done something worth while, and felt that he was becoming part of the Martian community. The identification was now nearly complete, and the fact that Mars had already made one attempt on his life had merely strengthened his determination to stay. If he returned to Earth, he would not be going home—he would be sailing into exile.

"Enthusiasm isn't enough, you know," said Hadfield.

"I quite understand that."

"This little world of ours is founded on two things—skill and hard work. Without both of them, we might just as well go back to Earth."

"I'm not afraid of work, and I'm sure I could learn some of the administrative jobs you've got here—and a lot of the routine technical ones."

This, Hadfield thought, was probably true. Ability to do these things was a function of intelligence, and Gibson had plenty of that. But more than intelligence was needed; there were personal factors as well. It would be best not to raise Gibson's hopes until he had made further enquiries and discussed the matter with Whittaker.

"I'll tell you what to do," said Hadfield. "Put in a provisional application to stay, and I'll have it signalled to Earth. We'll get their answer in about a week. Of course, if they turn you down there's nothing we can do."

Gibson doubted this, for he knew just how much notice Hadfield took of terrestrial regulations when they interfered with his plans. But he merely said: "And if Earth agrees, then I suppose it's up to you?"

"Yes. I'll start thinking about my answer then."

That, thought Gibson, was satisfactory as far as it went. Now that he had taken the plunge, he felt a great sense of relief, as if everything was now outside his control. He had merely to drift with the current, awaiting the progress of events.

The door of the airlock opened before them and the Flea crunched into the city. Even if he had made a mistake, no great harm would be done. He could always go back to Earth by the next ship—or the one after.

But there was no doubt that Mars had changed him. He knew what some of his friends would say when they read the news. "Have you heard about Martin? Looks as if Mars has made a man out of him! Who'd have thought it?"

Gibson wriggled uncomfortably. He had no intention of becoming an elevating object lesson for anyone, if he could help it. Even in his most maudlin moments he had never had the slightest use for those smug Victorian parables about lazy, self-centred men becoming useful members of the community. But he had a horrible fear that something uncommonly like this was beginning to happen to him.

FOURTEEN

"Out with it, Jimmy. What's on your mind? You don't seem to have much appetite this morning."

Jimmy toyed fretfully with the synthetic omelette on his plate, which he had already carved into microscopic fragments.

"I was thinking about Irene, and what a shame it is she's never had a chance of seeing Earth."

"Are you sure she wants to? I've never heard anyone here say a single good word for the place."

"Oh, she wants to all right. I've asked her."

"Stop beating about the bush. What are you two planning now? Do you want to elope in the *Ares*?"

Jimmy gave a rather sickly grin.

"That's an idea, but it would take a bit of doing! Honestly though —don't you think Irene ought to go back to Earth to finish her education? If she stays here she'll grow up into a—a——"

"A simple unsophisticated country girl—a raw colonial? Is that what you were thinking?"

"Well, something like that, but I wish you wouldn't put it so crudely."

"Sorry—I didn't mean to. As a matter of fact, I rather agree with you; it's a point that's occurred to me. I think someone ought to mention it to Hadfield."

"That's exactly what——" began Jimmy excitedly.

"—what you and Irene want me to do?"

Jimmy threw up his hands in mock despair.

"It's no good trying to kid you. Yes."

"If you'd said that at the beginning, think of the time we'd have saved. But tell me frankly, Jimmy—just how serious are you about Irene?"

Jimmy looked back at him with a level, steadfast gaze that was in itself a sufficient answer.

"I'm dead serious; you ought to know that. I want to marry her as soon as she's old enough—and I can earn my living."

There was a dead silence, then Gibson replied:

"You could do a lot worse; she's a very nice girl. And I think it would do her a lot of good to have a year or so on Earth. Still, I'd rather not tackle Hadfield at the moment. He's very busy and—well, he's already got one request from me."

"Oh?" said Jimmy, looking up with interest.

Gibson cleared his throat.

"It's got to come out some time, but don't say anything to the others yet. I've applied to stay on Mars."

"Good Lord!" exclaimed Jimmy. "That's—well, quite a thing to do."

Gibson suppressed a smile.

"Do you think it's a good thing?"

"Why, yes. I'd like to do it myself."

"Even if Irene was going back to Earth?" asked Gibson dryly.

"That isn't fair! But how long do you expect to stay?"

"Frankly, I don't know; it depends on too many factors. For one thing, I'll have to learn a job!"

"What sort of job?"

"Something that's congenial—and productive. Any ideas?"

Jimmy sat in silence for a moment, his forehead wrinkled with concentration. Gibson wondered just what he was thinking. Was he sorry that they might soon have to separate? In the last few weeks the strain and animosities which had once both repelled and united them had dissolved away. They had reached a state of emotional equilibrium which was pleasant, yet not as satisfactory as Gibson would have hoped. Perhaps it was his own fault; perhaps he had been afraid to show his deeper feelings and had hidden them behind banter and even occasional sarcasm. If so, he was afraid he might have succeeded only too well. Once he had hoped to earn Jimmy's trust and confidence; now, it seemed, Jimmy only came to him when he wanted something. No—that wasn't fair. Jimmy certainly liked him, perhaps as much as many sons liked their fathers. That was a positive achievement of which he could be proud. He could take some credit, too, for the great improvement in Jimmy's disposition since they had left Earth. He was no longer awkward and shy; though he was still rather serious, he was never sullen. This, thought Gibson, was something in which he could take a good deal of satisfaction. But now there was little more he could do. Jimmy was slipping out of his world—Irene was the only thing that mattered to him now.

"I'm afraid I don't seem to have any ideas," said Jimmy. "Of course, you could have my job here! Oh, that reminds me of something I picked up in Admin the other day." His voice dropped to a conspiratorial whisper and he leaned across the table. "Have you ever heard of 'Project Dawn'?"

"No; what is it?"

"That's what I'm trying to find out. It's something very secret, and I think it must be pretty big."

"Oh!" said Gibson, suddenly alert. "Perhaps I have heard about it after all. Tell me what you know."

"Well, I was working late one evening in the filing section, and was sitting on the floor between some of the cabinets, sorting out papers, when the Chief and Mayor Whittaker came in. They didn't know I was there, and were talking together. I wasn't trying to eavesdrop, but you know how it is. All of a sudden Mayor Whittaker said something that made me sit up with a bang. I think these were his exact words: 'Whatever happens, there's going to be hell to pay as soon as Earth knows about Project Dawn—even if it's successful.' Then the Chief gave a queer little laugh, and said something about success excusing everything. That's all I could hear; they went out soon afterwards. What do you think about it?"

"Project Dawn!" There was a magic about the name that made Gibson's pulse quicken. Almost certainly it must have some connection with the research going on up in the hills above the city—but that could hardly justify Whittaker's remark. Or could it?

Gibson knew a little about the interplay of political forces between Earth and Mars. He appreciated, from occasional remarks of Hadfield's and comments in the local press, that the colony was now passing through a critical period. On Earth, powerful voices were raised in protest against its enormous expense, which, it seemed, would extend indefinitely into the future with no sign of any ultimate reduction. More than once Hadfield had spoken bitterly of schemes which he had been compelled to abandon on grounds of economy, and of other projects for which permission could not be obtained at all.

"I'll see what I can find out from my—er—various sources of information," said Gibson. "Have you mentioned it to anyone else?"

"No."

"I shouldn't, if I were you. After all, it may not be anything important. I'll let you know what I find out."

"You won't forget to ask about Irene?"

"As soon as I get the chance. But it may take some time—I'll have to catch Hadfield in the right mood!"

As a private detective agency, Gibson was not a success. He made two rather clumsy direct attempts before he decided that the frontal approach was useless. George the barman had been his first target, for he seemed to know everything that was happening on Mars and was one of Gibson's most valuable contacts. This time, however, he proved of no use at all.

"Project Dawn?" he said, with a puzzled expression. "I've never heard of it."

"Are you quite sure?" asked Gibson, watching him narrowly.

George seemed to lose himself in deep thought.

"Quite sure," he said at last. And that was that. George was such an excellent actor that it was quite impossible to guess whether he was lying or speaking the truth.

Gibson did a trifle better with the editor of the "Martian Times." Westerman was a man he normally avoided, as he was always trying to coax articles out of him and Gibson was invariably behind with his terrestrial commitments. The staff of two therefore looked up with some surprise as their visitor entered the tiny office of Mars' only newspaper.

Having handed over some carbon copies as a peace offering, Gibson sprang his trap.

"I'm trying to collect all the information I can on 'Project Dawn,'" he said casually. "I know it's still under cover, but I want to have everything ready when it can be published."

There was dead silence for several seconds. Then Westerman remarked: "I think you'd better see the Chief about that."

"I didn't want to bother him—he's so busy," said Gibson innocently.

"Well, I can't tell you anything."

"You mean you don't know anything about it?"

"If you like. There are only a few dozen people on Mars who could even tell you what it is."

That, at least, was a valuable piece of information.

"Do you happen to be one of them?" asked Gibson.

Westerman shrugged his shoulders.

"I keep my eyes open, and I've done a bit of guessing."

That was all that Gibson could extract from him. He strongly suspected that Westerman knew little more about the matter than he did himself, but was anxious to conceal his ignorance. The interview had, however, confirmed two main facts. "Project Dawn" certainly did exist, and it was extremely well hidden. Gibson could only follow Westerman's example, keeping his eyes open and guessing what he could.

He decided to abandon the quest for the time being and to go round to the Biophysics Lab, where Squeak was the guest of honour. The little Martian was sitting on his haunches taking life easily while the scientists stood conversing in a corner, trying to decide what to do next. As soon as he saw Gibson, he gave a chirp of delight and bounded across the room, bringing down a chair as he did so but luckily missing any valuable apparatus. The bevy of biologists regarded this demonstration with some annoyance; presumably it could not be reconciled with their views on Martian psychology.

"Well," said Gibson to the leader of the team, when he had disentangled himself from Squeak's clutches. "Have you decided how intelligent he is yet?"

The scientist scratched his head.

"He's a queer little beast. Sometimes I get the feeling he's just laughing at us. The odd thing is that he's quite different from the rest of his tribe. We've got a unit studying them in the field, you know."

"In what way is he different?"

"The others don't show any emotions at all, as far as we can discover. They're completely lacking in curiosity. You can stand beside them and if you wait long enough they'll eat right round you. As long as you don't actively interfere with them they'll take no notice of you."

"And what happens if you do?"

"They'll try and push you out of the way, like some obstacle. If they can't do that, they'll just go somewhere else. Whatever you do, you can't make them annoyed."

"Are they good-natured, or just plain stupid?"

"I'd be inclined to say it's neither one nor the other. They've had no natural enemies for so long that they can't imagine that anyone would try to hurt them. By now they must be largely creatures of habit; life's so tough for them that they can't afford expensive luxuries like curiosity and the other emotions."

"Then how do you explain this little fellow's behaviour?" asked Gibson, pointing to Squeak, who was now investigating his pockets. "He's not really hungry—I've just offered him some food—so it must be pure inquisitiveness."

"It's probably a phase they pass through when they're young. Think how a kitten differs from a full-grown cat—or a human baby from an adult, for that matter."

"So when Squeak grows up he'll be like the others?"

"Probably, but it isn't certain. We don't know what capacity he has for learning new habits. For instance, he's very good at finding his way out of mazes—once you can persuade him to make the effort."

"Poor Squeak!" said Gibson. "Sometimes I feel quite guilty about taking you away from home. Still, it was your own idea. Let's go for a walk."

Squeak immediately hopped towards the door.

"Did you see that?" exclaimed Gibson. "He understands what I'm saying."

"Well, so can a dog when it hears a command. It may simply be a question of habit again—you've been taking him out this time every day and he's got used to it. Can you bring him back inside half an hour? We're fixing up the encephalograph to get some EEG records of his brain."

These afternoon walks were a way of reconciling Squeak to his fate and at the same time salving Gibson's conscience. He sometimes felt rather like a baby-snatcher who had abandoned his victim immediately after stealing it. But it was all in the cause of science, and the biologists had sworn they wouldn't hurt Squeak in any way.

The inhabitants of Port Lowell were now used to seeing this strangely assorted pair taking their daily stroll along the streets, and crowds no longer gathered to watch them pass. When it was outside school hours Squeak usually collected a retinue of young admirers who wanted to play with him, but it was now early afternoon and the juvenile population was still in durance vile. There was no one in sight when Gibson and his companion swung into Broadway, but presently a familiar figure appeared in the distance. Hadfield was carrying out his daily tour of inspection, and as usual he was accompanied by his pets.

It was the first time that Topaz and Turquoise had met Squeak, and their aristocratic calm was seriously disturbed, though they did their best to conceal the fact. They tugged on their leads and tried to shelter unobtrusively behind Hadfield, while Squeak took not the slightest notice of them at all.

"Quite a menagerie!" laughed Hadfield. "I don't think Topaz and Turquoise appreciate having a rival—they've had the place to themselves so long that they think they own it."

"Any news from Earth yet?" asked Gibson, anxiously.

"Oh, about your application? Good heavens, I only sent it off two days ago! You know just how quickly things move down there. It will be at least a week before we get an answer."

The Earth was always "down," the outer planets "up," so Gibson had discovered. The terms gave him a curious mental picture of a great slope leading down to the Sun, with the planets lying on it at varying heights.

"I don't really see what it's got to do with Earth," Gibson continued. "After all, it's not as if there's any question of allocating shipping space. I'm here already—in fact it'll save trouble if I *don't* go back!"

"You surely don't imagine that such commonsense arguments carry much weight with the policy-makers back on Earth!" retorted Hadfield. "Oh, dear no! Everything has to go through the Proper Channels."

Gibson was fairly sure that Hadfield did not usually talk about his superiors in this light-hearted fashion, and he felt that peculiar glow of satisfaction that comes when one is permitted to share a deliberate indiscretion. It was another sign that the C.E. trusted him and considered that he was on his side. Dare he mention the two other matters that were occupying his mind—Project Dawn and Irene? As far as Irene was concerned, he had made his promise and would have to keep it sooner or later. But first he really ought to have a talk with Irene herself—yes, that was a perfectly good excuse for putting it off.

He put it off so long that the matter was taken right out of his hands. Irene herself made the plunge, no doubt egged on by Jimmy, from whom Gibson had a full report the next day. It was easy to tell from Jimmy's face what the result had been.

Irene's suggestion must have been a considerable shock to Hadfield, who no doubt believed that he had given his daughter everything she needed, and thus shared a delusion common among parents. Yet he had taken it calmly and there had been no scenes. Hadfield was too intelligent a man to adopt the attitude of the deeply wounded father. He had merely given lucid and compelling reasons why Irene couldn't possibly go to Earth until she was twenty-one, when he planned to return for a long holiday during which they could see the world together. And that was only three years away.

"Three years!" lamented Jimmy. "It might just as well be three lifetimes!"

Gibson deeply sympathised, but tried to look on the bright side of things.

"It's not so long, really. You'll be fully qualified then and earning a lot more money than most young men at that age. And it's surprising how quickly the time goes."

This Job's comforting produced no alleviation of Jimmy's gloom. Gibson felt like adding the comment that it was just as well that ages on Mars were still reckoned by Earth time, and not according to the Martian year of 687 days. However, he thought better of it and remarked instead: "What does Hadfield think about all this, anyway? Has he discussed you with Irene?"

"I don't think he knows anything about it."

"You can bet your life he does! You know, I really think it would be a good idea to go and have it out with him."

"I've thought of that, once or twice," said Jimmy. "But I guess I'm scared."

"You'll have to get over that some time if he's going to be your father-in-law!" retorted Gibson. "Besides, what harm could it do?"

"He might stop Irene seeing me in the time we've still got."

"Hadfield isn't that sort of man, and if he was he'd have done it long ago."

Jimmy thought this over and was unable to refute it. To some extent Gibson could understand his feelings, for he remembered his own nervousness at his first meeting with Hadfield. In this he had had much less excuse than Jimmy, for experience had long ago taught him that few great men remain great when one gets up close to them.

But to Jimmy, Hadfield was still the aloof and unapproachable master of Mars.

"If I *do* go and see him," said Jimmy at last, "what do you think I ought to say?"

"What's wrong with the plain, unvarnished truth? It's been known to work wonders on such occasions."

Jimmy shot him a slightly hurt look; he was never quite sure whether Gibson was laughing with him or at him. It was Gibson's own fault, and was the chief obstacle to their complete understanding.

"Look," said Gibson. "Come along with me to the Chief's house tonight, and have it out with him. After all, look at it from his point of view. For all he can tell, it may be just an ordinary flirtation with neither side taking it very seriously. But if you go and tell him you want to get engaged—then it's a different matter."

He was much relieved when Jimmy agreed with no more argument. After all, if the boy had anything in him he should make these decisions himself, without any prompting. Gibson was sensible enough to realise that, in his anxiety to be helpful, he must not run the risk of destroying Jimmy's self-reliance.

It was one of Hadfield's virtues that one always knew where to find him at any given time—though woe betide anyone who bothered him with routine official matters during the few hours when he considered himself off duty. This matter was neither routine nor official; and it was not, as Gibson had guessed, entirely unexpected either, for Hadfield had shown no surprise at all when he saw who Gibson had brought with him. There was no sign of Irene; she had thoughtfully effaced herself. As soon as possible, Gibson did the same.

He was waiting in the library, running through Hadfield's books and wondering how many of them the Chief had actually had time to read, when Jimmy came in.

"Mr. Hadfield would like to see you," he said.

"How did you get on?"

"I don't know yet, but it wasn't so bad as I'd expected."

"It never is. And don't worry. I'll give you the best reference I can without actual perjury."

When Gibson entered the study, he found Hadfield sunk in one of the armchairs, staring at the carpet as though he had never seen it before in his life. He motioned his visitor to take the other chair.

"How long have you known Spencer?" he asked.

"Only since leaving Earth. I'd never met him before boarding the *Ares*."

"And do you think that's long enough to form a clear opinion of his character?"

"Is a lifetime long enough to do that?" countered Gibson.

Hadfield smiled, and looked up for the first time.

"Don't evade the issue," he said, though without irritation. "What do you really think about him? Would *you* be willing to accept him as a son-in-law?"

"Yes," said Gibson, without hesitation. "I'd be glad to."

It was just as well that Jimmy could not overhear their conversation in the next ten minutes—though in other ways, perhaps, it was rather a pity, for it would have given him much more insight into Gibson's feelings. In his carefully probing cross-examination, Hadfield was trying to learn all he could about Jimmy, but he was testing Gibson as well. This was something that Gibson should have anticipated; the fact that he had overlooked it in serving Jimmy's interests was no small matter to his credit. When Hadfield's interrogation suddenly switched its point of attack, he was totally unprepared for it.

"Tell me, Gibson," said Hadfield abruptly. "Why are you taking all this trouble for young Spencer? You say you only met him five months ago."

"That's perfectly true. But when we were a few weeks out I discovered that I'd known both his parents very well—we were all at college together."

It had slipped out before he could stop it. Hadfield's eyebrows went up slightly; no doubt he was wondering why Gibson had never taken his degree. But he was far too tactful to pursue this subject, and merely asked a few casual questions about Jimmy's parents, and when he had known them.

At least, they seemed casual questions—just the kind Hadfield might have been expected to ask, and Gibson answered them innocently enough. He had forgotten that he was dealing with one of the keenest minds in the Solar System, one at least as good as his own at analysing the springs and motives of human conduct. When he realised what had happened, it was already too late.

"I'm sorry," said Hadfield, with deceptive smoothness, "but this whole story of yours simply lacks conviction. I don't say that what you've told me isn't the truth. It's perfectly possible that you might take such an interest in Spencer because you knew his parents very well twenty years ago. But you've tried to explain away too much, and it's quite obvious that the whole affair touches you at an altogether deeper level." He leaned forward suddenly and stabbed at Gibson with his finger.

"I'm not a fool, Gibson, and men's minds are my business. You've no need to answer this if you don't want to, but I think you owe it to me now. *Jimmy Spencer is your son, isn't he?*"

The bomb had dropped—the explosion was over. And in the silence that followed Gibson's only emotion was one of overwhelming relief.

"Yes," he said. "He is my son. How did you guess?"

Hadfield smiled; he looked somewhat pleased with himself, as if he had just settled a question that had been bothering him for some time.

"It's extraordinary how blind men can be to the effects of their own actions—and how easily they assume that no one else has any powers of observation. There's a slight but distinct likeness between you and Spencer; when I first met you together I wondered if you were related and was quite surprised when I heard you weren't."

"It's very curious," interjected Gibson, "that we were together in the *Ares* for three months, and no one noticed it there."

"Is it so curious? Spencer's crewmates thought they knew his background, and it never occurred to them to associate it with you. That probably blinded them to the resemblance which I—who hadn't any preconceived ideas—spotted at once. But I'd have dismissed it as pure coincidence if you hadn't told me your story. That provided the missing clues. Tell me—does Spencer know this?"

"I'm sure he doesn't even suspect it."

"Why are you so sure? And why haven't you told him?"

The cross-examination was ruthless, but Gibson did not resent it. No one had a better right than Hadfield to ask these questions. And Gibson needed someone in whom to confide—just as Jimmy had needed him, back in the *Ares* when this uncovering of the past had first begun. To think that he had started it all himself! He had certainly never dreamed where it would lead. . . .

"I think I'd better go back to the beginning," said Gibson, shifting uneasily in his chair. "When I left college I had a complete breakdown and was in hospital for over a year. After I came out I'd lost all contact with my Cambridge friends; though a few tried to keep in touch with me, I didn't want to be reminded of the past. Eventually, of course, I ran into some of them again, but it wasn't until several years later that I heard what had happened to Kathleen —to Jimmy's mother. By then, she was already dead."

He paused, still remembering, across all these years, the puzzled wonder he had felt because the news had brought him so little emotion.

"I heard there was a son, and thought little of it. We'd always been—well, careful, or so we believed—and I just assumed that the boy was Gerald's. You see, I didn't know when they were married, or when Jimmy was born. I just wanted to forget the whole business, and pushed it out of my mind. I can't even remember now if it even occurred to me that the boy might have been mine. You may find it hard to believe this, but it's the truth.

"And then I met Jimmy, and that brought it all back again. I felt sorry for him at first, and then began to get fond of him. But I never guessed who he was. I even found myself trying to trace his resemblance to Gerald—though I can hardly remember him now."

Poor Gerald! He, of course, had known the truth well enough, but he had loved Kathleen and had been glad to marry her on any terms he could. Perhaps he was to be pitied as much as she, but that was something that now would never be known.

"And when," persisted Hadfield, "did you discover the truth?"

"Only a few weeks ago, when Jimmy asked me to witness some official document he had to fill in—it was his application to start work here, in fact. That was when I first learned his date of birth."

"I see," said Hadfield thoughtfully. "But even that doesn't give absolute proof, does it?"

"I'm perfectly sure," Gibson replied with such obvious pique that Hadfield could not help smiling, "that there was no one else. Even if I'd had any doubts left, you've dispelled them yourself."

"And Spencer?" asked Hadfield, going back to his original question. "You've not told me why you're so confident he knows nothing. Why shouldn't he have checked a few dates? His parents' wedding day, for example? Surely what you've told him must have roused his suspicions?"

"I don't think so," said Gibson slowly, choosing his words with the delicate precision of a cat walking over a wet roadway. "You see, he rather idealises his mother, and though he may guess I haven't told him everything, I don't believe he's jumped to the right conclusion. He's not the sort who could have kept quiet about it if he had. And besides, he'd still have no proof even if he knows when his parents were married—which is more than most people do. No, I'm sure Jimmy doesn't know, and I'm afraid it will be rather a shock to him when he finds out."

Hadfield was silent; Gibson could not even guess what he was thinking. It was not a very creditable story, but at least he had shown the virtue of frankness.

Then Hadfield shrugged his shoulders in a gesture that seemed to hold a lifetime's study of human nature.

"He likes you," he said. "He'll get over it all right."

Gibson relaxed with a sigh of relief. He knew that the worst was past.

"Gosh, you've been a long time," said Jimmy. "I thought you were never going to finish; what happened?"

Gibson took him by the arm.

"Don't worry," he said. "It's quite all right. Everything's going to be all right now."

He hoped and believed he was telling the truth. Hadfield had been sensible, which was more than some fathers would have been even in this day and age.

"I'm not particularly concerned," he had said, "who Spencer's parents were or were not. This isn't the Victorian era. I'm only interested in the fellow himself, and I must say I'm favourably impressed. I've also had quite a chat about him with Captain Norden, by the way, so I'm not relying merely on tonight's interview. Oh yes, I saw all this coming a long time ago! There was even a certain inevitability about it, since there are very few youngsters of Spencer's age on Mars."

He had spread his hands in front of him—in a habit which Gibson had noticed before—and stared intently at his fingers as if seeing them for the first time in his life.

"The engagement can be announced tomorrow," he'd said softly. "And now—what about *your* side of the affair?" He'd stared keenly at Gibson, who returned his gaze without flinching.

"I want to do whatever is best for Jimmy," he had said. "Just as soon as I can decide what that is."

"And you still want to stay on Mars?" asked Hadfield.

"I'd thought of that aspect of it too," Gibson had said. "But if I went back to Earth, what good would that do? Jimmy'll never be there more than a few months at a time—in fact, from now on I'll see a lot more of him if I stay on Mars!"

"Yes, I suppose that's true enough," Hadfield had said, smiling. "How Irene's going to enjoy having a husband who spends half his life in space remains to be seen—but then, sailors' wives have managed to put up with this sort of thing for quite a long time." He paused abruptly.

"Do you know what I think you ought to do?" he said.

"I'd be very glad of your views," Gibson had replied with feeling.

"Do nothing until the engagement's over and the whole thing's settled. If you revealed your identity now I don't see what good it would do, and it might conceivably cause harm. Later, though, you must tell Jimmy who you are—or who he is, whichever way you like to look at it. But I don't think the right moment will come for quite a while."

It was the first time that Hadfield had referred to Spencer by his christian name. He was probably not even conscious of it, but to Gibson it was a clear and unmistakable sign that he was already thinking of Jimmy as his son-in-law. The knowledge brought him a sudden sense of kinship and sympathy towards Hadfield. They were united in selfless dedication towards the same purpose—the happiness of the two children in whom they saw their own youth reborn.

Looking back upon it later, Gibson was to identify this moment with the beginning of his friendship with Hadfield—the first man to whom he was ever able to give his unreserved admiration and respect. It was a friendship that was to play a greater part in the future of Mars than either could have guessed.

FIFTEEN

It had opened just like any other day in Port Lowell. Jimmy and Gibson had breakfasted quietly together—very quietly, for they were both deeply engrossed with their personal problems. Jimmy was still in what could best be described as an ecstatic condition, though he had occasional fits of depression at the thought of leaving Irene, while Gibson was wondering if Earth had yet made any move regarding his application. Sometimes he was sure the whole thing was a great mistake, and even hoped that the papers had been lost. But he knew he'd have to go through with it, and decided to stir things up at Admin.

He could tell that something was wrong the moment he entered the office. Mrs. Smyth, Hadfield's secretary, met him as she always did when he came to see the Chief. Usually she showed him in at once; sometimes she explained that Hadfield was extremely busy, or putting a call through to Earth, and could he come back later? This time she simply said: "I'm sorry, Mr. Hadfield isn't here. He won't be back until tomorrow."

"Won't be back?" queried Gibson. "Has he gone to Skia?"

"Oh no," said Mrs. Smyth, wavering slightly but obviously on the defensive. "I'm afraid I can't say. But he'll be back in twenty-four hours."

Gibson decided to puzzle over this later. He presumed that Mrs. Smyth knew all about his affairs, so she could probably answer his question.

"Do you know if there's been any reply yet to my application?" he asked.

Mrs. Smyth looked even unhappier.

"I think there has," she said. "But it was a personal signal to Mr. Hadfield and I can't discuss it. I expect he'll want to see you about it as soon as he gets back."

This was most exasperating. It was bad enough not to have a reply, but it was even worse to have one you weren't allowed to see. Gibson felt his patience evaporating.

"Surely there's no reason why you shouldn't tell me about it!" he exclaimed. "Especially if I'll know tomorrow, anyway."

"I'm really awfully sorry, Mr. Gibson. But I know Mr. Hadfield will be most annoyed if I say anything now."

"Oh, very well," said Gibson, and went off in a huff.

He decided to relieve his feelings by tackling Mayor Whittaker —always assuming that he was still in the city. He was, and he did not look particularly happy to see Gibson, who settled himself firmly down in the visitor's chair in a way that obviously meant business.

"Look here, Whittaker," he began. "I'm a patient man and I think you'll agree I don't often make unreasonable requests." As the other showed no signs of making the right reply, Gibson continued hastily:

"There's something very peculiar going on round here and I'm anxious to get to the bottom of it."

Whittaker sighed. He had been expecting this to happen sooner or later. A pity Gibson couldn't have waited until tomorrow: it wouldn't have mattered then. . . .

"What's made you suddenly jump to this conclusion?" he asked.

"Oh, lots of things—and it isn't at all sudden. I've just tried to see Hadfield, and Mrs. Smyth told me he's not in the city and then closed up like a clam when I tried to ask a few innocent questions."

"I can just imagine her doing that!" grinned Whittaker cheerfully.

"If you try the same thing I'll start throwing the furniture around. At least if you can't tell me what's going on, for goodness sake tell me *why* you can't tell me. It's Project Dawn, isn't it?"

That made Whittaker sit up with a start.

"How did you know?" he asked.

"Never mind; I can be stubborn too."

"I'm not trying to be stubborn," said Whittaker plaintively. "Don't think we like secrecy for the sake of it; it's a confounded nuisance. But suppose you start telling me what you know."

"Very well, if it'll soften you up. Project Dawn is something to do with that plant genetics place up in the hills where you've been cultivating—what do you call it?—*Oxyfera*. As there seems no point in keeping that quiet, I can only assume it's part of a much bigger plan. I suspect Phobos is mixed up with it, though I can't imagine how. You've managed to keep it so secret that the few people on Mars who know anything about it just won't talk. But you haven't been trying to conceal it from Mars so much as from Earth. Now what have you got to say?"

Whittaker appeared to be not in the least abashed.

"I must compliment you on your—er—perspicacity," he said. "You may also be interested to know that, a couple of weeks ago, I suggested to the Chief that we ought to take you fully into our confidence. But he couldn't make up his mind, and since then things have happened rather more rapidly than anyone expected."

He doodled absentmindedly on his writing pad, then came to a decision.

"I won't jump the gun," he said, "and I can't tell you what's happening now. But here's a little story that may amuse you. Any resemblance to—ah—real persons and places is quite coincidental."

"I understand," grinned Gibson. "Go on."

"Let's suppose that in the first rush of interplanetary enthusiasm world A has set up a colony on world B. After some years it finds that this is costing a lot more than it expected, and has given no tangible returns for the money spent. Two factions then arise on the mother world. One, the conservative group, wants to close the project down —to cut its losses and get out. The other group, the progressives, wants to continue the experiment because they believe that in the long run Man has got to explore and master the material universe, or else he'll simply stagnate on his own world. But this sort of argument is no use with the taxpayers, and the conservatives are beginning to get the upper hand.

"All this, of course, is rather unsettling to the colonists, who are getting more and more independently minded and don't like the idea of being regarded as poor relations living on charity. Still, they don't see any way out—until one day a revolutionary scientific discovery is made. (I should have explained at the beginning that planet B has been attracting the finest brains of A, which is another reason why A is getting annoyed.) This discovery opens up almost unlimited prospects for the future of B, but to apply it involves certain risks, as well as the diversion of a good deal of B's limited resources. Still, the plan is put forward—and is promptly turned down by A. There is a protracted tug-of-war behind the scenes, but the home planet is adamant.

"The colonists are then faced with two alternatives. They can force the issue out into the open, and appeal to the public on world A. Obviously they'll be at a great disadvantage, as the men on the spot can shout them down. The other choice is to carry on with the plan without informing Earth—I mean, planet A—and this is what they finally decided to do.

"Of course, there were a lot of other factors involved—political and personal, as well as scientific. It so happened that the leader of the colonists was a man of unusual determination who wasn't scared of anything or anyone, on either of the planets. He had a team of first-class scientists behind him, and they backed him up. So the plan went ahead; but no one knows yet if it will be successful. I'm sorry I can't tell you the end of the story; you know how these serials always break off at the most exciting place."

"I think you've told me just about everything," said Gibson. "Everything, that is, except one minor detail. I *still* don't know what

Project Dawn is." He rose to go. "Tomorrow I'm coming back to hear the final instalment of your gripping serial."

"There won't be any need to do that," Whittaker replied. He glanced unconsciously at the clock. "You'll know long before then."

As he left the Administration Building, Gibson was intercepted by Jimmy.

"I'm supposed to be at work," he said breathlessly, "but I had to catch you. Something important's going on."

"I know," replied Gibson rather impatiently. "Project Dawn's coming to the boil, and Hadfield's left town."

"Oh," replied Jimmy, a little taken aback. "I didn't think you'd have heard. But you won't know this, anyway. Irene's very upset. She told me her father said good-bye last night as if—well, as if he mightn't see her again."

Gibson whistled. That put things in a different light. Project Dawn was not only big, it might be dangerous. This was a possibility he had not considered.

"Whatever's happening," he said, "we'll know all about it tomorrow—Whittaker's just told me that. But I think I can guess where Hadfield is right now."

"Where?"

"He's up on Phobos. For some reason, that's the key to Project Dawn, and that's where you'll find the Chief right now."

Gibson would have made a large bet on the accuracy of this guess. It was just as well that there was no one to take it, for he was quite wrong. Hadfield was now almost as far away from Phobos as he was from Mars. At the moment he was sitting in some discomfort in a small spaceship, which was packed with scientists and their hastily dismantled equipment. He was playing chess, and playing it very badly, against one of the greatest physicists in the Solar System. His opponent was playing equally badly, and it would soon have become quite obvious to any observer that they were simply trying to pass the time. Like everyone on Mars, they were waiting; but they were the only ones who knew exactly what they were waiting for.

The long day—one of the longest that Gibson had ever known —slowly ebbed away. It was a day of wild rumours and speculation: everyone in Port Lowell had some theory which they were anxious to air. But as those who knew the truth said nothing, and those who knew nothing said too much, when night came the city was in a state of extreme confusion. Gibson wondered if it was worth while staying up late, but around midnight he decided to go to bed. He was fast asleep when, invisibly, soundlessly, hidden from him by the thickness of the planet, Project Dawn came to its climax. Only the men in the watching spaceship saw it happen, and changed suddenly from grave scientists to shouting, laughing schoolboys as they turned to race for home.

In the very small hours of the morning Gibson was wakened by a thunderous banging on his door. It was Jimmy, shouting to him to get up and come outside. He dressed hastily, but when he reached the door Jimmy had already gone out into the street. He caught him up at the doorway. From all sides, people were beginning to appear, rubbing their eyes sleepily and wondering what had happened. There was a rising buzz of voices and distant shouts; Port Lowell sounded like a beehive that had been suddenly disturbed.

It was a full minute before Gibson understood what had awakened the city. Dawn was just breaking: the eastern sky was aglow with the first light of the rising Sun. The eastern sky? *My God, that dawn was breaking in the west.*

No one could have been less superstitious than Gibson, but for a moment the upper levels of his mind were submerged by a wave of irrational terror. It lasted only a moment; then reason reasserted itself. Brighter and brighter grew the light spilling over the horizon; now the first rays were touching the hills above the city. They were moving swiftly—far, far too swiftly for the Sun—and suddenly a blazing, golden meteor leapt up out of the desert, climbing almost vertically towards the zenith.

Its very speed betrayed its identity. This was Phobos—or what had been Phobos a few hours before. Now it was a yellow disc of fire, and Gibson could feel the heat of its burning upon his face. The city around him was now utterly silent, watching the miracle and slowly waking to a dim awareness of all that it might mean to Mars.

So this was Project Dawn—it had been well named. The pieces of the jig-saw puzzle were falling into place, but the main pattern was still not clear. To have turned Phobos into a second sun was an incredible feat of—presumably—nuclear engineering, yet Gibson did not see how it could solve the colony's problems. He was still worrying over this when the seldom used public-address system of Port Lowell burst into life and Whittaker's voice came drifting softly down the streets.

"Hello, everybody," he said. "I guess you're all awake by now and have seen what's happened. The Chief Executive's on his way back from space and would like to speak to you. Here he is."

There was a click; then someone said, *sotto voce:* "You're on to Port Lowell, sir." A moment later Hadfield's voice came out of the speakers. He sounded tired but triumphant, like a man who had fought a great battle and won through to victory.

"Hello, Mars," he said. "Hadfield speaking. I'm still in space on the way home—I'll be landing in about an hour.

"I hope you like your new Sun. According to our calculations, it will take nearly a thousand years to burn itself out. We triggered Phobos off when it was well below your horizon, just in case the initial radiation peak was too high. The reaction's now stabilised at exactly the level we expected, though it may increase by a few per cent during the next week. It's mainly a meson resonance reaction, very efficient but not very violent, and there's no chance of a fully fledged atomic explosion with the material composing Phobos.

"Your new luminary will give you about a tenth of the Sun's heat, which will bring up the temperature of much of Mars to nearly the same value as Earth's. But that isn't the reason why we blew up Phobos—at least, it isn't the main reason.

"Mars wants oxygen more badly than heat—and all the oxygen needed to give it an atmosphere almost as good as Earth's is lying beneath your feet, locked up in the sand. Two years ago we discovered a plant that can break the sand down and release the oxygen. It's a tropical plant—it can exist only on the equator and doesn't really flourish even there. If there was enough sunlight available, it could spread over Mars—with some assistance from us—and in fifty years there'd be an atmosphere here that men could breathe. *That's* the goal we're aiming at: when we've reached it, we can go where we please on Mars and forget about our domed cities and breathing masks. It's a dream that many of you will live to see realised, and it'll mean that we've given a new world to mankind.

"Even now, there are some benefits we'll derive right away. It will be very much warmer, at least when Phobos and the Sun are shining together, and the winters will be much milder. Even though Phobos isn't visible above latitude seventy degrees, the new convection winds will warm the polar regions too, and will prevent our precious moisture from being locked up in the ice caps for half of every year.

"There'll be some disadvantages—the seasons and nights are going to get complicated now!—but they'll be far outweighed by the benefits. And every day, as you see the beacon we have now lit climbing across the sky, it will remind you of the new world we're bringing to birth. We're making history, remember, for this is the first time that Man has tried his hand at changing the face of a planet. If we succeed here, others will do the same elsewhere. In the ages to come, whole civilisations on worlds of which we've never heard will owe their existence to what we've done tonight.

"That's all I've got to say now. Perhaps you may regret the sacrifice we've had to make to bring life to this world again. But remember this—though Mars has lost a Moon, it's gained a Sun—and who can doubt which is the more valuable?

"And now—good night to you all."

But no one in Port Lowell went back to sleep. As far as the city was concerned, the night was over and the new day had dawned. It was hard to take one's eyes off that tiny golden disc as it climbed steadily up the sky, its warmth growing greater minute by minute. What would the Martian plants be making of it? Gibson wondered. He walked along the street until he came to the nearest section of the dome, and looked out through the transparent wall. It was as he had expected: they had all awakened and turned their faces to the new Sun. He wondered just what they would do when both Suns were in the sky together. . . .

The Chief's rocket landed half an hour later, but Hadfield and the scientists of Project Dawn avoided the crowds by coming into the city on foot through Dome Seven, and sending the transport on to the main entrance as a decoy. This ruse worked so well that they were all safely indoors before anyone realised what had happened, or could start celebrations which they were too tired to appreciate. However, this did not prevent numerous private parties forming all over the city—parties at which everyone tried to claim that they had known what Project Dawn was all the time.

Phobos was approaching the zenith, much nearer and therefore much warmer than it had been on rising, when Gibson and Jimmy met their crewmates in the crowd that had good-naturedly but firmly insisted to George that he had better open up the bar. Each party claimed it had only homed on this spot because it was sure it would find the other there.

Hilton, who as Chief Engineer might be expected to know more about nucleonics than anyone else in the assembly, was soon pushed to the fore and asked to explain just what had happened. He modestly denied his competence to do anything of the sort.

"What they've done up on Phobos," he protested, "is years ahead of anything I ever learned at college. Why, even meson reactions hadn't been discovered then—let alone how to harness them. In fact, I don't think anyone on Earth knows how to do that, even now. It must be something that Mars has learned for itself."

"Do you mean to tell me," said Bradley, "that Mars is ahead of Earth in nuclear physics—or anything else for that matter?"

This remark nearly caused a riot and Bradley's colleagues had to rescue him from the indignant colonists—which they did in a somewhat leisurely fashion. When peace had been restored, Hilton nearly put *his* foot in it by remarking: "Of course, you know that a lot of Earth's best scientists have been coming here in the last few years, so it's not as surprising as you might think."

The statement was perfectly true, and Gibson remembered the remark that Whittaker had made to him that very morning. Mars had been a lure to many others besides himself, and now he could understand why. What prodigies of persuasion, what intricate negotiations and downright deceptions, Hadfield must have performed in these last few years! It had, perhaps, been not too difficult to attract the really first-rate minds; they could appreciate the challenge and respond to it. The second-raters, the equally essential rank-and-file of science, would have been harder to find. One day, perhaps, he would learn the secrets behind the secret, and discover just how Project Dawn had been launched and guided to success.

What was left of the night seemed to pass very swiftly. Phobos was dropping down into the eastern sky when the Sun rose up to greet its rival. It was a duel that all the city watched in silent fascination—a one-sided conflict that could have only a predetermined outcome. When it shone alone in the night sky, it was easy to pretend that Phobos was almost as brilliant as the Sun, but the first light of the true dawn banished the illusion. Minute by minute Phobos faded, though it was still well above the horizon, as the Sun came up out of the desert. Now one could tell how pale and yellow it was by comparison. There was little danger that the slowly turning plants would be confused in their quest for light; when the Sun was shining, one scarcely noticed Phobos at all.

But it was bright enough to perform its task, and for a thousand years it would be the lord of the Martian night. And thereafter?

When its fires were extinguished, by the exhaustion of whatever elements it was burning now, would Phobos become again an ordinary moon, shining only by the Sun's reflected glory?

Gibson knew that it would not matter. Even in a century it would have done its work, and Mars would have an atmosphere which it would not lose again for geological ages. When at last Phobos guttered and died, the science of that distant day would have some other answer—perhaps an answer as inconceivable to this age as the detonation of a world would have been only a century ago.

For a little while, as the first day of the new age grew to maturity, Gibson watched his double shadow lying upon the ground. Both shadows pointed to the west, but though one scarcely moved, the fainter lengthened even as he watched, becoming more and more difficult to see, until at last it was snuffed out as Phobos dropped down below the edge of Mars.

Its sudden disappearance reminded Gibson abruptly of something that he—and most of Port Lowell—had forgotten in the last few hours' excitement. By now the news would have reached Earth; perhaps—though he wasn't sure of this—Mars must now be spectacularly brighter in terrestrial skies.

In a very short time, Earth would be asking some extremely pointed questions.

SIXTEEN

It was one of those little ceremonies so beloved by the TV newsreels. Hadfield and all his staff were gathered in a tight group at the edge of the clearing, with the domes of Port Lowell rising behind them. It was, thought the cameraman, a nicely composed picture, though the constantly changing double illumination made things a little difficult.

He got the cue from the control room and started to pan from left to right to give the viewers a bit of movement before the real business began. Not that there was really much to see: the landscape was so flat and they'd miss all its interest in this monochrome transmission. (One couldn't afford the bandwidth for colour on a live transmission all the way to Earth; even on black-and-white it was none too easy.) He had just finished exploring the scene when he got the order to swing back to Hadfield, who was now making a little speech. That was going out on the other sound channel and he couldn't hear it, though in the control room it would be mated to the picture he was sending. Anyway, he knew just what the Chief would be saying—he'd heard it all before.

Mayor Whittaker handed over the shovel on which he had been gracefully leaning for the last five minutes, and Hadfield began to tip in the sand until he had covered the roots of the tall, drab Martian plant standing there, held upright in its wooden frame. The "airweed," as it was now universally called, was not a very impressive object: it scarcely looked strong enough to stand upright, even under this low gravity. It certainly didn't look as if it could control the future of a planet. . . .

Hadfield had finished his token gardening; someone else could complete the job and fill in the hole. (The planting team was already hovering in the background, waiting for the big-wigs to clear out of the way so that they could get on with their work.) There was a lot of hand-shaking and back-slapping; Hadfield was hidden by the crowd that had gathered round him. The only person who wasn't taking the slightest notice of all this was Gibson's pet Martian, who was rocking on his haunches like one of those weighted dolls that always come the same way up however you put them down. The cameraman swung towards him and zoomed to a close-up; it would be the first time anyone on Earth would have seen a real Martian—at least in a live programme like this.

Hello—what was he up to? Something had caught his interest— the twitching of those huge, membranous ears gave him away. He was beginning to move in short, cautious hops. The cameraman chased him and widened the field at the same time to see where he was going. No one else had noticed that he'd begun to move; Gibson was still talking to Whittaker and seemed to have completely forgotten his pet.

So *that* was the game! This was going to be good; the folk back on Earth would love it. Would he get there before he was spotted? Yes— he'd made it! With one final bound he hopped down into the little pit, and the small triangular beak began to nibble at the slim Martian plant that had just been placed there with such care. No doubt he thought it so kind of his friends to go to all this trouble for him. . . . Or did he really know he was being naughty? That devious approach had been so skilful that it was hard to believe it was done in complete innocence. Anyway, the cameraman wasn't going to spoil his fun; it would make too good a picture. He cut for a moment back to Hadfield and Company, still congratulating themselves on the work which Squeak was rapidly undoing.

It was too good to last. Gibson spotted what was happening and gave a great yell which made everyone jump. Then he raced towards Squeak, who did a quick look round, decided that there was nowhere to hide, and just sat still with an air of injured innocence. He let himself be led away quietly, not aggravating his offence by resisting the forces of the law when Gibson grabbed one of his ears and tugged him away from the scene of the crime. A group of experts then gathered anxiously around the airweed, and to everyone's relief it was soon decided that the damage was not fatal.

It was a trivial incident, which no one would have imagined to have any consequences beyond the immediate moment. Yet, though he never realised the fact, it was to inspire one of Gibson's most brilliant and fruitful ideas.

Life for Martin Gibson had suddenly become very complicated—and intensely interesting. He had been one of the first to see Hadfield after the inception of Project Dawn. The C.E. had called for him, but had been able to give him only a few minutes of his time. That, however, had been enough to change the pattern of Gibson's future.

"I'm sorry I had to keep you waiting," Hadfield said, "but I got the reply from Earth only just before I left. The answer is that you can stay here if you can be absorbed into our administrative structure—to use the official jargon. As the future of our 'administrative structure' depended somewhat largely on Project Dawn, I thought it best to leave the matter until I got back home."

The weight of uncertainty had lifted from Gibson's mind. It was all settled now; even if he had to make a mistake—and he did not believe he had—there was now no going back. He had thrown in his lot with Mars; he would be part of the colony in its fight to regenerate this world that was now stirring sluggishly in its sleep.

"And what job have you got for me?" Gibson asked a little anxiously.

"I've decided to regularise your unofficial status," said Hadfield, with a smile.

"What do you mean?"

"Do you remember what I said at our very first meeting? I asked you to help us by giving Earth not the mere facts of the situation, but also some idea of our goals and—I suppose you could call it—the spirit we've built up here on Mars. You've done well, despite the fact that you didn't know about the project on which we'd set our greatest hopes. I'm sorry I had to keep Dawn from you, but it would have made your job much harder if you'd known our secret and weren't able to say anything. Don't you agree?"

Gibson had not thought of it in that light, but it certainly made sense.

"I've been very interested," Hadfield continued, "to see what result your broadcasts and articles have had. You may not know that we've got a delicate method of testing this."

"How?" asked Gibson in surprise.

"Can't you guess? Every week about ten thousand people, scattered all over Earth, decide they want to come here, and something like three per cent pass the preliminary tests. Since your articles started appearing regularly, that figure's gone up to fifteen thousand a week, and it's still rising."

"Oh," said Gibson, very thoughtfully. He gave an abrupt little laugh. "I also seem to remember," he added, "that you didn't want me to come here in the first place."

"We all make mistakes, but I've learned to profit by mine," smiled Hadfield. "To sum it all up, what I'd like you to do is to lead a small section which, frankly, will be our propaganda department. Of course, we'll think of a nicer name for it! Your job will be to sell Mars. The opportunities are far greater now that we've really got something to put in our shop window. If we can get enough people clamouring to come here, then Earth will be forced to provide the shipping space. And the quicker that's done, the sooner we can promise Earth we'll be standing on our own feet. What do you say?"

Gibson felt a fleeting disappointment. Looked at from one point of view, this wasn't much of a change. But the C.E. was right: he could be of greater use to Mars in this way than in any other.

"I can do it," he said. "Give me a week to sort out my terrestrial affairs and clear up my outstanding commitments."

A week was somewhat optimistic, he thought, but that should break the back of the job. He wondered what Ruth was going to say. She'd probably think he was mad, and she'd probably be right.

"The news that you're going to stay here," said Hadfield with satisfaction, "will cause a lot of interest and will be quite a boost to our campaign. You've no objection to our announcing it right away?"

"I don't think so."

"Good. Whittaker would like to have a word with you now about the detailed arrangements. You realise, of course, that your salary will be that of a Class II Administrative Officer of your age?"

"Naturally I've looked into that," said Gibson. He did not add, because it was unnecessary, that this was largely of theoretical interest. His salary on Mars, though less than a tenth of his total income, would be quite adequate for a comfortable standard of living on a planet where there were very few luxuries. He was not sure just how he could use his terrestrial credits, but no doubt they could be employed to squeeze something through the shipping bottleneck.

After a long session with Whittaker—who nearly succeeded in destroying his enthusiasm with laments about lack of staff and accommodation—Gibson spent the rest of the day writing dozens of radiograms. The longest was to Ruth, and was chiefly, but by no means wholly, concerned with business affairs. Ruth had often commented on the startling variety of things she did for her ten per cent, and Gibson wondered what she was going to say to this request that she keep an eye on one James Spencer, and generally look after him when he was in New York—which, since he was completing his studies at M.I.T., might be fairly often.

It would have made matters much simpler if he could have told her the facts; she would probably guess them, anyway. But that would be unfair to Jimmy; Gibson had made up his mind that he would be the first to know. There were times when the strain of not telling him was so great that he felt almost glad they would soon be parting. Yet Hadfield, as usual, had been right. He had waited a generation—he must wait a little longer yet. To reveal himself now might leave Jimmy confused and hurt—might even cause the breakdown of his engagement to Irene. The time to tell him would be when they had been married and, Gibson hoped, were still insulated from any shocks which the outside world might administer.

It was ironic that, having found his son so late, he must now lose him again. Perhaps that was part of the punishment for the selfishness and lack of courage—to put it no more strongly—he had shown twenty years ago. But the past must bury itself; he must think of the future now.

Jimmy would return to Mars as soon as he could—there was no doubt of that. And even if he had missed the pride and satisfaction of parenthood, there might be compensations later in watching his grandchildren come into the world he was helping to remake. For the first time in his life, Gibson had a future to which he could look forward with interest and excitement—a future which would not be merely a repetition of the past.

Earth hurled its thunderbolt four days later. The first Gibson knew about it was when he saw the headline across the front page of the "Martian Times." For a moment the two words staring back at him were so astounding that he forgot to read on.

HADFIELD RECALLED

We have just received news that the Interplanetary Development Board has requested the Chief Executive to return to Earth on the *Ares*, which leaves Deimos in four days. No reason is given.

That was all, but it would set Mars ablaze. No reason was given—and none was necessary. Everyone knew exactly why Earth wanted to see Warren Hadfield.

"What do you think of this?" Gibson asked Jimmy as he passed the paper across the breakfast table.

"Good Lord!" gasped Jimmy. "There'll be trouble now! What do you think he'll do?"

"What can he do?"

"Well, he can refuse to go. Everyone here would certainly back him up."

"That would only make matters worse. He'll go, all right. Hadfield isn't the sort of man to run away from a fight."

Jimmy's eyes suddenly brightened.

"That means that Irene will be going too."

"Trust you to think of that!" laughed Gibson. "I suppose you hope it will be an ill wind blowing the pair of you some good. But don't count on it—Hadfield *might* leave Irene behind."

He thought this very unlikely. When the Chief returned, he would need all the moral support he could get.

Despite the amount of work he had awaiting him, Gibson paid one brief call to Admin, where he found everyone in a state of mingled indignation and suspense. Indignation because of Earth's cavalier treatment of the Chief: suspense because no one yet knew what action he was going to take. Hadfield had arrived early that morning, and so far had not seen anyone except Whittaker and his private secretary. Those who had caught a glimpse of him stated that for a man who was, technically, about to be recalled in disgrace, he looked remarkably cheerful.

Gibson was thinking over this news as he made a detour towards the Biology Lab. He had missed seeing his little Martian friend for two days, and felt rather guilty about it. As he walked slowly along Regent Street, he wondered what sort of defence Hadfield would be able to put up. Now he understood that remark that Jimmy had overheard. *Would* success excuse everything? Success was still a long way off; as Hadfield had said, to bring Project Dawn to its conclusion would take half a century, even assuming the maximum assistance from Earth. It was essential to secure that support, and Hadfield would do his utmost not to antagonise the home planet. The best that Gibson could do to support him would be to provide long-range covering fire from his propaganda department.

Squeak, as usual, was delighted to see him, though Gibson returned his greeting somewhat absentmindedly. As he invariably did, he proffered Squeak a fragment of airweed from the supply kept in the Lab. That simple action must have triggered something in his subconscious mind, for he suddenly paused, then turned to the chief biologist.

"I've just had a wonderful idea," he said. "You know you were telling me about the tricks you've been able to teach Squeak?"

"Teach him! The problem now is to stop him learning them!"

"You also said you were fairly sure the Martians could communicate with each other, didn't you?"

"Well, our field party's proved that they can pass on simple thoughts, and even some abstract ideas like colour. That doesn't prove much, of course. Bees can do the same."

"Then tell me what you think of this. Why shouldn't we teach them to cultivate the airweed for us? You see what a colossal advantage they've got—they can go anywhere on Mars they please, while we'd have to do everything with machines. They needn't *know* what they're doing, of course. We'd simply provide them with the shoots—it does propagate that way, doesn't it?—teach them the necessary routine, and reward them afterwards."

"Just a moment! It's a pretty idea, but haven't you overlooked some practical points? I think we could train them in the way you suggest—we've certainly learned enough about their psychology for that—but may I point out that there are only ten known specimens, including Squeak?"

"I hadn't overlooked that," said Gibson impatiently. "I simply don't believe the group I found is the only one in existence. That would be a quite incredible coincidence. Certainly they're rather rare, but there must be hundreds, if not thousands, of them over the planet. I'm going to suggest a photo-reconnaissance of all the air-weed forests—we should have no difficulty in spotting their clearings. But in any case I'm taking the long-term view. Now that they've got far more favourable living conditions, they'll start to multiply rapidly, just as the Martian plant life's already doing. Remember, even if we left it to itself the airweed would cover the equatorial regions in four hundred years—according to your own figures. With the Martians *and* us to help it spread, we might cut years off Project Dawn!"

The biologist shook his head doubtfully, but began to do some calculations on a scribbling pad. When he had finished he pursed his lips.

"Well . . . I," he said, "I can't actually prove it's impossible; there are too many unknown factors—including the most important one of all—the Martian's reproduction rate. Incidentally, I suppose you know that they're marsupials? That's just been confirmed."

"You mean like kangaroos?"

"Yes. Junior lives under cover until he's a big enough boy to go out into the cold, hard world. We think several of the females are carrying babies, so they may reproduce yearly. And since Squeak was the only infant we found, that means they must have a terrifically high death-rate—which isn't surprising in this climate."

"Just the conditions we want!" exclaimed Gibson. "Now there'll be nothing to stop them multiplying, providing we see they get all the food they need."

"Do you want to breed Martians or cultivate airweed?" challenged the biologist.

"Both," grinned Gibson. "They go together like fish and chips, or ham and eggs."

"Don't!" pleaded the other, with such a depth of feeling that Gibson apologised at once for his lack of tact. He had forgotten that no one on Mars had tasted such things for years.

The more Gibson thought about his new idea, the more it appealed to him. Despite the pressure of his personal affairs, he found time to write a memorandum to Hadfield on the subject, and hoped that the C.E. would be able to discuss it with him before returning to Earth. There was something inspiring in the thought of regenerating not only a world, but also a race which might be older than Man.

Gibson wondered how the changed climatic conditions of a hundred years hence would affect the Martians. If it became too warm for them, they could easily migrate north or south—if necessary into the sub-polar regions where Phobos was never visible. As for the oxygenated atmosphere—they had been used to that in the past and might adapt themselves to it again. There was considerable evidence that Squeak now obtained much of his oxygen from the air in Port Lowell, and seemed to be thriving on it.

There was still no answer to the great question which the discovery of the Martians had raised. Were they the degenerate survivors of a race which had achieved civilisation long ago, and let it slip from its grasp when conditions became too severe? This was the romantic view, for which there was no evidence at all. The scientists were unanimous in believing that there had never been any advanced culture on Mars—but they had been proved wrong once and might be so again. In any case, it would be an extremely interesting experiment to see how far up the evolutionary ladder the Martians would climb, now that their world was blossoming again.

For it was their world, not Man's. However he might shape it for his own purposes, it would be his duty always to safeguard the interests of its rightful owners. No one could tell what part they might have to play in the history of the universe. And when, as was one day inevitable, Man himself came to the notice of yet higher races, he might well be judged by his behaviour here on Mars.

SEVENTEEN

"I'm sorry you're not coming back with us, Martin," said Norden as they approached Lock One West, "but I'm sure you're doing the right thing, and we all respect you for it."

"Thanks," said Gibson sincerely. "I'd like to have made the return trip with you all—still, there'll be plenty of chances later! Whatever happens, I'm not going to be on Mars *all* my life!" He chuckled. "I guess you never thought you'd be swapping passengers in this way."

"I certainly didn't. It's going to be a bit embarrassing in some respects. I'll feel like the captain of the ship who had to carry Napoleon to Elba. How's the Chief taking it?"

"I've not spoken to him since the recall came through, though I'll be seeing him tomorrow before he goes up to Deimos. But Whittaker says he seems confident enough, and doesn't appear to be worrying in the slightest."

"What do *you* think's going to happen?"

"On the official level, he's bound to be reprimanded for misappropriation of funds, equipment, personnel—oh, enough things to land him in jail for the rest of his life. But as half the executives and all the scientists on Mars are involved, what can Earth do about it? It's really a very amusing situation. The C.E.'s a public hero on two worlds, and the Interplanetary Development Board will have to handle him with kid gloves. I think the verdict will be: 'You shouldn't have done it, but we're rather glad you did.'"

"And then they'll let him come back to Mars?"

"They're bound to. No one else can do his job."

"Someone will have to, one day."

"True enough, but it would be madness to waste Hadfield when he's still got years of work in him. And heaven help anyone who was sent here to replace him!"

"It certainly *is* a peculiar position. I think a lot's been going on that we don't know about. Why did Earth turn down Project Dawn when it was first suggested?"

"I've been wondering about that, and intend to get to the bottom of it some day. Meanwhile my theory is this—I think a lot of people on Earth don't want Mars to become too powerful, still less completely independent. Not for any sinister reason, mark you, but simply because they don't like the idea. It's too wounding to their pride. They want the Earth to remain the centre of the universe."

"You know," said Norden, "it's funny how you talk about 'Earth' as if it were some combination of miser and bully, preventing all progress here. After all, it's hardly fair! What you're actually grumbling at are the administrators in the Interplanetary Development Board and all its allied organisations—and they're really trying to do their best. Don't forget that everything you've got here is due to the enterprise and initiative of Earth. I'm afraid you colonists"—he gave a wry grin as he spoke—"take a very self-centred view of things. I can see both sides of the question. When I'm here I get your point of view and can sympathise with it. But in three months' time I'll be on the other side and will probably think you're a lot of grumbling, ungrateful nuisances here on Mars!"

Gibson laughed, not altogether comfortably. There was a good deal of truth in what Norden had said. The sheer difficulty and expense of interplanetary travel, and the time it took to get from world to world, made inevitable some lack of understanding, even intolerance, between Earth and Mars. He hoped that as the speed of transport increased these psychological barriers would be broken down and the two planets would come closer together in spirit as well as in time.

They had now reached the lock and were waiting for the transport to take Norden out to the airstrip. The rest of the crew had already said good-bye and were now on their way up to Deimos. Only Jimmy had received special dispensation to fly up with Hadfield and Irene when they left tomorrow. Jimmy had certainly changed his status, thought Gibson with some amusement, since the *Ares* had left Earth. He wondered just how much work Norden was going to get out of him on the homeward voyage.

"Well, John, I hope you have a good trip back," said Gibson, holding out his hand as the airlock door opened. "When will I be seeing you again?"

"In about eighteen months—I've got a trip to Venus to put in first. When I get back here, I expect to find quite a difference—airweed and Martians everywhere!"

"I don't promise much in that time," laughed Gibson. "But we'll do our best not to disappoint you!"

They shook hands, and Norden was gone. Gibson found it impossible not to feel a twinge of envy as he thought of all the things to which the other was returning—all the unconsidered beauties of Earth which he had once taken for granted, and now might not see again for many years.

He still had two farewells to make, and they would be the most difficult of all. His last meeting with Hadfield would require considerable delicacy and tact. Norden's analogy, he thought, had been a good one: it would be rather like an interview with a dethroned monarch about to sail into exile.

In actual fact it proved to be like nothing of the sort. Hadfield was still master of the situation, and seemed quite unperturbed by his future. When Gibson entered he had just finished sorting out his papers; the room looked bare and bleak and three wastepaper baskets were piled high with discarded forms and memoranda. Whittaker, as acting Chief Executive, would be moving in tomorrow.

"I've run through your note on the Martians and the airweed," said Hadfield, exploring the deeper recesses of his desk. "It's a very interesting idea, but no one can tell me whether it will work or not. The position's extremely complicated and we haven't enough information. It really comes down to this—would we get a better return for our efforts if we teach Martians to plant airweed, or if we do the job ourselves? Anyway, we'll set up a small research group to look into the idea, though there's not much we can do until we've got some more Martians! I've asked Dr. Petersen to handle the scientific side, and I'd like you to deal with the administrative problems as they arise —leaving any major decisions to Whittaker, of course. Petersen's a very sound fellow, but he lacks imagination. Between the two of you, we should get the right balance."

"I'll be very glad to do all I can," said Gibson, quite pleased with the prospect, though wondering a little nervously how he would cope with his increasing responsibilities. However, the fact that the Chief had given him the job was encouraging: it meant that Hadfield, at any rate, was sure that he could handle it.

As they discussed administrative details, it became clear to Gibson that Hadfield did not expect to be away from Mars for more than a year. He even seemed to be looking forward to his trip to Earth, regarding it almost in the light of an overdue holiday. Gibson hoped that this optimism would be justified by the outcome.

Towards the end of their interview, the conversation turned inevitably to Irene and Jimmy. The long voyage back to Earth would provide Hadfield with all the opportunities he needed to study his prospective son-in-law, and Gibson hoped that Jimmy would be on his best behaviour. It was obvious that Hadfield was contemplating this aspect of the trip with quiet amusement. As he remarked to Gibson, if Irene and Jimmy could put up with each other in such close quarters for three months, their marriage was bound to be a success. If they couldn't—then the sooner they found out, the better.

As he left Hadfield's office, Gibson hoped that he had made his own sympathy clear. The C.E. knew that he had all Mars behind him, and Gibson would do his best to gain him the support of Earth as well. He looked back at the unobtrusive lettering on the door. There would be no need to change that, whatever happened, since the words designated the position and not the man. For twelve months or so Whittaker would be working behind that door, the democratic ruler of Mars and the—within reasonable limits—conscientious servant of Earth. Whoever came and went, the lettering on the door would remain. That was another of Hadfield's ideas—the tradition that the post was more important than the man. He had not, Gibson thought, given it a very good start, for anonymity was scarcely one of Hadfield's personal characteristics.

The last rocket to Deimos left three hours later with Hadfield, Irene, and Jimmy aboard. Irene had come round to the Grand Martian Hotel to help Jimmy pack and to say good-bye to Gibson. She was bubbling over with excitement and so radiant with happiness that it was a pleasure simply to sit and watch her. Both her dreams had come true at once: she was going back to Earth, and she was going with Jimmy. Gibson hoped that neither experience would disappoint her; he did not believe it would.

Jimmy's packing was complicated by the number of souvenirs he had gathered on Mars—chiefly plant and mineral specimens collected on various trips outside the Dome. All these had to be carefully weighed, and some heartrending decisions were involved when it was discovered that he had exceeded his personal allowance by two kilogrammes. But finally the last suitcase was packed and on its way to the airport.

"Now don't forget," said Gibson, "to contact Mrs. Goldstein as soon as you arrive; she'll be expecting to hear from you."

"I won't," Jimmy replied. "It's good of you to take all this trouble. We really do appreciate everything you've done—don't we, Irene?"

"Yes," she answered, "we certainly do. I don't know how we'd have got on without you."

Gibson smiled, a little wistfully.

"Somehow," he said, "I think you'd still have managed in one way or another! But I'm glad everything's turned out so well for you, and I'm sure you're going to be very happy. And—I hope it won't be too long before you're both back on Mars."

As he gripped Jimmy's hand in farewell, Gibson felt once again that almost overwhelming desire to reveal his identity and, whatever the consequences, to greet Jimmy as his son. But if he did so, he knew now, the dominant motive would be pure egotism. It would be an act of possessiveness, of inexcusable self-assertion, and it would undo all the good he had wrought in these past months. Yet as he dropped Jimmy's hand, he glimpsed something in the other's expression that he had never seen before. It could have been the dawn of the first puzzled surmise, the birth of the still half-conscious thought that might grow at last to fully fledged understanding and recognition. Gibson hoped it was so; it would make his task easier when the time came.

He watched them go hand-in-hand down the narrow street, oblivious to all around them, their thoughts even now winging outwards into space. Already they had forgotten him; but, later, they would remember.

It was just before dawn when Gibson left the main airlock and walked away from the still sleeping city. Phobos had set an hour ago; the only light was that of the stars and Deimos, now high in the west. He looked at his watch—ten minutes to go if there had been no hitch.

"Come on, Squeak," he said. "Let's take a nice brisk walk to keep warm." Though the temperature around them was at least fifty below, Squeak did not seem unduly worried. However, Gibson thought it best to keep his pet on the move. He was, of course, perfectly comfortable himself, as he was wearing his full protective clothing.

How these plants had grown in the past few weeks! They were now taller than a man, and though some of this increase might be normal, Gibson was sure that much of it was due to Phobos. Project Dawn was already leaving its mark on the planet. Even the North Polar Cap, which should now be approaching its midwinter maximum, had halted in its advance over the opposite hemisphere—and the remnants of the southern cap had vanished completely.

They came to a stop about a kilometre from the city, far enough away for its lights not to hinder observation. Gibson glanced again at his watch. Less than a minute left; he knew what his friends were feeling now. He stared at the tiny, barely visible gibbous disc of Deimos, and waited.

Quite suddenly, Deimos became conspicuously brighter. A moment later it seemed to split into two fragments as a tiny, incredibly bright star detached itself from its edge and began to creep slowly westwards. Even across these thousands of kilometres of space, the glare of the atomic rockets was so dazzling that it almost hurt the eye.

He did not doubt that they were watching him. Up there in the *Ares*, they would be at the observation windows, looking down upon the great crescent world which they were leaving now, as a lifetime ago, it seemed, he had bade farewell to Earth.

What was Hadfield thinking now? Was he wondering if he would ever see Mars again? Gibson no longer had any real doubts on this score. Whatever battles Hadfield might have to face, he would win through as he had done in the past. He was returning to Earth in triumph, not in disgrace.

That dazzling blue-white star was several degrees from Deimos now, falling behind as it lost speed to drop Sunwards—and Earthwards.

The rim of the Sun came up over the eastern horizon; all around him, the tall green plants were stirring in their sleep—a sleep already interrupted once by the meteoric passage of Phobos across the sky. Gibson looked once more at the two stars descending in the west, and raised his hand in a silent farewell.

"Come along, Squeak," he said. "Time to get back—I've got work to do." He tweaked the little Martian's ears with his gloved fingers.

"And that goes for you too," he added. "Though you don't know it yet, we've both got a pretty big job ahead of us."

They walked together towards the great domes, now glistening faintly in the first morning light. It would be strange in Port Lowell, now that Hadfield had gone and another man was sitting behind the door marked "Chief Executive."

Gibson suddenly paused. For a fleeting moment, it seemed, he saw into the future, fifteen or twenty years ahead. Who would be Chief then, when Project Dawn was entering its middle phase and its end could already be foreseen?

The question and the answer came almost simultaneously. For the first time, Gibson knew what lay at the end of the road on which he had now set his feet. One day, perhaps, it would be his duty, and his privilege, to take over the work which Hadfield had begun. It might have been sheer self-deception, or it might have been the first consciousness of his own still hidden powers—but whichever it was, he meant to know.

With a new briskness in his step, Martin Gibson, writer, late of Earth, resumed his walk towards the city. His shadow merged with Squeak's as the little Martian hopped beside him; while overhead the last hues of night drained from the sky, and all around, the tall, flowerless plants were unfolding to face the sun.